THE ANGKOR MASSACRE

THE ANGKOR MASSACRE

—— *a novel by* ——

Loup Durand

TRANSLATED FROM THE FRENCH

BY HELEN R. LANE

WILLIAM MORROW AND COMPANY, INC.
New York   1983

F
D

Library of Congress Cataloging in Publication Data

Durand, Loup.
The Angkor massacre.

I. Title.
PQ2664.U6734A84   1983   843'.914   82-18818
ISBN 0-688-00487-3

Printed in the United States of America

First Edition

1 2 3 4 5 6 7 8 9 10

Book Design by Ellen Logiudice

9845

To Roger, murdered
   one twenty-third of January
not far from Angkor Thom.

To all the others.

Part One

THE
WARLORD

1

THE PLANTATION WAS—AND DOUBTLESS STILL IS—IN THE NORTH of Cambodia, above and slightly to the left within an inverted triangle whose lower point would be represented by Phnom Penh and whose two sides would be formed by the Mekong River flowing down from Laos, and by the axis Phnom Penh–Siem Reap. There was no road leading to it, just a trail of laterite and then sand which continued north beyond the plantation, in the direction of the ancient temples of Prah Vihear and the Thai border. The low mountains of the Dangrek Range are a few dozen miles away as the crow flies; a more humid atmosphere makes one aware that they are there, but not even the foothills of the range are visible because of the forest growth, which is dense and tropical here, a real jungle. When Oreste Marccaggi arrived—most likely early in the afternoon on January 17, 1948—it was almost exactly two years to the day since Pierre and Nancy Lara and their little daughter Elisabeth had been murdered, and in all probability Kamsa and his gang of cutthroats, who had been responsible for the massacre, were still somewhere in the vicinity. So a man had to be either completely out of his mind, or eager to die, to go to the plantation alone.

Oreste Marccaggi stopped the Peugeot a few yards short of the arroyo before trying to cross it. He got out of the car and walked over to the bridge to make sure that the two huge teak beams that formed both its span and the roadway across it were still solid enough to support the car. He stamped on them and checked the spacing between them, exactly the proper width to fit the wheels of a passenger car or a light truck. Oreste Marccaggi was a stout man who at that time was forty-seven years old, five feet eight inches tall, and weighed around 240 pounds, with a leonine face, crew-cut gray hair, and heavy cheeks furrowed by two deep vertical wrinkles resembling scars. He had met Pierre Lara's son in Hanoi, and what Lara said to persuade him will always remain a mystery. Lara was not yet eighteen at the time, he had never set eyes on Oreste before in his life, and he had no money of his own; what was more, he wasn't even Corsican, since that would at least have created a tie between him and the former bodyguard of the Governor General of Indochina. Nonetheless, the very next day Oreste was on his way. On the fourteenth of January, he managed to get himself a seat on a military transport plane flying the route linking Hanoi and Saigon; on the fifteenth, he left Saigon at the wheel of a car most likely lent him by a Corsican from Cho Lon; on the seventeenth at dawn, he took off from Phnom Penh.

When he stopped at the bungalow in Kompong Thom, where he drank a couple of beers, he was still wearing his khaki bush jacket; he had now taken it off and was wearing only shorts, his paratrooper boots, and a cartridge belt with a pearl-handled Colt .45 and a machete tucked into it.

He strode boldly out to the middle of one of the planks and jumped up and down with an agility that was surprising for a man of his weight; below him was a forty-foot drop. The water flowing past at the bottom of the little stream was perfectly clear, not that muddy ocher color of most Indochinese rivers. It was making a pleasant splashing noise, and above the splashing Oreste made out, very distinctly, the sound of bodies gliding through the dense forest, the breathing of men who were watching him, not only on the opposite shore but on this very shore where the Peugeot was standing. He could even identify the click of an old Mas-36 rifle being cocked. He heard these sounds but didn't bat an eye, his face, with the two crevasses furrowing his cheeks, impassive; he chewed on one of those cigars of his that he always made himself, starting with an ordinary Caporal cigarette as a base around which he rolled the leaves of various trees, following his inspiration of the moment.

Having reassured himself that the beams would hold, he climbed back behind the wheel and cautiously crossed the bridge, leaning out the window at regular intervals to make sure that his four wheels were well centered. Once across, he was on the plantation proper. He drove slowly along for some three hundred yards, following a red dirt track and humming "*Vous qui passez sans me voir*" in a sweet tenor voice that certain Corsican singers have. Behind him, around him, the tall grass that had grown in wild profusion for two years closed again with no sound save a slight rustling, and Kamsa's men began moving, invisible but surrounding him on all sides, content to keep close watch on him as he drove on but doing nothing to stop him. They may well have been dumbfounded by his heedlessness, or perhaps they were merely obeying orders. Or then again, perhaps they thought that a man would have to be completely mad to be doing what Marccaggi was doing. And they doubtless wanted to see just how far his madness might take him.

He finally turned into a square courtyard. Facing him was a long building with a zinc roof that had been painted bright yellow before the fire. To his left was the little factory with its aluminum coagulation tanks, the rolling press, the boiler, the vat for making crepe rubber, the long troughs, the heaps of galvanized tin buckets used by the latex collectors. Everything in the factory was blackened by the fire; the latex melted by the flames had spread everywhere like a black leprosy, and still stank terribly.

To his right, beyond a double screen of lemon and sandalwood trees, was the house, apparently intact. Intact with the exception of a heavy wooden shutter half torn off and hanging from one last twisted hinge: That was how the assailants had gotten in after a siege that had lasted for thirty-three hours. The house was built of teakwood, but the massive pilings that raised it three feet above the ground were anchored in a cement foundation.

The Peugeot rolled to a stop. Oreste's gaze fell on the veranda, some eighteen feet wide and sixty feet long, shaded from the sun by a roof made of fan-palm leaves. A man sat there in proud solitude, lolling voluptuously in one of the two outsize peacock-fan Manila rattan rocking chairs. Oreste turned off the ignition and a total silence fell. He got out of the car, walked up to within ten feet of the steps, and asked in Khmer:

"Is that you, Kamsa?"

"Yes, it is," Kamsa replied, not budging from the chair. He was wearing a colonial cork sun helmet, a sarong, and a white smoking jacket over his bare chest, and was paring his toenails with a knife more than a foot long.

Behind Oreste's back there was the sound of gliding footfalls, pounding feet, and the silent presence of many men. There was also a peculiar noise, a sort of hissing sound, produced by machete blades whistling through the air.

"How come you're not wearing a shirt?" Kamsa asked inquisitively.

Oreste shrugged.

"Too hot."

The very next second he felt the first machete blow; with a breathtaking lightness of touch, the blade delicately nicked his shoulder, slicing off several ounces of flesh. He did not turn around or even show the slightest reaction. Without letting go of his cigar he spat, hitting a bottle on the ground four yards away. When it came to spitting or drawing a bead with his Colt, Oreste Marccaggi's aim was incredibly accurate.

"Do you know why I've come here?" he asked.

Kamsa shook his head, laughing. His head moved but not his helmet, which was too big for him.

"Why did you come?"

Oreste smiled in turn. "To kill you," he answered.

Kamsa laughed even more heartily. Oreste shook his head, like someone who has just told a great joke and is happy to note that it is properly appreciated. He held out his left fist and opened it, revealing the two ivory dice that he was holding.

"But first we're going to have a game of dice," he said.

At that point he received two more machete blows, delivered with as delicate a touch as before, one of them nicking his right thigh after having slashed through the cloth of his shorts, the other making a very fine cut in his back, below his shoulder blade. Without turning a hair, Oreste rattled the dice in his left hand.

"Dice, eh?" Kamsa said thoughtfully.

"They told me about you in Hanoi," Oreste said. "They told me you're the biggest cheat in Indochina. But I'm a big cheater too. A better one than you are. I can beat you anytime I please."

"Unless I kill you."

"Naturally," Oreste replied calmly.

A silence. Mingled with the stagnant stench of the burned latex was another odor, equally overpowering, rich and stifling, almost sticky: that of the rotting Cambodian jungle, creeping day by day over the abandoned plantation in a monstrous process of digestion. Oreste's back was bleeding profusely now.

"You're a Warlord," Oreste went on. "But you don't really know how to play a game of dice. I can beat you anytime I please."

Kamsa roared with laughter again, in bursts that resembled gunfire. There was a wild gleam in his eye.

"You're a Warlord, but I can beat you at dice and at something else as well," Oreste added.

Kamsa's head tilted to one side. "What else exactly?"

"At *chum*,"* Oreste said. "I can drink more of it than you can."

Oreste turned around for the first time. Behind him were perhaps thirty men, standing stock-still; they had an interested, attentive look on their faces. They were dark-skinned men, with the shiny, oil-dark hair of Samrés, the Khmers of the forest, or of Phnongs, wild mountain-dwellers. A number of them had rifles and all of them had machetes. Oreste turned around again to face Kamsa.

"I can beat you whenever I please, Warlord. And when I've beaten you, I'm going to kill you."

And in fact they began the game, sitting opposite each other in the two peacock-fan chairs, rolling the dice on the amazingly smooth black floor of the veranda, as the onlookers, squatting on their heels with elbows on knees, their hands with open palms dangling loosely, settled down to watch in a respectful, grave half-circle. Not a one dared even to set foot on the steps of the veranda, leaving those entirely to the *louk thom*, the great lords and masters, the notables in their eyes: their leader Kamsa and the foolhardy *Barang*.† Little by little, growing bolder, women appeared; their *sampots* clung to their round, full hips and long thighs. Unlike those of Vietnamese or Chinese women, who for the most part are flat-chested, their naked breasts were well-developed.

Hour after hour went by. As they played, the two men on the veranda steadily emptied, one after the other, the hundred-some bamboo jugs filled

---

* Alcohol distilled from rice
† Abbreviation of *Barangsès*, meaning *Frenchmen* in Khmer; a term used to designate any white

with *chum* that the Corsican had brought with him in the trunk and on the back seat of the Peugeot.

"I'm a Warlord," Kamsa said in a voice that had become thicker and thicker. He had downed enough alcohol to float a sampan. "I'm a great Warlord, a Communist, a revolutionary, fighting for the independence of Cambodia."

"*Eccu, eccu,* that's what you are, all right," Oreste Marccaggi replied in a soft, nonchalant tone of voice. He was leading at that point by a score of 42 to 3. On his huge torso, the pink skin dotted with freckles in the places that weren't suntanned, the blood had finally dried. But because he had drunk such enormous quantities, he was literally dripping with sweat.

Around seven o'clock, the usual squadrons of flying foxes appeared in the darkening sky, and giant bats measuring up to a foot and a half long, as black as nightmares, beat the air with a sound of rustling silk. They were returning from the Mekong, from the Kratie Falls, to their dark towers at Angkor. Night fell on the game of dice in progress without a soul budging from the spot: neither the two men on the veranda who were rolling the dice and downing one drink after another as they stared intently into each other's eyes, nor the some fifty onlookers awaiting the end and knowing that it was rapidly approaching.

Acetylene lanterns, bearing the trademark of the French National Small Arms and Cycle Factory of Saint-Étienne, were then lighted and began to hiss in the damp night buzzing with insects. The onlookers were invisible in the dark. Only the veranda was bathed in light.

There came a moment when, having agreed to take time out from their game, Oreste Marccaggi and Kamsa, preceded by lantern bearers, left the veranda arm in arm, fingers intertwined, united by an eternal friendship that would last till the moment they slit each other's throats, to take a tour around the plantation. They began to sing, their way of driving away their fear of each other. Almost with one voice, they gave a rendition of *"Marie chez nous soyez reine"* and also *"Viens Poupoule,"* because these were the only two songs they knew the words of. At heart they were very much alike, both wild men who acted on instinct, and they had now sized each other up perfectly. Still chewing on the same cigar, Oreste saw the door of the barn that Kamsa had nailed Nancy to; he also saw the bedroom, still miraculously in order, that had been little Elisabeth's—she was six years old when she was murdered—and was able to see the closet where the child had hidden for a time. And finally, he saw the already rusted wreck of the Citroën-45 truck to whose bumpers Pierre Lara had been tied, to be dragged over the ground till he was dead.

"But you didn't kill the boy," Oreste said. "You missed that one."

"He got away," Kamsa explained regretfully. "He died in the forest. He was hurt, hurt bad. They cut off half his head but he got away anyway. He died in the forest."

"He isn't dead. The Neak Ta, the Guardian Spirit of the Forest, watched over him. And he's sent me here to kill you."

Kamsa roared with laughter and Oreste joined in. The others all laughed confidently, several naked children rolled on the ground in a hilarious fit of the giggles, and the old women with shaved skulls grinned from ear to ear, exposing tooth stumps blackened by betel. With tears of laughter the two men went back up onto the veranda, where they ate gummy rice wrapped in banana leaves, fish seasoned with *prahoc** and ginger, watermelon and papayas, the whole washed down with generous quantities of *chum* fortified by the addition of the last remaining bottle of Mont-Saint-Michel cologne. One after another, the lamps went out with a final sputter, and the last ones still burning were placed on the veranda, where the two men again found themselves surrounded by the aura of proud solitude befitting *louk thom.* Oreste tried to keep the atmosphere friendly and festive, but his staggering partner was beginning to lose all interest in doing so. Kamsa kept making heavy-handed jokes for the benefit of his audience down below, swallowed up in the darkness of night and invisible now, but greeting each of his crude jests with roars of laughter.

Soon there were only two lighted lanterns left on the veranda, and then just one, which finally sputtered out. Just before the last beam of light flickered out, Oreste Marccaggi sat down in his peacock-fan chair again and began to rock back and forth as regularly as a metronome, with a characteristic little creak marking each movement to and fro. His beady black eyes never left Kamsa, who had collapsed in his chair and was sound asleep, wide-open lips baring gleaming white teeth.

The darkness completely enveloped the veranda. It was not so much that the night was a particularly dark one: Without the palm-leaf roof, without the huge trees next to the house, the onlookers would doubtless have been able to make out what one or the other of the two men was doing, but the roof and the trees were there and no one could see anything. For hours on end, the faint creak of the Corsican's rocking chair could be heard. At one point it ceased, and those of the onlookers who had not fallen asleep themselves held their breath. After a few minutes, the creaking sound began again, with the same regularity.

When dawn broke, those present spied Kamsa first: He was hanging from the master-beam, his neck obviously broken, his feet dangling three feet above the floor. The Corsican finally decided to get up from his chair. He rose ponderously to his feet and walked over to the edge of the steps. He began to speak in Khmer in his booming voice. He said that the plantation now belonged to Monsieur Lara once again, that Monsieur Lara would be coming back, and that work on the plantation would begin again.

* Fermented fish sauce, similar to Vietnamese *nuoc-mam*

The men and women bowed, their palms joined at the level of their foreheads.

But that happened on January 17, 1948. The real story does not begin until twenty-one years later.

2 MATTHEW KINKAIRD SUDDENLY REMEMBERED THE FIRST TIME HE had met Lara. The memory came back to him with astonishing vividness. For a few seconds it was as if Lara were standing motionless inside the living-room doorway, tall and thin, with a lock of hair tumbling over his forehead, his gaze fixed on the Laotian teakwood statue, his right hand mechanically massaging his left shoulder (a tic whose origin had been known to Matthew even before the two of them met). "I hesitated between buying this statuette and an elephant, but elephants eat too much," Lara was saying in that soft tone of voice he had when he spoke English. And then the image disappeared, and the living room was empty once again. Matthew was still holding the letter in his hand; he folded it in four, slipped it into the breast pocket of the shirt he was wearing underneath his heavy jacket. He glanced through the rest of the mail: nothing important. As he was about to leave, he went back inside, picked up the statuette, and this time did leave the house, locking the door behind him and slipping the key, as usual, through the slot in the mailbox.

The two-story, eight-room dwelling was built entirely of wood, painted pale green with white trim; it was located on Powder Cache Street in Colorado Springs. Outside, a light truck was waiting for him, with Peter Martinez at the wheel.

"Everything okay?" Pete asked him. "Are you sure you haven't forgotten anything this time?"

Matthew merely nodded in reply and climbed into the cab of the truck. It started off, heading west. *I should be feeling sad,* Matthew thought. *I really should.* But perhaps sad wasn't the right word. *Grief-stricken? Crushed? In any case I should be feeling* something. But he didn't feel anything. *I feel—just empty.*

"If it's all right with you, I'm going to take Manitou Avenue rather than Twenty-fourth and take a detour by way of the Garden of the Gods."

Matthew only nodded. He had just discovered that his hands were trembling as they held the statuette, and he vaguely wondered why. . . . *I must be in a state of shock. That's it: in a state of shock.* Oddly enough, the expression pleased him and somehow reassured him.

"You okay?" Pete asked him again.

They had left Powder Cache Street as planned at ten o'clock. Now the new skyscrapers of the Civic Center were behind them, and the Rocky Mountains filled the horizon. The permanent haze that had built up in recent years was still there, gray in places and in others almost orange in the early morning light, the sad result of the factories, the cars on the interstate highway that slices Colorado in two from north to south, the cars on the streets of Denver, Colorado Springs, Boulder, or Pueblo, cars everywhere on the roads that had been laid down following the traces of old Indian or French trails.

A day will come when the Rockies will disappear completely from men's sight, but thank God I'll be dead by then. It was Matthew's memory speaking to him, bringing back, with the particular clarity and sharpness it seemed to possess this morning, a short summer stay on that farm in Cheyenne Wells, on the Kansas border. He had been sixteen years old at the time, so the year had been 1915. What he was remembering now about Cheyenne Wells, in the heart of the Great Plains, was a brightness, an almost radiant light on the Rockies, even though they were more than a hundred miles away.

"You don't look like you're okay," Pete said. "You're not okay," he added.

Matthew's hands were ice-cold. They stroked the slanting eyes, the faint, enigmatic smile of the statuette that had come from Laos.

"I'm all right," Matthew said. "Why is it we're going by way of the Garden of the Gods?"

"I've got two crates of stuff for Allie Nillson. It won't take us any longer if we go that way."

"The last detour I made with you took us three days."

"You were the one who didn't want to go back home. I practically had to knock you out and drag you off bodily."

Matthew closed his eyes, struggling desperately to answer in an even tone of voice.

"You're not able to knock me out. You never have been. I've always been much stronger than you."

"Except once," Pete said. "Bam!"

"You caught me by surprise."

They spoke of the incident as though it were a fist fight they'd had just the night before, but it had happened some fifty-odd years ago. Matthew Kinkaird was thirteen years old at the time, and Pete Martinez the Chicano was eleven. The Anglo had punched the Chicano and then walked off, turning his back. . . . And when he came to, he was lying with his nose in the dust and a lump as big as a basketball on the top of his head.

"Come on, it wasn't all that big," Pete said.

He turned the radio on and tuned in a Spanish-language station. The two of them recognized at the same time, from the very first bar, *"El Niño*

Jesús de Chihuahua." Pete began to hum along. The truck was following Mesa Road, so that a little bit farther ahead the natural sandstone cathedrals of the Garden of the Gods suddenly loomed up in sharp outline against the green of the sage and the pines. They stopped for just a few minutes not far from the Garden of the Gods, and it was just past eleven when they left again, driving uphill through the strange outcroppings of rock that had given the place its name. They reached the crest-line road of Green Mountain, still heading north into the heart of the Rockies and gradually climbing higher, as the radio continued to pour out Chicano music. Patches of snow appeared on the shoulders of the road but the asphalt pavement was bare and black; the air became more bitingly cold and at the same time clearer: They were climbing up out of the layer of smog. On their right, Blodgett stood out distinctly, at the same altitude that they had now reached, almost 10,000 feet. On the left they could now see very clearly the path of the road—ordinarily enveloped in a cloud of red sandstone dust but for the moment buried in snow—that in summer allowed cars to drive to the summit of Pikes Peak, an altitude of just over 14,000 feet. Directly ahead of them were other mountains, hiding Aspen and other ski resorts from view, as well as the headwaters of the Platte River.

"I received a letter about Jon," Matthew Kinkaird suddenly announced. It was as though he had waited till he was in clean, clear air before he could speak.

Pete shot him a quick glance and without a word switched off the radio.

"He's accused of having killed one of his officers and deserted," Matthew said.

The road the Toyota was following had been paved thus far, but now it became a white trail winding its way through the tall snow-decked trees of Pikes Peak National Forest.

"He's disappeared somewhere in Vietnam and been listed as absent without leave for thirty-five days now. He may be dead."

Pete Martinez remained silent. He turned off to the right, in the direction of Wildcat Gulch. Finally he said, "It's that letter that's upsetting you?"

"That's right."

A house appeared amid the trees. Two chained dogs began yapping and jumping about. Pete braked to a stop, but left the motor running.

"They're claiming my grandson is not only a murderer and a deserter but a drug addict as well. They don't say that they'll shoot him on sight as soon as they've found him, but I presume that Army regulations allow them to do so. Pete, the letter's from Larry. He's covered with shame. He's Jon's own father and he says we should all be ashamed, that our entire family is dishonored forever. He hopes that Jon is dead, or if he isn't, that he'll never see him again. That's what my son has written me, and I can just see my dear daughter-in-law leaning over his shoulder as he wrote approving of every word."

He fell silent. After a moment, Pete Martinez turned off the ignition, jumped out of the truck, and began unloading the provisions he'd brought from Colorado Springs. Clutching the statuette to his chest, Matthew let the dogs loose and went into the house. It was a low wooden building; a vast living room took up half the space, and the other half was divided into a kitchen, a storeroom, and a bedroom with a small adjoining bathroom. But there was also a back door, which Matthew now opened.

All of a sudden, it was as if he'd crossed a distance of thousands of miles: A miniature jungle was before him, a humid profusion of vegetation, a mad, almost Amazonian luxuriance, though limited in fact to the dimensions of what was simply a conservatory, the first of the three that Matthew Kinkaird had built with his own hands over a period of twenty years. This first one, a hothouse, was seventy-five feet long and almost thirty feet wide; bougainvilleas, daturas, euphorbias, lemon trees, crotons, anthuriums, coffee shrubs, Florida poinsettias, and orchids filled its many tables and lath platforms, rising above a veritable carpet of iridescent ferns, pandanus, and festuca, while the far end of this first conservatory, screened off by fine wire netting, was given over to an aviary populated by tanagers and hummingbirds.

Matthew went on.

The second conservatory was kept at a lower constant temperature, around sixty-five degrees Fahrenheit. Slightly less wide than the first one but just as long, it contained pots of azaleas and African violets dotting a real vegetable garden with tomatoes, cucumbers, and lettuce. Matthew went on.

He entered the third conservatory, this one cantilevered out over the sharply sloping ravine below. This one contained spring plants, hyacinths and primroses grouped about at the foot of orange trees, mimosas, and myrtles, with a host of cactuses in the foreground. It was almost cold in this one, since the heat went on only when the temperature fell below forty-five degrees.

Beyond the glass panels mounted in red cedar framework was a gorgeous panoramic view—or what would have been one had it not been for the pollution. Without the smog, one could easily have seen Colorado Springs, twelve miles away and 4,500 feet below, and beyond it the Great Plains, stretching out across Nebraska and Kansas and Oklahoma.

Behind Matthew, the sound of footfalls and the rasping of the dogs' claws on the tile floor.

"It'll be ready soon," Pete said. "Lunch, I mean. Ruth has made us enchiladas."

Matthew retraced his footsteps, automatically checking each of the thermostats. The dogs followed along behind him, sniffing inquisitively at these unknown worlds that ordinarily they were not allowed to enter.

"I'm starved," Pete said. "I wouldn't like to have taken off again on an empty stomach. I'm sure I'd have passed out at the wheel. But you know Ruth—when she makes enchiladas there are enough of them to feed the entire country."

He waddled along behind his bushy mustache, as clumsy and affable as always. The moment they'd finished lunch, he left, though quite obviously reluctant to do so. Once the house had fallen silent again, Matthew sat himself down in front of the fire. The first Kinkaird had arrived in Colorado in 1858, along with the horde of prospectors heading for the gold of Pikes Peak as though it were a new Eldorado, ten years after the California gold rush. That Kinkaird had come from St. Louis, where he had already set up in practice as a lawyer. His profession had perhaps enabled him to escape the gold fever; in any event it had helped him acquire a solid reputation with cattle raisers and farmers as a negotiator of water rights. The state of Colorado is a veritable water tower, for the majority of the great rivers of the West rise there; if fifty farmers divert the course of fifty streams, a billion acres at the far end of the chain suffer a lack of water.

Matthew's remembered feeling for his grandfather was one of open-mouthed admiration. *Whereas I don't remember ever having had any sort of real communication with my own father. Or, for that matter, with my own son, Larry.* He was suddenly struck by the fact that in the Kinkaird family any real understanding seemed to skip a generation. *Between my father and Larry on the one hand, and between my grandfather and me on the other . . .*

And Jon.

He felt the heartache once again, in abrupt surges each more painful than the one before. He was obliged to get up from his chair. He paced up and down the vast living room. Larry was his only son. Larry had refused to study law, refused to be the fourth Kinkaird generation to try to arbitrate disputes over water rights. When he got out of the army in 1945, he had stayed on in San Francisco and found a job in television that brought in enough, he said, to feed his wife and his daughter, Lisa, who had been born in 1942. Jon had been born later, in 1949.

Matthew found himself in the hothouse once again, though he had not gone there deliberately. Just as mechanically, he leaned over the pond where the goldfish were lazily swimming back and forth and noted that Pete had planted, among the hart's-tongue ferns and the towering water iris, a number of impatiens whose bright red dotted the mass of green foliage. *He could have asked me first. It's my hothouse,* he said to himself, mildly irritated. Lost in thought there in the hothouse, he almost missed hearing the telephone ring.

"Grandfather?"

Lisa's voice; her calm, even, clear voice; her low-pitched, slightly muffled voice that never uttered anything but exactly the right, necessary words. Lisa with the violet eyes, the same eyes as her brother's, yet someone so different from her brother.

"I know what's happened," Matthew said. "Your father's written me."

"Something has to be done, and I have every intention of doing something."

The image of the young woman came forcibly to his mind. Why was it that for almost as long as he could remember, even when she was still only a little girl, Matthew had always had the impression when he was with his granddaughter that he was the child and she the grown-up?

"Where are you?" he asked.

"In New York. I called Colorado Springs but there was no answer. You shouldn't have gone up to the cabin. You're much too lonely up there all by yourself."

"Pete Martinez has just left," Matthew replied, on the defensive.

"I've been thinking matters over all night long," Lisa went on. "I don't see any other possible solution except to go to Saigon myself. If Jon is still alive, I'll find him and persuade him to turn himself in. Providing he's really done what he's being accused of, naturally."

For a moment Matthew was speechless.

"Please, I beg you, don't do that," he said finally.

"I need money. For the trip, and above all for after I get there. I may need to pay people off. Papa refused to give me any."

Matthew closed his eyes, struggling to keep tears from streaming down his face.

"Grandpa, did you hear me?"

"Yes."

"There's no other possible solution."

"I don't know if there is or not."

"That's the only possible one."

One of the dogs came over and laid its head against his thigh. *I've left the door of the hothouse open besides,* he said to himself.

"I can send you twenty thousand dollars," he said aloud. "Tomorrow morning. I'll go down to Manitou."

A silence.

"I feel like crying too, you know," Lisa said very softly.

"I know."

"I love you."

He didn't answer.

"Don't be too angry at Papa and Mama."

"All right, I won't."

"When I first heard, I had the same reaction they did. I was furious with Jon."

"I understand."

He hung up. The second dog—his name was Tige and his pal's Rover, from the names of two characters in Clifford Simak's novel *City*—also came over to be petted. Matthew went back into the dining room and then, changing his mind, went back out to the cold greenhouse. He sat down in the wooden armchair that afforded a panoramic view of the entire valley. He spent the remainder of the afternoon there, and watched night fall. The lights of Colorado Springs managed to penetrate the smog here and there. There was even a vague halo of reddish brightness in the northwest, which might well have been Denver.

He didn't decide to write till much later, around two o'clock in the morning.

In 1874 the first of the Kinkairds to arrive in Colorado was a widower of ten years standing with three children, one of whom was Matthew's father. The widower married again, the daughter of a Scottish businessman who had come to the American West to oversee the investments of his friends in Edinburgh. The second Mrs. Kinkaird, who had no children of her own, did have a niece, however, and this niece, Nancy, had married an Indochina planter named Pierre Lara. There was thus no blood relationship between the Kinkairds and the Laras.

The following day, April 4, 1969, Matthew Kinkaird sent two letters off from Manitou Springs. The first contained a certified check for $22,000 made out to Lisa Kinkaird-Trenton, leaving Matthew only $10,630 in his bank account.

The second letter bore an address in French, copied word for word from the one left by Lara eleven years before when he had spent a short time in Colorado: *Monsieur Lara, Boîte Postale 424, Phnom Penh, Cambodge.*

This second letter was a shot in the dark. Matthew had no idea whether the old address was still the right one. At the time he sent it, he had had no news of Lara for nine years. For all he knew, Lara might be dead or have long since left Cambodia.

3

SEVEN DAYS LATER, AT TWO O'CLOCK IN THE AFTERNOON, A Frenchman by the name of Roger Bouès opened his eyes, and in the very next second was persuaded once again that life was worth living. That is to say, he was persuaded of this in the same way that a person talks himself into buying a secondhand car: "Let's be frank, I still have my doubts," he said aloud. He gazed at the ceiling above his bed. From the floors below came the muffled sound of feet stamping in time with an earsplitting rendition of the immortal *"Cerisiers roses et pommiers blancs"* in its Sino-Koreo-Filipino-Japanese version blaring out of a half-dozen loudspeakers aimed directly at the street; this was the most definitive sign that the evening showing at the movie theater was just about to begin, in two or three hours at most. The Phnom Penh Cinema Lux was located at the corner of the Rue Dekcho-Damdin and the Boulevard Norodom; it had made a specialty of showing Indian films, which more often than not featured a fat Tarzan with a drooping chest who triumphed over a tiger only slightly smaller than a bus, his one aim being to save a heroine in jodhpurs and a blond wig.

Roger Bouès lived on the single floor above the movie house auditorium and his entire apartment consisted of just one room, though admittedly this one room was 150 feet long by 30 feet wide. His combination kitchen and bathroom was directly above the projection booth, with the same dimensions and even the same three round holes in the partition. A pure flight of fancy on the part of the architect, this architect being none other than Roger Bouès himself.

He was not an architect swamped with work, and this day promised to be like all the others: He had nothing in particular to do, except keep an appointment he'd made to meet someone, and in fact he hadn't yet decided whether or not he'd show up for it. Not that he never worked; as it happened, he did so several days a year, when the rising tide of his debts reached a figure that triggered off a disaster alert. He would then mount a counterattack on his laziness and dash off plans for a villa or the interior of a movie theater, a store even, whatever. His imagination would run wild; he would invent the most outlandish shapes and forms, and since his most important clients were Chinese, he mixed and contrasted colors with sly, deliberate spitefulness, until the garish results seemed frightful to him. At times, he carried his masochism to such an extreme as to visit a work site to see the result of the mad fantasies he had set down on paper. But most of the time he wisely refrained from doing so. Often people did not pay the fees due him, or else payment came his way as slowly as a desert caravan. This did not upset him terribly, and through an ingenious system of mental bookkeeping, he balanced the sums owed him against those he himself owed; having thus applied the principle of interchangeable creditors, he considered the problem resolved.

He got up out of bed. He was around forty, with the big eyes, the greedy mouth, the pointed nose, the thin mustache of Gascons. Wrapped in a light bathrobe, he looked like a musketeer who had found himself in the kitchen of a convent. On a shelf in his tiny kitchen he came across three plain Petit-Brun cookies and a bit of powder in the bottom of an old tin of Nescafé. He was making his breakfast when suddenly he became aware of a presence behind him. He turned and recognized Ieng Samboth.

"How the devil did you get in here?"

"By way of the roof and your balcony."

"You could have knocked at the door."

"With that music blaring down below, you wouldn't have heard anything anyway," Ieng answered with a shrug.

And it was true that the two men almost had to shout to make themselves heard. Roger contemplated the Nescafé powder in the bottom of the tin.

"There's probably enough for two cups. Would you like some?"

Ieng nodded, his mind elsewhere. He looked worn out. *What could have brought him to my place?* Roger wondered. The last time he'd heard anything about Ieng had been several months before, when the rumor had gone around that after Ieng—deputy to the Sangkum, the Khmer National Assembly—had been arrested by Lon Nol's police, he had managed to escape, though how he had done so and what had happened afterward had remained more or less a mystery. Some people had even claimed that Ieng and his companions, Khieu Samphan, Hu Nim, and Hou Yuon, had been executed. In any event, Ieng and Roger Bouès had never been particularly close friends.

"I thought you were in prison," Roger said. "Or dead. Or at the very least being sought by the police and strolling pensively about the impenetrable Khmer jungle."

"I'm still being searched for by the police."

"Thanks a lot for coming to my place," Roger said sarcastically. "As a matter of fact, I've always wanted to decorate the prison."

The kettle on the electric hot plate began to whistle and steam. Ieng turned on his heel and, stepping out of the doorway of the kitchen-bathroom, went back into the vast main room. This room had few furnishings, only a camp cot, a pile of foam-rubber cushions, a large plywood panel on sawhorses which Roger used as a drafting table, and two wooden crates that served as wardrobe chests; some thirty bottles, almost all of them empty, were lined up in one corner. But on a black marble base, in the heart of this desert, stood a stone Apsaras* of truly breathtaking grace and beauty.

Ieng sat down on the camp cot. After a moment, Roger joined him, bringing the two cups of Nescafé and the three cookies.

"Are you hungry?"

Ieng refused a cookie with a shake of his head.

"May I ask why it is you've come here?"

"Well, I can't just walk around the city streets," Ieng said. "I'd be recognized."

When he spoke French, he pronounced certain words with the trace of

* In Hindu mythology, a celestial water nymph or a dancer in Indra's heaven

a Parisian, almost working-class, accent, like many Indochinese who had
lived for a long time in France, particularly in Paris.

"Are you planning to stay at my place very long?"

"I'll be leaving tonight."

Roger nodded, absorbed in complicated mental calculations. *Let's see,
I smoked the last cigarette for yesterday this morning at around four-thirty,
just before leaving the Saint-Hubert. It's now two-fifteen in the afternoon. If
I don't have another cigarette besides the one I'm going to smoke right now,
I'll have nine left for the evening.* He'd made it a rule not to smoke more
than ten a day and discovered to his satisfaction that his getting up two
hours later than usual had put him one up on his timetable. (Naturally, he'd
never managed to come even close to following that.) He lit a Bastos and
asked, "And who was it who told you how to get into my apartment by way
of the roof?"

"Lara."

"Ah, I see," Roger said.

If anyone had told Roger Bouès that Lara had just left with two or
three men to conquer China and incidentally to reannex Tonkin on his way
there, Roger would have packed his bags immediately and gone to wait for
him in Peking.

"When did you last see Lara?"

"A couple of days ago."

"Is he all right?"

"Yes."

"And where did you see him?"

Ieng Samboth (in Khmer his first name was his family name) leaned the
back of his head with its long, glistening black hair against the white wall.
He closed his eyes. Thus silhouetted his face had a youthful look that Roger
had rarely seen. (*He must be thirty-seven or thirty-eight, if I remember
rightly.*) Something about Ieng had always troubled Roger, a sort of deadly
seriousness. He searched for the right word. *Fanaticism?*

"I'm going to take a shower," Roger said aloud. "Would you like to get
some sleep? It seems to me you're in bad need of some."

The loudspeakers in the street were now letting out hurricane blasts of
Chinese music. Under the warm shower, Roger began to sing at the top of
his lungs, counterattacking the cymbals and gongs with a rendition of *"Le
Temps des cerises."* But his heart wasn't in it. He was bothered by what he
had inferred about the secret complicity between Lara and the leftist ex-
deputy who'd been forced out of Parliament. *Lara even explained to Ieng
how to get into my apartment without knocking.* An image of the two men
scheming together somewhere in the forest, the many rumors about Lara
that had circulated in the past, and the even more numerous ones that had
been going around recently came forcibly to mind, with a sudden ring of

truth that they had never had before. It was an open secret that rubber planters had long been paying a tenth of their profits to the Viet Cong in Vietnam, and now in the southeast of Cambodia as well. Lara had been said to be one of those who were paying the Viet Cong off, even though his plantation was in the north and a very small-scale operation. But worse things still were being said about Lara; people were surprised at his peculiar and persistent immunity in a region into which very few people ventured, a region where anything could happen. *Come off it*, Roger thought to himself, *Lara's old enough to know what he should do*. He turned the shower water off.

"I'm going out, Ieng," he called. "I've got an appointment in Sihanoukville. Don't you want to leave here with me?"

No answer.

"Ieng?"

He got dressed, put on one of his wide-collared white starched shirts that he had delivered to him by the dozen and scrupulously forgot to pay for. He came out of the bathroom. Lying on the narrow cot with his face to the wall, the Khmer was sleeping, or pretending to be asleep.

"Okay, I'm leaving now," Roger said. "There's only one key and I'm taking it with me. If I knock and say it's me, you'll know for certain that it's somebody else. I'll be back very late tonight, or won't be back at all. Thanks for dropping by."

Maybe he's really asleep. All in all, I find his obvious trust in me quite upsetting. I'd even go so far as to say I find it downright offensive. Do I really seem like such a decent sort? He went out the door, double-locking it behind him.

Once outside on the street, he climbed behind the wheel of his car, an ancient sky-blue and white Studebaker station wagon that he had received as payment for decorating a combination bar and restaurant built by some Chinese on the Avenue Kampuchea Krom. The next fifteen minutes were devoted to the usual formalities: persuading the nearest gas station owner that he was going to pay his long-overdue bill very shortly. He finally got the gas tank filled, after promising to decorate the garage for the owner, an offer that was turned down in desperately forceful terms, if not in terror, when Roger said he was off to Sihanoukville, where a very important building project awaited him.

He decided that the next time he wanted his gas tank filled, he wouldn't *offer* to decorate the garage but threaten to do so.

Before taking to the road, Roger wanted to drop by the post office. It was more of a rite than a necessity; as a matter of fact, he wasn't expecting any mail. His mother, who lived in France somewhere on the banks of the Dordogne, was the only one who might have written him, but he hadn't had a

letter from her for seven or eight years now. He drove by the Banque d'Indochine and its garden courtyard, came out on the square in front of the
Main Post Office, and parallel-parked in front of the terrace of the Taverne.
He got out of the car, exchanged a friendly wave with the French pharma-
cist standing in the doorway of his drugstore, with the Frenchman from the
Auvergne who ran the Taverne, and the man from Lorraine who earned his
living as a male nurse and lived close by. He passed by two Corsicans and a
trio of his compatriots from the Ariège reading a two-week-old copy of
L'Equipe just arrived from Paris. He very nearly went directly into the
Taverne, but at the last second changed his mind and walked across the post
office square that had such a French air about it. He entered the post office
not by way of the main lobby, jam-packed as always with Chinese sending
off parcels to the families they'd left behind in China, but by the little door
on the side of the building. His post office box number was 424, and he
shared it with Lara. There was nothing inside for him, naturally, but there
was a letter for Lara, from the United States. Who the devil could be writing to Lara from Colorado? As he was going out the door, he very nearly
collided with Oreste Marccaggi, who quite plainly was just beginning to
come awake.

"Hey there, Oreste, how goes it? Did you sleep well?" Roger said
cheerily.

They'd run into each other the night before at Pilou's place, the Saint-
Hubert.

"Mrmmff," Oreste answered.

"There's a letter for Lara," Roger said.

The Corsican nodded, and said something like "I'll pick it up for him."
Roger stood in the doorway for a moment before going back outside in the
sun. Oreste nearly bumped into him again on his way out, vaguely nodded
or shook his head, as surly and taciturn as before, got into his Land-Rover
and drove off.

*He's going straight back to the plantation. I wonder where Lara is. I
haven't seen him for days.* Roger was suddenly overcome with pangs of
loneliness. *But where is there to go?* Forgotten images of his childhood
flooded over him, the Palais des Pyrénées in Pau, the basin where they
sailed toy boats, the time he'd fallen into it, to his great terror, and been
fished out with one hand by his father, who was laughing beneath his mustache. The father who had committed suicide in 1944. *And little Roger
leaving all by himself for Indochina on the great ocean liner. Stop this, you
idiot.* He went back to his car, cast a hesitant glance inside the dark main
room of the Taverne but didn't go in. Instead, he got back behind the wheel
and set out for Kompong Som, also called Sihanoukville, especially by Sihanouk.

✲   ✲   ✲

The work site that he had spoken about at the garage actually existed, but it wasn't an important project; the building under construction was just a little one-story villa, scarcely more than a hut. Moreover it was a commission passed on to him out of simple friendship, by Huoth, the Cambodian architect in charge of the overall design of the new casino that Sihanouk had decided to have built.

He followed the Rue Ang Non, turned left into the Boulevard Monivong. From here on out there were now as many Chinese shops as in the Rue Ohier, on the other side of the city. And those that weren't Chinese were Vietnamese. *Where in the world are the Cambodians then?* Roger wondered.

Phnom Penh at that time was a city of 600,000 inhabitants, 400,000 of whom were Chinese or Vietnamese. Moreover, Cambodia was a country without a single city that it could really call its own: The proportion of foreigners and the division of income-producing businesses and wealth were in fact the same, if not even more striking still, in Battambang, Kompong Cham, Kampot, Kompong Chhnang, Pursat, Kompong Thom, Takeo, or Prey Veng. The only typically Khmer city was Angkor Thom. But it was no longer a city, for it had been deserted and abandoned for centuries and the only men capable of interpreting its past were not Cambodians but the archaeologists of the École Française d'Extrême-Orient.*

In order to reach the shores of the Gulf of Siam, Roger Bouès had a choice between two roads: the one by way of Kompong Speu which was known as the American Highway because it had been built by the American aid mission ten years before, or the older road to the south which passed through Kampot and its famous pepper plantations. Roger chose to take the southern route. He drove along slowly.

Cambodia was a country at one and the same time rotten to the core and incredibly easygoing with sudden flare-ups of raging cruelty, a place where it was impossible to die of hunger unless one deliberately chose to do so, and hence a country that was a rare exception in Asia. The political system was based on a vaguely hereditary monarchy, plus a vast amount of graft and corruption. At its head, Samdech Euv, His Lordship-Our-Father, Monseigneur-Père, whose domestic as well as foreign policy were resolutely neutralist, out of both selfish motives and sincere inclination. That is to say, his foreign policy was aimed at counterbalancing Soviet, American, Chinese, and French pressures, while within the country he played off against each other the antagonisms of left and right, hatreds and special interests, cleverly maintaining an overall equilibrium and experiencing obvious plea-

* The French School of Far Eastern Studies, an institute under the patronage of the Paris Institut de France, for the study of Indochinese art, history, and language, formerly based in Hanoi

sure in so doing, dancing on a tightrope like a high-wire artist convinced that he would never fall.

Roger had been on the road for an hour now.

When you came right down to it, a purebred Cambodian in Cambodia couldn't be anything but a prince or a pedicab boy. There was nothing between the two. No middle class, except if you were of Chinese descent like Lon Nol, or Vietnamese like many another. On the other hand, there were cliques, at least four important ones: that of the Queen Mother, that of the military, that of the bankers and bigwig Chinese businessmen, and finally that of Samdech Euv's own wife. The cliques fought among themselves for control of the primary sources of revenue: the managing of nationalized business enterprises; the control of public markets or private firms headed by insiders from their clique; traffic in gold, foreign currency, precious stones for Païlin close to the Thai border, rice, opium; protection rackets putting the bite on stores and nightclubs; misappropriation of foreign aid funds; control of the arms traffic going to Viet Cong units set up in Cambodia, of gambling dens and casinos, of prostitution.

Roger was approaching Kampot. To get to Kompong Som/Sihanoukville, Roger should have gone straight on. Without even being aware that he had made a decision, he turned left, in the direction of the beaches of Kep, where a few years before he had designed and built a rotunda-style combination bar and restaurant. From one end of Cambodia to the other, there were thus striking proofs—very striking proofs in fact—that Roger Bouès worked now and then. One day he had even agreed to go up the Mekong to Stung Treng—twenty hours by steam launch and twenty hours back— just to design the plans for an annex to the local high school. He had only dim memories now of this expedition to the north; what he remembered best was meeting men of the high plateaus carrying woven baskets on their backs, bristling with lances and crossbows, looking a little like naked black Santa Clauses. There was something disturbingly furtive and animallike about them as they walked the streets—or rather the street (there was only one main drag in Stung Treng)—stopping to stare at a bicycle with the faces of Stone Age men suddenly breaking through a five-thousand-year time barrier.

Ieng Samboth was from Stung Treng. He had a master's degree in economics and history, but he had been born and had spent part of his youth among men such as these.

The beach of Kep and palm trees with trunks permanently slanted by the winds appeared within the rectangle of the windshield, sea-smells swirled in through the rolled-down windows of the Studebaker. Roger was overcome by a sudden sharp, almost painful rush of happiness. He adored Kep, especially as it was just now, almost deserted, swept by the warm monsoon wind from the southwest. He passed the rotunda-bar he had designed and drove along the road at the edge of the beach. Perched at the

very top of a steep sloping lawn was the bungalow, valiantly trying to resemble a grand hotel but probably empty, as it almost always was. Kep was
a seaside resort that nobody ever went to. The Westerners in Phnom Penh
preferred the pool at the Club Sportif or water-skiing on the Mekong. Occasionally a family of Cambodian government employees ventured there on
a Sunday, gravely pretending to be vacationing at Saint-Tropez; but invariably they soon fled, overwhelmed by the silence and the feeling that they
were not at home there, in either time or space.

Roger parked in front of a restaurant run by Chinese. On its menu were
stuffed crabs flamed in cognac. Roger gave his order to the impassive-faced
waiter drowsing under the arbor.

"Is way to eat in half-hour?" he asked.

"Is way," the Chinese replied laconically.

Roger got a pair of swimming trunks out of the back of the Studebaker.
A minute later he was floating on his back in the Gulf of Siam, facing the
open water, contemplating the familiar silhouette of the Vietnamese island
of Phu Quoc straight ahead of him. Ieng Samboth. And Lara. Why the devil
couldn't he think of anything else? For a minute, he made himself think of
nothing but Huoth, his architect colleague who had no doubt been waiting
for him in Sihanoukville for at least an hour. He almost managed to feel a
slight twinge of guilt. Ieng's face silhouetted against the white wall nonetheless continued to prey on his mind.

Ieng had left his native province for Phnom Penh at a very early age;
he had gone to secondary school at the Lycée Descartes—in all probability,
Roger was convinced, thanks to the financial aid of Pierre Lara. Once Ieng
had obtained his *baccalauréat* from the *lycée,* he had left for France, where
he'd studied first in Montpellier and then in Paris for seven or eight years.
Returning to Cambodia with his degrees, he had systematically turned
down all the posts offered him in various ministries and for a time had
even gone back to Stung Treng, where he had worked as a humble schoolteacher.

Then the 1966 elections had come along. These were not ordinary
elections: For the first time, out of one of those bursts of vanity, Sihanouk
had decided not to intervene in the choice of candidates. Using the argument that the country's only political party—the Sangkum Reastr Niyum,
of which he was the head—represented every possible political tendency,
he had up until then always selected the future deputies himself, in order,
he had explained, to maintain the proper balance between the left and the
right. But in 1966 he had suddenly decided to allow anyone who so desired
to be a candidate. This *reductio ad absurdum* merely proved that he had
been right all along. Business circles and the army had joyously greeted this
decision and gone to work with a will, putting pressure on voters or, failing
all else, buying votes. As a result only four leftist deputies had managed to
get around this formidable barrier: Hou Yuon, Hu Nim, Khieu Samphan,

and Ieng Samboth. Their parliamentary immunity hadn't lasted long. Hunted down by the police on all sorts of pretexts, the four men had disappeared.

The water of the Gulf of Siam was marvelously warm. Roger lay floating on his back. He was remarkably good at this and was of the opinion that his closest rival at this particular feat of skill was surely in Australia, if not even farther away. Lara didn't know how to float on his back; he'd never been able to do so, despite the fact that he was an excellent swimmer, and Roger had been delighted to discover that there was one thing at least that he could do better than Lara.

Moving his hands very slowly, with his arms straight at his sides, he paddled slowly backwards in the direction of the beach. Soon his shoulders touched the sand. He stood up and began walking toward the Chinese restaurant, where his two crabs ought to be ready by now. He would wash them down with a cognac-and-soda, even though ordinarily he never touched alcohol.

As a matter of fact, on this day in April Roger Bouès had a sudden intuition that some serious development in the country's situation might be in the offing. But for the moment this premonition had no more importance for him than a signal one might glimpse without having any idea of its meaning. He sat himself down underneath the arbor, with no need to. choose a place: He was the only customer and only one table had been set up.

"Monsieur Lara, he not be coming?" the Chinese asked.

"No," Roger answered. "I'm alone."

4   ORESTE MARCCAGGI WAS IN THE HABIT OF GOING TO PHNOM PENH once a month to spend four days in a row, during which time he drank beer. When it came to beer drinking, Oreste's capacity was truly impressive: He was able to down a good hundred bottles a day, even more, and down them he did, neither eating nor sleeping nor even leaving the bar counter except to answer the call of nature. The day that Roger Bouès had met him, he'd just made his monthly rounds to say good-bye to everyone and had hit the road the minute he left the post office. He thus arrived at the plantation that very evening, with the letter from Matthew Kinkaird.

"I remember you," Matthew Kinkaird had written. "And perhaps you remember me. Eleven years ago you came here to Colorado and stayed at my house. Not very long, it's true, and you said very little. Here at my house, you met an eight-year-old boy, my grandson Jon Kinkaird. Jon enlisted in the army to go off to fight in Vietnam. Yesterday I learned that he supposedly killed one of his officers and then deserted. Whatever the real story is, it is more than a month now since he disappeared and the army has informed me that it has no idea what has happened to him. They also claim that he's become a drug addict. I've hesitated to write you. I'm not even certain my letter will reach you, and even less certain that it will be possible for you to do something for Jon. Lisa, Jon's elder sister, who was not in Colorado when you were here, is on her way to Saigon at this very moment. She has money, if that can help any. I haven't spoken to her about you. Hence you are free not to answer me and I will never know whether you have chosen not to reply or whether you simply never received my letter. . . ."

They left at two o'clock in the morning on April 13, 1969, with Kutchaï at the wheel of the Land-Rover and Lara sitting in the seat beside him in a posture that was a habit with him: legs stretched out as far as the seat allowed, hands buried in the pockets of his bush jacket (the collar of which was always turned up, no doubt to conceal the scar made by Kamsa's men on the back of his neck and left shoulder), chin on his chest, and pale blue eyes, reddened by the dust from the crushed red-rock trail, staring into the night.

In this year 1969 Lara was thirty-eight years old. He was dark-haired, a little above average height, very thin, and seemingly enveloped in a cool reserve, a self composure difficult if not impossible to ruffle. His voice was very soft-pitched and gentle though very serious, and when he spoke he had a particular way of looking straight at the person he was addressing with a thoughtful, attentive expression in his light gray-blue eyes fringed with black eyelashes; he would then tilt his head slightly to one side, and in a gesture that was probably unconscious, the long fingers of his right hand would begin gently to massage the nape of his neck in the place where he had been wounded. He gave the appearance of moving slowly, but this impression was misleading. He was known to be generous, little inclined to confide in others, and above all patient and obstinate. He had been born in Indochina and had lived there all his life; the first of the Laras had landed in Annam with a nephew of Dupleix, in the spring of the year 1785. In addition to French and English, Lara spoke Khmer and Vietnamese fluently and understood the Chinese of Canton and several dialects of the high Cambodian plateaus quite well. He had been married, but his wife, who belonged to a rich Sino-Khmer family in Phnom Penh, had died in childbirth in 1966; they had been married ten years.

Kutchaï and Lara crossed the arroyo on a bridge that had been replaced since the first time Marccaggi had passed over it, emerged from what was real jungle, and drove on for thirty-five kilometers through open forest in the moonlight. They put to flight nightjars and wild peacocks hypnotized by the headlights, awakened as they passed enormous water buffalo wallowing in the yellow mud who stared at them with bloodshot eyes, and a little after three in the morning they arrived at Kompong Thom.

At Kompong Thom the slight stir of light occasioned by the departure of the bus for Phnom Penh had just subsided. But the lights of the market-place were still on, attracting clouds of multicolored moths that made the night air quiver gently. The Land-Rover made a quick stop, just time enough for an iced coffee, and then they took to the road again. Half an hour later, they caught up with and passed the Chinese bus; it had been slowed down by the countless stops it made, but after each of them it lighted out again in a suicidal burst of fury. It was an amazing contraption, the odometer of which would most likely have shown 300,000 or 400,000 kilometers if by chance it still worked; an unbelievably beat-up, wobbly old rattletrap, originally meant to hold thirty-two passengers but carrying at least seventy, not counting the dozen nonpaying passengers who had been allowed to hitch a ride clinging to the bales of rubber piled on the roof, along with a number of live chickens and various pieces of baggage. Towering twenty or twenty-five feet above the road with this vertical ac-cumulation of impedimenta and leaning far over to one side, the vehicle nonetheless hurtled along at close to sixty miles an hour, a veritable bomb that every so often ended up in a rice paddy, to the uncontrollable hilarity of all hands aboard.

At four A.M. Lara and Kutchaï crossed the Tonle Sap on the Prek Dam ferryboat. At four-thirty they reached Phnom Penh. Mueller, a Swiss liquor salesman who was just going home to bed after a business discussion at the Zigzag spied them around five o'clock in the Old Market, standing at a stall eating a bowl of Chinese soup. He exchanged a few words with them, ask-ing them what the hell they were doing that far away from the plantation, in Phnom Penh at such an ungodly hour.

Kutchaï's enormous spatulate index finger poked him in the chest.

"We're fed up with their fucking Vietnam war," Kutchaï said. "All those bombs exploding keep us from sleeping. We're going over to tell them to cut out the racket."

The Swiss insisted on paying for their Chinese soup. He was a six-foot-six-inch beanpole who, to everyone's utter stupefaction, somehow managed to find room for himself behind the wheel of his Triumph with his knees doubled up to approximately the level of his ears. Mueller was famous throughout Cambodia for having given his microscopic Vietnamese mistress a black eye one day, thanks to a sudden erection he'd had as they were fon-dling each other in the shower. He didn't believe for one second that Lara and Kutchaï were really on their way to Vietnam.

After leaving the market, the two men drove to a little street near the Olympic stadium. Kutchaï stopped the car in front of a two-story stone house. He glanced quickly at Lara; with his hands thrust in the pockets of his bush jacket and the nape of his neck resting on the top edge of the seat, Lara appeared to be asleep.

"I get it," Kutchaï said. "In other words, it's up to me to go in there?"

"And make it snappy," Lara said, yawning but not opening his eyes. "I was the one who went in last time. So it's your turn now."

The Jaraï got out of the car and knocked on the downstairs door. Here, two kilometers from the center of town and the noise of its markets, the night was remarkably quiet, with the exception of the toads offering their usual nocturnal recital. Kutchaï knocked once more, but again there was no answer. He looked at Lara.

"Yep, it's up to you," Lara said, his eyelids still closed.

Kutchaï finally screwed up his courage. He spied an outside stairway on the right side of the building leading to the upstairs floor. He climbed up it and found himself facing a second door. Taking great care not to expose himself in the line of fire bounded by the doorway, he knocked, and then quickly pushed the door open and ducked to one side. He heard the characteristic sound of a Colt .45 going off; a bullet whistled through the air and landed on the other side of the Tonle Sap, or perhaps even the Mekong.

"I'll get every one of you!" a voice cried in French with a strong Alsatian accent. "Every last one of you, you pack of jackals!"

Kutchaï sat down, huddled against the wall for cover. "You idiot from the Mekong," he said. "Get a move on and bring your parachute. We're going for a plane ride."

Boudin was a Frenchman who had for obscure reasons been nicknamed the Strasbourg Sausage. Employed as a chief mechanic by Royal Cambodian Airlines, he piloted a Cessna in his spare time for anyone willing to pay for his services. A man scarcely taller than a barstool, he had a very nasty temper most of the time, and the rest of the time he was in a foul mood. A few years earlier, during an argument after he'd had a lot to drink, he had bitten off and swallowed in one bite the first joint of the index finger that his adversary had pointed at him.

"You're going to kill somebody some day," Lara said to him in the Land-Rover, which was now heading for Pochentong Airport.

"There's nothing I'd like better," snarled Boudin. "And where is it you want to go?"

"To Saigon," Lara answered. "Via Bangkok. Unless, that is, you want to take the risk of landing at Tan Son Hut without authorization."

"A guy would have to be nuts to do that," Boudin said.

"Well, you're nuts," Lara said quietly.

"That's quite true," Boudin acknowledged.

"Well, we'll go by way of Bangkok nonetheless."

Lara was the one who, twelve years before, had found Boudin his job at Royal Cambodian Airlines, and it was also Lara who had advanced him the money to buy the old Cessna. Lara was the one person in the world who could tell Boudin to his face that he was a madman without setting off an explosion.

They arrived at Pochentong just as dawn was breaking and drove straight to the hangar where the Cessna was parked. As the Alsatian was making his flight check, a jeep drove up with a Cambodian in a captain's uniform behind the wheel. The officer braked to a stop, tires squealing, and spied Lara.

"What the hell are you doing here at this ungodly hour?"

"A business trip," Lara answered.

"Are you really going to take off in that junkheap?"

"What's that he said?" Boudin roared, raising his head from the engine, his eyes almost bulging out of their sockets.

"Yes, that's precisely what we're about to do: We're going to take off in this junkheap."

"You're out of your minds," said the captain.

Captain Kao was in charge of airport security; in other words, it was his own particular racket, exercised in the name of the queen. He and Lara had known each other for years but had never really been on friendly terms.

"Out of your minds," Captain Kao repeated. "Utterly out of your minds."

Kutchaï burst out laughing. When Kutchaï laughed, he first grinned literally from ear to ear, baring at least thirty-two gleaming white, perfectly spaced, perfectly aligned teeth suggestive of a wolf trap; there then followed a visible burst of light-hearted, gay laughter, marked by an increasingly fierce, intense joviality, though not one sound came from his lips. Despite Kutchaï's amazing mastery of French, there was something savage and animallike about him, and his silent laugh was most disturbing, especially in view of the fact that he ordinarily used it to express some violent emotion, such as rage.

"Tell him not to look at me like that," Kao said to Lara.

"Stop looking at him like that," Lara said to Kutchaï.

A sudden silence fell. As Boudin maintained that he wouldn't be ready to take off for another twenty minutes yet, Kao, perhaps to break the tension, invited Lara and Kutchaï to come have a drink with him. They climbed into the jeep and went off to the airport bar, which at this hour was normally closed but which Kao opened just for them by kicking ass here and there.

"How's Oreste these days?" Kao asked.

"He's showing his age," Lara replied.

"That depends on the day you meet up with him," chimed in Kutchaï, who worshiped the Corsican. "He's still capable of killing a captain of the Cambodian police with one blow."

Kao chose to pretend he hadn't heard.

"He's well over seventy, isn't he?"

"He's not all that old," Lara answered with a smile.

They downed their first cognac-and-soda of the day.

"And how are things at the plantation?" Kao asked. "The Khmer Rouge aren't making trouble for you?"

"What Khmer Rouge?" Kutchaï replied, laughing.

"There's your answer," Lara said, his pale eyes never leaving Kao.

They ordered three more cognac-and-sodas, with Lara paying for this second round.

"I can't stop you from taking off in that crate of Boudin's."

"Well then, don't stop us."

"You're perfectly free to crash into a rice paddy if you like. That would at least rid Cambodia of a madman." He pointed his finger at Kutchaï.

"Not possible kill Kutchaï, miselable Khmel wletch," Kutchaï said. "Kutchaï immoltal Khmel wletch."

They emptied their glasses and went back to join Boudin. A few minutes later they spied, below the silver wings of the Cessna, the neat checkerboard squares of jade-colored rice paddies and ocher embankments, and the graceful shadows of palm trees lengthened by the rising sun. Boudin flew two or three furious passes a few inches above Kao's head as he stood alongside his black-painted jeep. "A junkheap!" Boudin was foaming with rage. Then, having vented his spleen, he headed northwest. The forest soon appeared, encircling the temples of Oudong, the former capital of the kingdom and a royal burial site. Then, to the left of the plane, there loomed up the great masses of the Kirirom, and then of the Cardamome Range forming a barrier more than 4,500 feet high in places, uniformly covered with a dark green sea of trees and separating the flood plains of the Tonle Sap and the Mekong, to the east, from the coast of the Gulf of Siam.

They flew over Battambang, leaving Siem Reap and Angkor far behind in the distance to their right.

"We'll be in Bangkok in nine hours," Boudin cried, as though this fact personally filled him with fury. "And you'll be there in time to catch the plane to Saigon. Unless the Saigon plane crashes en route." He plainly hoped for some such catastrophic turn of events.

The sky was perfectly clear, almost unreal, as always in the first light of dawn. There would come a moment, however, when the air would begin to quiver in the heat; the light would then become diffuse, stagnant, etching the least shadows in an acid whiteness.

"The last one to get to the Continental pays for drinks," Kutchaï said.

Lara nodded, his heart suddenly gripped by his inordinate love for this country. Few men had loved or still loved Cambodia as much as he did; fewer still were as capable as he of surviving any event the future might bring. And not a one of them was as fiercely determined to stay in the country no matter what happened.

5

LISA KINKAIRD TRENTON HAD BEEN IN SAIGON ONE DAY. A WEEK earlier she had informed her grandfather, Matthew Kinkaird, of her intention to leave for Vietnam. Since that telephone call, she hadn't wasted a single minute.

She had begun her investigation by visiting the editorial offices of *The Washington Post*, where her husband's many friends clearly hadn't forgotten her. She had been given access to the paper's back files and for an entire day two journalists had briefed her on desertions by American Army personnel in Vietnam.

The Department of State then, and after that the Pentagon, each time with the necessary introductions. She had devoted another entire day to these two visits.

On the third day, she arrived in Paris in time for lunch with another journalist, a French one this time, who had done his best to sum up for her in four hours everything that he had learned in twenty-five years about Vietnam, Saigon, and the war that had begun in 1945 and, practically speaking, had gone on without letup ever since.

The following day she flew to Tokyo. She had spent only five hours in all in the Japanese capital, just long enough to question an officer of the Americal Division, who had personally known the lieutenant whom Jon Kinkaird was accused of having killed. "What in the world is the use of raking up that whole affair again? It's already past history. It happened in other places besides Anh Khé and it could have just as well happened to me. Ricket had chewed his men out because he found them asleep and because they were high on drugs. He left the bunker and got blown up with a hand grenade. They don't even know who threw it. Three of the men who were in the bunker at the time are dead now, and two others have deserted. Let me give you a piece of advice: Forget the whole thing. Let it drop."

Then she had made a final stop in Korea, where she had gone to Camp Casey, near Seoul. She had spoken with two wounded veterans there, one who'd had both legs amputated and the other one blind, and both of whom remembered Jon Kinkaird. But neither of them had the least idea where he might possibly be, nor the least name to suggest to her, nor the least clue, nor, quite obviously, the least desire to talk any more about the entire matter.

And then at last Saigon. And facing her a foreign service officer at the U.S. Embassy in Vietnam, an impeccably dressed functionary named Gaitskell, blond and tidy, in a clean and no less tidy office, so efficiently air-conditioned that it was freezing cold.

"Mrs. Trenton? I knew a Robert Trenton who was with *The Washington Post.*"

"He was my husband. He's no longer alive."

"I'm terribly sorry," he said. "He was a remarkable man."

"He's been dead for five years."

Gaitskell stared at her almost open-mouthed, fascinated by her eyes, by what he could see of her legs, by the open neck of her well-filled blouse.

"And you too are a journalist, like your husband?"

"Yes," she said, and added, "Not for *The Washington Post.*" She told him she worked for United Press and for a weekly on the West Coast. And that was true, though it was not the whole truth: She really had been accredited by UPI, but it had been agreed that she was to pay all of her own expenses. She explained the subject of the story she'd come to Vietnam to do. The effect of this revelation was spectacular: Gaitskell's face froze. The second before, he had quite clearly been on the point of inviting her to dinner, but now he was wondering if that was really such a good idea, no matter how strikingly beautiful this young woman was.

"Deserters? What an extraordinary idea! We don't have any deserters." He gave her a kindly smile that was just a touch condescending. She was only a woman, after all.

"Believe me, Mrs. Trenton, all the boys who are here know why they're here. They do good work, really good work. I can assure you that every American soldier is fiercely eager to fight."

Lisa rose from her chair, stubbing out her cigarette in the crystal ashtray.

"Thank you for receiving me," she said curtly.

She walked toward the door as Gaitskell hurried to open it for her.

"Have you just arrived in Saigon?"

And now he was going to invite her to have dinner with him. She looked him up and down almost in fury, but merely replied: "Yes, I've just arrived." She went out the door and he walked side by side with her down the hall, surprised at how tall she was.

"May I drop by at dinnertime? Could we at least have a drink together?"

She didn't even turn her head but left the embassy.

The man she met next was a colonel on the staff of the commander in chief of the American forces in Vietnam. This one was a jovial Texan. With the aid of a wall map with little multicolored flags stuck all over it, he demonstrated to her that there was absolutely no question that the war was already won. "All the last tricks are ours." The bridge term pleased him and he repeated it.

"Deserters? Where could deserters go?" He led her back over to the map. She should think about it for a minute: Where would deserters go? Was there any use in their trying to swim across the China Sea or the Gulf

of Siam? Or in their lighting out for Thailand on foot all the way across a
Cambodia that as everyone knew was in the hands of the Viet Cong, who
were pulling the strings of a puppet prince? "A man doesn't desert in
Vietnam, Mrs. Trenton. For the very simple reason that there's no possibility of doing so. Physically, geographically, I mean. Except for a few hotheads . . ."

"Exactly," Lisa said. "Those are the men who interest me."

"You're a woman," the colonel said.

"I've noticed," Lisa answered.

The colonel burst out laughing.

"And the prettiest one I've ever even dreamed of meeting. Have you
ever thought of going into the movies? But those hotheads I was speaking to
you about sometimes find a hiding place, a very temporary one, naturally,
in one of those establishments . . ." He was obviously searching for the
proper word.

"Brothels you mean?" Lisa asked.

Another peal of laughter, but then the colonel said in a paternal tone of
voice, "I hope you're not thinking of visiting them one by one."

"Who checks up on them? The American Military Police?"

"We're in a foreign country. It's up to the Vietnamese police. In close
collaboration, naturally, with our M.P.'s."

"I'd like the name of the Vietnamese police officer directly in charge of
inspecting them," Lisa said.

She was not only the most attractive young lady he'd ever met but also
the most persistent, he said. But he finally gave in. He mentioned a name to
her, gave in again when she pressed him to telephone to ask Monsieur
Dieu—"His name is really Dieu"; did she know that Dieu meant God in
French? Yes, she knew that—to ask Monsieur Dieu to see her.

Lisa then took from her purse a sheet of 8½- by 11-inch paper folded
in two and handed it to the colonel.

"I have five names here that were given to me in Washington. I know
the families of these five men; in each case, I've visited either their parents
or their wives. I'd like to know what's become of them. All five of them are
officially listed as AWOL—that is to say, deserters.* May I ask you to make
a special inquiry into the case of these five men?"

He promised, after she had made it a point to mention that she had

---

* According to Army regulations, an American soldier is not considered to be a deserter
until he has been absent without leave for thirty days. Desertion is a crime which may lead
to the death penalty in wartime if a court-martial decides, beyond all reasonable doubt,
that the serviceman listed as absent without leave had the firm intention of not returning to
his unit, regardless of the length of time that he has been AWOL. The official figures of the
Department of Defense are: Out of the 7,575,000 men liable for service or having served in
Vietnam, a total of 1,522,000 were at some time absent without leave; of this number
563,000 were considered to be deserters. Only 24 deserters were actually court-martialed.
No American serviceman was sentenced to death for desertion.

known through her husband, and still knew, the chief editors of *The Washington Post*, former Secretary of State Dean Rusk, and at least a dozen senators. This was blackmail, and she didn't even bother to hide the fact that it was.

The colonel read the names: John Paul Petit, Jon Kinkaird, Johnny Dee Williams, Harry Watson, Larry Menendez. Williams and Watson were blacks, the former from New York and the latter from Montgomery, Alabama; Menendez was a Chicano from New Mexico; Petit was from Louisiana; and Kinkaird came from San Francisco. Had she noticed that of these five men only two were Whites, and of these two Petit had a French name and could well be a Cajun? Yes, she had noticed. No, she was not free for dinner.

"I'm going to have a copy made of your list," the colonel said. His joviality had vanished little by little in the course of their interview.

"Keep it," Lisa said. "I have other copies. I'll come by to see you in forty-eight hours."

"I'll need more time than that."

Lisa smiled, her eyes cold.

"In forty-eight hours."

Outside, the stifling, humid heat made her stagger, as well as the veritable wall of smells topped off by the stink of exhaust fumes hovering in the air in a blue haze. She took a few steps along the sidewalk, and was immediately assailed by hordes of urchins, beggars of all sorts, pedicab operators, and taxi drivers. She looked at her watch, still set at New York time: a little after five A.M. Retracing her steps, she asked one of the Marine guards stationed by the embassy door what time it was: 12:10 P.M. Her meeting with the Vietnamese police official was scheduled for two o'clock the following afternoon. She climbed into a taxi and asked to be driven to the Continental Hotel, which had been suggested to her by a journalist she'd met in Paris: "Either there or at the Majestic, you'll be most likely to run into one or another of my colleagues who may be able to help you." He'd given her the names of some of them, the majority of them French. "If they're there."

Nothing in her room was working: There was no electricity for the moment, she was told. Nothing worked, that is, except the shower. She stayed under the warm water for a long time, not caring whether she got her hair wet or not (she always did her hair herself, almost indifferently), then stretched out naked on the bed, trying without success to sleep. She had dried off in just a few minutes, so she got back under the shower, and when she returned to the bedroom she began to count how much money she had. She expected to have to pay off the Vietnamese police officer, or one of his subordinates, or other men and women. She had $25,600 in all, plus around 100 French francs that she'd forgotten to change as she left Paris. And her plane ticket. On leaving New York she'd drawn out all the money she had in her bank account, just over $1,800, and had added to it the

$22,000 she'd received from her grandfather, plus $2,500 from the quick sale of her car. She mechanically spread the bills out on the bed in a checkerboard pattern. She had $25,000 to find Jon, and the remaining $600 would be more than enough to get her back to New York. She had no idea of what prices were like in Vietnam; she didn't even know how much the room she was occupying cost per day.

She was suddenly aware that she was being watched. She raised her eyes and saw a man's face peering through the transom of the door leading to the hall. She got up from the bed immediately, paying no attention to the fact that she was still naked. She walked hurriedly to the door, turned the key, opened it, and found herself face to face with one of the hotel boys, who had not even been quick-witted enough to hop down off the stool he was standing on.

"Go away," she said. "*Allez-vous-en!*"

He fled down the hall, dragging the stool behind him, bowing the while but keeping his eyes firmly fixed on her breasts. She finally closed the door and leaned her back against it, fighting down the rage that was making her shake from head to foot and the sudden urge to burst into tears. Later, just before she fell asleep, she wondered which had first caught the Peeping Tom's eye: the money spread out on the bed or her naked body.

"I'm sorry," Dieu said. "There's nothing I can do."

He was short and gave the appearance of being fat—that is to say, he had a round face and pudgy hands. At the very beginning of their conversation, when he was standing, he had seemed thin and nervous, but he was calm now and staring with an amused smile at the tall American woman sitting opposite him.

"We're a country at war, Madame Trenton, and I'm a very busy man. Moreover, deserters from the American Army aren't within my province, unless of course they break the laws of this country."

With his fingernail he flicked the sheet of paper with Jon Kinkaird's name on it along with four others. "To my knowledge, that is not the case with these men," he said.

"They're not being searched for then?"

"Not by my department."

"I'm prepared to offer a monetary reward to anyone who will help me find these men," Lisa said.

He leaned back, resting his elbows on the arms of his chair and delicately placing the fingertips of his two pudgy hands together. He stared at her, smiling, and for the space of a second she felt like getting up and leaving.

"I can go as high as five thousand dollars," she said.

She realized instantly that she had made a terrible blunder. No journalist in the world would be prepared to pay $5,000 for the mere satisfaction of writing a good article on deserters, at a time when there were thousands and thousands of them.

"It would seem that these men are much more important to you than you've been willing to admit thus far," Dieu said quietly.

"Let's say that it's a matter of professional pride with me."

"That's quite understandable," he said, still smiling.

He suddenly sat up straight in his chair again, picked up the paper with the five names from his desk top, and read aloud: "Petit, Kinkaird, Williams, Watson, Menendez. Which one of them, Madame Trenton?"

"I don't understand what you mean."

"Come, come, you understand me perfectly. It's obvious that these five men are not of equal concern to you. Which one is it you really want to know about?"

She looked at him intently, her big violet eyes darkening with anger.

"Please understand me, Madame Trenton. Five deserters among a goodly number of others don't interest me. As I've already told you, I'm a very busy man and my colleagues are swamped with work. However . . ."

He took a pad of paper and a solid gold pen out of a drawer and removed the cap of the pen. ". . . However, being personally of service to a pretty young woman who is looking for her husband is something else again."

"None of these men is my husband."

He shook his head regretfully. "We're wasting time, Madame Trenton. It wouldn't be very difficult for me to discover what you and one of these men have in common. I'm a policeman and I've been one for a long time. I was one in the days when the French were here and I'll be one after your compatriots have gone home. Moreover, I'm the man in the best possible position to have a search made for a man in Vietnam, by persuading certain of my colleagues to put in extra hours on the job."

"Kinkaird," Lisa said, acknowledging that she was beaten and surrendering at the same time. "Jon Kinkaird, my brother."

He nodded, satisfied, and spread his hands apart as if to say, "Isn't it better this way?"

"Would you like to give me a description of him? I presume that you prefer that this inquiry be made discreetly—that is to say, without contacting official agencies of your country?"

"Yes, that's correct," Lisa answered.

She took out of her purse two photographs of Jon, one of him in civilian clothes and the other in uniform, and a written description of him.

"The same color eyes as you?"

"Yes."

Dieu consulted a little memorandum book. "Six feet five inches tall: That would make him around a meter ninety-five. Tall enough to be a basketball player."

"He did play basketball before he went into the service."

"Does he know any other language besides English?"

"Spanish and a little bit of French, very little."

"How about women in his life?"

"No fiancée as far as I know."

"But is he normal?" He bowed his head. "Excuse me."

He compared the two photographs. "What about drugs?"

"No."

She looked him straight in the eye and repeated emphatically, "No."

"When did you last see your brother?"

This time she was taken by surprise. She lowered her head, staring at her trembling fingers.

"Around eight months ago," she finally answered.

They had met each other at the St. Francis on Powell Street. He'd come in to San Francisco from the other side of the bay, and she had arrived two hours before from New York. She'd seen her brother suddenly appear in the full sunlight of the square opposite the hotel, and almost hadn't recognized him after four years' separation. He'd grown like a weed and was extremely tall, walking along with that gait typical of basketball players: long, rather loping strides, as though he were readying himself to leap after a ball and catch it on the rebound at any moment. She could recall the precise feeling she had experienced in that second at the St. Francis: the sensation of being a hundred years old even though she was really only seven years older than he was, and a sense of guilt toward this brother she had left to his own devices for so long.

"How did he happen to come to Vietnam?" Dieu asked.

"He was called up for service."

They'd spent only one day together in San Francisco. Jon was too young to be able to order himself a drink before lunch (Lisa had been struck by that too; her brother was considered old enough to kill or be killed in Vietnam, but at the same time too young to be *legally* served a beer), and they'd gone directly to Kan's, in Chinatown, for lunch—the best way, Jon had said with a laugh, to begin to get acclimated to Asia. All during the meal Jon had been in unusual and almost unbelievably high spirits, launching into hilarious imitations of one or another of his superior officers or wild tales of basketball games, and in any case giving the impression of awaiting his departure for Saigon as the beginning of an exciting adventure. He may well have been putting on an act for her benefit. How would she have been able to tell? The brother she'd known had been a boy of twelve when she married Bob Trenton, and barely fourteen when Bob's plane had crashed.

After leaving the Chinese restaurant, they'd walked back up California Street, and then they'd run the tourist gamut: riding on the steps of a cable car, then down to Fisherman's Wharf, and after that a flight in a helicopter over Alcatraz and the Golden Gate, then wandering about the Cannery and up and down the different levels of Ghirardelli Square admiring the graceful maneuvers of a flotilla of soaring kites. That evening they had wanted to have dinner at Scoma's, but lacking reservations, they'd fallen back on Alioto's. And that night, Lisa had taken her brother back to his base at Oakland, in the car she'd rented when she got off the plane. "In heaven's name," Jon had said, "please don't say you're my sister. Let them think I've won the heart of the prettiest girl in California. They'll all die of jealousy." She went along with the game, smothering him with affectionate caresses beneath the sly gaze of the guards and servicemen on leave coming back to the base and finally giving him a big kiss on the mouth, like a girl friend, which aroused a chorus of admiring whistles and left her standing in a daze, overwhelmed by this fraternal love she had suddenly discovered.

"You haven't answered my question," Dieu said. "Even a humble police officer from Saigon knows very well that most, if not all, of the five hundred thousand U.S. troops who have come to fight in this country have come here because they had to. Even a humble policeman, a slob, a gook, a yellow dog, a slanthead, as your compatriots call us, Madame Trenton, knows that America has mostly sent its niggers and its halfbreeds, its Chicanos and its illiterates here. Your brother wasn't . . ."

"Don't talk about him in the past tense!" She got up, picked up her purse from the table, and walked to the door.

"I'll find him," Dieu said. "No problem."

Lisa's hand was on the door handle, but she didn't turn it.

"If he's still alive," Dieu said.

She stood there stock-still but didn't turn around.

"If your brother's still alive I'll surely find him," Dieu said. "But what do you want me to do after that?"

"I want to talk to him."

"That's all—just talk to him?"

She nodded and finally turned around, lowering her head to hide her tears. Dieu looked at her impassively. After a moment he opened another drawer and took out seven photographs, which he carefully laid out on the top of his desk.

"Look."

She raised her head.

"Come on over here, Madame Trenton. You should see these photos."

She came over to the desk, looked at the photos, and was overcome by a violent wave of nausea that shook her whole body.

"Do kindly excuse me," Dieu said. "These seven men are soldiers from the American Army. Their bodies were found during these last two weeks, four of them in the river and partially devoured by crabs, which explains the state they were found in. They were drug addicts who were robbed and then killed, or else died of an overdose."

She forced herself to lean over and look at the horrible photographs again. She finally straightened up once more, her face pale.

"None of these men is Jon," she said in a dull voice.

He nodded. "I know. But maybe there will be exactly the same sort of photograph of him tomorrow or in days to come."

"I wish I were a man so I could punch you in the nose," Lisa said.

He shrugged. "People have been punching me in the nose, literally and figuratively, for twenty-four years now, Mrs. Trenton."

He put the photos back in the drawer. "Five thousand dollars ob- viously won't be enough. And there are certain outlays I'll be obliged to make immediately."

She had a packet of bills amounting to $5,000 all ready. She laid it alongside the photographs and the list of five names she had given him.

"And what if I find the four others?"

She shrugged, and asked, "When will you have news for me?"

"Where are you staying—at the Continental? There's no point in your coming back here. I'll come by your hotel myself, or rather one of my de- puties will come by."

Once out in the street again, she was incapable for some time of doing any- thing but walking straight ahead, making her way through a moving sea of *ao-dais* and white, yellow, or purple tunics, of men in white shirts and black silk pants or else in shorts and cork helmets, flowing along the sidewalks laid out in little cement squares. The streets were a hell of cars making an ear- splitting racket, and here and there were traces of the fighting that had taken place during the Viet Cong offensive in January and February of the year before, when Saigon very nearly fell.

On the Boulevard Nguyen Hue, without even thinking or knowing where she was, she went into the first bar she saw and sat down on a stool at the counter. It took her about twenty seconds to realize that a sudden si- lence had fallen around her. Raising her head, she spied the prostitutes in miniskirts and the American soldiers gaping at her in embarrassed surprise. A master sergeant walked over to her.

"You shouldn't stay here, ma'am. This is no place for you."

She rummaged about in her purse, fished out a five-dollar bill, and laid it on the counter.

"I'd like a whiskey."

Amid complete silence she downed her drink in one gulp and left. She had taken only a few steps when the master sergeant joined her.

"Your change."

"Buy yourself a drink on me."

She walked off, leaving him standing there on the sidewalk, immediately surrounded by a horde of children who had noticed the bills in his hands and besieged him, like tiny grampuses leaping to attack a whale. Lisa walked on, still paying no attention to where she was going. *The bastard!* she thought to herself. She had no illusions: Dieu would milk her of her very last dollar.

Tiny hands clung to her skirt, begging for money. She freed herself, almost in fright.

By sheer chance she found herself in front of the terrace of the Continental. When she asked for her key at the reception desk, she was told that a man named Lara had come to see her, on behalf of Monsieur Kinkaird. And that he would be back at dinnertime.

It was just after six P.M.

6 HE WAS A CORSICAN FROM SAIGON NAMED JEAN-BAPTISTE MORRA-chini, one of the big-time operators among the Corsicans of Indochina who had landed there in the twenties or thirties to spread the gospel of gambling dens, bars, restaurants, hotels, dance halls, opium, brothels, among the local populace. He had the rather plump belly, the soft, almost feminine eyes, the offhanded way of speaking, of his native Ajaccio. Most any priest would have given him the communion wafer without confession—if only to keep him from helping himself.

He had firm, fast friends and two combination restaurant-dance halls in the Chinese quarter of Cho Lon; and he had very recently sold his interest in one of the largest gambling dens, immediately sending off to Switzerland, via Hong Kong, the million new francs he had thus realized, to be added to the other three million that he had accumulated in thirty years of hard and patient work. He was a man with a minimum of faith in human nature in general and men and women in particular, capable of providing you on a moment's notice with twenty pretty girls or an equal number of pretty boys, a hundred kilos of opium, assault rifles, dynamite, or machine guns. But at the same time he was a man who went to mass each Sunday and was incapable of cheating on his wife, a woman from Tourane who had brought his seven children into the world.

"Stop me if I'm wrong," Jean-Baptiste Morrachini said to Lara, "but all you're asking me to do is simply to find, in the space of a few hours, an American in the midst of hundreds of thousands of others, who's been missing for around forty days now, in a country of a million and a half square kilometers with a population of approximately twenty-six million other people about to smother each other to death, it being understood that the guy you want me to look for may very well be somewhere else entirely, in Outer Mongolia for example, or the suburbs of Stockholm?"

"That's it exactly," Lara said. "You've gotten the whole picture."

"He's out of his mind," Morrachini said to Kutchaï.

Kutchaï nodded with suspect enthusiasm.

"He clazy in the head," Kutchaï said. "Me miselable Khmel wletch, velly nervous. And aside from that, old pal, how are things going with you?"

"Okay," the Corsican answered. "We're packing up to leave."

"I'd be surprised if he's in Outer Mongolia," Lara remarked with a smile.

Morrachini nodded.

"But he may very well be in the suburbs of Stockholm. I've been told that there are quite a few American deserters who've fled to Sweden, where they not only don't extradite them but even look on them as heroes."

"Kinkaird should have left Vietnam. But I don't think he has."

"Some of those dumb bastards just go to Air France and try to fly out of the country. And they get caught."

"That's not what he did. I checked."

"And then there's that sort of Buddhist bonze at Mytho, on the delta, who hides deserters."

"Negative," Kutchaï said. "I've already looked into that possibility."

"The priest at Gia Dinh hasn't seen him either," said Lara. "Or that bunch of French teachers with panties and bras the same colors as the North Vietnamese flag."

Morrachini looked at the two men facing him. "And you just got here early this afternoon? You haven't lost any time."

He looked more closely at Lara, whom he had known since Lara was a little boy, in the days when Pierre and Nancy and their children stayed at the Continental on their trips to Saigon. He remembered a thin, withdrawn little boy who seemed to be lost in a daydream, his pale gray-blue eyes staring almost without blinking at whoever was speaking to him, a child who said very little, almost abnormally quiet for a boy his age, yet with a sweet smile and a friendliness that left you uncertain what to make of him. *And Kutchaï was already with him constantly, if I remember rightly. They've always been together.* Morrachini remembered that it had been Kutchaï who had helped his playmate escape and get out of the forest alive when Kamsa had attacked the plantation.

"For a time there was also that so-called American pacifist group that had organized an underground network to get deserters out of Vietnam. You had to knock on the door of a house near Arroyo Bridge, behind the Quai de Belgique. All the deserters who went there are in the clink now. Behind the door were the Mike Papas, the M.P.'s. But their little trick doesn't work anymore."

Lara took a sip of cognac-and-soda, holding his glass and his cigarette in the same hand. "So then, we know where Kinkaird isn't," he said calmly. "Can you take it from there? Your Chinese friends."

"You've got more Chinese friends than I have," the Corsican said.

"Not the same ones." Lara's tone of voice was polite but firm.

The gangster didn't press the point. "Are you staying in Saigon long?"

"I don't know yet." Lara looked at Kutchaï questioningly, but the Khmer gave a shrug, accompanied by dumb show indicating that he couldn't care less how long they stayed.

"And what if you leave and I have news for you?"

"Call Christiani in Bangkok, and he'll pass the word on." Lara rose to his feet, still holding his glass in his hand.

"Are you sure the two of you won't stay and have dinner here at my place?" Morrachini asked. "Or all three of us go out somewhere together?"

"I have an appointment," Lara answered. There was a thoughtful look in his eyes. "By the way, Kinkaird's sister has been here in Saigon since yesterday or the day before. She's already made the rounds of the American authorities, and even more importantly, she's been to see Dieu, they tell me."

"A dumb idea. Once Dieu gets mixed up in something the whole thing goes wrong—except for him. I've never liked cops in general, but that one is the worst of the lot."

Lara shook hands with the Corsican. "How's Li?"

"She's in Toulon with the three littlest kids. She wrote me again yesterday to tell me she's learning to make bouillabaisse. I fear the worst. She's sure to slip some *nuoc-mam* into it."

Li was Morrachini's wife. She was also a straitlaced Annamese Catholic who looked like a shy little mouse but had a disposition steely enough to knock out an entire armored division. "And she hasn't mellowed the least bit over the years." The Corsican sighed. "In her last letter she ordered me to get my ass back to France within forty-eight hours. But I can't leave just like that. Even though I'd like to . . ."

"And the kids?"

"Pierre and Dany are studying medicine, and Pascale's getting ready to take the *bac* exam. Michel's not doing anything, as usual, and the three others have the measles."

Morrachini accompanied his visitors to the garden gate. He hesitated a moment and then asked, "Do you know this Kinkaird girl?"

"Not yet," Lara answered.

7

AS ALWAYS, ROVER HEARD THE SOUND OF THE CAR ENGINE FIRST. He rose to his feet, and Tige did too. Matthew put the hoe down, walked back through the three conservatories and the house, and saw a man of about thirty-five, very elegantly dressed, standing alongside a black Lincoln.

"Jubal Wynn? I'm Matthew Kinkaird."

The two men shook hands.

"I was hesitant about turning up so early in the morning, but since you assured me that you'd be up at daybreak . . . And being an early riser myself, especially when I'm in the country . . ."

He glanced around him. "You're in a wonderfully quiet spot here."

"Some coffee?"

The two men sat down in front of the fireplace where a fire glowed, filling the entire house with the fragrant smell of burning wood. The peace and quiet of the place seemed incredible to Wynn. "You're at the end of the world," he remarked.

"Yes." Matthew Kinkaird ran his hand through his white hair. "Thanks for coming. And especially for coming so quickly."

"Two days' vacation in Colorado aren't to be sniffed at, even when one lives in San Francisco."

"Did you have a good trip?"

"Wonderful," Jubal Wynn answered.

Wynn lit a Gitane, taking his time. His intelligent brown eyes never left Matthew. "How old are you, Mr. Kinkaird?"

"Seventy."

"Have you traveled a lot in your life?"

"No."

"The boy told me it was his grandfather who had urged him to come see me. You're his grandfather?"

"Yes."

"You didn't think your grandson ought to go fight in Vietnam, is that it?"

"It's a dishonorable war," Matthew said.

Wynn exhaled a cloud of smoke. "You think that the United States ought to tend to its own business and stay home, the way you do here on your mountaintop—is that it?"

"I never said any such thing," Matthew said quietly. He got up to put another log on the fire.

"You asked me to come here for two reasons," Wynn said. "Or at least that's what you told me on the phone. The first reason, it would appear, is this: You'd like me to explain to you why your grandson is now in Vietnam. Am I wrong?"

"No, not at all."

"He spoke to me of his father, a hero of the war in the Pacific and all the rest. I remember that very well. Jon Kinkaird is my only failure, which is sufficient reason for me to remember him. A very tall boy, with amazing eyes, who was a basketball player, I believe? You see? I remember him very well."

"And so he left for Vietnam because of his father?"

"Don't ask me to explain his real reasons," Wynn said with a smile.

Matthew sat down again, gazing into the fire where the log he'd put on was beginning to sputter. "I don't know anything about this business of deferments," he said. "What did you advise Jon to do?"

"Oh, there were any number of solutions. He could have signed up for courses leading to a degree in education, with a ninety-five percent chance of getting a deferment. Or registered as a conscientious objector, or joined the National Guard or the Coast Guard. As a basketball player with a promising future, he would have had no trouble getting a deferment. These were all common ways of getting out of the draft. Does that shock you?"

"Yes."

"You nevertheless sent your grandson to me."

"I know."

The dogs were getting restless, obviously eager to be let out for a run.

"This is the hour of the day when I usually take them out with me," Matthew explained. "How about having lunch with me when I get back?"

"I was hoping you'd invite me," Wynn said.

"Do you know a movie actor by the name of George Hamilton? I saw him recently in a French film with Brigitte Bardot, *Viva Maria.* He wasn't shipped off to Vietnam because he supports his poor old mother, on an annual income of barely two hundred thousand dollars, poor devil. By law, if you have a parent you support who lives with you, that's sufficient cause to exempt you from military service, providing you've got a good lawyer."

Jubal Wynn was walking through the forest, on the slopes of Blodgett, with Matthew. He raised his head and looked about him:

"Let's see if I've got it all straight. We're in Wildcat Gulch; in front of me is Ute Pass and behind me is Devil's Kitchen. Good Lord, the man who invented all those names must surely have come from a New York ad agency!"

He lit another cigarette and went on: "Don't get the idea that I have a personal grudge against George Hamilton. The truth is that after August of 'sixty-four, the date of our military intervention in Vietnam on a grand scale, and generally speaking during the nine years that followed, the number of Americans subject to the draft was around twenty-nine million. Out of these twenty-nine million, twenty-seven million escaped, are escaping, or will escape being sent to Vietnam, in one way or another. And out of these twenty-seven million, sixty percent haven't done or will not do any sort of military service. Either because they're not fit to do so, or above all because they've known of ways to get out of it, or had advisers who did."

"Such as yourself."

"Such as myself."

"What fee do you charge your clients?"

"Five hundred dollars, on the average. Sometimes a thousand, somethings nothing at all. But I don't exactly carry on my practice all by myself in my law office; I have apprentice clerks and secretaries."

"I understand," Matthew said. "You're a philanthropist."

Wynn laughed. "Mr. Kinkaird, escaping the draft began in this country at the time of the Civil War. A man could decline the invitation to join the Army of the Confederacy providing he owned at least twenty black slaves; it was known as the Twenty Negroes law. On both sides, a man who'd been called up could buy himself a replacement. In our day, that's no longer possible, but there are any number of ways of getting out of being shipped to the jungles of Vietnam.

"I knew a boy who got out of serving in the Army by claiming to his draft board that going to Vietnam would interfere with his mission in life that he had chosen for himself: being the leader of a revolution. A number of others obtained the same result by unzipping their trousers and pissing on the table of the head of the draft board. There were others who got themselves exempted by claiming that they were regular drug-users; certain others were exempted because they'd stolen cattle or killed an eagle; others because they claimed to be homosexuals, or really were. In Baltimore, antiwar militants set fire to thousands of draft records in the space of a single night, using napalm. Others married the first girl that came along; others fathered children without really wanting to have a family. A famous football player downed a dozen pizzas a day for three months, so that he weighed over three hundred pounds on the day he turned up for his physical and was exempted; another one got himself tattooed all over with the worst sort of obscenities—he'll have that for the rest of his life.

"I won't mention the dozens who deliberately mutilated themselves, the thousands who, just before their eighteenth birthday, crossed the Canadian border, the ones who joined the Quakers, the Jehovah's Witnesses, the Mennonites, the Moslems, and other sects or religions that officially preach pacifism, or those who began studies to become ministers, priests, rabbis, imams, or heaven only knows what. A young draftee from the Samoas was exempted because he believed that the god who ruled over the volcano of the island where he was born would cause an eruption if he himself killed anyone. The total number of all these men who cheated the draft is sixteen million."

"An eloquent defense counsel's plea," Matthew said sarcastically.

Wynn jokingly raised his clasped hands above his head, like a boxing champion hailing his fans.

"Isn't it, though?"

He bent over a white flower with a yellow stamen and pistil.

"*Fragaria virginiana*," Matthew said. "It's a common wild strawberry. You should take nature walks more often on Sundays. And you ought not to have picked it: It won't bear fruit now."

"Don't forget that the law provides only that draft registrants are to appear for classification before their local draft board, so that by changing his residence, a registrant can in effect choose the draft board before which he will appear. In my office, one of my assistants keeps a map of all the local Selective Service committees in U.S. territory constantly up to date. This map is dotted with stars ranging in color from yellow to green. The closer to green a star is, the easier it is to get a deferment from the local draft board that it represents. The greenest place in the United States? Butte, Montana. The criteria on which selection is based are essentially a reflection of the registrant's social status and his economic and cultural level. The proportion of Harvard students of draft age who are actually inducted is one out of a thousand. In Wisconsin not a single youngster whose family's income was over five thousand dollars a year was sent to Vietnam. And forty-five percent of those who have died in Vietnam have been blacks, Chicanos, Indians, Puerto Ricans, Nisei, Micronesians, Guamanians, and even Aleutians."

"How would you like your steak?" Matthew asked.

"Rare," Jubal Wynn said. "Extra rare—really bloody."

"One of my friends brought me some bottles of California Cabernet. I think it's a red wine. Would you like to try it?"

"What a feast! Can I help you?"

"You can see if you can get the bottle open. I don't have a corkscrew."

Wynn went to work with a bowie knife he found lying on the mantelpiece alongside an old Winchester.

"I have the figures on desertions in Vietnam," he said. "More than half a million deserters. Your grandson's case isn't exactly unique. And rest assured, in the history of the United States, since 1864 only one man has ever been shot for desertion, in 1945."

Matthew came back with the steaks. "But how many of those deserters are accused of having killed an officer?" he said.

"An accusation isn't a final sentence," Wynn answered. "Thank heaven. What would lawyers be good for otherwise?"

He tasted the wine, which unfortunately was chilled.

"Your grandson may have left Vietnam, Mr. Kinkaird. It's possible, at least. There have been cases of deserters—not many, I grant you—who have succeeded in boarding an Air France plane in Saigon after having gotten their hands on enough money for the ticket and, above all, for false papers."

"If Jon were no longer in Vietnam, he would have gotten in touch with me."

Wynn nodded. "That seems obvious to me. Or else he'd have contacted his father. But he hasn't. I checked, last night. Most of the men who have managed to escape from the U.S. Army have done so after being sent to Hawaii, Hong Kong, Korea, or Japan for a week of R and R—Rest and Recreation. Thus far, thirty-five hundred boys have managed to desert that way. Not Jon: He's never been on official leave from Saigon."

He attacked his steak. Too well done, as usual.

"Mr. Kinkaird, my informers' opinion is that Jon's disappearance can be explained in one of three ways: Either he's hiding out in Vietnam, with a woman who's taken him in, or somewhere else; or he's taken refuge with the Viet Cong . . ."

"No. Absolutely not."

"Or else he's been killed. That's the third possibility. You did tell me, if I remember correctly, that your granddaughter has gone to Saigon?"

"Yes, that's right. Lisa is there right now."

"By herself?"

"She's not a child. Far from it."

"What is it exactly that you want me to do?" Jubal Wynn asked.

"Help Lisa, first of all, and above all, as soon as she's found Jon, defend him if you can, in every way possible. Legal or not. I'll pay whatever is necessary. I can give you ten thousand dollars immediately. I've put a house that I have in Colorado Springs up for sale, and I think it'll bring me thirty to thirty-five thousand dollars."

Wynn stared at him for a moment in open-mouthed amazement. Then he shook his head. "I've finally found somebody who's managed to leave me speechless," he said with a laugh. "For the first time in my life."

He rose to his feet and began walking about the living room, stroking with the tip of his index finger the spines of books piled up in orderly disorder.

"Mr. Kinkaird, you haven't asked me why I've chosen to help these boys. I've done so because I'm altogether opposed to this war, and I'm doing everything in my power to help put a stop to it. And contrary to what you seem to think, I'm now earning less money, far less, than I did four years ago with my usual sort of clients."

He walked back over to the coffeepot being kept warm over the coals in the fireplace and poured himself more coffee.

"I have a boat in San Francisco, a gorgeous ketch with a black hull. You should see it when it sails under the Golden Gate in the sunset. I have a very nice house on Telegraph Hill; I have three or four cars, a Monet, a Pissarro, and even an Andy Warhol to put me in a good mood when I wake up in the morning. I also have around one or two million dollars in available cash or invested in stock. Plus some money that I inherited from my father. I've never really felt like getting married—although I find women physically far more attractive than men—perhaps because I don't want to be responsible for bringing children that I've fathered into this world."

He raised the porcelain coffee mug to his lips.

"As soon as your granddaughter with the fascinating violet eyes manages to find her brother, give me a call. And I'll leave for Saigon on the very next junk."

8

THE HOTEL BOY WAS THE SAME ONE WHO HAD SPIED ON HER through the transom and seen her when she was naked. He stammered something in French.

"I don't understand," Lisa said angrily.

She spoke good French and ordinarily understood it well, but the way in which it was spoken by many Vietnamese threw her entirely off the track. The boy walked impassively away down the hall, turning around every so often to stare at her with the expression of a dreamer not yet completely awakened from his dream. Lisa locked the door of her room from the inside and lay down on the bed again. It was ten minutes to nine in the evening and she was hungry, but the mere thought of going downstairs to the restaurant, amid all those Frenchmen wilting in the heat, sitting there beneath the ceiling fans undressing her with their eyes for the rest of the evening . . .

She too was suffering unbearably from the heat, to the point that she was very nearly ill, and she was feeling the effect of the tension, the fatigue, all the disappointments that had followed one after the other for several days now. She was suddenly overcome by a dull, bitter depression, assailed by intermingled images of her exhausting search for information about Jon. But she was not a woman who gave in for very long to her depressive moods; she ordinarily fought them off very quickly, almost violently. Less than twelve hours after having learned of the death of Bob Trenton, whom she had loved deeply, she had begun looking for a job, and when they'd asked her what her marital status was she'd merely replied, "Widow," without the person who had interviewed her ever suspecting that this widowhood was at the time still causing her seriously to contemplate killing herself.

She reacted this time too. She hadn't complained to the management about being spied on by the hotel boy. She solved the problem on her own, by hanging a pillowcase over the transom so that no one could see through it. Her distress of a few moments before was gradually giving way to a cold rage, against this Continental Hotel that was so French, that bore so many traces of the colonization of this country, that colonization that had led to one war and then another, and in the final analysis to this situation in which she and Jon found themselves trapped. All these things were related.

She got undressed and took refuge under the shower, and was still there when someone knocked at the door of the room. The insistent manner of the knocking irritated her even more. She came out of the bathroom, slipped on a dressing gown, and opened the door. She found herself face to face with a thin European with pale gray-blue eyes. He was dressed in a bush jacket with the collar turned up.

"Mrs. Trenton? Are you Lisa Kinkaird?"

"Who are you?"

He smiled, his eyes gazing directly into hers.

"I know your brother, Jon. The last time I saw him was at your grandfather's, in Colorado Springs. My name is Lara."

Her hair was still wet and she tucked it up in a vague sort of bun at the nape of her neck, fastening it with a simple tortoiseshell barrette. In a beige linen dress that buttoned all the way down the front, with nothing underneath but her panties, the curve of her breasts was clearly visible above the low, square-cut neckline. She wore no jewelry or makeup, but slipped her feet into a pair of flat-heeled sandals, and left the room. He was waiting in the hall outside, leaning his back against the wall. When she appeared he didn't stir for a moment or so, merely looked at her with the same calm, thoughtful gaze as before.

"I haven't had dinner and I learned that you haven't either. May I ask you to have dinner with me?"

"I thought that all we were going to do was talk about my brother," she answered, more curtly than she had really intended.

"We'll talk with our mouths full, if you'll accept my invitation. And you can always throw the dishes in my face if you feel like it."

His imperturbability was exasperating, but she nonetheless fell into step with him. As they walked down the hall she noticed that they were exactly the same height.

"So you learned that I haven't had dinner. . . . Are you from the police or have you simply set spies to watching me?"

"Your second conjecture is the correct one. I have spies everywhere."

"Including the one who was watching me while I took a shower, I presume."

He gave her a somewhat surprised look, then began to laugh softly and said in his slow drawl, "I might not have been able to resist the temptation myself. But all joking aside, I've been coming to this hotel since I was a little boy and everyone on the staff knows me. And I'll grant you that they're very talkative, if not downright indiscreet."

They crossed the lobby and he showed her to a black Mercedes and slid in behind the wheel.

"Would you like to eat French, Vietnamese, Chinese food?"

She shrugged indifferently. He was about to start the engine when she said, "Wait."

His hand halted on the ignition key.

"I'm not having dinner with you because I want to," she said. "What I mean is, I have no desire to be with you. No desire to be with you at a dinner table, and even less desire to be in a bed with you. Do I make myself clear?"

He nodded. He opened the door on his side which he had just closed, stepped out of the car, rummaged around in the trunk, and came back with an object which he placed in Lisa's hands.

"What's this?"

"A crank," he said impassively.

He took her to a Chinese restaurant in Cho Lon. They were welcomed as though their arrival had been awaited for thirty years. He spoke Chinese with several men, and Lisa and he were the only Occidentals in the long rectangular dining room.

"So then, your name is Lara and you've visited my grandfather in Colorado," she said as soon as they were seated. "And besides that?"

"I thought my name might be familiar to you."

"It's not."

"My mother's name was Nancy O'Neill, and if I've got it all straight, her aunt married your grandfather's grandfather."

"So we're related," she said in an icy tone of voice.

"Not really. At least we're not blood relations."

The table in front of them was soon covered with all sorts of dishes. Lisa was hungry and began to eat, using the chopsticks at her place efficiently if not skillfully. Lara scarcely touched the food in front of them and looked at her.

"I met your grandfather eleven years ago," he said. "I visited what he calls his cabin, in Wildcat Gulch. I remember his two greenhouses."

"There are three of them."

"There were only two of them back then."

He appeared to remember something all of a sudden. He fished Matthew Kinkaird's letter out of the pocket of his shirt and handed it to her. She read it and remarked, "He seems to think that you can be of help to Jon."

"That's right," Lara said.

He gazed at her intently with a disconcertingly grave expression in his pale, calm eyes, as though everything that words could convey were of absolutely no importance to him. Lisa was suddenly overcome by an indefinable emotion. She lowered her head.

"And there's really a possibility of that?"

"Of my helping your brother? I can try."

"Because you live here in this country?"

"I don't live in Vietnam but in Cambodia. I arrived in Saigon only today."

"Simply because my grandfather wrote to you?"

"That's my one and only reason for being here."

Lisa had raised her head and was returning his steady gaze. And again she was overcome by the disconcerting feeling that the words they were speaking were not what was important; what was essential were Lara's eyes and hers, locked together as though spellbound. The emotion she had felt a few moments before gripped her once again, more powerfully this time. *What's happening to me?* she wondered.

"Do you know my grandfather well?"

"I saw him only once. I'd taken several months' vacation so as to be able to travel all through the United States and South America. When I arrived in Colorado, it seemed the natural thing to do to drop by and say hello to the Kinkairds my mother had told me about. Your grandfather made me feel more than welcome when I appeared on the scene. He's a wonderfully warmhearted man."

"And Jon was there with him."

Lara nodded. "A merry youngster, who kept eating one ice cream after another, with eyes . . ." He hesitated. "There was also a very fat man with a mustache there, a man with a Spanish name. . . ."

"Pete Martinez."

"Yes, that was his name all right."

A silence. She laid her chopsticks down on the table.

"Some dessert?"

"No, thank you," she said. "May I have a glass of whatever it is that you're drinking?"

"Cognac-and-soda?"

"Cognac-and-soda."

He barely raised one finger and the Chinese waiter came to the table instantly. Lara must have seen something in Lisa's eyes, for he immediately said with a smile, "Yes, I know: the white colonialist who merely waggles a finger or glances out of the corner of his eye and is obeyed instantly."

"Yes, that's it exactly," Lisa replied.

She fished around in her handbag for a cigarette and pretended not to see Lara's hand offering her a light, using her own lighter instead. "And simply because a man you met for a few hours ten or eleven years ago asks you to, you're all set to go searching for an American deserter?"

He, too, lit a cigarette. "You went to see a police officer named Dieu this afternoon." He raised one hand slightly, as though anticipating her probable reaction. "Don't be surprised that I know what's going on. I haven't had you trailed or anything like that. But you didn't exactly pass unnoticed at the Continental. Keeping an eye on the Long Noses has always been the favorite pastime of the hotel staff. And just before you went off to your appointment with Dieu, you asked for his address."

"And so?"

"Be on your guard against that man."

"Is he the only one I should watch out for?"

Again Lara's answer was one of his characteristic slow smiles.

"I'm sorry my grandfather wrote that letter," Lisa said in a firm tone of voice. "I'm sorry you went to the trouble of coming here. As a matter of fact, it seems to me that the police are in a better position to find my brother than anybody else is. All I'm asking them to do is to get me in touch with Jon, who will then give himself up to our country's military authorities."

"But I was the one your grandfather wrote to," Lara said softly.

"It was a mistake on his part to do so."

He looked at her in silence for a moment, then rose to his feet, went to pay the bill, and came back to the table. Her eyes followed him, and she struggled with all her might against the attraction, the fascination almost, that she felt for this man.

"Would you like me to take you back to the hotel?"

Her only answer was to get up from the table and make her way to the door ahead of him.

"Why is it you'd have a better chance of finding my brother than the police would?" she asked.

"I never said any such thing."

"But that's what you think."

"I think I have as good a chance as the police."

"And why is that?"

"Because I know a certain number of doors to knock on."

"Who are you anyway? A smuggler?"

He was driving very slowly, scarcely faster than a person could walk, as though he wanted to delay their return to the Continental as long as possible. Lisa looked away from Lara's profile and found herself gazing at his delicate, firmly muscled hands.

"I have a small rubber plantation in northern Cambodia," he said.

He explained how he made his living, how over the years he had little by little gotten the plantation, inherited from his father but actually first put into production by his grandfather, back into operation. He told her what had happened in January of 1946, the attack on the plantation, the murder of his parents and his sister; he recounted the entire story gravely, with no show of emotion, in an even tone of voice, wasting no words. He also said that he had lived in Hong Kong and in Singapore, where his grandfather O'Neill had lived for forty years and was buried.

The Mercedes stopped in front of the hotel.

"What other solution would my brother have?"

"It's a wide, wide world."

"Meaning?"

"He could leave Vietnam if someone gave him a helping hand."

"You, for instance?"

"If your brother asked me to."

"And where would he go?"

Lara shrugged. "To Cambodia first of all, and after that wherever he wanted to go."

He was sitting slightly aslant in the driver's seat, his left shoulder against the door frame and his arm resting on the windowsill with his elbow jutting outside.

"So then, that's all you can offer as a solution?" she said. "Turning my brother into a sort of international bum who won't ever be able to go back to his own country?"

"He'll have to decide for himself."

"Providing you find him before the police do."

"Obviously."

"And nothing that I could say or do will keep you from doing what you've made up your mind to do?"

He turned his head, his pale eyes examining her intently. "If the Vietnamese police find your brother before I do, he won't have any choice whatsoever. Dieu will bleed you white to begin with, and then he'll turn Jon over to the M.P.'s. You're out of your mind if you think there's any other solution."

She closed her eyes, trying desperately to control herself. "So what other favor are you offering to do for Jon? Giving him a leg up in the world of opium smuggling or trafficking in arms?"

"You're forgetting white slavery," Lara said in his drawling voice.

He turned the handle of the door on his side and got out, walking around the hood of the Mercedes to open her door for her, but she got out without waiting for him. She walked quickly up the stairs to the terrace of the hotel, went into the lobby, and only then turned around. Despite her fears, he had not followed her in. Nor had he waited outside. She asked for her key at the desk and the clerk handed it to her. Just as she was about to step into the red-upholstered elevator she hesitated for a moment. She then slowly retraced her steps, impelled by an emotion she didn't understand, had no desire to understand, and reproached herself for feeling. She walked to the edge of the terrace and looked down. Lara was there, standing in front of a very tall, solidly built Asian sitting at one of the tables. Lara must have realized she was standing there staring down at him, for he raised his head and gazed back at her. She turned around and this time went upstairs in the elevator.

The Jaraï's powerful, sinewy body gave every appearance of being about to cause the collapse of the chair in which he was sitting. "Aren't you going to sit down?" Kutchaï asked.

"Yes," Lara answered, but nonetheless stood as if rooted to the spot.

After a moment he sat down in the chair beside Kutchaï's. The terrace was practically deserted.

"Everything's all set," Kutchaï said. "All the Corsicans and Chinese in Saigon are on the trail of our pal. A real manhunt."

Lara sat there without a word, his legs stretched out, his chin on his chest, his eyes staring off into space.

"A good-looking woman," Kutchaï said warily.

"More than that," Lara replied.

9

SHORTLY BEFORE ELEVEN O'CLOCK, IENG SAMBOTH DECIDED TO STOP and rest. He was so exhausted his legs were numb; he stretched out on the ground in the shade of a grove of areca palms, ready to plunge into a denser patch of forest close by if danger threatened. He had left Phnom Penh and Roger Bouès' apartment at three in the morning the day before, hidden among wooden crates in the back of a flatbed truck headed for Pursat, where the truck driver had dropped him off as arranged near the high-school athletic field. He had found the hut he'd been told about, and the married couple who had agreed to take him in. He had spent the day with them watching the students play countless games of soccer in their bare feet. At nightfall, dressed in peasant clothes once again, he had set off in the direction of Leach, a small settlement some twenty kilometers to the southwest. He had skirted the village and, following the river, had walked on during part of the night, taken time out to rest, and then continued on his way.

And now he was waiting.

Ahead of him, in the distance, the Cardamomes rose above the tops of the trees. He was still a very long way from his destination, the little village deep in the forest where he had decided to establish his base. He hoped Ouk would turn up soon. Ieng was hungry and thirsty. Though he was quite tall, he weighed scarcely a hundred pounds, and outside of a little soccer he had played barefoot as a kid—and not very well at that—he had never devoted much of his time to physical activity. He leaned his head back against the trunk of the areca palm, positioning himself to keep close watch on the trail in both directions. He estimated that since leaving the hut alongside the soccer field in Pursat he had probably walked some forty kilometers. Six months earlier he would have been totally incapable of such a thing; during the last ten years it would never have occurred to him even to cross the street without getting into a car or hailing a pedicab boy, but since then this body had gotten tougher. Another Ieng was in the process of being born.

He closed his eyes for a second, opening them again immediately. He wasn't really sleepy, and besides it would have been dangerous to doze off even for a little while. Getting something to put in his belly was his most immediate physical need.

The forest around him was silent except for the continual buzzing of insects. Over and above the usual odors of growing things, however, Ieng's nose discerned the nearly indetectable smell of a wood fire. No doubt there was a hut somewhere close by. The image came forcefully to mind of a Cambodian family peacefully gathered togther, working at centuries-old tasks of wresting a living from the land, respecting the spirits of the forest and tradition. The only real Cambodia is rural, he thought; a people of patient peasants, asking only to live in freedom—a freedom they surely did not enjoy at present.

Once again, words repeated over and over during discussions in Paris, years earlier, came back to him: "The one chance for the survival of rural Cambodian society lies in a complete, final rupture of the economic ties created and forced upon it by foreigners, by the French obviously, but also by the Chinese since time immemorial, not to mention the expansionist aims of the Vietnamese and the Thais. There is no other solution except this total break; otherwise there is only the death, the disappearance of the Khmer people, of the Kampuchea of our ancestors. We must pitilessly cut all ties with the outside world, isolate ourselves, retreat within ourselves, reject the constraints and the needs that others have done their utmost to persuade us were fundamental. It is not true that the ultimate goal of a country, of a nation, ought to be to resemble the industrialized countries of the West as closely as possible. In reality that is a snare, a trap, and if we fall into it we will lose our identity; we will lose ourselves. We should not feel ashamed at being an underdeveloped country; on the contrary, we must re-

main one or, if need be, even go back to being one. We must become more
and more perfectly underdeveloped."

In his excitement, Ieng nearly failed to hear the sound of footsteps approaching.

He sat up straight, on the alert. *Ouk.* Most likely it was Ouk who was
coming. It couldn't be anything else. Ieng was on the point of calling out to
him. But, suddenly wary, he did not call out.

In fact, it was a band of about a hundred men approaching, somewhere
on his left behind the wall of dense vegetation, five hundred feet away from
him. In November 1966, on the initiative of the prime minister, Lon Nol,
the province of Battambang, scarcely more than a stone's throw away from
the spot where Ieng now was, had been invaded by the so-called Khmer
Krom, ethnic Cambodians who had been born and had lived up until that
time in Vietnamese territory, ever since the days long ago when the Khmer
empire had extended to the China Sea. The official pretext for this invasion:
providing a refuge for Cambodians living in Vietnam who were fleeing a
country at war. The real situation, in Ieng's view, was quite different. As he
saw it, this settling of Khmer Krom in Battambang was a maneuver on the
part of Lon Nol and the pro-American clique in Phnom Penh—in other
words, of the CIA. The Khmer Krom of Cochin China were for the most
part rabidly anti-Communist, and therefore capable of forming shock
troops that could be used against the Viet Cong based on Khmer soil, or
even against Cambodian neutralists and the Cambodian left. In fact, Ieng
was certain that this maneuver was the prelude to an even more important
campaign, aimed at putting an end to Khmer neutrality in the Indochinese
conflict, a neutrality that was driving the American experts out of their
minds.

The sound of footsteps was closer now. *That can't be Ouk.* The new arrivals were far too numerous, and above all were making too much noise,
not taking sufficient precautions, behaving in fact as though the forest belonged to them and could not possibly hold any surprises in store for them.
They were making their way like hunters, not like prey. Ieng lay down flat
on the ground, inched his way into the heart of the dense patch of forest,
and hid himself as best he could. *But the day will come when they'll be the
prey and we'll be the hunters,* he thought to himself.

Talk exchanged in a loud whisper, laughter reached his ears. *That's not
Ouk.* He was trembling, as much out of hatred as out of fear. He virtually
buried himself in the earth, became one with it. Ieng had always loudly
voiced his pride at being of peasant stock, at being a man born in the forest,
but deep down he knew very well that this was not altogether true: One is
not a member of Parliament in Phnom Penh, and even more, one does not
spend years and years studying in France without being radically changed.
In reality, this forest in which he was burying himself frightened him; he

pictured in his mind the snakes in it—which were by no means entirely the
product of his imagination—and swarming hordes of insects. This weakness
made him furious with himself. What a miserable excuse for a guerrilla
fighter he was!

The band of men passed within twenty yards of him. He waited more
than a minute after they had gone by, and in the deepening silence that
gradually came over the forest once again he finally generated the courage
to stand up. Peering through an opening amid the leaves, he could see in the
distance the backs of the men walking off down the trail. They were dressed
in combat fatigues in yellow and green camouflage colors, and were wearing American field helmets. He hadn't been mistaken: They were perhaps
regular soldiers from a FARK* unit or the Provincial Guard, or worse still,
Khmer Krom troops such as were beginning to be seen more and more frequently. Ieng imagined what would have happened had he been captured
by these men. They might have tortured him, or perhaps even executed him
on the spot, and at the very least they would have given him a terrible
beating and thrown him in prison. Somehow the certainty and the reality of
the danger he had just escaped put him at peace with himself. He was not
an experienced guerrilla fighter, not yet at any rate—far from it—but at
least his life really was at stake.

An hour later, almost imperceptible rustling sounds, minute stirrings of
leaves, and the inexplicable sensation of a human presence close at hand
alerted him once again. In the nearly total silence of the forest at this midday hour, he heard the prearranged signal very distinctly, repeated twice:
the palms of two hands rubbed together four times.

"I'm over here."

He rose to his feet and was startled to discover that Ouk was less than
three yards away from him. *I didn't hear him at all. He might very well have
sneaked up on me behind my back and slit my throat before I even realized
he was there!* Once again he was dumbfounded by the Jaraï's frightening
ability to move about in the forest without making the slightest sound.
"Walking without making any more noise than a leaf falling," as the Jaraïs
of the high plateaus of the East put it.

But Ouk was smiling at him. "Did you see them go by?"

"Yes, but they didn't see me."

"Luckily," Ouk said with a laugh. "You're the one they're looking for.
You and Khieu Samphan."

Ouk had the same disconcerting silent laugh, the same wolf's jaw, the
same big, black, slightly bloodshot eyes, the same wild, almost animal look
about him as his elder brother Kutchaï. He was not as enormously tall as his
brother, however, and lacked that unfathomable, disturbingly ambiguous

* Forces Armées Royales Khmères: Khmer Royal Armed Forces

quality so typical of Kutchaï, who was capable of speaking and thinking like a Barang behind what seemed to be the face of a primitive aborigine who had just left his native forest. Ouk raised one arm. Four other men materialized, emerging all of a sudden from their hiding places a dozen yards away.

"But there are only five of you!" Ieng exclaimed. "Where are the others?"

"There aren't any others," Ouk answered, shaking his head and laughing to conceal his embarrassment. "Some of them have gone back to Battambang or Pursat to take up their studies again; many of them have gone home to their villages because they have work to do there. They have to feed their families."

For the space of a few seconds, Ieng felt crushed and utterly discouraged. It had taken him weeks, if not months, to gather a hundred men together one by one. He had gone from village to village, often with his pursuers at his heels, on occasion escaping capture only by a miracle, spreading the word and preaching revolution. And now, after little more than three weeks' absence, everything had caved in. All he had left were five men. Five! He remembered the old proverb that the colonials staying at the Continental in Saigon or the Royal in Phnom Penh were fond of repeating in an ironic tone of voice: "In Indochina, a Vietnamese plants rice; a Cambodian watches it grow; a Laotian listens to it grow." For a moment hatred flared up within him. *But it was the supposedly easygoing, lazy Khmers who built the hundred temples of Angkor and at one time dominated all of Indochina,* he thought. *And we'll do it again.*

"They'll come back," Ouk said, trying to cheer Ieng up. "They'll come back when you need them."

Ieng relaxed.

"I'm hungry and thirsty," he said.

"I thought you might be," Ouk said with a smile.

After two hours the forest seemed suddenly to thin out ahead of the six men walking along in silence. They caught a whiff of the heavy, rich odor of the rice paddy, mingled with the fragrant smell of woodsmoke. The green wall parted and the village appeared: four or five huts perched on wooden pilings hugging the mountainside with a waterfall cascading down it. Stretching out in front of the huts was the rice paddy, marked off by the graceful trunks of *thnots,* sugar palms standing like sentinels posted outside a stand of teak. It was a poor village and a very small rice paddy, measuring a scant twenty *raïs.** Dripping with sweat, his legs feeling heavier and heavier with each step, Ieng was nonetheless intensely relieved at the sight of it. He spied two water buffalo.

* A *raï* is approximately 1,500 square meters.

"We stole them," Ouk explained, not mincing words. "We have to start getting things organized."

It must have been around two in the afternoon in Phnom Penh. In Phnom Penh but not here. Here time didn't count. *Time is our friend. I'm in the heart of the forest, with a handful of practically unarmed men, but time is on my side, on our side,* he thought. Ieng was totally convinced that they would win in the end; any other outcome was inconceivable.

Ouk was speaking. While Ieng had been gone, he and his men had had a brief engagement with a patrol from the Provincial Guard. It hadn't really been a battle, just an exchange of shots fired more or less at random. "But we killed one of their men and got ourselves a rifle."

One man and one rifle. That's nothing! Ieng thought. "We ought to avoid any engagements with them," he said in a weary voice. "It's not our role to fight, not yet. We must simply stay here, in the forest, and wait for all those who are certain to join us eventually, peasants driven from their land by the Khmer Krom, and students who want to fight the revolution with us."

Suddenly his imagination ran wild: He saw an army of shadows emerging from the forest, an army of men dressed in black, the color of peasants, of tough, fanatic, implacable men—*and therefore young men above all*—spreading out over the Khmer countryside like the floodwaters of the Tonle Sap, rooting out every last trace of foreign influence, of that culture and that civilization, of that so-called technology they had tried to force upon the Cambodian people. *And we'll destroy the cities. They're overrun with Chinese, Vietnamese, and Europeans; they're corrupting us. We'll empty them and burn them to the ground. The Cambodia that we're going to create doesn't need cities.* Hou Yuon and Khieu Samphan had convinced him of that. They thought it would even be necessary to eliminate in one way or another those Cambodians who were too deeply marked by urban civilization. Khieu went so far as to speak of eliminating them physically. But Khieu had always been something of a wild-eyed extremist. He seemed almost capable of coldly envisaging the prospect of eliminating one Cambodian out of every three or four, a million and a half people at least. Ieng, naturally, couldn't go along with him that far. Moreover, Khieu couldn't be serious when he spoke of such a thing.

Ieng opened his eyes again. "Ouk," he said, "we'll destroy the cities some day. And we Khmer Rouge will come out of the forest by the thousands, by the tens of thousands."

10

THE SECOND INDOCHINESE WAR—THE FIRST BEING THE ONE waged and lost by the French—had officially begun in early August of 1964. North Vietnamese vedettes had had the audacity to open fire on two American destroyers, the *Maddox* and the *C. Turner Joy,* as the destroyers were supporting ("though playing no part in the conduct of operations," in the words of General William Westmoreland) attacks launched against North Vietnam by South Vietnamese commandos under the orders of the aforementioned General Westmoreland. President Johnson had then asked Congress to authorize him to take all necessary military measures "for the protection of the United States." The House of Representatives had granted him this authority by unanimous vote; in the Senate there were only two dissenters.

On February 7, 1965, aerial bombings north of the seventeenth parallel—that is to say, the bombing of North Vietnam—began, aimed at "dragging North Vietnam to the negotiating table on its knees within six weeks."

In the spring of this same year, American troop strength in Vietnam— which would eventually go over 500,000—numbered 75,000 men.

The U.S.S.R. had not intervened, nor had China, where the advocates of intervention such as Liu Shao-chi and Lo Jui-ching, the Army chief of staff, met with a veto on the part of Mao and Chou En-lai.

In January of 1968, General Westmoreland asked Washington for reinforcements of precisely 206,000 troops "in order to end the war once and for all." The Viet Cong, he announced, were at the end of their rope. On the thirtieth of that same month, during Tet, the Sino-Vietnamese New Year, the Viet Cong "at the end of their rope" launched an attack, invading all the cities, pounding their enemy's defenses to bits, advancing on Saigon and reaching even the U.S. Embassy, which they proceeded to occupy.

The American-South Vietnamese counterattack was not long in coming; it rolled the enemy back. But Washington's will to go on with the war had been broken, and at the end of March 1968, Lyndon Johnson announced that he would not seek a second term as President, that he was stopping the bombings outside of the so-called combat zone (between the seventh and the twentieth parallels), and that he was willing at last to enter into unconditional peace negotiations with North Vietnam.

The negotiations began on May 13, 1968, in a building on the Avenue Kléber in Paris. They became more broadly based the following January, when the representatives of the National Liberation Front were seated at the negotiating table after agreeing to participate in the peace talks on

condition that all bombing of any sort be stopped. The negotiations pro-
gressed to the point that a peace agreement seemed close at hand in the
early days of 1969.

But not for long. And for two essential reasons, the first being the
obtuse stubbornness of the North Vietnamese, mad with pride and hence
convinced that they could force America to accept what amounted to a veritable capitulation, and the other being Richard Nixon's succession to the
presidency. It was Nixon who, during his term as Vice President in the Ei-
senhower administration, had been the most ardent proponent of American
military intervention in Vietnam. Nixon had a very personal version of the
form that the withdrawal from Vietnam—which American public opinion
was demanding in more and more forcible terms—ought to assume: This
process of disengagement should be counterbalanced, step by step, by the
so-called process of Vietnamization. For every American infantry unit
withdrawn from combat, two South Vietnamese units ought to take over,
supported by the overwhelming firepower of the United States Air Force
and the United States Navy.

This Vietnamization, moreover, ought to be complemented by three
operations deemed absolutely indispensable: It was necessary, first of all, to
seal off the forty-five-kilometer boundary line between North and South
Vietnam: it was necessary, secondly, to seal hermetically the border between South Vietnam and Laos.

And it was necessary, thirdly, to pay serious attention to Cambodia.

And there was only one solution to the problem of Cambodia: a coup
d'état ousting Norodom Sihanouk, who had held the reins of power in the
country of the Khmers for twenty-eight years.

Roger was dreaming.

To his vast surprise, he discovered that he was dreaming of women,
something he hardly ever did. He had never been much of a womanizer. He
searched his memory, counted on his fingers, and realized that it had been
at least seven months since he had found himself in the same bed with a
woman. "Damn! How time does fly!"

By a quite logical association of ideas, he managed to fish up from his
memory the face of his own wife, a Frenchwoman he'd wed in Saigon for
what must have been the briefest marriage in the history of Indochina and
neighboring territories: thirty-one days, including the divorce. A record. On
the second day of their honeymoon, spent at Kep, Roger had gone off for a
quarter of an hour to have a drink at the bar of the bungalow with a couple
of friends, and coming back unexpectedly the following morning, he had
found his wife in what had very recently become their marriage bed with a
crane operator from Saint-Jean-de-Luz named Barnebougle, who had happened to pass by that way under circumstances that were not at all clear.
Roger had thrown his spouse out the window (with no harm done, since it

was only one floor up with lots of bougainvillea beneath). He had then attempted to defenestrate the crane operator in like manner. *A fatal error.
He was twice as big as I was.* The crane operator had sent him flying out the
window, thus reuniting the ill-starred couple in the bougainvillea below.

The telephone rang.

After glowering at it for some time, Roger finally picked up the receiver and recognized Christiani's voice almost immediately. Christiani was
a Corsican, naturally, but one who lived in Bangkok, having left Cambodia
some ten years before and settled in Thailand to manage an import-export
business he'd gone into fifty-fifty with Lara. Roger thus knew what the ties
were between Christiani and Lara. Or at least he thought he knew. But did
anyone ever really know what Lara was up to?

"I have a message for you, Roger," Christiani said.

Roger didn't ask who the message was from; it could only be from
Lara.

"We have a friend who would like to visit Cambodia, and perhaps
even spend a fair amount of time resting there and touring the country. He
appreciates how calm and peaceful it is in Khmer country."

"I see," Roger replied, translating the message in his mind: *A man who
wants to hide out, mayhap one fleeing Vietnam. I wonder what's up.*

"We thought he might like to go tiger hunting," Christiani went on.
"Perhaps you could arrange something along those lines. I've been told
you're an expert at tiger hunts."

"Well, I wouldn't say that," Roger said, utterly dumbfounded.

"And that you've even run into a few at your construction sites. You
could organize a hunt at the last place you saw one."

"Do you think so?" Roger said, completely puzzled.

Roger had never hunted a tiger in his life; in fact, he'd never hunted
anything, even though he'd tramped through a good many kilometers of forest following Lara and Kutchaï in the days when the two of them still went
on hunting trips. As a matter of fact, his only contact with a wild animal
bigger than a mongoose had been . . . All of a sudden he caught on to what
the Corsican was trying to get across to him.

"I understand perfectly."

"And our friend will doubtless want to see Cambodia from the air. Try
to find a private pilot. Boudin, for instance. He'd be just the right man for
the job. I would have phoned him myself, but you know how hard it is to get
in touch with him. You'll probably have better luck. And the sooner the
better."

"I follow you."

"Sorry to let you know at the last minute. Really the very last minute."

In other words, it's very urgent, Roger thought to himself. "Anything
else?" he asked.

"No, that's all."

Roger hung up, thinking things through. It was three in the afternoon on a Thursday. "It's going to be touch and go." He ran downstairs. Four minutes later he was driving down the Boulevard Monivong at the wheel of his fifteen-year-old Studebaker. He went to Boudin's place first, found the pilot's two Cambodian wives and their eight kids there, along with various nephews, nieces, grandparents, uncles, and aunts all merrily chatting together, but not a sign of Boudin. He couldn't quite see himself making the rounds of all the countless places in Phnom Penh where Boudin might be, so he decided to try his luck at the airport. "The fool may be working."

Boudin was indeed working, his nose buried in one engine of his plane.

"Not here, for heaven's sake," Boudin said before Roger had even opened his mouth.

Boudin led him outside the hangar to the edge of the runway and sat him down inside a Peugeot 404 that he was probably more attached to than he was to all of humanity put together, spending an hour each day polishing it and inspecting every single one of its mechanical parts thoroughly twice a week.

"What the hell's wrong with you anyway? Are you crazy or what— talking in front of all those guys?"

Roger had always been vastly amused by Boudin. The explosive Strasbourg Sausage's fits of utter rage delighted him. And Boudin was so short that in order to see the road when he drove, he was obliged to peer *underneath* the rim of the steering wheel.

"Have you by any chance heard about someone going to cross the border into Cambodia on the sly?"

"Naturally."

"Agent X-13 in Bangkok, that is to say Christiani, has just phoned me, and if I understood his message correctly, that someone is to arrive in Cambodia today. Do you know the former plantation of Ang Chan near Kampot?"

"Yes, I know it."

"That's where it'll be," Roger said. "What I mean is, that's where the unknown person will be arriving."

Ten years earlier, the Cambodian government, doubtless annoyed to see that all the rubber plantations on Khmer soil were in the hands of foreigners, Frenchmen for the most part, had decided to create a national plantation. The officials had chosen a spot near Kampot, not far from the Vietnamese border, and begun the project by constructing a splendid building to house the director. Roger had been commissioned to draw up the plans for it. Some hundreds of dwarf rubber trees had been set out, and the government had proceeded to hold the official inauguration of the plantation, attended by the Chief of State, ministers, secretaries of state, ambassadors, and consuls yawning like oysters; by several hundred bureau-

crats; and by the inevitable brigade of cheering, applauding spectators, recruited from the neighboring villages to stage a "spontaneous" demonstration, proving to Samdech-Father the depth of his people's love for him. Just
as the first words of the first speech were delivered, a huge tiger had suddenly appeared, and in the 400-meter race that ensued, the diplomatic
corps had shown itself to be noticeably less fleet of foot than the government authorities, with the Minister of Information establishing on this occasion the new Cambodian record for that distance. Roger for his part had
immediately taken refuge in the stand-up toilets that he had had the fore-
sight to include in his building plans. As far as he knew, the plantation had
then been abandoned.

"What unknown person?" Bourdin roared. "It's me and my junkheap
that are going to set down there. If there's enough room to land."

Everything's becoming clear, Roger thought; he no longer had the
slightest idea of what was going on. "There's enough room. I think so anyway. There's a large flat cleared space where workers' shacks were to be
built, but as far as I know they never were."

"I certainly hope not," Boudin said threateningly. "What I didn't
know was what day it was going to be. He did say 'at the last minute,' right?
Are you absolutely certain of that?"

"I'd swear to it on a stack of Bibles," Roger answered. "Is that all? Can
I go back home now?" *I shouldn't have said that,* Roger thought.

Boudin exploded. "What do you mean, 'Is that all'? You're to go
straight there and get the landing strip ready for me."

The pilot did at least deign to explain what Roger was supposed to do:
Take thirty or so cans of gas, load them on a truck, get behind the wheel of
the aforementioned truck, and take all of them to Ang Chan. Once there, he
was to set the cans out along the edge of the improvised landing strip and be
ready to light the wicks of them—"Obviously they have to have a wick, you
cretin!"—and then wait. And where was he to find the cans, the gas, and the
truck? Everything was all taken care of, naturally: Roger was to stop in
Takeo en route and go see the Vietnamese who ran the garage on the Chau
Doc road, who would provide him with everything he needed.

"Now listen carefully," Boudin added. "And try to understand what
I'm saying. You'll hear my engine first. I'll follow the river, keeping the
lights of the city to the south-southwest. I'll make a first pass over the strip,
very low, at less than three hundred feet, with all my lights out. The minute
you hear me, light a fire, a big fire, at the end of the runway. Then count to
fifty and light the gas cans. Have you got that straight? The fire, count to
fifty, and then the gas cans."

Roger looked at the little man with new respect. He hadn't the vaguest
idea of what was going on, but he could tell that it involved a great many
risks, the majority of which were going to be taken by the Alsatian. *It's bet-*

*ter not to ask him any more questions. He might very well hit me over the
head with his jack.*

Roger nonetheless did ask him one question: "Is it Lara who's organized this whole thing?"

Boudin closed his eyes, like someone finding it very difficult to repress
an overpowering urge to commit murder:

"No," he answered in a curiously gentle voice. "It was Snow White."
Then, becoming himself again, he roared: "And now clear your ass the hell
out of here!"

Shortly before six-thirty, Roger Bouès turned off the paved road onto a trail
gullied by the rains of the season before. He was somewhat reassured to see
that the ground bore no traces of another car having passed that way; quite
obviously the place was far off the beaten track. Behind him, on the bed of
the truck, some forty little metal containers made from the bottoms of old
gas cans were piled up, plus half a dozen jerry-cans full of gas. After twenty
minutes or so he came out onto a plateau where the building he had designed ten years before, which clearly had not been occupied since, was still
standing, silent and dreary. A little farther on some rusty steel beams reminded him that the plans had also called for a hangar that had never been
built. And of the several hundred young rubber trees set out once upon a
time, barely two or three dozen had grown to maturity, without anyone apparently ever having bothered to collect the sap from them.

As he had driven along, Roger had worried that he might come across
someone who would politely question what he was doing there. But his
fears proved groundless: The plateau was deserted and there was nothing
else in sight except the thickly wooded slopes of the Elephant Range and
the round silhouettes of a few isolated *phnoms,* or hills.

He set to work marking out what seemed to him the best possible axis
for an emergency landing strip. He lined up the metal containers, one every
twenty yards, in two parallel rows also twenty yards apart. He went off to
gather all the wood he could find and made a pile big enough to burn a
dozen Joans of Arc to death. Then he went back and sat in the cab of the
truck, eating a banana or two simply to while away the time. He felt lonely,
naked, vulnerable, completely at the mercy of heaven only knew what. A
few years earlier, bandits had roved about the region, sometimes attacking
the rare passenger cars that happened by, or even the Chinese buses. And
then there were the Khmer Rouge and the mosquitoes, the leeches, and the
snakes.

He settled down to wait, alternately glancing at the darkening sky and
his watch, whose hands pointed to just eight o'clock.

11

"WE'RE LUCKY," JEAN-BAPTISTE MORRACHINI SAID. "IT COULD HAVE taken forever, but we made it in just a few hours."

The Corsican's Mercedes had now left behind the takeoff runways of Tan Son Hut, the Saigon airport. The rectangular windshield framed a world hugging the ground as far as the eye could see, a mind-boggling jumble of shanties jammed one against the other, with walls and roofs of wooden planks, cardboard cartons, the remains of wrecked cars and trucks and even of airplanes and tanks, of food tins and beer cans slit apart and then patiently rolled out flat and held together with dried mud. The vast slum swarmed and stank in the stifling heat. Here and there, real houses rose above this chaos, little besieged islands, some of them with pointed canvas roofs jutting up out of the sea of putrefaction. A hundred thousand human beings, perhaps more, were huddled together there.

"The Americans call this Soul Alley. There was a time when people went hunting here. Things have changed a bit since then."

Morrachini maneuvered the car slowly and cautiously through the teeming streets to a sort of little public square. He rolled to a stop alongside a Vietnamese police jeep parked there, with four armed men in helmets inside. He went over to talk with the policemen, and finally signaled to Lara and Kutchai to join him.

"These men are friends of mine. They'll keep an eye on the car for me."

The three men entered what was virtually an alleyway, full of hordes of bare-assed kids with crafty, glittering eyes and dogs so scrawny their ribs were nearly sticking out through the skin, all of them, kids and dogs alike, avidly rummaging through heaps of refuse. Here and there razor blades gleamed in the fingers of one or another of the children, some of them barely five or six years old, who would use the blades to cut the straps of a camera slung around a neck or to slit a pocket bulging with a fat wallet.

The only light in the alleyway came from bare bulbs suspended on wires strung up every which way, an installation so dangerous it would have given any electrician heart failure. These bulbs produced feeble halos of light, but also disquieting zones of deep shadow. Passing from light to shadow at a slow, almost ritual pace, an occasional Annamite stood out amid the crowd in rags and tatters; clad in mandarin tunics and white pants, the traditional headbands of Hue encircling their foreheads, they made their way along like ghosts from another time, immured in a contemptuous indifference toward the ignominy surrounding them. Most often they were

followed by their wives, trotting after them at the customary distance of
three paces, their heads bent forward beneath the weight of their heavy,
meticulously coiled chignons.

As Morrachini hesitated, pondering which direction to take, a woman
suddenly appeared in front of him and nodded her head to signal that they
were to follow her. Walking ahead, she led the three of them first into a labyrinth that they were obliged literally to creep through, then into a sort of
burrow where transistors, stereo systems, television sets, Akaï, Sony, Zenith,
or Nikon cameras and optical instruments, sat alongside air conditioners,
typewriters, bound volumes of *Playboy*, car tires, batteries, almost all of
them brand-new.

A pause. The woman motioned with her head again: "Wait," and disappeared. In the semidarkness Kutchaï made out three or four faces turned
toward them. But no one moved.

"It's enough to make you wonder how come there's anything left on
American bases," Morrachini said, lowering his voice, no doubt also impressed by the strangeness of the place. "The guy we're going to see now is
a deserter himself, a former regular-army sergeant. He's set up a vast network and serves as an intermediary between his pals who are still stationed
on the bases and his customers. He's convinced that the world's his oyster,
that he's got it all taped, the war, the Vietnamese, the Chinese. He has
money, all the women he wants, all the drugs that he and his pals can possibly consume. He believes in the brotherhood of colored people, black and
yellow. The poor bastard. He's a prisoner for life. A day will come when the
Chinese he works for and who keep him in drugs will drop him and replace
him with somebody who's not such a loudmouth. Or else the cops he pays
off will have had enough of him. One way or another, sooner or later, somebody will turn him in to the Mike Papas, and as a matter of fact that'll be
the best thing that could possibly happen to him. Otherwise he'll simply get
his throat cut one of these days, or o.d., and they'll find his dead body in the
arroyo. He doesn't have the ghost of a chance. But it's better not to tell him
that."

The woman eventually came back. Another labyrinth. The heat, the
stench of the night became unbearable. Finally they went down a short
flight of stairs and ended up in a real room, in a real house, with a wooden
floor covered with straw mats, walls hung with photos of naked women,
alongside an enlarged photograph of the Superdome—the roofed stadium
in New Orleans—and a framed portrait of Martin Luther King, Jr., across
whose intelligent face the word *sucker* was scrawled in red ink. Sitting in an
armchair was a gigantic Black. He rose to his feet as the three men entered
the room, and stared haughtily down at them. Like his two bodyguards,
both also Black and obviously armed, he was wearing a long, gaudily colored silk robe, earrings, jade and gold bracelets, and a headband.

"You're on my turf here," he said. "Even the police can't be of any help to you here."

"You talk to him," Morrachini said to Lara in French. "My English . . . But watch your step—don't let him try to get any money out of you. I've already taken care of that with Huong."

"What's the name of the man you're looking for?" the Black asked.

"Kinkaird. Jon Kinkaird."

Lara took out of his pocket the little identification photo Matthew had enclosed in his letter and held it out to him. The Black glanced offhandedly at the snapshot without making the slightest move to take a closer look at it.

"And who are you?"

"One of his friends. My name is Lara. I've come here from Cambodia to see him and talk to him."

"You're American."

"No."

"What is it you want from him?"

"I've already told you: I just want to talk to him."

"Don't let him try to make a deal with you," Morrachini said to Lara in French. "He knows where the kid is—Huong's certain of that. The only thing he has to do is take us to him."

"What's he saying," the Black asked, looking angrily at Morrachini.

"He was talking to me about Huong," Lara explained.

"Kinkaird doesn't want to go back to the Army," the Black said.

"I couldn't care less," Lara said. "I've come here because his grandfather asked me to."

A silence. The Black glared at him and finally said: "If there's dirty work afoot, we'll shoot you and the two others down in cold blood."

Lara shrugged.

"Come with me," the Black said. "Just you. The other two stay here."

Kutchaï shifted position.

"Cool it," Lara said to him. "There's no point in starting a fight."

He followed the Black, who had opened a door. Beyond it was another room, furnished with the sort of camp beds provided by the American Quartermaster Corps; two young women were lying on them, one stark naked, the other white and clad in a sarong. Her eyes followed Lara, their pupils reduced to a pinpoint from heroin. On a gorgeous lacquered table from Bien Hoa was a metal tray with syringes. The Black passed through the room without stopping and entered a narrow, three-foot-wide passageway with corrugated tin walls. A little farther on he entered a smoking room. Very young American soldiers in uniform, some of them Black and some White, were lying there in an atmosphere heavy with the overpowering sweetish odor of opium. Smoking room wasn't really the right word for this den: Evidently not having the patience to smoke the opium, the youngsters were simply chewing and swallowing it. The Black passed through this room and finally stopped some twenty yards farther on, in front of a sort of shanty made of cardboard and corrugated tin.

"If he blows you sky high, it's not my fault."

With these words, the Black turned on his heel and left, his enormous basketball player's shoulders touching both sides of the narrow passageway.

Lara waited until he had disappeared from sight. He glanced about and spied an elderly Vietnamese squatting on his haunches a dozen paces away, observing him with an utterly blank expression in his eyes.

"What's inside here?" Lara asked him in Vietnamese.

The man didn't so much as blink an eye for a good ten seconds, then shrugged. "A man with a hand grenade."

"Thanks," Lara said.

He walked over to the sort of door, which had neither frame nor lock and in fact was simply a cardboard panel. Very slowly, he pushed the panel aside and entered. He found himself this time in almost total darkness. He squatted down on his heels, waiting for his eyes to accommodate to the very dim light. Finally he was able to make out a silhouette lying at the far end of this redoubt, feet facing him.

"Jon?"

There was no reply, but a change in the rhythm of the silhouette's breathing assured him that his voice had been heard.

"Jon, my name is Lara. Some ten years ago I went to Colorado, and I met you at your grandfather's. You and I took a long walk together in the forest. I showed you how the Moïs in Cambodia make crossbows."

Silence.

"May I smoke? There's no one with me, of course."

Still receiving no answer, he slowly fished his package of Bastoses out of his breast pocket, and then his lighter. The flame flared up, and the first thing he saw, outside of Jon Kinkaird's eyes staring at him, was the grenade the youngster was holding against his chest.

The flame went out.

"Do you remember me, Jon?"

"Yes."

"I can get you out of here. Not only out of this place, but out of Vietnam. You can come to Cambodia with me. Over there, you won't have to see anybody at all. You'll be able to do whatever you like and go wherever you want to. Do you understand what I'm saying? Jon?"

"Yes."

"Your sister's in Saigon. She's looking for you. Do you want to see her?"

"No!"

Lara's hand, searching along the floor, finally found the electric cord and slowly crept upward along it.

"I can see your every move," Jon said. "You've seen the grenade. I'll blow myself up if you turn the light on." Jon Kinkaird's voice was hoarse, like a hiss at times, but very slow, as though he were half asleep.

"Okay. I've got all the time in the world. I have no intention of forcing you to do anything. Especially not with that grenade you're holding. If it were to go off, I'd be blown up with it. You don't have any reason to kill me. I came here to help you get out of this country. I've arranged everything: a plane is waiting to take you to Cambodia. You're free to make up your own mind. You know very well that you can trust me."

Prolonged silence.

"I warn you," Jon said, "I'm not letting go of this grenade. Not for one minute."

"That's okay by me," Lara said. "Keep it if you want to. But please be careful with it."

"I don't want anybody to touch me. I don't want anybody to come near me."

"You should talk to your sister. Just talk with her, that's all. She deserves it."

"No, I said." Again the same zombielike voice.

Lara slowly rose to his feet and backed out of the room. The old Vietnamese was still there and again stared at him with blank eyes.

"Okay, Jon, come on out," Lara said in his gentle voice.

In the room where Lara had left Kutchaï and Morrachini, the situation was nearly the same as before, except that someone had turned on the stereo and soft music was coming out of its four speakers. When Lara came back into the room, Kutchaï suddenly relaxed, but the Corsican's eyes opened wide when he spotted the grenade that Jon Kinkaird was clutching to his stomach.

"Well, that's that," Lara said to the Black.

The Black's eyes traveled from Jon to Lara. "You're taking him away?" he asked.

"He's coming with me," Lara corrected him. "Of his own free will. Just ask him."

Turning around as he spoke, Lara had his first real look at Jon Kinkaird. The youngster was scarcely more than a living corpse: His beard had grown out, swallowing up an emaciated face in which only the eyes showed any sign of life. He was staggering, blinded by the light, blinking. He was so filthy he was repulsive, stained with vomit and with what must have been his own excrement.

The Black approached Jon with lithe, dancing footsteps, planted himself directly in front of him, and asked in a surprisingly warm tone of voice, "Do you really want to take off with this guy, Jonnie?"

A sudden gleam appeared in Jon Kinkaird's amazing violet eyes. "It's okay, Harry," he said.

"There's nothing forcing you to go with him if you don't want to. Me and my pals can defend you."

"I know," Jon said. "But it's okay. Everything's really cool."

The Black hesitated. He turned his head toward Lara. "This kid's a really great basketball player," he said in a curious tone of voice, at once proud and threatening.

"Come on, Jon," Lara said.

As he turned to head for the door, his eyes met Kutchaï's and he immediately saw a tension, almost a warning, in them. "What's wrong?" Lara asked in Khmer.

Kutchaï shook his head: "I don't know."

They went out the door and walked through the same narrow passageway they'd entered by, Morrachini leading the way, followed by Kutchaï, with Lara drawing up the rear at Kinkaird's heels.

"Put the grenade under your shirt at least," Lara said to him.

They went back through the sort-of-den that looked like a pawnshop and finally came out into what was almost a street.

"The car isn't very far from here," Morrachini said. "I'll be damned— that whole scene wasn't so bad after all! What do you want us to do now, Lara? We could go to Ferrari's place—it's not far."

"We're going straight to where Boudin's waiting for us," Lara said.

"Have you seen the state the kid's in?" Morrachini asked. "He's apt to collapse any minute now. That thing he's got in his hand is a grenade and he's pulled the pin. If he lets go of it, there'll be a real bloodbath. We'll be all blown to smithereens with him."

"There's no other solution." Once again Lara looked into Kutchaï's eyes. The indefinable sensation that something was about to happen.

"Yes," the Khmer said in his own language. "Me too."

"What kind of a game are you two playing anyway?" the Corsican asked in an anxious voice.

"Keep walking," Lara said. "Fast."

But Jon, who was beside him, was dragging himself along, about to collapse, his eyelids heavier and heavier, his mouth desperately gasping for breath.

"Listen, Jon. All I'm going to do now is take your other arm to hold you up. I won't do anything else, just hold you up. Okay? Just keep calm."

He slid his hand under Jon Kinkaird's right armpit, held his tall body more or less upright, and forced him to walk. Jon's hand holding the grenade had disappeared underneath his shirt. *He might very well let go of it without even realizing it,* Lara thought.

"We're almost there, Jon. You can make it."

"The car," Morrachini said.

The little square where they'd parked. The Mercedes was still there all right, but it looked somehow oddly isolated: The few people passing by a while before had all disappeared, as had the jeep with the four policemen in it.

"Something's not right," Morrachini said. "What's happened to those damned cops?"

"Get in front," Lara said to Kutchaï. "I'll take care of Jon."

"I don't like this at all," Morrachini said. "I smell a rat."

Lara sat down in the back seat, still holding Jon's arm.

Morrachini had backed out of the parking space and was shifting into first when it happened: Car lights suddenly came on and police appeared, shouting orders. Lara dived for Kinkaird's hand just as he was about to open it, clutching the young American's fingers tightly in his two clenched fists. Jon and Lara rolled about on the floor of the back seat, wrestling with each other in a tangle of arms and legs. The Mercedes leapt forward as Morrachini gave its powerful six cylinders full throttle. The car hit something in front of it with a violent shock. A volley of shots rang out. The car skidded, collided with several unidentifiable obstacles, took off again each time with a roar, drove over something, and then through something. And finally a sudden miraculous quiet, with no sound but the hum of the tires on the pavement.

"Cool it," Lara said to Jon. "Everything's okay. Relax. Get up. Slow and easy."

IIe had not managed to get the grenade away from Jon. But at least he'd managed to keep him from dropping it. As the car passed through successive zones of light and darkness, young Kinkaird's striking violet eyes brought the memory of Lisa's to his mind, as vivid as a hallucination.

"Get up. Slowly. I'm going to let go of you."

Lara, too, got up off the floor. The first thing he saw was Kutchaï, laughing, his wolf's jaw with its formidable teeth gleaming in the dim light.

"We drove right through their shanties! Straight through! This car's a tank!"

Lara turned around to look through the rear window. It was true: The Mercedes had plowed an enormous furrow straight through any number of miserable shanties.

"Was anybody hurt?"

"I don't think so," the Khmer said. "But I'm not sure—it all happened so fast."

Not until they reached the highway again did Lara realize that Morrachini had been hit. The Corsican's head was leaning farther and farther forward, and his hands were falling slowly away from the wheel, as though letting go of it reluctantly.

"Jean-Baptiste!"

Lara reached out, touched Morrachini's shoulder, felt something damp beneath his fingers. Kutchaï realized what had happened at the same moment; he hurriedly leaned over, grabbed the steering wheel, and turned off the ignition key. The Mercedes rolled on for several dozen yards more, then stopped as Kutchaï pulled the hand brake on.

"Don't move, whatever you do!" Lara said to Jon.

He leapt out of the car, walked hurried around it, and opened the door on the driver's side. Kutchaï was already laying Morrachini down across the two front seats. He raised his head.

"A bullet in the throat. He's done for."

Brokenhearted, Lara leaned over the Corsican. Despite the spurting blood, the entry wound was perfectly visible, a hole just underneath his left ear. There was another wound as well, just above his heart. Lara closed his eyes. "Oh, no!" A wave of grief and pity engulfed him. "Not Morrachini! He was just trying to help us!"

"He's dead," Kutchaï said, deeply touched in turn by the look on Lara's face. "We'd better not stick around here. Dieu's men will be back any minute to finish off the job. Give me a hand."

He grabbed Morrachini by the shoulders and sat him up in the seat he himself had occupied till the moment before. He slid in behind the wheel and started the engine again. Lara just stood there outside the door on the driver's side, not moving, as the Jaraï slowly began to pull it shut.

"Come on," Kutchaï said softly. "Come on, get in. It's no use standing there eating your heart out."

The Mercedes took off again. Lara sat on the back seat, contemplating the lights of Tan Son Hut fading in the distance behind them and the night filled with moths. The air throbbed with the low rumble of a cargo plane landing.

"Did you see what happened?"

"It was Dieu. I got a good look at him, and I'm sure. He yelled to us to get out with our hands up. Morrachini put his foot to the floor then. Because of that damned grenade, I suppose—he probably thought we'd all be blown to bits if he stopped. That's all I saw, except that after that we drove straight through people's shacks."

Lara was deathly pale. Kutchaï glanced at Kinkaird in the rearview mirror. The young man had curled up in a ball on the back seat, as far as possible from Lara, his strange violet eyes staring into space. *He may not even have realized what happened*, Kutchaï thought. *In any case, he never once let go of his damned grenade.*

In a low-pitched, pitiless tone of voice Lara said to Jon in English, "That man who's dead was worth as much as you are. And maybe even more. And he was my friend."

They drove along for several minutes in silence.

"What should we do?" Kutchaï asked. "We'd be out of our minds to go back to Saigon now. Dieu can call out all his cops to hunt us down. And they'll be watching for this car and spot it immediately."

"We're going to Mytho, to Ferrari's place. He'll lend us another car."

Kutchaï glanced at the clock on the dashboard, noting that it showed exactly the same time as his watch: 9:50 P.M.

"And once we get there, our only hope is that that crazy fool of a Boudin will be there too."

Still looking in the rearview mirror, Kutchaï glanced at Lara. He was slowly massaging his shoulder, his pale eyes filled with sadness.

12

SOMEONE HAD PASSED THE STORY ON TO MATTHEW KINKAIRD, swearing that it was absolutely true: It had happened in the fall of '68, on the campus of the University of Denver. A man of about fifty who gave every appearance of being a veteran of the Second World War in the Pacific, wearing a ruptured duck button in his lapel that confirmed this impression, had aggressively confronted a youngster less than twenty years old and had silently contemplated for a moment the boy's empty sleeve.

"You lost your arm while you were doing your military service?"

"Yes."

"In Vietnam?"

The young man smiled timidly at him, touched that someone had taken an interest in what had happened to him. "Yes. I lost it at Tam Ky. I was in the First Corps."

"Serves you right," the veteran of Guadalcanal or Iwo Jima replied. "You had no right to be there in the first place."

At the time, Matthew couldn't believe the story was true. He'd repeated it to Jubal Wynn, and the San Francisco attorney had stated categorically that he was convinced that if the story was not literally true, it might as well have been, and had added that he had personally witnessed similar confrontations, or heard Vietnam veterans recount the same experience. That the Vietnam war was turning America rotten to the core was gospel truth as far as Wynn was concerned.

Matthew Kinkaird was mulling such stories over in his mind as he waited for the piercing voice of the Vietnam telephone operator at the far side of the world to inform him, in almost incomprehensible English, that his granddaughter was on the other end of the line at last. And then the miracle happened, and he heard Lisa's voice: "Grandfather?"

"Oh, thank God!" Matthew exclaimed with a great sigh of relief. "I've been waiting for hours and hours trying to get in touch with you, I had despaired of ever getting a call through."

"What's happening there at your end?"

"I've gotten a cable from Lara. I don't think I've said anything to you about him, but ..."

"What did the cable say exactly?"

"He's found Jon."

A silence. Then Lisa's voice, incredibly calm: "When was that? When did the telegram arrive, I mean?"

"Three hours ago. They telephoned it to me from Colorado Springs." Again a silence.

"That's good news," Lisa said.

"Do you mean to say you didn't know?"

"That's right."

"I don't understand. I thought you could fill me in on all the details."

"I don't know anything about it," she said. "Nothing at all."

It was now Matthew's turn to remain silent for several seconds. Finally he said, "Lisa, what in the world is happening there? Something's wrong. I can tell by your voice."

"It's ten-thirty at night here," she answered, as though he'd asked her specifically what the time difference was. "I haven't the least idea what's going on, Grandpa. I don't know where Jon is. I'm still trying to track him down."

"Lisa ..."

"Everything's all right, Grandpa. Please don't worry. I'll call you again as soon as I have any news."

"Lisa!" He had a sudden intuition. "Lisa, you're not alone, is that it?"

"Yes."

"The police?"

"Yes."

"But is everything really going all right?"

"Yes. I love you, Grandpa. Good-bye."

It was Lisa who hung up first. Then she turned around and confronted Dieu.

13

IT WAS A SHORT STRIP WITH JUST ENOUGH ROOM FOR THE CESSNA to land. It had been laid out twenty-five years earlier to serve the two adjacent plantations, but it had been overrun with vegetation in the intervening years. In fact, Ferrari couldn't manage to drive his car all the way to the runway.

"I can't go any farther. If I remember rightly, the strip is more or less straight ahead of us. Behind those three tall trees over there."

Ferrari was a rough-voiced Corsican in his fifties, marked forever by his twenty-five years in the colonial infantry; he was short, thin, and tough, and did his best to appear even tougher than he really was. He hadn't batted an eye on spotting Morrachini's dead body and had listened without a word to Lara's story and his explanation of how it had all happened. Ferrari knew Lara only slightly, mostly through what Jean-Baptiste Morrachini had told him about him, and apparently that was all he needed to know. "In any event, you've brought his body and his car here to my place, and it's up to me to take care of things. I really owe that to Jean-Baptiste. I'll see to everything." He'd refused the money that Lara had offered him. "It's not a question of money."

Ferrari turned around toward Lara, who was sitting in the back seat of the car.

"And you're sure there's a plane ready to take off? Even though it's pitch-dark?"

"It should be there," Lara answered.

Kutchaï got out. "I'm going to take a look around," he announced.

He disappeared into the dark, moving as usual without making a sound. Ferrari also got out, and sat down a dozen yards from the car, probably because of the grenade that Jon Kinkaird was still holding. After a moment Lara joined him, panting with barely contained rage. Ferrari raised his eyes and looked at him.

"And what if the plane isn't here?"

Lara shrugged. There were clouds in the night sky, but the moon appeared now and again, shedding enough light so that they could see thirty or forty feet ahead of them.

"Jean-Baptiste had bought a villa at Carqueiranne," Ferrari said, speaking very softly. "Do you know where Carqueiranne is?"

Lara shook his head.

"It's not far from Toulon. A nice place. Jean-Baptiste was planning to retire there. He told me he was going back there to live and spend all his time following rugby matches. He was crazy about rugby. That's really funny—a Corsican in Indochina who dreams of nothing but rugby. He was absolutely nuts about it."

"You should leave soon," Lara said. "You're running a risk by sticking around here."

"And what if the plane's not here?"

"I'm going to get that youngster out of the car," was Lara's only answer.

Jon Kinkaird had assumed exactly the same position in Ferrari's Renault as in Morrachini's Mercedes: all huddled up in one corner of the back seat.

"Get out," Lara said.

The young man didn't budge.

"Get out or I'll drag you out and so much the worse if we both get blown up."

Kinkaird at last decided to get out of the car. As he stood up in the darkness, he looked all at once gigantic.

Ferrari came back over to the car.

"Clear out of here," Lara said to him. "Don't put yourself to any more trouble for us. You've never seen us before in your life. Thanks. I'll remember what you've done for me."

"But I can't just leave you here like this."

"Go on."

They shook hands. The Corsican got behind the wheel, turned the car around and took off, driving very slowly, not daring to turn his headlights on yet. After a moment the sound of the engine died away and silence fell once again. Lara sat down on the ground, lit a cigarette, shielding his lighter with his jacket and then holding the cigarette in his cupped hand to hide the glowing tip of it.

"I'm so sorry." Jon Kinkaird's voice, oddly enough much firmer than at any other point thus far, echoed dangerously in the silence of the night.

"Shut up."

"I didn't ask anybody to help me," Jon went on. "But I'm . . ."

"Shut your trap," Lara said.

He rose to his feet, peering anxiously through the tall weeds as he waited for Kutchaï to return, seized once again by that panting rage that had come over him a few moments before.

"Listen," Kinkaird said. "When you arrived . . ."

Lara bounded forward. In two steps he was on top of Jon, this time grabbing not the hand that was holding the grenade but the youngster's wrist, jerking it away from his body and forcing him to stretch his arm out.

"Go ahead!" Lara panted. "Let go of it! Come on! Let's see you drop it!"

Time seemed to stop. Then Jon Kinkaird shook his head.

"I'm sorry," he said. "Really sorry."

But he was whispering now, with closed eyes. After a moment, Lara relaxed. The silence enveloped them. Kinkaird opened his eyes again.

"Are we really going to Cambodia?"

"We're going to try at least."

Several minutes went by. Then there was a slight rustling sound in the tall grass three yards from them and Kutchaï appeared.

"The two of you were yelling so loud you could be heard for miles. . . ." He glanced in the direction Ferrari had taken, and went on: "Boudin's here. I happened on him by chance as I was crawling around an ant. He managed

to flutter down like a dead leaf just as night was falling and he's been waiting since. The guy's hopping mad."

He walked over to Kinkaird and noted that the grenade was still in his
hand.

"Maybe it's time he got rid of that thing, what do you say? Papa Boudin's never going to let anybody come aboard his supersonic transport with
a thing like that."

"Throw it away," Lara said to Jon in English.

The violet eyes stared at him.

"Throw it away or we'll leave you here."

Lara was obliged to take the grenade away from Jon, loosening his
tightly clenched fingers one by one.

They had to walk more than four hundred yards before they reached the
spot where Boudin was. The little Alsatian suddenly appeared in front of
them as though he'd popped up out of the ground, somehow managing to
scream without raising his voice above a whisper:

"Don't hurry! Oh, certainly not! I'm at your beck and call—is that
what you think? I'm at your entire disposal—is that what you think? Do you
think I'm doing all this for my pleasure—landing in the dark and taking off
in the middle of the night? Is that what you think?"

Venting his rage in a furious hiss, he pushed and tugged them toward a
clump of trees that turned out to be frangipanis, and what they might easily
have mistaken for an ordinary straight branch was suddenly transformed
into an airplane wing.

Kutchaï had hurried off at a run.

"Get aboard, for Christ's sake," Boudin screamed in a whisper. "Did I
ask you to do anything? It's my plane. Kutchaï's gone off to light a fire. Do
you think I'd know where the damned airstrip is otherwise?"

He scampered about in all directions like a mad mouse. Finally he sat
down in front of the controls and the tiny lights on the dashboard lit up the
round face screwed into a fierce scowl.

"What was that explosion I heard a minute ago?"

"Nothing important," Lara answered.

A giant shadow appeared and Kutchaï climbed aboard. Five or six hundred yards ahead, a fire was burning.

"Make it quick," he said. "It's not going to last long."

"Go to hell," Boudin said.

He turned the ignition switch on. Despite the fire glowing in the distance, the night was so dark that he was unable to make out a single thing
by the light of it. It seemed impossible to take off in a plane at a speed of
over a hundred miles an hour.

"Boudin, what a stupid ass you are," Boudin said. "Really too stupid for words. You have to be an ass like Boudin to try and pull off a trick like this!" He glared at Kutchaï as the roar of the revving engine grew louder and louder.

"Hey, listen, I didn't say a word!" Kutchaï said. "It's your plane."

The Cessna throbbed, screamed, headed down the strip, gradually picked up speed, and finally got off the ground, just barely clearing the glowing flames that marked the end of the airstrip. Suddenly it was airborne, a minuscule cell barely lighted by the reddish glow of the dials on the dashboard and suspended in an utter void.

"God damn it to hell. How I hate flying," Boudin said.

Roger, who had been searching the sky for more than five hours, heard them before he saw them, a sort of humming sound, a few minutes before one in the morning. He even thought he could make them out, in the form of a dark dot flying over the little lights and the dimly lit bridge of Kampot. The humming sound died away and then, after a silence, became a dull roar as the Cessna appeared, its red and green lights on, flying so low it nearly brushed the top of his head.

"One, two, three, four, five, six . . ."

At the count of fifty, he ran over to the wicks and lit them.

A little later he asked Lara, "Did everything go all right?"

"No," Lara answered.

Roger caught sight of the young American, who seemed, especially in the dark, to be at least six and a half feet tall. They got into the truck and drove back to Takeo, exchanging the truck for the Studebaker there. It was two-thirty in the morning when they arrived in Phnom Penh.

As for Boudin, he hadn't even switched off the engine of the Cessna but had taken off again by himself, heading for Pochentong, where he had landed a few minutes before 1:20 A.M.

14

DIEU LOOKED AT LISA. "YOU DON'T HAVE TO TELL ME WHO CALLED you, naturally."

"My grandfather, phoning me from the United States. He's worried."

The outside door of Lisa's room was open. Dieu sighed.

"Which name should I call you—Mrs. Trenton or Mrs. Kinkaird?"

"Whichever you like."

"We very nearly found your brother," Dieu said. "As a matter of fact, we just barely missed him. Somebody kidnapped him, right under our very noses. We were able, of course, to identify the kidnappers' car. It belongs to a Corsican who's well known in Saigon, whom we're bound to track down in just a short time. Does the name Jean-Baptiste Morrachini mean anything to you?"

"Absolutely nothing."

"I personally recognized Morrachini at the wheel of his car. But he wasn't alone. There were three other men with him: two Occidentals, one of whom was your brother, and an Asian who might very well be a Cambodian. You still don't have any idea what's going on?"

"Not the slightest," Lisa answered.

"Who else besides me did you ask for help in finding your brother?"

"Nobody."

At that moment Gaitskell, the foreign officer from the American Embassy, appeared in the doorway, silhouetted against the light in the corridor.

"I came just as soon as I could," he said to Lisa.

It turned out that he was not alone. Another American and a Vietnamese had come with him. Gaitskell, his two companions, and Dieu all stepped out into the corridor, where they talked together for a long time in low voices. Then Gaitskell came back into the room alone.

"The story that Dieu's just told me is pretty incredible. Why didn't you tell me from the very first that you were looking for your brother?"

Lisa shrugged. It was 2:40 A.M., Saigon time, by her wristwatch. "Don't be ridiculous," Lisa said. "This whole thing is none of my doing. I'm somebody who works in an ad agency in New York, not a lieutenant in the Mafia."

Gaitskell shifted from one foot to the other, scratching his forehead at the hairline every so often with the nail of his little finger. "An incredible story, really incredible."

He moved a step or two toward the corridor as though he were about to leave, then changed his mind. "Listen, if you know something, tell me. The ambassador himself is going to be obliged to look into this whole affair."

"I know absolutely nothing about it," Lisa said. "And I'd like to get some sleep. You and the ambassador and anybody else can interrogate me for days and weeks, but I still couldn't tell you anything except: I don't know one thing about it." She sat down on the edge of the bed. "And if you or anyone else is still here in my room one minute from now, he'll have the pleasure of seeing me stark naked. Because I have every intention of getting undressed and going to bed."

At these words from her, all of them left.

The next morning around nine o'clock she was awakened by the telephone ringing. She picked up the receiver and was told there was a call for her from someone in Bangkok. The someone in question didn't give his name, and though he spoke very good English, he was obviously French. He was calling simply to pass on a message he'd been given for her. The message advised her to go to Phnom Penh. No further details.

She got dressed, unable to decide whether she felt more angry than relieved or vice versa. The telephone rang again. This time it was Gaitskell, who just wanted to know how she was and whether there were any new developments since he'd left her the night before. She replied that the situation was still exactly the same.

She went downstairs to have coffee on the terrace, watching the colorful spectacle in the street below without really seeing it, and then, having come to a decision, went straight to the reception desk.

"May I put in a call to the U.S.?"

As usual, the Vietnamese answered yes, but it was plain to see he hadn't understood one word of the question she'd asked him in English. She repeated it in French and then, changing her mind at once, asked where the Air France office was. They gave her the address. At Air France she was informed that to get to Phnom Penh she would have to go by way of Bangkok, since there was no direct flight between South Vietnam and Cambodia. She bought a ticket, paying cash for it.

On her return to the hotel, she began a letter to Matthew Kinkaird, in which she told him everything that had happened: how Lara had intervened in the situation, and what the consequences of this intervention had been, for herself first of all and then for Jon, who, according to what Lara had hinted, must now be in Cambodia, where she was going herself if the Vietnamese police didn't interfere. She was just writing the last lines when there was a knock at her door. She walked over and opened it, and found herself face to face with Dieu.

"Let's get all of this straight," Dieu said. "Last night one of my men was seriously injured when he was run over by the car of this Corsican whom you claim to know nothing about. I've already told you that deserters from the American Army don't interest me as long as they don't break the laws of my country. My man has a broken leg and a fractured rib cage. I therefore have every reason to intervene in this whole affair."

The police official glanced about the room and his eye fell on the suitcase that Lisa had almost finished packing.

"There's another thing," he said. "You came to see me to ask for my help in finding your brother. Last night, just as I was about to satisfy your wishes in this regard, this incident that we both know about occurred. And a few hours later, what happens? You go to the Air France office and purchase a plane ticket for Phnom Penh via Bangkok."

"You can't stop me from leaving," Lisa said.

"Certainly not, in the final analysis. But I can delay your departure for a considerable length of time." He smiled. "You can take my word for that."

Lisa shrugged and, as proof of her perfect sangfroid, sat down at the writing desk and finished her letter to her grandfather. Dieu watched her, still smiling. She signed it, added the little x's and o's that mean love and kisses, slid the letter into an envelope, sealed it, and was about to rise to her feet.

"Lara," Dieu said.

She froze.

"You had dinner with him night before last, in a Chinese restaurant the name of which I don't know; my informer failed to mention it. On the other hand, a great many people on the staff of this hotel know Monsieur Lara. Lara and the very tall Cambodian who's always with him, whenever he comes to Saigon. And everybody knows that Monsieur Lara lives in Cambodia."

Dieu joined his two pudgy little hands, glancing at his wristwatch, a gold chronometer, as he did so. "Your plane will be leaving in a little less than three hours."

Lisa lowered her head and then raised it. She reached for her handbag on the writing desk next to her. She opened it.

"Ten thousand dollars."

"For a broken leg and a fractured rib cage?" He shook his head.

She turned the handbag upside down and poured everything in it out on top of the writing desk. "Count up for yourself," she said. "Twenty thousand one hundred dollars. It's every cent I have left."

Dieu took one step forward.

"On one condition," Lisa said. "You're to escort me, personally, to my plane. And I'm not going to hand over the twenty thousand dollars to you till after I'm past the passenger check-out."

He nodded his head, an amused expression on his face. "In other words, you'll be putting me in a very compromising situation."

She placed the twenty thousand-dollar bills in another envelope.

"Precisely," she said.

She got off the plane in Bangkok on the sixteenth of April 1969, in the late afternoon, only to be informed that the next flight for Phnom Penh, via Royal Air Cambodia, would not be leaving till the following morning. Having considered the possibility of spending the night at the airport, she found a TWA flight crew that drove her into town to the Hotel Erawan, where she shared a room with a stewardess from Wyoming.

She took off for Phnom Penh the following day, the seventeenth, with only seventy dollars left to her name. And a hundred French francs.

Part Two

THE PLANTATION AT PRAH VIHEAR

1 THAT MORNING, AS ON THOUSANDS OF OTHER MORNINGS IN THE PAST, Charles and Madeleine Korver left their villa in Phnom Penh together. It was a villa in a quiet little street lined with overhanging tamarinds, behind the Phnom and the former French Embassy. They left on foot, as they did every day, starting their walk by heading down the left-hand sidewalk of the Mona Vithei, the Avenue of the French, for several hundred yards. It was eleven A.M.

Charles and Madeleine Korver had lived in Phnom Penh since July 21, 1933. They both remembered the exact date they had moved there, for the simple reason that both their birthdays were on the twenty-first of July and it had been their wedding date as well. Charles Korver was seventy and Madeleine sixty-eight. He had been born in Shanghai and she in Hanoi, and it was in this latter city that they had met, and an annual ball given by the Tonkin Coal Corporation, from which both their families derived a large part of their considerable fortunes. Both of them had Alsatian grandfathers who had arrived in Tonkin at practically the same time, immediately following the Franco-Prussian War, after having hesitated between the Far East and Algeria.

On the first day of their married life, once their immediate effusions of joy had passed, Charles and Madeleine had taken stock of their assets and discovered that their combined fortunes—provided they were managed with meticulous care—would permit them to live a life of leisure and also to satisfy their common passion: collecting Chinese and Indochinese objets d'art. In fact, they would be able to devote most of their time to collecting, even if Charles Korver—who had nonchalantly gone through law school, making excellent grades, and received his law degree—occasionally agreed to take on work as a consultant. But with a few rare exceptions (among them the constitution of Cambodia, which he had personally drafted) his advice had not usually been followed. Who could trust an attorney who refused to accept any sort of fee for his services, claiming he had no need of money?

In fifty years of marriage they had scrupulously fulfilled their contract: They had devoted their time and energy so exclusively to collecting art works and traveling that they'd even neglected to start a family. When their villa in Phnom Penh was full to overflowing with treasures, they had started to ship their subsequent purchases to a large country mansion they owned in France, in the Bordelais, and naturally they had planned to end their days there. In 1959, they had in fact left Phnom Penh, taking with them on the boat almost a ton of bibelots, porcelains, ceramics, pieces of furniture, a thousand things each more precious than the last. They had paid the import duties of some 11 million old francs levied on their collection, but after only four months of French life, homesickness for Indochina had overcome both of them and they had returned to Phnom Penh, bringing the majority of their treasures back with them. And people in Phnom Penh once again saw their two small, frail silhouettes walking with tiny footsteps along the Boulevard Norodom each morning, hand in hand, invariably cheery and smiling, two people become a single person, one of them beginning a sentence and the other finishing it.

Leaving the Avenue des Français this morning, they came out on the esplanade of the Phnom, walking across it in a direction that would take them by the Palais du Gouvernement, whose Neo-Greco-Indian architecture with a slight flavor of the Exposition Universelle of 1900 always put them in a joyous mood.

This was apparently a morning like any other, except that there were clouds in the sky to the west and also, Madeleine claimed, a sort of chill in the warm air, though the temperature must have been in the mid-eighties. "I'm not intelligent," Madeleine Korver often said of herself. "I'm not as intelligent as Charles, who knows everything, but I'm like cats: I intuitively sense tidal waves, epidemics, earthquakes, gas leaks; and I'm certain I'd sense a revolution brewing if by chance there was one in the offing." Charles' unfailing answer to this was a derisive "meow."

They arrived at the Boulevard Norodom, having made their way around the esplanade of the Phnom to their left. Madeleine sniffed the air, delicately touched her hair with the tips of her fingers (it was tinted an azure blue and arranged in a style that hadn't changed since 1925, a coiffure with a part on the side and a wide wave over her right temple), and said in her little-girl voice:

"Charles, I think there's a revolution brewing."

"Really, my darling?" Charles replied offhandedly.

He contemplated the Boulevard Norodom and could detect no sign of anything out of the ordinary. As far as he could see, it looked the same as it always did: cars, very few of them, proceeding nonchalantly down the boulevard, a few trucks, a bus, pedicab boys pedaling with one leg and chewing a length of sugar cane, people sauntering along the sidewalks; in short, the usual Phnom Penh, fragrant, easygoing, peaceful. Unbelievably pleasant, languid, serene.

Charles Korver knew Cambodia like the palm of his hand; he knew each and every thinker in the country, or at least every man who believed himself capable of thinking. The intimate of most of the ministers and above all of the Palace, to which he still had easy entrée, thanks to his long-standing friendship with the Queen Mother, he'd watched Samdech Euv's clown act for years and had a connoisseur's appreciation of it, feeling sympathy and something close to affection for the little Chief of State who had once been king. He had seen him struggle desperately to keep his country from being involved in the fighting in Indochina, to try to remain friends with everyone. He had been witness to the bloody crushing of the coup d'état that the right, financed by the CIA, had attempted in 1959, and the no less brutal suppression of a second plot, this time staged by the left.

For some time, however, Charles Korver had had the feeling that Samdech Sihanouk was no longer in top form. When had he first had that feeling? In 1965, when the breaking off of diplomatic relations with the United States and the sacking of their embassy had taken place? In '66, at the time of the elections, in which, curiously enough, Sihanouk had taken no interest—he who up until then had always run everything, refereeing soccer matches, writing the music for films of which he was also the producer, the scenarist, the director, and even the leading actor? Or was it in '67? In '67 there had been that disappearance, that retreat into the forest, so rumor had it, of the four leftist deputies who had been legally elected but, after being pursued by Lon Nol's police, had chosen to go underground. *And among them that madman, Ieng Samboth, with his incendiary theories. A fine young man all the same, with close ties to Lara. Maybe the open air will help him get his head screwed on straight. . . .*

Charles Korver didn't really believe that the four leftists represented any real danger for the regime; at any rate, not as long as Sihanouk remained at the helm. And in fact . . . It was in that same year, 1967, that the differences between Sihanouk and Lon Nol had begun to be quite apparent, to the eyes of insiders; in 1967 that the Khmer refugees from Cochin China, and anti-Communist Khmer Krom, had begun to settle on Cambodian soil, clearly constituting a possible weapon, or even a potential army, for Lon Nol's right; in 1967 that the American bombing of Khmer villages accused of sheltering Viet Cong (*an accusation, moreover, that is undoubtedly true*) had begun, and the first violations of the border by troops from Saigon exercising their so-called "right of pursuit." Disturbing developments, all of them.

"Charles," Madeleine said in her little piping voice, "I assure you that something's brewing. It's not something that's going to happen today, or in the next few days. But there's definitely something brewing."

"I believe you, my love. You know very well that I always believe you."

"You're just saying that to please me."

"I swear to you I'm not."

They were walking along the Boulevard Norodom now, following the same itinerary they had followed every morning for some twenty-five years, and which they would no more have dreamed of changing than they would have contemplated divorce.

Charles was certain that the totally unexpected success of the Viet Cong offensive against Saigon in 1968, the near-collapse of the South Vietnamese and American armies, had saved Cambodia from a coup d'état by Lon Nol, who in turn was being prodded by Sirik Matak, the Cambodian prince on extremely friendly terms with the CIA. But this had merely been a respite: The installation of Richard Nixon in the White House in January 1969, three months ago, the new President's avowed determination to maintain the American presence in Vietnam—even if only indirectly, by way of the "Vietnamization" of the war—had doubtless reassured the conspirators. In fact, the slow and relentless orchestration of events intended to eliminate Sihanouk had begun again. And neither the intensification of the American bombing of southern Cambodia, nor even the spraying of defoliants from the air over certain Khmer rubber plantations suspected of hiding Viet Cong troops, had prevented the reestablishment of diplomatic relations between Cambodia and the U.S. during this month of April, 1969. *Which means, in effect, that it won't be long now before the coup d'état is launched. How long? Six months? A year?*

Still hand in hand, the Korvers passed by the coral trees of the Ministry of National Education, which, with the Phnom Penh fondness for acronyms and abbreviations that was rapidly becoming a mania, was called the Minéducanal.

"Yet Phnom Penh is so marvelously peaceful," Madeleine said. "They surely won't change our city, will they?"

"Phnom Pĕnh will never change."

They turned left into the Rue Khemarak Phoumin, then again to the right, into the Ruc Yukanthor, and there straight ahead of them were the terrace and balcony of the Taï-San restaurant, their goal.

A year, Charles Korver thought to himself. *It will take them at least a year. Providing Sihanouk lets them get away with it.* It seemed impossible to believe that Sihanouk was being taken in, that he was unable to see that a coup was in the making.

They sat down on the terrace of the Taï-San, a Chinese restaurant whose principal merit was that it was in the very heart of the city. Charles and Madeleine preferred it to the Taverne, which was too French to suit them. They ordered iced coffee in a tall glass, in Chinese *sut café naï li poui,* this being more or less the sum total of their knowledge of Cantonese.

At the next table was a Cambodian magistrate, a pot-bellied, likable man who presided over one of the courts in Phnom Penh—at least he did in theory; no one had ever seen him in a courtroom—and whose principal claim to fame was a bizarre perversion: He always wore a handkerchief perfumed with human excrement in his breast pocket, and would sniff its effluvia with voluptuous pleasure. He smiled at the Korvers, who returned his smile.

What troubled Charles Korver most about the situation in Cambodia in this spring of 1969, and what was to trouble him even more in the months to come, was Sihanouk's attitude. Just as they had helped to thwart the attempted pro-American coup d'état in 1959, the French intelligence services had alerted Samdech to the possibility of a coup being staged by Lon Nol and Sirik Matak; the Australians and the Chinese had done the same. Besides that, there had been no lack of warning signs: It was more or less a matter of common knowledge, for instance, that Sirik Matak had received a payment of some $3 million through the intermediary of a supposed banker who had come with the money from Bangkok, a certain Song Sakd; and then there were the trips to Indonesia, in November of '68 and January of '69, made by officers loyal to Lon Nol—in order to study on the spot the techniques that had ensured the success of the coup that toppled Sukarno from power. *And what is Sihanouk doing? Nothing. The weariness of the high-stakes player? Overconfidence?* Charles Korver didn't understand.

They were served the iced coffees and he relaxed, looking over at his wife, who seemed a bit tired, he decided. This walk they took every morning was perhaps beginning to be just a little too long for her. For a moment he gave way to his emotion, to all the love and tenderness he had felt for her for more than half a century. Around them, the terrace of the Taï-San was filling up with Chinese and Cambodians flocking in for their noon cognac-·and-sodas. Cops rode by on bicycles, in sloppy uniforms and looking touchingly clumsy on their vehicles of another era: a far cry from the image of the policeman as a stern, well-disciplined guardian of law and order. And then a familiar two-toned car appeared and Charles Korver recognized Roger Bouès' sky-blue and white Studebaker. But good old Roger wasn't alone. Lara was with him. Lara, who got out and walked over to the Korvers with his usual odd, slow gait, massaging his shoulder.

2

"WATCH OUT!" OUK WHISPERED.

The whole group hit the dirt, their fingers on the triggers of their rifles. After some twenty seconds they too heard the sound that had alerted the tall Jaraï: Soldiers were approaching. Again Ieng felt a sudden shock of fear But Ouk was already getting to his feet, a big toothy smile on his face.

"They're our men."

Bent over from their struggle up the steep slope, seven men appeared, their faces drawn after the hard climb. It was the detachment that Ieng, when he pulled the rest of his men out, had left in the rear to slow down their pursuers or throw them off the track, after the engagement that Ieng had done everything possible to avoid, without avail.

"They have a prisoner. An officer."

Ouk's smile turned into an impossibly broad grin. Ieng felt a shiver of fierce joy, the joy of the prey long hunted that suddenly has the hunter at its mercy.

The detachment cleared the crest, crept beneath the shelter of boulders, and lay there panting for breath. The prisoner fell to his knees, his hands free but his elbows bent back and tied behind him. In Jaraï fashion, a thin cord with a slipknot had been looped around his neck: With one jerk the man could be instantly strangled to death. Ieng walked over to him.

"Where were you born?"

"Phnom Penh."

"He's lying," a hate-filled voice snarled. "He's a Khmer Krom. I saw him burn a village down."

The peasant who had spoken came forward, swinging a machete.

"Wait," Ieng ordered, with a brusqueness that he reproached himself for the very next second. *I should give orders more calmly. Quiet authority,* he told himself.

He began to interrogate the prisoner, a lieutenant who looked to be about twenty-six or twenty-seven years old, and who replied without bothering to search for words, with a sort of dispirited indifference that was not even scornful. *He knows very well that we're going to kill him.*

The lieutenant said that his unit had been based for the last few days in Leach, some twenty kilometers southwest of Pursat. He gave them information regarding the number of men—approximately two companies—the weapons they had, their disposition as far as he knew. His eyes met Ieng's. "You're the one they're looking for," he said in French. "They know you're somewhere in this region. Ieng Samboth, the former deputy."

"Is there a price on my head?"

"Ten thousand riels."

He answered the questions that followed with the same lack of hesitation, describing the way in which the search for Ieng had been organized. He realized almost immediately what was on Ieng's mind. "If you try to go east, you won't get through. They're watching all the roads."

Ieng's plan was in fact to lead his men to the provinces in the East, toward the high plateaus of Laos. This maneuver, the aim of which was to put the guerrilla forces in a position where they could eventually be supplied with arms via the Ho Chi Minh trail, had been decided on several days earlier, at the meeting that had taken place in Phnom Penh. *If this man is tell-ing the truth, we're not going to get through, not without a fight at least,* Ieng thought to himself. He decided to regard the information he had just re-ceived as trustworthy. Instead of heading directly eastward, he would swing north first, then northeast, the very next night, thus skirting the upper edge of the great lake of Tonle Sap. With a double obstacle to get around: the road linking Pursat and Battambang, and the one farther north leading from Kompong Thom to the Thai border via Siem Reap.

He stared intently at the lieutenant he had just interrogated. "Are you really a Khmer Krom?"

"No."

The peasant was perhaps mistaken. The man didn't have the char-acteristic accent of Cambodians who lived in Cochin China.

"We found this on him," Ouk said, holding out a transparent plastic sack. Ieng searched through it and found, in addition to identity papers, several photos of a young woman and two children; it also contained letters and a small sum of money.

"Your family?"

"Yes."

"She's French?"

The young woman in the photographs was blond, short and dumpy, not very pretty, wearing thick glasses.

"Yes," the lieutenant said.

"Where is she?"

"In France."

That was more certain to be the death of him than the peasant's accu-sations. Ieng's eyes left the prisoner's face and took a quick look at the men surrounding him. An inexplicable feeling of pity came over him. Thus far in his life, he had never killed anyone, had never in fact seen a human being die. He forced himself to raise the barrel of his Kalashnikov, to aim it at the lieutenant, knowing in the same instant that he probably wouldn't have the courage to pull the trigger.

"No shots," Ouk said. "Too much noise. But you can strangle him if you want to." Squatting on his heels, keeping his balance by leaning on his assault rifle with the butt resting on the ground, the huge Jaraï looked at Ieng impassively. He held out the end of the little cord looped around the prisoner's neck.

"Pull hard," he said in his hoarse booming voice, so untypical of a Khmer. "It's best if you stretch him out on the ground. Then put your foot on his face and give the cord a good hard jerk. Unless, of course, you want him to suffer." His almost animal face betrayed no sign of emotion. If his words had been meant to convey either sarcasm or pity, there was no hint of either in his tone of voice.

Ieng shrugged, unable to go through with it. "Do it yourself."

Ouk burst into silent laughter. For several seconds he shook his head, laughing without a sound. He sank the butt of his rifle in the ground several times, leaving parallel marks; he had an air of intense concentration, as though nothing in the world were more important than to leave a long line of these imprints in the earth. Finally he raised his head.

"I only kill what's at the end of my rifle," he finally said.

"I'll kill him." Rath, the former schoolteacher, stepped forward, separating himself from the group of men who up to that moment had stood motionless. He was a stocky little man with round cheeks and short crew-cut hair; there was something Chinese about his face, despite his dark brown skin. From the very beginning, of all the men who had rallied around Ieng, he had been the one who had posed the most difficult problem. Rath came from Kampot or Kompong Speu, Ieng had forgotten which; at any rate, he was from southeast Cambodia. Rath had been a left-wing teacher. The majority of other left-wing teachers in the country had been tortured and then murdered by personal order of Sihanouk—who, moreover, had officially boasted of having had these executions carried out. Some of the teachers had been tied together in twos or threes and thrown to the bottom of the great cliff of Bokor, others had been put to death less dramatically, by simply slitting their throats. Rath was one of the very few who had managed to escape the massacre. He had wandered about in the forest for a time, and then, just a few weeks ago, he had volunteered for Ieng's unit. He had immediately assumed a special role in it, acting more or less as the former deputy's lieutenant, even though Ieng had taken no steps whatsoever to name him second in command. In certain respects, Ieng was not sorry to see a recruit such as Rath arrive: He was a cold, taciturn sort, but efficient; to this day, he was the only man in the detachment really to have come under sustained enemy fire—and returned it.

But his silences, the look in his eye, his attitude as a whole, suggested that while he accepted Ieng's authority, he was doing so only temporarily and out of necessity. Ieng felt himself being continually sized up, judged, weighed in the balance. Sometimes he was so annoyed by this that his irritation bordered on rage, but sometimes he discovered that he felt ashamed of his anger, which he decided had its roots in scorn—the scorn of the intellectual, the veteran of the resistance that he was, toward a mere schoolteacher who probably didn't even have a high-school diploma and was not yet twenty-five years old.

At moments that were rarer still, Ieng could not hide from himself the fact that he was afraid of Rath.

Rath took the little cord out of Ouk's fingers, then appeared to change his mind. A trace of a smile appeared on his tiny, thin-lipped mouth. He looked down at the plastic sack that had contained the lieutenant's personal belongings and picked it up off the ground. He suddenly slipped it over the prisoner's head, loosened the slipknot in the cord for a second and then tightened it again so that it held the sack in place around the man's neck, not tightly enough to strangle him, but tightly enough to prevent air from getting in.

No! Ieng silently screamed to himself in horror.

Rath stepped away and squatted down. The eyes of the whole group were riveted on the lieutenant's face. They saw his mouth open, but not the slightest sound came through the sack. His terror-stricken eyes opened wide, the prisoner suddenly threw himself on the ground and crawled along it rubbing his face against it in the hope of tearing the plastic that was smothering him to death. For two or three endless minutes he writhed and twisted and struggled, his eyes bulging now, drooling at the mouth, plainly still screaming, though no sound penetrated the transparent hood that stuck to his face and made it look more frightening still.

At length, after one last series of spasms his body stiffened. Ieng had closed his eyes at the last. He opened them now and met Rath's eyes, gleaming with excitement.

Rath rose to his feet. He bent over the corpse, undid the little cord, pulled the sack off. He showed it to Ieng.

"Not a sound," he said, in his odd piping voice, with the precise articulation of a schoolteacher. "Not a sound. And the same sack can be used over again. You can kill thousands of men and women with the same sack. Thousands."

3 "ARE YOU AWARE THAT THERE'S A REVOLUTION BREWING?" MADEleine Korver asked Lara.

"That's wonderful," Lara answered. "I hope to take advantage of the occasion to kidnap you and flee with you to a desert island. You know very well that I'm just waiting for the chance."

Madeleine laughed delightedly, gracefully patting her blue locks.

"I'm going to rush out and buy a revolver," Charles said. "And you can show me how it works."

"Will we go about stark naked beneath the mangroves?" Madeleine asked ecstatically.

"You guessed it," Lara replied. His eyes sought Charles Korver's.

"Excuse us for a few moments, will you please?" Charles said to his wife. "We'll leave you Roger to keep you company. Behave yourselves, you two."

"And you, Roger? Are you aware that there's a revolution brewing?"

"I'm an expert when it comes to revolutions," Roger answered. "Ask me all the questions you like."

Lara and Charles Korver headed down the street along the sidewalk, passing in front of Chinese shops whose owners, perched on tiny wooden stools, were clad only in short white linen trousers that were sometimes downright indecent.

"Here's what's happening," Lara said. "Last night, I brought a young American deserter back with me from Vietnam. Obviously he's in this country illegally. He has no identity papers. But that isn't all: He's a drug addict. He eats opium and doubtless takes other sorts of junk. In any case, he cracked up in the car as we were coming back to Phnom Penh after the plane landed. We had trouble calming him down, and finally had to drive him to Cheng's for a shot. Cheng doesn't think he'll have another attack like that; he thinks it was due mostly to psychological causes. And it's true that the boy must have been through quite a lot. His name is Jon Kinkaird. Jon in three letters: J-O-N."

As they walked on, they encountered a superbly well-endowed, curvaceous young woman from Martinique who owned a dress shop on the Boulevard Norodom, accompanied by her Portuguese lover, who divided his time equally between taking siestas and making love to his mistress. Behind the couple came Mueller the Little Swiss, walking along with his great six-foot strides, preceding his tiny five-foot, eighty-pound concubine, who was trotting along feverishly to keep up with him, but without moving her entire upper body at all. At the tail end of the procession came Boudin the pilot, who merely glared furiously at Lara. All of them were heading for the Zigzag, a bar just a few steps away in the Rue Dekcho Damdin, to have their apéritif, smoked meat, and brochettes prepared by Albert Vandekherkove, the proprietor.

"And what would you like me to do to help?" Charles asked Lara when all of them had gone past.

Charles Korver was obliged to tilt his head nearly all the way back in order to see Lara's face. He had always felt a rather paternal affection for this slender, secretive man, whose habitual mildness of manner served as a nearly perfect mask concealing an almost frightening emotional intensity. Charles Korver had known him since Lara's earliest childhood, and it was at the Korvers' that the young boy had first taken refuge, in February of 1946, after the murder of his parents and his little sister. "Taken refuge" was perhaps not the proper term. *No one can claim ever to have seen Lara overcome by self-pity. Let's say that he stayed for a time with us.* In fact, nearly five weeks had gone by between the day the Korvers had learned of the death of Pierre and Nancy Lara and their daughter and the day the boy had appeared at the garden gate of the Korvers' villa in Phnom Penh, literally dragging himself along, frightfully thin, with a foul-smelling makeshift bandage over the horrible wound in his neck, but fiercely fending off the slightest gesture of solicitude or consolation. He had told the story of the butchery that had taken place before his eyes in an inhumanly calm tone of voice, without once giving way to his emotions. He had offered them a detailed account of his escape: how the assassins had searched for him, how he had managed to elude them with the aid of a boy his own age, a tall, fiendishly clever black Jaraï named Kutchaï. After days and days the two young fugitives had managed to get to Kompong Thom, where there was a French Army post— though, curiously, they hadn't bothered to go to it. "Why was that?"

"Because there wasn't any point in going there. There wasn't anything I needed them for. My mother and my father and my sister were already dead."

The youngster had stayed at the Korvers' for nearly three months, recovering his strength in an incredibly short time and doing his level best to behave in every respect like an ordinary guest, speaking Vietnamese with the servants, Cambodian with the pedicab boys; disappearing for days on end, doubtless wandering about the markets, the huts in the native quarter; getting together every so often with his Jaraï friend, who was obviously a bosom pal of his; but at the same time reading, asking questions, taking a lively interest in the Korvers' art collection. He had a keen, searching, almost cold intelligence and, at that time, a sort of aggressiveness, a nervous wariness in his eyes and his demeanor. As the weeks went by, the Korvers had seen him struggling with himself and slowly but surely mastering his violent inner feelings.

And then one day he had disappeared completely, leaving behind a few words written in a small, steady hand: "I'm going off to join my uncle in Hanoi. Don't worry about me. Thank you."

Four years had gone by without any word from him, though the Korvers had been able to keep track of him through friends of theirs in Tonkin, learning from them that Lara had taken up his studies again in the Tonkinese capital, prepared for his *baccalauréat* exams and passed them, and then signed up to fight and, in the company of his inseparable friend Kutchaï, taken part in the battles against the Viet Minh in the Clear River area.

Toward the end of the fourth year he had reappeared all of a sudden, accompanied not only by his Jaraï but also by a huge Corsican with the chest of a gorilla. "The name of the man who murdered my mother and my father and my sister was Kamsa. He's dead now and we've taken over the plantation again. These two are my partners; their names are Kutchaï and Oreste Marccaggi. The three of us are working together now. I'm very happy to see you again."

He had grown taller in those four years, though he was as thin as ever. He had plainly won the fight against himself, the fight to master himself completely: From that time on his outward manner was unfailingly mild and gentle, the shedding of his former self a *fait accompli.* He had embraced Madeleine so affectionately that she had burst into tears then and there, and Charles himself had found tears welling up in his eyes.

"You've missed me. I should have written to you. Please forgive me for not doing so. I assure you I thought of you, very often." He had held out a package clumsily wrapped in ordinary brown paper. "None of the three of us is very good at gift-wrapping. I hope you'll like this. The shopkeeper in Hong Kong swore to me that it's a plate with the coat of arms of Ch'ien Lung manufactured in 1785, the very year the first of the Laras arrived in this country. I seem to remember that you're fond of old objets d'art." Words accompanied by a smile. And naturally the plate was authentic.

On the sidewalk of the Rue Yukanthor, at the corner of Dekcho Damdin, following on the heels of the dress-shop owner and her Portuguese, Mueller and his mistress, and pint-size Boudin, there now filed by feisty little Filipino sailors, an English journalist, another from New Zealand, and a Frenchman officially both in the import-export business and also the consul for Monaco, who in point of fact lived off the charms of two or three young girls that he brought in from France and rotated—three months in Phnom Penh, six in Saigon, three in Bangkok—for the delectation of Chinese notables with a preference for white skin. He pretended not to see Lara, who had once bashed in several of his teeth.

"And what is it you'd like me to do to help?" Charles said.

"Put Jon Kinkaird up for a while."

"Hide him, in other words."

"You hit the nail on the head."

"I'm certain that Madeleine will be overjoyed if they throw the two of us in jail."

"I'm certain of it too," Lara said.

On the other side of the street, almost directly across from the two men, workers outside the Kampuchea Theater were taking down enormous gaudy posters advertising a Chinese film from Hong Kong and pasting up another for the coming attraction: *The Naked Jungle,* a Charlton Heston film. *It's one they've already shown,* Charles sighed to himself with irritation. He loved going to the movies.

"I had no choice," Lara went on. "I can't take him to the plantation. It's not exactly the last word in comfort, and what's more I can't be there all the time. Roger offered to take him in at his place but you know Roger: You can't ask him to look after a sick man. All I need is somebody to take care of him for a few weeks till he's well enough to travel and I can get him the necessary papers."

"And you went to Vietnam to bring him here?"

Lara nodded.

"How are things in Saigon?"

"Awful."

Charles Korver searched his memory for the name of Charlton Heston's leading lady in the film. A marvelous redhead . . . He managed to fish it up at the very moment it appeared on the poster: Eleanor Parker.

"Do you share my thoughts as to what's likely to happen in Cambodia?"

Lara's thoughtful gaze met his.

"I'm referring to what Sirik Matak and Lon Nol are probably up to," Charles explained.

Lara shrugged. Charles turned part way around so as to have the terrace of the Taï-San in full view. Madeleine was laughing heartily as Roger Bouès told some story or other with a great many animated gestures, and once again Charles marveled at how wholeheartedly his wife embraced life.

"Have you seen Ieng recently?"

He sensed Lara's irritation at the question. "Yes," Lara finally answered. And at that very moment, in the distance, above the rumble of traffic in the streets of Phnom Penh, a sort of low roar began to fill the air. It was coming from the south of the city, from the Monument to Independence at the far end of the Boulevard Norodom, at the spot where the Tonle Sap and the Mekong meet; it was a rhythmical sound, like a giant's breathing.

"Lara, there's a question I've been dying to ask you for months, if not longer," Charles Korver said. "I'm going to ask it, and as always, you needn't answer unless you want to. . . ."

He paused for a moment, listening to the low roar grow gradually louder and louder.

"Lara, are you helping Ieng and his friends—Khieu Samphan and the others?" Charles asked.

"Ieng's my friend."

"We had that Australian journalist Walter Brackett for dinner last night. You know what he's like: always ready to belch fire and flames at American imperialism. He swears the Americans are plotting to get Sihanouk ousted from power. He says it's only a question of months now. What's your opinion?"

"I'm not interested in politics."

The roar now became slogans, shouted in unison.

"I have a strange presentiment," Charles said. "A grave apprehension, in fact, if not a downright fear. Let's suppose for a moment that Sihanouk has been chased out of the country, that a Lon Nol and a Sirik Matak have taken over. . . . What would Ieng and his friends do in that case?"

"Fight."

"And do they have enough men and enough arms to wage a war?"

"Not for the moment."

Above the slogans came the sound of a huge crowd marching.

"But do you think they might have eventually?"

"Perhaps," Lara replied in his calm voice and added: "Come on. We'd better not stay out here on the street."

He took Charles Korver's arm and led him back to the terrace of the Taï-San. Roger and Madeleine and all the other customers had risen to their feet.

"It's a revolution brewing, just like I told you, right?" Madeleine said triumphantly.

"We'd best go to your place," Lara said to Roger.

The latter nodded. The four of them went into the restaurant, walked through the kitchen, and reached a long narrow courtyard where kitchen boys were deboning future glazed ducks on wooden chopping boards. They crept under five lines of washing hung out to dry, then down a corridor to their left, and then, after losing his sense of direction for a moment, Charles Korver finally recognized the stairway leading up to Roger Bouès' place. Upstairs, despite the thick walls, they could still hear the roar of the demonstrators drawing closer and closer. They entered the single giant room that constituted Roger's entire apartment and the Korvers, as always, stood stock still in front of the Apsaras standing with empty eyes on its black marble pedestal.

"I hope those demonstrators won't set my car on fire," Roger said. "My insurance agent detests me. He says I never pay him."

Lara was already outside, nimbly climbing a little metal ladder up to the flat roof, where the metal arms supporting the neon lights of the Lux movie theater formed a sort of guardrail beyond which one could see the city. Charles Korver followed him, surprised at his own agility. He leaned out over the Boulevard Norodom far below and spotted the crowd, some four to five thousand people, most of them men and most of them young. The leaders, though they were dressed in civvies, looked like army men. He listened to the slogans the crowd was chanting, in Cambodian and also, more curiously, in English.

"Who is it they're demonstrating against?" Charles too was forced to shout. The procession had now reached the intersection of the boulevard and the Rue Dekcho Damdin.

"Hanoi, the North Vietnamese, the Communists. They're demanding the evacuation of Cambodia by the Viet Cong. Have you noticed the placards and the banners?"

For a moment Charles didn't understand. Then he realized what Lara was getting at: Nearly all the signs were in English instead of Cambodian, or at least in French, the second language of the kingdom.

"They're solely for the benefit of the American photographers," Lara said. "Their aim is to make it clear to America, whose embassy staff has just come back after having been gone for years, that even though Cambodia is still officially neutral, it won't be for much longer. This is nothing other than a carefully staged demonstration for the American mass media."

"Where is Ieng now?"

"In the forest."

"Is Hanoi helping him and Khieu Samphan?"

"Not really."

The tide of demonstrators swept toward the Phnom. Lara lit a cigarette.

"I can't believe it," Charles Korver said thoughtfully. "I can't believe that someone, anyone, could ever dream of putting this country to fire and sword, for whatever reason. Good Marxist that he is, Walter Brackett talks of the meaning of history, of historical necessity. Good Lord, how I do detest that meaningless jargon!"

"There's no such thing as history," Lara said. "There's only chaos, sound and fury signifying nothing. Trying to predict the future of it, deducing rules of conduct from it is stupid. Your Brackett is an idiot."

Charles stared at him in amazement. In the twenty years or very nearly that he'd known him, he could never remember having heard Lara indulge in abstract speculation or engage in philosophical discussion of any sort. He started laughing. "Did you know that we're of exactly the same opinion?"

Lara smiled back at him. "Well then, what's the use in even talking about it?"

The crowd of demonstrators was breaking up; no one was following it now except some kids shouting and yelling as though they were kicking up a rumpus in a classroom. Heat rose from the roof as the midday sun beat down on it. Charles Korver turned away from the spectacle on the boulevard below, and started back down the ladder.

"I think that sooner or later Cambodia's going to be a country at war," Lara said.

Charles stopped dead in his tracks.

"Those who are fighting in Vietnam will start fighting here," Lara went on. "And they'll lose—the Americans, I mean. You and Madeleine ought to think about leaving."

Charles' mouth gaped open in amazement. At that moment, Roger stepped off the little ladder onto the rooftop.

"Would anybody like a drink?"

"Where is this American you've been telling me about?" Charles Korver finally managed to blurt out to Lara.

"At your house, of course," Lara answered. "You don't imagine the thought would ever cross my mind that you might refuse, do you?"

"I've some rosé from Provence," Roger said. "Not very cold, I grant you—my refrigerator detests me too."

"We'll be right down," Charles said.

Roger nodded and left.

Charles Korver looked at Lara. "What about you? Would you leave?"

He was later to remember the look that came into Lara's eyes at that moment.

"Absolutely not," Lara said. "No one's ever going to make me leave this country that's mine."

For a brief instant, he seemed totally self-absorbed, gently massaging the scar on his neck with his bony hand. Then he raised his head and his slow, warm smile reappeared.

"Come on," he said to Charles. "The show's over. In any event, it was just a prologue. And if we don't go downstairs, Madeleine might decide we don't love her anymore."

To please Roger, they all drank a little of his rosé wine, well past tepid on the warm side, and then left. As they came out of the building, the Rue Dekcho Damdin was deserted, but they had taken only a few steps when a metallic clanking rang out. All three of them turned around at the same time and saw the Chinese merchants, smiling as usual, raising the iron grilles they had lowered over their doors and windows as the demonstrators passed by. There was no sign of the demonstration now, except for a dull rumble from the north, somewhere around the Palais du Gouvernement, gradually growing fainter and fainter, and a torn, trampled banner lying in the middle of the pavement on the Boulevard Norodom. Two little shoeshine boys walked by, unconcernedly bantering back and forth and drumming their brushes against their wooden boxes out of force of habit. There was a smell of smoke in the air, drifting by in intermittent whiffs that masked the delicate fragrance of the tamarinds. Beyond that, nothing at all out of the ordinary. Everything was calm once again and Phnom Penh looked exactly as it did every day. *And nothing will ever change,* Charles Korver thought.

4

DURING THE NIGHT OF APRIL 16 AND THE EARLY MORNING HOURS OF April 17, Ieng Samboth and his detachment managed to cross, in one push, the road and rail line linking Phnom Penh with Battambang and the Thai frontier.

Around three o'clock in the morning, having arrived at the northwest tip of the great lake of Tonle Sap, they finally reached more solid ground and followed a road leading directly north for several kilometers till they came to the Stung Seng, a rust-colored river that flows down from the Dangrek Range, looping westward as it passes round Siem Reap. They followed the river upstream and arrived at dawn on the outskirts of a village deep in the forest, not much bigger than the one the Provincial Guard had driven them out of two days earlier. It consisted of no more than five or six huts grouped around a modest *sala khum,* the communal building. Half a dozen families lived there, subsisting by gathering kapok and by doing the worst sort of work there was in Khmer country: collecting the sap from sugar palms. Ieng had done a bit of it when he was a child but had very soon given up. You had to go up to the very top fronds of the tree, either by climbing along the rough trunk which ripped your belly and thighs, or by means of a bamboo ladder more than sixty feet tall which required a balancing act worthy of a circus performer. Once up there, you crushed the flowers, with round pincers if they were male flowers, flat ones if they were female; then you cut the ends off them and set in place an *ampong,* a hollow length of bamboo that had to be changed morning and night so that it didn't get clogged. You thus obtained, with luck, fifteen to twenty glasses of sap per tree. You could drink this juice, but that was a luxury that poor peasants didn't allow themselves; you either made wine of it or else you boiled it in kettles, made sugar of it, and rolled it in palm leaves, which could then be sold for a few riels. In Ieng's early youth, three days of exhausting and dangerous work would enable you, in principle, to collect enough sugar to buy a chicken. In actual fact, the sugar palms rarely belonged to those who did this work, being as a general rule the property of notables and Chinese.

The village where Ieng and his men arrived on the morning of April 17 was almost rich: There were ducks, three pigs, *prahoc* (the fermented fish sauce made by the Vietnamese fishermen of Tonle Sap), several jars of palm wine, some lotus seeds, some rice. The mayor, the *chausangkar,* was a man with white hair who claimed to have once been a soldier with the Barangs, and after that an insurgent fighting against them, twenty years earlier. The sudden intrusion of this guerrilla band of some thirty men in rags and tatters, armed with four or five Kalashnikovs, three ancient Garand rifles, one Colt, and machetes, did not seem to throw him into a panic. He told Ieng that most of the provisions they had accumulated in the village were for the *bhikkus,* the monks in the nearby temple (which in fact was an hour's march from there), but if Ieng and his men would be content with some rice with *prahoc* and some watermelon, he could feed all the men without the venerable bonzes being any the worse off. It was his way of saying that the visitors should accept what the village offered and not take whatever they wanted.

I would need only give the order and this entire village would disappear, Ieng thought wearily. *And it would not be long before the forest swallowed up the ruins.* But before he'd decided what his reply would be, Rath had stepped forward and begun to speak.

"We're Khmer Rouge, not bandits," he said. "We don't make war on peasants. On the contrary, we're fighting in their name. We're not going to steal your rice or your pigs. We won't touch your women."

He went on speaking this way, in a slow and simple—deliberately simple—Khmer, without raising his voice, as though he were in his classroom addressing children. *And they're listening to him,* Ieng thought to himself. Reassured by Rath's voice, the villagers were in fact drawing closer. *Would they have listened to me in the same way? I would have had to remember to tell them simple things like that.* More sharply than ever, the sense of guilt he'd carried for years assailed him, along with the despairing, painful feeling that he would never be able really to communicate with his compatriots of the rice paddies and the forest for whom he was risking his life, but from whom, it seemed, everything separated him. He glanced toward Ung and Suon, the two former students from Battambang: They too were listening to Rath with shining eyes.

Ieng's eyes met those of the mayor, the man who had been a soldier in the ranks of the French Army, and he read in them a sort of complicity that annoyed him, as though the fact that he and the *chausangkar* had rubbed shoulders with Westerners for such a long time sufficed to create a bond between them and make them outsiders without hope of inclusion in the community formed by Rath and the villagers.

Suddenly filled with rage, he stepped forward to Rath's side. The second before, he had been intending to set up camp here in this village for two or three days and get some rest. But he interrupted the former schoolteacher in a deliberately peremptory tone of voice.

"We're leaving," he said. "This minute. And we don't need their rice."

They might have skirted Siem Reap and the temples of Angkor from the south, following the upper edge of the Tonle Sap. That would have meant taking the risk of going through the many villages of Vietnamese fishermen who had settled along the shores of the lake, and also the risk of coming dangerously close to the Kompong Thom–Siem Reap road often traveled by columns of soldiers. Despite the dangers, this route would have been shorter.

Ieng chose instead to follow the northern route and ordered his men to follow the course of the Stung Seng in the direction of the Dangrek Range, through rolling countryside covered for the most part with open forest and dotted everywhere with *phnoms,* hills that formed what looked like islands covered with dense vegetation. This involved a march of nearly two hundred kilometers, which they made in six days, eating dry rice and roots and drinking river water. Ieng felt the effects of this forced march much more than any of his men, all of whom were younger and less removed from life in the raw than he was; what was more, he alone knew that the only reason for making it was his own need to punish himself. Rath marched at his side most of the time, and it had become obvious that this simultaneous presence of two men at the head of the column implied joint command of the detachment.

Having gone ahead with three men to reconnoiter, Ouk reappeared one afternoon loaded down with rice and dried fish. He announced that there were no soldiers in the area (Ieng's detachment had now reached the border between the provinces of Prah Vihear and Siem Reap) even though they were very close to the Thai border, and the abandoned pagoda that was their rendezvous point was now only two hours' march away. According to the plan of operations drawn up in Phnom Penh, Ieng's unit was to join up there with a group from Stung Treng, and there Ieng was to begin organizing a sort of guerrilla command force, grouping around him not a maximum number of recruits but rather the future cadres of the revolutionary army.

"There's a village not far from here that has a radio set," Ouk said. "According to one of the villagers, there's been a demonstration in Phnom Penh. Crowds marched in the streets demanding Lon Nol's return to power and above all the departure of the Viet Cong. They also demanded the death of Khieu Samphan, Hu Nim, and Hou Yuon. And yours."

Ieng nodded indifferently. Some sixty or eighty yards farther on, Rath was marching off, with the column following in Indian file behind him, already disappearing in the distance. Ieng fell in step behind the last of his men, with Ouk at his side.

"You're tired," Ouk remarked. "Or at any rate, you look as though you were. Why did you have us march so fast? There's no hurry. I went as far as the pagoda. The others haven't arrived yet and won't be arriving till three days from now. We have plenty of time."

Ieng shrugged.

"I don't like Rath," Ouk went on. "I don't like him at all. I didn't like the way he killed that officer."

"You should have killed him yourself then."

Ouk burst out laughing, tossing his head up and down like a horse. He took a mango and a papaya out of a canvas knapsack he was toting on his back. "Here, these are for you."

The trail they were following began to climb steeply, through a veritable wall of vegetation. The musty smell of the forest assailed their nostrils.

"There are troops at Kompong Thom," Ouk said. "Around five hundred of them. They have trucks and two armored cars."

"Why didn't you say so before?"

"You're the one who's in command. Not Rath. You know now and he doesn't."

"Do you have any idea what those troops are up to?"

"No."

The vegetation grew denser, the open forest turning into jungle. The humidity rose as the light turned a darker and deeper green. The trail became steeper and steeper.

"We don't have much farther to climb," Ouk said. "We'll be going downhill very soon. Up ahead there are only big hills, one after the other, and then a gently sloping plateau, and the arroyo you know very well."

The Jaraï's last words were a revelation to Ieng. Why hadn't he thought of it before? He took out his map, a rough one dating back to the time of the French, with spellings that were often so wild as to make place names unrecognizable, having been phonetically transcribed by cartographers with no knowledge whatsoever of Khmer.

"That's right," Ieng said, laughing. "The plantation is just behind those hills, within ten or twelve kilometers of us. But I don't know if Lara and my brother are there or not. Maybe Oreste is there alone."

5   ALMOST THE MINUTE SHE GOT OFF THE PLANE AT POCHENTONG, THE Phnom Penh airport, Lisa had been approached by a giant Cambodian, or at least a native of some sort—she'd never seen a Cambodian in her life before—nearly six and a half feet tall, who told her that Lara had sent him to meet her. Later on, she was to get to know Kutchaï better. At the time, she found him quite scary. Because of his jungle-savage face; because of his silent, more or less continual laugh.

"What proof do I have that it was really Lara who sent you?"

A burst of soundless laughter. "None. Except, I know that your name—your real one, not the one you're traveling under—is Kinkaird, and that you've come to Phnom Penh to meet your brother. Come on, I'm going to take you to him. He's all right—as well as could be expected under the circumstances." He spoke a very pure French, and without an accent as far as she could tell; in any case, she could understand every word he said.

Like many others before her, she was struck by the contrast between Kutchaï's features, build, and backwoodsman's look and the amazing fluency with which he expressed himself in French. It was like those cowboy movies of the thirties, forties, and fifties, in which Indian chiefs who'd never set eyes on a white man before answered them in impeccable Harvard-accented English; it was the same effect of lack of synchronization, like a bad job of dubbing.

"Do you work for Monsieur Lara?"

"I work with him."

They had gotten into a Land-Rover spatted with yellow mud and had driven through the center of town. Lisa had barely looked at Phnom Penh. She had come here to meet Jon and that was all that counted. She was feverish with excitement. The car had finally stopped in front of a huge, gorgeous three-story villa, surrounded by a luxuriant garden full of bougainvillea and coral trees as well as hibiscus, jasmine, and red and yellow cannas more than three feet tall.

"Monsieur Lara lives here?"

"No."

"But he lives in Phnom Penh?"

"No, not in Phnom Penh."

The moment the Land-Rover stopped, a couple had come out of the garden and she met Charles and Madeleine Korver, both of them practically midgets alongside her. She had barely set eyes on them and said hello when, with that instantaneous change of scene one ordinarily experiences only in dreams, she found herself at last with Jon, who said to her:

"You shouldn't have come."

He was sitting in an armchair in a bedroom on the second floor. He was wearing a Chinese silk bathrobe, a little too small for him even though it was brand-new and had obviously been bought especially for him; the long sleeves of it did not reach quite far enough to hide the bandages around his arm.

"Were you wounded?"

"No."

"How come the bandages then?"

Their eyes met, both of them experiencing the familiar feeling that they were seeing their own double. He was looking at her with the same expression that he always had as a child when she forced him to own up to something naughty he'd done.

"My arm's full of abscesses."

She didn't understand immediately, and he noticed. "I took drugs," he explained. "And the needles weren't always clean."

There was a silence, followed by a grim, unpleasant laugh from Jon. He stared into Lisa's eyes again for several seconds, then abruptly looked away toward the window. It had no glass panes, only a mosquito netting over it. Finally his eyes met his sister's again.

"I thought for a moment there that you were going to give me a good hard slap in the face. It wouldn't have been the first one. You gave me a good many over the years."

"You deserve one," she said, her voice hoarse and tense with emotion.

"You're the only person who's ever hit me."

"I've always been a terrible sister to you."

He nodded. "And how."

A silence.

"I deserve a good slap," Jon agreed. "And even worse. But I've had more than I can take lately."

His voice broke on these last words and he lowered his head, staring intently at his hands resting on his knees. Thus far, Lisa had remained standing in the doorway. Suddenly she gave way to her emotions, came over and knelt down next to her brother, put one hand over Jon's and her other arm around his neck. She kissed him on the forehead, and he began to weep softly, without a sound, like a child. She gently stroked his hair and hugged him, comforting him as she had not done for more than fifteen years. *As I've probably never done before.* She searched her memory in vain for a moment when she had taken her young brother in her arms like this, and couldn't remember a single one. In New York there were at least ten men whose lives and temperaments she knew better, whose needs she had paid more attention to.

They began talking of Colorado, of San Francisco, of New York. She told him a few anecdotes about the world of advertising in New York, and avoided even mentioning the circumstances under which she had made the trip to Saigon and then to Phnom Penh. Thus it was Jon who first uttered Lara's name, and despite the drowsiness that was coming over him little by little, he noted that his sister immediately tensed.

"What's the matter?"

She explained the disagreement she and Lara had had in Saigon, a disagreement that was bound to become even more violent now that Jon was in Cambodia. She thought it obvious that Jon's fleeing to Cambodia instead of turning himself in immediately to the American authorities in Vietnam was going to complicate matters considerably.

"Grandfather had even found a lawyer who specializes in cases like yours and he'd agreed to take you on as a client. By intervening in the whole affair and getting you to change your mind, Lara . . ."

"Oh, no, you're wrong," Jon interrupted her. "I was the one who made up my mind to come here. Me and nobody else. It's all my fault."

He finally decided, not without one last moment of hesitation, to tell her the story of the grenade and the death of a man, a Corsican friend of Lara's, who had helped them. "I'm responsible for that too."

His eyelids were drooping from the effects of the sedative he'd taken. Lisa helped him back to bed, holding him up bodily, horror-stricken at how thin and weak he was. He lay down on the bed. He was wearing an Asian-style sarong under his bathrobe. She covered him with a sheet.

"Lisa, that Lara's an extraordinary guy. He had to be to come get me the way he did. Did you know he came to Colorado when I was nine? I remember his visit very well."

Jon was having difficulty speaking distinctly now: "I remember . . ."

He fell silent and she thought he'd dropped off to sleep. But he managed to open his eyes halfway and added, in an astonishingly clear voice, "Lisa, don't try to persuade me to go back there. Don't try to persuade me to give myself up. Not ever."

She kissed him on the forehead.

"We'll talk about it later. You sleep now."

"Not ever," Jon said. "Not ever."

When he saw her coming back down the stairs, Charles Korver wasn't quite certain but he thought she'd probably cried at one moment or another. As she came out of Jon's bedroom he'd heard her stop briefly by the bathroom next door, and she had evidently rinsed her face with cold water. In any event, he found her breathtakingly beautiful. He had been struck by how beautiful she was when she had stepped out of the car with Kutchaï.

"He's falling asleep," Lisa said. "I think he's asleep already."

She spoke in French, not remembering whether her hosts spoke English. The Korvers came barely up to her shoulder. *Miss Gulliver*, she thought.

"The doctor's prescribed all sorts of sedatives for him. He's a very good doctor, who's often treated . . ." Charles Korver hesitated.

"Drug addicts," Lisa said, finishing his sentence for him.

"That sort of thing, and soldiers who've been wounded or are suffering from shock," Charles Korver said with a smile. "He's a former Army doctor who was at Dien Bien Phu. As for your brother, don't worry about him: He's going to recover very quickly; it's just a matter of days—two weeks at most. Would you like some tea?"

As a matter of fact, both the Korvers spoke English, and spoke it remarkably well. They were sitting next to each other on one of the couches. They were both frail, fragile little things, whose manner was so polite as to be just a trifle precious, yet at the same time engaging, gracious, reminding one of the exquisite courtesy of past centuries. They sat there holding hands and smiling at Lisa, behaving toward her as though they had always known her, as though she were a young friend who had surprised and pleased them by paying them an unexpected visit, as though they were overjoyed at her being there with them.

"Thank you," Lisa said, deeply touched. "Thank you more than I can say."

"Tsk, tsk, tsk," Madeleine Korver said. "But perhaps you'd prefer orangeade? Ti Aï makes very good orangeades. Heaven only knows what she puts in them. Oranges maybe. Why not? There's nothing I'd put past her. Or perhaps you'd rather have a drink? A cognac? Or some whiskey?"

"I'd love some orangeade," Lisa said with a smile, suddenly discovering that she was dying of thirst.

A Vietnamese maid with a superb, heavy chignon appeared and disappeared in a flash, gliding across the marble floor in her bare feet.

"Have you been in Cambodia before?"

She said she hadn't, and the Korvers began to talk about the United

States, which they had visited five or six times, beginning in the early twenties. One of Madeleine Korver's great regrets was that she'd never been able to exchange a few words with Al Capone, though she had nonetheless been "fortunate enough to catch a glimpse of him, he was no farther away from me than you are right now, my dear child, so close I could almost have reached out and touched him, just as he was leaving the Hawthorne Hotel in Chicago surrounded by his bodyguards.

"He looked straight at me," Madeleine said. "Right into my eyes"—she made a V with a middle and index finger, raising it to her face to point to her two eyes—"like that. His gaze was absolutely hypnotic."

Charles Korver laughed, his own bright eyes, beaming with intelligence, fixed on Lisa. "My wife is prevaricating," he said. "The truth of the matter is that we were hidden behind a fireplug."

He went on, in a perfectly matter-of-fact voice, as though it were a foregone conclusion: "Your room is all ready for you. Of course, my dear, we're naturally expecting you to be our guest. Did you think we were going to let you leave? We're delighted to have you. And besides, this way you'll be able to be with your brother."

The distressing thought of her money that had gone down the drain crossed Lisa's mind again, but this invitation solved her problems, at least for the time being. She answered that she would let them know the very next day if she had definitely decided to stay on in Phnom Penh. She thanked them warmly, drank her orangeade, and for the first time since her arrival at the Korvers', really looked around her. She spied three or four vast, luxuriously furnished rooms downstairs, decorated and crammed almost absurdly full of objets d'art from China and Japan and others whose origins she could not even guess. Quite obviously, this collection represented the investment of enormous sums of money and countless hours of patient research.

"What a marvelous house."

"But we don't have room enough left now to add even so much as a thimble. Madeleine and I are a wee bit mad when it comes to things like this."

She learned that the Korvers had guests coming for dinner that night, French people from the embassy, Cambodians who had just come back from New York where they'd been their country's delegates to the United Nations, and an Australian couple from the aid mission, whom Charles and Madeleine described as lively, fun-loving people, always the life of the party, whose stay in Cambodia was coming to an end. Around seven o'clock, Lisa went upstairs to her room and lay down for a few minutes. Neither Charles nor Madeleine Korver had so much as mentioned Lara's name and it was Lisa's impression that this was not a chance omission, especially on Charles' part, since he seemed to be able to read her face like an open book. She ought to have brought up his name herself; it would have been only natural for her to do so. After all, Lara had saved Jon, and had been responsible for the death of one of his friends in so doing. But she hadn't been able to bring herself to mention his name, without knowing precisely why.

When she lay down, she was afraid she'd give in to her exhaustion and fall dead asleep, but she soon discovered that she was much too tense even to drowse off. She got up, went into Jon's room next door, and saw her brother peacefully sleeping just as she had left him, hands stretched out at his sides, yet with a look of toughness, of maturity on his emaciated face that she had never seen there before. She went back to her own room, where the Korvers had thoughtfully left a few books in English for her to read; she began to leaf through one of them, published in Calcutta in 1955 and entitled *Angkor Empire*, by a certain George B. Walker. The illustrations in it were dreadful, apparently ruined temples photographed in a thick fog with a camera whose settings the author had forgotten to adjust properly. The accompanying text was almost as bad, but she read a few pages of it and learned that, according to the author, the Khmers had arrived on the shores of a certain Lake Tonle Sap around the fifth century B.C.—*in the morning or in the afternoon?*—and that their ancestors had perhaps been Mongols or Negroids, or proto-Malayans, or else Scythians, Sumerians, or even Aryans or Greeks. *And why not New Yorkers?* Lisa thought to herself, beginning to be amused.

Around eight o'clock cars arrived and she hurriedly changed and went downstairs.

The French guests talked a lot, in self-confident voices. They had seen everything, read everything, heard everything; they babbled venomously on and on, taking obvious pleasure in saying nasty things about everyone, with that love of sarcasm that had so irritated Lisa on her first trip to France. But they were often very amusing. The Cambodians were timid and likable, making a courageous effort to speak rather broken English. They told Lisa that what they liked most about New York was the skating rink in Rockefeller Center and the pizza served in a restaurant on Thirty-eighth Street.

The Australians' names were Peter and Ronda Soames. They indeed had a marvelous sense of humor, and were already homesick for the Cambodia they were about to leave; they were obviously almost in despair at the mere thought of having to go back to Canberra for at least two years, claiming that the capital city of their country possessed, the year round, all the lively charm and mad gaiety of a Scottish cemetery in a November rain. They made Lisa laugh by telling her of their dealings with their houseboy who, on being asked to make the "dog's soup" (the canine in question being a sorry mutt they'd found roaming the streets of Phnom Penh; it had wheedling eyes, though, and sometimes answered to the name of Trafalgar), had promptly made the soup, but he'd made it *with* the dog. They spoke of the temples of Angkor, which they adored, and advised Lisa to be sure not to miss seeing the superb little building at Bantaÿ Sreï, a veritable jewel made famous in 1923 by a certain André Malraux, who had ended up in a Cambodian jail for having stolen some bas-reliefs from it.

"It's been restored by French archaeologists since then," Charles Korver remarked. "But you should also see Bayon, of course, and Angkor Wat, and the Prah Palilaÿ, the Phimeanakes, the Kleangs and the Prasats, Neak Pean, Phnom Bakheng, the Tep Pranam, Roluous, Bantaÿ Samré. . . ."

"He's forgetting quite a few," Madeleine said.

The names had a ring to them at once musical and forbiddingly strange.

It must have been twelve-thirty A.M. before the guests left. Madeleine Korver went off for a few moments to confer with the Vietnamese servants who were being shepherded home by Monsieur Bê, officially the chauffeur but in reality the majordomo of the entire household staff. Lisa found herself alone with Charles Korver for the first time. She began to walk about the largest of the rooms that served both as reception rooms and private art gallery, halting before an object that she was unable to identify.

"A reliquary of the Buddha Shakyamuni," the old Frenchman said softly, in answer to her unspoken question.

"Is it gold?"

"No, just gilded bronze. But it's worth very nearly as much as if it were solid gold. It's not the material it's made of that makes it so valuable. Like many other things. Men and women, for instance. Except that when it comes to women . . ."

Lisa turned around to face him and was about to say something.

Charles raised his index finger, with an impish gleam in his kind eyes. "I know," he said. "I saw the question on your lips all evening. But I assure you that I've no idea where he is."

He tilted his head to one side. He looked like a very sweet little bird, or a very wise cat. She thought of the Cheshire cat in *Alice in Wonderland*, whose grin continued to hover in the air long after the rest of it had disappeared.

"May I call you Lisa?"

"You should have from the very beginning."

He laughed. "We French of a hundred years ago are rather formal."

"I adore your wife," Lisa said.

"I do too."

He smiled again, but suddenly a more serious look came over his face. "And I—we—Madeleine and I are very fond of Lara."

She understood immediately what he was trying to tell her. She shook her head. "My brother explained the whole thing to me. And I also know that a man is dead because he helped Jon."

Charles' eyebrows shot up in surprise. "Well then, you know more about the whole affair than I do."

"You didn't know that?"

"Lara isn't the most expansive person in the world . . . To tell the truth, we were expecting him this evening. We thought he'd be here for dinner. He must have been detained."

She began walking slowly about the room again, halting from time to time in front of one piece or another.

"There's something else that's bothing you," Charles Korver remarked. "Besides Lara's absence, I mean."

She nodded. "The fact that you speak of him as Lara and never by his first name."

"We've always called him Lara. And yet we've known him since the day he was born. Anything else?"

"No, nothing else."

But there was something else. When she had seen Lara for the first time, his impassive self-assurance, his evidently perfect knowledge of all of Indochina had led her to conclude that he was one of those dealers in contraband goods—Corsicans for the most part—that the French journalist in Paris had told her about. Therefore the obviously intimate ties between Lara and the Korvers puzzled her, since they didn't fit her preconceived idea of who and what Lara was.

Madeleine Korver came back into the room. "At this late hour, Charles, you ought to be in bed instead of flirting. As for you, Lisa . . ." Madeleine came over to her and slowly walked all around her, her nose tilted upward every so often, like an admiral inspecting an airplane carrier in drydock.

"You have marvelous eyes, Lisa Kinkaird. And the rest of you is absolutely ravishing. If I were a man, I'd already have kidnapped you. With a hoist. How in the world did you ever get to be so tall?"

"It's because she eats popcorn," Charles explained. "Shall we all take ourselves off to bed?"

About an hour later, there was a gentle knock on Lisa's bedroom door. She laid George B. Walker and his lucubrations aside and went to the door.

"I know," Lara said. "This is no hour to come calling on you—and it's the second time I've done so. But I saw your light. Don't be too angry with me. Or if you are, don't scream at me in too loud a voice. You'd wake up Charles and Madeleine."

In the dim light on the second floor of the perfectly silent house, his eyes seemed to Lisa to be an even paler grey-blue than in Saigon. He looked bone-tired and even a little sad as he stood with one shoulder leaning against the doorframe.

"We can go downstairs to one of the living rooms. Or else you can come with me. My car's outside." He smiled. "I'll give you the crank."

She lowered her eyes, violently torn between feelings of furious annoyance and relief at seeing him there. She raised her head.

"I'll get dressed."

He drove slowly, one hand on the steering wheel and the other on the gearshift, sitting slightly slantwise, with his left shoulder raised a little and leaning against the door pillar. She noticed that he had a Y-shaped scar on the back of his right hand. He hadn't said one word since they'd left the Korvers'. The Phnom Penh night was unbelievably silent and peaceful. There wasn't another single car on the streets and the only living souls about seemed to be two gangling, ghostly pedicab boys in duck shorts and open-necked shirts, their heads covered with funny, battered little skullcaps; they were biking along, one behind the other, pedaling with one leg and resting on the other nonchalantly on the handlebars. A pedal on one of their bicycles squeaked slightly each time it went around.

Lisa looked at the trees lining the avenues and the sort of pointed hill, a pagoda at the very top, which the car was driving slowly around.

"Where are we exactly?"

"The Phnom. A *phnom* is a hill in Khmer. This one once belonged to a certain Mrs. Penh. Hence the name of the city: the *phnom* of Mrs. Penh."

"Absolutely fascinating," Lisa said sarcastically. "I'm overawed by your knowledge."

"I can see how impressed you are."

He took a package of cigarettes out of the breast pocket of his shirt with his right hand and held it out to Lisa, who shook her head. The click of Lara's lighter and the faint odor of ignited lighter fluid. The car entered a fairly narrow street, bordered by what seemed to be government buildings. The river appeared, though Lisa didn't so much see it as feel its presence. She was unable to make out the water itself, for it was at a low level, but she could glimpse the other shore, stretching along the horizon, bristling with black trees, with here and there the sort of hard-edged, sharp-pointed shapes that formed the backgrounds of Burne Hogarth's illustrations of the Tarzan books.

"The Mekong, I presume?"

"The Tonle Sap. The Mekong joins it a little farther on. What's there opposite you is really the Chrui Chang War Peninsula."

"I thought the Tonle Sap was a lake," Lisa said, remembering what she had read in George B. Walker's book.

"It's both a lake and a river. At times it flows in one direction, and at other times in the opposite direction. The water level of the lake rises or falls, depending on the season, on whether it's filling up or emptying. When it fills up, it overflows its banks. And the snakes climb the trees to keep from drowning. Then the peasants come along in boats, catch the snakes with their bare hands, stuff them in a sack, and take them off to sell them."

She turned her head and stared at him, dumbfounded. But his face was impassive.

"And that's not all," he went on. "Beginning in October, the water level drops and the lake empties. Not completely, but almost. And as the waters retreat, the fish don't always have time enough to follow the lake as it empties out. So they race after it. You can see them crossing the roads. On foot, so to speak. Lots of them end up in what are just little pools of water, whose muddy surface dries out in the sun. And do you know how they catch them?"

"No," Lisa answered.

"With a pickaxe," Lara said imperturbably. "A pickaxe. That's the very best way."

Out on the river, lights were moving slowly from place to place. Soon Lisa was able to make out that they were the lights of sampans gliding along without a sound, propelled by silhouettes pushing against the river bottom with poles. Some of the sampans had cabins on their decks, and others were merely pirogues with pointed bows and sterns, sitting very low in the water, most of them with a man and a woman wearing black Vietnamese pants and cone-shaped hats standing at either end.

"How's your brother?" Lara asked.

"He's very weak."

"He'll recover quickly."

The car slowed down still more and stopped. At the very edge of the water, in the light of electric bulbs hanging by their cords from poles stuck in the ground, men were busily working despite the late night hour, loading a sort of long rectangular barge with yellow jars, amphorae somewhat narrower in shape than Mediterranean ones. The jars gave off an almost unbearable smell of fish, so overpowering that the stale odor of the river was nearly unnoticeable by comparison. *Asia is above all a smell*, Lisa thought. *A thousand smells, stronger than its lines and colors.* But the smells of Cambodia were, beyond doubt, those of a country at peace.

"Maybe you'll manage to persuade your brother to give himself up at the U.S. Embassy," Lara said. "And maybe not. Do you think you're going to be able to talk him into it? I asked him that same question myself—without getting any answer, I'll admit."

Lisa hesitated. "I haven't given up yet."

He nodded his head. "The contrary would have surprised me."

He suddenly leaned over, almost touching her, and opened the door on

120

her side. He got out on the driver's side and walked around the hood of the car. He looked at the dockers struggling with the jars, and the harsh light coming from the riverbank accentuated the clear-cut features of his thin face, the particular contours of his mouth. She got out of the car and joined him. They were practically the same height.

"In any event, if Jon wants to leave Cambodia on his own, other than through official channels, I think I've found a solution," he said. He tossed away the cigarette he had just finished and immediately lit another. "He might get out by plane, but the controls are relatively strict, though there's always a way of getting around them."

"Smuggling him out."

"That's right," Lara answered. "I could also get him on board one of the freighters that go downriver toward the China Sea, but they pass through Vietnam en route and they're watched very carefully. So I thought instead of the Cambodian port on the Gulf of Siam: Sihanoukville, also known as Kompong Som. In about three weeks, a Norwegian freighter is scheduled to call there. Jon can get out of the country aboard it, if he wants to."

"And go where?"

"To Sweden. I've found out that the Swedes not only don't refuse to allow American deserters from Vietnam to enter the country, but even welcome them almost as heroes."

A wave of rage swept through Lisa. She had already turned halfway around to face Lara, but at the very last second, she managed to control herself. Accepting the idea that Jon should flee to Sweden amounted to the same thing as accepting the idea that he would thereby become a fugitive for the rest of his life. But this man standing next to her wasn't responsible for what had happened. All she said was: "Why not Canada? My grandfather and I will pay whatever is necessary."

"I made inquiries. Canada doesn't take in deserters; it turns them over to the American authorities. It lets in only young Americans less than eighteen years of age, and then considers them as immigrants who are obliged to become Canadian citizens. Jon is over eighteen and he's a deserter."

The dockers below had spied them. One of them made a remark in Khmer. Lara answered something in the same language that sent the men into gales of laughter, whooping hilariously and loudly slapping their thighs.

"Come on," Lara said.

She didn't move.

"Won't you please be so kind as to come with me?"

She finally got back into the car, feeling ridiculous, furious at being made to feel that way, furious at herself and at this man and at Jon. And at everybody else in the world. *If I were a man, I could at least punch somebody in the nose,* she thought.

"And I presume that I was the object of that huge joke they were all laughing at fit to kill?"

"Who else?" He started the car and asked, "Would you like me to take you back to the Korvers'?"

She turned her head, looking him straight in the eye for a long moment, then turned away again and looked at the wharves, where a freighter flying the Japanese flag was docked. She still didn't answer.

Finally she said, "I couldn't sleep if I did go back."

They drove by the Casino, following the Quai Sisowath past the entire center of the city as far as the Palais Royal. They finally stopped in front of a gate marked Club Nautique. Everything was dark inside but a watchman appeared the moment they approached the gate. He recognized Lara, who reassured him in a few words, and let them inside. They walked to a marina where motorboats were tied up.

He looked at her. "You game?"

"For what?"

"A little boat ride on the river."

I'm mad, she thought to herself. "Okay, I'm game," she said.

He very quickly got the boat up to full power and immediately there was something extraordinarily intoxicating about this wild rush into the heart of the night. But there was just enough light from the sky to be able to make out both banks of the river, and moreover there were lights twinkling almost everywhere. To her left . . .

"Are we going up the river or down it?"

"We're going upriver."

. . . To her left, Lisa recognized the rectangular yellow lamps lining the avenues and the streets laid out in a star around the pagoda of the Phnom; she thought she could even more or less locate the Korvers' villa. Farther on along the same bank, the unmistakable silhouette of the bell tower of a Christian church stood out, topped by an illuminated blue cross.

The opposite bank was darker; she could make out lamps however, and in their white halos of light she could see the insides of huts where people were sleeping, curled up on mats, and black latticework floors. The general impression of peace, of a calm, pleasant way of life was striking: Within less than a hundred kilometers the war in Vietnam was raging.

"And where is it we're heading?"

"Nowhere in particular." He pointed to the wheel. "Would you like to try your hand at it? Just steer straight ahead."

She slid behind the controls and accelerated. The 150-horsepower engine roared, the double edges of the wake behind them grew taller and broader. After two or three minutes, however, Lisa gradually throttled back and reduced the roar of the engine.

"Does this boat belong to you?"

"Yes."

"I suppose you own half of Cambodia?"

"A little bit more than half. How long are you planning to stay?"

"I don't know yet. That man who died in Saigon—who was he?"

"A friend."

"That's awful."

He lit another cigarette.

The lights of Phnom Penh grew fainter and the river darker and darker, with no lighted dwellings on its banks now.

"I'm so sorry," Lisa said. "I can't tell you."

"Let's go back now," Lara answered.

He took over at the controls to turn the boat around, and then cut the power altogether, allowing it to drift on the current, leaving no sound to be heard except the quiet flow of the river. Instead of returning to her seat, Lisa went and sat down on the little bench at the bow. She stared at Lara, confused. What had she expected? He did not even turn around, as though there were no one else aboard. The church with the lighted bell tower reappeared, on their right this time, and the row of lights along the dock. The sound of music could be heard, coming from one of the dancehalls on the riverbank along which they were gently, slowly drifting with the lazy current.

They docked at the marina and walked back to the car.

"Would you like to go have a drink somewhere?"

"I'd rather go back to the Korvers' now."

He nodded without a word, and drove her back to the villa. She didn't wait for him to open the door for her, and got out.

"Thanks for the boat ride. And thanks for what you did for Jon."

He stared at her with his thoughtful eyes.

"Try not to be in too big a hurry to leave this country."

She nodded her head, turned away, and entered the garden of the villa. Lara must have waited for the light to go on in her bedroom, for it wasn't till then that she heard him drive off.

6

CAPTAIN KAO, IN CHARGE OF THE SECURITY AND THE POLICING OF the airport of Phnom Penh, was a man of about forty, tough and rawboned, with prominent cheekbones jutting out above hollow cheeks. A career officer, he had been a sergeant in the French Army. He loved weapons and was passionately fond of hunting, though the one and only species of game he ever went after on his hunting expeditions was roe deer, which he always killed in the same way: with a 12.7 machine gun, which he had had mounted on the hood of his personal jeep so as to be able to shoot almost without leaving the driver's seat once he'd lowered the windshield. When he managed to bring down his deer, and he seldom missed, it was not so much a feat of marksmanship as an outright slaughter. But that was what he liked most about hunting: the total destruction of the life of a graceful creature, rather than the dubious pleasure of bringing back game that he would never deign to eat.

Few things that happened at the airport escaped his notice. He had been there on the spot when Boudin had taken off in his Cessna, with Lara and Kutchaï aboard, supposedly for a routine business trip to Bangkok. Supposedly. He hadn't believed their explanation for a minute; the flight had not been planned in advance and was obviously being made on the spur of the moment, and Lara's business affairs in the Thai capital, so far as he knew, involved nothing really urgent.

He had later seen Boudin fly back into the airport. Alone.

Questioned in a friendly manner, the little Frenchman had begun swearing his usual blue streak. Captain Kao hadn't pursued his questioning any further. Then, two days later Boudin had taken off again as night was falling, still alone, maintaining that he was going to Siem Reap but reappearing the following morning without any sign of a passenger, screaming at the top of his lungs to anybody who cared to listen that he had had fuel problems, that his plane was a shitbox, that the engine was rusting away, that the fuselage was falling to pieces, that a man had to be crazy to take off in a junkheap like this, and finally that he, Boudin, would brain, there and then, anybody who dared to agree with him.

In any other circumstances, Kao would have tried to satisfy his curiosity in every possible way. He would have asked Boudin what emergency landing field he had used, would have then checked to see whether the field in question showed any signs of such a landing, whether there had been any witnesses, and whether this landing field was made of the red earth, characteristic of plantations, of which there were still traces on the wheels of the Cessna. He would certainly have done all that, even though it might have gotten him nowhere, simply because Lara was obviously involved in the matter. And above and beyond his conviction that Lara enjoyed close relations with the Palace, though he had no proof of this, Kao also felt a certain respect, even a certain warm regard, for the planter from the province of Prah Vihear. As a matter of fact, Lara had always impressed him.

In any other circumstances, therefore, Kao would have conducted an inquiry. He did not do so for the one reason that for some time another matter, much more important in his eyes, had been occupying his thoughts and all his free time. Kao was one of the key men who, in this spring of 1969, were laying the plans for a coup to oust Norodom Sihanouk from power.

Sihanouk had ascended the Cambodian throne in 1941, at the age of eighteen, and had not left the helm since, securing the independence of his country as early as 1953, almost a year before the Geneva Accords, without ever having had any sort of armed conflict with the French. Moreover, he was venerated like a god throughout the country. That Captain Kao should be involved in such a serious and spectacular undertaking as this overthrow had not been the result of a sudden decision. In reality, Kao's involvement went back ten years. A second lieutenant at the time, he had played a role in the Dap Chhuon affair.

In 1959 Dap Chhuon had been governor of the province of Siem Reap, north of Lake Tonle Sap, the province in which the temples of Angkor are located. A sort of local potentate surrounded by his own personal bodyguards, Dap Chhuon had been contacted by the Central Intelligence Agency, in those days the fief of Allen Dulles, and the South Vietnamese secret services. The objective of the maneuver: staging a coup d'état that would have thrown Cambodia into the U.S. camp, along with South Vietnam, Thailand, South Korea, and other countries belonging to SEATO, the South-East Asian Treaty Organization. The coup had miscarried, thanks largely to information passed on to Sihanouk by the French intelligence services (Kao was of the opinion that Lara had played a personal role in the securing of this information), who had zestfully thwarted the designs of their American colleagues.

Two hundred seventy kilograms of pure gold, in sixteen-ounce ingots bearing the impress of Fort Knox, had been recovered, piled up on banana leaves in the middle of a jungle clearing. Weapons and radio sets had been seized; South Vietnamese officers in civilian clothes had been arrested and joyously sliced to ribbons. Dap Chhuon had been killed, literally butchered, his body savagely hacked to pieces. A number of his accomplices had also had their throats cut and photos of all of them after the massacre, quite stomach-turning photos, had been pinned to the wooden walls of all the *sala khum,* the communal halls, throughout the country. The great majority of Dap Chhuon's co-conspirators, however, had mysteriously managed to slip through the net spread for them by the superior officer Sihanouk had sent from Phnom Penh to apprehend and punish the guilty parties.

This superior officer was then a colonel; his name was Lon Nol.

Kao was based at Kompong Thom at the time. He had learned of the plot six months earlier and agreed to take part in it. The night he saw the troops arriving from Phnom Penh and realized that he had just bet on the wrong card was one of the worst in his life. For a few moments he thought he was done for. He was only a young junior officer at the time, intelligent certainly, undoubtedly ambitious (even going so far as to take night courses in English and history given by the French teachers at the Kompong Thom high school), and admirably untroubled by qualms of conscience, but alas, possessed of no friends with influence who could protect him. In other words, a man condemned, for he had no lack of enemies among his own men. He very quickly collected his wits however. One of his buddies in the little garrison at Kompong Thom, also a second lieutenant, was named Ung Sath; he was a good sort, with eight or nine kids at home to feed, a kindly, easy-going man, quite convinced that now he'd made second lieutenant he was bound to become a field marshal some day, and very pleased to be on his way up. Kao was certain, absolutely certain, that Ung Sath had never been involved, either directly or indirectly, in any sort of plot whatsoever, that the thought of opposing Samdech Euv had never once crossed his mind. Kao had gone to Ung's place as the trucks arriving from Phnom Pen began unloading their troops in the market square. He had lured Ung outside and coldly put a bullet through the middle of his forehead. He had then cut off Ung's head and brought his trophy to Lon Nol's headquarters.

"I've personally killed one of the treasonous accomplices of the ignoble henchmen, the spittle-driveling toads of American imperialism. He dared to ask me to help him get away and I was blinded both by anger and indignation."

Lon Nol hadn't believed Kao for a single instant, naturally, and Kao for his part was immediately aware that Lon Nol knew exactly what was going on. But the two men had understood each other instantly. Kao had been congratulated for his zeal and promoted to the rank of full lieutenant on the spot, with the right to confiscate, for his own use, from among Ung Sath's earthly possessions, the one he coveted the most: his Vespa scooter with a radio antenna but no radio.

And now Kao was a captain, about to be promoted to the rank of major; he had his own personal Peugeot 404, bought secondhand from a French teacher; he had his own apartment with a bathroom in a new building on the Rue Pasteur in Phnom Penh; and he had just recently deposited $25,000 in a bank in Hong Kong, thus bringing the balance of his little savings account up to 88,000 U.S. dollars. His functions at Pochentong Airport netted him approximately five or six times what he would have pocketed as a minister, with far fewer inconveniences. Obviously this sum did not represent his official salary, which would not have sufficed to feed a fakir following an ascetic diet. Kao levied personal taxes on almost everything, including, of course, the opium traffic carried on by the confederation of Corsicans and Chinese working hand in glove, planes taking off and landing—or at least the great majority of them—the profits of the bar and the restaurant, even the airport toilets. He resold merchandise confiscated on the flimsiest and most farfetched pretexts and appropriated the money, levied a reasonable 10 percent duty on packages sent by Chinese in Cambodia to their families in China, and supplied a shop on the Rue Prey Nikor, near the Central Market, with supposedly lost baggage, taking his cut of the profits.

On certain days, at hours when he gave himself over to self-contem-

plation, he dreamed with poignant melancholy of what a man of his stamp
might have made of himself had he been the head man at a really important
airport like O'Hare in Chicago, Kennedy in New York, or Orly in Paris.

He had other dreams as well, which struck him as having more chance
of coming true: dreams of becoming a colonel and even a general.

Hence his involvement in the plot against Sihanouk.

The coup d'état being planned now had a scope and aim quite different
from those of the folkloric one that Dap Chhuon had tried to carry off, with
its hundreds of gold ingots meant to look like a pile of forgotten bananas.
Captain Kao was certain of it. This time the game was being played for very
high stakes, and the men holding the cards, as he saw it, were in a position
to be real movers and shakers. At their head was Sirik Matak, a prince of
royal blood and the former Cambodian Ambassador in Washington, Peking,
and Tokyo, who thought, with all due modesty, that he would have made a
much better King of Cambodia than anyone else. Behind him, but also in a
certain sense ahead of him—since this corpulent, slow-moving, elephantine
man who believed in heaven and the stars and their influence on men's des-
tinies, served in fact as a sort of shock-absorbing front bumper—was General Lon Nol, the number two man, whose thoughts no one was ever certain
of (perhaps because he didn't think very often); who consulted his personal
astrologers the moment he got out of bed each morning; who dreamed of
setting up a great federation of the non-Vietnamese peoples of Indochina,
being fearful of the expansionist aims of Hanoi and of Saigon alike, the former striking him for the moment as being much more dangerous than the
latter; and who, because of his Chinese origins, had strong and intimate ties
with Chinese business circles and therefore was more or less kindly disposed
toward their efforts to exert pressure on him.

Lon Nol had been impressed by the successful coups d'état staged by
Ne Win in Burma in 1962, and above all by the one led by Suharto in Indonesia in 1965. He had sent certain of his faithful followers, among them
Captain Kao, to consult with these victorious generals in order to learn
their secrets of success. With the patience of a filing clerk, or of a Mah-
Jongg player, he had slowly pushed his pieces forward on the game board,
while at the same time never missing an opportunity to proclaim his un-
swerving devotion to Samdech Sihanouk. The establishment on Cambodian
soil of camps of fanatically anti-Communist Khmer Krom refugees from
Cochin China was one of these pieces. He thus had at his disposal several
thousand men who could join forces, when the right moment came, with
the partisans of the country's former prime minister in the days of the Japanese occupation, Son Ngoc Thanh, who had fled to Thailand. In all, ten to
twelve thousand combatants, whom the American special units and Green
Berets of South Vietnam were training.

As for funding the coup, Kao had no worries on that score either. Charles Korver had been quite right: It was common knowledge that a businessman from Bangkok by the name of Song Sakd had arrived in Phnom Penh and caused many an eye to gleam by vaunting the merits of judicious investments—which, moreover, did not require the investors' tying up their own money, since the obliging Sino-Thai assured them it would not be necessary. "You'll repay me out of the profits," he had said, to Kao in particular. It was as plain as day that Song Sakd had connections with the CIA. It was even a bit too obvious. Threatened with arrest, but fortunately warned in time of this possibility, the banker had finally fled the country—Kao had personally escorted him to his plane—absent-mindedly taking with him 400 million riels, a sum amounting at the time to 9 million U.S. dollars, belonging to the Royal Khmer Bank. Or at least that was the sum he was officially said to have taken out of the country with him. In reality, a large part of this enormous sum of money had remained in the pockets of certain individuals.

Around eight o'clock on an April morning, Captain Kao left his apartment on the Rue Pasteur, more to escape from his wife than to hurry to his job. Nuba, his one and only lawfully wedded wife, was the sole cloud on Kao's glowing pink and blue horizon. Nuba was a fiercely, even pathologically jealous woman. She had twice turned up suddenly at his office at Pochentong, brandishing a carving knife the first time, and the second time a Smith & Wesson .38 that he had made the mistake of leaving in the wardrobe chest of their bedroom. The two bullets she had fired shattered a windowpane and spent themselves out of doors, luckily without hitting anybody, but Kao had been obliged to knock his wife unconscious with a chair. After this incident, their relations had been a bit strained. Oddly enough, despite Nuba's vehement accusations, Kao did not have at the time—had never had—a mistress or even a passing affair with another woman. Beyond question he had attended certain private banquets in the company of a minister or two, several high officials, and a few hospitable young women, but that was all, and he had done so only for professional reasons; he was definitely not a womanizer. More surprising still, he loved his wife, though he would have preferred her to be less demonstrative. In actual fact, all his absences and late nights, which Nuba attributed to scandalous philandering on her husband's part, had been occasioned by confidential meetings of a political nature. Captain Kao considered himself more or less a martyr to politics.

He had another of these confidential meetings this very morning. He was scheduled to meet a South Korean, a Filipino, and, in all likelihood, a Chinese from Formosa who ordinarily traveled on a Malaysian passport and a cover identity as a specialist in the air-conditioning of airports and other public buildings. The man who had organized this meeting, an American whom Kao knew only as Price, would doubtless not be present, first of all because it was a routine meeting, scheduled for beginning the study of the steps to be taken on D-Day, and secondly because Price, with touching tactfulness, preferred to leave the direction of operations to his Asiatic comrades as often as possible. "Decide among yourselves," he would say with a friendly smile. This "among yourselves" infuriated Kao. As if a Korean, a Filipino, a Chinese, and a Cambodian had something in common . . .

In the glove compartment of his 404, Kao had a 9 mm German Luger, one of his favorite handguns. And under the back seat, in a specially built cache, was one of his jewels: a very recently manufactured Beretta 70.223 automatic assault rifle that had come out of the factory a bare two months before. Taking chargers of thirty cartridges, it would fire no less than 670 rounds per minute. It was a 5.6 mm-caliber rifle, which placed it in the latest generation of weapons of the same type, despite a design that in the final analysis was quite traditional. Kao hadn't yet had a chance to try it out, and wondered whether it was the equal of the American Armalite 18 that he was particularly fond of. He looked at his watch: 8:25 A.M. The Formosan disguised as a Malaysian was scheduled to land at 11:40 A.M. and the meeting would not begin before noon. He gave in to temptation. He would find a quiet spot on the road to Takeo and fire off a few clips.

Aimed at a tree, alas. Too bad there was nothing else to shoot at. Nothing that was alive.

7 LISA SPENT THE THREE DAYS FOLLOWING HER NOCTURNAL BOAT RIDE on the Tonle Sap doing absolutely nothing. She naturally kept an eye on Jon and had endless chats with him, which reminded them both of vacations they'd spent together at Matthew Kinkaird's cabin when they were little. Or at least they pretended to have nostalgic memories of them. In reality, they had never been close when they were youngsters. There was seven years' difference in age between them; when you're fifteen that's a world of difference, and even more so when you're eight. They now re-created a common adolescence, like travelers who have gazed out at the same landscape from different trains, and thanks to the imaginary color and texture one can impart to memories if one takes the trouble, they even managed to rediscover some sunny days in their past, along with a number of shared experiences that sent them into hysterical giggles. They were becoming a brother and sister again.

Jon was making a spectacular recovery. That is to say, he was rapidly putting on weight and regaining his strength. He still had crises, though they became fewer and further between and less violent as the days went by; but there were times when the acute mental and physical stress brought on by the sudden withdrawal of the drugs he had been on—he had mixed opium and methadone—sent him into convulsions or he lost consciousness. One afternoon, when the prescribed sedatives were not enough to calm him down, the doctor—whom Charles Korver had called in to treat Jon the moment he had come to stay at the Korvers'—had to rush to the house and give Jon a series of injections. He was a former army doctor who had lived through the last hours of the siege of Dien Bien Phu and acquired there an amply deserved fame. He undressed Lisa with his eyes, quite obviously regretting that she was not the one he had been called in to treat.

"Are you certain you're all right?"

"Absolutely certain," Lisa said with a laugh. "I'm terribly sorry."

"Not as sorry as I am."

Jon and Lisa never once spoke of what had happened in Vietnam, Lisa because she thought that the right moment hadn't yet come along, and Jon because he appeared to have blotted out the entire experience from his memory. The general atmosphere at the Korvers', above all Charles' and Madeleine's attitude, their warm friendship, their outright affection almost, the sensation that he had always lived there, also contributed to prolonging this truce. Lisa willingly allowed herself to relax and spend her time as she pleased, for the first time, really, since Robert Trenton's death five years before. Her surroundings gave her every reason to feel she didn't have a care in the world, and on the third evening after her arrival she even agreed to accompany her hosts to a good-bye party for Peter and Ronda Soames given by the Australian Ambassador.

But on the morning of April 22 she woke up, literally and figuratively. Despite the Korvers' vehement protests—they seemed to think that she'd be staying on with them for the next ten or twenty years—she realized it was impossible for her to go on living this carefree existence. It was necessary, first of all, for her to resolve the problem of money. She dared not say a word to Charles or Madeleine about her financial difficulties, for she was certain they would immediately offer her whatever sum she cared to name. Her first thought, of course, was to phone the United States.

"I'd like to reassure my grandfather," she said to Charles.

"I'd be curious to see the look on the Cambodian operator's face when you ask her to get you a line through to Colorado Springs. It'll take her three or four days to get over the shock."

Charles was the one who suggested that she ask the American Embassy to help her out. Curiously, she hadn't thought of that, accustomed as she was to solving her problems all by herself.

"I'm not surprised you didn't think of it," Charles remarked, misjudging the sort of help she was going to ask for. "Your embassy here was shut for such a long time. You're lucky, come to think of it: If you'd arrived a little earlier, just last month for instance, you'd have found it closed."

She stared at him. "The embassy closed?"

"You didn't know?"

"One doesn't hear much about Phnom Penh on Madison Avenue."

"Diplomatic relations between Cambodia and the United States were broken off in May of '65; it's only in the last few days that they've been reestablished."

"And there weren't any Americans at all in Cambodia during all that time?"

"Not officially. I'm going to tell Bê to get the car out of the garage and drive you to the embassy."

If Bê, the chauffeur, wasn't stretched out in the back of the car sleeping, he could usually be found dozing in the front seat. If his eyes were open, he was usually occupied in slowly walking around his vehicle in majestic circles, with the haughty air of a bullfighter from Seville entering the bullring.

"Is it all that far?" Lisa asked.

"You could walk it in the time it would take you to cross Central Park along the lake on a fine summer day."

Lisa set off on foot. It was her first real contact with the Cambodian capital, in daylight and by herself. She found it not only a beautiful city but a charming one. *Cleaner than New York—though that's not a very difficult feat.* She saw a city that had almost nothing Asiatic about it, in the quarter she was walking through at least, laid out along broad avenues lined with superb, luxuriantly flowering trees, a city in which time clearly didn't mean very much, where peace and calm reigned and the pace of life was slow and easygoing. On one of the boulevards, which she recognized as Norodom, she caught sight of an elephant in gold and purple trappings, like in the movies, and she decided it was a white one, or very nearly so. *A sacred elephant, no less. All that's missing is the Thugs who strangle you to death. But they must be from a different film.* The elephant, sacred or not, had a jolly keeper who waved at his admirers on the sidewalks, and was preceded by a jeep with four policemen majestically seated in it. The elephant had only one tusk, the other broken off almost at the root; it snuffled angrily, its little beady eyes glaring at the cars that hastily moved aside to let it by. A little farther down the boulevard, she turned to her right and caught sight, as Charles Korver had said she would, of the star-spangled banner and the inevitable Marine guards in white shoulder belts, starched shirts, and dress helmets.

"If you have the courage, go on to the Central Market," Charles Korver had said. "Don't be put off by the smells, which are overpowering, or by the crowd, which will be friendly or at worst indifferent. You'll be safer there than on Fifth Avenue at night. The spectacle is worth the trouble, and as a beginning it will be less disconcerting than the Psa Tia, the Old Market, whose smells would knock over a jackal not used to them."

It was just past 9:30, and she knew from experience that foreign service officers were not early risers. At the end of a street lined with European-type stores, many of them run by Westerners or Indians, she could see the curious cupola, built of successive tiers of concrete, which Charles had described to her. Sixty yards farther on, as she entered the market square the smells leapt at her throat. They were like an invisible wall that grew thicker and thicker with each step she took; they clung to her skin, they dizzied her and turned her stomach, and the next second intoxicated her like alcohol.

There was everything imaginable in the Central Market, amid a deafening chaos that reminded her of a railway station just before a holiday. Fruits: mangoes, mangosteens, sapodillas, papayas, oranges with green skins, so-called pig bananas, so starchy as to be inedible and used only to feed domestic animals, delicious little yellow bananas only a few inches long, coconuts, limes, litchis. All the usual market produce and other things that were less common: betel nuts and leaves to be chewed, mint, green Kampot peppercorns that can be crushed beneath the tongue, the best in the world, freshly gathered soy or bamboo sprouts, hot peppers and ginger, secondhand bicycles that must have dated from the first days of the Tour de France, pans marked "Made in Germany" in English, and Vietnamese *québat* calabashes, hardware and basketry, Japanese thong sandals competing with cans of sweetened condensed Nestlé milk, checkered sarongs in blue and white or red and white, black *sampots*. There were ortolans and roasted crickets threaded on bamboo rods, incubated eggs with chicks inside buried beneath ashes, hot red peppers swimming in oil, rice, sticky or dry, already cooked and to be eaten immediately, each takeout portion rolled up inside a leaf. Meats, smoke-cured or raw hunks freshly butchered, were laid out in bloody displays covered with swarms of brilliant flies. The butchers were naked except for a pair of undershorts, their arms blood-spattered up to their biceps, and they looked like jovial, swarthy-skinned Jack the Rippers. Chickens more or less everywhere, all of them live, but some of them both live and completely plucked with the exception of the head and neck, thus exposing a baby-pink flesh that would have taken away the appetite of a legionnaire. In nearby stalls, fish, either still wriggling or dried, alongside jars of the *nuoc-mam* fish sauce of Phu Quoc or Phan Thiet, and *prahoc* from the Tonle Sap.

Lisa had reached the heart of the building, better organized, oddly enough, than the approaches to it. The heat inside was suffocating. She headed outside again, wandering about more or less at random, as vendors scarcely taller than their stands cheerfully called out to her.

"I don't have any money." And she spread her hands apart as a sign to show she had no money, as she had seen customers do at the street market on the Cours Lafayette in Toulon when she had gone there with Bob Trenton who adored the South of France.

She finally found herself out in the open air again. Outside, women in black *sampots,* their upper torsos clad in tight-fitting colored bodices, were squatting on their heels, selling pitifully small pyramids of rice, a bit of fish, a single banana laid out in front of them, their bare broad toes clinging to the cement like suction cups. There were also vendors selling marvelously tasty Chinese soup such as no restaurant could offer, vendors of sugar-cane juice and palm wine and *chum* in bamboo containers. A bit homesick for American ice cream, Lisa stopped without thinking in front of a big aluminum tray with an assortment of Chinese pastries laid out on it. The vendor hastened to her side, overjoyed. He chose one of the cakes, placed it on half a banana leaf, and handed it to her with the exquisite politeness of a mandarin.

"I don't have any money," Lisa said, smiling and shaking her head.

The man—iron-gray crew-cut hair, affable and homely, a mere seventy pounds of skin and bones plus seven or eight gold teeth—insisted.

"No money," Lisa said in French.

"Eat today, pay *sahec*—tomorrow," the vendor said with touching kindness.

A little crowd was forming around them and everyone began to laugh, evidently finding the scene irresistibly funny.

Lisa picked up the cake, as she would have picked up a live cobra.

"Eat, eat," the vendor said. "Pay *sahec.*"

Lisa put the cake in her mouth: Socrates swallowing his hemlock.

"Much good," the vendor said.

"Mmmm, much good," Lisa said, trying to get her jaws unstuck.

"Madame much beautiful," the vendor said.

Lisa smiled. "Thank you. I'll come back tomorrow and pay you."

The Khmer clapped his hands, slapped his thighs, laughed till tears came to his eyes. *What in the world did that monster give me to eat?* she wondered. She walked off amid peals of laughter from the crowd, laughing too, without quite knowing why. She crossed the square again, having by some miracle come out of the market directly opposite the street by which she had come. The cake tasted terribly sweet, with a flavor of mint, anise, and coconut, and left her mouth dry. But suddenly, despite the more and more stifling heat, despite the sea of smells still surrounding her, she felt carefree and gay. In the shade of the arcades, Malabar Indians with eyes like a woman's were sitting with their rolls of cloth piled up or spread out before them, their insistent gaze caressing her hips and her breasts. In retaliation, she merely smiled at them. And she was suddenly overcome with an indefinable feeling of regret as she stepped across the threshold of the U.S. Embassy after a courteous but firm discussion with the Marine guards.

This was April 22, the day she first met Thomas Aquinas O'Malley.

8

THE NAME OF THE COUNTER AGENT AT AIR FRANCE WAS HUBRECHT. He was as surprised to see Roger Bouès entering his agency as he would have been to see a ghost walk through the door.

"Well, I'll be damned," Hubrecht said. "I thought it was ten in the morning."

"It is ten in the morning," Roger said in an ominous tone of voice. "Let's have none of your sly sarcasm, please. I'm a customer."

"Don't tell me you want to buy a plane ticket."

"As a matter of fact, that's precisely what I'm planning to do: purchase a plane ticket. I'm not joking. I never joke at ten o'clock in the morning. At ten o'clock in the morning, I'm fast asleep."

"A ticket to where?"

"France. What's the price of one?"

Hubrecht slowly laid down the ball-point pen he was holding in his hand. "France?"

"France. Sweet-France-land-of-my-childhood. Ah! *les-p'tites-femmes-de-Paris. Oh-là-là, c'est l'amour*—and all that jazz. France."

"Round trip?"

"One way," Roger said impassively.

"Three thousand six hundred forty-five francs, tax included."

Roger shook his head. "Thanks anyway, old pal," he said.

"Three hundred sixty-four thousand five hundred old francs."

Roger shook his head again. He turned on his heel and left. He'd gone only a few steps down the sidewalk when Hubrecht came from behind the counter and joined him.

"Is something wrong, Roger?"

"Everything's fine. I'm in great shape. I'm full of vim, vigor, and vitality."

"Let's go have a drink somewhere on me."

Roger smiled. "Some other time, old pal."

He bade Hubrecht good-bye with a debonair little wave of his left hand and began walking straight ahead, paying no attention to which direction he was heading in. He was seeing in his mind's eye a poster hanging on one wall of the Air France ticket office: a photograph of one of the châteaux of the Loire, Chenonceaux. He remembered the time he'd visited Chenonceaux, and Chambord, Blois, Amboise, Cheverny, Azay-le-Rideau, Valançay as well. He remembered that spring of '43, the front-drive Citroën that had taken him there, him and his father and his mother, with him sitting in the back seat, listening to his mother talking on and on endlessly, if you could call it talking, in her dull, hard, pitiless, almost masculine voice. He remembered his father's delicate hands on the steering wheel, his father's sly, conspiratorial gaze meeting his in the rearview mirror, his father's silences, the enormous, heart-rending wave of happiness that had come over him at a certain moment when he felt his father's hand on his shoulder, as they stopped to rest for a few minutes along the roadside not far from Semblançay, and his father's voice saying: "Don't hold it against her. It's my fault. I should be with you more often. When the war's over . . ."

Three thousand six hundred forty-five francs. Or in old francs, in which he had once made all his mental calculations, the francs of those days, 364,500.

His mother's voice, his mother holding the telephone receiver and forgetting to hang up, in the entry hall of the house in Pau on the tree-lined Allées de Morlaas, in the entry hall smelling of wax, darkness, cold, his mother staring at him with her hawkeyes and saying to him, on that day in September 1944: "He's killed himself. Your idiot of a father has just killed himself."

He walked past the grounds of the Hotel Raja, heading toward the Rue des Orfèvres leading to the Royal Palace. Three hundred sixty-four thousand five hundred old francs, as Hubrecht had put it: It seemed like an utterly fantastic sum. *Even if I sold my car. And in the first place, who'd want it? It's unfortunately too recent a model to interest a museum; it'll be a couple of years yet before it's old enough for that. Keep calm, Roger. First of all, you don't even own a revolver. And you'd miss. What's more, let's face it. Let's imagine that you're in Paris, walking along the Champs-Elysées. You don't even have a decent suit, not to mention a tie. What restaurant worthy of the name would let you in without a tie? So you see . . .*

He stopped outside a shop that sold gold and silver jewelry, jade and ebony statues, some of them from Laos, women's heads with fiendishly complicated chignons, with smiles on their lips beside which the Gioconda's smile had the transparent innocence and naturalness of a spring morning in the countryside around Tours. Years before, he and Lara had gone into this same shop and bought one of these heads in black wood, carved to order by a Laotian craftsman from Saravane. Lara had taken it home with him, and had finally given it as a gift to an American friend whose name Roger had never known.

Three thousand six hundred forty-five francs. It did seem less expensive in new francs.

He began walking again, retracing his footsteps, this time skirting the Old Market, the smell of which hadn't gotten much better over the years. He reached the Rue Dekcho Damdin again, with the Onalom pagoda on his left. Dentists were working in the open air on the sidewalk in front of the temple, with no other equipment except a pair of tongs, a knife, a not neces-

sarily new Gillette Blue Blade with which to slit gums, and ready-made
gold teeth, carefully laid out on checkered handkerchiefs spread out on the
sidewalk. A little farther on an itinerant barber: a chair, a razor, a pair of
scissors, a pocket mirror hanging from a nail on the nearest tree. Young
bonzes in saffron robes were haughtily standing in line, waiting to have
their heads shaved. The enormous cutlass-size straight razor scraped their
skin, not only along their scalps but also across their foreheads and eyebrows, and sliced off in one last broad sweep, with the precision of a scalpel,
any hairs growing in their ears.

He walked by the door of the Zigzag without stopping, resisting almost
furiously the tempting odor of the brochettes that Vandekherkove was beginning to prepare for the noon apéritif crowd. Roger was hungry, since as
far as he could recall he hadn't eaten a thing since the night before.

A few steps farther on he met the Portuguese.

"You're up early, aren't you?" he greeted Roger.

"Work," Roger answered. "I'm swamped."

"How are you?"

"In great shape."

"See you in a while," the Portuguese said, heading for the Zigzag,
doubtless to await his mistress, the dress shop owner.

Roger smiled. He liked the Portuguese. *In fact, is there anyone I don't
like?* he thought. *Apart from myself, naturally.* Present company always ex-
cepted. He climbed up the three flights of stairs and entered his apartment.
He rummaged around in the closet that served him as a kitchen and finally
came up with three or four lumps of sugar that were a bit sticky from the
dampness. The tin of Nescafé was empty, except for a few granules in the
bottom. *Why couldn't I add some water and boil the whole thing, tin and
all?* He went back into the enormous room, put a record on the turntable,
and then remembered that the sapphire needle was definitely *hors de combat.* He sat down on the floor, with his back to the wall near the door,
directly opposite the stone Apsaras on its black marble pedestal. He didn't
have the right to sell it; it belonged to the Cambodian government and he
would not even be allowed to take it with him if he left the country, but
would have to give it back to the National Museum. All he enjoyed was the
right to safeguard it temporarily, the usufruct of it, so to speak.

"You wouldn't have three thousand six hundred forty-five francs to
lend me, by chance? In new francs?"

9

THE SHOTS GREW FEWER AND FURTHER BETWEEN, THEN CEASED AL-
together. Silence came over the forest once again, a total silence in which
there was not even a sound of birds or insects, a tense, unreal silence. After
perhaps thirty seconds, Ieng Samboth warily raised his head an inch or so
and risked taking a peek around. There, where the enemy ought to be, two
hundred yards straight in front of him, all his eye could see was an enigmatic wall of greenery, without a single leaf stirring. Ieng glanced quickly
to his right and his left, where his own men were hiding, and was able to
make out many of them, all of them suddenly, strangely, absolutely motionless, as in a freeze-frame shot in a film.

Some twenty men had finally arrived at the rendezvous at the abandoned pagoda, joining his own detachment, so that it now numbered around
fifty combat troops. Combat troops in a manner of speaking: Most of the
newcomers had no weapons at all, and five of them were armed with nothing but hunting rifles dating from the thirties. But almost all of them were
wearing *kramas* around their necks—red scarves, with prayers and invoca-
tions written on them, which had been blessed by the bonzes, so that they
had the property of protecting those who wore them, and their comrades
fighting with them, from enemy bullets or blows.

Other men were carrying on their persons a little statuette of the Buddha, or simply a pebble or a bit of wood whose talismanic value stemmed
from their having been picked up in the immediate vicinity of the old dead
tree trunk representing the Neak Tâ, the Spirit of the Forest, of their pos-
sessors' native village. Two or three of the guerrillas were even clad in duly
blessed magic shirts, even more efficacious, if that were possible, than any
krama.

Ieng silently spat out the remains of the stalk of sugar cane he had been
chewing on. The existence of these superstitions, the unconscionable place
occupied by the bonzes in Cambodian life, in the countryside especially,
were problems that would have to be resolved some day. The problem of
the bonzes in particular, those Buddhist monks whom Ieng thoroughly detested because of what he regarded as their arrogance, their laziness, their
cupidity. *You shave your head and don a saffron robe, and all you have to
do for the rest of your life is sponge off poor devils such as these who ruin
themselves and go into debt to make you richer and richer.* Ieng's hatred of
the bonzes was all the more violent in that he remembered the gestures of
respect that he himself had made, the powerful emotion he had felt in days
gone by in the presence of the venerable of Phnom Penh who had blessed
him before his departure for Europe. *"Celui qui croyait au ciel et celui qui*

n'y croyait pas"—"He who believed in heaven and he who did not"—that verse by Louis Aragon, his and Khieu Samphan's favorite poet, came back to him. Ieng was not really sure whether he was a believer or a nonbeliever; he was too intelligent, and above all too self-observant, not to recognize that his violent hostility toward those who wore the habit was the hatred of the apostate who experiences pangs of remorse at having renounced his faith.

He looked at Rath, squatting on his heels a few yards away. He was certain that Rath did not suffer from any sort of metaphysical anguish. Rath, thickset and tough, indefatigable, capable of living for days on a handful of rice. Rath, sure of himself and of the reasons why he was fighting. Rath, with whom peasants identified much more than they did with Ieng. Rath, who killed as naturally as other men breathed.

Only the night before, he had put three persons to death in that little village that Ouk had said lay ahead: three executions carried out in exactly the same way, with his plastic sack. The victims had been a Chinese, Teo Chin, the owner of a kapok plantation, and the two Cambodian hirelings who represented him in the village, a husband and wife, both of whom were moneylenders, and the husband the mayor as well. Curiously enough, it was the woman who had struggled and thrashed about the longest. She had crawled along the ground, among the legs of her former charges, for an incredibly long time, and there had been bursts of laughter as they stepped aside from the woman writhing in her death-agony. But laughter in Khmer country was not necessarily a sign of mirth; it could also mean that a person was so disconcerted, so taken aback that he was unable to express his emotion or his profound fear in any other way.

Rath was signaling to him, pressing him to issue an order. Ieng hesitated—not to give an order (he had already made up his mind), but to give that order to Rath. At that very moment, as though he had instinctively felt his presence necessary, Ouk appeared, his huge body slipping through the branches as silently as a shadow.

"We can counterattack," he whispered. "I don't think there are very many of them. No more of them than there are of us, at any rate. They're Kroms and they've got Thais with them. They have a heavy machine gun over there on the left, at the foot of the areca palm that's fallen over. But I can take a few men with me and take them by surprise from behind."

Ieng shook his head. Never engage forces; refuse to do so as often as possible; never strike a blow at the adversary unless there was no question that he was definitely at a disadvantage and could be taken by surprise, and then strike for only one reason: to capture as many weapons as possible, to be used later when precisely the right opportunity presented itself. In the meantime, survive. Those were the orders that he had received, general orders that he himself had helped draw up.

"We're moving out. We're pulling back toward the ruins of Prah Khan."

Withdrawing to the northeast, in other words, a dozen kilometers from there, to an extension of the little road linking Siem Reap and the town of Rovieng. Ouk nodded and took off into the forest again as silently as a leaf falling. Ieng's eyes sought Rath's again; he raised his right hand, forefinger and middle finger uplifted, moving them in a circle, and concluding with a forthright backward jerk of his thumb: "We're pulling back." Rath nodded. For the moment he was obeying orders and thus causing no particular problems from that point of view. For the moment at least.

Ieng watched Rath leave his post, crawl forward a few yards, and disappear. To left and right, as the order to pull back reached them, the guerrilla fighters began moving back, abandoning with surprising agility their posture of hunters rooted to the spot awaiting the prey. Everything appeared to be going perfectly. *They had no idea that the enemy was right there in front of them,* he thought. At that very instant the heavy machine gun and other automatic weapons began firing. *It was too good to be true,* Ieng said to himself as he huddled behind a tree trunk for cover.

He heard bullets landing in the rich earth around him and felt the usual fear come over him. But he somehow found the courage to raise the barrel of his Kalashnikov and gently squeeze the trigger. With a quick glance to his right he saw two of his men in the rear guard—whose duty it was to cover their retreat—firing their weapons as he himself was doing, their faces tense and glistening with a film of sweat that had nothing to do with the heat. *Five minutes more and we'll pull out too.* He looked at his wristwatch, a gift presented to him by the German Democratic Republic on his second trip to East Berlin. *Once upon a time, Blacks and Indians were given glass-bead necklaces as presents. Nowadays we Cambodians are given a day-date stopwatch chronometer. . . .*

Four minutes.

He took out another clip from the green canvas sack hanging from his belt and inserted it in his Kalashnikov. He fired two or three bursts, being careful not to let his finger freeze on the trigger. Then he immediately took cover. *And what if I'd gone to Washington instead of East Berlin—what would they have offered me? A Cadillac?* Another watch, no doubt. Ieng was not particularly anti-American. He wasn't anti-anything, nor was he pro-anything. *All I want is to be a Cambodian.* Why was it impossible to be Cambodian the way a person was Swiss?

One minute.

A grenade launcher was firing somewhere to his left, around four hundred yards away, but happily the grenades were all landing even farther away, in a spot where he doubted very much that any of his men were.

Twenty seconds.

He quickly inserted a new clip into his rifle, even though there were still a few bullets left in the previous one.

Okay, I'm leaving too.

With fear clutching his belly he crawled backward, his assault rifle cradled in the hollow of his arm, making his way along on his outstretched elbows and the insides of his knees. After seven or eight yards, once he'd entered the deep brush, he decided to stand up. He gradually started to run, his head tucked between his shoulders, his legs bent, covering twenty or thirty yards in this fashion. He saw his comrades running along parallel to him; some of them had already reached denser cover.

The first bullet hit him in the back of the right thigh, spun him halfway around, and made him stumble. The second one hit him when his feet were in the air, entirely off the ground; struck him somewhere around the nape of the neck. It was as though he had taken a massive blow to his shoulders and head. He lost consciousness before he hit the ground.

And then there was Lara's voice, slow and grave even when he spoke in the high-pitched tones of Cambodian. Lara's voice pierced the fog and reached his ears.

"He should be coming round soon now."

Ieng instinctively translated into French the words uttered in Khmer, a language that, as it was generally spoken, did not lend itself to nuance. *It's not only our temples that are in ruins. Our language too,* he thought. He opened his eyes.

"Hello there," Lara said in French. "Have you finished your nap?"

Ieng tried to sit up and felt the bandages across his chest and around his skull.

"What's the matter with me?"

"You've got a bullet in your thigh, one in your shoulder, and another that's more or less made a hole in your head. But don't worry: There's not much danger that what's inside your noggin is going to leak out. What were you doing anyway? Walking about on all fours?"

"Maybe he was looking for mushrooms," a hoarse booming voice commented.

"Who picked me up?"

"Ouk."

"Did he get out all right himself?"

"Ouk pool wletch of an immoltal Khmel, he little blother Kutchaï, all same," the other voice said.

Ieng didn't need to turn his head to recognize the possessor of that voice: Kutchaï. *Who else? Since Lara's here too.*

He looked past Lara, recognized the long shelves lined with books,

shelves made of the same smooth black wood as the wall they were attached
to. "Have I been here at your place for a long time?"

"Since yesterday."

"Have you seen any soldiers?"

"Not yet."

"And what about the others?" He said "the others" to avoid saying
"my men," a turn of phrase that embarrassed him.

"They regrouped first some ten kilometers west of Rovieng, a little to
the north of the ruins of Prah Khan. But they were attacked again last night
by another column from Siem Reap and they pulled out. I don't know exactly where they are right now. They may not be far away. There was gunfire in the distance this morning."

"Were you here when I arrived?"

"Phnom Penh. Oreste sent me word when Ouk brought you here."

"Are there soldiers at Kompong Thom?"

"Yes."

"At Rovieng?"

"Yes, there too."

"You're taking risks."

"I know, I know," Lara answered.

Ieng closed his eyes. "Colonialist."

He managed a smile. When he was living in Paris, he'd once gone to a
dentist who'd given him a shot in the jaw before extracting a tooth; he felt
the same sensation of rigidity, of something missing, but extending this time
to a good half of his body. And the same feeling as then of light-headedness,
intoxication almost, began to overtake him.

"I don't hurt anywhere."

"He big Khmel Louge chief not one bit clybaby," said Kutchaï's
booming voice, so like his younger brother's.

But Ouk isn't a clown. Ieng had never been really fond of Kutchaï.
That perfect coexistence in this elder of the two Jaraï brothers of an aggressive, insolent humor and a latent savagery, capable of anything, that too-
intent, almost animal look in his frequently bloodshot eyes, and his very odd
laugh, had always disconcerted Ieng. Then, too, Kutchaï was on such intimate terms with Lara that at times the two of them seemed to be one person. Although he had known them both for more than twenty-five years,
Ieng had never heard Lara and Kutchaï exchange more than ten words at a
time with each other, as though words between them were needless and
their thought processes identical. Moreover, few Cambodians spoke French
as perfectly as Kutchaï. Almost all of them, including Sihanouk, had a slight
accent. Even he, Ieng, despite his years in France, still had a trace of Cambodian accent, that slightly syncopated rhythm, that tendency to stumble
over certain words, those sudden high-pitched notes in his voice. And Ieng
had diplomas that Kutchaï didn't have.

"Opium and a local anesthetic," Lara said in his quiet voice. "That's all I had here. But they'll wear off. Try to get some sleep."

Ieng obediently closed his eyes. He was still thinking of Kutchaï, a wild giant who'd come out of his native forest and who could express himself, if he cared to, like an intellectual born in Touraine. *He's an extraordinary creature, when you come right down to it.* Ieng fell into a deep sleep.

10

SHE BURST OUT LAUGHING. "THOMAS AQUINAS O'MALLEY? DON'T tell me that's your real name!"

He glanced all around, leaned over his desk toward her, and whispered confidentially. "I'm here under an alias. It's all been fixed. That's even the name on my passport. Are you X-23?"

"X-24," Lisa answered. "X-23 had the flu."

She invented a story about money that had disappeared, between Bangkok and Phnom Penh, claiming she hadn't noticed that the money had been stolen till she arrived in Cambodia, which she was visiting as a reporter, intending to write a series of articles—not on the political or military situation, she wasn't qualified for that—but on the Cambodian people.

"I'm not working for any paper in particular," she said. "I'm a freelance journalist, and pay my own travel expenses."

"Any relatives?"

She hesitated again, realizing she must be giving him a very curious impression of herself. "My grandfather, who lives in Colorado. And my parents, in San Francisco."

He looked at her with a thoughtful, friendly air, but at the same time with that particular gleam in the depths of his eyes of the civil servant who has just heard about a money problem.

"Tell me all about yourself."

He was wearing one of those light suits with narrow blue and white pinstripes that apparently are the official uniform of the American foreign service in a tropical country, and a bow tie with pink and black polka dots. From one of his inside pockets he took a little notebook and a silver pen with a clip in the shape of a shamrock.

"I must take a few notes. Nothing serious, nothing official."

"I live in New York. I was working in an ad agency on Third Avenue but I've quit my job, even though they don't know it yet. As a matter of fact, I left New York on a sudden impulse."

Her explanations were beginning to involve increasingly acrobatic leaps as she became more deeply entangled in her own lie. But Thomas Aquinas O'Malley didn't bat an eye.

"I'm also an accredited United Press correspondent."

"Credentials like those are more than sufficient as far as I'm concerned."

He took down the number of her passport and various other information. "All right. We'll no doubt be able to help you out. How much money would you like?"

"A thousand dollars?"

He laughed. "Why not? And while you're waiting for all the arrangements to be made, would you like a hundred dollars?"

They had lunch together the next day, Wednesday, April 23, at the restaurant of the Hotel Royal. It was almost directly opposite the Club Sportif, where the evening before, Lisa had attended a cocktail party she'd been invited to by the French people who had come to dinner with the Soameses and the Cambodian couple on the night she arrived. It was not until the middle of the lunch—avocado stuffed with crab and leg of roe deer—that O'Malley, after recounting a number of hilarious anecdotes about his stay in Morocco just before coming to Cambodia, brought up the subject of Lisa's situation.

"Somebody's been talking with us about you, Lisa. A certain Sussmann."

"The head of my ad agency."

"As far as he knows, you're on vacation. But he's concerned about you. First of all because you took off from New York like a rocket, and secondly because he misses you. It seems that you're his best account executive, if that's your proper title."

"That's right."

"Is it an important position?"

"Fairly important. But not really, especially from the perspective of Phnom Penh."

He smiled back at her and shook his head. "You told me stories, didn't you, Lisa Trenton?"

He gave her no chance to reply.

"No, don't say anything. And it's not Sussmann who gave you away. According to the information I've received, your brother, Jon Kinkaird, is in Vietnam. And has deserted. He apparently got himself into a lot of trouble: They say he threw a grenade at one of his officers. . . . Though admittedly it's not entirely certain that he was the one who threw it; several other men are under suspicion as well. Don't tell me you didn't know that."

"I don't know any of the details," Lisa said, telling the truth this time.

"You went to Saigon, is that right?"

"Yes."

"And did you see your brother there?"

"No." She looked him straight in the eye, with a self-assurance that astonished her. And now O'Malley was going to ask her if she knew where Jon was, and why, after she'd gone halfway around the world, she'd ended up here in Cambodia. And she didn't think she'd be able to go on lying much longer.

But instead of that, he said, "Listen, I'm a cultural attaché. My grandfather was on the New York police force, and my two uncles as well. It seems to me that I spent my childhood in a police station, and I saw so many uniforms around me when I was six that when people asked me what I wanted to be when I grew up I answered, 'a nudist.' Policemen give me the creeps, secret agents irritate me no end, diplomats make my hair stand on end, and bureaucrats in general make me break out in pimples. Last night, our first secretary had a guy named Dieu, a high police official in Saigon, on the phone. Dieu saw you, and he claims you didn't meet your brother on Vietnamese soil. He swears it, taking Dieu as his witness. Amen. Your case is closed. But may I add that you have the most fantastic violet eyes in this entire world? When I see them I feel like hanging from the blades of that ceiling fan overhead and howling like a coyote. How much longer will you be staying in Cambodia to finish that series of articles you're doing?"

("The Norwegian freighter will be making port in two or three weeks," Lara had said. Lara, whom she hadn't once set eyes on since their boat ride on the Tonle Sap; even the Korvers hadn't heard a word from him.) She said, "A few weeks. I don't know exactly how long."

He grinned so broadly he practically dislocated his jaw. "More than enough time to have an unforgettable love affair."

"Far more."

He looked at her in amazement. "You speak French, I believe?"

"More or less."

"Where did you learn it?"

"In Paris. I studied art history there for two years."

It was in Paris that she'd met Robert Trenton.

He opened his eyes wide in astonishment and threw his arms up. "And you didn't even tell me. But that's fantastic!"

That very evening, he found an excuse to arrive at the Korvers' just as they were about to have their usual before-dinner cognac-and-soda. He tried his very best to appear embarrassed at turning up at that inopportune hour, without succeeding in the slightest. He immediately charmed Charles and Madeleine by telling them an amusing, involved story about his great-great-grandfather's heroics one night when he was making his rounds as a cop on the beat in Prospect Park. He flirted shamelessly with Madeleine, who was forty years older than he was.

He finally managed to have a word alone with Lisa, and offered her a job as his assistant at the embassy. It was within his power, he explained, to recruit personnel on the spot if he came across suitable candidates, in theory native-born Cambodians. And Lisa was obviously a native, as any fool could plainly see. He didn't know how much she would be paid, doubtless not very much, but after all she could leave when she pleased and it would be truly marvelous to work with her, and in this way she could partially pay back the thousand dollars she was borrowing from the embassy, perhaps even the entire sum if she stayed long enough, and so everybody would benefit all the way around. . . .

She accepted, dizzied by this flurry of decisive arguments, and it was agreed that she would begin work the following Monday, with a flexible contract that could be renewed automatically from week to week. The next day, a Thursday, he came to dinner at the Korvers' and had a long conversation with them about Chinese art, about which he knew a fair amount while claiming to know nothing at all. And he and Lisa saw each other again that Saturday, when they took a trip by car with an American couple from the embassy, Bert and Shirley Staltman, to visit the tombs at Oudong, where the ancient Khmer kings are buried.

And on Monday the 28th, Lisa began her job in a little office alongside Thomas Aquinas O'Malley's. It had now been ten days since she'd seen Lara, and despite herself she found she was both annoyed and worried by this silence. Even Charles Korver could no longer hide the fact that he found such a long silence not at all like Lara.

11

AROUND THREE O'CLOCK IN THE MORNING KUTCHAÏ WAS AWAKened by an inexplicable feeling of danger. At least he didn't try to explain it to himself; he had almost an animal instinct for that sort of thing.

It was the second night after Ieng had been brought to the plantation after being wounded.

Kutchaï did not turn a light on. The moon was bright enough for him to be able to make out a silhouette ten yards away. He went out onto the veranda and saw that Lara was already there, nodding at him as if to say, "Yes, me too."

Kutchaï had a sarong wrapped around his loins, but Lara, who always slept in the raw, was naked, in his left hand, however, was a package of Bastos cigarettes and a lighter. For a few moments the two men stood side by side without a word, listening, searching the dark with wide-open eyes. That was doubtless what had awakened both of them: the silence. There wasn't a sound from the forest; all they could hear was the familiar rush of a little stream over a waterfall close by, where they were in the habit of showering. Then something else caught their attention, the almost imperceptible low rumble of an engine turning over very slowly, far off in the distance. Kutchaï looked at Lara. "Oreste?"

His lips formed the word without really saying it aloud. Lara nodded. Kutchaï ran toward the traditional hut, a hundred yards away, which the Corsican had lived in ever since his arrival on the plantation twenty years before. He found Marccaggi there, sleeping with his three women, like an enormous beached whale with its calves. He touched Marccaggi's foot.

"We need you, Napoleon."

With a superb sense of timing, the innumerable dogs of the latex collectors' village, a few hundred yards away, began to bark.

"Soldiers," Oreste said, buckling on his cartridge belt as he broke into a run. "There are soldiers coming."

"Thanks for the information," Kutchaï said. And he laughed, hard, his huge bloodshot eyes almost phosphorescent in the dark.

Back at the house, Lara had put on a sarong and tucked the cigarette pack and lighter in the fold at his waist. He watched the two men as they ran toward him. "Make it snappy, you hired hands."

Lara did not appear to have budged from the veranda. Inside the house, on a low table, he had nonetheless laid out three hunting rifles, a pouch of cartridges, electric torches clipped to strips of cloth so they could be tied to their foreheads, a haversack containing a few provisions, and Kutchaï's clothes.

"You can get dressed as you go."

"Yes, bwana," Kutchaï said with a laugh.

They laid the rifles and all the equipment on the stretcher where Ieng was lying, still unconscious, and Oreste and the Jaraï each picked up one end of it. Lara watched the two men disappear into the forest, carrying the wounded man. He checked that everything was in order in the house. Then he stretched out on the bed again, waiting.

In April of 1969, Lara's house bore almost no resemblance to the building that Oreste Marccaggi had discovered on his first visit, when he had come to the plantation to settle a score with Kamsa in single combat. The lines of it had changed: It was, or appeared to be, bigger and lower; even the layout of it was different. Almost all the partitions separating the various rooms had been removed, most of the door and window openings had been enlarged, and the veranda had also been considerably extended, running around all four sides of the rectangle now and uniformly screened overhead by fan-palm thatching. Lara had left the smooth black wood, which was similar to ebony and used for the timber work and outside walls, completely exposed everywhere. The result was a structure so light it was almost unreal, entirely black, most of it taken up by one room measuring nearly fifty by forty feet, continuing out onto the veranda, with something Japanese about the way it opened on all sides onto the surrounding vegetation, but no kitchen and bathroom.

Very few Occidentals had seen it. Roger Bouès was one of these privileged few, and he found the house so stunningly beautiful it had taken his breath away.

The sound of footsteps of several men. Shouts. A rifle butt pounding on the black floor of the veranda. More shouts. Lara finally got up, went outside, and found himself facing some fifteen men in the uniform of FARK troops, the Khmer Royal Armed Forces, under the command of a major.

"Didn't you hear us coming?"

Lara yawned. "With all those yapping dogs in the village . . ."

"We're looking for a man, Ieng Samboth, the former deputy. He was wounded when he attacked one of our detachments and got away."

"I'd be surprised if you found him here," Lara said.

The officer tilted his head upward, trying to get a better look at the face of the man addressing him. "Are you Monsieur Lara?"

"That's right."

"I've heard of you."

"You must have heard that I don't dabble in politics."

"Ieng Samboth isn't being sought for political reasons. He's a criminal," the officer said in a stern voice.

"It seems to me you might have waited till tomorrow morning to pass on that piece of information to me," Lara remarked quietly. "Do you know what time it is?"

All at once screams came from the village and a shot rang out. Lara stepped forward one pace, his pale eyes suddenly cold as ice.

"Those people in the village have nothing to do with the man you're looking for. I'm holding you responsible for anything that happens to them."

"We're questioning them."

"Kindly see to it that you go no further than that."

The sound of tramping feet. Another group entered the courtyard via that path from the village: a good twenty men or more dragging along three swollen-faced black-clad prisoners by cords around their necks. One of the prisoners was wearing a red *krama*.

"You know them, Monsieur Lara."

"I've never seen them before in my life. They don't belong to our settlement."

"They say the criminal Ieng Samboth came here."

Lara leaned against the wooden post behind him in such a way that his head tilted slightly backward, his eyes glancing downward through eyelids three-quarters lowered.

"I don't believe they said that," he replied in his quiet voice, "but you may search the house."

He stepped aside two paces, thus more or less allowing them access to the veranda, and with an indifferent expression on his face went over and leaned against the outside wall of the house, with one hand between the wall and his back. As though it were independent of him, his other hand took a Bastos out of the package tucked in the fold of his sarong, lit it, and then slowly toyed with the hinged cover of the lighter. In the half-shadow he looked taller than he really was. His torso and arms were slender but the muscles were spectacularly lean and sharply defined; his body emanated an aura of tenseness rigorously held in check, of latent nervous energy liable to explode at any moment. His thin, handsome face as perfectly expressionless, with two piercing, pale gray-blue eyes staring into space.

The officer came back after a few minutes. "I've been told about a Frenchman named Oreste and an employee named Kutchaï."

"Kutchaï isn't my employee; he's my partner," Lara said, still staring into the dark. "The two of them have gone out hunting."

"In the middle of the night?"

"They have flashlights, I presume."

A cry rang out. One of the prisoners fell to his knees but was almost immediately jerked backward by the cord knotted tightly around his neck. One of the soldiers struck him again, square in the belly with the butt of his rifle. The officer sat down on the steps. He looked tired, but his impeccably polished American Army paratrooper's boots gleamed in the glow of the lanterns lighting the veranda. He wore a carefully knotted white scarf around his neck, and his hair was cropped very short. He lit a Lucky Strike.

"Do you speak Cambodian?"

"Yes," Lara answered.

A silence. The major looked Lara up and down. "And you live here alone?"

"Not exactly alone."

"I've been told that your family was murdered here in this house. Your father, your mother, and your sister. Tortured and murdered. Aren't you afraid the same thing will happen to you some day?"

Lara's pale, piercing eyes met his. "No."

"Why not? What makes you so certain of that? Bands of Khmer Kraham—Khmer Rouge—friends of the Viet Cong, very often come through this region you live in. The Khmer Rouge are savages, Communists who are trying to free Cambodia from North Vietnamese imperialism. They don't like Europeans. They might very well kill you too."

As he spoke, the officer took a little rectangle of suede cloth out of his pocket and began wiping off the slightest trace of dirt from his boots.

"Anybody can kill you here in your house, Monsieur Lara, and no one would ever know what really happened. No one would know who killed you. They'd naturally think in Phnom Penh that it was the Khmer Rouge. If anything were to happen to you, I myself could do nothing more than make out a report, and all I would be able to say in it would be: 'Monsieur Lara was killed by the Khmer Rouge and unfortunately we arrived too late to save him. We simply found his tortured body. Horribly tortured.' I've already told you: Those Khmer Rouge are savages. Do you understand the risk you're running?"

He stretched out both legs simultaneously, to size up the polish job he'd done on his boots, which now shone spotlessly. He raised his eyes toward Lara and smiled. "Do you understand?"

Other soldiers were now arriving in a steady stream, pouring into the clearing around the house and the larger courtyard around the little factory, behind the thick curtain of lemon and sandalwood trees that towered above a sea of bougainvillea. There were at least a hundred of them, equipped with American matériel: M-1 rifles, M-16 submachine guns, M-39 grenade launchers, and also M-14 automatic rifles whose ammunition clips were fastened together end-to-end with adhesive tape to give them a more rapid-fire action. And a unit of perhaps equal size was doubtless positioned north of the house, in the latex collectors' village.

The accents of these men left no doubt as to their origin: All of them, or almost all of them, were Khmer Krom, brought in from Cochin China. They had the tough, lean faces of men trained for combat, their movements were adroit and self-assured, and they obviously respected the discipline that had been inculcated in them. There is always something childlike about a Vietnamese in uniform, as though he were dressed up in a costume, particularly if he is from the South but also if he's from Tonkin—an impression attributable largely to his small stature. A Cambodian, on the contrary, being usually taller and more solidly built, almost instinctively adopts the gestures of the warrior, his attitudes and his reflexes. The French in the 1950s knew this, and when they assigned soldiers under their command to man observation posts along the roads, they always sent both Khmers and Vietnamese, with one Khmer for each three or four Vietnamese, thus assuring that no one would spend his tour on duty sleeping instead of standing guard. The French were well aware of the ancestral hatred the two races bore each other, and above all of the visceral, physical, atavistic fear that, man for man, a Vietnamese feels toward a Khmer. But in what was once French Indochina, there were forty million Vietnamese as against four million Khmer.

"When will your friends be back from their hunting expedition?" the major asked.

"They didn't set any special time. Usually they come back at dawn, but sometimes they stay out longer."

"How does it happen you didn't go with them?"

"I haven't gone hunting for fifteen years now," Lara said indifferently.
"Do you mean to say it's a matter of principle with you?"
"That's right."

Three other low-ranking officers approached. The major lithely rose to his feet, walked over to them, and drew them aside out of Lara's hearing. The four men conferred for a minute or two in low voices. Then the major came back to where Lara was standing.

"My men have marched all day long and part of the night. If you have no objection, we'll pitch camp just outside. We may even stay on for a few days."

He stared Lara straight in the eye and added, "That will no doubt give me a chance to meet your partner and the Frenchman who lives here with you as well. I was also told in Siem Reap how he got you your plantation back some years ago. A man who's rather out of the ordinary, it would appear."

Lara yawned and moved away from the wall. He headed for the central room, and just as he stepped into it, he turned and asked with a smile, "Cognac or coffee?"

More than two days went by after that, during which time neither Kutchaï nor Oreste Marccaggi reappeared.

During the night following his boat ride on the Tonle Sap with Lisa Kinkaird, Lara had driven north in his car. His intention at the time was to spend no more than two or three days at the plantation, and then to drive back to Phnom Penh, perhaps to see Lisa again. Oreste Marccaggi's call, telling him of the wounded Ieng's arrival at the plantation, had reached Lara at the Taverne, just a few minutes after he'd gotten back to Phnom Penh. He had immediately headed for the plantation once again.

Ieng Samboth had been wounded on the morning of April 22, at almost the same moment that Lisa Kinkaird met Tom O'Malley for the first time, and at almost the same moment that Roger Bouès realized, without any great surprise, that he didn't have—probably never would have—the money to buy himself a plane ticket to France, his native land that he hadn't seen in more than twenty-three years.

"Oreste Marccaggi is a man who feels really alive only in the forest," Lara said. "He's a Corsican, of course. He's told me that on the island where he was born, he spent his entire childhood and adolescence in the heart of the mountains. He probably learned to use a hunting rifle before he learned to walk—that's what he claims at any rate. He's an exceptional marksman, an instinctive, born sharpshooter. The best I've ever seen."

Lara smiled. "Don't make any bets with him on that score. You'd lose."

"All right. I won't even try," the major replied.

Most of the soldiers had gone. There were only some twenty men and the officer left in the vicinity of the house. Using the plantation as a base camp, the major had sent out patrols in every direction; none of them had come back as yet. A person would have had to be simpleminded not to have seen a real danger sign in the fact that the major had thus gotten rid of a good hundred witnesses—his own troops—keeping with him only men he knew he could trust. Lara was not simpleminded. He knew full well that he was now at the mercy of the Khmer Krom officer, who in his estimation was perfectly capable of committing murder in cold blood.

"You have a huge estate."

"No. On the contrary, it's very modest. The Chhuup plantation with its eight million rubber trees is a thousand times bigger than mine. There's no possible comparison. This is a very small-time operation."

The major had also expressed his surprise at the extremely rudimentary furnishings of the house. It wasn't at all his idea of what a planter's manor house was like. There was nothing in it, outside of a few hundred books, an ancient turntable and some sixty or so records, a few pieces of rattan furniture and two hammocks. In a shed outside were two cars: a Land-Rover and a Peugeot 504, plus the generator. And in the bedrooms—veritable cells— the beds, or rather the simple wooden sleeping platforms that served as such, didn't even have mosquito netting over them.

."What's the word Europeans use: Spartan?"

"That's right."

"And you and that Cambodian are partners?"

"Yes."

"Co-partners?"

"Yes."

"Since when?"

"Since 1949."

"You were just a kid at that time."

"The plantation came to me by inheritance."

The three Khmer Rouge prisoners had been tortured. During the first night that he spent talking with the major, Lara heard them screaming and was later to learn that though the major's men had been content merely to burn the first two slowly to death, they'd used a more sophisticated technique in the case of the third one: They had first peeled him, in the literal sense of removing his skin, and then they had sprinkled the great patches of raw flesh thus exposed with a mixture of salt and red pepper. Perhaps it was this prisoner who had talked and revealed that Ieng Samboth, brought wounded to the plantation, had been carried off again on a stretcher borne by two men, one of whom was European.

"The man named Oreste," the major said.

"No."

"Monsieur Lara, there aren't that many Europeans in this part of Cambodia."

"There are a number of them in Kompong Thom and Siem Reap."

"Teachers or archaeologists."

"It wasn't Oreste Marccaggi. He's gone off hunting with Kutchaï."

During the second night, Lara heard more screams, coming this time from the latex collectors' village and followed by shots from automatic weapons. Lara tried to leave the plantation and go down to the village, but the soldiers prevented him from doing so, pointing their rifles at his chest.

"Calm yourself, Monsieur Lara. You may be certain of one thing: I am not going to leave this area until I've gotten to the bottom of this affair."

At dawn Lara spied a column of smoke rising from the village. And around nine in the morning Kutchaï reappeared, escorted by soldiers, covered with wounds and blood, staggering, his face drawn with fatigue.

But he was alone.

The major conducted the interrogation himself. Only once did he allow anger to get the better of him, hitting Kutchaï square in the face and ripping his cheek with the barrel of his pistol. But Kutchaï stuck to his story: He had gone off hunting with Oreste Marccaggi around the place where the Stung Sen, which flows past Kompong Thom before emptying into the Tonle Sap, makes an east-west bend. On the first night, he and the Corsican had run into a Khmer Rouge patrol that had opened fire, no doubt taking them for soldiers pursuing them. Kutchaï and Oreste had returned their fire with their hunting rifles and had managed to get away, but in their headlong flight they had taken off in different directions and lost each other. Kutchaï hadn't seen Marccaggi since, though he had scoured the forest for a long time trying to find him once things had quieted down again. He himself had ended up in a little hamlet called Phnom Pnong, where the villagers had dressed his wounds and given him food. He had then come back to the plantation, and been taken completely by surprise when soldiers leapt upon him just as he was coming in sight of it.

His wounds were unquestionably real. A bullet had gone through his left arm, luckily leaving only a flesh wound, and he bore the marks of at least ten machete blows as well as a wound in the head.

The major consulted his map: Phnom Pnong was about forty kilometers northwest of the plantation.

"When were you there?"

At the beginning of his interrogation he had addressed Kutchaï in the familiar *tu* form; he was now using the formal *vous* form. The interrogation had taken place in French, a language that the Krom officer spoke better than he did Khmer.

"I left the village day before yesterday, late in the afternoon," Kutchaï answered.

Lara looked at him without understanding what he was up to. The officer was bound to check his story out.

"We're going to verify all the statements you've made, and check if you were really where you say you were," the major said.

Kutchaï didn't appear even to have heard him. With the tips of his blood-smeared fingers he was cautiously exploring the wound in his cheek. His face was ashen and the constant rain of blows from the butt of the major's pistol which he had been receiving for the last thirty minutes had left him without strength enough to get to his feet. He was crouching on his knees on the ground, just in front of the bottom step of the veranda. He couldn't possibly be pretending to be that worn out; Lara knew him too well. Kutchaï was really utterly exhausted.

"I'll go to Phnom Penh," Lara said in a voice trembling with rage. "I'll tell them about you and your methods. I'll go see Monseigneur-Père Sihanouk and General Lon Nol."

A few minutes earlier, half-mad at the sight of Kutchaï about to be beaten to death, he had struggled with the major, who had hit him square in the belly with the butt of his pistol. But the rhythm of the blows raining down on the Jaraï had slowed down and finally stopped.

The major gave a toss of his head and carefully put his pistol back in the leather holster on his hip. There was a dull thud: Kutchaï had fainted dead away.

"If he's seriously hurt, I swear to you that you'll have me to deal with," Lara said.

The officer stepped aside, contemplating a spatter of blood on his boots. He wiped it off, and said to Lara, "I'm going to go personally to Phnom Pnong to check whether this man has lied to me or not. If he's told the truth, the villagers should be able to confirm that he passed by that way, and that the Khmer Rouge that we're searching for are in that area. And perhaps we'll also find your Corsican friend."

He straightened the knot in his white scarf. "For his sake and yours, I hope he hasn't been lying to me. You're to remain here, of course. I'm leaving some of my men to see that you're . . . protected."

Lara pushed aside the barrels of the submachine guns aimed at him, went down the stairs, and picked Kutchaï up off the ground. No one made a move to help him. He lifted the 220-pound Jaraï, carried him in his arms to one of the bedrooms, and laid him down on the sleeping platform. Then he got some water and began to wash Kutchaï's wounds. There were a great many of them, but they were all superficial—unless he had some sort of internal injury after that hail of blows from the major's pistol butt.

Approximately a quarter of an hour later, the major and his men took off in two half-tracks, leaving only fifteen men posted around the house under the command of a sergeant. The sound of the engines had just died away when Kutchaï opened his eyes. He looked at Lara.

"It's okay to talk," Lara said.

"Oreste is at Prah Khan. Do you remember that little moat where we found the Apsaras that you gave Roger? He's there with a bullet in the abdomen. It was Ieng's adjutant who shot him, a guy named Rath, a madman. I'll be hunting him up again one of these days."

"How come you're so worn out?"

"I went to Phnom Pnong, as Ieng and I had agreed. It was necessary to draw that bastard of a Krom up there."

From the plantation to Prah Khan, from Prah Khan to Phnom Pnong, then from Phnom Pnong to the plantation, Kutchaï had covered more than 120 kilometers, carrying a man on a stretcher through the forest over rough terrain for a part of that distance. And all that despite his wounds . . .

"Who cut you up like that with machetes?"

"Rath's men."

. . . And all that despite his wounds. That explained why he was exhausted. Nobody but Kutchaï could have accomplished such a breathtaking feat.

"What about Ieng?"

"He'll pull through all right. He's tougher than he appears to be, or than he himself thinks he is. Did he tell you about Rath?"

"Yes."

"A shit. I'll find him again, I swear I will."

"I believe you. I just want to be sure there's nothing seriously wrong with you."

The Jaraï managed to shake his head, his long black hair matted with sticky drying blood. He smiled as he slowly closed his eyes.

"Kutchaï pool wletch of a Khmel in gleat shape," he stammered. "It's Oreste who needs your help."

He was already half asleep. Lara went outside and summoned the sergeant of the small detachment assigned to guard him.

"I have to go to Kompong Thom to make a phone call."

The sergeant shook his head.

"Five thousand riels."

"Até. No," the sergeant replied.

"Ten thousand then. Five thousand now, five when I get back. You and some of your men can come with me. You can keep your eye on me every second."

He got behind the wheel of the Land-Rover, with the sergeant in the seat alongside him and three soldiers sitting in the back. He went to the village first. The storage cellar he had built and filled with rice hadn't been discovered, but several huts and the communal hall had been razed, and above all there were eight men dead and a dozen seriously wounded, none of them as yet in really critical condition, however. The little dispensary was still intact and the two nurses, a married couple whom he paid out of his own pocket, were hard at work. They explained that they had been forbidden to go up to the plantation house and that the soldiers had left only a few moments before. The bloody butchery had begun when several of the village women had been raped by the soldiers.

Assuring himself that their stock of sulfanilamide and bandages would suffice, Lara took off again. He crossed the arroyo and headed down the trail leading to Kompong Thom.

On the twelfth ring, Roger Bouès picked up the receiver.

12

ON APRIL 28, MATTHEW KINKAIRD RECEIVED THE FIRST LETTER Lisa had sent from Cambodia. Up until then, Matthew had had no definite news, save for a cablegram relayed to him, curiously enough, by the Department of State. Its point of origin, no less curiously (since as far as Matthew knew his granddaughter was still in Saigon), was Phnom Penh. (He never received Lisa's letter telling him she was leaving for the Khmer capital.) The cablegram read: "Everything okay. Have solved all my problems. Love, Lisa." The phrase "have solved all my problems" obviously had to do with Jon. At least that was how he interpreted it. Her letter cleared up this point, and several others, but at the same time gave rise to other mysteries.

In her small, regular handwriting Lisa informed him that Jon was now in Phnom Penh, though she did not explain the circumstances that had brought the boy there. Lisa wrote that Jon was all right, as she was, and that there was no reason for him to worry about either of them. The young woman seemed to have weighed each of her words, and moreover she never once mentioned Jon by name. She simply referred to her brother as "he" or "him" and did not go into details. But at the end of the first paragraph she had plainly thought it necessary to reassure her grandfather once again that there was no need for him to be concerned: "All you have to do now is take care of your flowers in your greenhouses and watch your waistline. You know how many pounds you put on eating Ruth Martinez's Mexican food. Outside of those two things, there's nothing, absolutely nothing, you need worry about."

Good lord, she must think I'm senile, Matthew thought to himself. *I got the message the first time around: Jon's safe and sound.*

He took time out to pet Rover and Tige, who once again had managed to slip into the greenhouse. Then he went on reading the letter from his granddaughter, the second part of which left him lost in thought. In it she spoke of staying on in Phnom Penh and announced that she'd found a job— apparently she intended to spend several years there—as an assistant to the cultural attaché, who answered to the ridiculous name of Thomas Aquinas O'Malley. "But Tom is absolutely adorable," Lisa wrote. "He's an Irishman with a marvelous sense of humor, a sweet, cultivated man. Moreover he has absolutely nothing to do here at the embassy, and since I'm his assistant that leaves me with a fair amount of free time for myself." Then she described Cambodia, or at least what she'd seen of it, and mentioned French friends who had taken her in out of sheer kindheartedness. They had a huge house and lots of room—"so Jon feels very much at home there"—and were even more adorable than the famous Thomas Aquinas O'Malley.

And then she spoke of Lara.

She had remarkably little to say about him. "He's a really unusual man. I've never met the likes of him before. He's done things that few men would be capable of doing." That was all she had to say about him. And simply because this description of him was so laconic, it intrigued Matthew, who found himself unable to decide on the basis of these two ambiguous sentences whether the things Lara had done were heroic or horrendous.

Matthew had never really understood his granddaughter. He knew she was intelligent, even unusually intelligent, and more than capable—in his opinion at least and above all by comparison with him—of choosing and organizing her own life. He regarded her as a young woman with a will and a mind of her own, and had only to recall how she had immediately recovered from the shock of Bob Trenton's death, finding a job entirely on her own and very soon making a name for herself at it. He even thought her a bit overbearing, not exactly cold, but in any case not in the habit of easily giving her heart away. As a child, she had already been possessed of the gift of creating around herself an aura of imperturbable calm into which few adults ventured. Matthew was extremely fond of her, but at the same time he had always been just a little disconcerted by those violet eyes of hers, apparently so like Jon's and yet so different, eyes that looked straight at you almost without blinking, with a serious, sometimes mocking expression in them.

He read the letter over again two or three times, and then hunted up an atlas, opened it, and located Phnom Penh. He wondered what in the world a Cambodian looked like exactly.

Matthew showed the letter, or at least the first page of it, to Pete Martinez, who was working in the hothouse. Pete—not surprisingly—drew the same conclusion from it that he himself had. "Jon's gotten out of the mess he was in. I told you he would. He's left that country full of Chinese and is now dancing with naked girls beneath palm trees. If I were you, I wouldn't worry a minute more. At least not about Jon. Just about those girls maybe. He's going to show them what a real man is like here in Colorado."

Then, in the afternoon, after Pete and his wife had left, Matthew phoned Jubal Wynn in San Francisco. The lawyer listened without interrupting as he read the first paragraph to him and summed up the contents of the rest of the letter.

"What do you think?" Matthew asked.

Wynn used almost the same words Pete Martinez had. "It's quite clear: in some way that I don't know the first thing about and that personally leaves me dumbfounded, he's managed to cross the border between Cambodia and Vietnam, and not only reach Phnom Penh but find a safe hiding place there. Either he's a genius or he has incredibly clever friends. The minute he ascends the throne in Cambodia in Sihanouk's place, please let me know. I'll send flowers."

"Who's Sihanouk?"

Wynn told him. Then Matthew asked, "What advice would you offer my grandson?"

"Certainly not to give himself up, not when he's gotten this far. I think I'd tell him to get himself to Sweden however he can. Even though Cambodia and Sweden aren't exactly next-door neighbors."

"Would he really be out of his mind to turn himself in at the American Embassy in Phnom Penh?"

"In the first place, the embassy has just reopened. They need the case of a deserter about as badly as they need an attack of yellow fever. Secondly, every journalist in Southeast Asia will latch on to him. They'll offer him thousands of dollars to tell the story of his life, and the court-martial judges will be four times as hard on him, simply because the papers will have made a big thing of his case and because they'll be out to make an example of him. You pay dearly for the publicity you get. Not to mention the fact that if he gives himself up, he risks embarrassing—though that's not a strong enough word for it—the person or persons who helped him. They'll throw the book at him."

"Even with you to defend him?"

"Even if Abraham Lincoln were his defense attorney. No, believe me—Sweden. Stockholm's a very nice place, in the summertime."

Matthew thanked him and hung up. Why Sweden and not Canada? He hadn't dared ask the question, out of fear of appearing to be an utter ignoramus. A doddering old fool. Except when it came to problems involving the water rights of beet farmers . . .

He stared at the colored page of the atlas, reading the strange names: Phnom Penh, Siem Reap, and Sway Rieng, and Kompong Thom, and the Mekong. . . .

But Jon and Lisa were in no danger. A recent issue of *Time* magazine
that he'd read at the dentist's had said Cambodia was a country at peace.
The exact words were, "an oasis of peace."

13

GOING TO THE AIR FRANCE OFFICE TO ASK THE PRICE OF A TICKET
to Paris was a step that Roger Bouès had not contemplated for long. It had
really been an impulse of the moment. Or that might be what it had been.
He wasn't quite certain. He thought his gesture might have been the end-
result of a subconscious process that had been at work within him for weeks
and months, or even longer still. Roger didn't believe in plans calmly
worked out to the last detail, in long-term projects, or even in short-term
ones, and he'd never been able to plan even little things in advance. On the
other hand, he was absolutely convinced that every great turning point in a
person's life comes as the result of a sudden, irrational impulse; he was of
the opinion that a person spends more time choosing what to order in a restaurant or what tie to wear than he does carefully pondering such matters
as whether to get married, to quit his job, to leave his family, to take off
for Australia. Or for Indochina. In his view the big decisions, the ones that
affect a person's entire life, are always the result of a sudden whim, an
unexpected meeting, a word that is one too many or one too few, an aching
corn.

In any event the cost of the ticket to France was so far beyond his financial means that it bordered on irony. *I'd have just enough to pay the airport taxes. If that.* Of course, he could have borrowed money from Lara or
from Charles Korver. Either one would have advanced him the sum he
asked for, and more besides, without hesitating, and they would have done
so without requiring—without the thought even crossing their minds, in
fact—that he pay it back. But he would far rather have swum back to Mar-
seilles than go to them for money. In his entire life Roger had never borrowed a single cent from a friend; the only debts he had ever owed were to
people he found thoroughly unlikable, downright grotesque, or just plain ridiculous. He considered that he was making them pay ransom, so to speak,
for their stupidity, their insignificance, or their ugliness; and who would
even think of giving back money received as ransom unless forced to do so?

Unfortunately, no one in Cambodia was stupid, insignificant, or ugly
enough to lend him 364,500 French francs. Old francs.

Nevertheless, during the sleep from which Lara's telephone call had
awakened him, he had dreamed for the first time in years that he was in
France. In his dream he wasn't in Paris or on the shores of the Loire, but in

Pau; he was walking down the Rue Serviez, enjoying a *canougat de Josuat,* and then the next moment, with the marvelous illogic of dreams, a pepper sausage from Biben's. Then he was strolling majestically (Savorgnan de Brazza returning to his native land after having conquered the Congo) down the Rue Guichenné or the Rue Maréchal-Foch, and crowds were standing everywhere, watching in awed amazement as he passed by, opening their arms and their hearts to him, pressing him to their Gasco-Béarnais bosoms, offering him board and room, a man surrounded by people who loved and admired him.

"You're going to have to ask Boudin for help again," Lara's voice said at the other end of the line.

At times, if he really cared to, Roger Boués was capable of acting with the formidable efficiency of those who were experienced idlers, professional lazybones so to speak. In a flash, he rallied around him the doctor from Dien Bien Phu and the volcanic little Boudin (who had sworn, a bit too late, that he'd shoot Roger on sight the next time he laid eyes on him). At two-thirty in the afternoon, all three of them were in Siem Reap.

A quarter of an hour later, having left the Strasbourg Sausage sulking alongside his plane, Roger and the doctor were driving past the temples of Angkor, hailing the great state temple of Bayon as they passed by, and heading east in a light truck borrowed from the Temple Preservation Commission, thanks to the French administrator, to whom Lara had also telephoned. It took them an hour and twenty minutes to cover the 120 kilometers or so between the eastern face of the wall and the moat surrounding Angkor Thom and the little separate group of temples of Prah Khan, an hour's drive from Rovieng. The doctor from Dien Bien Phu, whose lost youth was being restored by this escapade, bounced about in the back of the truck like a cork bobbing on the waves, shouting that his bottles of plasma would not withstand all the jouncing and jolting.

Once they'd arrived at the appointed spot, Roger at first found nothing but the heavy, oppressive silence of the forest in the burning sun. He got out of the truck, reciting Lara's instructions like a litany, his nostrils filled with the omnipresent odor of rotting vegetation given off by the jungle. As he turned this way and that to orient himself, he finally found a moat, or what seemed in all likelihood to be one, a stone rectangle that had held no water for centuries and whose bottom was carpeted with moss in the places where it had not been completely overgrown with vegetation. A platoon of tanks could easily have been hidden there—certainly a man could. *If Oreste is unconscious, calling out to him will be useless, and heaven only knows who and what might be around us.* He felt eyes spying on him, he felt presences, but perhaps it was only his imagination. He hesitated, overcome by a sense of helplessness and his eternal and obsessive certainty that he was incapable of acting.

"Oreste! Oreste! It's me, Roger."

Long seconds of silence, and then something moved. All at once two men appeared, Cambodians dressed entirely in black, with dark, thin faces and huge, incredibly bright eyes. They were armed with rifles of some sort that bristled with shoulder pieces and chargers—Roger knew nothing whatever about firearms, either for hunting or for combat. The two apparitions stared at Roger and uttered a few words in Khmer.

"I not understand," Roger said in French. And he wondered why they called spooks dressed all in black Khmer Rouge.

They repeated what they had said and this time he caught the word *barang* in passing.

"Barang? Where's the Barang?"

He followed them through a veritable tunnel, half filled in places with fallen building stones. He finally came out in a kind of underground chamber with an opening at the top like an air shaft which let in a greenish light.

"Bring any beer?" Oreste asked.

"You analphabet of a Corsican you," the doctor from Dien Bien Phu said. "They didn't get you this time. All my hopes have come to nothing."

"What's an analphabet?" Oreste asked worriedly.

"A guy that kills wild boars with one bullet between the eyes," Roger said. "How about shutting your big mouth for a while?"

Helped by Ieng Samboth's two men, they had made the opening in the roof of the chamber bigger and taken Oreste Marccaggi back up to the surface through it. They carried him to the little truck, where they laid him down on two mattresses that Roger had also borrowed, this time from the Auberge des Temples. They didn't see the two Khmer Rouge guerrilla fighters leave. At one point they simply weren't there anymore, having vanished into the forest without a sound, leaving no trace of their passage. *Impressive.* The former army doctor gave Oreste two shots of something that soon put him to sleep, and fixed the bottles of plasma so they wouldn't bounce around.

"Maybe it's not worth the trouble trying to make a record Monte Carlo Rally run on the way back. Take it slow and easy, please," he said to Roger.

They reached the little airport at Siem Reap, then Phnom Penh, and finally the French Hospital there, where Oreste Marccaggi was immediately operated on. At ten that night, they came to tell Roger that the Corsican was completely out of danger.

"They removed this bullet from him. How old is he anyway? Over sixty? He's got such a hard sheath of abdominal muscles we nearly had to use an electric drill on him."

Roger went off to his favorite garage, in the Rue Kehmarak Phoumin, threatening this time to come back shortly to redecorate the front of it in the colors he was fondest of: navy blue and violet, plus a third one that even he didn't know quite what to call. Giving in to this blackmail, to his feelings of friendship for Roger, and also to his impression that there was something urgent about the situation, the French garage manager filled his tank with gas and gave him two full twenty-liter jerry-cans as well.

Roger left Phnom Penh around eleven P.M. When Lara had called him from the bungalow in Kompong Thom, where he could no doubt be over-heard, he had simply mentioned a hunting accident. Naturally, Roger hadn't believed a word of it. "You're not able to go there yourself?"

"Not at the moment."

"You're not hurt, are you?"

"There's nothing wrong with me. Or with Kutchaï either."

It was this remark about Kutchaï that had really put Roger on the alert. Later on, Oreste had told him the whole story: how Ieng had been wounded and taken in at the plantation by Lara and Kutchaï, how soldiers had suddenly appeared in the middle of the night, how Kutchaï and he had taken to the forest, how that assassin Rath had shot at them and would doubtless have finished them off if Ieng, who'd come to, hadn't intervened.

"I'll go get Oreste out of trouble and then come up there right away," Roger had said to Lara on the phone.

"As a matter of fact, I'd been planning to invite you up for the week-end. It's sort of lonely here at times," Lara had answered.

As he drove in the moonlight along the banked road above the rice paddies, Roger again had that same premonition of impending catastrophe that he'd had on the beach at Kep. And this time, something was really up.

At least that's my opinion. And I'm sticking to it. A hundred percent, he said to himself.

As it turned out, he did not arrive at the plantation straightaway. One of his tires, which weren't exactly brand-new, had a flat about ten kilometers out-side Kompong Thom, at the bottom of one of the few steep grades in this section of what had once been known as Colonial Route 1. He swore in the silence of the night and mounted the spare tire, which gave up the ghost less than two kilometers farther on. After waiting in the middle of the road, without much hope, for another car to pass by, he set out on foot, and about 2:30 in the morning reached the bungalow from which Lara had telephoned the night before. Lara had naturally left long since, but the rooms were oc-cupied by ten or so French *co-opérants,* young men doing community ser-vice work in lieu of military service, all of them teachers at the local high school. Roger woke up one of them, a certain Cornet, who was from Mar-seilles and who, despite being rather rheumy-eyed, had a more or less intel-ligent air about him—for a *co-opérant* at least. Roger was not overly fond of *co-opérants;* he had never quite seen the point in passing on to so-called underdeveloped countries a technology, and above all a "civilization," that did not strike him as having wrought many miracles in the countries where they had originated, especially in view of the fact that this "aid" inevitably entailed the destruction of indigenous cultures that were as valuable as any other.

After indignantly shouting at the top of his lungs, carrying on for a good fifteen minutes, Cornet in the end willingly agreed to drive Roger back to his car and to help him roust from his straw mat a mechanic who would be able to repair two tire tubes or, failing that, provide him with two other fairly new ones.

"But I don't happen to have any money," Roger said blandly. "I must have left my wallet somewhere."

Cornet was even willing to dip into his own pocket to pay the man. He also told Roger that he had indeed seen Lara the evening before, at dinnertime. Lara had arrived in his Land-Rover with four soldiers who'd dogged his every footstep and never let him out of their sight; he had made two phone calls and then left immediately. How had the soldiers acted? As though they were protecting him or guarding him. Yes, soldiers in FARK uniforms.

"You're not going to leave like this in the middle of the night. Your tires wouldn't hold up on the trail to the plantation. Get some sleep here in the bungalow and I'll take you up there tomorrow. Just between you and me, I'd be curious to have a look at Lara's place, like all the rest of us here."

"That can be arranged," Roger answered.

"It's sort of lonely here at times," Lara had said, and Roger had translated that as meaning: "Bring people here with you." He slept very little that night and dragged Cornet out of bed at dawn. Then, with Cornet's help, he woke up all the rest of the teachers, including the two women, and announced to one and all that they were invited to have lunch and dinner with Lara at the plantation, since it was Saturday and there were no classes. He made them down their morning coffee as quickly as possible, and they reached the arroyo a few minutes before nine. They crossed it and were immediately stopped by soldiers in camouflage helmets bucolically decorated with leaves, who ordered them not to go a single step farther. Roger negotiated with them, and finally a sergeant who spoke fluent French appeared on the scene.

"We're friends of Monsieur Lara's. He's invited us here as his guests."

The three-car convoy that had left the bungalow was finally allowed to proceed. They parked in front of the house, alongside the Land-Rover and an army truck. And the first person Roger spied was Lara, sitting on the top step leading to the veranda, smoking a cigarette.

"You forgot to bring along the majorettes," Lara said.

"He's been operated on and is as solid as the Cape of Corsica," Roger said. "He's asking for beer. Watch out for that schoolmarm on my left—she's a man-eater."

Roger introduced all of them. Lara smiled his usual calm smile, as though the presence of ten teachers, fifteen soldiers, and a machine gun mounted on the roof of the warehouse of his plantation were the most natural thing in the world.

"I'd be very happy if you would all be my guests," he said. "There are two bedrooms and the rest of us can sleep in hammocks or on straw mats."

Roger realized then that he had guessed rightly, that his feelings of apprehension had been justified after all.

For the moment, that was all he grasped of the situation. Until the following day, Sunday, when Kutchaï appeared, walking as stiffly as a robot, with a patch of adhesive tape on his cheek and bandages around his chest and arm.

"Another hunting accident?" Roger asked.

"I turned over in the jeep crossing a ravine," Kutchaï explained.

He looked more as if he'd been trampled on by elephants.

Lara took Roger aside.

"We're not free to talk right now. Just remember that I called to ask you to intercede with Lon Nol, because one of his officers was making trouble for me. As for Oreste, you learned that he'd been wounded and intervened when Faber, the head of the Temple Preservation Commission at Angkor, telephoned you immediately after I did."

"But I didn't even see Faber!"

"I know. But as for everything else, just tell the truth."

The sergeant scarcely left their side. The French teachers didn't either, though in their case it was because they were fascinated. Lara showed them through the little factory, explained to them how they treated the latex and the rubber crepe, but this time did not take his visitors to the latex collectors' village as he usually did. Roger noticed and was surprised that he hadn't, though he didn't go so far as to ask Lara why—just as the teachers noted the absence of Oreste Marccaggi, whom they knew because they'd drunk more than one beer with him when he came to Kompong Thom to buy rice for the latex collectors.

On Sunday afternoon, a large motorized column of soldiers appeared. The commanding officer, a major, seemed thunderstruck at the sight of this concentration of Europeans who cheerily invited him to have a cognac-and-soda with them. He spent the first few minutes doing just that, then went off with Lara for a discussion that lasted around a quarter of an hour, the officer showing all the signs of suppressed anger, while Lara remained as cool and collected as usual. Finally Roger was summoned to join them, and he came into the room with his heart pounding, afraid he'd say too much, or else not enough. But the major asked him only a few simple questions, as though he were acquitting himself of a task that he no longer found of much interest.

"Monsieur Lara informs me that Oreste Marccaggi was taken to the hospital in Phnom Penh, thanks to you, is that correct?"

Roger gave a brief account of his rescue mission.

"And it was someone at the Preservation Commission that got word to you, if I understand rightly. He's seriously wounded?"

"A bullet in the stomach," Roger answered, not daring to look at Lara.

"Marccaggi didn't tell you any of the details as to how he got wounded?"

"He was more or less unconscious and in great pain."

And that was all. A short time later, the soldiers climbed back in their trucks and the column took off, soon followed by the French teachers heading back to their bungalow. Thus, within the space of a few minutes, the three men, Lara, Kutchaï, and Roger, found themselves alone, sitting on the wooden floor of the veranda with the shadow of the cook silently padding back and forth preparing the evening meal, as overhead the first bats flew back to their base.

"Come with me," Lara said to Roger.

The two of them drove off in the Land-Rover, heading for the latex collectors' village. Night was falling.

"I'd really like to . . ." Roger began.

"Later. You're sure Oreste is going to pull through?"

"No question, the surgeon said."

Lara shook his head, his chin on his chest, driving with one hand, the other massaging the back of his neck.

They arrived in the village and Roger saw the razed huts and the dead bodies laid out in a row. He was horrified. He had no idea that things had reached such a point. On the way back from the village, he exclaimed, "And that's how it's going to be? Men dead and wounded, women raped! Kutchaï nearly killed! What about you—what are you going to do?"

"Nothing."

"I can't believe you mean it."

"There's nothing to do. Cambodia is changing. Lots of things are changing."

"You, first of all."

Lara nodded. "Me, first of all."

He then related the entire Ieng Samboth affair, explaining it to Roger as though he were trying to explain it to himself.

Roger shook his head. "And why did that major let the whole thing drop all of a sudden?"

"Because he went to the village of Phnom Pnong, where he discovered that Kutchaï had really been by that way and that just a few hours after Kutchaï had been there, the villagers had also seen a detachment of Khmer Rouge carrying Ieng Samboth on a stretcher. So the story that Kutchaï had invented gave every appearance of being true. And the major let the whole thing drop because Oreste had indeed been wounded by a bullet, which he certainly didn't fire at himself. The major knows it wasn't his men who wounded Oreste. So it was the Khmer Rouge. And from that point on he could no longer accuse Oreste of being their accomplice. Or Kutchaï or me either. And since he didn't have the least desire to pursue Ieng into an area where there are perhaps Viet Cong as well, he decided to go back to Siem Reap, where he'll have a really impressive scorecard to turn in: the three Khmer Rouge he captured and tortured, plus those seven latex collectors, poor devils. Ten of the enemy killed. He's a great leader, a Warlord."

"Who exactly is that Rath fellow who shot Oreste?"

"I don't know him."

Or else he knows him and isn't talking, Roger thought. There had always been a side of Lara's life kept hidden even from Roger. And that Sunday night he was more secretive than ever. What amazed Roger most was how calmly Lara took everything that had happened; Lara acted as though adventures of this sort were the most ordinary everyday thing in the world. *And after all, how do I know that isn't true?* Living in Phnom Penh, never straying off the main highways, Roger had only come to the plantation from time to time, the way a city dweller goes to the country to spend the weekend.

They went back to the house and settled themselves in the rattan peacock-armchairs, Roger drinking iced tea and his two companions cognac-and-soda. To all appearances it was an evening no different from hundreds of others that Lara and Kutchaï had spent there over the years. Some twenty yards away the cook was leaning over the glowing coals of the outdoor charcoal brazier. The smell of grilled meat mingled with the fragrance of the frangipanis, and a silence that might have been that of the beginning of the world.

Or of the end of the world.

"What did you mean when you said to me, 'Lots of things are changing'?"

"Let's talk about something else," Lara answered. He raised his glass. "Thanks."

"Up yours and cheers," Roger said.

Kutchaï stretched out his legs, contemplating his toes as though he'd just been reunited with them after a long absence. "The prettiest feet in Cambodia."

"In Indochina," Lara said.

They sat down at the table, bringing their glasses with them.

"I won't be leaving for Phnom Penh till Thursday or Friday," Lara said at one point in a drawling, almost drowsy tone of voice. "Somebody has to take Oreste's place here, and since this lout"—he pointed at Kutchaï— "seems bent on being pampered . . . Do you want to stay on here till then?"

"My car's at Kompong Thom," Roger said. "Two flat tires, one right after the other. That damned rattletrap's about done for."

It took him a moment to realize he hadn't answered Lara's question. He looked at the two men sitting across from him. He suddenly discovered a sort of resemblance between them he'd never noticed before and which was plainly not a physical one. *The two of them are one person. Kutchaï is Lara's Khmer half.* He scratched his head. *I'm utterly out of my mind,* he thought.

"No," he said aloud. "I won't stick around that long. All you need to do is drive me back to Kompong Thom."

Lara nodded. He had buried himself in an armchair, leaning the nape of his neck against the back of it, completely oblivious to the mosquitoes circling about in the light of the lamps, blowing smoke rings as his pale eyes, their pupils slightly dilated, contemplated the darker and darker forest.

"And how's business with you?"

"Things are going along all right," Roger said. "Better than at other times I can think of."

"You know that if you need anything . . ."

"I know," Roger said with a smile. "I'll keep it in mind. . . ."

The cook brought the leg of roe deer seasoned with mint to the table. They ate almost in silence, with Sidney Bechet's "Little Flower" as background music from the record player.

Roger left the plantation the following morning. And as things turned out, he never saw it agan.

14

THE NAME KHMER KRAHAM—KHMER ROUGE—WAS INVENTED BY Norodom Sihanouk. The term had first appeared in 1968, in the course of one of the long rambling speeches that Samdech was so fond of delivering.

In Cambodia it was easy to lose one's way amid the labyrinth of names of factions, cliques, parties, and ethnic minorities that succeeded each other or, more often, joined forces with each other without the latest one ever completely absorbing the one that had preceded it. In fact, when it came to the basic question of the origin of the Khmers, specialists who had studied the matter closely had not indulged in any of the flights of fancy of a George P. Walker which had brought a smile to Lisa Kinkaird's lips. They had advanced only the most cautious hypotheses: The Khmers, they maintained, were a Mongolian people with a strong Hindu admixture, religiously, culturally, and even racially, who had arrived in the Indochinese peninsula (they didn't say from where exactly) at the same time as the Khas from Vietnam and the Mois from Thailand. The Khas and Mois had lost their ethnic identity over the centuries, due to the effects of foreign migrations. But not the Khmers.

Things became even more complicated when it came to the precise details. For if one was simply a Khmer, with no admixture of foreign blood, despite the fact that one's ancestors had been born a thousand or two thousand years before on the alluvial plains of the Tonle Sap or the Mekong, one could also have become a Khmer Loeu—a Khmer from Up Above, a highlander living in the mountains—or more often a Khmer Pnong—a "savage," living either in the mountains or in the forest. In the latter case, one could well be a Khmer Brao, Kuy, Jaraï, Souch, or Pear, depending on the region one lived in. Unless, that is, one were a Khmer Islam, a Moslem from Malaya who had somehow landed in Khmer country.

And politics had also complicated the picture. From the first days of the war against the French, a sort of resistance movement had sprung up in the Cambodian forest. Its roots were not in Cambodia itself but in South Vietnam, in the region of Cochin China. A certain Nguyen Thanh Son had organized the Nambo, the rival and counterpart of the organization directed by Ho Chi Minh in the North, in the region of Tonkin. Among the adjutants of this Nguyen Thanh Son was a man named Sieu Heng, a Vietnamese of Cambodian descent, who had become the leader of the Issarak— "Free"—Khmers. The movement had spread rapidly, to the point that between 1950 and 1960 three separate factions of Issarak Khmers had made their appearance: The first had turned Communist and sworn allegiance to the Viet Minh; the second had taken a curious turn to the right and been taken in hand by Bangkok, where the former Cambodian prime minister during the Japanese invasion, Son Ngok Thanh, had taken refuge; and the third, known as "pirates," were pure and simple bandits who lived off rapine and racketeering (Kamsa and his band had belonged to this faction). After the Geneva Accords of 1954, the first had been dissolved and a number of their cadres had gone to Hanoi to complete their training; and the third had quite simply been eliminated once peace had been restored. The second, the rightist anti-Sihanouk Issaraks, had survived, later on becoming the Khmer Sereï—sereï, like issarak, meaning "free." In this year 1969, as part of the groundwork for their coup and in the guise of bringing about national unity, Sirik Matak and Lon Nol had just integrated these Khmer Sereï with FARK, the Khmer Royal Armed Forces, along with the Khmer Krom from South Vietnam.

As for the Khmer Kraham, they themselves did not call themselves by that name. They preferred to be known as Khmer Rondom, *rondom* being yet a third word meaning "free."

The first Khmer Rouge, even though no one called them that yet, had appeared in April of 1967, in the province of Battambang. They were simple peasants, embittered at seeing their best lands handed over to the "repatriates" from South Vietnam. An insurrection had broken out which had been brutally put down by troops sent from Phnom Penh with orders to shoot the peasants in cold blood. The most aggressive survivors had instinctively obeyed an age-old Khmer tradition: As Corsicans take to the maquis, they had taken to the forest, forming an underground network that little by little became a veritable peasant uprising. The same cause had the same effect in the provinces of Stung Treng, Ratanakiri, and Mondolkiri, whose populations were largely wild mountain Khmers—that is to say, second-class Cambodian citizens. But in addition to having the advantage of a wooded, mountainous terrain with which they were extraordinarily well acquainted, these mountain Khmers held another high trump card: the immediate proximity of Viet Cong divisions, rifles at hand, ready and waiting for orders to attack Saigon and the Mekong delta. A trump that for the moment was only a potential winning card. Anxious not to provoke a violent American reaction, Hanoi had ordered its troops not to intervene in Cambodia....

... As long, at least, as Sihanouk remained in power in Phnom Penh.

A sort of peasant uprising then, not yet really politicized, not yet really organized, even though a few students, high school kids for the most part, were in the forest playing at being Cambodian versions of Robin Hood. The principal consequence of the expulsion by Lon Nol or Khieu Samphan, Hu Nim, Hou Yuon, and Ieng Samboth from the country's official political life, and the escape of these hounded deputies to the forest, had been to furnish the peasant rebels with the leaders they had previously lacked.

The march led by Ieng Samboth from the foothills of the Cardamome Mountains to the northern part of the province of Prah Vihear in April of 1969 in fact represented the first attempt to unite and pool the forces of underground rebels from the west and those from the east, the latter operating from bases just across the border from the Viet Cong armies. In a matter of a mere three weeks, Ieng found himself in command of not five men, but a hundred.

On June 9, after several days' rest in a hut located some fifteen kilometers southeast of the temples of Prah Vihear, which thirteen years before had been the object of violent disputes and very nearly a war between Cambodia and Thailand, Ieng Samboth entered his native province of Stung Treng.

On the night of the fourteenth, he crossed the Mekong, accompanied by 127 men, only a third of whom were equipped with combat weapons.

Rath was among these men, the officer second in command of the unit.

15

O'MALLEY AND LISA HAD MADE PLANS FOR THE FOLLOWING WEEK-
end. O'Malley was scheduled to visit the town of Kompong Cham with a
representative of the Cambodian Ministry of Cultural Affairs, and had proposed that Lisa join them. "An excellent chance to see something of Cambodia besides Phnom Penh and its environs. Till we have a little free time to
visit Angkor."

Lisa had readily accepted the invitation. In just a short time, her
friendship with the Irishman from New York had grown by leaps and
bounds, thanks in large part to the many hours they spent together at work
and to O'Malley's unfailing high spirits and sense of humor, not to mention
his cultivated mind, his way of never taking himself too seriously, and his
extraordinary kindness. Thomas Aquinas O'Malley's parody of Irish drama-
tist J. M. Synge's *Deirdre of the Sorrows* was hilarious. But in addition to
knowing nearly all of Deirdre's lines by heart, and all the dialogue of
The Playboy of the Western World, O'Malley could also quote Whitman or
Villon and was passionately devoted to his job as cultural attaché, in circumstances that to say the least were difficult. It would have been hard to
imagine, in the Cambodia of this period, anything more useless than an
American cultural attaché. O'Malley was well aware of this, yet showed not
the slightest sign of discouragement; on the contrary, he made superhuman
efforts to do his job well, without ever losing heart, with a cheerful good
humor that bordered on the miraculous.

If Lisa detected certain premonitory signs on his part of more affectionate feelings toward her, far from encouraging them in order to enhance
her own self-esteem, she chose to ignore them. In the five years that she had
been a widow, she had only once given way to her feelings and allowed
herself to have a brief love affair, in New York, with a young executive who
was one of her agency's clients. She had agreed to spend three days with
him in that traditional romantic spot, the Bahamas. As soon as they returned to New York she had broken off with him, gently but firmly, despite
his pleading—he was ready, willing, and eager to marry her. That she had
ended the affair had nothing at all to do with any feeling of respect on her
part for Robert Trenton's memory, though that respect was quite genuine;
in this regard, she considered herself as free as a man would have been in
her place. Moreover, she had felt no vocation for remaining celibate. From
the first days of their marriage, Bob Trenton, who was fifteen years her se-
nior, had proved to be an experienced and skillful lover, and with her usual
forthrightness she had never sought to conceal the purely physical pleasure
their lovemaking brought her.

And now the climate of Indochina, its soothing, sensual warmth, was having its effect on her. She duly noted the fact, without being either surprised or overly disturbed by it. It was as though she were waking from a long sleep.

Their plans were for O'Malley to come by the Korvers' to pick her up in his car at nine-thirty A.M. She rose at dawn, awakened by the light streaming through the windows, which had neither shutters nor curtains. She took her morning shower, packed a little travel case with another dress, a pair of pants in case they would have to hike on foot, and two swimsuits in case there was a pool. And what if O'Malley suggested they share the same room for the night? This was the first time since they had met that she would be free of the obviously discreet, indeed hypothetical guardianship of the Korvers. She smilingly toyed with the idea of allowing O'Malley to become her lover, but was certain in advance she would refuse, with all her usual wariness and gentle politeness, for the same reason she had refused to see the New York executive again—in the same bed at least: She really didn't want to.

Despite the early morning hour, she could hear the quiet murmur of voices downstairs. Charles and Madeleine slept very little and Lisa was beginning to be familiar with their daily routine of getting up at the crack of dawn to work together in the garden in the hours when it was still relatively cool, and then spending the rest of the day indoors, sitting at a table going over the archives of their collection.

She headed downstairs, and on the stairway, even before she saw him, she recognized Lara by his voice.

She felt a quiver run down her spine that for a second made her freeze motionless on the step. Then she continued downstairs.

"Good morning," he said on catching sight of her. "I came to ask you to go swimming with me in the Gulf of Siam. Would you like to come with me?"

Naturally she said yes.

16

"I KNOW VERY LITTLE ABOUT MY FOREBEARS," HE SAID. "ON MY FAther's side at least. I do know, however, that the Lara who landed in the bay of Tourane—now known as Da Nang—with a nephew of Dupleix's, came from India. And that he didn't land there by chance: Another Lara, no doubt his great-grandfather, had already come to Cochin China, around 1690, on a French India Company ship with a group of explorer-settlers led by a certain Véret. Hence I gather that as early as the seventeenth century there were already Laras in the East Indies, but don't ask me where their

roots were before they arrived in Pondicherry. They obviously came from
Europe—there seems to be no doubt of that—but I have no idea what country they were from originally."

She looked at his face in profile and was almost fascinated by the contours of his lips.

"And that makes how many generations?"

"Of Laras in Indochina? Eight."

"Longer than my family's been in America."

"There you are." He smiled. "Two hundred eighty years. But it doesn't
take that long to sink deep roots in a place."

"Without their ever going back to Europe?"

"What for? Did the Kinkairds ever go back to Europe?"

"That's different."

"How is it different? Or rather, there is one difference, I'll grant you:
The Kinkairds and the Johnsons and the Cabots and the Lodges took over
the country they'd settled in, so that after that it belonged to them. The
Laras, on the contrary, settled in Indochina with the aim of becoming an
integral part of the country. So Cambodia doesn't belong to them; they belong to it. In our family we've never been jingoist flag-wavers. I'm a Cambodian."

"You don't look like one."

He laughed. "There's a Cambodian general whose name is Sósthenes
Fernández; he has Portuguese blood. After how long a time does a person
become a colonizer? When the Khmers first arrived in the Indochinese
peninsula, they doubtless fought for their place in the sun, weapons in hand.
The Arabs conquered all the southern shores of the Mediterranean in the
seventh century; the Turks took over Turkey; the Russians, Siberia. There
are countless similar examples. What can the Laras be blamed for—not
having come in sufficient numbers to exterminate all the prior occupants of
the country? At what moment does one become an original inhabitant, a
native? Take the case of Algeria. Before Mohammed it was Berber, often
Christian, and often Roman. Today it's Arab and Moslem, and convinced
that it has always been so. When did the scales tip?"

Lisa jokingly put her hands to her head. "Good heavens, before our
next picnic I'll have to bone up on my world history."

"Am I boring you?"

Their eyes met.

"You surprise me," she answered.

"I've got my act down pat, wouldn't you say?"

She was the one who laughed this time. "Not a bad performance, I'll
have to admit."

"My grandfather visited Paris only once in his life, for the Universal
Exposition. Forty years later, he still used to laugh at the memory of the
Cambodian pavilion that the French had built for it. As for my father, he

never ventured any farther than the Philippines and Japan. And Hong Kong, of course, where he met my mother."

"I know," Lisa said with a smile. "You and I are cousins."

"Not in the same family line. Luckily."

There was a sudden break in the wall of vegetation on both sides of them and the sea came into view. The car rolled on for a few more yards along the rutted, bumpy brick-red road, then stopped. Lisa saw a sandy beach, absolutely transparent water, and in the distance the irregular outline of a dark green chain of islands. Lara switched off the ignition, and the chirring and buzzing of the insects in the forest around them immediately filled the car.

"Well, here we are," he said in his drawling voice. "I'd like to ask you something now. We have a choice. We can spend the day here on this beach and have a picnic. I've got a big enough lunch in the trunk to feed a dozen starving American women. And as soon as night gives signs of being about to fall, I'll turn the car around in one of those skillful maneuvers that are a special secret of mine and we'll head straight for Phnom Penh, where you'll be back in time for supper."

He had placed his thin suntanned hands on the leather-covered steering wheel and was slowly clenching and unclenching his long fingers, his eyes fixed on the islands of the Gulf of Siam on the horizon. Lisa's pulse suddenly quickened.

"And what's the other alternative?" she asked, almost in a whisper.

"If we continue along this same little road for a few hundred yards more, we'll find on our right a tiny village of Malay fishermen. They catch sharks for their fins, which are a great delicacy among Chinese gourmets. They have great streamlined black pirogues, with a single triangular sail, that go like the devil. A lot of them are friends of mine. I'm certain they'd agree to take us to one of those islands out there on the horizon. All of them are deserted, or at least all the smaller ones. But on one of them there's a sort of house. And a spring. I built that house a dozen years or so ago, but nobody's ever lived in it. I go there sometimes when I want to be by myself."

A silence.

"And when would the fishermen come back to get us?" she asked.

He looked at her.

"Whenever we asked them to. Tomorrow, for instance."

The pirogue was indeed black and streamlined, less than four feet wide but ten feet long, with a plank deck. It cleaved the waves rather than riding above them, its white sail at times blending into the pale blue of the sky. Lisa clung to the mast, the only place she had been able to find a handhold, at once excited by the sensation of incredible speed and terrified of losing her balance each time the narrow deck tilted too far to one side. But she saw the island gradually grow bigger, and as soon as the craft sailed past a long, narrow, rocky cape sticking out into the sea like a tongue, the water before the bow immediately became miraculously calm. And the deck returned to the position of any trustworthy deck: horizontal.

"We've arrived. But we weren't in all that great danger. You looked like Captain Carlsen during his very last moments aboard the *Flying Enterprise*. Haven't you ever been sailing before?"

"Yes, on a real sailboat. Not on a thing like this."

The fishermen laughed uproariously, self-confidently, despite the fact that they didn't understand a single word. There were three of them, one a youngster about ten years old, and all of them were wearing the black headdresses of Moslem Malays.

With a hissing sound, the bow sank into the sand of a beach at the mouth of a cove and finally came to a stop.

"Your island," Lara said with a smile.

Lisa hesitated. By walking to the very end of the deck, she could have jumped down onto the beach without getting her feet wet. But she chose to take off her sandals and leap into the water, taking a primitive, childlike pleasure in getting the hem of her white linen dress wet. She immediately found herself in water up to mid-thigh, and it was warm. One of the fishermen cracked a joke; the Malays burst out laughing, and even Lara joined in.

"And what's more, they're making fun of me."

"He said that if he was a shark, he'd already be upon you. He's paying you a compliment."

She stood there not moving, her eyes closed and her head thrown slightly back the better to feel the sun on her face, pleased to be close to shore again, sensing the fine sand give beneath her feet and trickle between her bare toes.

"There aren't any sharks," she said smugly.

"Oh, no? There's one just behind you."

She turned around, not believing him for an instant. She caught sight of a long black shape cleaving the water. The next second she was up on the beach. The Malays laughed till tears came to their eyes.

"Keep calm," Lara said. "It's only a baby shark, two feet long at most. He's much more scared than you are. What you should really watch out for is *méduses*, what you call in English Portuguese men-of-war."

Lisa stretched out on the sand, in the shade of the trees at the water's edge.

"And I suppose the island is literally teeming with snakes, scorpions, and tigers? Not to mention cannibals who drop by every Friday for breakfast?"

"Not so much as a mosquito. And no *boumaques* either." He explained that *boumaques* were little black and white insects, the size of mosquitoes, which sometimes swooped down on the coasts when the wind was right; they could almost eat you alive, and their bites itched terribly afterward.

"But there aren't any here. There never have been. Don't ask me why."

"Political reasons perhaps?" Lisa suggested. "What creature would dare tackle eight generations of Laras?"

"That's surely the explanation."

The Malays had finished unloading the pirogue and disappeared in the trees. A sudden overpowering silence came over the beach, finally broken by Lisa, who was feeling almost ill at ease, for Lara's eyes never once left her. She had suddenly realized that they would soon be all by themselves.

"Where are we?" she asked.

"We've just left the Cheko Peninsula, which is about forty kilometers away. That big island over there in the distance is Rong. It lies at the entrance to the bay of Kompong Som, where the only Cambodian port on the Gulf of Siam is located. Those mountains way off there on your left are the Cardamomes. Facing you is the Kirirom Range, and to your right is the Elephant Range. And this island that we're on is called Sré."

"Does it belong to you? The island, I mean."

He shook his head. "Oh, no," he said, laughing. "It's just that very few Cambodians care to venture out to sea. The only fishermen in these waters are Malays and there are at most only about thirty of them. Do you want to see the house?"

There wasn't even a path leading up to it. One simply clambered up over a series of flat rocks, warmed by the sun, and then, after making one's way through a thick curtain of pellitories, one emerged amid a tiny palm grove hugging the single summit of Sré, a cone of earth and rocks which, like very nearly all the rest of the island, was covered with vegetation consisting of a mangrove swamp at the bottom, and then ferns, eucalyptus, and palms of all sorts as one gradually went higher. The highest spot on the island was probably about a hundred feet above sea level. What Lara called the house was a wooden platform with some twenty posts supporting a roof of fan-palm thatch. The principle was the same as the one used in the construction of the house at Prah Vihear.

"The spring flows directly into what would be the kitchen or the bathroom, if the house had either one."

There was little furniture, just two long planks several inches thick that served as a table, with other planks running along either side serving as benches; the only other furnishings in the room were thick pads of foam rubber brought from the plantation. The Malays were busy spreading colored *sampots* out on top of them. Feeling embarrassed, Lisa walked over to the spring and put one hand under the water dripping down from it just above her head; it was almost cool. She wet her temples and her lips, which still had a slight taste of salt after the crossing in the pirogue. She heard Lara speaking to the fishermen in what could perhaps have been Khmer, and then they left.

"Are you dying of hunger or would you like to go swimming first?"

She turned around. Lara was uncovering large rattan hampers.

"Go swimming," Lisa said.

He nodded, gazing intently at the end of his cigarette.

"There are several beaches on the island where we could go, not counting the ones facing the open sea—it's better to stay away from them. Real sharks sometimes turn up on that side, but the water isn't deep enough for them to venture close inshore on the side facing the mainland. I suggest we go back down to the beach where we landed. I'll leave you here to change into your swimsuit and wait for you down below."

She waited till he'd gone off and then opened her travel case, which contained, in addition to the other clothes she had packed for her trip to Kompong Cham, the two swimsuits, one of them more or less an ordinary bathing suit and the other so tiny it practically fitted into the palm of her hand. After hesitating for a moment she chose the latter, though she had never worn it since the day she had bought it, almost two years before, in a boutique in Saint-Tropez on the French Riviera. She doubted she could manage to tie its thin ribbons, doubted that the ridiculous minuscule triangles would even cover her breasts. *And what's more, since the thing's white, it's going to be transparent the minute I come out of the water. . . .*

She was obliged to go through all sorts of contortions to get it tied properly, seized with a fit of nervous laughter she was barely able to control. Again she was overcome with the extraordinary sensation of giddy lightheadedness, of dizziness almost, that had come over her when she left the Central Market of Phnom Penh.

She left her sandals behind and headed toward the beach, feeling practically naked—dressed as she was, the difference was minimal—and in any event completely indecent, altogether too conscious of her breasts and her nipples, which had suddenly become hard and erect. As she emerged from the curtain of ferns, in sight of the sea and the beach, she caught sight of the black spindle-shaped Malay pirogue, already several hundred yards out to sea.

"Where are you?"

The sea, just a few feet away, was fabulously transparent and she could see the multicolored coral formations on the bottom, on either side of the tongue of sand stretching out underwater from the beach. Lara was nowhere in sight. Then she spied a shadow slowly gliding beneath the surface and Lara emerged from the water. He was wearing a sort of sarong.

"Are you coming in? The sharks swore to me that they wouldn't bother you."

He taught her to dive. Not to plunge into the water with a big noisy splash, but to immerse herself in the water slowly, without a sound, almost without a ripple, and to descend almost imperceptibly beneath the surface, something she'd never done before without giving herself a big push off the bottom. In the beginning, since she was unable to master immediately the trick of jackknifing her body and simultaneously working up just the right amount of momentum by pushing with her arms, he helped her, pulling her downward with one hand or pushing her with his fingers resting on her hips.

She finally flopped down on the sand, out of breath; she stretched out on her belly, the warm waves lapping halfway over her body. She felt him stretch out alongside her but did not raise her head. She lay there with her cheek resting on her arm, her eyes closed, breathing in the smell of the warm sand perfumed by the sea and the more acrid odors of the vegetation. The heat enveloped her like a cape and the air was completely still.

"Cigarette?"

She shook her head. The scent of tobacco mingled with the other odors. A long minute elapsed in total silence.

Then Lara said softly, "If you hadn't come to Cambodia, I would have gone back to find you in Saigon. I would even have gone to New York."

She did not answer, panting for breath. An extraordinary feeling of well-being and certainty came over her, and she waited without the least impatience, savoring each second of this anticipation.

"You should take off that thing that's tied too tightly around your breasts," he said, even more gently. "I'll give you a *sampot* to wear in a little while."

She waited for a few moments more, simply to prolong her pleasure, with no doubt in her mind as to what she was going to do. Finally, without a word, she raised her breasts almost imperceptibly from the sand and felt Lara's fingers gently undoing the fastenings of the top of her bikini. He pulled it slowly away and the ridiculous little bits of cloth came away from her breasts. Her hard, burning nipples sank back into the cool sand.

"I couldn't get to Phnom Penh any sooner," Lara said. "It just wasn't possible. On the other hand . . ."

He dug a hole in the sand and buried his cigarette in it.

"On the other hand, these few days that I was obliged to wait before I saw you again . . ."

He didn't finish his sentence. Lisa's lips parted halfway and her breath was burning hot on the skin of her arm. She licked her skin with its fine crust of dried salt. She felt like moaning very softly.

"You had other plans for this weekend, isn't that right?"

She nodded, unable to speak. Another long silence. Lara's hand came

to rest on her shoulder and one of his fingers slowly stroked the mark left by the top of her bikini. Then, very slowly and deliberately, she turned over onto her back. Lara was very close to her, leaning on one elbow. His eyes ran over her naked breasts, then met hers, and she saw in them a tenderness that overwhelmed her, an amazing blend of violence and gentleness, of strength and of something close to defenselessness, that she had never seen in any other man's eyes before. She stretched out full length, her arms above her head. Then she closed her eyes again and, taking Lara's hand in hers, guided it to her breast.

"I would never have gone back to the United States without having seen you again. I had to know," she said.

"And do you know now?"

"I think so. Yes, I think so."

He leaned over and kissed her lightly on the lips, almost cupping her breast in his hand and then gently stroking it above the nipple, just brushing the tip. She raised up so that he could slide the bottom of her swimsuit down over her thighs, and finally she sent it flying into the sea with a toss of her legs.

"Now?" he said in a whisper.

She opened her eyes again and smiled at him. "Mmmmm."

She raised one hand and gently stroked the horribly scarred flesh where he had been wounded long ago. Then, leaning on her elbow, she kissed him on the chest, on the scar itself, on the cheek, and finally on the mouth, in a slow and almost ceremonious succession of soft little kisses, breathing in the smell of his skin and gently nibbling his lower lip. And it was she who untied his sarong, stripped him naked, and drew him on top of her.

They ate lunch on the rocks, stark naked, their hips touching, but they were obliged to interrupt their meal when they were once again overcome by their terrible, fierce desire for each other. This time it was almost a battle; they were nearly black and blue when it was over, with swollen lips and panting breath. They went back into the sea and swam about, searching each other out again and again, avidly, their bodies intertwining as they met. They dived beneath the water, so clear it was invisible, swimming above the red, yellow, and blue-violet coral in the midst of incredible armies of fish of all shapes and colors that approached them as though to sniff at them and, with a total absence of fear, even touched them.

They spent the remainder of the afternoon walking all the way around the entire island. Sré was no more than three hundred yards in diameter at any point, with a coastline made up of an endless succession of tiny dry coves, most of them with a bottom of coral sand so blindingly white it hurt their eyes and so hot it was impossible to walk barefoot on it except in the shade of trees or amid the mangrove roots. To the south, their island ended in a low sand spit gleaming with millions of silvery microscopic shells,

where the waves from the bay and those from the gulf mingled. While to the left the water was shallow and bristling with fantastically colored coral reefs, on the side facing the open sea it was much darker, a sumptuous and almost frightening midnight blue, so deep it was impossible to see the bottom.

"And way off there in the distance opposite us is Malaysia," Lisa said drowsily, her head resting on Lara's shoulder.

"Your sense of geography . . ."

She bit his shoulder. "Say it in French. *En français!*"

"Your sense of geography strikes me as terribly rudimentary."

"I couldn't care less," Lisa said. "I just like that word: Malaysia."

"Malaysia is much farther south. What we're seeing there opposite us is Thailand."

"I thought it was Siam."

"They're the same thing. And if it's not Thailand, it's Burma. And it's over four hundred kilometers away."

"I love you," Lisa said. *"Je t'aime."*

She removed his inevitable cigarette from between his fingers and took a puff that made her cough. "You smoke too much," she said to him.

"So you're starting in on me already, are you?" Lara asked with a smile.

For no reason at all they were overcome with a fit of helpless mad laughter that stopped as abruptly as it had begun, and they sat there gravely looking at each other. Then they walked out along the sand spit as far as they could, hand in hand, naked and completely alone, flirting with the very real danger of being sucked down by the quicksand and drowned. They finally stretched out full length in the shallows, and then, staring into each other's eyes as though it were some sort of dare or in order to prove how much they trusted each other, they ventured into deep water, swimming above an unknown, black abyss, from which at any moment the razor-sharp silhouette of a shark might emerge.

That evening they fell asleep in front of a wood fire, and decided they wouldn't get dressed for dinner.

In the afternoon of the following day, Sunday, the Malays' pirogue reappeared at the hour agreed upon, a little before nightfall, and they reached the mainland just as the sun was setting in the sea. They arrived in Phnom Penh around ten o'clock that night, having made the entire trip almost without exchanging a word. At one point they considered dinner and dancing at a place on the shore of the Tonle Sap, but they soon realized that would be a mistake and, giving in to their need to be alone together, went to spend the night in a room at the Hotel Raja.

On Monday, Lisa told Jon, and wrote Matthew Kinkaird, that she intended to marry Lara.

Which she did, on July 2, 1969.

17

THE MARRIAGE TOOK PLACE BEFORE THE CONSUL AT THE FRENCH
Embassy and was simultaneously made a matter of record in Cambodia and
in the United States.

Thomas Aquinas O'Malley did not attend the wedding ceremony. He
had been invited by Lisa, and at the moment had been so surprised that he
had accepted, but then he had changed his mind, claiming that a trip he
was obliged to take to Bangkok and Rangoon—one he could easily have
postponed—would make it impossible for him to be in Phnom Penh during
the first days of July. In Bangkok, all by himself in his room at the Hotel
Erawan, he went on the most fantastic, and surely the most solitary, drinking bout of his entire career—he who had always boasted of never drinking
alone.

Kutchaï didn't attend the wedding either. "You know very well that I
don't like official ceremonies," he said to Lara.

"Cool it," he went on, squarely meeting Lara's gaze. "Don't get the
wrong idea into your head. Lisa Kinkaird is an extraordinary woman. She's
as beautiful as the temples of Angkor at sunrise and she's the best thing in
the world that could happen to you."

"Well why won't you come then?"

"I'd be out of place."

He refused to give an inch. Besides, he explained, somebody had to be
around to look after the plantation, since Oreste, who was now back but
still convalescing, was in no condition to do so. He stubbornly resisted all
Lara's arguments, countering each of them with the same warm, friendly
laugh. His attitude simply left no room for a fight—which would have been
their first in some thirty years—though Lara would have been ready and
willing to go that far.

"You and Lisa don't need me. As a matter of fact, you don't need anybody. Especially not a consul." He laughed. "I didn't ask you to come to all
my wedding ceremonies."

To Lara's knowledge, though even he didn't know all there was to
know, Kutchaï, had at least three wives scattered about here, and there, and
an impressive number of children.

Charles and Madeleine Korver were present at the wedding, however,
as was Roger Bouès.

For Roger Bouès, those first days of July 1969 marked the beginning of
a new period in his life. The turning point came after a late-June drinking
session in a bar called the Saint-Hubert, run by a Frenchman who'd pulled
up stakes in Hanoi and come to Phnom Penh. Roger started talking shop

about photography with a man who turned out to be a professional photo-journalist working mostly for *Paris Match;* he had lost a foot when, in one and the same parachute jump, he'd landed in a Dien Bien Phu surrounded by enemy troops and on top of a land mine. Roger had always been interested in photography, mostly as a hobby, though he had also sold an occasional photo, in particular some he'd taken as the last French troops were pulling out of Indochina. He had given up taking pictures only when he'd found himself so hard up for cash one day that he'd stopped selling photographs and sold his camera instead.

The journalist—whose name was Legros—suggested he take it up again.

"I don't even have a camera anymore," Roger said.

"I happen to have a Rolleiflex and a backup Canon that I'm not using. They're yours."

Roger burst out laughing. "I don't have any money either."

"Who said anything about money?" Legros responded. "I'll lend them to you. With enough film to last you ten months."

"I get it: You're bombed out of your mind, as usual."

But he was tempted. And for once Legros hadn't drunk a whole lot. He was famous, in Cambodia and elsewhere, for the amazing amount of alcohol he could consume: One day he'd made a bet that he could down, without stopping, fifty whiskeys lined up on the counter of the Zigzag; he had drunk them and was still on his feet when he reached the other end, though along the way he'd started smashing the empty glasses with his fists and they'd had to take him to the hospital to get the cuts on his hands sewed up.

Two days after their meeting at the Saint-Hubert, Legros brought Roger the cameras and the film.

And two days after that, Roger learned that Legros had just taken the plane for France, going home for good. It was only then that Roger caught on. He rushed over to Lara's room at the Raja.

"Who paid Legros?"

"I don't have the least idea what you're talking about."

"Legros can't afford to give me a gift like that. Above all with enough film to take a picture of every last Chinaman in China, one at a time."

"I really don't have any idea," Lara said impassively. "I swear to you on a stack of Bibles and Lon Nol's head."

"You swine of a rotten planter you."

"While I think of it, Legros left me this for you," Lara answered nonchalantly.

"This" was the receipt for the sale of the two cameras, made out in Roger's name.

"I still wonder why he left it with me to give to you," Lara said. "Those press photographers are all mad." His bright eyes twinkled.

"Let me remind you that you're having dinner with Lisa and me tonight. And I also remind you that you're my best man. If you could manage to be at the wedding, it'd be a big help. I may be there myself."

Jon Kinkaird didn't attend the wedding ceremony. Since he was in the country illegally, he obviously didn't dare show up for it. And yet it was precisely on his account they had chosen the date of July 2, for two days later, on the fourth, he was to leave on a Norwegian ship that would first call at Singapore and Bombay, then round the Cape of Good Hope and enter the Atlantic, whereupon it would head directly for Oslo—or else it would make for Argentina or the Antilles, with that poetic vagueness of itinerary of certain tramp freighters. From Oslo, Jon could easily get to Sweden, where in principle he would have no difficulty assuming his real nationality again. In the meanwhile, Christiani, Lara's Corsican partner in Bangkok, had managed to produce a splendid fake Australian passport for him for the trip, thanks to a series of mysterious transactions.

After the wedding Lara and Lisa spent the night of July second and the day and night of the third in Phnom Penh, at the Hotel Raja. Early on the morning of the fourth, before daylight, they left the capital for the port of Kompong Som/Sihanoukville, with Lara at the wheel of the Peugeot 504. Jon was with them. Christiani, who had made a special trip from Bangkok in order to be there, followed them in another car. Christiani was a man of average height, broad-shouldered, intelligent and energetic, fiendishly sly and cunning, who claimed he had missed his chance at a magnificent career as a great swindler. He had long been an unswervingly devoted friend of Lara's, and moreover had held him in great respect ever since the day, fifteen years before, when Lara had placed him at the head of the import-export company in which they were co-partners.

It was Christiani who very efficiently managed the operation of getting Jon Kinkaird aboard the freighter. Lisa's expressions of concern as to how her brother was going to fit in with, and act as though he had always been a member of, a Norwegian crew he had never set eyes on, were greeted by Christiani with a pitying, even slightly mocking smile.

"My little lady, that's my problem. First of all, your little brother is a big boy now. And secondly, the captain is a friend of mine. A brother, you might say. He talks to me in Norwegian and I answer him in Corsican. And we understand each other very well." He rubbed his thumb and index finger together in an unmistakable gesture.

Christiani kept answering Lisa as "little lady" despite the fact that she was nearly a head taller than he. "However, the quicker he gets on board, the sooner he'll be safe. We'd better not dawdle."

This left no time for an emotional good-bye scene between brother and sister. By these first days of July, Jon had more or less recovered his strength. He was still a bit pale, but that was only natural after his long stay at the Korvers', when he had almost never left the house except at night.

Jon Kinkaird shook Lara's hand. "I'm not worried about Lisa," he said. "But I do worry about you. She has a really nasty disposition. Don't hesitate to hit her. A good thrashing from time to time."

"I can't promise anything," Lara said. "But I'll do my best."

Jon kissed Lisa, hugging her almost timidly. "It's fantastic how things have changed in just a few weeks. I'm certain you've done the right thing."

"I'm certain too," Lisa said.

"Take good care of the guy. I'm fond of him."

"Me too."

The freighter lifted anchor early on the afternoon of the fourth. Lara waited till the ship had disappeared off Rong Island, heading out to sea, before leaving the dockside. He took Lisa and Christiani to lunch at a restaurant run by a Corsican named Battesti, a man as expansive and lively as a wild boar from his native island; his menu consisted of roe deer with buttered noodles or of buttered noodles with roe deer. As soon as lunch was over, Christiani climbed into his car to go back to Phnom Penh, and from there to Bangkok.

Lara had proposed to Lisa that they spend their honeymoon in Hong Kong, in the Philippines, in Ceylon, Java, even in French Polynesia. She had laughingly rejected all these proposals.

"All I want is to go back to Sré. Nowhere else."

And so they went directly from Kompong Som to the island. This time they spent three weeks, their perfect solitude interrupted only twice, when the Malay fishermen came to bring them more provisions.

Later, after they'd returned to Phnom Penh, Lara rented a villa in the Rue Phsar Dek from a Cambodian minister of state; it was a three-bedroom, two-story house, painted white, with flowers all about it, smaller than the Korvers' villa, and just on the other side of the Avenue des Français. And in the first days of August of that same year, 1969, Lisa heard the doctor confirm that she was pregnant; if it was a boy, she and Lara agreed they would name him Mathias.

Part Three

THE AMERICAN HIGHWAY

1 THE ROUND SIGHT OF THE LARGE 12.7 MACHINE GUN ROSE WITHOUT the slightest jerk. When it was centered on the doe's head and slender neck, Captain Kao squeezed the trigger and the huge bullets roared like thunder, slashing and hacking the animal to bits and decapitating it. The terrified fawn leapt straight in front of him and began to run across a patch of grass. The thundering rain of bullets caught up with it, blowing it to bits in turn.

As soon as he was certain he had butchered the fawn, Kao turned the gun back on the mother, though she was already no more than a bloody pile of flesh. He fired again, scattering bits of meat about for a dozen yards, stubbornly tracking the severed head as it bounced from the impact of the bullets till it landed in the black water of the swamp. Only then did he cease firing, breathing in great hoarse gasps, his pulse pounding, overcome by a sense of pleasure so acute it was painful. He started the engine of his jeep again, turned it around, and started down the steep winding trail.

The massive bulk of Elephant Mountain looms above the port and bay of Kompong Som, the city of Kampot, the beach of Kep; it lies to the south of the Cardamome and Kirirom ranges, separated from them by a narrow plain across which, a dozen years earlier, the U.S. aid mission built a high-way linking Phnom Penh and the Gulf of Siam.

Where the trail Kao was following ended, replaced by the asphalt of the American Highway, he turned right without hesitating, toward Kom-pong Speu and Phnom Penh. Kao glanced at his watch and noted that it was just after six A.M. He checked in the rearview mirror and then turned his head back over his shoulder to see if the trucks were already on the high-way, but it was deserted. It was still too early; he would be on time. His American instructors had kept harping on the importance of keeping to schedules, to a point where they'd annoyed him a little. It was quite plain they'd taken him for an ignorant savage.

After he'd gone on a dozen kilometers or so, he saw the two men along the roadside signaling to him. He stopped long enough to allow them to climb aboard the jeep.

"Have you been waiting for me very long?"

"Two hours."

"Has anyone been by this way?"

"The bus and two Chinese taxis. But Price came to ask us where you were."

Despite their peasant dress, the two men were really second lieutenants, shavetails barely twenty years old.

"Shit on Price," Kao said.

The jeep went five or six kilometers more, then started up the gentle curves leading to the top of Phnom Pich Pass, where Price and his detachment should be if nothing untoward had happened. And there they in fact were, hidden behind a fold in the terrain.

"It's about time," Price said.

He was a tall, blond American, with long sideburns to compensate for the fact that he was almost bald, though he was only a little over thirty. He had big, heavily muscled arms covered with golden hair, and a tattoo—a star with an arrow through it—on his left biceps. In addition to French, which he spoke perfectly with a pronounced Parisian accent, he had a fair command of Khmer.

Without leaving the seat of his jeep, Kao took a look around him. There were half a dozen vehicles there, plus some forty men, all wearing the dress of peasants from the rice paddies, all in black trousers and jackets, all armed. In reality they were paratroopers from the Second Battalion who had moved in the evening before, leaving their billet in Phnom Penh as though going out on a nighttime practice maneuver. Most of them were Kroms from Cochin China.

Price was fiddling with the dials of a radio set. He stood up. "The convoy left Kompong Som an hour ago. They'll be here shortly."

The American was sweating heavily despite the early morning hour, and chewing on a Philippine cigar that had long since gone out. Addressing Kao in the familiar form, as he always did when speaking to him in French, Price said, "Your men have already had something to eat and to drink. They're all set to go. Are you hungry?"

Kao shook his head. He leaned forward and patted the barrel of the machine gun mounted on the hood of the jeep. The metal had cooled off by now.

"Have you fired it this morning?"

"I did a little hunting," Kao answered.

They exchanged glances and a smile. Kao had a mental picture of the big blond American, so sure of himself, running in a panic across a dry rice paddy and he, Kao, driving along slowly behind him, the sight of the machine gun trained on the hollow of Price's back, tracking him relentlessly. They were right in the middle of the dry season and the temperature was rising very fast, as though they were inside an oven.

❈   ❈   ❈

A few days earlier, at the beginning of this year 1970, on January 10 to be precise, Norodom Sihanouk had left Cambodia for France, where he was to take the waters. Princess Monique, a second-rank wife of his who had become his official wife, and serene old Penn Nouth, doubtless Sihanouk's most trusted intimate, had left with him.

Sihanouk would have been hard put to it to choose a worse moment to be out of the country, from which, according to the official plans, he would be absent for several weeks.

He had gone off, however, without a worry in the world, despite the urgent warnings of the French and Chinese secret services (working hand in hand, as they often did). He had taken off for Paris, and from there, after a short stay, he was scheduled to go on to Moscow—a dreary task, for the Russians struck him as lacking a sense of humor, and in his opinion their expansionist aims were as much of a threat as all the others put together, especially since Moscow was using Hanoi as a cover. Then on to Peking, where he was scheduled to meet with his great and dear friend Chou En-lai, the man whom, after De Gaulle, he admired above all others. He conceded that something serious might take place during his absence, and probably even expected that it would. But it could be argued that he was persuaded that the best way to deal with Sirik Matak and Lon Nol was, in the final analysis, to let them "stew in their own juices," as he himself put it. That would not definitely get rid of them—in his view their existence and that of a pro-American rightist faction represented an essential element in the delicate balance he intended to maintain in the country, this balance being, as he saw it, Cambodia's one and only chance for survival—but it might calm their ardor. Backed by his Franco-Russian-Chinese ties of friendship, which would be reaffirmed by the trip he was now embarking upon, there would always be time enough, if a crisis came along, to call upon his country's people to support him. In short, time enough to make his own June 18, 1940, appeal to his nation, like a latter-day De Gaulle.

If this was not in fact his line of reasoning, his lack of concern would be difficult to explain.

Sihanouk was forgetting only one factor: the Khmer Rouge.

Price's radio set crackled.

"They're arriving."

Through his binoculars, Captain Kao saw the lookouts falling back from their posts eight hundred yards away, on both sides of the road.

"Eleven trucks," Price said. He hesitated, his pale eyes suddenly thoughtful. "Are you sure we really have to kill some of them?"

Kao gave an exasperated shrug. "We've already discussed that. If we were real Khmer Rouge, we'd shoot. And besides, stealing trucks belonging to Chinese, and what's being transported in them, isn't going to bother anybody in Cambodia. The Chinese aren't very popular here in our country—they're too rich. But if we kill a few poor buggers who are just Khmers hired to drive trucks, and if we do a good job of it, everyone will know and say that the Khmer Rouge are savages. Which is true."

What did he mean by "doing a good job of it"? Price didn't waste too much time pondering his own question, perhaps because he already knew the answer. He looked at the machine gun mounted on the hood of the jeep, and then at Kao's face.

"You're all savages," he said.

Kao smiled, nodded, broke into an even broader smile. "And you're helping us," he said in English. "Very much."

About four years before, Sihanouk had entered into a secret agreement with the North Vietnamese military authorities and their theoretical, if not imaginary, allies in the Provisional Republican Government of South Vietnam, allowing Viet Cong divisions to utilize Cambodian territory full time for their operations. That had been like entering into an agreement with rain before it began to fall and even after it had begun to fall, for the Viet Cong had been in Cambodia before 1966. Their first detachments had appeared in the fifties, during the war against the French—barefoot, almost invisible men furtively stealing in Indian file across the high plateaus at night. In principle, after the signing of the Geneva Accords there had been no further point in sending this trickle of men across the border. But on the outbreak of the Second War of Indochina the infiltration had soon begun again. The columns had grown larger, the Ho Chi Minh trail had become a main highway, and Cambodian soil a veritable staging area, extending all through the eastern provinces of Ratanakiri and Mondolkiri, through the south of the provinces of Kratie and Kimpong Cham, to the famous Bec de Canard of Svay Rieng. The Sanctuary.

The arrival of Richard Nixon in the White House, his determination to cut the Viet Cong off from their bases so as to facilitate the process of "Vietnamization," had resulted in a slowdown in the flow of arms, ammunition, and various supplies being sent to the Viet Cong divisions. In 1969, Hanoi had found a way out: A part of these necessary supplies were simply shipped via the port of Kompong Som/Sihanoukville. In addition to ensuring the safe arrival of the supplies, since the convoys were beyond the range of the American bombers, the new formula had the further merit of furnishing Princess Monique and her friends with a source of profit, for they immediately levied a transit tax on the supplies entering the country.

As always in Cambodia, the organization of operations had been entrusted to Chinese. Thus it was Chinese who owned the eleven trucks that were heading eastward with arms unloaded from a Soviet freighter during the night, eleven trucks that at this moment, starting to climb the Phnom

Pich Pass, were looming larger and larger every second in Captain Kao's field glasses.

Price was lying on the ground two hundred yards from the road, and the heat waves rising up from it interfered at times with his vision. He saw Captain Kao raise one arm, and the paratroopers rise halfway to their feet, crouching over ready to make their move. Then the first of the Chinese trucks appeared, and the detachment's panel truck, as planned, drove up into the pavement to collide with it head on.

The men leapt out from both sides of the road, and for a brief second Price did not recognize them in their black clothes and their scarves which made them look entirely different, like real Khmer Rouge. The first shots rang out, and each truck cab was attacked by three or four men, according to the plan that Price himself had devised. But none of the rest of his plan was carried out.

Contrary to all the tactics worked out beforehand, Kao's jeep leapt forward from its hiding place. And the massacre began. The truck drivers, stunned with surprise, were cut in two by the machine gun; others were hacked to pieces in their cabs with machetes; still others dragged from their seats, drenched with gasoline, and set on fire, in an access of insane savagery.

The worst was yet to come, however. Price saw Kao chase a man, forcing him to run and then catching up with him; Kao then made him lean his back against an areca palm, and as the bumper of the jeep slowly closed in on the poor wretch—hypnotized by the barrel of the machine gun aimed straight at his face—Kao flattened him against the trunk and slowly crushed him to death, amid a deafening roar of racing engine.

The paratroopers meanwhile leaned over the panting bodies of the truck drivers and slit their bellies open with knives so as to remove from them bloody trophies: the men's livers.

Price turned away and began to vomit.

After a few moments, Price straightened up again and walked over to his own vehicle, a panel truck borrowed from the embassy. He got out a bottle of whiskey and gulped some down. He sat there in the shade, sick with heat and disgust, waiting. Several minutes went by. Then a dull roar made him raise his eyes and he spied Kao's jeep. Price looked at the bumper spatted with loathsome bits of flesh and bone.

"And how many of them did you kill?"

"Nineteen," Kao answered. "But remember—*we* didn't kill anybody. It was the Khmer Rouge. We left one of them alive. We just knocked him unconscious. He'll say he saw Khmer Rouge."

"We agreed that five of them were to be killed."

"What's the difference?" Kao said with a smile.

"And how come you mutilated them like that?"

"The Khmer Rouge are savages. They cut out the livers of their enemies and eat them. Everybody knows that. It's an age-old custom."

Kao leapt nimbly out of his jeep and began calmly wiping the bumper
with a handful of grass. Turning around at one point, he spied the bottle of
whiskey.

"May I?"

Price handed it to him. "Keep it," he said.

Kao took a swig from it and belched. He winked at Price. "I'll take you
hunting with me one of these days. I know all the best spots."

"A good idea," Price said, feeling as though he were about to vomit
again.

Kao drank some more, his huge, black, wide-open eyes staring at the
Elephant Range in the distance.

"I've been in the army for years and years now," he said. "And there's
never been any sort of war. Cambodia has always been at peace. Do you
think that things are maybe going to change? This is better than hunting
anyway. Lots better."

2

"AT THE BEGINNING OF THE NINTH CENTURY, KING JAYAVARMAN II ES-
tablished, or to be more precise, reestablished royal hegemony over all of
Cambodia," Charles Korver said. "He died in the year 854. On about the
seventeenth of July, at approximately two fifty-two P.M., local time. But he
wasn't the one who built Angkor. Since he was a decent sort, he left that
glory for his successors to enjoy."

"I honestly couldn't care less," Lisa said.

She contemplated her bulging belly and was horrified. *I look like an ei-
derdown.* And she was dying of the heat despite the air coming in through
the open window of the Land-Rover. Bê, the Korvers' Vietnamese chauffeur, was at the wheel, and Charles and Madeleine were sitting in the back
seat, gently waving straw fans in front of their faces. The car was going
along very slowly, its engine nearly silent, swerving mildly from time to
time to avoid bumps in the ill-paved road which the rains cut ever-deeper
gullies in each year. Now and again a branch lower than the others lashed
against a door, setting it to vibrating. Stifling air seemed to rise from the
ground, bringing with it whiffs of damp rot and moss, masked the next second by the powerful odor of stone heated white-hot. The light, too, changed
drastically from one moment to the next: at times sea-green, as though they
were underwater in an aquarium, it would suddenly take on a yellow

tinge and then brighten to a blinding, acid white as they passed, from beneath the heavy cover overhead, into a clearing.

Madeleine Korver leaned forward and put her little hand on Lisa's shoulder. "Are you all right?"

"Yes, let's go on," Lisa said.

This was her third visit to Angkor. The other two had been with Lara, the first one at the end of July the year before. They had wandered about among the temples together in a pouring rain, big fat drops, incredibly warm and pleasant, that made the black paving stones of the great high road of Angkor Wat glisten and hid the fleecy tops of the trees in a violet haze. She remembered a bare-naked little boy, clutching his sandals and his sarong which he had taken off to keep them from getting soaked through, running over the paving stones with a burst of joyous laughter. She also remembered the two young monks with impassive faces and haughty air, awaiting the hypothetical end of the rainstorm, their saffron-colored robes lighting up the darkness of the gallery where they had taken refuge. She remembered, too, the dizzying climb up the steep flights of steps, many of them eaten away, where it was better not to look at the abyss opening up behind them as they clambered higher and higher, and their aimless strolls amid stones that had crumbled away or were still intact.

They had shared an obstinate determination to make not the slightest attempt to learn who had built what, or when and how and why, but simply to enjoy being in this dead city besieged by the jungle, welcoming even the constant rain as an ally because it discouraged ordinary tourists and thus gave them the feeling that the place was theirs alone to explore. They had scrupulously walked all around the three concentric enclosures of Angkor Wat, had peered into the semidarkness of each gallery and room where countless statues lay, often mutilated, with hauntingly beautiful blind eyes and frozen smiles. As the rain beat endlessly down, they had spent entire days wandering along the trails that linked one temple to another, had climbed the pyramids of Pre Rup, of Phnom Bakong, and of Phimeanakas, and ridden the great stone horse of Neak Prean. Lisa had kissed the Leper King on the lips before creeping through the narrow passageway leading to the Elephant Terrace, then bent over to thread her way through the series of alternating dark and light doors of Prah Khan at Angkor, where dark clouds of bats hung suspended from each ceiling like harmless, quivering vampires waiting for nightfall.

"There's nothing in the world like Angkor," Lara said. "Greek monuments and medieval cathedrals speak to your mind. Angkor reaches out to touch your skin and your blood. Angkor is something you breathe in with your body as well as see with your eyes."

They had come back again at the end of October, this time beneath a sun that never stopped shining and an ultramarine blue sky. They had stayed in the same modest room at the Auberge des Temples as before, and rediscovered the same familiar elephant that knocked on their shutter with his trunk each morning, begging for a share of their warm breakfast brioches with a pleading look in his tiny eyes.

"I can see that you find my background lecture absolutely fascinating," Charles said. "I sense you are hanging upon my every word, panting with suspense. I've always had amazing talents as a storyteller. After Jayavarman II there was another king, and then yet another, the great Yaçovarman who built the first city of Angkor, in the form of a square whose sides measured four kilometers. At that time, the kingdom of Cambodia extended almost to Yunnan in China and to Burma. It was during Yaçovarman's reign, and after him, for two centuries, that the temples began to be built in ever-increasing numbers, over an area of dozens of kilometers, at a time when in Paris they were building Notre-Dame. It would take ten years to really know all of them, a century and all the gold of the Great Mogul to restore them, for as soon as you've put one stone back on top of another and turned your back for a moment, the jungle creeps in and starts devouring everything all over again."

"He gets on your nerves, doesn't he?" Madeleine said to Lisa. "And he could go on like this for weeks, night and day. That's why I married him. I've always liked background noises that allow you to pursue your own thoughts as you please."

Coming from the Grand Hotel in Siem Reap, where the Korvers always stayed when visiting Angkor, rather than the much too new Auberge des Temples, the Land-Rover had skirted the southern edge of Angkor Wat and headed for the eastern *barai*—a huge reservoir that had once been seven kilometers long and two kilometers wide, where the land had gradually reasserted its rights and encroached upon the waters of the basin.

"Have you seen Ta Prohm?" Charles asked.

"Yes, in October."

Of all the temples of Angkor, Ta Prohm, built around 1180, was perhaps the one that had most impressed Lisa. A hundred years before, in 1868, the sailors under a French lieutenant-commander named Delaporte had been terrified by what they took to be incredibly huge snakes: the gigantic white roots of kapok trees over 130 feet high, which over the centuries had pierced, overgrown, or toppled stone walls weighing many tons, and then run freely along the ground for a distance of sometimes twenty or thirty yards, in an unreal sea-green light like that of an ocean bottom many fathoms deep. At Ta Prohm, the archaeologists of the École Française d'Extrême-Orient had not tried, as they had everywhere else, to fight against the irresistible invasion of the jungle, first of all because nowhere else had this sort of giant milk-colored octopus so completely taken over the stone, so enveloping in its tentacles a five-hundred-foot-long building that the labor of rooting them out would have been colossal; and secondly because they had decided to leave Ta Prohm as a dramatic example of the terrible grip of the forest, of that fantastic and irrepressible digestion that the jungle unendingly engaged in.

"In that case, it seems pointless to go out of our way to visit it. It would be better if we headed directly for Bantéay Sreï."

"I apologize," Lisa said. "But I'd like to go back to the hotel."

Madeleine leaned forward again, put her arms around Lisa, and kissed her. "An excellent idea," she said. "It's so hot and I didn't dare ask my ogre of a husband myself."

"We're heading back, Bê," said the ogre, who weighed at most a little over a hundred pounds.

They went back by way of the Gate of the Dead at Angkor Thom. Charles Korver had begun his lecture again, his eyes fixed on Lisa's face, or at least on what he could glimpse of it from the back seat, overwhelmed as always by the beauty of this young woman, and talking mostly to fill a silence that had become decidedly too oppressive.

"Angkor died a first time in 1177, following an attack by the Chams, a mixed breed of Indonesians who had settled on the coast of Annam. The Chams arrived by sea, via the Gulf of Siam, and plunged Cambodia into a sea of troubles, according to the chronicles. But the Khmers were not really vanquished, not yet: Under the leadership of one of their princes, they took refuge in their traditional hideout, the forest. And they emerged from it four years later, driving out the invaders, reconstructing dikes, ponds, and fountains, rebuilding temples, reopening the pilgrimage route, that Royal Way so dear to the heart of André Malraux. The prince who led them became King Jayavarman VII. He's the Louis XIV and the Queen Victoria of Cambodia. You've seen, of course, the statue of the Leper King? Well, that's him. Or perhaps it is."

The Land-Rover was heading for Siem Reap.

"Jayavarman VII reigned for many years. After him, total collapse. A gradual one. The baraïs filled up with land, the dikes fell into ruin, the hydraulic system clogged up. The city of a million people, famous even in far-off China, was finally and definitely deserted by its last inhabitants when the region was overrun by Thais, invaders from South China. In the fifteenth century, the story was ended. Though he was crowned at Angkor, the last king of this era preferred to establish his capital at the junction of the Tonle Sap and the Mekong. And he, or one of his successors, was murdered by mistake by a gardener. Like the Great Inca, the God-Kings of Angkor vanished in the night of time. Angkor was dead."

The car stopped in front of the Grand Hotel.

"Come on," Madeleine said to Lisa. "He can go on talking to himself. Let's pretend we don't know him. Come and lie down."

"Dead forevermore," Charles said, sitting quietly in the back seat. "It's a sad story, terribly sad. And it's a true one."

Lisa smiled at him. "You're a marvelous storyteller," she said.

"I always knew I was," Charles said gloomily.

The downstairs floor of the Grand Hotel in Siem Reap was made up of enormous formal rooms with great high ceilings lost in shadow. The lobby was decorated with repoussé work, achieved by applying sheets of rice paper on top of inked bas-reliefs and then gently tapping them with mallets, and by reproductions of statues. The most pleasant spot was the bar, whose massive counter of carved wood resembled a slightly flamboyant Gothic altarpiece; it ordinarily hid from sight a tiny bartender, who trotted back and forth behind it like an old rat, suddenly popping up when one had given up expecting him ever to appear or else reaching up over his head to hand you your glass, so that it seemed to be coming up out of the floor. At the slightest signal, six or seven hotel boys revealed their presence behind the armchairs where they were hiding, most likely taking a little nap. They took your order with a visibly interested air and then disappeared again, apparently to be dispatched on unknown missions that kept them from reappearing.

"I'm so sorry," Lisa said as she sat down on the bed in her room. "I've kept you from driving on to Bantéay Sreï."

"My dear child, we've visited Bantéay Sreï between thirty and forty times before, if my calculations are correct. Even though we adore those stones, the prospect of seeing them yet another time doesn't make us exactly feverish with excitement. Lie down and stretch out all the way.... No, wait, you're dripping with sweat. Take your shower first, a warm one please, and then come lie down. Don't look at me with your big eyes like that. I know you're bad-tempered. Come on now! Where does it hurt? Your back? That's from the ride in the car. Come on, on your feet."

Madeleine helped her get undressed, then literally pushed her under the shower and regulated the temperature of the water herself. Then she sat down in one of the armchairs on the balcony, making sure she could still see Lisa from there, smiling at her every now and again with that graceful way she had of cocking her head to one side, like a bird. Only after Lisa had come back to her bed did Madeleine come back into the room.

"Well, then. In a little while you're going to try to sleep till dinner time. Turn over on your side; I'm going to massage you."

She began kneading Lisa's back with surprisingly strong fingers.

"I've always dreamed of being one of those special masseuses who do all kinds of things to men, in Bangkok. I wanted to practice on Charles, but he'd have none of it, claiming that all I was managing to do was tickle him. You're laughing!"

Madeleine stopped for a moment and went over to turn off the ceiling fan. "I detest those things that go round and round and give you bronchial pneumonia. And I can't bear those awful air-conditioners either. Do you feel better now?"

Lisa flopped over onto her back. "Yes."

Madeleine covered her with a sheet. "What a belly!" she said. "The baby's surely going to be a giant."

Lisa began to cry.

"Well, it's about time!" Madeleine exclaimed. "Poor Charles didn't know what else to say, there in the car."

A silence. Then the little old lady asked, "How long since you last saw him?"

"Twelve days."

"Did he tell you where he was going?"

"No."

"He never says anything. That's how he is. He's always been like that. Did you two have a fight?"

"No . . ."

She had all too obviously hesitated before answering.

"A lovers' quarrel? Though you're not the type for that sort of thing, either of you. You're not children anymore. The two of you have equally nasty tempers however. You don't have to answer my questions."

"I hate that plantation," Lisa burst out, in such a vehement tone of voice that it surprised even her.

"Ah, so that's it," Madeleine said.

Her little hand flitted about amid her blue locks. There was one very striking thing about Madeleine Korver: her bright, lively blue eyes. They were young eyes in the face of an old doll.

"I could say all sorts of things to you," she went on. "What one usually says in such cases: that you knew what the plantation means to him, above all what this country means to him, the way he lived before he knew you, and the impossibility of ever changing him. Just for examples."

Her eyes gleamed. "You don't think he's taken up with another woman, do you?"

"No, no."

Madeleine nodded her head. "That's already a big point in your favor. And I can tell you something else: Lara's no ordinary man. But you already knew that too. Otherwise you wouldn't have come all the way from the United States. You wouldn't have stayed on here to marry him. You could have married that nice, amusing Thomas Aquinas O'Malley, who would have worshiped you like a saint in a niche all the rest of his life. You chose Lara instead, and you're mad about him, just as he's mad about you. Yes, that's true, and you know it. You didn't marry him on a sudden whim; you're much too sensible for that. You thought things over carefully, calmly, coldly. You wanted him and you were ready to do anything to get him. I'm certain you make love wonderfully well, both of you, wildly and tenderly.

My god; my dream woman! And don't look at me as though your violet eyes were a pair of dueling pistols. Well then, what else is wrong? You're afraid for him? You're mad. Nothing can happen to him. What do you expect him to do? Burn his plantation down and chop down his rubber trees one by one so as to go off fishing for salmon trout in Colorado? That's insane. Lara without Cambodia would no longer be Lara."

Madeleine opened her eyes wide, staring into space with a puzzled expression. "That's odd: Charles and I have always called him Lara. Never by his first name . . . And yet you can be sure that we love him too. . . ."

She stood up, joined her two hands, fingers pressed tightly together. "I'm going to tell you what you're going to do: You're going to sleep for an hour or two. Then after that you're going to push your big belly in front of you to the dining room and we're going to drink a vintage Bordeaux that we had shipped specially from France and that probably won't have any bouquet in this heat."

She leaned down and kissed Lisa. "Lisa, he'll be back, with the tired look of a very thin cat who's a night prowler, affectionate and tough, that touching look we know so well and that melts our hearts. You'll take him to your bosom—the Good Lord knows it's ample enough at the moment—and you'll console him for being so worn out. I even bet that it'll be you who'll make love to him. Go on, sleep. We're at Siem Reap for a few days. He knows that and he'll come join us here sooner or later and he'll find you ravishingly beautiful. What's more, you are. Just look at yourself in a mirror."

With those words she left, gently closing the door behind her.

3   FOR FIVE DAYS NOW, THEY HADN'T SEEN ANOTHER HUMAN BEING; they had walked for miles through a forest that was deserted and yet teeming with life. In these five days they had come across every possible species of animal, as though the jungle were determined to present them with a sample or two of each of its products. They had seen civet cats with silver coats and black stripes holding their big bushy tails haughtily erect; lazy, self-assured badgers; porcupines and gleaming gold cock-pheasants; iguanas drowsing on a rock, just above buffalo toads; crested chameleons, motionless as stones, suddenly coming to life and snapping up a dragonfly; and wild boar and deer of all sizes, some of them miniature species scarcely bigger than newborn roe deer, though full-grown adults. They had even spotted a tiger and two panthers, had kept clear of elephants and gaurs—enormous dark-colored buffalo with huge horns and curious white feet, as though they were wearing socks—and kept clear above all of the countless snakes, among them an absolutely superb royal cobra over twelve feet long. And Lara had rediscovered forgotten sensations, dating back fifteen years, from the time when he still went hunting.

By a change in Kutchaï's demeanor, a certain relaxation of the tension he had given signs of up till then, Lara intuited that his companion was experiencing the same flood of memories suddenly returning, the same nostalgia. The Khmer smiled at him. "They make your trigger finger itch, right?"

Lara nodded.

"Gleat white hunter back on tlail of gleat wild beasts to kill."

"Idiot."

A quarter of an hour earlier, they had hesitated as to whether or not to halt in a little clearing, curiously centered around an old tree stump on which strikingly beautiful wild orchids were growing. A little stream close by would have provided them with water. But precisely because of this little stream, they had hoped to find an even better spot and had gone on, following the current. The forest offered them proof that they had made the right choice by bringing them the sound of a waterfall, which they came upon some hundred yards farther on. The water fell six to ten feet after flowing through a jumble of huge blocks of pink granite; it formed a natural, limpid basin below, its surface covered with a delicate, almost crystalline moss. On one side of the basin, a lovely little sandy beach had slowly formed, sloping gently upward to a first screen of bamboos and high grasses marking the edge of the forest.

"There wouldn't be much point in going any farther," Kutchaï said. "We'd be hard put to it to find a better spot. And they'll find us here just as easily as they would anywhere else."

As proof of his firm intention not to go a step farther, he removed the ranger boots he was wearing without socks and his duck pants and delightedly plunged his huge toes in the water of the basin. The afternoon was drawing to a close. As always at that hour, there was a sort of throbbing in the air, a progressive acceleration of sounds and their rhythm, as though the entire jungle were gathering together, tuning up for a last concert before nightfall.

After leaving the plantation, Lara and Kutchaï had gone first to Stung Treng, where they had found a nervous garrison, the men huddled together within its walls plainly convinced in advance that there was no point in defending it if it became the object of a really determined attack. They had asked Lara and Kutchaï no questions, and had viewed their departure with the same gloomy indifference.

The two of them had next reached the colonization center of Kantuy Ko, where nine months earlier buses rented from Chinese by the minister in charge of the Plan had deposited—amid countless patriotic anthems and ministerial speeches—several dozen families who had arrived either from Cochin China or from the provinces of the South. These families had been persuaded, with the greatest of difficulty, to come settle in the North by the promise of monthly allotments that amounted to more than they were earning at the time: six hundred riels for a bachelor, a thousand for a family with three children. A promise which, as usual, had very soon ceased to be kept, the bureaucrats in charge of distributing the allotments having preferred to spare themselves the trouble of handing them out. For a year or two the thirty or forty men who had suddenly found themselves woodcutters had conscientiously supplied the brand-new sawmill with logs, and had continued to do so even when the machines of the sawmill had been sold on the sly by their director. The director had then hastened back to Phnom Penh, where one could at least live in a civilized manner, and where, incidentally, luck had turned against him: He had lost all his money at the gaming tables of the casino that Samdech-Father had generously offered his people. In a manner of speaking, the government had robbed the robber who had robbed it.

From Kantuy Ko, Kutchaï and Lara had headed northeast. A Chinese merchant had transported them to the little settlement of Voeune Saï, where they had gathered the first intelligence that they needed. On the five following days, they had gone deep into the jungle, more or less following the line of successive mountain crests, sometimes in Laotian territory, sometimes in Cambodia, feeling the ground tremble beneath their feet every so often as, thirty or forty kilometers away, the giant fleets of American B-52's dumped their thousands of tons of bombs and napalm on the countryside.

"Are you hungry?"

"No."

The smoke from Lara's cigarette rose straight up in the dead-still, stifling air. He had sat down on a rock with his back leaning against another, indifferently aware of the presence close at hand of a snake which he couldn't see but could hear softly hissing in a nearby cleft in the rocks. He seemed thinner than usual, perhaps because he hadn't shaved since they'd left Voeune Saï.

Kutchaï was stretched out in the water, moving about very slowly, careful to make not the slightest splash. Suddenly he stopped moving altogether, and his eyes sought Lara's.

Lara nodded.

"We've been spotted, my brother," Kutchaï said.

He came out of the water and got dressed again. An entire hour went by, however, before they discerned, above the hiss of the waterfall, the first distinct sounds of several men approaching.

There were about twenty of them, Braos and Jaraïs, several of them stark naked, some dressed only in blue loincloths and wearing around their foreheads red and black headbands studded with little pearls, exactly like the ones they made their necklaces and bracelets of. The group included five or six women serving, as usual, as beasts of burden, carrying their traditional beautifully woven baskets with a pattern of alternating black and fawn-colored squares. For centuries these baskets had been used to transport opium or rice, but these contained chargers for assault rifles. In like fashion, their companions—who ten years earlier would have been equipped with spears or crossbows or even those curious rifles with very long barrels manufactured in their jungle forges—were now armed with Kalashnikovs.

Lara left it up to Kutchaï to conduct the negotiations, though his knowledge of the dialect they were speaking permitted him to follow all the ins and outs of the long-drawn-out conversation. They finally came to an agreement. They would all leave together at dawn, since night was now falling. They drank bitter black tea through clenched teeth, as custom dictated, accompanied by a bit of rice that had the green taste so characteristic of dry rice fields in the mountains, wrested from the forest by carefully setting fire to little patches of it.

The next morning, after four hours of marching on the double, they arrived at a village whose inhabitants had strained their ingenuity to make it invisible from overhead, scattering the huts about beneath the palms and banana trees so that they could not be spotted by American helicopters coming over from the Plain of Jars (which had been retaken from the Pathet Lao and the North Vietnamese during the offensive of September 1969).

On spying the first dwellings on pilings, Lara and Kutchaï had the impression that they were more or less uninhabited. It was not until they were almost on top of them that they realized that the village was in fact a veritable entrenched camp, around which many times more than the traditional number of *chamrongs*—traps consisting of sharp-pointed bamboo stakes smeared with poison—had been set out. Even more importantly, several hundred combatants, uniformly dressed in black and nearly all of them wearing scarves with little red and white squares, were billeted in the village.

Ieng Samboth came out to meet them.

"There were easier ways to join me," Ieng said. "And I might not even have been here. Two months ago I was around Kratie. In October I returned to Pursat. I travel freely these days, from one end of Cambodia to the other. We have friends and collaborators everywhere. The Phnom Penh army is just barely able to direct traffic on the Boulevard Norodom and to extort money from the pedicab operators."

"I've found you nonetheless."

Ieng nodded his head, stared inquisitively at Lara, and as the minutes went by, the warm glow of friendship appeared once again in his dark eyes.

"I've never thanked you for your help last year when I was wounded."

"How is your leg wound?"

"A mere memory. How's Oreste?"

"He's all right."

The truth was, however, that old Oreste had changed. It was not so much that he was suffering from physical aftereffects of his abdominal wound, for he had recovered from it completely. But something had happened to the Corsican: he had lost a lot of weight too fast and the skin over his powerful muscles had become loose and wrinkled. Lara had twice seen him so drunk he'd passed out—which had never happened before despite the enormous quantities of beer Marccaggi regularly downed.

Ieng's eyes met Kutchaï's and he read the unspoken question in them.

"Rath isn't here," Ieng said. "He has his own group and operates on the other side of the Mekong, to the east of Kompong Thom. Just forget that he exists."

"Okay," Kutchaï said, laughing his great silent laugh. "I'm just going to forget him once and for all. That's precisely what I'm going to do."

His bloodshot eyes gleamed fiercely. Ieng shrugged and turned back to Lara.

"I know why you chose to come all this way, even though it would have been easier to get a message through to me: You wanted to prove to yourself that there's nowhere in Cambodia you, Lara, can't go. You're proving this country is still yours and always will be."

"Right you are," Lara said impassively. He stared thoughtfully at the lighted end of his cigarette. At length, he raised his eyelids and his pale eyes stared at the Khmer Rouge leader.

"Do you want those arms? Yes or no?"

"What reason would you have to furnish me with weapons?"

"Because you need them. I know that Hanoi is refusing to arm you Khmer Rouge. Hanoi doesn't want anything to do with you, nor Moscow either. Hanoi and Moscow want Cambodians who are at their beck and call, the way Souphanouvong's Pathet Lao are in Laos. And I don't think you're at anybody's beck and call. Not you personally at any rate."

"Almost all the Occidentals in Cambodia are probably ready to accept a Lon Nol regime," Ieng·said. "If Lon Nol and·Sirik Matak succeed in eliminating Sihanouk, the system they set up ought to please the Whites a lot. Banks and middlemen have already been given free rein. Lon Nol and Sirik Matak will go even further than that. And a Cambodia where baksheesh is the ruling·principle has something to please just about everyone: It's picturesque, it's profitable, and it's amusing."

"I'm not an Occidental in Cambodia," Lara said in a soft voice, with eyes closed.

"But you're a White."

Ieng was disconcerted by the look Lara gave him. Unable to bear it, overcome with emotion in his turn, he rose to his feet, paced slowly around the hut, whose black wooden partitions still gave off the powerful, persistent odor of the opium that had been stored there for years and years. For a long moment Ieng contemplated the spectacle of the camp, all the men he had brought together under his command and to whom he would one day give the order for the final attack. If the day ever came for a final attack.

There had been a time when the smallest gathering of Cambodians immediately became an excuse for singing, music-making, retelling traditional tales, merrymaking. On the slightest pretext, the tiniest village in the forest or the mountains could get together some sort of orchestra, the instruments varying from region to region—hurdy-gurdies, *tro ou* with two or three silk strings strung across a sound box made of a simple hollowed-out coconut shell, lutes or flutes, *roneats,* Indian xylophones, Takhe or Chapey guitars, all accompanied by the cymbals and the clear-toned transverse horns typical of the peoples of the forest.

But these black-garbed Khmers that Ieng could see before him spoke little and did not sing. They had not even one guitar among them. They were another Cambodia, a new one, perhaps the Cambodia that everyone had thought dead for centuries, now coming back to life, awakening from its slumbers and re-creating itself in the forest. Perhaps. On certain days, Ieng's imagination was fired and he was ready to believe in this renaissance. But not at the present moment. *Perhaps we're merely in the process of creating a monster.* Through an association of ideas he couldn't possibly have explained, his thoughts took him back to France, and street names, cafés, meetings surged up out of the depths of his memory, along with the recollection of wildly impassioned discussions in that little hotel room on the Rue de l'Estrapade, where that French friend of his had taken him in for such a long time. All that was so far away....

He waited till his eyes were no longer clouded with emotion and then came back and sat down opposite Lara.

"All right then," he said. "It's true that I need those arms. More than I need anything else. How are you going to go about getting them?"

"Christiani in Bangkok."

"He's in a position to furnish arms?"

"Yes."

"And who's going to pay for them?"

"I am."

"You aren't that rich."

Lara shrugged. A silence. Ieng glanced at Kutchaï, who hadn't turned a hair, as though the conversation had nothing to do with him.

"What I need most are individual weapons. Seven-six-two caliber."

"Russian and Czech ones. But Austrian ones as well. Whatever we can turn up."

Ieng thought for a moment. He unfolded a map and spread it out on the floor of the hut. "Look. Here, approximately halfway between the headwaters of the Stung Sangker and the headwaters of the Stung Tamyong. It's a spot way off in the mountains."

"I know it."

"I know you do."

Images of hunting expeditions returned to mind: years and years before, with Lara and Kutchaï; he, Ieng, being the least able to endure physical hardships, the least resourceful, the worst shot of the trio. Images of sleeping in the open in the moonlight after all-day hikes in the gentle, endless rain of the Cardamomes.

"You follow the border," Ieng said. "Straight south-southwest. To here, to this point on the coast. If Christiani can bring the arms there, I'll have men there to get them."

"They'll have to go through Thai territory, both going and coming."

"That's my problem, not yours."

At the spot Ieng was pointing to, the Cambodian border lay barely a dozen kilometers from the coast of the Gulf of Siam, separated from it by a narrow tongue of land that belonged to Thailand and ran parallel to the foot of the Cardamome Range for almost seventy kilometers.

"I want to try to get together all the money I can lay my hands on," Ieng said. "Even if it means holding up banks"—he suppressed a smile—"or at any event holding Chinese up for ransom. There's no reason for you to ruin yourself financially. When do you think Christiani could be ready?"

"Not before the fifteenth of March. At the very earliest."

Another silence.

"When do you want to leave here?"

"Just as soon as possible," Lara said.

Ieng shook his head. "Not today though. There are North Vietnamese detachments moving up from south to north. At the moment, they're between the Mekong and us. The Viet Cong aren't fools. They've found out what's happening in Phnom Penh or what's about to happen, just as we have, and they know very well that if Cambodia were to cease to be neutral and side with Saigon, what American journalists call the Sanctuary would no longer be one. And so they're pulling out, or beginning to. They've been on the move for nearly ten days now."

He smiled. "Sell that information when you get back to Phnom Penh."

"I'll consider it."

"If you wanted to go back the same way you came, you and Kutchaï, you'd be certain to run into their advance patrols, or you'd find yourselves getting napalmed by the Americans, who spray anything that moves. I'll get you through tomorrow, or day after tomorrow."

❂   ❂   ❂

The day that followed was strange, and remained engraved on Kutchaï's memory. He for his part spent it without ever really going far from the hut where Ieng Samboth had set up his command post, stepping out of it, so as not to appear to be eavesdropping, only when the guerrilla chief's aides came in to consult with him. While he did exchange a few words with some of the men quartered nearby, it was only because they too were Jaraïs, though a whole world now separated them. He didn't ask them a single question, not even about Ouk, his own brother; nonetheless he learned that Ouk was farther south at the moment, near the former Deshayes post. In the final analysis, what most amazed the men he spoke with was his height, really extraordinary for a Jaraï, especially in view of the fact that he was four inches taller than his younger brother, himself a good six feet four.

But Kutchaï's mind was elsewhere. His attention did not wander for a single instant from Lara, who with touching persistence eagerly made the rounds of the entire camp as though nothing or no one could have possibly convinced him he was out of place there. Lara walked among the various groups of guerrilla fighters, sometimes recognizing a face or a particular local accent or remembering a name, whereupon he would smilingly strike up a conversation, in the most natural way in the world, the warmth of his smile and his perfect mastery of Khmer compelling the man thus addressed to answer him. And he got results, managing to create a certain immediate rapport with the men, or at least an air of cordial good feeling, and at times even provoking outright smiles and laughter. Who else, Kutchaï thought, would be capable of doing what he's doing?

Lara would join a group, squat down on his haunches, and say to one of them: "You there, you're from Kompong Cham. I've met your father and your elder brother." And he would go into detail in his slow, grave voice, in perfect local Khmer dialect that even Kutchaï was not able to speak that fluently. With another man, who was from the province of Kratie, he spoke of a *bikkhu*, a bonze who had long been a teacher at the local Buddhist school and a friend of his. "I was there the day they cremated him. He was my friend and I was honor bound to be there. You were there too." The man nodded, remembering now the Barang who had traveled halfway across the country just to attend the cremation of an old bonze who was completely unknown outside the borders of his province.

Or else he recalled a soccer match he had taken part in some years before, played barefoot on a day so stifling hot it made you pant for breath, and he mentioned the players on both teams by name—Kim Samith for instance, who had had the makings of a world-class star and would perhaps have become one if he hadn't been as lazy as a sated python.

He also told the story of a certain provincial governor, an old Issarak leader who had eventually rallied to Sihanouk's cause but had nonetheless kept at his side his faithful followers from the time of the guerrilla campaigns against Samdech. The governor was a fanatic soccer fan. He had formed a team, personally choosing each of the players, from the goalie to the center forward. He witnessed all the matches from his very own dismountable box, with room for only one spectator, that by his order was transported from one playing field to another, and he solemnly warned each player that he would personally settle the fate of anyone who turned in a bad performance. A warning that rightly struck terror into the hearts of the team: A penalty kick that failed to score was worth a hundred lashes, and it was even rumored, though there was no definite proof of the story, that he had a goalie beheaded with one saber blow because the man had had the misfortune to see the ball sail past under his belly as he dived for it, thus causing his teammates to lose the match. (One thing was certain: The goalie in question had disappeared from the scene overnight, though he had perhaps simply emigrated to Brazil.) And any forward who failed to score a goal he apparently couldn't possibly miss ran immediately to the goal line and knelt down in front of the governor/chief-referee/trainer/team-manager all rolled into one seated on his throne-tribunal and smote the ground with his forehead in terror that was not feigned.

The men all laughed as they listened to Lara. That was the sort of story Cambodians loved to tell of an evening, at once tragic and funny, full of the aggressive black humor that betrayed the ever-latent violence of the Cambodian people, the humor and violence that so disconcerted the Vietnamese and the Thais, for example, despite the fact that they far outnumbered the Khmers.

Joining another group, who at first greeted him with cold or averted eyes, Lara spoke of the slow, meticulous, absorbing labor of cultivating the irrigated rice paddies, of the necessary endless treading of men and water buffaloes in the ocher, almost burning-hot waters of the rice field beneath a sun of molten lead, of the seasonal round of the monsoons, of waiting for the rains, of the furtive miracle of the Mango Rain, of the reversal of the currents of the Tonle Sap, of that other recurrent miracle of green stems at last emerging, of the fragrant scent of mangoes, of the drunken orgies brought on by drinking palm wine once the day's work was over. And to Braos just barely emerged from the Stone Age, he spoke in their own dialect of communal hunts, their tracking of a man-eating tiger for many long days and nights, the rush for the spoils that followed the kill, the death of a monstrous python that had settled down as a squatter in the refuse of their village, or that of an old elephant that had gone mad.

Kutchaï knew Lara too well to believe for a single moment that he was putting on an act, that, as the French expression had it, he was "doing a number." Though at first it wrung his heart to witness an effort he thought doomed to failure, Kutchaï found himself little by little becoming spellbound too, and rediscovered at one and the same time the passionate love this country of his could inspire, and a friendship bordering on tender affection, stronger than ever, for Lara, whose faith he began to share then and there.

"So you're going to Siem Reap? What route will you take to get there?"

"I'll go by way of the plantation," Lara answered.

He and Ieng exchanged a long look, and Kutchaï had a foreboding that things were going to go sour once again. He expected them to have a bitter fight. He had seen how Lara had acted all during the day and he could guess how much new strength Lara had drawn from his conversations with the men in the camp, how much his faith in himself had been renewed. But there was no fight, merely an apparently polite, almost academic discussion, to which Kutchaï attached little importance at the time.

"Do you hold it against me that I own that plantation?" Lara asked Ieng calmly.

"Certainly much less, a hundred times less, than I hold it against those who carved out Chhuup, Mimot, and others, or against the Terres Rouges d'Indochine, or against the bank of the same name."

Night had now fallen on the camp, where, despite the presence of several hundred men, there were very few fires, two or three at most, so that it looked like no more than a simple open-air encampment of a little group of mountain dwellers, or perhaps a tiny village.

"I'm not the only owner of the plantation," Lara said. "It's as much Kutchaï's as it is mine. And don't talk to me about written evidence of our joint ownership."

"I know." Ieng smiled. "I know how close you and your latex collectors are. And I know above all that anybody would have to be crazy to try to come between you and Kutchaï."

"Kutchaï miselable Khmer wletch. Kutchaï velly lich lubber pranter," the Jaraï said in a feeble effort to ease the tension.

But Lara's eyes never left Ieng. "What is it you hold against me, then?"

Ieng shook his head. "Let's talk about something else."

"There are very few things in the world that interest me as much," Lara said, in the same calm voice.

Now that it was dark, the odor left in the room long ago by the opium had become stronger, a sickly-sweet, persistent smell.

"Colonization," Ieng said. He stretched out one hand and, without even removing the package from the breast pocket of Lara's bush jacket, fished a cigarette out of it. "Why not talk about colonization, for example? I know your theory on the subject: Colonization is simply a matter of power relations, and the situation might well have been the reverse. The Javanese might have colonized Flanders or the Rhine Valley, just as the Dutch colonized Indonesia. Perhaps so. But that in fact didn't happen, and on a global scale the consequences are quite clear: In every case the best lands have been confiscated from the native people who worked them so as to pave the way for the monoculture of products for export that were indispensable to the economy of the colonizing countries. And a country reduced to monoculture is a country doomed to be permanently blackmailed. Its independence is illusory."

"You've always like playing around with words," said Lara. "You're reciting to me from a book."

"Books are sometimes right."

"Talking about Cambodia in terms of a monoculture of hevea is idiotic."

"I'm not talking of hevea in particular, nor of Cambodia in particular either. But rubber trees are symbols. Even yours. After all, before the arrival of the French, the English, the Dutch, there wasn't a single hevea in all of Asia."

Kutchaï became aware of a slight buzzing in the air, like an angry swarm of bees slowly drawing closer. Of the three men on the wooden steps of the hut, he was the only one—or at any rate the first—to hear it, doubtless because he was not involved in the conversation his two companions were having.

"I don't give a damn about what's happened in Africa, in South America, or anywhere else," Lara said. "I don't give a damn about Western civilization, just as I don't give a damn about symbols. This country is not any more yours than it is mine merely because your ancestors arrived here before mine did."

"At least twenty centuries before," Ieng remarked. "Surely that counts for something."

"And I don't want to be held accountable for something I didn't do, and that my father, my grandfather, or some ancestor even further back didn't do."

The sound like buzzing bees began to fill the air, and the floor and steps of the Moï hut began to vibrate. At that point both Lara and Ieng heard it too.

"Lara, the world has been White for four hundred years. You yourself wouldn't be here if that weren't so. Most likely you would never have come to Indochina. Willy-nilly, you were part of the wave. The development of White civilization, of its technology, was made possible only by raiding all the world's resources for the benefit of Whites only, by deflecting the normal development of what are known as the nonindustrialized countries. It's as though it were some sort of hereditary defect not to be industrialized. We've lagged behind Europe, the United States, the Soviet Union? Well, what of it? Maybe we've had good reason to lag behind. In any event, we had the right to. That's what your plantation means to me."

The buzzing gradually turned into a thundering roar, making even the ground and the trees in the forest tremble, to the point that any sort of conversation became impossible.

"B-52's!" Ieng cried, gazing up at them in wide-eyed amazement, a note in his voice that might well have been taken for sad self-satisfaction. "But they're not for us, Lara. Not yet anyway."

Lara and Kutchaï left the following morning before first light, escorted by a detachment of twenty men under orders to get them safely through to a spot on the Mekong a dozen kilometers north of the little settlement of Sambour, where the detachment was to see them across the river to the province of Stung Treng on the other side. Without needing to discuss the matter, neither Lara nor Kutchaï was taken in by this apparent solicitude: By thus providing them with an escort, Ieng was simply making certain they would not meet up with Rath. Ieng was convinced such a meeting would lead to bloodshed.

As a matter of fact, they did not meet.

4 "I'M GOING TO PLUNGE MY ALABASTER BODY BETWEEN THE LINENS," Roger Bouès said.

Thomas Aquinas O'Malley stared at him hesitantly. There were moments such as this when his mastery of the French language proved insufficient.

"Meaning?"

"I'm going to bed," Roger explained, with a certain hauteur.

The two men left the Zigzag bar, in the Rue Dekcho Damdin in Phnom Penh, together.

"I'll stand you a bowl of Chinese soup," O'Malley said.

He was quite sure that, as usual, Roger didn't have a cent in his pocket, though he was being careful to hide the fact. They sat down at a tiny table, which their knees kept bumping into, and exchanged friendly smiles with pedicab operators who were having their breakfast. "If anyone from the embassy sees me here, eating native food that definitely hasn't been sterilized and is doubtless infested with sneering amoebas with slanty eyes, they're going to ship me back to New York on the first hospital plane, claiming I've had a tropical sunstroke."

But the soup was delicious. The broth had the marvelous aroma that legend attributed to it, and the soybean sprouts were crisp and crunchy. "These amoebas deserve three Michelin stars." He smiled at Roger. "I've seen your latest photos at the Korvers'. You have real talent."

"I'm so full of talent that it makes even me a little sick," Roger replied. "I'm the most talented architect-photographer on this side of the Mekong. I said as much just the other day to my pedicab boy. He agreed with me, no doubt because he thought I was going to tip him."

"I'm serious. Have you ever thought of selling them?"

"My photos?" Roger's mouth gaped open in surprise, whereupon his right hand took advantage of the opportunity and stuffed it full of the transparent noodles and black mushrooms trapped between his chopsticks. "And to whom would I sell them, may I ask?"

"You haven't even tried."

"I have indeed, sir. You're wrong there."

"Come on. Indochina's very popular these days."

"Indochina at war. Not Cambodia. Who's going to pay good money for a photo of a Khmer peasant bent over double in a rice paddy or a bare-assed kid chewing on a sugar-cane stalk?"

O'Malley shook his head. "You're wrong, Roger. And what's more, I've never seen as many reporters trooping into Phnom Penh as I have in these last few months. Saigon is beginning to pall on the gentlemen of the press: too much noise, too many gasoline fumes in the streets, too many mutilated men brandishing hand grenades, too many kids begging, too many corpses, soldiers, whores. And too many articles. All the exoticism is gone."

Roger sat lost in thought.

"I can't promise you anything," O'Malley said. "But right offhand, I can think of two sorts of openings for you. The press first of all. I'd be vastly surprised if all those reporters disguised as paratroopers who keep coming around to bother me didn't need photos at one time or another. Moreover, I can contact agencies or wire services in the U.S. directly. That's the first solution. As for the second . . ."

"You're plastered to the gills," Roger said, laughing.

"I never get drunk. In fact, I don't drink—at least never between glasses. As for the second solution, I'm thinking more in terms of something for a publisher, a real book. Three years ago I collaborated on an art book on Degas. I know publishers in New York and California who'd be interested."

The truth of the matter was that he was making all this up as he went along, wondering at the same time how in the devil he was going to keep a promise that had been made in all sincerity. And then, so as to hide, or try to hide, his real aim, which was to give his friend a helping hand, he had the nerve to add: "Set your mind at rest. I'm acting out of pure selfishness. You're looking at the man who's going to write the text to go with the photos. I love getting royalty checks."

Indeed there was something miraculous—and at the same time inevitable, inescapable—about the fact that just a little while after that, at the end of January 1970 or the beginning of the following month, a whole bunch of Americans claiming to be journalists, a number of whom just happened to be the real article, turned up in Cambodia. Keeping his promise, Thomas Aquinas O'Malley put them in touch with Roger Bouès, whom he described as the best photographer there had ever been in all of Southeast Asia, with the result that the ex-architect was hired on the spot to accompany the new arrivals on their tour of the country, serving them as a guide and taking all the photos they needed.

One of these Americans told an English journalist and foreign correspondent named Donaldson—whose nickname was the Black Shadow despite the fact that he was a redhead—about Roger.

From that time on, and until the end, that was how Roger Bouès made his living, and he suddenly found himself the possessor of something that up until then he had known only by hearsay: money. He hastened to spend it with exuberant prodigality, offering monumental rounds of drinks in bars and renting the entire dining room of the Wa-Kuan, reputed to be the very best Chinese restaurant in Phnom Penh, for a Pantagruelian repast to which he invited at least sixty people, among them the Laras, the Korvers, O'Malley (who was in Saigon at the time and unable to come), and even his favorite pedicab operator, to whom he owed sixteen or seventeen years' worth of tips.

It was about this time that O'Malley met a compatriot of his who introduced himself as Price. And Thomas Aquinas suddenly tumbled to the reason for the unprecedented and growing journalistic interest in the little kingdom of Cambodia, which up until then had been more or less ignored by the big-name international reporters and correspondents.

From the first moment he laid eyes on him, O'Malley detested Price.

"You're Irish," Price said to him.

"No, I'm Spanish," was the answer immediately forthcoming from O'Malley, who regarded himself as American through and through. "Spanish, with Maltese ancestors."

But O'Malley's sarcasm slid off Price, off what was left of his strawberry-blond hair, off his sideburns and his pale blue eyes, like water off the proverbial duck's back.

"I've been told that you might be able to help me," Price went on with exasperating equanimity. "But naturally, everything I'm about to tell you is highly confidential. You must not mention our conversation, or any part of it, to anyone."

O'Malley smiled. "The door is behind you, on your left. You turn the handle to the right and it opens. It's a device I invented myself."

"I've been told that of all the American citizens in Cambodia at the present time, you are beyond a doubt the one who's established the best contacts with the autochthonous elements."

"With *what?*"

"With the natives."

"You mean those people who wear bones in their nostrils? I've never seen a one of them. They've all gone off to Hollywood, to play themselves in a movie."

It wasn't the best joke he'd ever made; it was even a pretty feeble one, but he had the satisfaction of seeing the man who called himself Price impatiently tap the arm of his chair with his fingertips.

"I'm talking about Cambodians," Price said. "You know more about them than any of our compatriots. We're expecting . . ."

"Who exactly do you mean by 'we'?"

"The government."

"Pleased to meet you," Thomas Aquinas said. "My name's O'Malley."

"We're expecting you to furnish us with a list of all the Khmers that you think are secretly anti-American, that you think are likely to oppose, by the use of violence or any other means, a modification of the Cambodian position vis-à-vis Hanoi and Saigon, of its abandonment of its present neutrality, of its membership in SEATO, the Southeast Asian Treaty Organization."

"You don't want a list of those opposed to contraception?"

"No," Price answered patiently. "Just the other things I've mentioned."

I detest these spies, whatever side they're on, whatever it is they're after, O'Malley thought to himself. *I could obviously hit this one over the head with a chair. But that wouldn't change anything. And besides, have you noticed what bulging arm muscles this guy's got? So that's what's up: They're getting ready to stage a coup d'état.* With regard to this prospect, he had no particular opinion. Politics interested him even less than non-Euclidian geometry.

"I know a Cambodian who's capable of doing everything you've mentioned. And even worse. As far as he's concerned, I'm absolutely certain. As for others, I'd have to give it some thought. But there's no doubt about this one. He'll oppose to his last dying breath any change in Cambodia's policy."

"Don't mention any name aloud," Price hastened to say. "Write it down on a piece of paper."

Thomas Aquinas wrote: "Norodom Sihanouk."

The expression on Price's face was nearly as well worth seeing as the sight of dawn breaking above the Brooklyn Bridge.

5 IN FEBRUARY, FOR THE FIRST TIME IN MONTHS AND EVEN YEARS, THE
loading and unloading of Soviet arms destined for the Viet Cong were interrupted.

In the course of an unofficial interview between the representatives of
Hanoi in Cambodia and those of the Sirik Matak government, the Cambodians explained that there were certain reasons, all of them excellent, for
this interruption. First, this supplying of arms and their transport across
Khmer soil obviously presented a serious threat to Cambodia's policy of
neutrality. Secondly, the reestablishment and strengthening of diplomatic
relations with the United States of America made it necessary to take certain precautions. And finally, with each passing day the convoys leaving
from Kompong Som were running a greater and greater risk of being attacked by bands of Khmer Rouge. After all, there had already been one such
attack, amid incredible carnage! The way the Khmer Rouge had massacred
the poor truck drivers before making off with all the arms! To run any further risk of allowing those mad Khmer Rouge to gather strength was simply
unthinkable.

On this point at least, Hanoi and the Cambodian right were in agreement, though to quite different degrees.

Moreover, for the entourage of Sirik Matak and Lon Nol (the latter had
just returned from Europe, where he had met and greeted Sihanouk in
Rome with all the marks of deepest respect), stopping arms and supplies
from reaching the Viet Cong had another merit above and beyond its polit-
ico-military advantages: It put an end to the juicy racket being carried on
by Sihanouk's wife and her clique. In short, it was another maneuver in the
gang war that brought to mind Chicago in the 1920's, when Bugs Moran
and Al Capone had fought it out.

But things did not go so far as to lead to another Saint Valentine's Day
Massacre in Phnom Penh. In the absence of the princess, who had gone off
with her husband to France, a campaign was launched against her two most
loyal supporters, the least faithful followers of Norodom Sihanouk in the
power spheres of the Khmer capital: Oum Mannorine and Sósthenes
Fernández, both quite capable of opposing the impending coup d'état by
force, since the former was head of the Provincial Guard and the latter the
head of police. As for the charges to be brought against them, their corruption was so well known that it was difficult to choose which of their malver-
sations to focus on. In the end it was decided to accuse them of smuggling, a
charge that in fact was true. (Just as it was also true that if all the high-

placed officials guilty of graft and dereliction of duty in the Phnom Penh of that time had had to be clapped into prison, there wouldn't have been much of anyone left to slam the doors shut on them.)

In February of 1970, the likes of Sirik Matak or Price could consider the situation satisfactory: The Provincial Guard and the police were now taking orders from them. There was no further danger of their doing battle with the army, which was under Lon Nol's control, nor with the gendarmerie, headed by Lon Non, his brother, who ran little risk of being overwhelmed by his own powers of intelligence. The flow through Kompong Som of arms for the Viet Cong had ceased. The Chinese merchants supplying them with rice had been brought into line, on occasion arrested but more often merely fined, yet at all events had stopped their deliveries. The members of the royal family suspected of fidelity to Sihanouk had been placed under house arrest. The ten thousand or so anti-Communist Khmer Krom and Khmer Sereï, who had been officially integrated into FARK, were on the move and, arriving for the most part from the province of Battambang or else directly from Thailand, were taking up positions around the capital. And finally, things were in hand in the National Assembly as well: Cheng Heng, who presided over it (with every qualification for so doing, having formerly been the warden of the state prison), personally vouched for the conduct of a chamber from which all the troublemakers had been expelled.

In short, everything was ready.

In addition to eliminating Oum Mannorine and Sósthenes Fernández, along with all their rich friends, the anti-corruption campaign audaciously launched by the anti-Sihanouk cabal had allowed its members to deliver themselves of their usual emphatic remarks when addressing the foreign press: They spoke of a restoration of law and order, of an economic revival, and in more guarded but nonetheless clear terms, of a new Cambodia about to be born.

Even the World Bank, playing a most ambiguous role in this affair, let it be understood by its representatives visiting Phnom Penh in the course of this same month of February 1970 that any substantial aid to Cambodia could be granted in the present circumstances only if "important changes" were forthcoming.

There remained only one obstacle, albeit a major one: the astonishing, irritating, spectacular popularity of Norodom Sihanouk among "ordinary Cambodians," those who were not in the army or the gendarmerie, those who were not public functionaries with a place in the hierarchy of graft, those who were neither pro-American nor pro-Communist, neither pro nor anti anything at all, the average, typical Cambodian, the one laboring in a rice paddy, most often for a usurer, or the one in the forest whom no one had ever interviewed—in brief, the Cambodian nobody gave a damn about.

For these people—the majority—Sihanouk continued to represent the unspoiled Cambodia of bygone days. French and American journalists could lampoon him endlessly, gleefully poke fun at the Gaullist "clown" whose like no longer existed even in France, a real oddball, capable of citing Mao Tse-tung and the Sapper Camembert in the same sentence, enlivening his revelations concerning the troubles he was having with Washington and Hanoi with bits of juicy bedroom gossip. But for all that Sihanouk remained Sihanouk, the Prince, His Lordship, Samdech, Snookie, under whose reign, whether by chance or as a result of his clever and skillful hand on the reins of power, the people of Cambodia had enough to eat— something not often the case in Asia or many other parts of the globe—and lived in peace. And this had been true for twenty-nine years, ever since Si- hanouk had ascended the throne (later handed over to his own father) in 1941. The great weeklies of the West then knowingly explained (in the East, nobody ever explained anything) that the sole cause of this popularity that bordered on idolatry was the chronic brutishness of the typical, ordinary, average Cambodian, who of course had assembled the billion blocks of stone that were Angkor out of only the blind obedience of the slave.

The truth was that Sihanouk, even absent from the country, even com- prised by the trafficking of his wife or his mother, remained an enormous, fundamental problem. Ieng Sary, Saloth Sar, Khieu Samphan, Hu Nim, Hou Yuon, Ieng Samboth, all the Khmer Rouge leaders, knew this. They them- selves would not have been mad enough (though some of them were quite mad) to dare to attack the myth.

The plotters and their American, South Korean, Formosan, Philippine, and Indonesian advisers thought they had nonetheless found the answer: They would exploit the visceral, centuries-old, irrepressible hatred of Khmer for Vietnamese. The campaign had begun even before Sihanouk's departure for France on January 11, 1970, being limited at first to repeti- tions of the long-standing recriminations of Sihanouk himself with regard to the North Vietnamese presence in the country, uttered in a low-pitched Cambodian key at first and gradually becoming shriller and shriller.

In February the pitch mounted even higher. They spoke of the Com- munist-atheist Vietnamese (it was necessary to make a distinction between the Vietnamese of Hanoi and those of Saigon, since the plans called for the latter to become friends), and they made it a point to stress the expansionist aims of the Tonkinese. As for the expansionism of Hanoi and its iron deter- mination to conquer the entire Indochinese peninsula, no Cambodian, whatever his camp, had the slightest doubts on the subject. One had to have a peculiar blind spot—when one was, for instance, a famous and highly re- spected French journalist and a specialist on the subject—to disregard com- pletely this aspect of the problem.

And soon, as the hate campaign was stepped up on the radio and in the press, it was not even necessary to know Cambodia like the palm of one's hand, as Charles Korver did, to have a strong inkling that the country was heading straight for large-scale race riots.

In the best of causes.

6

LISA WAS FAST ASLEEP, DREAMING. SHE DREAMT KNOWING SHE WAS dreaming, finding herself in that state halfway between sleeping and waking one sometimes experiences during an afternoon nap on a hot summer day, perhaps, when dozing in an upstairs bedroom with a bittersweet taste in one's mouth, one hears familiar voices downstairs yet cannot recognize them, and has no desire to recognize them because the state one is in is so pleasant. She was dreaming of herself, with a flat belly and looking very slender, and of Lara, at her side on a beach in Hawaiian colors, and mistaking the ghostly shadow of the mosquito netting in her bedroom in the Grand Hotel at Siem Reap for a white sail. And then the slight noise of a key turning in a lock—only a vague sound in her dream—became a conscious perception, and Lara was there beside her.

"Did I wake you up?"

She had vowed to herself to greet him coldly, to have things out with him. She stretched out her arms and drew him to her, and for long moments all she could do was weep silently. He caressed her gently, seeking only to quiet her.

"I hate you," she finally said in English, turning her face away.

"So do I," Lara said.

The room was still in shadow. He kissed her: each of her fingers first, then her wrist, the tip of her shoulder, her cheek.

She drew away. "You were with Kutchaï?"

"Yes." He placed his thin hand over Lisa's mouth. "I know. You hate Kutchaï," he said in English.

She pulled away, opening her eyes wide to try to see his face, barely visible in the dim light filtering through the balcony shutters.

"Oh, no!" she said. "Not Kutchaï. You and he are much too close to each other for me to hate him."

She slid one hand through the opening in Lara's shirt front and ran it lightly over his chest. "You've gotten thinner still."

"May I turn the light on? Open the shutters?"

"What time is it?"

"It's six. In the evening. It's still light out."

She closed her eyes again.

"Shall I open the shutters or turn the light on?"

"No. Yes."

"Yes or no?"

"I guess there's no way around it," she said.

He switched the light on, and she pulled the sheet up under her chin and raised her knees to hide the outline of her swollen belly.

"How did you get in? The door was locked."

"I persuaded the hall porter that I was your lover. He believed me."

"You were. Years and years ago. But we've broken up, remember?"

"Too bad," he said. "I liked things the way they were."

He looked her up and down, very slowly, an amazed look on his face. She clutched the edge of the sheet under her chin even more tightly.

"Clear out of here or I'll scream."

"It's barely six o'clock. Do you think you could get up and come visit Bayon?" His eyes were now fixed on Lisa's hands. "Charles and Madeleine told me you've been sleeping all afternoon, and what's more they told me you've spent almost all your time here sleeping."

Sitting down next to her on the edge of the bed, he stretched out his hand and tried to loosen the fingers desperately clutching the sheet.

"Don't touch me," she said in a distant voice.

"Charles also told me that you finally went to Bantéay Sreï. It's the only great temple we've never seen together. Very handsome. Bantéay Sreï, I mean, not Charles."

She struggled with her last ounce of strength. "Superb," she said, between clenched teeth.

One of her hands let go. He kept hold of it with one of his as he fought to loosen her grip with the other hand.

"It was from Bantéay Sreï that Malraux carried off stones and sculptures. Did Charles tell you that?"

"He didn't stop talking for one minute, I swear," Lisa said. She was struggling still, panting now.

"One of these days we'll go to the temples of Prah Vihear. There aren't many people who have seen them."

"I dream of seeing them," Lisa said, torn between rage and uncontrollable laughter.

All at once she gave up the fight, joined her wrists above her head, stared at Lara as though challenging him. He hesitated. Then he slowly pulled the sheet back, sliding it down little by little, uncovering her entire body. He leaned over and gravely kissed her on the tips of her breasts and on her taut belly.

"Forgive me. I'm mad. I should never have left you for a moment. I won't ever leave you again."

She pulled him down next to her and this time returned his kisses with a passion at least the equal of his, kissing his body all over.

A little while later, she said, "I'd really sort of like to go see Bayon in the moonlight."

Something amazing always happened as night was falling on the jungle, and in particular on the jungle around the temples. During the day it was, if not completely silent, at least quiet, uniformly filled with a murmuring sound made up of millions of chirps and faint cries which blended together and eventually formed a background sound one was no longer even aware of. In the minutes just before darkness fell, however, there came a moment when all the many sounds began to die away as though obeying some sort of signal. A total, almost unbearable, silence followed, lasting thirty or forty seconds, rarely longer. And then, with the same extraordinary simultaneity, all the birds began to give their characteristic call, as loudly as they possibly could, their throats nearly bursting, in a deafening din that gradually spread till it seemed to extend for kilometers of jungle in all directions. Again the phenomenon lasted a very short time and then suddenly stopped, in the space of a second, like a radio that had been turned off. And when it stopped, one discovered that in the meantime night had fallen, the tops of the trees were enveloped in darkness, and the jungle was already full of the snarls of carnivores on the prowl.

"Not to mention snakes," Lisa said. "*I hate* snakes."

"And sharks."

"And sharks."

"And me."

"And you. *I hate* you. *I hate you particularly, specifically,*" she said in English.

She pressed her hip against Lara's as they walked.

Angkor Wat with its five main towers was a rectangular structure, its long axis measuring about a kilometer and a half; Angkor Thom was twice as large and very nearly square. Bayon lay at the exact center, its sixteen quadrangular towers, each decorated with four faces, two meters high, overlooking a world of galleries, of dark and disquieting labyrinths that no one dared enter. By daylight Bayon was merely beautiful, exotic, with its sixty-four giant smiles carved in silver-gray and green stone, in the heart of a huge clearing crisscrossed with walkways. But it was at night that Bayon assumed its real dimensions. In the moonlight the smiles came to life, and the subterranean world took on strange overtones as the smell of mold and eroded sandstone grew stronger. Bayon by night, with its wild romanticism and the oppressive atmosphere of its cypresses, both frightened and fascinated Lisa. She sat down on a step and took the cigarette Lara offered her. They were completely by themselves.

He began to tell her about his travels through the east of Cambodia, in Moï country, and his meeting with Ieng Samboth; he repeated to her, almost word for word, what the Khmer had said to him, except that he made no mention of arms.

"Why was it you went to see him?"

He shrugged. "I wasn't taking any great risks. As proved by the fact that I'm back safe and sound."

"He's one of those so-called Khmer Rouge, isn't he?"

"One of their leaders. Not the most important one. But one of the higher-ups."

The step that Lisa had sat down on was too narrow for both of them to sit side by side, so Lara sat on the step just below, one shoulder leaning against the moss-covered wall and the other between his wife's knees.

"And you really aren't running any great risk by going to see him, or simply by having friendly relations with him?"

This was the first time since they'd been married that she had asked a question having to do with the strictly Cambodian side of Lara's life. He felt a tremendous nervous tension. The moment had come.

"Not really," he answered. "Not so long as the news isn't broadcast over loudspeakers and spread by the press throughout Southeast Asia."

Lisa slowly ran her fingers through her husband's hair. Her hands moved lower and she began to massage his shoulder and the nape of his neck, rubbing her thumb back and forth across the old scar. *He'll come back to you like a cat who's been out on the prowl, thin and affectionate,* Madeleine Korver had said, and that was exactly the way it was. Except that Lisa, faithful to herself, had no intention of confining herself to the role of consoling wife, of being a permanent, cozy warrior's rest. She wanted to size up precisely what future awaited them, not just Lara and herself, but Lara and herself in Cambodia. She realized that she had just envisaged, for the very first time, the prospect of leaving this country for good. She felt ice-cold, despite the sultriness of the warm, humid night.

"But you took risks," she said. "Why? Why get mixed up in their quarrels?"

"Because those quarrels are my quarrels, because they affect me and can turn our lives topsy-turvy."

She leaned her shoulder against the stone. She had nearly answered: "That's not true. You're not Cambodian, not really." But just as she was on the point of saying it, she had intuited that those were exactly the words she should not utter, at least not yet. As she glanced through a series of corridors illuminated by the moonlight, she saw the car that had brought them parked at the end opposite her with its lights out; its very presence there in the middle of the jungle, in front of these dead stones, struck her as incongruous. *We're acting as though we were in a park, somewhere in New York or in Paris, chatting in the moonlight. But we're not in a park. What's around is a jungle, full of all sorts of dangers, from the wild beasts that haunt it to the men who might come leaping out of it.* She gave a start as a nightjar screamed its strange raucous cry.

"Do you want to go back to the hotel?"

"No." She bent down and kissed the nape of Lara's neck. "Explain to me."

"Explain what?"

"Who the Khmer Rouge are and why a man like Ieng Samboth, who's your friend, has joined them and is even leading them. Who are they? Communists?"

"Some of them. Some of them much more so than others. But things aren't that simple."

"And Ieng Samboth?"

"He was one. He's less of one now, and in fact may no longer be one at all, to the degree that being a Communist means total submission to Moscow or Peking and subservience to another form of imperialism."

She hesitated. Imagine asking such a question after seven months of married life! "And how about you?"

Though she could not see his face, she could tell he was smiling.

"No," he answered. "And I never will be. I'm simply someone who was born in this country and wants to stay here."

"No matter what happens?"

His fingers gently squeezed Lisa's thigh. He lit another cigarette.

"I love you," Lisa said. "More than I thought I could ever love anyone."

He tilted his head slightly back and rested it against his wife's breast. After a moment, he began telling her what was going on in Phnom Penh, as he saw it: the plot, the groundwork being laid for a coup d'état, and the worrisome prospect that Sihanouk might be ousted. "The result of which would be that sooner or later Cambodia would enter the war."

"And you've chosen to be on Ieng Samboth's side?"

"I don't have any choice."

"I don't understand."

"If there's really a coup d'état one of these days, if Sihanouk is driven out, the regime that will replace him will be the same sort of one that's in power in Saigon now: pro-American."

"I don't see what's so terrible about that."

"Neither Moscow nor Hanoi nor even Peking will be willing to accept such a regime. It'll mean war. A war that Lon Nol won't be able to carry on without American aid. But a day will come when the Americans will pull out, just as the French did."

"You could be wrong."

"There's nothing that would please me more."

A cloud passed overhead, hiding the moon, and for a few moments the night shadows grew even darker. Lisa was overcome by a flood of violent and contradictory emotions: jealousy of Lara's love for this country; her need, for reasons of pride, to explain and defend those of her compatriots who had decided to intervene in Vietnam and were now turning their eyes toward Cambodia, pushing pawns whose names were Lon Nol or Sirik Matak; a poignant sadness at the thought of the marvelously peaceful and pleasurable way of life in Cambodia, soon to be destroyed by the same war that had nearly destroyed Jon. And finally, cold feminine anger at what she considered the insane, stupid games men play, maintaining each time that they have the best of reasons for playing them. For a brief moment, her anger against men in general included even Lara.

And then she closed her eyes, struggling fiercely to recover a semblance of self-control, aware of the fact that her pregnancy was making her more edgy, more vulnerable than she had ever been before in her life.

"And you'd still want to stay on, even if one day those men they call the Khmer Rouge won out and took power?"

"I'm not going to leave."

"Not under any circumstances?"

"No."

She took a deep breath. "Well, at least everything's out in the open." She stood up. "I'd like to go back now."

He held out his hand to help her down the steps, but she pretended to be unable to see it in the darkness. They got back into the Peugeot.

He started the engine and turned on the headlights, the bright beam reflected in the gleaming violet eyes of nightjars.

"And what about the plantation?" she asked.

It was not the words themselves so much as the impassive tone of voice in which he spoke them that stunned her:

"I've decided to get rid of it," he said.

Back in their room at the Grand Hotel, they ordered dinner sent up and did not even touch it. Lara lay down beside her without a word. Lisa dropped off to sleep, but after an hour or two, the repeated double note of a gecko awakened her, and she could tell by the rhythm of his breathing that Lara was still awake. After a violent struggle with herself she stretched a hand out underneath the sheet and laid it on Lara's hip. Their fingers intertwined, and this time they dropped off to sleep together.

On seeing them the following morning, Charles Korver, with his usual subtle insight, intuited that something had happened, something that was not only the result of Lara's long, upsetting absence and of the slight depression that Lisa, ordinarily so thoroughly in control of her feelings, had let herself fall into. But Charles Korver did not venture to guess what had gone wrong, and very nearly crossed swords with Madeleine, who was dying of curiosity and was on the point of subjecting Lisa to one of those searching interrogations—Madeleine maintained they were tactfulness itself—that were a specialty of hers.

"My dear friend, if you ask one question, just one, I'll whip you within an inch of your life with a banana," Charles said to his wife.

They left Siem Reap in two cars, with Lara at the wheel of the 504, Charles in the seat next to him, and the two women in the back seat, while Bê followed along behind all by himself in the Land-Rover. They stopped to have lunch, a dreadful repast, at the bungalow in Kompong Thom, where they were warmly welcomed by the French teachers who boarded there. The reasons for this cordial reception did not become clear to Charles Korver until later, when Roger Bouès told him, in more or less rough detail, the story of how Oreste Marccaggi had been wounded; at the time, Charles was puzzled by this reception, especially when he realized in the course of the lunchtime conversation that all the *co-opérants* had spent a weekend at the plantation. Since he himself hadn't set foot there for ten years at least, Charles was very nearly jealous.

They did not reach Phnom Penh till late afternoon, first of all because Lara drove almost at a crawl, as though he feared his wife would give birth at the foot of some kilometer marker along the edge of the road. (*And yet he took off for three weeks without a single word of explanation! That's Lara all over,* Charles Korver thought to himself.) Secondly, there were long lines of FARK trucks, transporting soldiers who, curiously enough, were less lighthearted and cheerful than usual, all along the road between the capital and the ferry at Prek Dam that crossed to the other side of the Tonle Sap.

They had dinner at the Korvers', one of those legs of lamb impossible to find in Cambodia that Charles had shipped to him directly from France by air freight. And at the end of this dinner, on the evening of February 16, Lara announced he was giving up the plantation. Charles Korver was thunderstruck, but had enough presence of mind to glance in Madeleine's direction as a sign to her not to do or say anything. For a moment he feared that his impulsive wife might embrace Lisa as one congratulates a winner. But Madeleine held her tongue of her own accord.

"And that's not all," Lara added. "Lisa and I have come to another decision."

He mentioned Sré, something he had never done before. The Korvers knew vaguely of the existence of this island. They knew the couple had spent their honeymoon there, but knew nothing more about it than that and thought it was an island like any other, or at any rate quite different from the one Lara now described to them, with a house, a spring, and everything necessary for a long stay.

"We're going to improve and enlarge the house at Sré," Lisa said. "We'll buy a boat so we can get out there and back on our own, without needing to call on the services of those obliging Malay fishermen each time." And she added with a laugh, "Besides, those boats of theirs are more or less just dugout canoes—they terrify me. I have the feeling I'm astride a shark."

"You mean to say you won't be living in Phnom Penh anymore?" Madeleine asked, so distressed she was almost at a loss for words.

"No, I don't mean that at all. But we'll be dividing our time between the two places."

Lara explained that he would be going off to Bangkok every so often, to buy the boat first of all, and then after that and more importantly, to resume a more active part in the import-export firm in which Christiani was his partner.

"Lisa can't travel right now, but as soon as she can, she'll come with me."

"It's true that you've scarcely even seen Bangkok," Charles said to Lisa.

"I stopped overnight there on my way here from Saigon."

"You'll like it, I'm sure."

Charles, too, was a little taken aback by these developments. His eyes kept traveling back and forth between Lara's face and Lisa's. He read in them a deeply shared understanding and, although he mistrusted that sort of word, happiness as well. When he thought back on it in the days that followed, he became more and more convinced that whatever happened at Siem Reap had had as an end result a readjustment in their relations as a couple, a definite strengthening of the ties between them. Charles Korver, who was equally fond of both of them, had always been vaguely worried about their considerable differences in temperament, upbringing, background, and way of life. Only one small step separated the noting of these differences and envisioning the possibility that they might some day cause a terrific quarrel between the Laras, even a total break—a threshold that Charles' mind had crossed more than once. But now the situation had completely changed. He sincerely believed that, and was overjoyed.

Lara did go off to Bangkok a few days later. He was gone no more than forty-eight hours and came back announcing that he had found, thanks to Christiani, a boat that exactly suited their needs. He described it as a sort of junk that was not altogether a junk but nonetheless more or less resembled one, some twelve meters long, with a cabin spacious enough to sleep four and even cook meals in. Charles Korver's most recent contact with life at sea dated back to a crossing from Le Havre to New York aboard the Normandy. He offered his services as a ship's boy and learned, without taking the slightest interest in the fact, that the junk which was not really a junk could make its way across a body of water either under a sail or by motor.

Apart from this brief trip to Bangkok, Lara remained on the scene,

meeting from time to time with Kutchaï for long talk-sessions. It was Kutchaï who took off to Sré in order to oversee the improvements that had been
planned. Lara himself never once left Phnom Penh or his wife's side, even
though there was every sign that the birth of the baby would be an entirely
normal one, according to the two French doctors who were looking after
Lisa.

The two specialists had even made bets with Madeleine Korver. They
were both quite certain that Lisa would have her baby on the fifteenth of
March.

7

ON THE EIGHTH OF MARCH, AS DAWN WAS BREAKING, CAPTAIN KAO
returned from Svay Rieng in his personal jeep, leading a small convoy of
four trucks and two armored vehicles. Svay Rieng is the southernmost city
in Cambodia, just a few kilometers from the South Vietnamese border. Kao
had spent an entire day there, holding several meetings, first of all with
high-school students and a number of their teachers whose loyalties he had
no doubts about, and then with a group of about fifty men whom he himself
had dispatched there and who, despite the fact that they were dressed in
civilian clothes, were really Khmer Sereï soldiers, a fair number of whom
had already established themselves in Thailand two years before, awaiting
the moment to mount an attack aimed at setting up in Phnom Penh the
rightist regime they had been persuaded was worth sacrificing their
lives for.

Assisted by a teacher of history and geography at the Sisowath High
School in Phnom Penh, Kao had addressed these two groups in almost the
same words and repeated the same orders, ending his speech in each case
with his favorite slogan: "We must hit hard." Kao was not an orator—far
from it. In this regard the teacher, who took himself to be Robespierre and
Washington rolled into one, with just a touch of the Spanish Falangist José-
Antonio Primo de Rivera—the bugger had a lively imagination—easily
outdid Kao. His descriptions of the imminent resurgence of the legendary
splendors of the Khmers were eloquence itself; and his vibrant anathemas
against the Thmils (the atheists) with gleaming white teeth—in other words
the Viet Cong—were well worth traveling miles to hear. But Kao's "We
must hit hard," though less original, had the advantage of being a model of
concision. It was Kao who had made his hearers' eyes gleam.

He had left the Robespierre of the Mekong there in Svay Rieng, in the
company of Khmer Sereï officers also dressed in civvies, with complete confidence that they could be counted on when the time came, and had gone
on his way in the darkness.

He arrived in Phnom Penh at five o'clock.

Reaching the vast esplanade circling the Monument to Independence, he hesitated. The Boulevard Norodom stretched out before him, beginning in a garden planted with coral trees and traveler's trees and ending far in the distance at the Phnom; behind him the Tonle Sap broadened out, doubled in size after joining the upper Mekong, and the great river thus formed divided again a little farther down into the lower Mekong and Tonle Bassac at a spot called Quatre-Bras.

Just for the fun of it, Kao drove all the way around the traffic circle, very slowly, and was amused to note that the convoy obediently followed along behind him. He ended up facing the Boulevard Norodom gain, totally deserted at this early morning hour. He stopped the jeep and issued orders: As planned, trucks and armored cars were to take up positions at the approach to the cement bridge connecting the downtown section to the peninsula of Chrui Chang War, on the other side of the Tonle Sap. He kept only two soldiers with him, installing them in the back seat of his jeep with their M-16 assault rifles, chargers engaged, between their knees, ready to fire. They were both Kroms with light skin and big impassive moonfaces. Kao liked to listen to them when they were off duty, the one playing the guitar, the other singing heart-rendingly sad songs. If so ordered, they would have slit the throats of an entire village.

Five-thirty. He headed home, taking savage pleasure in driving down the very middle of the deserted avenue, from time to time aiming the barrel of his machine gun at a door or a window chosen at random, as though it were some sort of game. He drove with his left hand, keeping the index finger of his right hand on the trigger of the machine gun; if he had pulled it back just one millimeter farther it would have fired a hail of bullets, blasting everything to bits. He'd never yet fired at human beings, not even during that ambush in the Phnom Pich Pass with Price. He had been too young to join the Issarak guerrillas fighting the French, and since independence, seventeen years earlier, there hadn't been even one little war to have fun in. What rotten luck! To think that he might have been born a Vietnamese!

He let the jeep coast to a stop in front of the door of the building. If his bitch of a wife was still sleeping, it was better not to wake her up.

"Wait for me," he said to the soldiers.

The elevator was the pride of his life. He lived in a building with an elevator!

As an extra precaution, he stopped it at the third floor instead of the fourth floor, where he lived. He walked up the last flight of stairs, and put his key in the lock with the delicate touch of a professional housebreaker. He had taken only three steps on tiptoe across the tiny entry hall onto which all the rooms of the apartment opened when Nuba suddenly appeared from the kitchen where she had been lying in wait for him, foaming at the mouth and brandishing the cleaver she used to cut up chickens. The weapon whizzed through the air, nicking him in the left shoulder just as he reflexively raised his arm to defend himself. He stepped back, bumping his heel against a low table, and fell backward. The fall saved his life, her slash with the cleaver just barely missing his face.

"Where were you? Where were you, you bastard?"

He rolled over on his side, a deliberate move on his part this time, and ran into the dining room, which he had insisted be European-style. He dived between the chairs, got the table between Nuba and himself, and drew his Colt .45.

"Put that thing down or I'll kill you," he said to her.

She flung herself upon him, paying no heed to the automatic. At the last second he took his index finger off the trigger, stepped aside, dodged the cleaver blow, grabbed the Colt by the barrel, swung wildly, and hit her square in the face with it.

She collapsed to the floor.

Kao waited, thinking she was about to get to her feet again. He'd often hit her, and even beaten her so severely he'd almost killed her, but she had always returned to the charge. This time she didn't stir. He walked to where she was lying, wary of a trick on her part. He finally bent over her. *Well, at least she isn't dead.*

He picked up the cleaver, which had dropped from her hand, went into the bedroom, and locked it in the drawer of his bureau where he kept his reserve handguns.

I should have pulled the trigger when she came at me. Legitimate self-defense. But the formalities would have taken time and he would not have been able to participate in the events that were about to happen. He went into the bathroom, removed his uniform shirt, and examined the gash in his shoulder: The wound was impressive but clean and, though bleeding copiously, not in fact very deep. He'd had a close one.

"I nearly killed her this time," he said to his reflection in the mirror.

He took a shower, contemplating his own blood as it flowed down the drain, mingling with the water in pinkish rivulets on the white porcelain. He then put a prepackaged gauze bandage over the gash, and wound strips of adhesive tape around his arm to hold it in place. A few drops of blood still oozed from the wound but it was no longer bleeding badly. It would soon stop altogether. He finished changing, put on a pair of dark cotton pants and a shirt with a red and black flower pattern which he'd bought at Gimbel's in New York. Even if blood seeped through the bandage it would not spot the cloth, or if it did, the spots would be invisible.

Completely dressed, wearing nothing now that would give away the fact that he was an army officer, he came back into the dining room. Nuba was lying on her side, moving slightly and moaning. The pistol blow had caught her cheekbone and temple, slightly tearing her cheek as well. A little blood was oozing out of the wound but there was no sign of swelling. *I must have broken a bone*, Kao thought.

The red *sampot* she was wearing had come undone, baring her surprisingly firm breasts. She was a purebred Khmer whom he had married when she was seventeen years old. Her skin was dark, with a velvety texture that had always made him go weak in the knees. She was not beautiful and never had been, even when she was very young; she had always been half-crazy, with something savage and primitive, animallike, about her, but she was the only woman he had ever truly desired, despite her craziness—or perhaps because of it. She had given him five children, seven in fact, but two of them had died shortly after their birth, one of them perhaps deliberately smothered to death by Nuba. He had taken her children away from her, fearing she would kill all of them some day during one of her fits of madness, and had entrusted them to the care of his own mother, his sisters, and sisters-in-law, all of whom still lived in the village where he had been born, near Kompong Speu.

He leaned down, grabbed Nuba under the shoulders and knees, picked her up in his arms, and carried her to their bed. He brought a soaking wet washcloth from the bathroom, wrung a little of the water out of it, and folded it before putting it on Nuba's cheek. She was no longer moving but she was breathing, her eyes shut tight, conscious but not wanting to look at him. She was calm now, as though her spirit were broken. Kao saw a tear well from beneath one of her eyelids. He was overcome with sudden emotion, but like all the other times, he did not ponder the miracle that made this woman rouse his feelings, this woman among all others, this woman and no other—he, who looked upon the possibility of killing or even of being killed with truly inhuman, cold-blooded indifference.

With amazing tenderness he knelt at the edge of the bed, tugged gently at the *sampot*, stripped Nuba naked, breathing in the odor of that black flesh, licking it. Straightening up again, he got undressed and lay on top of her. She let him enter her without reacting at first, and then in a rush of passion buried her fingernails in his back.

He left his apartment at 6:42 A.M. The soldiers waiting down below had not budged.

At 6:57 the jeep with the machine gun mounted on the hood entered the vast rectangular courtyard of the general headquarters of the Khmer Royal Armed Forces.

The Vietnamese quarter in Phnom Penh was a city in itself. The tens of thousands of people who lived there came from almost everywhere in Indochina, from Hanoi to Saigon. The basic sector of the population was made up of men of the delta, certain of whom came from families who had lived in Cambodia since time immemorial, though they had nonetheless kept their original language and ethnic identity. A second wave had arrived with the French, whose policy had generally been to give to Vietnamese, rather than to Khmers, those minor administrative posts which Europeans could not accept without losing face. A third wave, a much more recent one, had arrived at the time of the first battles between the troops of Ho Chi Minh and Giap and the French Expeditionary Corps; this third wave was made up largely of Tonkinese and Annamites who had fled a war in which they had little desire to take sides, and even less desire to risk their lives.

The Vietnamese influx was not limited to Phnom Penh; it had affected other Khmer cities, especially in the south—cities like Takeo and Svay Rieng—just on the border between the two countries. These Vietnamese colonies became less important the farther north one went in Cambodia, with one exception: On the shores of the great lake of Tonle Sap, Vietnamese fishermen had lived for generations, steeping fish to make *prahoc*, an indispensable condiment in the Khmer diet, just as their cousins on the island of Phu Quoc made *nuoc-mam*.

Between the two communities, Vietnamese and Khmer, the differences—in theory at least—were striking. There was the difference in language, first of all, even though everyone more or less spoke Cambodian, whose syntax and vocabulary, bastardized for centuries, were not all that difficult to learn. Customs, secondly—the differences in dress, for instance: Vietnamese women wore wide pants and tunics rather than the *sampot* of Khmer women. Religion, thirdly, for Cambodians were Buddhists, while most Vietnamese were Catholic and buried their dead, whereas the Khmers cremated theirs.

Admittedly, there had been a fair admixture of the two communities over the decades and the centuries; when they did not have Chinese blood in their veins, a goodly number of officially Khmer bureaucrats or technicians had ancestors who were Vietnamese. But the contacts between the two communities had never really brought them together, and they persisted in eyeing each other suspiciously, like a pair of porcelain dogs, or at best looking upon each other with total indifference. There was obvious jealousy in the way Cambodians viewed their neighbors: If he was not Chinese, an automobile mechanic, a radio repairman, a chief cook, a maître d'hôtel, a shoemaker, a goldsmith, a restaurant owner, a hotelkeeper, an important merchant, or a vendor with an open-air stall was most likely a Vietnamese. As for the servants employed by the European colony, apart from a Chinese amah to look after the children, one spoke of having a *bep* (cook), a *ti-aï,* a *ti-nam,* a *ti-ba,* in descending order of their importance in the hierarchy of domestics, all of these Vietnamese words corresponding to a given household function, used even when the employee was Khmer—which was almost never the case unless the employer himself was Cambodian.

The Korvers' five servants were Vietnamese, not by a deliberate decision to exclude Cambodians, but because Charles and Madeleine had simply yielded to the insistent pressure of Bê, the chauffeur, who had been in their service since 1934 (he was around sixty now) and who had been eager to surround himself with members of his own family, thus creating a sort of consortium, with himself as president. Sometimes the Korvers wondered whether it was Bê or themselves who really gave the orders around the house. The car would mysteriously break down every time Bê decided that the errand he was being asked to run was either futile or inconvenient for him; and the quality of the dinners served varied in the most surprising way, depending on the quality of the guests, whose appearance, manners, and social rank (Bê was a terrible snob) had to meet with the approval of Bê and his assistants. In the first rank of assistants was Monsieur le Bep, who defended the approach to his stove with all the valor of a pirate confronting Francis Garnier, the French conqueror of the Song Koi Delta. As for the books in the library, the Korvers had finally conceded, despite a rearguard action on Madeleine's part, that they were to be placed on the shelves upside down, so that the best way to read the titles was to stand on one's hands.

With the exception of these minor details, Bê's fidelity and devotion were total. During the Japanese occupation, the Korvers had been placed under house arrest in their villa surrounded by barbed wire and were unable even to have money sent in to them. That they did not die of hunger was only because of the courage and friendship of their chauffeur, who, braving the guards outside and the Nipponese exhortations to brotherhood among all Asian peoples and eternal enmity toward white colonials, had for months and months brought them each night provisions he had bought out of his own savings.

Differences of race, customs, religion, language, of wealth in certain cases, Khmer jealousy in the face of the obviously greater ability on the part of the Vietnamese to find their place in the sun in an Indochina attempting to become a Western-type industrial nation, the inferiority complex of a minority group: All these factors explained the strained relations between the two communities. Elsewhere, throats had been slit with far less reason. But in addition there was the sometimes transparent scorn of the Vietnamese toward the "lazy, barbarian" Khmers, and above all the centuries-old Khmer suspicion of Vietnamese imperialist ambitions. After all, armed Vietnamese—in other words, invaders—were already on Khmer soil. Even Samdech-Father had said as much. The fact that these invaders were Communists, whereas the majority of Vietnamese who had settled in

Cambodia were Catholic and hence opposed in principle to Communism, and in fact in many cases had come to Cambodia as refugees from Communism, didn't count. A Vietnamese was still a Vietnamese.

The Indonesian intelligence services and the experts of the American Central Intelligence Agency had explained to Lon Nol and Sirik Matak what had to be done. It was necessary to exploit the hatred of the Khmers for their neighbors (and if need be to reawaken that hatred) in the same way that the hatred of the Indonesians toward the Chinese had been brought into play to eliminate Sukarno in Djakarta. It was necessary to organize not only a demonstration but an insurrection. It was necessary to bring about the irreparable. It was necessary to cause bloodshed. "At least a hundred dead—a number in three figures. It's more spectacular in a wire-service bulletin."

For such a delicate task, they could not simply depend on the crowd, not even an unruly one stirred to white-hot fury. A crowd is capable of anything, even (who can ever tell?) benevolence. The fifty soldiers disguised as civilians whom Kao had brought to Svay Rieng were on hand to see that everything went right: to start the insurrection, to keep it going and make certain it ended as planned—that is to say, to slaughter the victims themselves. Often cut off from their families for years now, men without a country so to speak, and carefully trained, they were to be the leaders and the butchers. But while there were a mere fifty of them at Svay Rieng, there were eight or nine hundred of them in Phnom Penh on this early morning of March 8, 1970. Everything had been planned: Price had personally written the texts for the placards and banners to be carried by the demonstrators; he had written them not in Khmer, which nobody would have understood, or even in French (that was not the audience he was aiming at), but in English, so that television networks all over the globe could show them to their viewers. Naturally, the plotters had made it a point to allow a maximum of news teams to enter Cambodia, and when necessary had whispered an ultraconfidential piece of information in their ears. And Price, who was a perfectionist, had deliberately made a few spelling mistakes, even a grammatical error or two, in the slogans he had written for the placards and banners, errors that a Cambodian incensed at North Vietnamese imperialism but having had only an elementary course in English might have made.

The spontaneous demonstration of the Cambodian people expressing their righteous wrath at the invasion of the sacred soil of their fatherland by hordes of Viet Cong was scheduled for precisely 8:04 A.M.

8

AT DAWN ON MARCH 8, MADELEINE GOT UP FIRST, AS CALLED FOR BY the rite established over a half-century of married life. It had taken twenty-two years of patient representations on Charles' part to convince her that it was up to her to fix their morning coffee, before the arrival of the servants (who officially began their duties at nine o'clock but were never really operational till ten, after Bê had had a meeting with his staff and issued the orders for the day).

Dressed in a flowing black silk dressing gown with a red dragon spitting orange flames and an advertising slogan for Kawasaki motorcycles on the back of it, Madeleine went down, not to the kitchen, which she would not have been allowed to enter in the absence of Monsieur le Bep, but to a little room, slightly smaller than a phone booth, reserved for her use through the sheer magnanimity of the consortium, with a shelf on which were three dozen boxes of ground coffee, an alcohol burner, some sixty packages of rusks, and a little refrigerator. Madeleine made the coffee, buttered two rusks, one for Charles and one for herself, put everything on a tray, and went back upstairs to have breakfast with her husband.

The evening before, they had received a large packet of letters from Europe, from nephews and nieces, grandnephews and grandnieces, of whom they had an incredible number, a good many of whom lived in Bordeaux or in Landes or in Chalosse. Oddly enough, this couple of Alsatian origin had no family at all left in Alsace.

Sitting side by side on their big bed, over which the mosquito netting held up by an elegant teak frame formed a sort of canopy, they sipped their coffee and nibbled their one rusk apiece as they read the letters. They had been to a dinner at the British Embassy the evening before and had had to put off reading this mail. These first hours in the morning, without servants, in a deserted house, were the hours they were fondest of. They loved the peace and quiet of them, but above all else the marvelous, reassuring certainty they brought, when on awakening from the sleep that had separated them, they again found themselves together, alive and still able to smile at each other after so many years.

"Well, well!" Madeleine exclaimed. "Christine's married a certain Jean-François Suffert. What's an *énarque* exactly?"

"A graduate of the ENA—the French National School of Administration. Who's Christine?"

"Charlotte and Bernard's daughter."

"Ah, I see," Charles said, wondering who the devil this Charlotte and

Bernard, whose names he was hearing mentioned for the first time in his life as far as he could recall, could possibly be.

"Charlotte's Louis-Léopold's niece, and Louis-Léopold is Jacques's cousin. And Jacques is your grandnephew, since he's Henri and Sophie's son. As for Bernard, his relationship to you is even easier to figure out, and I'm surprised that you don't even seem to know that he exists: His brother-in-law is Françoise's uncle, and Françoise is married to Georges, who's a second cousin of Paul's, the one who married Annick. Not the Annick who lives in Lons-le-Saulnier but the other one, Michel's sister, and Michel, along with Yves and Claudie, are Janine's children by her second marriage, to Robert."

"And who turns out to be the murderer in the end?"

"That'll be enough of your clever jokes," Madeleine said. "And stop wolfing down your rusk like that. You'll have a stomachache again."

There was also a letter, the fourth he'd sent them, from Jon Kinkaird, mailed from Stockholm. Jon was rather laconic as usual, expressing his concern about their health and writing that as far as he was concerned things couldn't be better. His Swedish was improving by the day and he'd changed jobs, but he didn't say what sort of job he'd left nor what his new one was.

Around seven o'clock, still following their daily ritual, they put on their gardening outfits and went out to stroll among the flower beds. Neither of them knew the least thing about gardening, yet this didn't bother them in the slightest. Tam, Bê's nephew, if they understood correctly, was the one who was officially responsible for the garden, and with kindly generosity he had allowed Charles and Madeleine to have a minuscule patch of soil of their own which they hoed, spaded, harrowed, and worked however they felt like it, without ever troubling their heads as to proper garden technique, since they never expected their plot to produce anything. And in that respect they were not disappointed: Nothing ever grew there.

The first sounds reached their ears around eight o'clock in the form of a vague murmur, far off in the distance at first, coming from the south, well beyond the Phnom. They noticed it but paid little attention to it. At that moment the two of them were in the vast salon-library on the ground floor, absorbed in what was their principal occupation outside of doing nothing in particular: making out, for each of the objets d'art in their collection, an extremely detailed filing card, indicating not only the origin of the piece but also, insofar as was possible, the precise date and exact place where it had been produced, the historical circumstances surrounding its creation, and even the name of its creator, plus a description of the era in which it had first seen the light of day. Their collection, which would have amazed any specialist in the world, included objects from Japan, Java, China, Burma; it was an absolutely miscellaneous collection, with no guiding principle whatsoever, assembled as their fancy and a series of sudden irresistible impulses had dictated. The task of drafting these cards, calling for familiarity with a period of more than twenty centuries and an area representing almost a third of the globe, had kept them occupied for forty years, without their being as yet anywhere near finished.

Perhaps twenty to forty minutes later, the murmur having meanwhile become a tremendous rumble punctuated with indistinct cries and even shots, they realized that something out of the ordinary was happening. They regretfully tore themselves away from their silent research. Charles went out into the garden but saw nothing except the little Rue Chey Chetha, which was deserted at that hour, but no more deserted and no quieter than usual.

"From the balcony perhaps?"

They went upstairs and out onto it together, hand in hand, leaning on each other for support. The trees blocked their view, but they could see clouds of smoke to the northeast, to the southwest, and also directly above the peninsula of Chrui Chang War.

"Whatever can they have thought of now?" Madeleine asked, in the tone of a mother speaking of her fractious and rather mischievous children.

Using the telephone in their bedroom, Charles called the first number that popped into his head, that of the Taverne, opposite the Main Post Office. There was no answer. It occurred to him to phone the French Embassy. The line was busy. The British Embassy. The line was busy. The U.S. and Australian embassies. Busy.

"Keep calm," Madeleine said in her little-girl voice. "Do you see me getting upset?"

Just in case, following one of her processes of reasoning that never failed to stagger Charles, she had changed clothes, appearing now in a yellow dress with a big gray and white flower print of the sort she wore to cocktail parties. She had taken off the hairnet she wore over her blue locks in the morning. She looked admirably well turned out.

Roger Bouès: The phone rang and rang but there was no answer. The police station across from the main Post Office. Busy. The French Embassy again. Busy.

The tremendous steady din of the demonstration was closer still.

"Perhaps I could walk over to the Laras', since they don't have a phone—what do you think?"

"You could also go water-skiing on the Mekong. When there's a demonstration going on, Charles, one stays at home."

He dailed Roger Bouès' number for the third time: The phone rang and rang with still no answer.

The minutes went by. They became quite concerned when, though it was well after nine o'clock, they still had not heard the usual sound of Bê's motorbike arriving. In and of itself, the absence of the chauffeur-and-head-of-the-household-staff would not have been enough to upset them thoroughly, but none of the servants had arrived yet and this failure of the entire staff to show up, or their delay, was becoming really alarming. It was not possible to believe that all five Vietnamese servants, even though they were all more or less related, could have been taken ill on the very same day. They didn't even all live in the same place; the young Ti-Ba lived south of the city on the road to Pochentong, and Bê and the others north of it, out toward the Malay village.

Charles went back into the garden, and this time walked out to the street. The other villas appeared to be empty; all the ones that had shutters had closed them. Their neighbors had either shut themselves up inside or had fled. The usual quiet of the French quarter suddenly became ominous. For a brief moment Charles Korver saw Madeleine and himself from the outside, so to speak: a very elderly couple, physically frail, holding hands and waiting to be murdered in a house that was much too big and looked like a museum. But his sense of humor soon got the better of him again. *We'll hole up here in the villa and hold out for fifty-five days, the way they did in Peking, driving off the enemy by firing rusks at them.* He went back inside and joined his wife upstairs.

"Listen," Madeleine said. "It sounds as though they're not coming this way."

There was indeed a strange feeling in the air. The entire city seemed to have been taken over by rioters, by arsonists, by people firing shots—the entire city, that is, except the place where they were.

"Have you called Roger Bouès?"

"I've tried again and again."

"Try just once more."

"He must not be home. There's no answer."

It was 9:10.

"Just once more, to please me," Madeleine said softly, gracefully tilting her little head to one side and fingering her blue curls.

"Hello," Roger's voice said after one ring.

"The servants," Charles said. "They didn't come this morning. We're all alone."

A silence.

"I'll be right over," Roger replied.

9 BETWEEN EIGHT AND ELEVEN O'CLOCK, CAPTAIN KAO ALMOST WENT out of his mind. Not because something happened to him, but on the contrary, because he had nothing at all to do. The colonel in command wanted, he said, to keep him in reserve and had threatened to shoot him down if his jeep with the machine gun mounted on the hood moved one inch. For three

hours, Kao was like a hunting dog that has been left behind in the kennel
and hears his companions barking as they close in for the kill. He pawed the
ground, writhed with rage as he listened to the distant gunfire and the fierce
roar of demonstrators swarming in the streets somewhere, everywhere—
without him.

At one moment, he even hoisted himself up onto the roof of the headquarters building and spied the multiple columns of smoke the Korvers had
seen rising from quarters of the city burned to the ground, from razed
churches, clouds of smoke that the wind drove downriver, toward the south,
toward Vietnam, like a funeral announcement.

But Kao soon climbed down off the roof again. While he had been gone
they might have needed him—that is to say, freed him, let him loose. Not a
chance. He begged the colonel and was told where he could go—to hell.

"You and your fucking machine gun!"

The two moonfaced soldiers in the back of the jeep still hadn't budged,
living images of impassivity in the middle of this courtyard swarming with
messengers endlessly coming and going. All around Kao men were shouting,
telephoning, bustling about. He was just sitting there. He saw trucks bringing in arms, and he knew where these arms came from.

The *Columbia Eagle* affair was far from an ordinary one; it was evidence of the nature of the plot as a whole, at once cunning and naïve, daring and carefully planned. The ship, flying a U.S. flag and loaded to the
gunwales with M-16 assault rifles and ammunition, mortar, machine guns,
and grenades, was not officially scheduled to land at the Cambodian port on
the Gulf of Siam. Its cargo manifest showed that it was carrying sanitary
equipment for the wretched hordes in Saigon.

But by chance, just as it was heading along the Khmer coast, a sort of
mutiny had apparently broken out aboard. Part of the crew had suddenly
revealed its "hostility to the policy being followed in Vietnam by the
United States of America." The terrified captain had hurriedly made for the
nearest port, which happened to be Kompong Som, where the same Cambodian stevedores who a month earlier had been offloading cases of Russian
Kalashnikovs being sent to the Viet Cong, had immediately unloaded the
cases of M-16's manufactured by Colt, as well as mortars, machine guns,
grenade launchers, and several tons of ammunition.

The only common feature of the two operations: the trucks used to
transport the arms. They were the property of Chinese traders and businessmen in Phnom Penh, who were not exactly brokenhearted at the prospect of seeing their Vietnamese business rivals suffer an attack or two at the
hands of protesters.

"Kao!"

He had been waiting for the order for so long that he very nearly
missed hearing it. He leapt from his seat.

"Take your fucking jeep and head for Chrui Chang War," the colonel said. "With or without those two statues you've got there in the back seat."

The colonel unfolded a hand-drawn map of the peninsula. He drew a red circle on it. "Here, in one of these houses. It would appear that they've hidden arms, Soviet arms destined for the Viet Cong, there. You're to go there and organize everything for the arrival of the foreign photographers and cameramen that they'll be bringing to you around one or one-thirty. Give or take a few minutes. Get going."

Kao leapt behind the wheel of his jeep. A wild beast let loose. But before he had time to turn the key in the ignition switch . . .

"And what about the truck?" the colonel said.

"What truck?"

"The one with the Soviet arms in it. Where were you planning to get them? If you don't take them with you, how do you expect to find them there when you arrive? You can take ten men with you."

"These two are all I need," Kao answered.

On reaching the bridge leading to Chrui Chang War, he saw the first corpses: two women, three men, and a boy of about twelve. Poorly dressed Vietnamese. The bodies were lying less than twenty yards from one of the armored cars that Kao himself had positioned on the bridge when he returned from Svay Rieng. He stopped, bent over the wounds covered with flies, inhaling the stale smell of blood in deep, almost avid, breaths. But the wounds had not been made by bullets. Some of them were from machetes, others perhaps from truncheons.

"Iron bars," said a young sergeant who'd climbed down from his armored car. "Our orders were not to budge, not to do anything, just watch. And we didn't do a thing; we just watched. The demonstrators killed them before our very eyes."

He looked like a university student, or perhaps even a high-school student. For a moment, blinded by his own emotions, Kao thought the youngster was trying to express what he himself felt: frustration at the sight of the results of this hunt he had been prevented from participating in. But that was not it. The young sergeant was really horrified, sick with disgust at what he had seen.

"I knew one of them," the young sergeant said. "The one with his head cut off. He sold little cakes in the Central Market. Why did they kill him? He surely wasn't a Viet Cong."

Kao examined the body curled up in a ball. It was quite true: The man had been half decapitated and beaten to a pulp with iron bars as well, in a murderous frenzy. He saw that it was an old man, thin, with close-cropped iron-gray hair and a homely but nonetheless friendly, likable face.

"How do you know?" Kao said savagely. "How do you know?"

"I just don't think he was a Viet Cong," the youngster said stubbornly.

"I knew him. If he took a liking to you, he'd sometimes give you one of his little cakes."

Kao grabbed him by the shoulder and shoved him toward the armored car, so violently he nearly sent him sprawling. "You stupid little shit! Get back where you belong. Where do you think you are anyway? You're a soldier! Get the hell out of my sight. *Tao.* Go on!"

He started to climb back into the jeep. He had already hoisted himself halfway into the seat when he froze. Some of the soldiers in the trucks posted at the approach to the bridge had climbed down onto the roadway of the bridge and were leaning over the railing laughing. Kao went and leaned over the railing too. Down below he spied dozens and dozens of corpses being carried downstream by the viscous, ocher waters of the Tonle Sap. Some of the dead were floating face up on the surface; others, a number of them stripped naked, were turning slowly in circles; others still were caught motionless for a moment against the pilings of the bridge, resisting the current with the senseless obstinacy of dead things, though it nevertheless eventually swept them on. Almost hypnotized for a minute, Kao finally turned away, his gaze seeking in the distance, on the shore of the river that lay to his right, the site of the Vietnamese Catholic village, one of the principal targets assigned the rioters. He saw smoke and could even make out flames. He went back to the jeep to get his field glasses and focused them on the village. The whole thing was in flames, including the site of the Catholic girls' school, run by nuns who for the most part were Tonkinese. A sudden fit of rage overcame him. *That's where I should have been, from the very first!* He stood there foaming at the mouth, his eyes filled with images of nuns scattering in all directions, caught one by one in the cross hairs of the round sight of his machine gun. The very thought made him tremble with excitement.

The gears of his jeep screeched as he took off, and almost regretfully avoided running over the leg of a corpse lying across his path on the roadway of the bridge. Farther on, along the entire length of the bridge in fact, lay other dead bodies. He drove off the bridge onto the peninsula itself and stopped again, both to consult the map the colonel had given him and also because he realized he was overwrought and needed to get better control of himself. The houses circled on the map were five or six hundred yards farther on at most, beneath a clump of tamarinds, directly within sight of a little chapel on fire.

He took off again, deliberately driving slowly. A group of people appeared in front of the jeep, Cambodians who had nothing to do with the slaughter but who had witnessed it without taking part. Probably that had been the reaction of the vast majority of the Khmer population of Phnom Penh—and of Svay Rieng, where the same sort of butchery had undoubtedly taken place. They had watched the demonstration taking shape, had seen more and more people joining it, had even shouted and screamed along with the rest, but at the moment the outright violence had broken out, most of them had hesitated and left the actual butchery up to the professionals who had come from Thailand, aided by a few scattered groups of overexcited students and the inevitable hooligans drawn to the scene. Kao knew this; he had had proof of it in the reports that had come to the general headquarters during the morning as he himself champed at the bits in the courtyards. From that point of view, the uprising had been a failure: It had not succeeded in bringing about the "sacred union" of all Cambodians against the Vietnamese community, or against anything else for that matter. The ordinary Cambodian hadn't lifted a finger, or at the very worst he had looted, timidly venturing into houses whose occupants had fled or been massacred.

The crowd in front of the hood, their backs to him, didn't move. Kao raised the barrel of his machine gun and aimed a short burst of fire at the smoke-darkened sky.

"Tao!"

The crowd immediately cleared out of his way. He drove on for a few yards and arrived in front of the little group of wooden houses that was his objective, according to the orders he had received. He saw three or four traditional thatched huts that had more or less undergone improvements, standing on pilings with the space between ground and floor being used as poultry yard or, in one case, as a pigsty for three or four pigs.

It must be that one.

He very nearly stepped on the corpses. There were about fifteen of them, among them seven or eight children, several of them mere infants, apparently three families who had been surprised in their houses by the attack and had tried to barricade themselves behind ridiculously flimsy bamboo screens, paper-thin barricades that had immediately given way. Yet despite three braziers that still had white-hot coals in them, the dwellings hadn't caught on fire. By chance? Or because the so-called demonstrators who had operated there had received strict orders not to destroy the houses? Kao favored the second explanation. To the mind of a soldier it was reassuring, satisfying, to believe that every detail of the operation had been conceived, foreseen, planned in advance by his superiors.

Among the bodies were those of several women, one of them a pretty young thing dressed in black pants and a pink silk *ao-daï* who had probably been a waitress or a hostess somewhere; her face was vaguely familiar to Kao. On her wrist was a silver bracelet of the sort made by the jewelers in the Rue du Palais, and someone, either as he was hacking at her with his machete to kill her, or afterwards, had slit the *ao-daï* down the front, and the European-style brassiere enveloping her little pink-nippled ivory breasts as well. Kao bent over and covered the woman's naked breast. The fact that she was dead, butchered like an animal in a slaughterhouse, didn't move him in the least, but this indecent show of a bare bosom made him feel uncomfortable.

The other women had superb, heavy black hair tucked up in meticulous chignons. All of the victims of the massacre, men, women, and children, were unquestionably Vietnamese. And a Vietnamese remains a Vietnamese. *We must hit hard.* They had hit hard, and this was only a beginning.

Kao turned around. The two Buddhas from Cochin China were still sitting in the back seat of the jeep awaiting his orders, the truck loaded with Russian arms was a short way behind it, and at a respectable distance but nonetheless still forming part of the same half-circle, the Cambodian spectators were staring in turn at Kao and at the corpses of their former neighbors who had been murdered. Kao suddenly remembered that he was not in uniform but in civvies. *For all the good's that done!* he thought bitterly.

"I'm a captain in the Khmer Royal Armed Forces. I want this place cleaned up."

He hesitated. Should he remove the dead bodies from the scene or leave them where they were so the foreign journalists could see them when they arrived? The matter hadn't been mentioned in the orders he'd been given. He chose to adopt a compromise solution.

"I want volunteers." He pointed his index finger. "You, you, and you. And you two over there. And I need a cart. You're to take these bodies away. Not all of them. Leave all the men over twenty and one of the women. This one."

He touched the body of an old woman with the tip of his shoe to indicate the one he meant. He stepped back a few paces, trying to visualize the tableau he was about to offer the journalists, thinking, *Yes, that will do. It's better to leave one dead woman; it makes the whole thing look more natural. A slip. Someone no doubt killed her by mistake.*

He was asked what should be done with the bodies.

"Dump 'em in the river."

He had one last vision of the pleasing face of the young girl in the pink *ao-daï. I wonder where I've seen her before?* It bothered him a little not to be able to remember; usually he never forgot a face.

"All the rest of you clear out of here. *Tao!* I don't want to see a one of you left here. *Tao, tao!*" he ordered.

He motioned to his two helpers, who immediately jumped out of the jeep and cleared everyone out in a few seconds, their icy eyes sufficient to command the instant respect of the crowd of onlookers. Only then did Kao order the truck to move forward. He had the driver back it around against the particular house he had chosen, the one with the pigsty. *The gentlemen of the press will have to get their feet dirty. And that will keep them from thinking the situation over too carefully.* Kao did not underestimate the importance of such little details as this.

The corpses he had ordered carted off were gone now, leaving only six dead, five men and one woman. But bloodstains were visible here and there. Kao grabbed the dead bodies by the hands and feet himself and disposed them in such a way that each bloodstain was explainable. His men had dug a hole in the middle of the pigsty underneath the floor of the house above and aided by the truck driver, they were now finishing putting the arms in it, AK-47's in good condition for the most part, with or without metal breeches, plus a few old Simonov SKS-46's. Kao even spied two or three bayonets. They had put mats down in the hole to keep the rifles from touching the ground, and the pigs, as stupid as the rest of their kind, were trying to eat the mats as Kao's men laughingly kept them from doing so. The hole they had dug was plainly a little too small to contain all the arms.

"That doesn't matter," Kao said. "Leave a few of them scattered around the hole. We can say we took them out when we discovered the cache."

His watch showed twenty-five minutes to twelve. He therefore had at least an hour's wait ahead of him before the arrival of the journalists. *What's more, they may not come at all,* he thought. He imagined that his superiors had arranged other fake caches such as the one he had just stage-managed. He made a sudden decision.

"You men stay here. Don't move from the spot under any circumstances. Don't let anybody come near, except if the journalists arrive by some chance before I get back. But I'm sure to be here."

He got into his jeep and drove back over the Tonle Sap. As planned beforehand, the Chinese quarter on the Rue Ohier and the nearby streets was intact and everything was quiet, though all the iron grilles of the shop-windows had been lowered. For it had been definitely decided that the demonstrators should in no case attack the Chinese community or subject it to any sort of annoyance. Much less the Occidentals, who above all were to be left entirely alone. It was impossible, however, to predict how far men trained to commit acts of violence might go.

Kao took a swing around the center of the city, perfectly calm and orderly now with the one exception of the Boulevard Norodom, down which the demonstrators had passed, remaining there long enough to be photographed and leaving behind them a few tattered banners as proof of their having passed that way. Patrols of soldiers were making the rounds of the streets, and the atmosphere was more or less the same as on an ordinary Sunday morning.

Kao headed back down toward the river via the Rue Khemarak Phoumin and began to drive along the wharves, irresistibly attracted by the column of smoke mounting vertically from the Catholic village along the highway leading north.

A few minutes later, he recognized Charles Korver.

10

IN ORDER TO AVOID THE RIVER WHARVES, WHERE IT SEEMED TO him that the uproar of the demonstration was worst at that moment, Roger chose to drive around behind the Olympic stadium, heading around it to the west along the very end of the Boulevard Monivong, not far from the French Hospital.

It seemed like a good idea at first. For a few minutes, Roger and the Korvers thought the ancient Studebaker was going to manage to reach the Catholic village, not by following the national highway leading to Siem Reap and Battambang but by approaching the settlement from the rear and getting to Bê's house that way.

When Charles and Madeleine had told him of their determination to go to Bê's house, Roger had hesitated at first. He had no idea then that the demonstration had in fact turned into an uprising, and of course no idea that it had been carefully planned in advance that it would turn into one. From the roof of his building on the Boulevard Norodom, he hadn't seen anything except people bearing placards, which oddly enough were all written in English. He had thought it was just another demonstration for or against something and had scarcely bothered to read the historic texts Price had dreamed up. He had felt that at worst this one might go as far as the one several years before, when the demonstrators had ended up burning down the U.S. Embassy, a few hundred yards from his place. This time it was the right instead of the left that was filling the streets, but to Roger the difference was minimal. He had been in Paris the last time Pétain had marched down the Champs-Elysées; he was still there when some time later it had been De Gaulle's turn. Standing on the sidewalk, he had seen the same faces, cheering with the same enthusiasm, in both cases.

Even Charles Korver's phone call hadn't really upset him, though he had been aware of a sort of polite anguish in the old man's voice.

"Charles, you're worrying too much. Especially about Bê. That old squid certainly wouldn't let himself, or any of his family, get caught up in this sort of thing. And it'd be hard to mistake him for a pal of the late Ho Chi Minh.* But if it would reassure you . . ."

---

* Ho Chi Minh had died in September 1969.

They drove past the dizzyingly high wall of the huge stadium with its tens of thousands of seats—built at the express wish of Sihanouk—which Cambodia had needed about as badly as it needed an epidemic of yellow fever. Beyond the stadium, asphalt and cement disappeared, their place taken by little dirt streets and huts laid out every which way. They wandered about for many long minutes in a veritable labyrinth of shacks without spotting a single inhabitant.

"It looks as though there's a fire over by the Church of the Sacred Heart," Roger suddenly said.

The Korvers didn't answer. Huddled up next to each other on the front seat of the ancient car, they were staring intently at the tall column of smoke rising straight up before it slowly swirled southward. Through the lowered windows, the recent din seemed less deafening now. That reassured Roger. "Things are calming down." He drove on a few hundred yards farther and arrived in front of a pagoda that even the yellow-robed bonzes had deserted, just as the huts they had passed had all been deserted.

Roger started the engine again and drove around the temple.

He stopped dead.

The mob was there, less than thirty yards from the hood, unmoving and strangely silent. There were probably thousands of people there, but not one of them seemed to be paying the slightest attention to the Studebaker. Roger was suddenly filled with apprehension. *What in the world is happening?* he wondered. He shifted into neutral, ready to put the car in reverse. He turned his head and his eyes met Charles Korver's.

"I don't know," Charles said in answer to his unspoken question.

But Madeleine said imperiously, "Why don't you honk the horn? They'll get out of the way. I'm certainly not going to go back home before I have news of Bê and the others, who may need us, who surely need us. You know Cambodians: They shout and scream, but they're not vicious. We've lived with them for forty years now."

Roger hesitated.

"Honk, Roger," Madeleine said. "Go ahead and honk!"

Charles nodded.

"Here we go!" Roger said gaily, leaning on the horn button. The car crept forward and the mob moved to either side, as though reluctantly. Three hundred yards farther on, just as the car wheels touched the asphalt of the road to Siem Reap again, they had to stop once more, lost in the midst of a veritable human sea which not only would not let them through but closed in around them, surrounding them on all sides.

There was nothing to do but stop.

"Honk again, Roger," Madeleine said.

The horn sounded, a ridiculous beep that failed to produce the slightest result. Except to cause thousands of strangely blank eyes to stare intently at the three of them inside the car. There were certainly armed men, dressed like peasants or pedicab operators though they were neither, present in the crowd; but something else impressed Roger much more—those sullen faces with dull eyes fixed on the car and himself and his two friends, without seeming really to see them.

The memory of a scene dating back fifteen years flashed through Roger's mind. It was morning, one of the mornings like any other at the Central Market, with the usual hundreds of peasant men and women in black *sampots* and turbans, come to the market to sell their produce. Everything was as full of life, as colorful, as easygoing and relaxed as always. But then a group had entered the market from the end of the Rue Prey Nokor. It was made up of eight men bound together by a little steel chain attached to their hands and ankles. Half a dozen policemen were escorting them. At the time, Roger, who just happened to be passing by the market on his way home to bed after a night at the Saint-Hubert, had no idea who these prisoners were. He found out later: They were a group of outlaws, of "brigands," who among other misdeeds had kidnapped two children of a merchant to hold for ransom. The ransom had been paid but they had killed the children anyway. . . .

The group of bandits was being marched to the prison. Roger had first heard the silence that fell over the crowd, suddenly rooted to the spot, a complete, overwhelming silence. Then, leaving the stalls, people had little by little moved in on the child-killers. Very soon a human wall had formed as they passed by, had slowly closed in on them, making it impossible for them to move, to take another step forward. The faces of the crowd were curiously lifeless, like those wax dummies in the show windows of department stores in empty streets at night. Their eyes had gone blank and dull. The policemen escorting the prisoners had realized what was about to happen and had taken to their heels. And the butchery had begun. In a few moments, nothing was left of the eight men; in a terrifying orgy of violence, they had been hacked to pieces.

Today the faces surrounding the car were the same, the silence the same, the pupils of the eyes of the mob equally lifeless. Roger tried to talk with them, stringing together the few paltry words of Khmer that he knew: *"Kniom Barang . . . Kniom tao . . ."*

He didn't know how to finish the sentence. To have lived so many years in this country and be unable to put across even a simple idea, since its inhabitants didn't speak French! What a disastrous failure!

"Look!" Charles Korver said.

Roger looked in the direction Charles was pointing in, and his heart leapt. The dense crowd in front of them had irresistibly started to move aside. A silhouette appeared, clearing a rectilinear path before it, heading straight for the car. The voice was speaking Khmer, but it was nonetheless familiar, grave and slow. Lara reached the Studebaker.

"Drive ahead very slowly. They'll get out of your way."

He spoke again in Cambodian, in the calm, quiet voice of an animal tamer addressing wild beasts. The opening he had cleared for himself as he made his way to the Studebaker widened as if by magic. Roger shifted into first and accelerated very slowly, with Lara walking alongside, one of his thin, tanned hands resting on the windowsill of the car door and the burning-hot metal body. He went on talking to the mob, which continued to move aside.

"You can accelerate now. Head out of this mob and park up ahead next to my Land-Rover."

Roger did as he was instructed. The mob disappeared behind him in his rearview mirror. He drove on for two hundred yards. They had now come out on a long free stretch of highway, just beyond the Sacred Heart school, where the gate appeared to have been ripped off its hinges and at least two of the buildings set on fire.

"Well, that's that."

Lara had simply opened the front door of the Studebaker on Roger's side, put one foot inside, and ridden out through the mob in that way. He now stepped down again and searched automatically in the breast pocket of his jacket for a cigarette.

"I was looking for you," he said. "How come you came directly here? You should have gone by my place first. They'd have given you the message I left for you there."

There was a pained, sad expression on his tanned face.

"What about Lisa?" Roger asked.

"She's all right. Kutchaï's with her."

"We're anxious to know what's happened to Bê and his family," Madeleine said in her tiny voice. "It's obvious that something's happened to them."

Lara gave her a long look. "I'm terribly sorry," he said. "I got there too late."

Roger found the silence unbearable.

"Oh, my God," Charles finally said.

The old man opened the door of the Studebaker and got out, looking suddenly more frail and fragile than ever. "I have to go there."

"It's not necessary," Lara said. "Truly not. It wouldn't make any difference at this point."

"I have to go there."

"I do too," Madeleine said, trembling all over.

At a glance from Lara, Roger intervened. He quickly leaned across the front seat and, before Madeleine could get out of the car, closed the door Charles had left open. At that very moment a jeep braked to a stop, tires squealing. There was a machine gun mounted on the hood and Roger recognized Captain Kao.

That's all we needed—this madman showing up, Roger thought.

But Kao paid no attention to any of them except Lara, and the eyes of the two men seemed riveted on each other.

"What are you doing here?" Kao asked.

"Certainly not the same thing you're doing," Lara answered.

It was Lara who turned away first. He helped Charles into the Land-Rover and sat himself down behind the wheel. As he started the engine, his eyes stared into the captain's one last time. "Can you take care of them and make sure nothing happens to them?"

Kao contemplated the Catholic school in flames. A dozen yards or so away were five or six dead bodies of adolescent Vietnamese girls, in black skirts and blood-soaked white blouses.

"I'm counting on you," Lara said.

"Sure thing," Kao said. "No problem."

He seemed to have a vague smile on his face, the pupils of his eyes were gleaming, and the movable barrel of his machine gun appeared, as if by chance, to be aimed more or less in the direction of the Land-Rover.

"Thanks," Lara said. "I'll remember that."

Kao nodded his head.

The Land-Rover took off.

There were fifteen people dead at Bê's house, among them Bê himself. The elderly chauffeur must have been one of the first killed. His thin body, all skin and bones, lay on the threshold of the stone veranda with towering rectangular columns and old red-ocher walls. This house, in the thirty years at least since he had bought it, had always been his pride and joy. Here he had gathered his whole family around him, reigning over it like a patriarch.

His skull had been crushed. His features were surprisingly calm, crowned by his delicate fleece of black and silver hair cropped very short, and bearing that characteristic expression, at once sarcastic and dignified.

With a look of horrified surprise on his face, Charles Korver was wandering about from one corpse to another, from one room to another, recognizing a granddaughter of Bê's here, a nephew there. Over the years, he had come to know all of Bê's family, discovering that he was able to follow its ramifications and meanders far more easily than those of his own relatives in France.

"There's somebody missing. The *ti-nam.*"

Of his five servants she was the youngest, the one who had most recently entered his service, and the one occupying the lowest place in the household hierarchy. She was around seventeen or eighteen years old, a tiny little thing, always smiling and gay, a shy creature who cheerfully accepted the tyranny her compatriots and relatives exerted over her by virtue of tradition and seniority.

And then Charles suddenly remembered that the *ti-nam* had married a few months earlier, that she had followed her husband to another of the Vietnamese communities of Phnom Penh, on the other side of the city, along the road out to Pochentong airport.

Monsieur le Bep, however, was there in the house. He had tried to make his escape through the back door, taking with him his wife and four children, no doubt when the assailants had burst into the dwelling. The murderers had caught up with him. They had caught up with all six of them, and not one of them had been spared. Lara knelt alongside their bodies, examined them, made sure that none of them was still alive.

He rose to his feet, wiped the sweat from his forehead, leaving a trace of blood on his own skin. "Come, Charles. What use is there in staying here at this point?"

"But someone should see to it that they're decently buried!"

"I'll see to it. Come on now."

From in front of the house came the noise of a motor and the more characteristic sound of tank treads. The army was arriving, too late, to keep order, having obviously waited until it was too late to do so. Charles Korver was too shaky to stand on his feet and sat down on a wooden bed partly covered with a mat. He contemplated the altar of the family ancestors, with its yellowed photographs, its sticks of incense, its mangoes and papayas laid upon it as an offering, and next to a pastel pink and blue statue of the Virgin, the gaudy, motley-colored images of Vietnamese tutelary deities that he knew nothing whatever about.

"Come on, let's go," Lara repeated.

Despite the presence of all the dead bodies, the dominant odor was of frangipani and incense, mingled with the persistent, oppressive smell of *tortillons*, the little spirals set out on tables to burn very slowly and supposedly drive mosquitoes away.

Lara put his arm around Charles Korver's shoulders and led him off. Outside a lieutenant in a helmet questioned them: "Any survivors?"

"Not a single one."

The officer shook his head, visibly ill at ease. Lara helped Charles back into the Land-Rover. He was about to get in himself, but then turned back to the lieutenant. "What are you going to do with the bodies?"

"Our orders are to burn them. If nobody claims them."

"I'm claiming them. My name is Lara."

"I know you. Nobody will come near this house or these bodies. I'm going to leave two of my men here to guard them."

"What's your name?"

"Mey Seap. I'm from Prey Veng."

"I knew a Mey Kom who was a schoolteacher."

"My uncle. I'll take care of them, Monsieur Lara."

"Thank you."

The Land-Rover took off again, heading toward Phnom Penh. At one moment, hordes of children surrounded it, yelling and shouting. A few words from Lara sent them scattering. They ran off, looking back with disappointment in their eyes, but still mentally incapable of confronting the Barang with the pale eyes.

"Do you realize we don't even know their names?" Charles said. "Except for Bê. We always called the others the *bep*, the *ti-aï*, the *ti-nam*, the *ti-ba*. They'd worked for us for years and we didn't even know their names." Charles Korver shook his head slowly, clasping his astonishingly white little hands together, unable even to weep.

11

IT WAS EVEN MORE DIFFICULT TO ARRIVE AT AN EXACT ESTIMATE OF the number of Vietnamese massacred on March eighth—perhaps a thousand in Phnom Penh alone and a hundred in Svay Rieng—since the race riots went on all during the ninth, tenth, and above all the eleventh of March.

March 11 marked the high point of the "spontaneous" demonstrations. The evening before, in Paris, shortly before his departure for Moscow, Norodom Sihanouk had announced the imminent visit to Cambodia of the North Vietnamese Prime Minister, Pham Van Dong. To the conspirators planning the coup, who were doing their utmost to provoke a vast uprising of the entire population against the Viet Cong, such an announcement took on the proportions of a slap in the face. They responded with a maneuver that was even more "spontaneous" than the preceding ones: the sacking of the embassy of the Republic of North Vietnam and of the Provisional Republican Government of South Vietnam, which in theory at least was to replace the "Puppets of Saigon" as soon as the United States had abandoned them.

Once again, the incident was carefully stage-managed, and every step was taken to permit foreign correspondents, particularly the English-speaking ones, to witness the event in the most comfortable circumstances possible. Roger Bouès, for his part, learned at precisely two o'clock in the morning of the eleventh—well in advance—that an attack was imminent. His informant was a barmaid at the Saint-Hubert. He received confirmation of this piece of news less than an hour later at the Zigzag, his last stop of the night before heading home for bed. As he enjoyed Albert Vandekherkove's brochettes, a traditional repast at that hour, he passed the news on to the journalist with whom he was working, a Britisher by the name of Donaldson. The news left Donaldson completely cold. He hadn't been sober for two or three days and by this time was quite uninterested in the outside world with just two exceptions: the low neckline of a Chinese girl with a pleasantly plump bosom, and his recital, for the twelfth time that night, of the way he had almost played in the Five Nations championship rugby tournament, with the Rose Team—England. He had been chosen as a third-string wing, but unfortunately hadn't been called upon to replace anybody at all, since none of the players had fallen ill before the match.

"Otherwise I would have played against the Boniface brothers," he explained to the Chinese girl. "Do you realize what it means to play against the Boniface brothers?"

"Yes, sir," the Chinese girl said in English; she could also say *I love you* and *Give me money for the water closet* in that tongue.

Usually based in Hong Kong, Donaldson often went to Indochina on reporting assignments, thus far mostly to Saigon and the Vietnamese battle-fields. He had arrived in Phnom Penh four days earlier, already several sheets to the wind. He was a man who for ten years had regularly drunk a bottle of whiskey a day—never more than that; he didn't want to overdo it—till he had eventually began to suffer from vague sickish feelings. He had scientifically determined that it was, beyond all possible doubt, the soda in his whiskey-and-sodas that made him feel ill. By a valiant effort, he had managed to eliminate soda water from his diet. But without the pleasant tingle of Perrier bubbles on the tongue, his straight scotch had seemed rather a dreary portion to get down. Through a stroke of genius that surprised even him, he had conceived the idea of replacing the harmful soda water in his drinks with champagne. He adored the mixture, to the point that he could no longer do without it.

Roger suspected him of being an alcoholic.

On the morning of the eleventh, Roger turned up at the Hotel Royal at an early hour, and after a Homeric tussle that for a few moments took on the proportions of a free-for-all on the playing field at Twickenham, he managed to drag the Great Reporter into the shower and even to rouse a faint glimmer of consciousness in him. Then they joined a party of American, French, British, and other journalists (among these others was a Brazilian who claimed that his only real interest was the situation in Angola, but that somewhere along the line he'd made a mistake and boarded the wrong plane), and all of them left in a body to witness the spontaneous demonstration.

They grumbled at first at having had to get up so early in the morning. These Cambodians didn't seem to be acquainted with the customary practice these days, which dictated that a political event of any importance, if it were to have a chance of being covered by world-famous correspondents, absolutely had to take place after eleven o'clock in the morning and before six in the evening.

"In our day, every organizer of a revolution worthy of that name must keep such details in mind, for they are of inestimable importance," an eminent French journalist explained to Roger. "There are revolutions meant for the evening news roundups on TV at eight P.M., and those for the evening papers, which as anyone ought to know hit the streets at noon. Both have their particular clientele. Coups d'état launched at dawn ought to be forbidden by universal law. I'm thinking of a decision to that effect by the World Court at The Hague."

"Not to mention the differences in local time. They don't help any," Roger chimed in.

Everyone around him agreed: Time zones were the plague of modern revolutions. The eminent French reporter who was holding forth to Roger had now completely recovered from his early-morning daze; encouraged by this unanimity on the part of the international press, he let himself be carried along on his own momentum. Very soon, as usual, he got around to speaking of his personal enemy: a novelist-journalist and former paratroop officer who, according to him, had been explaining Indochina to his readers purely on the basis of his own personal dealings and difficulties, all more or less imaginary.

"According to him, it's because he refused to shake Ho Chi Minh's hand that the latter declared war on France; Dien Bien Phu fell because he missed his plane that day; Ngo Dinh Diem was placed in power by the CIA and then assassinated by order of the CIA because of articles that *he* had written; Souvanna Phouma owes his downfall in Laos to one of his novels, and Norodom Sihanouk is not long for this world because he made him wait thirty-five minutes for an interview he'd demanded. I wouldn't be surprised to learn that the Second World War broke out because the mother of our hero turned the Führer down when he asked her for a dance."

The eminent French reporter was a leftist and was ardently hoping for a Viet Cong victory in Vietnam, and for progressive Laotian and Khmer leftist factions to win power in Laos and Cambodia. He detested military men, present, past, and future, but only if they were Occidentals, and particularly if they tried their hand at writing and thus gave him competition.

The sacking of the embassies was a complete success. There was only one minor snag: One of the rioters, who doubtless lacked experience, stupidly tried to set fire to the North Vietnamese flag at the precise moment that an American television cameraman was changing reels. Fortunately, another Hanoi flag was found at a nearby Chinese merchant's (he had a stock of national emblems of all the countries likely to intervene in Cambodia, just in case there was an unexpected invasion). The rioter was asked to begin all over again, and he willingly agreed. His apologies were accepted.

Two days later, on March 13, the Lon Nol/Sirik Matak government denounced all the accords, whether official or secret, concluded by Sihanouk with Hanoi. A formal demand was made that the Viet Cong troops retire immediately from Cambodian soil. At the same time, as the result of a prearranged agreement with Saigon carefully worked out by Price and his colleagues in the CIA, important forces of South Vietnamese Rangers in white scarves moved toward the Cambodian border, ready to march on the Bec-de-Canard and sooner or later on all the Viet Cong bases in the Sanctuary.

On March 17, playing the role of the faithful and respectful lieutenant to the very last second, Lon Nol had public prayers said for the recovery of Samdech-Euv Norodom Sihanouk, whose health was failing. Sihanouk was in Moscow at the time and scheduled to leave the next day for Peking, the last stop on his tour of the officers' messes of global politics before his return to Phnom Penh to bring his mischievous replacements to heel, his confidence renewed by reiterated promises of support from Pompidou, Brezhnev, Mao, and, above all, his beloved friend Chou En-lai.

And finally, on March 18, the decisive session of the Khmer National Assembly took place, in the course of which Lon Nol demanded that the Chief of State and former King of Cambodia, Norodom Sihanouk, be removed from office by the vote of the Assembly for having authorized the invasion of the sacred soil of the fatherland by the Atheists with Gleaming Teeth. In the thinking of Lon Nol and Sirik Matak, as well as of their American and Indonesian advisers, Sihanouk's reaction would doubtless be the same as that of all deposed sovereigns (for example, of the ex-emperor Bao Dai in 1955, after having been ousted by Ngo Dinh Diem): He too would retire to France, since he was so fond of that country, to the Côte d'Azur, where he had a villa—a modest one to be sure—there to devote himself to composing his dreadful music at his leisure.

Only one incident marred the orderly proceedings. To give the removal of Sihanouk as Chief of State the appearance of vast popular backing, several hundred people specially trained as spontaneous demonstrators had been called in to parade before the Assembly, shouting at the top of their lungs for the removal of the Chief of State. Unfortunately, out of force of habit and a reflex that went back twenty-nine years, these demonstrators began to shout "*Vive* Samdech" and "*Vive* Sihanouk," thus causing a near-panic among the deputies, who leapt to the conclusion that they were being confronted with a genuine demonstration. The organizers of the demonstration managed to shut them up and make them change their collective political will in the space of a few seconds. They thereupon began to yell "Throw the Viet Cong out of the country," "Down with Sihanouk," and "Cambodia for Cambodians." But the deputies had sweat bullets for a few minutes.

Cheng Heng, the president of the National Assembly, was a man with experience: He had long held the post of director of the central prison. The rules he set for the vote about to be taken left no room for chance. There were admittedly three ballots handed to each deputy. He was to use a blue one if he voted for Sihanouk's removal from office, a white one if he voted against it, and a white one ruled off in squares if he abstained. But Cheng Heng, who considered any man at liberty a prisoner who does not realize he is one, ruled that every ballot must be signed with the name of the deputy casting it.

As a consequence, the removal of Norodom Sihanouk from office was passed by unanimous vote.

12

THOMAS AQUINAS O'MALLEY REREAD THE LETTER ALOUD AND looked Douglas Fairbanks straight in the eye. "What's your opinion on the subject?"

Douglas Fairbanks did not answer. He was hanging suspended from the chandelier and eating a banana as he nonchalantly swayed back and forth, perhaps contemplating his next move.

Douglas Fairbanks was a little wou-wou gibbon about six months old, with ash-blonde hair, a black muzzle, and two bristling white eyebrows— O'Malley was of the opinion that he resembled a frisky double of Lionel Barrymore. Douglas Fairbanks was only two feet tall but his arms appeared to be twice that long and ended in great clawed fingers that were amazingly strong. Because of him, O'Malley had been obliged to redo the entire ceiling of the living room of the villa he had rented for his stay in Phnom Penh: He had installed big wooden bars more or less all over it, amid which Douglas Fairbanks—like the film star of the same name in *The Mark of Zorro* or *The Black Pirate*—leapt about with stunning virtuosity. The spectacle was all the more astounding in that the creature's face remained impassive, no matter what position he assumed or how suddenly he took off. At times, such as the present moment, the little primate remained absolutely motionless, abruptly turning into a statue after a session of effortless gliding. Then he would take off again in the most unpredictable fashion. He rarely came down from the ceiling, and when he did he looked clumsy, using his huge arms as balance poles with his curved fingers just touching the floor. O'Malley had not yet succeeded in getting close to him, much less petting him. At best he was able to get him to accept the dried fruits he bought in wholesale quantities just for him. But Douglas Fairbanks quite clearly preferred spiders, which he ate, with visible delectation, only if they were still alive.

Thomas Aquinas folded the letter in three and slid it into an envelope which he did not seal, merely tucking in the flap. He put the envelope in an inside pocket of his suit coat. Still hanging suspended by one hand, with the air of a dead leaf reluctant to fall, Douglas Fairbanks watched him intently.

"If anybody calls, tell them I've gone out."

As a matter of fact, O'Malley didn't have a phone. He left, closing the door behind him without bothering to lock it. He walked a few hundred yards down the Boulevard Monivong, then finally gave in to the engaging smile of a pedicab boy who had been pedaling along a yard or so behind him.

"*Tao*, American Embassy."

"Me know where is," the pedicab boy said.

"Tell that to the Marines," O'Malley said.

"Me not know Marines," the pedicab boy said.

It was almost eleven in the morning when he arrived at the entrance to the embassy. He gave the pedicab boy twenty riels, knowing it was far too much for so short a ride. The Marines in their dress helmets solemnly looked him up and down and decided to offer a smile of recognition only after he'd shown his pass, even though they'd seen him every morning for almost ten months now. But orders were orders, and they had recently become even stricter.

The Frenchwoman who had replaced Lisa as his assistant was already in the little room adjoining his own office and was reading the latest issue of *Réalités Cambodgiennes,* whose editor-in-chief was that well-known journalist Norodom Sihanouk.

"You've had two phone calls," the young woman informed him. Her name was Francine and she was the wife of a Cambodian technician whose field, as far as Thomas Aquinas could remember, was either petroleum or telecommunications.

"The first one was from Monsieur Charles Korver, the other one from Mrs. Ford. You are to call them both back."

"Thank you, Francine." He sat down in his chair, thoughtfully contemplating the immense photographic reproduction of the Avenue of Demons at Angkor Thom on the wall panel opposite him; the photo was by Roger Bouès and was extraordinary, so lifelike it was overwhelming.

Maggie Ford was the ambassador's secretary. *Whom should I call first? His Excellency the Ambassador or Charles?* He dialed the number himself, using the cap of his pen.

"You called me, Charles?"

"Could you come to lunch? If you've nothing better to do . . ."

Thomas Aquinas had a lunch date with the head of the British Council library, an Irishman from Belfast.

"Even if I searched for a long time, I could surely not find anything better to do," O'Malley said. He had been told of the massacre of the Korvers' Vietnamese servants, and the entire affair had so sickened him that he had vomited.

After hanging up, he took time for another long look at the Avenue of Demons, slowly turning his swivel chair first in one direction and then the other. His desk top was completely clear as usual, without a single file folder visible, contrary to the long-established tradition common to junior functionaries, American or other, of keeping one's desk piled high with pointless papers for the sole purpose of proving that one is swamped with work. Thomas Aquinas O'Malley had always refused to go along with this little game, and was even less inclined to do so now. He had next to nothing to do and his desk top ostentatiously proclaimed the fact.

He decided to phone Maggie Ford.

"The ambassador wanted to see you," Maggie said. "You asked to see him, didn't you? If you'd been around, he would have given you a few minutes of his time. But it's too late now. He's got a whole bunch of people in his office."

"Thanks anyway."

"Wait a second! Because of your Irish charm, and only because of it, I'll try to get you in to see him this afternoon if your many duties don't detain you elsewhere. Was it something urgent you wanted to see him about?"

"I just wanted to give him a letter. It can wait."

"Around five o'clock," Maggie said. "I'll do my very best."

"Great."

He called the British Council to cancel his lunch date with the Irishman from Belfast, and then, since it was barely past eleven when he left the embassy, he walked to the Korvers', taking his time, going the long way around through the Palace grounds.

Arriving at the Korvers', he discovered that Lara and Lisa were there too. For a moment his heart sank. If he had known the Laras were coming for lunch too, he would doubtless have turned down Charles' invitation. O'Malley had no illusions: He was desperately in love with the young woman, and one of the happiest periods in his life had been the few weeks he had spent with Lisa working at his side, till the day she had told him she was going to marry a man named Lara, whom he knew absolutely nothing about. This love of his was an evident fact, as inescapable as having red hair or being too short. He had become aware of it after a genuine depression that had lasted for several days, and had tried to make fun of himself for being in love with her, without much success.

He hadn't seen Lisa for more than two months, not since a New Year's party at the Hotel Raja. He thought she looked dazzling today, so beautiful it broke his heart. Her pregnancy, which would soon be over, had not clouded her face in any way, despite the climate; on the contrary, she was radiant. Thomas Aquinas had known her to be completely calm and collected; at present she was Olympian and he was intuitively aware, physically certain, of how deeply attached she and Lara were to each other now—which did nothing to make him feel less ill at ease.

He said hello to Lara and shook hands with him. O'Malley had always been of two minds about Lara: He appreciated, certainly, the man's very strong personality, his intelligence, his unfailing courtesy, even his humor when he let it show. Lara impressed him, and O'Malley almost admired him, in the way one admires an elder brother—after all, there must have been ten years' difference in age between them. But the difficulty was that behind the man's perpetual courteous calm, the mild-mannered self-assurance of the man who knows and has no need to prove it, O'Malley thought he detected too much violent passion. Lara made him uncomfortable because he suspected he was a man given to extremes. This was also Roger Bouès' opinion, expressed on the one occasion when Lara's name had come up in conversation; but Roger accepted Lara just as he was, without the slightest mental reservation, on simple faith, a faith that O'Malley did not share and moreover was incapable of acquiring.

"The *ti-nam* is alive," Charles Korver said. "She and her husband happened to be on the other side of the city at the time of the first demonstration, the one on March eighth. There where they were, the rioting was less violent, at least on the first day. Lara was able to find her in the afternoon and bring her back here to the villa, where we're hiding her and her husband, whose name is Tung. We don't know if they're going to stay. Tung is talking about going back to Vietnam. In their case, 'going back' is just a manner of speaking: Both of them were born in Cambodia."

The young Vietnamese in question entered at precisely that moment, carrying a tray. On hearing his name mentioned, he greeted everyone with a bow. He had the face of an adolescent. Once again O'Malley wondered how Lara or Charles, or others who weren't Asians either, could tell the difference between a Khmer and a Vietnamese, between a Laotian and a Chinese, or for that matter between a Japanese and a Korean. Of course, Cambodians were usually taller, darker-skinned, with something almost Indian about their build and their faces, whereas the Vietnamese were—or seemed to Thomas Aquinas to be—more Chinese. Those at least were the guiding principles. But as for applying them in practice . . .

"What do you expect?" Charles was saying. "We couldn't do anything else for those poor people. . . ."

He had waited until the young Vietnamese had headed off to the kitchen again before going on. "The entire family of the *ti-nam*—her real name is Lieu—was killed in the massacre. She's alone in the world now. As for Tung, he lost his parents and his two younger sisters, and he's had no news of his elder brother. They're safe here at least, until things calm down again. And then too, Madeleine and I are well along in years and we've never been alone. Furthermore, Lieu herself wanted to come back to work and she asked us to take her husband on too."

"You did exactly the right thing," Thomas Aquinas said. He was still thoroughly disconcerted at this unexpected meeting with Lisa and her husband.

He took advantage of the silence that followed, with no sound but the tinkle of ice in their glasses. "I had a talk with our ambassador a few days ago and asked him to accept my request for a transfer. He suggested I wait another week and think it over. Well, the week has gone by. I'm probably going to leave Cambodia."

"Oh, good heavens, what a terrible shame!" Madeleine exclaimed with sincere dismay.

O'Malley managed a feeble laugh. "I have the feeling that I'm absolutely useless. It's more or less a general rule that a cultural attaché isn't good for much of anything, but in my case I've probably set a record."

"You're exaggerating," Lisa said with a smile. "I've seen with my own eyes how hard you work."

Her kindness overwhelmed O'Malley, who was feeling more and more ill at ease. It was Lara who finally came to his rescue, by asking him what his next post after Phnom Penh would be.

"If I'm offered one," Thomas Aquinas answered. "They may just toss me out the door. But they're more likely to give me a desk in Washington, along with the usual air-conditioner, wastepaper basket, and pencil sharpener."

"I've been to Washington and know the city a bit," Lara said in his slow, grave voice, gazing at O'Malley with a thoughtful look in his eyes.

They began to talk about the United States, and the lunch didn't go too badly. When Thomas Aquinas, on the pretext that he had an appointment back at the embassy, said he ought to be leaving, Lara left with him, offering to drive him back downtown in the 504.

"Why are you leaving Cambodia?"

O'Malley was so taken aback by the question that he remained silent for a long moment. Weighing his words carefully, he finally answered: "Not for personal reasons."

Lara nodded. As usual, he gave the impression of being exceptionally, almost abnormally, calm. *This man has what's called presence. I think I'd be able to feel him next to me even if I were deaf and blind,* O'Malley thought.

"Well, why, then?"

O'Malley hesitated again, almost annoyed by Lara's persistence. But he finally decided to answer by asking a question in turn: "Do you know a man named Price?"

"I've heard of him."

"There are certain people whom you dislike intensely on first sight. They can be of almost any nationality."

"I've felt that sometimes."

"I'm not the least bit interested in politics," O'Malley said.

"I'm not either," Lara said. He smiled. "I'm even less interested than you are, if that's possible. But even if one isn't at all interested in rain, it falls nonetheless. And it gets you wet."

"An apt analogy."

"Isn't it, though?"

Lara smiled again, turning his head toward O'Malley this time, and there was great warmth in his smile, as though it were an offer of friendship. Instead of heading directly back downtown, he had veered off to the right at the Phnom and they drove by the Club Sportif and the Lycée Descartes.

"Do you have time to have a drink with me?" Lara asked.

He had put the question in a casual, offhanded tone of voice. It might have been no more than an invitation for politeness' sake; later on, however, much later, O'Malley became convinced this was not the case, that on that day, which in fact was the only time the two of them had had any sort of real contact, even if only for a few moments, Lara had wanted to talk to him. But O'Malley never knew what it was he might have wanted to talk to him about. At the time, letting his nervousness, his obvious jealousy (which he knew was absolutely ridiculous), his need to be alone after a lunch during which he had felt supremely uncomfortable, get the better of him, he had turned down the invitation.

"I really do have an appointment back at the embassy."

Lara nodded politely and did not insist. A few minutes later the 504 stopped outside the embassy. Regretting it later, O'Malley managed to get out of the car in such a way as to avoid shaking hands with Lara. He simply gave a wave of his hand to bid him goodbye. Not only was it the first time the two men had exchanged more than the usual polite small talk of cocktail or dinner parties, it was the only time. As it turned out, they were never to see each other again.

13 LARA HAD GONE TO BANGKOK AROUND THE MIDDLE OF FEBRUARY. He left again the day after he arrived and thus had remained in Thailand only some thirty hours, which was more than enough time to explain to Christiani what he expected of him. The Corsican received the news that he was henceforth to involve himself in the business of supplying arms without turning a hair; he wasn't the sort to work himself into a panic over such a trivial matter, and in all truth, since his arrival in the Far East in 1946 on a French freighter (not as a passenger but as a cabin boy), he had had a great deal of experience at smuggling all manner of contraband goods. He had trafficked a bit in cigarettes and especially in gold, and at one time had even seriously considered going in for smuggling opium and other drugs in a big way. The fact that he was working for Lara, and later on with him as his co-partner, had kept him from doing so. Lara had made himself perfectly clear on the subject of opium and drugs of any sort.

"The minute I find out, or even hear talk, that you're involved in drug smuggling, I won't have one thing more to do with you. Except to come and settle accounts with you. And there's to be no more smuggling of any sort. I want an import-export business that's absolutely legitimate, without the slightest shadow of suspicion. Take it or leave it."

Lara hadn't raised his voice or made a great dramatic scene out of this announcement of terms. As usual, he had spoken calmly and quietly, his pale blue-gray eyes staring straight into Christiani's. But the Corsican, who was far from stupid, had understood perfectly. And things had gone along just fine for him. Lara's Chinese friends—Christiani was well aware of these friendships, though he had no idea how they had come about—had gone out of their way to give the little import-export business a helping hand in any way they could from the very beginning, and not without success: In ten years the company had become an amazingly prosperous enterprise, and Christiani, who had meantime been named Lara's partner, had made piles of money. And even though the drug market had expanded enormously, especially after the Americans had begun to arrive in ever-increasing numbers in Vietnam, and despite the fact that the profits from the drug traffic, controlled by the Chinese and by certain of Christiani's compatriots in Saigon and elsewhere, had become fantastic, Christiani had scrupulously avoided becoming involved in it.

And now, arms smuggling.

Christiani knew where to get his hands on some. (If Lara had asked him to hunt up angels for him, the Corsican would have rushed off to locate some, and no doubt found them.) As for arms, Christiani knew somebody who knew somebody who probably knew somebody else. He told a first contact about his problem, and the party in question thereupon set up a meeting with a second, who arranged an appointment with a third, who saw to it that Christiani met a fourth. The fourth was in Hong Kong, with a passport in the name of Holek which was no proof whatsoever of his real identity. Holek made no secret of the fact that he had long been active in Latin America, particularly in Central America, where he had been at one and the same time the dealer supplying arms to the left-wing president of Guatemala, a certain Arbenz Guzman, to whom he had sold, for four dollars apiece, Garand rifles and Sten guns that he had bought for fifty cents apiece, and the supplier of Arbenz Guzman's adversaries in Honduras, Nicaragua, and El Salvador, financed by United Fruit and Standard Oil, who hated Arbenz Guzman's guts. At the time, Holek had been working under another name for a famous arms dealer from Philadelphia. After that, Holek had set himself up in business on his own.

"What sort of arms?" he had asked Christiani.

"Individual ones above all. Assault rifles and submachine guns mostly. And maybe some mortars, some grenade launchers, and some rocket launchers."

"Do you have a preference as to the nationality of the manufacturer?"

"In principle, I couldn't care less," the Corsican answered. "As long as they're 7.62 millimeter weapons."

"The standard NATO caliber, eh? Bah, weapons of that caliber are beginning to be outmoded. Everybody's adopting small-caliber ones of the 5.56 type and lighter weapons. Do you know why? Because the main thing isn't so much to kill as to wound, contrary to what almost everybody thinks. You can rest assured that humanitarian sentiments don't enter into it, luckily; it's simply that a unit armed for combat is far more inconvenienced by its wounded than by its dead. But I'm not going to give you a lecture on the subject.

"To make a long story short, I have two sorts of suppliers. The first is in the West, and the other one is the Czech Omnipol. Let's take a look at the available assault rifles first. The West offers you G-3's manufactured by Heckler and Koch, Swiss SIG Neuhausen M-57's, or the classic Belgian FAL made by Herstal. I can deliver you the latter in its heavy version, with a thicker barrel and a bipod that converts it into a Bren-type light machine gun. It uses NATO 7.62's. In the East, we have the weapons manufactured by the Czechs of course, but I suppose that like everybody else you'd rather have that damned Automat Kalashnikov 1947, which is simply a slavish copy of the Mauser Stürmgewehr 44. But then there's the fact that the 7.62 by 38.6's of the AK-47 are also standard ammunition for the SKS carbine and the Deqtyarev light machine gun, and that has its advantages. If your clients have any sort of contacts with people using Soviet arms—I'm just supposing—the AK-47's are preferable. And I haven't mentioned M-16's. . . ."

"Too expensive."

"We won't talk about them then."

At no time had Christiani said who his clients were, so that Holek could pretend not to have any idea who they were.

"One last word nonetheless about assault rifles. At this very moment Heckler and Koch in Germany and the Spanish Special Matériel Research Center, the CETME, are in the process of cooking up a little marvel for us. They've gone even farther than the Americans with the M-16 that weighs only three kilos and fires 5.6 by 45 Remington 223's. They're developing a tungsten bullet for us, that's beveled so that it turns at the moment of impact with a body: it's going to make wounds that are real beauties. And it's only a 4.56 caliber at that. But in my opinion, they're going to have fouling problems."

Holek pursed his lips. You would have thought he was master chef

Paul Bocuse speaking of the lark mousse with juniper berries served at the Troisgros brothers'.

"Submachine guns now. For close combat, they're obviously superior to assault rifles."

He proposed Italian Beretta M-12's, Franchi LF-57's used by the Italian Navy, Danish Modsens, Swedish Carl-Gustavs, German Ermas, Australian Owens, Spanish Parincos, Swiss SIG MP-310's, Luxembourg Solas, old English Stens, Israeli UZIs, Austrian Steyrs, Finnish Suomis, long-outmoded Japanese Nagoya 100's—"you'll get them for nothing"—not to mention all sorts of Czech ZK's.

His head swimming at this inventory that was not even complete, Christiani finally chose classic Russian P.P.S.M.'s because he knew the Chinese had enormous numbers of them and could doubtless supply Ieng Samboth with ammunition. And since French culture, after all, had left some traces in Indochina, he also placed an order for some good old MAT-49's, used at Dien Bien Phu.

"The only submachine gun in the world especially designed to be used as a beer-bottle opener," Holek remarked, fishing up the hoary old joke that always surfaced when MAT-49's were mentioned.

As a matter of fact, it was true, or very nearly so: The front of the trigger guard designed at Châtellerault and manufactured by the French government arms factory at Tulle had no equal as a bottle opener.

"It's the MAT's chief merit," Holek said.

Christiani gave up the thought of ordering any mortars: much too expensive. As for the rocket launchers, he decided he'd eventually purchase some, but put off placing an order for them till later. Procuring weapons wasn't everything; one had to be sure of having a steady supply of ammunition for them, and he had a few doubts on this score.

He went back to Bangkok, and three or four days later a Chinese from the influential colony firmly established in Thailand came to see him and announced that he could place at Christiani's disposal, for whatever use he might care to make of it, the sum of 235,000 American dollars, payable in Bangkok, Hong Kong, Manila, Tokyo, or even in Switzerland. Through mysterious though apparently most effective channels, Ieng Samboth, and perhaps other Khmer Rouge leaders as well, were doing their part to finance the purchase of arms. This sum of $235,000 was added to the $65,000 that, despite Christiani's disapproving shakes of the head, Lara contributed out of his own pocket, drawing very heavily on his liquid assets of the moment.

Christiani had arranged with Holek that the first delivery of arms would be made by a freighter flying the Japanese flag, most probably between the twentieth and thirtieth of March. More exact information would be furnished when the time came, at least ten days before the operation. These were extremely short lead times, as Holek had proudly pointed out, explaining that the situation in Southeast Asia, in Indochina as well as in Malaysia for example, allowed him to stockpile arms right there in the area—he didn't say where—so as to ensure rapid delivery.

At the beginning of this same month of March 1970, Christiani made two reconnaissance flights along the Thai coast at the foot of the Cardamomes. He found the place Ieng had chosen satisfactory, but no more than that. Both times, the plane was piloted by the Strasbourg Sausage—that is to say, Boudin.

Christiani returned a third time to the place where the arms were to be unloaded, arriving this time in a big cabin cruiser that belonged to him. This last inspection was no more reassuring. He who was imperturbability personified, for whom smuggling was second nature, was beset by a gnawing anxiety he couldn't explain.

In a word, he was scared. And he became even more so when on the afternoon of the eighteenth, he learned of the coup d'état that had taken place in Phnom Penh.

After mid-February, when he returned from Bangkok, Lara left Lisa only once, to go to Sré to check on the improvements being made there. At his request and Lisa's, Kutchaï was overseeing the project, and the work was being done by a small team of Cambodians in whom the Jaraï had complete confidence.

The house on the island had been enlarged; three rooms had been added, two of them, as well as a sort of large storeroom, having been dug directly out of the earth and rock that formed the island's main rise, on which the building abutted. The result was odd. It somewhat resembled Robinson Crusoe's house as seen by a movie set designer: half troglodyte dwelling, half forest hideaway. One thing was certain in any case: It was invisible from the mainland, from any point at sea around the island, and from overhead as well. Far from clearing away the vegetation growing all around the house, they had made more plantings, and very soon the luxuriant tropical growth had done the rest, covering the ebony railing running around the veranda, which could be reached only by a narrow, winding path that looked like a tunnel hollowed through the greenery. Even the latania roof had been invaded and was now entirely covered over; its too-severe geometrical lines had thus been softened, becoming natural, and the few square meters of the house that might still be visible—from a plane overhead, for example—lay in the shadow of the hillock.

In one of the little coves on the island, Kutchaï had dredged a channel of exactly the same size as the boat they now referred to as the junk, or even the sampan. The boat, bought by Lara in Bangkok, could now slide into it as snugly as a sword into its sheath and—just for fun, he said—Kutchaï came up with a sort of camouflage net which, once the mast of the boat had been lowered to the deck, completely hid the craft

Just for fun. The entire project, in fact, was to some degree a game. They were playing, like children who build a cabin in the woods or at the far end of the garden, acting out the old myth of the desert island entirely cut off from the outside world, a place that cannot be taken by storm, a refuge all the more safe in that not a soul knows about it. And it was true that outside of the Korvers—to whom Lara and Lisa had mentioned the name of the island and its existence, as well as the use to which they intended to put it—no one except Kutchaï knew of it. Not even Roger Bouès ever heard a word about it. As for Charles and Madeleine, since Lara and Lisa said no more to them about it, and since they themselves were completely preoccupied by what was happening around them in Phnom Penh and were still shocked by the death of Bê and his family, they carefully refrained from asking questions and never visited Sré; no doubt they had decided that it was more or less Lisa and Lara's secret garden, treasured above all for sentimental reasons.

Lisa was later to remember the eerie atmosphere that reigned in Phnom Penh in the course of these weeks, the endless discussions that she, Lara, and Kutchaï had about Sré and the project going on there, the uncontrollable fits of laughter that sometimes overcame all three of them as they dreamed up heaven-only-knew-what mad plans, from an underground swimming pool with water feeding directly into it from the sea which could also be used as a bathtub, to an underwater gallery built all around the island and glassed in on one side so one could walk about in it contemplating the species of coral and fish that in few other places in the world are as colorful and abundant as they are in that particular spot in the Gulf of Siam.

Nothing was too far-fetched.

Lisa had become used to Kutchaï's ways. Not without difficulty in the early days. The first thing she had been struck by was the Jaraï's profound air of mystery, what with his colossal physique of a wild man from the jungle and the speech of a cultivated European just landed in Cambodia. She had come to enjoy the fierce, mordant humor of the Khmer and had finally had to bow to the fact that the complicity, the fraternity linking Kutchaï and her husband were a *fait accompli* that nothing could ever change. And immediately she began to allow herself to give in, more and more often, to her warm feelings of friendship toward him. At other times she was suddenly aware, despite herself, of the difference between the two men, of the abnormal gleam in the pupils of the Jaraï's huge, bloodshot eyes, of his mute, rather disturbing laugh, of an attitude. And at such times she would see Kutchaï as a wild animal, in whom a latent danger always lurked.

She discovered to her surprise that he was, or had been, married, not just once but three times, inasmuch as he had at least three wives. He did not appear to have very steady relationships with them, though he must have gotten together with them from time to time, since he had ten or twelve children by them. With one exception, Lisa never saw any of these children; one day, however, the Laras did happen to find their friend in the company of a boy of fifteen. With his usual laugh, Kutchaï explained that the youngster was one of his sons, that the boy was studying to be an architect or a doctor some day—he wasn't sure yet just which. Whereupon the Jaraï had changed the subject, and from that day on, whenever Lisa asked him anything about the boy, he would invariably answer that Seap, his eldest son, was just fine, as were all the rest of his family. That was absolutely all Lisa could get out of him. She confided this to Lara, who took refuge in a more or less deliberate vagueness and replied that Kutchaï's private life was none of their concern, that it had never been his concern, that he didn't know a thing about it, that it was Kutchaï's problem and nobody else's, that this or these families she'd suddenly discovered the existence of lived, he thought, one out toward Kompong Thom, the second one somewhere in Phnom Penh, and the third, if in fact he had only three, in Pursat maybe or perhaps Battambang or Kompong Chhnang.

"Or Stockholm," Lisa said, piqued.

"Why not? He can do as he pleases."

Lara pointed out to his wife that, as his partner, Kutchaï must be quite well off financially, even though he continued to live without any apparent earthly possessions.

"What in the world does he do with his money then?" Lisa asked.

"That's a question you'll have to ask him."

"Don't *you* have any idea?"

"Not the slightest. A few years ago I offered to make him a partner in the import-export business in Bangkok, along with Christiani and me. All he would have had to do was put up a small amount of money. He refused, and I didn't press the point."

Kutchaï remained as mysterious a figure as before.

Lara left in the morning on his one trip to Sré and came back that night. Otherwise, he did not leave Lisa. In fact, during the last weeks of February and the first weeks of March, the couple seldom left the villa on the Rue Phsar Dek. Twice they accepted dinner invitations they received, the first from French friends who worked at UNESCO, and the second from a rich Chinese trader named Liu.

Since she had first thought that Liu was simply on old friend of Lara's, Lisa was greatly surprised to learn that he was really her husband's uncle-in-law by Lara's first marriage. Her initial surprise was tempered by a sort of embarrassment that she suddenly felt a little ashamed of.

"Why didn't you tell me sooner?" She was not referring to the marriage itself—Lara had told her about it during their first stay on Sré—but to the existence of this Asiatic uncle.

Lara had shrugged and answered, "I didn't think of it."

She had to be content with this reply. In any event, she found Liu to be an extremely affable, remarkably cultivated man, who spoke both English and French perfectly. She was charmed by him, especially by his way of speaking of China, which remained his country even though he was definitely not a Communist. If and when they visited Hong Kong, he offered to place at their disposal a villa he had there—a "modest villa," as he put it.

Lara later gave her the word about these supposedly modest accommodations. "The Liu family owns a good part of Star Heights, and a few other similar little properties all over Southeast Asia, and in London and in California as well."

Aside from these two evenings out, the only people they saw during this time were the Korvers, Thomas Aquinas O'Malley on the day he informed them he was leaving Cambodia, and, naturally, Kutchaï. Roger Bouès paid them just one visit, speaking with his usual high spirits of his new line of work as a photographer.

In the villa on the Rue Phsar Dek they had only one servant, a Cambodian by the name of Seng, who wore a permanent smile on his face but was otherwise impassive and seldom said a word. Seng prepared them succulent fish dishes and a Cambodian soup that Lisa adored, *samla men tiou,* a sweet-and-sour soup with beef and vegetables, seasoned with ginger, citronella grass, and saffron. He went off home each night, leaving them by themselves, and they spent their evenings—they always went to bed very late—playing gin rummy or *jacquet,* a game that Lisa decided was more or less the same as American backgammon, fierce games, in the course of which Lara cheated with a smiling, joyous shamelessness that made Lisa furious, though usually not for long; she simply hated losing. They also listened to music, playing the same old jazz records of the thirties and forties over and over again, intermingled with Jacques Brel or Sinatra and classical music, the last mostly German. The villa on the Rue Phsar Dek was neither especially beautiful nor especially comfortable, quite different in this respect from the Korvers'. They really didn't care, and outside of more or less properly furnishing a living room and two bedrooms, they'd hardly even bothered putting furniture in the other rooms.

They were so withdrawn from the world, so wrapped up in their life together from day to day that even the death of Bê and his family, whom they had thought highly of, did not really bring them out of their cocoon. In the days following the expedition he had made with Kutchaï to bring back the *ti-nam* and her husband, Lara did not set foot outside except to cross the Avenue des Français to call on the Korvers. He devoted all his time to his wife, with a sweetness and a tenderness that Lisa was to remember all the rest of her life. He seemed to have given up even those long confabs in Khmer with Kutchaï that had so annoyed her in the past. In front of her at least, the two men never mentioned the current situation. Of course, Lisa would have had to be both blind and completely insensitive to have been unaware of how distressed Lara was at what was happening in Phnom Penh. But he made such a valiant and almost pathetic effort not to show it that she thought it best to appear not to have noticed a thing.

Moreover, the fact that she was very close to term tended to make her more self-absorbed than usual. On March 15, she thought she was beginning to go into labor and announced to Madeleine, who had immediately been alerted by Seng, that the two doctors had won, hands down, the bet they had made with the little old lady that March 15 would be the exact date. Lara rushed his wife to the French Hospital, where she arrived just in time to realize she no longer felt even the slightest twinge; the blessed event was not going to take place until later.

It took place on March 17, 1970, just after nine P.M. It was a boy, as Lara and she had hoped, and they named him Mathias.

"The ninth generation of Laras in Indochina," was the first thing Lisa said on regaining consciousness.

14

IENG SAMBOTH HAD BEEN ON THE MARCH FOR FOUR DAYS NOW. HE was leading a small detachment of seventy-two men he had chosen himself, one by one, using as his criterion the indifference and near-antipathy he felt toward each of them. They were all Samrés, taciturn, gloomy forest-dwellers, a number of whom had no idea that such things as trains, television sets, telephones, even existed; almost all of them were very young, fanaticized, immured in their faith in a single cause, ready for anything, and able to march for hours and hours on end, for entire days in the heat without the least fatigue and without leaving behind them the slightest trace of their passage. All of them were dressed in black and wore, either around their necks or wrapped about their heads, the large red and white checkered scarves, the *kramas,* that had become their emblem. Ieng was convinced he had absolutely nothing in common with them, a fact that nearly drove him to despair and caused him to reproach himself bitterly. Moreover, he scarcely said a word to them, outside of giving them a few orders that were hardly necessary, since they were as well aware as he was, perhaps even more aware, of what they had to do.

On March 14, at first light, they crossed the Mekong at approximately the same spot where, a few weeks earlier, Lara and Kutchaï had passed over to the other side. On the afternoon of that same day they had met up with another detachment of Khmer Rouge, sent out to establish contact with them by Rath, who was directing operations in at least half the province of Kompong Thom. The two detachments, curiously identical, had said very little to each other. Certain information was exchanged, whereupon Ieng and his men had left. On the night of the fifteenth, between two patrols of the armored FARK column whose schedule had been reported on by the scouts, they had crossed the highway linking Kompong Thom and Kompong Cham. On the sixteenth they had advanced all day toward the northwest, leaving Kompong Thom behind on their right and managing to avoid, thanks to information furnished by villagers, another column of troops heading eastward from Phnom Penh. They had halted for only a few hours' rest after more than thirty hours of marching without a pause, and had then set out again. The night of the seventeenth found them well past the highway to Siem Reap, advancing rapidly on Rovieng, whose outskirts, if not the village itself, they had reached late on the morning of the eighteenth.

Another five-hour halt.

After the five hours were up, Ieng ordered the men to begin marching again. He himself was exhausted, despite the training he had undergone in recent months. It was pride alone that kept him on his feet, for he had never been very strong physically or possessed of great endurance. But he was fiercely, desperately determined to attain his objective: the spot on the Thai coast, just below the first foothills of the Cardamomes, where sooner or later the arms that Lara had purchased would be unloaded. "The delivery by sea will take place between the twentieth and the thirtieth, doubtless around the twenty-fifth," Kutchaï had informed him. By sea and not by land: That meant there would also be a delay while the arms were reloaded aboard Christiani's motor launches. But Ieng could not take any risks, particularly the risk of not showing up in time to meet the Corsican.

He had been delayed. Just as he was preparing to descend from his refuge on the plateau in Moï country, Khmer Sereï units had launched an offensive from Stung Treng. Faithfully following the tactical plan agreed upon with the other Khmer Rouge leaders, Ieng had immediately withdrawn, to avoid a pitched battle. And no doubt he would have been held up even longer if large Viet Cong units had not begun to retreat en masse toward the north from their southern sanctuary, thus abandoning the terrain to Rangers and Marines from Saigon who, as everyone knew, were about to launch an attack.

A curious war, all in all, in which for the moment all parties were trying their best to avoid doing battle with any other. The Khmer Sereï and Khmer Krom under the command of Lon Nol chose not to confront North Vietnamese troops seasoned by twenty-five years of constant fighting. These same Vietnamese troops were electing to cut and run in the face of the fu-

ture advance of the Saigonese, because they had decided that the moment
of final reckoning lay far in the future. At the same time they refused to
confront the Khmer army, no matter what its composition, because as long
as Sihanouk remained in power and the fiction of Khmer neutrality was
maintained, their orders from Hanoi were not to appear officially in Cambodian territory. As for the Khmer Rouge, they considered themselves, not
without good reason, far too weak to attack anyone at all; they were still
only a few scattered bands who lacked sufficient arms and whose only
chance of survival lay in their mobility and their determination not to be
forced into open combat.

Yet this very situation had been Ieng's salvation: The movement
northward of the Viet Cong units had forced the Khmer Sereï who had set
out in pursuit of him to pull back in turn, thus opening up the route to the
west to Ieng.

The open forest through which they had been advancing almost from the
moment they crossed the Mekong began to grow denser. They were approaching not only the road linking Rovieng and Siem Reap but also the
little group of temples of Prah Khan, where Oreste Marccaggi had taken
refuge after being wounded in the abdomen almost a year earlier.

Soon the forest became jungle and Ieng felt relieved. *We're returning
to our natural habitat.* The strap of his assault rifle was sawing painfully into
his shoulder. He shifted it to the other shoulder, knowing he was simply exchanging one pain for another, exactly the same as the first; he was so thin
now that the strap had worn the skin off both shoulders down to the bone.
To keep his mind from dwelling on the pain, he turned around as he
marched to have a look at the tail end of the detachment. At that very moment, a warning whistle sounded from back there in the rear. As one man,
the entire detachment deployed, ready to vanish under cover. But this time
the towering figure of Ouk, arriving at a run, did not mean that danger was
close at hand. Kutchaï's younger brother was waving his arms in the air. All
out of breath, he finally joined Ieng.

"There's been an announcement over the radio. The Assembly in
Phnom Penh has removed Sihanouk from power. Cambodia is to be a republic, with Lon Nol as President."

He was still panting from the mad marathon he'd run to bring them the
news. For several long seconds, there was no other sound save for his panting. One by one, the black shadows of the men who had scattered into the
forest reappeared. They drew closer, forming a silent circle around Ieng
and his lieutenant.

"Repeat what you told me."

Ouk did so.

"There's no possible mistake about it?"

Ouk shook his head. "A peasant told me the news. I didn't believe it and wanted to hear it with my own ears. I went to the pagoda to listen to the bonzes' radio. And I heard it, three times."

He looked all around him and repeated: "I heard it myself. I heard Lon Nol speaking."

With the butt of his rifle planted in the ground, Ieng leaned back against the trunk of the tree and then let himself slide gently to the ground. He had an empty feeling inside. "So they've dared to go that far."

He didn't even know whether what he felt was anger, joy, or simply a tremendous dull indifference brought on by his terrible fatigue. Perhaps also a dazed stupor.

"When?"

"This morning," Ouk answered. "The two chambers voted unanimously to remove him as Chief of State. Sihanouk is ousted, forever."

Ieng gazed one by one at the faces surrounding him. What had Sihanouk meant, what had he ever meant to these wild Samrés, most of whom weren't even twenty yet? *But I've known him all my life. I've never known any other Cambodia than one under his rule,* he thought. He fought the tears welling up in his eyes and forced himself to meet all the eyes fixed upon him. He was amazed to see in them sadness, dazed stupefaction, and, mounting little by little, an anger powerful yet cold, and thereby all the more impressive. *They've dared.* The words of Saloth Sar—who was beginning to use the name Pol Pot—and Khieu Samphan came back to him: "For the moment, touching Sihanouk is out of the question. We'll never have a popular base if we officially oppose him, him personally. Let's go ahead and attack and criticize his régime when we speak in the villages; let's attack those surrounding him and even the monarchical principle that we'll throw overboard one of these days. But not him, not Sihanouk. Obviously, the best thing that could happen would be to have somebody get rid of him for us. But let's not waste time dreaming: Lon Nol and Sirik Matak will never dare attack Norodom Sihanouk. Unfortunately for us. Because that would be the best way of pressuring all the Cambodian people of the forests and the rice paddies to join us."

"And it's happened," Ieng said aloud. "It's happened."

He closed his eyes, overwhelmed by the most powerful emotion he had ever felt. He breathed deeply, instinctively taking in the faintest odors of the forest, of the earth, the humus that had been decaying for thousands of years, with a new, almost painful intensity. And suddenly an entire shadow theater began to move beneath his eyelids, thousands and tens of thousands of mute, implacable combatants, slowly emerging from the mother forest as from a womb, dressed in black, irresistibly advancing, pursuing and crushing everything in their way.

It had happened. It was no longer just a question of time now. And he realized then, very clearly, that what he was feeling was joy, a grave, fierce joy, as dazzling as a sun.

Part Four

THE BOOBY GANNETS

1 PETE MARTINEZ WAS SWARTHY; OF AVERAGE HEIGHT, HE WAS RUNNING to fat—in fact to downright obesity. He had a mustache that had once been jet-black but was now salt-and-pepper. He was wearing jeans just a little too big for him, fancy leather rodeo-champion boots, a broad-brimmed cowboy hat, a checkered wool shirt, and a leather jacket with faded elbows. On March 22, 1970, he was in the waiting room of Stapleton, the Denver airport, waiting for a flight to arrive from New York. He had been there more than an hour already, although the plane was not scheduled to arrive for several minutes yet. Generally speaking, Pete Martinez didn't trust airplanes; he considered them completely unpredictable, and wouldn't put it past them not only to arrive late but to show up ahead of schedule, just to surprise a person. To while away the time, he had gone to the bathroom twice to piss, visited each of the airport shops three times, and eaten a chile con carne at the snack bar, keeping his eyes and ears open both for the announcement of the flight and the arrival of Ruth, his wife, who had strictly forbidden him to eat between meals.

Ruth arrived first.

"You see," she said. "I was right: We had plenty of time." She looked at him suspiciously. "I'm certain you stuffed yourself with chile con carne while I was gone."

"You're always right," Pete said. "We had plenty of time. I should have gone with you to do those errands."

"Don't change the subject. You didn't answer me about the chile con carne."

"What chile con carne?"

With a superb sense of timing, the loudspeakers at that moment announced that the plane from New York was arriving.

"You puffy-faced, pot-bellied Mexican, you, don't I feed you enough?" Ruth asked.

"I'm not a Mexican. I'm of Spanish origin," Pete answered with a hurt look.

Taking his wife's arm, he walked with her to the mouth of an endless corridor leading to the terminals, and soon, in the middle of a multitude of passengers, the tall silhouette of Matthew Kinkaird appeared, almost un-recognizable in the hat and overcoat with fur collar that he'd bought for his trip to Europe.

"We're terribly glad to see you again," Pete said in his usual expansive way, sincerely moved, almost with tears in his eyes. "How was Sweden and how's Jon?"

"They're both fine. Thanks for coming. Thanks, Ruth."

"I had some errands to do in Denver; otherwise I surely wouldn't have come," Ruth said grumpily. Ruth Martinez loved to grumble and the more she liked a person the grouchier her tone of voice became. With Pete and Matthew Kinkaird, who along with her three sons were the people she loved most in the world, she outdid herself. She asked, in a seemingly grudging voice, "You're sure Jon's all right?"

"Of course," Matthew answered.

As they waited for Matthew's bags to be delivered on the carrousel, Pete took a big packet of letters out of his pocket. "I picked up your mail on the way here. There was some junk mail I didn't bring."

There were only three really interesting letters: Two were from Larry Kinkaird, his son, written from San Francisco, and the third from Lisa. Matthew began reading that one first. It began: "By the time you read this letter, it's certain you'll already have a great-grandson or great-grand-daughter. Due to circumstances beyond my control, I can't tell you which for the moment. . . ." The letter was dated March 8; it was light and gay, but very short.

"Your baggage checks?" Pete asked. "What did you do with your plane ticket? The baggage checks are stapled to it."

Matthew held out the ticket, then opened the two letters from his son. They both repeated the same news, in more or less the same words. As the father of a deserter, Larry had been obliged to resign his membership in the American Legion and for the fifth time in a year FBI agents had come around to question the neighbors, checking to see that Jon hadn't made a surprise visit to his parents' home. The agents had even appeared on Christmas day, again for the same purpose, knowing well that a goodly number of deserters and especially conscientious objectors who had taken refuge in Canada couldn't resist coming home to spend the holidays with their families.

It was Ruth Martinez who got behind the wheel of the Chevrolet. Avoiding the downtown section of Denver, she drove round the city via the Aurora bypass and then headed down Interstate 25 to Colorado Springs. In the car Matthew began to talk about Jon. He had found his grandson in much better shape than he had expected.

Jon's first days in Sweden had been terribly difficult. For reasons that Matthew didn't understand very well, the relay system set up by Lara and

Christiani for Jon's arrival in Stockholm hadn't worked, apparently because he hadn't followed to the letter the advice he'd been given. Jon had nonetheless soon gotten work, though he found himself competing with unskilled foreign laborers like himself, emigrants from the British Antilles, Yugoslavians, Italians, or Portuguese, and what work he'd managed to get consisted of such menial jobs as washing dishes in restaurants, polishing floors, sweeping snow off sidewalks. He had lived for several weeks by begging in the streets and collecting empty bottles for the return fee he could get for them. Jon admitted he had even stolen, attacking an old man who was crossing a park at nightfall, luckily without doing his victim any real harm. Because his papers weren't in order, it was weeks before he could collect the money that Matthew Kinkaird—along with Lara—had been trying to get to him, and for a long time he had not even known that anyone was trying to come to his aid; since he had no proper documents, and no residence or work permit, it had been impossible for him even to receive mail. In one sense, that had almost been a good thing: He had also failed to receive the letter in which his father, after violently upbraiding him for having dishonored the family, informed him that he had burned Jon's birth certificate and his insurance policy.

The youngster had hung on. And at the beginning of December the miracle had happened, in the form of a basketball, just when he had lost a temporary job as a taxi driver. Without a cent left to his name, he had broken into a building he had chosen by chance, simply to keep warm for a while. It turned out to be a gymnasium, where a basketball team from the university was practicing. Some students had found him there asleep, and in the next hour he had proved to them how skillful he was at putting a basketball through a hoop. Less than three weeks later, with the help of the father of one of his new friends, he had managed to get the proper documents and a job had been found for him.

"And now he can more or less speak Swedish, is a member of a basketball team and the best player they have, and is going to become a Swedish citizen. He even introduced me to a girl he's been going out with regularly. He's gotten taller still and has put on twenty-five or thirty pounds of sheer muscle. You wouldn't recognize him. Wait a minute—I've got a picture of him."

He took the photographs out of his wallet and showed them to Pete and Ruth.

"It's true—we wouldn't have recognized him. He's a real giant now. He looks like he's over six feet six," Pete said.

"He is," Matthew said. "And he's hoping he'll grow even taller. He says that if he does, he'll then be able to play center rather than guard. He'd like to play center."

The question virtually burned Pete Martinez's lips: Could Jon come back to the U.S. some day? Perhaps he would have asked it if Ruth hadn't glared furiously at him through the rearview mirror.

Some fifty minutes after leaving Stapleton International Airport, they arrived in Colorado Springs. They did not go into town but turned right on Filmore Street so as to go through the Garden of the Gods and head directly for Matthew's along the crest-line road.

They found the telegram the moment they arrived at the house, the Cabin, cantilevered out over the abyss of Wildcat Gulch. "Happy to advise you of birth of your great-grandson Mathias. Lisa in perfect shape. Lara."

The Martinezes were struck by the look on Matthew's face. "Is something wrong?"

Matthew had to sit down, laughing and crying at the same time.

"Oh, heavens no!" he said in a trembling voice. "No, everything's just fine. Lisa's had a boy."

2

IT WAS FROM ALEXIS KOSYGIN HIMSELF THAT NORODOM SIHANOUK learned the news of his removal as Chief of State, just as he was about to leave the Soviet capital for Peking. Like the cuckold husband, he was the last to know; the Khmer dignitaries accompanying him on his tour had known for several hours about the unanimous vote of the Cambodian parliament, but none of them had had the courage to pass the news on to Samdech.

In the plane flying over the part of Central Asia under Russian domination, Sihanouk, far from allowing himself to be disheartened, soon rebounded with his usual breathtaking ability to bounce back like a rubber ball just as everybody thought his cause hopelessly lost. By the time the Ilyushin began its landing approach on the outskirts of Peking he was ready, having already planned in his mind the ways and means and the various stages of his counterattack. Not for an instant did he consider the famous Bao Daï solution—retiring to the French Riviera—which the strategists in Phnom Penh had so fondly predicted he would adopt. The even warmer welcome than usual accorded him by Chou En-lai as he set foot on Chinese soil further strengthened his will to fight.

Three days later, North Vietnamese Prime Minister Pham Van Dong, Ho Chi Minh's successor, made a lightning-quick trip to Peking, officially kept secret, whose express purpose was to assure Samdech that his country would join China in supporting him in his campaign to regain power.

On March 23, 1970, Norodom Sihanouk launched his own version of De Gaulle's famous Appeal of June 18, 1940. It was a five-point appeal that accused Lon Nol of high treason and decreed the immediate dissolution of the regime set up in Phnom Penh by the vote on March 18; it announced the formation of a government "uniting all tendencies," including progressivist elements—that is to say, the Khmer Rouge; it called for the creation of an army of national liberation; it convoked a constituent assembly; it demanded the establishment of a United National Front of Kampuchea, the FUNK.

In his piercing high-pitched, panting, cracked voice—which any Khmer was able to recognize at his first words—Sihanouk called upon his people to revolt and overthrow the Lon Nol/Sirik Matak regime.

Recorded by Radio Peking and Radio Hanoi, picked up and broadcast throughout Cambodia by tens of thousands of radio sets, by pagoda loudspeakers and by clandestine relay transmitters, the appeal was repeated every hour all during the day of March 23 and part of the following day, reaching the most remote villages.

Its effect was amazing. The apathy with which the speeches of Lon Nol on the national radio network had been received disappeared like a veil of tulle set on fire.

The following day another announcement was made that finished the job of electrifying the entire population: Khieu Samphan, Saloth Sar, Hu Nim, Ieng Samboth, Hou Yuon, and others, all the men who had gone underground three years before, certain of them after having been forced to give up their seats as deputies—all these men, who were believed by many to be dead, made a joint statement confirming that they were still alive and reaffirming their will to fight and their total support of Norodom Sihanouk, whom they unconditionally recognized as Chief of State.

The Land-Rover rented by Donaldson was heading for Kompong Cham, with Roger at the wheel. They should really have left Phnom Penh in the early hours of the morning, but rousing the British journalist from his slumber had presented the usual difficulties, so that it had been the middle of the afternoon before the two men had finally left, after a dip in the pool of the Hotel Royal.

Kompong Cham was no more than a dozen kilometers away. The idea of going there had been Donaldson's—an idea did occasionally occur to him, between one bottle of whiskey and the next. He had learned that this was the district from which Hu Nim—one of the Khmer Rouge leaders who had just thrown in their lot with Sihanouk—had been elected deputy and even reelected in the famous elections of 1966, despite the extraordinary campaign to bribe and intimidate the voters that had been waged by representatives of Lon Nol. Donaldson thought it might be interesting to interview some of these voters. What was more, it was a way of seeing something of Cambodia besides the capital.

"What did that guy at Prek Dam say to you?" the Englishman asked

Roger. "I can never manage to understand your French. You have a really odd accent."

Donaldson was persuaded that he himself spoke admirable French and that his constant failure to understand it stemmed from the faulty command of the language of the persons he was speaking with.

"It's not because of my accent," Roger answered. "It's my hollow tooth: It makes my voice echo. He was telling me about a fellow he'd met, a certain Kao, a very nice young man whom I met when he was a captain and who's just been promoted to major or is just about to be, I don't remember which exactly. The other day Kao killed off almost two hundred people, men, women, and children, all by himself, by letting them loose in a big dry rice paddy, chasing them in his jeep, and mowing them down with the machine gun mounted on it. It seems that it was a fascinating spectacle. I regret not having seen it. I would have taken some superb photos."

"I wouldn't have bought them from you," Donaldson said placidly. "My paper wouldn't have wanted them: not typical enough. And who are all these fellows anyway?"

Roger turned his attention back to the road and spied a dense crowd of grown men and adolescent boys blocking their path and waving placards and banners. "Oh damn, now what?" He slowed down, shifted into first, and crawled ahead, his stomach suddenly knotting with fear. He had always been afraid of crowds, Cambodian ones or any other sort. He saw in his mind's eye another crowd, this one in Pau, screaming "Down with collaborators!" underneath his windows. *Verily, verily I say unto you, I have always been afraid of everything, of crowds and of being all alone, of my mother and of the policemen in the Parc Beaumont in Pau, of a telephone ringing or a knock at my door, of women and of drunks. And even of children and of dogs,* he thought bitterly. He felt thoroughly sick and tired of himself. The surprising, raging anger he had felt a moment before toward Kao or other men whom he did not even take the trouble to identify, that anger and that hatred so uncharacteristic of him, had disappeared just as suddenly as they had mounted within him. He glanced over at Donaldson, who was sitting there not moving a muscle, his interlaced fingers resting on his pot belly, the smoke from the cigarette between his lips rising straight up in the stifling, unbelievably humid, motionless air. Donaldson looked like a blond, pink-skinned Buddha with pale blue eyes and albino eyelashes.

Roger's gaze shifted back to the placards, most of which were written in French. He read them, recognizing the face endlessly reproduced on all of them. The crowd had already surrounded the car, stopped it, engulfed it, and their knees and elbows and the wooden staffs of flags brushed against the body or thudded against it; the car swayed back and forth, as though shaken by a gale-force wind. Faces approached and were framed in each of the car windows.

"For or against? Who are you? Are you for Sihanouk?"

"We're for Sihanouk," Roger said, trying his best to smile.

"Well then, you should shout: '*Vive* Sihanouk!' "

"*Vive* Sihanouk!" Roger shouted.

"And what about him?" They pointed at Donaldson.

"Oh, he's for Sihanouk too, no question about it," Roger said.

"He should shout then."

"In the name of heaven, give them that pleasure!" Roger said to Donaldson.

The Englishman had stuck another cigarette right in the middle of his smiling pink lips. His blue eyes, so pale they were almost white, slowly surveyed the sea of faces, and his features, his entire demeanor, suggested that he was experiencing the profoundest satisfaction, a gluttonous sensual delectation even, as though the dream of his life had been to find himself in this precise spot, on this Cambodian highway with the sun beating down mercilessly, surrounded by these fanatics.

"All right, then," Roger said. "What risk are we running, after all? At the very worst, they'll set fire to this damned jalopy. And maybe they'll let us climb out of it before they do. If only the better to bash our heads in or cut our balls off. So what's the problem? There's really nothing to worry about."

"*Vive* Sihanouk," the Englishman said phlegmatically, managing to get the words out without letting the two-inch-long ash at the end of his Players Navy Cut cigarette fall.

He raised his right hand, his index and middle finger forming a V. *Good Lord*, Roger thought to himself.

Among the demonstrators, university and high-school students in white or colored T-shirts and leather shoes mingled with barefoot peasants dressed in black.

"I know you," one of the students said to Roger. "You're Monsieur Roger Bouès, the architect from Phnom Penh. But who's this guy with you? An American?"

"An Englishman," Roger answered. "A bastard son of Winston Churchill's."

"Ah, is that so?" the student said, impressed. "And you're going to Kompong Cham?"

"To Kompong Cham. I'm not an architect any longer—I'm a journalist. And Churchill Junior here is a journalist too. Are there lots of people out demonstrating for Sihanouk in Kompong Cham?"

"The whole town," the youngster said proudly. "And not only the town—the whole province. The whole country. We've heard Samdech's appeal; everybody's heard it. We've already taken to the streets to demonstrate and we'll go on demonstrating. We may all go to Phnom Penh. We're

going to demand that Lon Nol leave the country and that the National Assembly be dissolved."

The crowd around him nodded in agreement, interrupting his im-
promptu speech with cries in Khmer and repeated shouts, in French, of
"*Vive* Sihanouk!", "*Vive* Samdech!"

"We're going to march on Phnom Penh and drive Lon Nol out," the
student went on, as though he were suddenly discovering the obvious and
well-founded reasons for his own behavior. "That's right. That's precisely
what we're going to do," he added.

Young high-school students with a pot of paint and brushes were now
daubing something on the doors and hood of the Land-Rover. Roger finally
made out what it was they had written: "*Vive* Sihanouk." Obviously.

"And may we leave now?"

"You may."

The crowd moved to either side of the car, clearing the road ahead.
And Roger said to Donaldson, whose index and middle finger were still
raised in a V, "You can stop making a fool of yourself now, okay? What's
more, we're doubtless going to run into soldiers loyal to Lon Nol who are
going to shoot us on sight because of what's written on our car."

But they entered Kompong Cham without seeing a single uniform. The
small city was nonetheless in an uproar, tense and restless, teeming with
groups of people continually gathering and then moving on to form new
groups. Of all the Khmer cities outside of Phnom Penh, Kompong Cham
and Battambang were the most important. Kompong Cham was also the
center of the rubber plantation area, in the heart of great spreads of heveas,
perhaps the least foreign of all Cambodian cities when all was said and
done, situated on the banks of the Mekong with its tire factory and its little
textile mills. It had always struck Roger as an elegant city, full of flowers,
with a personality all its own.

The moment they arrived, Donaldson wanted to go interview the governor of the province. His name was Tien Kien Chieng, and Roger knew he
was a devoted supporter of Lon Nol's. After long palavers with the detachment of the Provincial Guard entrenched with rifles at the ready, they were
finally received by the governor and found a man plainly on the verge of
panic who spoke to them of "peasants and high-school students led astray
by the propaganda of Communist agents backed by Hanoi."

"Furthermore, all the leaders are Vietnamese," he stated.

"We didn't see a single one," Roger said.

The interview more or less ended on that note. Roger took a few photos
of the governor and was roughed up a bit when he started to photograph
the Provincial Guards in their posture of Texans at the Alamo awaiting
the Mexican attack. He was able to make his escape with all his equipment intact, though he was limping slightly after being struck on one hip

with a rifle butt. Outside, he separated from Donaldson, who had met up
with an American journalist who turned out to be the brother-in-law of
Dean Rusk, the former Secretary of State.

Roger went to spend this evening and night of March 27 at the home of
a Cambodian friend who was a graduate of the French École des Arts et
Métiers and worked at the tire factory. His friend was torn by political
doubts, hesitating to choose between Lon Nol and Sihanouk, feeling no particular attraction to either one. On the one hand, he was attracted by the
prospect of more rapid Westernization that, according to him, a pro-
American regime would make possible, and on the other he was aware that
Sihanouk (of whose own personal integrity he was convinced, though he
had grave doubts concerning that of his entourage) represented legitimate
power in the country, or more simply, the Cambodia hallowed by tradition.
By common accord, he and Roger tried their best to talk of other things and
to appear to ignore the restlessness that, despite the fall of night, continued
to grip the city.

"And Lara?"

"He's fine," Roger said. "You know, don't you, that he's married and
had a son a few days ago?"

"Kutchaï told me. He was here the other day. And what's become of
their plantation?"

"Heaven only knows," Roger answered, having been wondering for
some time about Kutchaï and his discreet trips all over the country.

The evening was noisy and the night full of commotion. Groups kept
passing back and forth continually below the windows of the engineer's little apartment on the edge of the Mekong, at the highway exit leading to
Mimot and Saigon. Roger, who had nonetheless managed to drop off to
sleep, was suddenly awakened around five o'clock in the morning by the
sound of great bursts of automatic rifle fire and the screams of men whose
throats were being slit. He had been sleeping in the children's room—a boy
and a girl had been bedded down on a mat in the hall so as to leave Roger
the room to himself. His window overlooked the highway and the river. He
got up, looked out and saw nothing, and then everything was quiet once
again. But he knew very well he hadn't been dreaming.

He left his room and found the engineer and his wife leaning out over
the little balcony of the living room, with all the lights out. He joined them
and looked out too. There were three men with their throats slit down
below, ten yards away at most, in the yellow halo of a streetlamp, all three
of them in the uniform of the Provincial Guards. One of them was still
crawling along, leading Roger to believe he had merely been superficially
wounded. And then, in the yellow light projecting immense shadows, the
man stopped crawling. Turning over extremely slowly, he raised himself up
on his elbows in a desperate effort to stand. They saw his throat then, slit

from one ear to the other, with the blood gushing out in great pounding spurts. After a few seconds his elbows holding his back up off the ground spread apart, and his entire body collapsed, with the chin thrown backwards. The man did not move again.

It's beginning, Roger thought, not knowing exactly what he was referring to.

3

"THERE'S A SPOT I REMEMBER VERY WELL," ORESTE SAID. "IT'S A mountain pass called the Insecca. I used to go hunting there with my father and my uncles. There's a little river, the Fium'Orbo, at the entrance; after that the pass starts climbing, with lots of boulders of all colors and all sorts of vegetation. There's grass, real grass. It's been so long since I've seen honest-to-goodness grass. The road is very narrow, and as you go up it you may meet woodcutters taking their pine trunks down along it on carts. You have to be very careful; the road doesn't have any sort of safety rail."

"I understand," Lara said with a friendly smile.

The old Corsican was sitting in Pochentong Airport, gazing at the flat horizon of the rice paddies beyond the runway. But his eyes were really staring into empty space, searching for images almost half a century old, trying to fish up from his memory a Corsica that he'd left in the year 1921 and had never once been back to. He hadn't given a thought to the question of what the Corsica he was going back to would be like; in his mind, it couldn't possibly have changed.

"I remember the inn at Pinzalone. To the right of it is the road that goes to Vezzani. The food's very good in that inn. The owner's a fine, upstanding man, who looks you straight in the eye. . . . Hmmmm, I've forgotten his name! But it could be that he's dead now; that was forty years ago at least. . . ."

"But you're not from around there, are you?" Lara asked, trying to remember some of the things Oreste had told him about his youth during the long quiet evenings on the plantation.

Marccaggi shook his head. "No, I'm not. I'm from mountain country, real mountain country. I'm from Piedicorte di Gaggio, where the finest boars in all of Corsica come from. In the wintertime it snows. And in the spring when you go to the very end of the village, out on the rocky point, you hear thousands and thousands of birds in the valley of the Tavignano down below. They sing, and the sound comes up to you. It's very beautiful."

"I'm certain it must be," Kutchaï said, his booming voice gruffer than usual.

The passengers for Bangkok, Delhi, Karachi, Tehran, Athens, Rome, Paris, were summoned to board the plane. Lara picked up Oreste's suitcase and put his arm around the Corsican's shoulders, his long thin fingers squeezing the nape of the old man's neck.

"Well," he said. "In that case you won't need to shoot tourists, because you'll have boars close at hand to hunt."

"What tourists?" Oreste asked indignantly. "There aren't any tourists in Corsica, outside of two or three Englishmen."

Kutchaï, who had gone off for a moment, joined them again, holding a package in his hands. "Your cigars."

"Thanks," Oreste said. "Thanks a lot. You're great guys, both of you."

He tried to say something more but there was a lump in his throat and all he could do was spread his hands apart helplessly.

"Oh, shut your big mouth," Kutchaï said, with tears in his eyes.

Lara lowered his head, his right hand mechanically massaging his shoulder and the back of his neck.

"Well then, I'm off," Oreste said, with a toss of his big head like an old lion.

"When you arrive in Bastia, don't forget to go by the bank to sign the paper. Otherwise you'll have to go back there to get your money. You won't forget?"

"I won't forget."

He shook hands with both of them and then, hesitating for one last moment, turned and left abruptly, his suitcase in one hand and in the other the brand-new tweed jacket that was the first he'd ever worn in his life.

Lara and Kutchaï waited till the plane had taken off, then went back outside into the muggy air. Standing in the beating sun of the parking lot, the car was like an oven inside. Lara got behind the wheel, seeming not even to notice the heat, his face completely expressionless. Kutchaï lit two cigarettes at once and handed one to Lara?

"In a way, it's worse than if he were dead."

Lara closed his eyes. "Oh, damn," he said softly.

He opened the car door again, stepped out, and began to pace up and down the parking lot, his hands thrust in the pockets of his bush jacket. After a while he came back to the car, got behind the wheel again, and started the engine. They drove to Phnom Penh, being obliged to stop twice at military checkpoints where soldiers had blocked the road with wooden barricades and were standing with the barrels of their submachine guns and M-16's trained on them. There was so little traffic that it took them only a few minutes to cross the city. With the exception of two or three passenger cars, all with diplomatic plates, the only vehicles in sight were army trucks, though the majority of them were sitting motionless at various intersections. At the northern exit of the city they had to go through exactly the same sort of check, conducted by officers whose impassive faces belied their obvious nervousness. Asked where they were going, they answered Kompong Thom. The officers nodded each time, but said nothing. They were allowed through.

Once on the open road again, Lara put his foot to the floor, in a raging fury.

4

"A MAJOR," KAO SAID. "I'M A MAJOR. DON'T YOU KNOW HOW TO TELL an officer's rank?"

"Excuse me," the youngster said, looking scared to death. "Excuse me, I didn't know."

"I didn't know, *sir.*"

"Yes. Sir."

Kao gave the youngster an almost kindly look, though he was convinced he would never manage to make a soldier of this boy. Or only with considerable difficulty.

"Do you know your own rank at least?"

"I'm a second lieutenant." A pause. "Sir."

"How old are you?"

"Nineteen."

"And what's your name?"

"Suon Phan."

"Come with me. Come on, get in!"

Kao got behind the wheel of the jeep, gave a nonchalant wave of his hand to signal to the column to follow him, and took off, driving along the Toulé Bassac for a few minutes before leaving it and heading in the direction of Kampot. The column consisted of two light tanks and eleven trucks full of soldiers. As he drove, Kao took a little Sony transistor radio from under the seat and turned it on. The set was tuned in to Saigon, which was broadcasting a jazz piece. Kao didn't particularly like jazz but he was of the opinion that pretending to like listening to it was part of his image.

"Do you like this sort of music?"

"Yes, sir."

"How did you happen to become a second lieutenant? How the devil did you end up in the army?"

"I was a law student at the university and my professors told me to sign up."

At least he didn't pretend that it had been his own idea to volunteer.

"When was that?"

"On the twentieth of March."

A week before. Suon Phan's story was a classic one: He had joined up when Lon Nol had called for a general mobilization immediately after discovering his army didn't exist, if one discounted the Sereïs and the Kroms. Suon had been speeded through basic training—the verb was something of an understatement—in just four days, during which time he had been vaguely taught to load and unload a rifle, to march in step, to remove the pin of a grenade, and above all to bawl out patriotic songs celebrating traditional Khmer courage and vituperating the shameless effrontery of the Communist North Vietnamese, invaders of the sacred soil of the fatherland. Whereupon he had been precipitately promoted to the rank of second lieutenant. He had just learned that he was now supposed to take on the responsibility of commanding thirty or forty peasants dragged away from their rice paddies and doubtless about as thoroughly trained as he himself was, and also, with this unit at his command, he was to mow down any and every Viet Cong force of whatever size within range.

Suon Phan had the feeling he was living a nightmare.

He didn't so much mind being in uniform; that might have had its charms, even been rather intriguing. Like every young Cambodian his age, Phan had been enrolled in the Khmer Royal Socialist Youth—Royal and Socialist!—since childhood and had therefore worn the uniform of that organization, halfway between that of a hotel porter and Lord Baden-Powell in campaign dress. But a second lieutenant's gold braid was something else altogether (he had been made a second lieutenant and not a sergeant because his uncle worked in the Planning Ministry). Parading about the streets of Phnom Penh with gold braid hadn't been unpleasant—quite the contrary—especially since the three days that duty had lasted had given him a glimpse of what an ideal military career could be like. The moment the braid had been sewed on, he'd presented himself at FARK headquarters, though no one had ordered him to do so. At headquarters, they had stared at him in surprise, perhaps even irritation.

"We'll send for you."

"And what about my pay?"

They'd given him such nasty looks that he hadn't pressed the point. Furthermore, his uncle had promised to arrange for him to continue to receive his full stipend as a scholarship student, and so in the final analysis nothing had changed all that much, except that he was wearing an officer's uniform and was no longer obliged to attend his courses at the university. And Phnom Penh was getting to be more and more fun, with new bars, new nightclubs, more brothels opening up every day. Because they were expecting the Americans to arrive at any moment. The time had finally come to get a share of the manna that up until then had fallen only on those awful, lucky Vietnamese.

As for the military situation in general, who in the world cared? The legendary pleasantness of life in Phnom Penh went on.

With regard to the coup d'état itself and the changes it had brought about, Suon Phan's views were amazingly indifferent. He had taken part, in a rather aloof way, in discussions on the subject with his fellow students. Almost all of them spoke of revolution; but while some of them called the upheavals provoked by Lon Nol and Sirik Matak by that name, others were of the opinion, expressed in more guarded words, that the real revolution was the one to come, the one that preparations were being made for in the forest, by Khieu Samphan, Ieng Samboth, and the others who had rallied round Sihanouk. The massacre of the Vietnamese, the expulsion from the university of students who were Khmer nationals but of ostensibly Vietnamese origin, had admittedly troubled a number of the students. For some of them—the minority—the Vietnamese richly deserved what was happening to them; as the time-honored French expression had it, *"C'était bien fait pour leur gueule"*—it served them right. For many whom this carnage had disturbed, it had simply been one of those unfortunate episodes that are a concomitant of all the great events of history (another time-honored French expression: "You can't make an omelette . . ."). And after all, it was true that the damned Vietnamese had always dreamed of grabbing Laos and Cambodia and even a good bit of Thailand. On this latter point Suon Phan, who wasn't exactly a fanatic, definitely sided with the hotheads.

And then, after three days of perfect happiness in his handsome uniform, everything had suddenly changed. On the afternoon of March 27, as he was beginning to get really used to the *dolce vita* of Phnom Penh, the sky fell in on him, in the form of a call-up. "You are assigned to duty in the defense of Kampot, beginning on Thursday, March 28, at 0600 hours. . . ."

In a panic, he had rushed to his uncle, who had managed to protect him so well up till then. His uncle had regretfully confessed that there was absolutely nothing he could do. The order had come from General Sósthenes Fernández in person, the former chief of police who had been imprisoned for smuggling and extortion but who had just spectacularly recovered his power and prestige—betraying Sihanouk, whom he was now opposing after having defended him, in the process. "There's not a single thing I can do," his uncle had said; in the course of trafficking in government gasoline, which he had resold for his own personal profit, he had had a run-in with General Sósthenes Fernández, and since that time the two men had been more or less on the outs.

Already crushed by the news that he was being sent off to war, Suon Phan had received the *coup de grâce* on the evening of that same day: Not only was he to leave for the battlefield the following morning at dawn, but he was to be under the command of an utter madman whom he had heard all too much about (a number of people had told him about the two hundred Vietnamese mowed down with a machine gun and other mischievous pranks of the same sort), a madman everyone continued to refer to as Captain Kao even though he had officially been promoted to the rank of major.

And there, right in front of his nose this very minute, so close that he could reach out and pull the trigger, was the famous machine gun mounted on the hood.

"Have you ever killed anybody before?" Kao asked.

Phan shook his head, then hastened to add, "No, sir."

Kao patted him on the knee. "Don't be afraid, my boy. I'll teach you how."

5 IN THE EARLY HOURS OF THE MORNING OF MARCH 28, THERE WAS A sort of truce at Kompong Cham. There were telltale signs however: All the Chinese shops remained closed and not a single peasant came to the market. A threatening silence hung over the city, and Roger, who was walking over to the hotel to see if Donaldson was still in this world, at one point found himself completely alone in a little deserted avenue lined with the elegant villas of plantation managers.

As he had expected, he found the Englishman sleeping like a log, snoring like a buzz saw, and impossible to rouse. Roger finally threw in the towel and went downstairs to the restaurant on the ground floor, where he met two young assistants from the Chhuup plantation drinking cognac-and-sodas. They cheerily invited him to share their breakfast. They told him they were tight as ticks, and what was more, eight o'clock in the morning was very late in the day, since their work consisted almost solely of getting up out of bed in the dead of night to deal out impartial kicks in the ass to the latex collectors to start them off on their day's round.

"But we don't have any more latex collectors. Which really isn't too serious a situation, since we don't have any rubber trees either. Have you ever seen eight million heveas sprayed with defoliants?"

Roger replied that no, he'd never seen a thing like that, or at least not yet. He roundly refused the cognac-and-soda they urged upon him but accepted a cup of coffee.

"If you don't have either latex collectors or rubber trees left, what in hell are you sticking around here for?" he asked them.

"Our contract," the younger one explained in a thick voice. He spoke in the solemn tone of drunkards and the accent of Castelnaudary. "Our contract specifically stipulates that we are to get up at three-thirty A.M. every morning except Sunday. It isn't Sunday. We're up."

"Otherwise those goddamned fucking bastards would refuse to pay us our vacation bonuses," the older one explained.

The first one took Roger in his arms and kissed him on the right cheek. "I really like you a whole lot. And so I'm going to tell you a secret: We hate those frigging rubber trees, when you come right down to it."

"When you come right down to it, we're overjoyed that they've all died. Whammo! just like that!" the other one said. With his arms dropping and his mouth gaping open, he imitated a rubber tree that was dying or completely dead.

"Take the first plane back to France," Roger said.

Two pairs of blurry eyes stared at him as though he'd just said something outrageous.

"This country's done for," Roger went on wearily, with the feeling that he was a hundred years old. "There's nothing left here for you to do."

He expected they would answer, "Well then, what about you?" but at that moment the roar of the engines of several vehicles and the din of a loudspeaker brought him to his feet.

"Take my word for it and get the hell out of here," he said. "While there's still time."

He left, not even touching his coffee. He spied a truck and two black Renault 16's slowly advancing toward him, the truck following the cars. A loudspeaker was mounted on the cab of the truck, and a shrill voice poured out of it, speaking in Khmer. The vehicles had bumper flags with three horizontal stripes, blue, red, and blue, with the white towers of Angkor Wat on the red stripe in the center. On the off chance that he could sell it, Roger took a photo and then, after a moment's hesitation, began to walk behind the truck, which was driving along at a crawl, the bed of it empty.

Then something odd happened which at the moment struck him as almost funny. One, then three, then ten, then dozens of Cambodian men and women emerged from the nearby streets and houses and joined him, some of them marching at his side but most of them behind him and none falling into line ahead of him. The crowd kept getting bigger and bigger. The loudspeaker kept blaring. *If only I could understand what it's saying!* Roger thought, feeling vaguely like bursting into laughter. In his mind's eye he saw once again the marvelous scene from Chaplin's *Modern Times* in which the hero, having politely picked up a red warning flag fallen from a truck, finds himself a moment later at the head of a strikers' demonstration.

Roger became aware that nobody was falling into line ahead of him, and only then did it occur to him to take a look at the faces of the people surrounding him. When he saw the blank expression in their eyes, he was suddenly frightened. He turned to the man closest to him and asked, "What's happening?"

He touched the man's arm, but the man slowly moved away from him, not even turning his head. Roger's heart began to pound, warning him of danger. *Get out of here, you idiot,* he said to himself. He halted in his tracks, clutching his cameras to his breast and automatically hunching his back.

Those following immediately behind him bumped into him, not anticipating his abrupt stop, but he stood his ground and little by little the crowd parted, passing on either side of him and joining ranks again beyond him. Roger watched the truck draw away as the loudspeaker continued to blare.

What the devil's going on anyway? Are they acting out the Pied Piper of Hamelin bit? The truck blaring out something in a language incomprehensible to him, and the people silently following after it struck him as extraordinary and very disturbing. Elbowing his way through the crowd, he reached the sidewalk and hoisted himself up onto the low wall surrounding a little three-story residential building. At the level of his knees, a veritable forest of heads was moving forward. Suddenly all of them halted at once. The din from the loudspeaker abruptly stopped, and in the silence the only sound was the shuffling of thousands of feet, without so much as a whisper of a voice. Roger felt a shiver run down his spine.

"What's happening?"

Not a single face was raised to look at him. But a voice rang out behind his back: "It's two deputies who've arrived from Phnom Penh. They're saying they have an important announcement to make."

Fumbling about in the big pockets of his canvas vest for another roll of film, Roger turned and saw a Cambodian of about fifty, wearing glasses, standing at a second-floor window of the building, three yards away from him.

"Something important? What?"

The man with glasses shrugged without answering. Roger reloaded his Canon, raised the viewfinder to his eye, trying in vain to focus on the truck; a coral tree was hiding it from view. He took a few steps along the low wall without finding a better angle. The loudspeaker was still silent.

Roger turned around toward the man with glasses. "May I come upstairs to your place?"

The man didn't answer, and what Roger found more irritating still, he was watching, spellbound, a spectacle that Roger was unable to see at all without climbing back down into the crowd, which he could not bring himself to do.

"Sir," Roger said, his voice pitched high in the total silence, "may I come upstairs to your place? Or else up onto the roof?"

The man in glasses gave him the annoyed look of someone whose concentration has been disturbed. "Come on up. I'll let you out onto the roof."

Roger met him on the second-floor landing. They climbed to the top of the stairs together and came to a locked metal door. The man produced a key and they went out onto the flat roof of the building.

"You're French?"

"Yes, of course," Roger replied.

"How did you find out?"

Roger skirted two little round chimneys and reached the edge of the roof. He leaned out over it. Thirty or thirty-five feet down, directly below him, was the truck.

"Find out what?"

"That the deputies were going to come here."

On the bed of the truck, two men in light-colored suits and ties were waiting for a third man in a short-sleeved shirt to finish setting up the microphone. Roger couldn't see their faces, just the tops of their heads, but. . . .

"I didn't know they'd be here. I just happened to come to Kompong Cham."

. . . But he could see the crowd. "All of Kompong Cham is here."

"Several Provincial Guards were killed during the night," the man with glasses said. "They seized their weapons." Nothing in his tone indicated whether he approved or disapproved of these murders. He added, "The deputies have come to explain why the government removed Samdech Sihanouk as Chief of State."

Roger made sure that the Rollei was loaded, then at the last moment decided to use the Canon. He took several shots of the square, of the streets swarming with people dressed in black. He went back to the Rollei to photograph the bed of the truck. The loudspeaker suddenly boomed out, but it was the technician testing.

"*Mouï, pi, baï, boun, pram* . . ." One, two, three, four, five . . .

Roger could recognize numbers at least.

"It's hard to make peasants understand," the man with glasses said.

"Are you for Lon Nol?" Roger asked, his companion's last remark having shed light on the man's political views.

"I'm anti-Communist," the man said. "I'm against those Viet Cong who are invading Kampuchea. What's happening in Phnom Penh . . ."

He didn't have time to finish his sentence. One of the deputies had begun to speak and his voice, amplified by the loudspeaker, drowned out everything else. He spoke for almost a minute and then the first boos and catcalls began.

"This is going to end badly."

Roger was all at once ridiculously glad to be on that rooftop, out of reach. The human sea below, some fifty yards away, began moving, leaving an empty space. Through his viewfinder Roger caught a quick glimpse of a man as he threw a stone. The catcalls gave way to screams. The loudspeaker roared, struggling to drown out the uproar. With his eye glued to the viewfinder, Roger swept his camera over the crowd and it was not till a shout from his companion alerted him that he realized the real drama was taking place elsewhere. He looked down at the truck again, just in time to catch sight of dozens of hands gripping the metal rails around the truck bed like claws. He watched the crowd rush forward, and in the second that followed the truck bed directly below him was invaded by a screaming horde. The deputies were lifted off their feet and flung down into the crowd, which greeted them with savage cries. At first all they received was a rain of blows from people's fists. They staggered backward and fell to the ground, but again and again they managed to struggle to their feet. Soon, however, the fine-honed, gleaming gouges with wooden handles that latex collectors use to nick the bark of the heveas appeared, and the blood began to flow. Those who did not have gouges used clubs, knives, machetes, their fingernails, their teeth, with everyone trying to get in at least one good blow, as though it were essential, a sacred ritual, for each one of them to have a share in the slaughter. The two deputies ceased to struggle, and very soon ceased even to resemble human beings.

6

AT KOMPONG THOM, AT THE SAME HOUR, THE BUNGALOW WAS SILENT and deserted, except for a Cambodian waiter who, because of the disappearance of the former Vietnamese manager and the flight of the *bep*, now found himself responsible for both managing the place and doing the cooking. He served the beers that Lara and Kutchaï ordered, and thereafter appeared unaware of their presence, going off to sit on the steps in the shade, his black face nearly invisible, overwhelmed perhaps by his promotion.

Lara and Kutchaï left after their twenty-minute break, but got no farther than the bridge over the Stung Sen. Sereï paratroopers had taken up positions around the high school to the left of the road, and had even begun to transform the central building into a little fortress.

"Where are you going?"

"To Rovieng."

The officer was a captain with a crew cut. He had a smooth, guileless face. He shook his head. "I can't let you go there. You'd be risking your lives."

The conversation had taken place in French thus far. Lara began to speak Cambodian. "I was born in this country. I belong in it as much as you do. My house is north of Rovieng. I'm going to go there and return. You can always shoot me in the back."

He re-joined Kutchaï in the 504, drove resolutely around the chevaux-de-frise, and accelerated. A minute later he was rushing down the laterite trail at whirlwind speed.

"It may not be worth wrecking the car," Kutchaï remarked in a wary tone. "We're going to need it to go back in."

"You can always get out if you want to."

Kutchaï clapped his hands. "Bravo! Me Kutchaï pool Khmel wletch what's got bad case jittels."

But a little farther on Lara slowed down to a normal speed. He banged on the leather-covered steering wheel with his fist.

"I know," Kutchaï said. "Me too." The Jaraï lit their fifteenth cigarette apiece in three hours and asked, "Any news from Christiani?"

"No."

The unloading of the arms was scheduled to take place on the night of March 28.

"He may have had difficulties. That was a tall order you gave him."

Lara nodded. He was his calm self again. The cloud of dust raised by the car, white for a time, resumed its red color as the sand of the trail gave way to laterite once more.

"As for Roger, he's at Kompong Cham with his Englishman. I've forgotten his name," Kutchaï said.

"Donaldson."

"That's right, Donaldson. He's got a terrible reputation. Especially for bringing bad luck to the photographers he takes with him. That's why they call him the Black Shadow. According to what I've been told, he lost one in Korea, another in Malaysia, and a third a year ago in Vietnam. Maybe you ought to tell Roger that."

"He already knows it."

"And what did he say when you told him?"

Lara's cool stare.

"Okay, okay," Kutchaï said. "If I get on your nerves, don't hesitate to tell me."

The open forest, vast stretches of yellow grass dotted with coconut palms, gave way to jungle. The dry heat became humid without becoming any more bearable: on the contrary.

Kutchaï went on talking, as though to himself. "According to Ieng, there are no more than four to five thousand Khmer Rouge in Cambodia at present. And they don't have nearly enough arms to go around. One rifle for every two men, roughly speaking."

"*Grosso modo.*"

"If you prefer to put it in Latin. And they're not even in agreement among themselves. There are those whose one allegiance is to Hanoi and Moscow—Ieng calls them the Stalinists, and I'd be surprised if he means the term affectionately. And then there are the pro-Chinese. And to quote Ieng again, there's a third category: himself."

Kutchaï had met Ieng Samboth four days earlier, a few kilometers west of Pursat, as Ieng and his detachment were headed toward the rendezvous point with Christiani on the Thai coast.

The 504 came to the little wooden bridge above the arroyo. Lara stopped the car, got out, and went to inspect the pilings and the planks of the roadway. He hadn't been to the plantation for several months, since the day, in fact, when he and Kutchaï had been arrested there, on their return from the Moï plateaux of Ratanakiri, where they had seen Ieng Samboth.

He came back to the car and leaned on the windowsill. "You can put away your artillery, Jungle Jim. But the pilings have been sawed partway through. If we'd tried to cross, we'd have landed up in the arroyo."

Kutchaï got out to inspect the damage: The four enormous teak pilings had been carefully sawed almost through at the bottom, with only a few inches of wood holding them upright. The weight of a man on a motorcycle would have been enough to make them collapse, not to mention a Peugeot 504 or a Land-Rover.

"Rath."

"It's nice to know that somebody's thinking of you," Lara said impassively. He took his elbow off the windowsill. "Let's go."

They had to make a long detour to get across the arroyo. One look had sufficed to assure Kutchaï that he and Lara had reacted the same way to the silence and the deserted air about the plantation as they approached. Normally, in the middle of the day like this, they should have heard the barking of dogs and other familiar sounds coming from the latex collectors' village and seen the smoke of cooking fires. And signs of the presence of the cook and his family should have come to them from the house built of black wood that perched like a huge insect amid the trees and flowers.

They couldn't see or hear a thing.

As the car stopped in the shadow of the trees just before the open ground, Lara stopped Kutchaï from getting out with a gesture of his hand. "Wait for me."

"Why you?"

"Because I'm two months older than you."

"If you get yourself killed, I warn you I'm going to be mad as hell at you."

They were whispering, and keeping their eyes peeled. Lara reached out his arm and his fingertips touched Kutchaï's. He crossed the last few yards of forest and stepped out into the blinding light, dotted with gleaming dust motes suspended in the air. *If Rath has been watching us, now is the time he'll attack. But I wonder why he's waited this long.* Kutchaï's eyes never left Lara's tall, thin figure walking very, very slowly toward the veranda, and climbing the steps just as warily. One, two minutes went by in deathly silence. *What in the world is he doing?* Kutchaï wondered.

Lara finally came out of the house. He waved vaguely as a signal to the Jaraï to join him, then leaned his back and even the nape of his neck against the outside wall, his eyes staring into space.

Kutchaï left cover, putting his feet exactly where Lara had put his. He, too, noted the fine wire attached to the second step, and as Lara had done, he avoided setting foot on that step. He knew how stairs could be booby-trapped. The technique was very simple: One merely detached the step from the upright supporting it, and the moment anyone set foot on it, it sagged and stretched the wire attached to it, thereby detonating the grenade fastened to the other end of the wire and hidden underneath the steps.

Kutchaï joined Lara on the veranda, stopping to have a look at him. Lara did not turn his head, holding his hands behind his back between the wall and himself, his face ghastly pale, his lips set in a thin, tense line. Kutchaï entered the house and saw the cook's wife first, lying with her arms and legs sprawled out in the middle of the floor and a hideous bloody mass of flesh stuffed into her wide-open mouth. Bath's four children were also pinned to the floor, with latex-collectors' gouges serving as stakes. And finally, Bath himself had been strung up by his feet, legs apart, the wire used to hang him having been threaded through his flesh. Obscene and frightening, it had taken as much imagination as it had diabolical patience to do what they had done to him. His wounds were black with blood that had coagulated and dried; they were old wounds, going back perhaps two or three days, all except for one, in the throat, where the carotid artery had been severed. This wound was recent, made a minute before at most, and Kutchaï saw, lying on the floor, the knife that Lara had just mercifully used to finish off the hideously tortured man.

Outside of the six dead bodies, at first glance nothing seemed to have been touched, not the records nor the books nor the few knickknacks. For an instant Kutchaï was tempted to go all through the house, to stop by his room especially, where he would have liked to pick up a few personal belongings. But he knew the risk was too great: There was probably not a single spot in the house that hadn't been booby-trapped. There was every sign that they'd done a thorough job of it. Threads strung in all directions, fine traces of sawdust on the floorboards, a book or a record just a fraction of an inch out of line on the shelves. . . . Perhaps even more than Lara, Kutchaï was familiar with the techniques. It was probable that a number of the only-too-apparent booby traps were fake; but he had also seen at one time or another a great many of those strange, fantastically complicated devices that his Jaraï compatriots, or the Braos or the Kuys, were capable of inventing and setting up to kill an enemy. And he had witnessed the horribly painful death of an elephant or a tiger or even a man pricked by minuscule poisoned arrowheads.

He came out of the house again, as cautiously as he had entered it. Lara hadn't moved, and his face was only slightly less pale now. *Oreste and now this,* Kutchaï thought. *That's a whole lot for just one day.*

He said aloud: "The less time we stay here the better. It's possible that

Rath's had the word passed to him that we've arrived, and that madman may well be already on his way here to greet us with one of his affectionate big hugs and kisses. I don't really feel very much like waiting for him."

He left the veranda, carefully choosing the places where he set his foot down. He took a few steps, then turned around. Lara still hadn't stirred.

"Come on, damn it!"

He began to walk in the direction of the rubber-processing buildings, and Lara finally joined him. They didn't try to go inside the factory, and using an old shovel and a wooden pike, they began to dig along the cement wall.

"Did Ieng say anything to you about Rath?"

"Just that he was head of the Khmer Rouge in the province of Kompong Thom. Rath and he don't get along any too well, I take it. But Rath would seem to be a great pal of Saloth Sar's, who protects him. There's nothing surprising about that, though: The one is as insane as the other."

When they'd dug some sixteen inches down they spied planks. Lara and Kutchaï lifted them up and uncovered the cache, consisting of four twenty-five-liter cans of gasoline, three SIG-530-1 assault rifles, each with twenty chargers of thirty cartridges, a tiny Skorpion submachine gun with a silencer, and finally an Israeli UZI submachine gun with a big bolt handle, plus twenty clips for each of the two last.

"It seems that Saloth Sar has changed names, is that right?" asked Lara.

"Yes. He now calls himself Pol Pot."

"Do you know why?"

"No idea," Kutchaï said with a shrug.

It took the two men half an hour to transport all the arms and ammunition to the 504. They left the cans of gasoline near the house.

"I'd like to do it myself, if you don't mind," Lara said.

"Symbolic?"

"Right," Lara answered.

"May I at least help you carry the gas cans?"

"You may."

Kutchaï went off to place a can of gasoline at each corner of the house and then stood off at a distance, holding the UZI, which he had cleaned and loaded. He watched Lara sprinkle gasoline on all four sides of the veranda. There were the usual subtle signs that night was coming on, and the usual squadrons of giant bats were beginning to appear in the sky. A poignant feeling of sadness came over the Jaraï; he realized that before his eyes, something was dying, and nothing would ever be the same again. The house that was about to burn down had been built—not in its present form, but that was not what mattered—by Lara's great-grandfather. Kutchaï's father and Lara's had grown up together, the wild Jaraï and the Barang already bound by ties of friendship that were not at all common in that era. *And not only in that era. Even today,* he thought. How many Frenchmen—though nationality was not the point; the same remark could have been made with regard to the British in India, the Dutch in Indonesia, or an Occidental anywhere—how many Frenchmen born in this country, having lived here all their lives and unquestionably loving it, could cite the names of real Cambodian, Vietnamese, Laotian friends?

Ieng Samboth's words came back to Kutchaï's mind, words Ieng had spoken to Lara in the half-shadow of the Moï hut as the American B-52's flew over it: "Lara, there's never been a real dialogue between you Westerners and us. Never. Nothing but a monologue, in which we've only rarely been able to get a word in edgewise. I've read your history books: They recount nothing but the history of the West. They say, for example, that the West invented democracy. When was democracy invented? In Greece, where nine inhabitants out of ten were slaves and half-breeds? In Rome, where only Roman citizens enjoyed the freedom of the city? In the British Isles where it was better not to be an Irish Catholic? At the time of the so-called American Revolution, after which blacks had to wait a hundred years and more to share the benefits of it—if in fact they really share them even today? If not in those times and places, then when and where? With the establishment of the so-called popular democracies in the West? Or the French Revolution, the immediate result of which was an empire constantly waging war, followed by a regime dominated by the industrial *grande bourgeoisie?*"

Lara came over to where Kutchaï was standing, his features as rigid as a mask in his effort to let none of his emotions show. The smell of gasoline was overpowering. Lara was holding a torch he'd improvised, using the rag the weapons had been wrapped in. He took out his cigarette lighter with his left hand and lit it. The greasy rag began to burn with an almost invisible blue flame.

Kutchaï's eyes followed the arc of the firebrand as it slowly sailed through the air. He saw it fall on the veranda and for a few seconds allowed himself to think that nothing was going to happen. Then a flame ran along the black wood, blue at first and then bright red-orange. There was a sort of dull explosion, and then everything caught fire at precisely the same moment, the flames leaping high in the darkening sky—higher than the tops of the towering teak trees in the forest. Fascinated by the inferno, Kutchaï could not tear his eyes away, but finally he resolutely stopped gazing into the flames. He turned his head. Lara had disappeared from sight. Kutchaï began to run, carrying the metal shoulder stock and barrel of the UZI that he had neglected to fold up.

One last time, just before he started off into the trees, he allowed himself to look back and saw only an immense red-orange blaze which had now almost swallowed up the subtle geometric forms of the house built of black wood. He could smell the first whiffs of roasted flesh, and as a silence fell over the forest, all he could hear was a soft, sad, crackling sound. Disappointing: In a confused sort of way, Kutchaï had expected a sort of great funeral pyre befitting the end of a world, burning with a thundering roar, but the death agony was very quiet, almost mute.

"And you didn't meet anyone?" they were asked by the officer who had installed his command post in the Kompong Thom high school, occupying what must have been the principal's office. Curiously enough—perhaps he hadn't thought of it—he had failed to remove the portrait of Sihanouk on the wall.

"Not a soul."

"You're Monsieur Lara."

It was not a question but a statement. He picked up the pistol he had laid down on the table and put it back in its holster. "And now you're headed back to Phnom Penh?"

Lara nodded.

"What condition did you find your house in?"

"Burned to the ground," Lara answered in an indifferent tone of voice.

The officer preceded him to the door of the office and saw him to his car. He looked closely at the dusty Peugeot and for a few moments Kutchaï was afraid he would ask them to open the trunk where the weapons were.

But the captain's mind was on something else: "I've heard about you," he said to Lara. "Everyone around here knows you. I've also heard about another European, who looked after your plantation. A Corsican."

"He left for France today."

"He won't be back?"

"No."

It was now pitch-dark out. The buffalo toads of the Stung Sen held forth with hoarse, rhythmic croaks, and in the intervals when they fell silent, the crickets managed to make themselves heard. It was still just as hot as it had been during the day, a stifling, muggy heat.

"I've been told that you and your family have been in this region for a very long time."

"A very long time."

A silence.

"Perhaps you'd have dinner with me," the officer suggested, almost shyly.

"Thank you for the invitation," Lara said in his slow, soft voice. "But I'm expected back in Phnom Penh. My wife would worry."

＊　＊　＊

They arrived in Phnom Penh a little before eleven that night, having had to pass through only one routine inspection in the course of which no one had bothered to look in the trunk.

"Would you like to come and sleep at my place? Lisa and Mathias are at the Korvers'. I didn't want to leave them by themselves, and besides, I'm waiting for news from Christiani, who's supposed to phone me. There's nobody at the house on Phsar Dek."

Kutchaï shook his head. "No, thanks anyway. Give Lisa and Mathias a kiss from me."

"Are you sure?"

"Yes, I'm sure."

"Then where shall I drop you off?"

"Right here will be okay."

They were entering the Rue Kol de Monteiro, at the far end of which, in the light of the rectangular streetlamps, they could see the massive silhouette of the Olympic stadium. Lara parked along the curb. There was a silence. Kutchaï searched through his pockets for a cigarette.

"We should have bought some at Kompong Thom."

"Look in the glove compartment," Lara said. "There must be an old pack in there."

The old pack in question contained five cigarettes, crumpled and damp.

"Take your clothes off when you get in the shower," Kutchaï said.

The cigarette lighter on the dashboard hadn't worked for at least two years. The click of Lara's Zippo.

"What a day!" the Jaraï said.

Lara had thrown his head all the way back and his pale eyes were staring at the roof lining.

Kutchaï went on: "And Bê is dead, along with almost everyone in his family. They were Vietnamese, I grant you. But Bath wasn't. I know what you're going to tell me: Rath is a madman. You'd have to be mad to do what he did to Bath and his family. But it happened nonetheless. You know as well as I do that even with the pilings of the bridge sawed through, all those booby traps, Rath wasn't really expecting to get us. And he didn't have it in for Bath either. He wanted to warn us, to warn you. That's probably why he didn't bother to be there when we arrived. Of course, it may be because he wasn't told of our arrival in time. Maybe. I know that five days ago he was east of Kompong Thom. Right now I don't have the faintest idea where he's hiding. And when I say hiding, it's a manner of speaking: Half of Cambodia is in the hands of the Viet Cong and for the moment the Khmer Rouge have nothing to fear from the guys from Hanoi. No, Lara, that's the real truth of the matter: Rath wanted to warn you. What he did at the house means: Lara, clear out."

Kutchaï stretched his hand holding the cigarette out in front of him. He had almost abnormally large, unbelievably strong hands, with broad spatulate fingertips.

"Damn!" he said. "I didn't want to talk to you about it. Talking never gets you anywhere. On the contrary, it gets everything all muddled up. What counts is what a person feels."

The stub of his cigarette was beginning to burn his fingers. Holding it between his thumbnail and the nail of his index finger, he took one last drag on it and then tossed it out the window, watching it burn to the very end in a crack in the sidewalk.

"Anyway, as long as I'm at it . . . Ieng talked to me about you. Among all his other problems, you're also one. He asked me if I knew what you'd do in case the Khmer Rouge came to power some day."

Lara was still staring at the roof lining. "When did he ask you that?" he said.

"The last time I saw him, near Pursat. He was on his way to the rendezvous with Christiani."

"After the coup d'état then," Lara said quietly.

"Yes, after. So he knew at the time that Sihanouk had just been ousted. Does it matter?"

"It changes quite a few things. The Khmer Rouge have thrown their support to Sihanouk. If they win out someday, they'll bring him back to Phnom Penh."

Kutchaï shrugged. "Maybe."

"It's certain," Lara said. He threw the stub of his cigarette out the window and took another, as did Kutchaï.

"And what did you answer when he asked you that?"

"You know very well what I answered, you bastard," Kutchaï said gently. "You don't even need to ask me. I told Ieng he didn't know you very well if he was hoping you'd solve his problem for him by voluntarily leaving here. I told him there will always be only one way of getting you out of this country. . . ."

His huge hand moved toward Lara, his thumb pointing straight up and the tip of his index finger resting on Lara's chest.

"Bang!"

He turned his head.

"And they'd have to kill me first," Kutchaï said.

From the nearby pagoda came the piercing, monotonous sound of the bonzes chanting their *chiyantho* prayers. An old joke had it that the monks simply tirelessly repeated the French words *Y en a, y en a pas*—there are things, there are no things. And in fact the resemblance was striking.

Kutchaï put one of his big paws on the door handle. "When are you and Lisa leaving for Sré?"

"In three weeks, a month—as soon as Lisa is able to travel again."

"You're taking Mathias with you?"

"Of course."

"How's the amah working out?"

The amah—the title designated her function, that of nursemaid—was a Chinese woman who'd come to live in at the villa on the Rue Phsar Dek as soon as Lisa returned from the hospital. She was a robust woman of about fifty, recommended by Liu.

"Just fine," Lara said. "She's perfect."

"A month." Kutchaï seemed to be calculating something. "There's a danger that the situation will have changed by a month from now," he said thoughtfully.

He opened the door and seemed about to get out of the car. But he changed his mind, leaving the door halfway open.

"The Rangers and the Marines in Saigon have problems on their hands. When they invaded the provinces of the South, with the agreement of Lon Nol, it was a real cakewalk at first; the Viet Cong had pulled out. But now they're beginning to have their troubles. They're encountering resistance and are going to be encountering more and more. According to what I've been told, Hanoi is going to launch a counterattack. In your opinion, how long will Lon Nol's army hold up against the North Vietnamese? A month? Even a month seems much too optimistic an estimate to me. As I see it, everything's going to fall apart within a few days. Unless somebody intervenes . . ."

He nodded his head. "Especially since Lon Nol is now going to have another problem: the peasants. The peasants are overwhelmingly in favor of Sihanouk. He's the only leader they know. The Khmer Rouge forces are attracting more recruits by the day; it's spectacular. And they wear little portraits of Sihanouk on their chests. All those guys plus the divisions from Hanoi would make it rough going for Lon Nol. His regime may well fall very soon. In any event, people are going to be shooting all over the place. War. We're heading straight for one."

He scanned Lara's face. Lara had stopped staring at the roof lining and had adopted a familiar position: sitting slightly crosswise in the seat, his left shoulder and temple leaning against the door pillar, his left hand outside the car and gripping the roof, his other hand lying flat on the steering wheel.

"Don't you think so too?"

"I don't know," Lara replied.

There was a silence. Then, making up his mind all of a sudden, Kutchaï got out of the car, closed the door behind him, and with a wave of his hand walked off.

7 AT THE KORVERS' VILLA, THERE WERE LIGHTS ON UPSTAIRS AND IN THE vast living room downstairs. Lara found Charles and Madeleine downstairs, working at their endless index cards, sitting opposite each other across a table piled high with books on art and history. As he came into the room they greeted him with a smile, as though he had spent the evening with them and was just coming inside after a stroll around the garden.

"I thought Kutchaï was with you," was all Charles said.

"He preferred to go spend the night heaven only knows where. You know Kutchaï."

"A woman in every hut," Madeleine commented acidly.

Lara smiled. "Ah, if only it were just one per hut."

He glanced toward the stairway.

"No, she's not sleeping. She was with us not five minutes ago. Have you had dinner?"

Lara shook his head. "I'm not hungry."

He hesitated, massaging his shoulder, staring off into space. He automatically reached for the pack of cigarettes in the breast pocket of his bush jacket, but then his hand fell back, empty.

"If it's cigarettes you're looking for, there's a whole drawerful behind you," Charles Korver said. "With all the packs you forget and leave behind here on each one of your visits, we could start a tobacco shop."

"In any case, he smokes too much," Madeleine said as she began writing again. "I've told him so a million times."

Lara took a pack from the drawer and fished a cigarette out of it. Then he changed his mind and walked toward the stairway, putting the cigarette back in the pack and moving with that seemingly slow, silent stride that was so typical of him and so striking.

He found Lisa sitting up in bed, one finger marking her place in the Signet pocket edition of Salinger's *Nine Stories*. She was wearing a thin nightgown that bared her arms and a good bit of her bosom. Her hair, which she had not had cut for months, now reached shoulder-length. Lara stood in the door for a few moments looking at her, and his gaze was so eloquent that she smiled, almost in embarrassment, and lowered her head for a few seconds.

"I heard you come in."

Lara's eyes finally left her and he glanced at the door, open just a crack, that led to the room where the amah and the baby slept. "Is everything all right?" he asked.

"Just fine," Lisa said in a gently mocking tone. "Marvelous. My man's back. Hallelujah!"

He sat down on the bed next to her, leaning his head against the headboard beside hers and placing one hand on her thigh.

"Tired?" she said.

"Mmmm."

She bent her head and kissed him on one corner of his mouth. "You might at least have said good evening."

He had closed his eyes. He opened one of them again. "Good morning, ma'am."

"And you might at least have gone to say hello to your son."

"I'm about to do just that."

But he closed his eyes again, as though he were about to drop off to sleep. There was a few seconds' silence, then: "Lisa, do you think you'd be able to travel right now?"

"Certainly, if it were necessary. I'm not made of sugar candy. And where would I be traveling to?"

"Bangkok or Hong Kong."

"With Mathias?"

He nodded, his eyelids still closed.

"With Mathias but without you, is that it?"

"Charles and Madeleine could go with you."

"Undoubtedly," Lisa said with the greatest calm. "Charles and Madeleine could undoubtedly go with me. And so could the amah, the *ti-nam* and her husband, and Seng, our cook, as well. Plus his family, of course. And I could also take Douglas Fairbanks with me, since Thomas Aquinas O'Malley left him with us before he went away. Plus several hundred women and children. Not to mention the dogs that this sudden evacuation of Phnom Penh would be certain to leave wandering around the streets all by themselves."

She felt Lara's hand on her thigh tense slightly.

"I hope I haven't forgotten anybody," she said, in the same calm voice.

He got up and walked to the door leading to the next room. The baby was sleeping peacefully, as peacefully as the amah lying on her mat. Lara leaned over the cradle, opening his eyes wide in the darkness to get a better look at the still-vague features of his son. He touched the wicker cradle. It rocked slightly and the amah immediately opened her eyes. "No, nothing's wrong. Sleep," Lara said in Chinese.

He went back into the bedroom, shutting the door behind him.

"I'm sorry," Lisa said, her finger still marking her place between the pages of the book.

He had stopped halfway between the door and the bed. He shook his head.

"What's happening? I haven't stuck my nose outside for days and days except to come home from the hospital, but everything seems calm. Madeleine and Charles say that Phnom Penh has never been quieter."

Meeting his steady gaze, she added, "They've naturally done their best to reassure me. And doubtless they've succeeded."

"There's a risk of a certain amount of unrest. Nothing really very serious."

"But you'd nonetheless prefer to make sure your wife and son were elsewhere."

He shrugged. "It's just a precaution."

She stared at the book of Salinger stories as though she had suddenly discovered she was holding it in her hand. She noted her page number, closed the book, and laid it down on the nightstand.

"There's one thing I'll never stand for, and that's being treated as though I were a delicate little creature that has to be carefully sheltered the minute a storm is brewing," she said in a quiet voice. "I am not a delicate little creature. *I am not,*" she repeated in English. "I'm strong enough to bear anything you can. If this country is good enough for you, it's good enough for me, and for our son. Or else it's no good at all for any of us and we should leave it—together. We've always agreed on that score."

He automatically rummaged in the breast pocket of his sand-colored bush jacket.

"I haven't had a cigarette all day long. I'd really like one now," Lisa remarked.

He was obliged to come closer to hand her the pack. She took him by the wrist and drew him toward her, gently but firmly.

"Don't you want to come sit down beside me?" There was a look of tenderness in the depths of her violet eyes once more, and she was resolutely smiling at him. He returned the smile and sat down on the bed. He leaned over and kissed her, gently at first, his lips barely touching hers, and then, putting a hand behind the nape of her neck, almost violently.

"Hey, watch it!" she exclaimed. "Take it easy!" But there was laughter in the eyes that brimmed with tears. She made a face. "Have I ever happened to tell you that you smoke too much?"

"You have said something to that effect, as a matter of fact. Once or twice."

A silence. She leaned her forehead on Lara's shoulder.

"So you and Kutchaï went to the plantation."

"Yes."

"What state did you find it in?"

"Deserted."

She moved away so as to see his eyes.

"They've killed Bath and all his family. Bath, his wife, and his four children. They've killed them and they've driven everybody out of the latex-collectors' village. There's not a living soul left," he said.

"Who's responsible? That man named Rath?"

"Yes, probably."

He told her everything, omitting only the tortures and the fact that he'd had to put Bath out of his misery himself. He told her that he and Kutchaï had burned the house. He talked to her of Ieng Samboth and of Rath, and of the differences he saw between the two of them. He described to her the situation in Cambodia in these last days of March 1970, as it looked to him at least, with a government in Phnom Penh that had real authority over no more than half the provinces at best; that had control only of the cities, the main highways, the axes linking the capital to Kompong Son on the one hand and Saigon on the other; that could really count only on the Sereï and Krom units and on the troops from Saigon that had just set foot on Cambodian soil.

"You mean to say that the Communist army could take Phnom Penh?"

"People have heard Sihanouk's appeal broadcast over the radio. According to Kutchaï, the peasants are readying themselves to march on Phnom Penh, tomorrow, to drive Lon Nol out. Lon Nol has done his best to exploit the age-old hatred of Khmers toward Vietnamese. But the international reaction has been such that they must now stop their racist campaign, at least for the moment. Its principal result has been to make the survivors of the massacres rally round the troops from Saigon, and they're out for vengeance. This isn't going to make matters any easier between Lon Nol and those same troops from Saigon, who are nevertheless his sole allies."

He got up to get an ashtray.

"You said a moment ago: if nobody intervenes."

"There are lots of people who think the Americans are going to intervene, the way they did in Vietnam."

"You mean"—Lisa said in English, and then immediately switched back to French—"military intervention?"

"Yes, military intervention."

They heard faint footsteps on the stairs.

"Good God!" Lisa exclaimed. "They're all utterly mad!"

The footsteps halted outside their room. There was a knock, and Lara got up to open the door.

"Am I disturbing you?" Madeleine Korver asked. "Please tell me frankly: Am I disturbing you?"

"No," Lara answered with a smile. "I can't think of anybody in the world who'd disturb us less."

"I have a terribly impolite suggestion to make to you," Madeleine went on. "Lisa hardly ate a bit tonight and you yourself admitted you hadn't had dinner. And Charles and I are hungry. We have two or three tins left of that foie gras we had sent to us from the Landes. With a little toast and even with that horrible Australian butter, it shouldn't taste too bad."

Lara turned around, looking at Lisa with a questioning gaze. Lisa lowered her head, then raised it and smiled. "I'm a delicate little creature who feels an overpowering desire for foie gras. And maybe even a wee drop of champagne. What's more, I adore impolite suggestions. I'm getting up out of bed this minute."

Madeleine took the time to cast a searching look at the couple; she obviously suspected they'd been quarreling. She then nodded briskly and turned on her heel. The moment the door closed behind her, Lisa got out of bed. She put on a dressing gown and walked over to her husband, who was still standing at the door. She slipped into his arms. Even in her bare feet, she was very nearly as tall as he was.

"You had an awful day, didn't you?"

"Kind of."

"And I leapt at your throat the minute you got here."

He held her close. "You were right to."

"You're going to miss Oreste."

"I certainly am. But less than he's going to miss Cambodia and Indochina."

She traced the contour of his lips with the tip of her tongue and whispered, "I keep wondering why I ever married you. A moment of inexplicable mental aberration."

"Some mystery!" Lara said mockingly.

She parted the neckline of her dressing gown and drew down the top of her nightgown, baring one of her breasts.

"Kiss it."

He did so and she moaned softly, her eyes closed. "And the other one? You forgot to kiss the other one. Do you think we'll be able to go to Sré?" she asked.

"Of course."

"I wish I were there already. I'd like to be able to make love to you there right now. The world's not made right. Why should we have to wait? I've been thinking about Sré all day long while I waited for you, wondering if you were going to come back, if you were going to come back alive. Every so often I told myself that it's mad to want to go to that island with a tiny baby. If a thing like that had been suggested to me a year ago, I'd have dismissed the thought with a shrug and not even listened. But now it's what I want most in the world. Being bare-naked and thin, and alone with you. I no longer recognize myself," she said in a low voice, kissing him. "I'm a pure and innocent American girl who's been perverted. It was you who perverted me. You."

"My ass," Lara said.

She slid her hands underneath his shirt. He backed away.

"I'm not exactly made of wood."

She smiled slyly, nodded in agreement, pulled up the top of her night-gown and closed her dressing gown. She went off to put on Japanese san-dals. She returned to his side, this time with a grave look on her face.

"Not Hong Kong and not Bangkok. Or else with you. Is that a deal?"

"It's a deal," Lara said. "I promise."

They went into Mathias' room together to have a look. Everything was quiet and peaceful. Lara put his arm around Lisa's waist and the two of them walked step by step down the stairs together.

8 "AND YOU DIDN'T TAKE PHOTOS?" DONALDSON ASKED.

"No," Roger answered. "I didn't take photos."

The Englishman's pale eyes stared at him. Finally he shook his head. "Never mind—it doesn't matter," he said kindly. "My paper wouldn't have used them anyway."

"Not typical enough," Roger said.

"Right."

"I took photos before and after, but none right at that very instant."

"It doesn't matter," Donaldson repeated. "And the two men were deputies?"

"Yes," Roger answered.

Donaldson yawned. They had left Kompong Cham during the morn-ing. Not exactly alone. On the road with them were hundreds, perhaps thousands of inhabitants of the province heading for the capital. Their Land-Rover in fact was now following, almost at a crawl, a veritable convoy of trucks and buses, private passenger cars, bicycles, and even carts: a magnificently miscellaneous convoy that was descending on Phnom Penh with no other weapon save countless portraits of Sihanouk. And not only Kompong Cham had taken to the road: Each village they passed added its contingent, while at the intersection of the highway from the North, delegations arriving from Kompong Thom and Siem Reap had joined the floodtide, as men and women from Kompong Chnang, Pursat, and even Battambang had done at Prek Dam. It seemed as though all of Cambodia had taken to the road to put its little prince back on the throne.

Creeping along behind all that, Roger felt a bit giddy with excitement. "We're going to invade Phnom Penh and take over the National Assembly, the Palace of Government, and the radio station, too, of course. We're going to occupy all the public buildings, the banks, the casino, the opium dens, and the brothels." He said "we" deliberately, thinking of all the men and women who were advancing alongside him and in front of him. This "we" was not at all inappropriate: Besides Donaldson and Roger, the Land-Rover was transporting seven other men, two of whom were sitting on the roof and another standing on the rear bumper, all of them grinning from ear to ear each time their eyes met Roger's. Roger didn't remember exactly when they had climbed aboard.

In his mind's eye he saw himself once again behind the truck with the loudspeaker the evening before, just as the two deputies arrived in Kompong Cham. *Roger Bouès, the famous revolutionary agitator. Roger the Red.*

Donaldson was slowly coming out of his stupor. He began to hum the first stanza of "Onward, Christian Soldiers." Along the edge of the road to his left, Roger recognized the first houses of the settlement that went by the name of the Malay Village, one of the rare places in Phnom Penh—if not in all of Cambodia—where one could buy fresh cow's milk.

The head of the convoy must have been a good kilometer farther ahead. Hence it took Roger several seconds to realize that the bursts of fire from automatic weapons that reached his ears just then were in fact aimed at this convoy he was part of.

The light dawned on him as all the vehicles in front of him braked to a sudden halt, all the chants and shouts abruptly ceased, and the human tide ahead began to flow back toward them. Donaldson had sized up the situation instantly. Taking advantage of the fact that the Land-Rover had been forced to stop, he leapt out with such uncharacteristic agility that he took Roger completely by surprise. Donaldson began literally dragging out the men sitting in the car and yanking off the ones clinging to the roof and bumper.

"Get out! Clear out of here! Go away!"

The rapid bursts of gunfire up ahead grew heavier and heavier. The crowd surging back in their direction broke into a run and the retreating tide became a chaotic general rout. Buses and trucks tried to turn around and in the confusion succeeded only in blocking each other, thus becoming motionless targets for the hail of bullets. The Englishman climbed back into the car.

"Okay, Roger? Go ahead!"

The Land-Rover started off again almost by itself. It left the road and jolted across the little drainage ditch alongside; it began to barrel over the yellow grass on the shoulder just beyond, making its way through the hordes of people fleeing in the opposite direction, many of whom collided with the hood of the Land-Rover in their blind flight.

"Keep going!"

And then after three or four hundred yards, the great wave suddenly subsided and Roger found himself confronting a veritable battlefield

stretching out before him. Dozens and dozens of vehicles had been set on
fire, and in one of them, a Chinese bus with windows that had been jammed
shut for ages, Roger saw a dense cluster of people fighting frantically with
each other as they tried to escape the holocaust. Then the entire bus was
enveloped in a great burst of red-purple flame.

The Land-Rover zigzagged amid all this debris and dozens of dead
bodies. Clutching the steering wheel in a death grip born of despair, Roger
felt the car run over and crush a number of corpses, but he nonetheless kept
his foot to the floor, half-blinded by tears.

"Keep going!"

Sitting at his side, Donaldson yelled, urged him on, gripped the steering wheel himself to keep the car headed in the direction of Phnom Penh,
no matter what. The din was deafening, but nevertheless Roger heard the
shrill, relentless whine of bullets fired at random all around them. He expected to die at any moment, and at one point indeed a star-shaped hole
appeared in the windshield, whereupon Donaldson, not ceasing for a moment to scream at him to keep going, opened the door on his side, leaned
out of the Land-Rover as far as he could, exposing his baby-pink skin and his
pale blue eyes, and waved them onward with his right hand.

The gunfire ceased, and all was silent once more. Just as miraculously,
the Land-Rover's wheels touched asphalt again. After they had driven on
for less than forty yards, soldiers loomed up, their automatic weapons aimed
straight at them.

"English journalist!" Donaldson shouted at them. "English journalist!"
His arm upraised, his middle and index finger formed the V-for-Victory
sign.

"Go ahead now, Roger." He climbed back into his seat, closed the door
on his side, lit a cigarette.

"Well, Roger, as you can see we got through. And you didn't take any
photos?"

9 THE PRINCIPAL CONSEQUENCE OF WHAT HAPPENED IN THE LAST TWO
days of March 1970 on the roads leading to Phnom Penh, outside of the
massacre of unarmed demonstrators by Khmer Sereï and Khmer Krom
units, was the elimination of any possibility of an immediate fall of the Lon
Nol regime and the return of Sihanouk—the two events that would almost
surely have enabled Cambodia to escape the holocaust, the martyrdom,
that was to follow.

In the beginning, the general mobilization decreed by Lon Nol had resulted in the birth of an army of thirty thousand men, a raggle-taggle bunch of high-school students and pedicab operators, vaguely headed by a handful of junior officers who had served in the French Army and, more importantly, by officers promoted in rank in direct proportion to their pull in high circles: A history teacher, for instance, who had accompanied the man who mistook himself for Robespierre at Svay Rieng, suddenly found himself a colonel. These thirty thousand men had been hastily sent off to do battle. Ten days later, there were scarcely half of them left. Few of those missing had been killed or wounded or taken prisoner by the enemy; they had simply gone home, generally taking their weapons with them. In one case, a battalion of eight hundred men had been surrounded and captured by twenty Viet Cong. Officers who suddenly discovered they had no men left had had to swim across the Mekong to inform their superiors of this news.

Giap's North Vietnamese divisions had not yet mounted an attack, however, or at least not a full-scale one. But as these forces withdrew toward the north and center of the country in order to avoid a pitched battle with the troops from Saigon entering Cambodia, they had been able to exert a fair amount of pressure.

As for the Khmer Rouge, they were lying low for the time being. The moment had not yet come and they knew it. Advancing, spreading out over the terrain taken by the soldiers from Hanoi, they had merely undertaken to administer the villages they had overrun. And thanks to the all-powerful portrait of Sihanouk, they had enlisted in their ranks the deserters from Lon Nol's army, especially when the renegades had brought their weapons with them, and all the young men who had taken refuge in the countryside to escape Lon Nol's orders for a general conscription, who were seeking vengeance for the massacre outside Phnom Penh, or who were simply fleeing the capital because the cost of rice, due to clever shady deals between certain ministers and the top Chinese traders, had gone up from two to twenty riels per kilo in a very short time.

Therefore, at the end of April, forty days after the coup d'état, the Lon Nol/Sirik Matak regime controlled only Phnom Penh and the other large Cambodian cities, a few isolated zones, and the communications network essential to the very survival of Phnom Penh: the links by river and road with Saigon, controlled by the South Vietnamese Rangers, and the highway and railroad leading to Kompong Som, the port on the Gulf of Siam.

The rest of the country—that is to say, four-fifths of it—was now officially in the hands of Sihanouk's representatives, or of men claiming to be such.

On April 30, Richard Nixon therefore announced in Washington that American and South Vietnamese troops were being deployed from one end of Cambodian territory to the other. Since the Dap Chhuon affair, which had occurred in 1960, it had taken the CIA ten years to turn Cambodia into another Vietnam.

But their efforts to do so had been a total success.

10

SUON PHAN HAD NEVER SEEN THE SEA, AND SETTING EYES ON IT WAS at least one consolation in these first weeks of his military career. After halting for a few days at Takeo, the motorized column led by Kao had arrived in sight of the Kampot River on the evening of April 4. The little post of the Regional Guard located in the city, on the other side of the bridge, was much too small to be used as quarters for the reinforcements that had already been sent out from Phnom Penh; in fact, the troops guarding the entire province had been billeted in a camp a kilometer or two from the river, immediately adjoining the road to Kep. In theory there was a reinforced battalion—nearly a thousand men—stationed there.

Being completely inexperienced, Suon Phan was not at first surprised by the spectacle that greeted his eyes: Very few men—practically none of them—were in uniform; almost all, officers and men alike, wore sarongs and nothing else, and carried no arms. There seemed to be more women, children, pigs, chickens, and ducks than soldiers. Pots of rice for the evening meal were cooking on little fires all over the camp. The atmosphere was peaceful, even bucolic, and Suon Phan thought, to his vast relief, that fighting a war was probably not so terrible after all. Two or three Chinese had set up temporary stalls where they sold ice cream, Tsing Tao beer, and *chum*, as well as such basic necessities as *prahoc* and soap. Suon noted with interest that there was even a group of prostitutes who weren't bad-looking. Well, he decided, things could certainly have been worse. . . .

Then the young second lieutenant, his peace of mind restored, looked at Kao and gave a start. Kao was quivering with rage, and it was plain to see that it would not have taken much for him to grab his machine gun and begin firing at will. Kao stopped the jeep and pointed his forefinger at a man holding a baby in his arms.

"You there! Come here!"

Visibly apprehensive, the man obeyed.

"Who's in command here?"

"I don't know," the man said.

"Are you a soldier or aren't you?"

Everyone around the jeep stood rooted to the spot. And little by little the feeling of apprehension spread throughout the camp.

"Yes, sir, I'm a soldier," the man answered.

"Go get me one of your superiors. And be quick about it."

A moment later a sergeant arrived in uniform. He was a man well past middle age, with gray hair, and the way in which he saluted Kao was proof that he at least had a certain amount of army experience. Under Kao's questioning he said he had been a lance sergeant in the French Colonial Army, and that the commanding officer of the camp was a colonel.

"And where is he?"

"In town, sir," the sergeant answered.

By that he meant Kampot. He explained that the colonel lived in town, as in fact all the officers did. How long had it been since the colonel, or one of his adjutants, had visited the camp? The sergeant hesitated warily before answering, and Kao did not pursue the question. But he did ask, "Have you received your pay?"

"There have been delays," the sergeant replied, with the same wariness.

In fact, he had not been paid for four months. Four months ago, that is to say, he had received part of the five months' pay owed him at the time. And the rest of the men? The same was true in their case. This explained the general appearance of the camp: Since they had not been given the pay that would have allowed them to feed their families—in theory at least, inasmuch as the pay in question was not exactly a princely sum—the soldiers had sent for their families to join them and had thus transformed the camp into a sort of kolkhoz. They had to eat, after all.

"And arms? Where are your arms?"

The sergeant allowed as how the arms in question, M-14's, were stored in a stone villa, and he was the only one who had a key to it. His standing orders were to keep them under lock and key during the day so as to prevent the soldiers from selling their rifles to Chinese traders; the going price was 1,000 to 1,200 riels. At nightfall however, according to the same standing orders, he took a hundred rifles and an equal number of chargers out of the villa and gave them out to those men whom he more or less trusted, so as to hold off the Khmer Rouge if they should attack. But naturally he rounded the rifles up again at dawn, counting them one by one. In any event, there weren't enough rifles to go around.

"Are there lots of Khmer Rouge around here?"

The sergeant pointed to the thickly wooded massif of Elephant Mountain, north of Kampot and separating it from the port of Kompong Som.

"They're there," he said. "But they don't attack us. There aren't very many of them."

As for the North Vietnamese Viet Cong, they were, if not fewer in number, even more harmless. The presence of Rangers from Saigon at Takeo and Svay Rieng, to the east, doubtless explained this situation. The sergeant admitted, however, that small detachments had been sighted from time to time, probably coming from South Vietnam, perhaps from the Camau Peninsula, slipping across a frontier that was more or less unguarded. They had been sighted but had not been attacked. Yes, they had been seen in broad daylight.

"Is there an agreement between your colonel and them?" Kao asked. The sergeant did not answer.

"And between your colonel and the Khmer Rouge?"

The sergeant bowed his head. "I don't know, sir."

"They come to get medicines, is that it? You let them have what they came for and in return they don't attack you, you're left in peace, you can grow your vegetable gardens, and your colonel can make himself a fortune."

Kao stroked the barrel of his machine gun. "Climb in," he said to the sergeant. "I want you to show me where your colonel lives."

The colonel lived in a villa belonging to some Chinese, the overall plan and architectural details of which had come from the drawing board of Roger Boués, so that the building resembled a blockhouse on the Siegfried Line ornamented with columns suitable for a Greek temple and huge portholelike apertures let into the thick walls and fitted with multicolored glass panes. As for the interior decoration, it also made a person shudder in horror. The predominant color was deep burgundy, applied to every wall in the house in a glossy finish so shiny you could see your face in it clearly enough to shave. Once it was finished, the villa had been deemed superb, even awe-inspiring, by the Chinese pepper-trader who had commissioned Roger to design it.

Kao ordered the soldiers on guard duty in the garden not to make a single move. He entered without knocking, with Suon Phan at his heels, leaving the colonel's bodyguards face to face with the ten commandos who customarily served Kao as an escort—commandos he himself had recruited and equipped with M-16's and Colt .45's, headed by the two Buddhas from Cochin China. The faces of these two men alone were terrifying enough, not to mention the icy impassivity of the group as a whole.

Kao found the colonel lying on a bed stark-naked, cavorting about with two Sino-Khmer half-breeds who were naked, too, one of them devoting herself to caressing his entire body, and the other paying more particular attention to the area between his thighs.

A few seconds went by before the colonel spied Kao's unquestionably martial silhouette, with all his weapons and even a hand grenade tucked into his belt. The colonel leapt to his feet.

"What are you doing here?"

"Sir," Kao said, saluting, "I have important information to communicate to you. Could you ask these ladies to leave the room?"

He waited till the door had closed behind the two damsels, then said, "And now, you shit, listen to me. If you say one word, a single one, I'll cut your throat on the spot. You're going to get dressed, leave this house with me, and come along with me. You're going to give me all the money you have here. Once outside, we're going together to see the Chinese friends of yours with whom you're trafficking and you're going to ask each one of them for all the money they have on hand. My men are outside. They'd kill their mothers if I asked them to. The slightest argument, the slightest resistance, and I'll have you all wiped out. I'm Kao; my name is familiar to you. Get going."

They made the rounds of the traders, collecting tens of thousands of riels which Suon Phan, scared stiff, stuffed into a big canvas sack as they went along. It took them almost four hours, so that it was already pitch-dark out when they left Kampot, the truckful of paratroopers following the jeep, via the highway leading to Kompong Som along the coast, at the foot of Elephant Mountain.

The colonel was completely distraught. "There are Khmer Rouge round about here," he managed to blurt out.

Kao burst out laughing. "I'm not afraid of the Khmer Rouge," he said. "I'm not afraid of the Khmer Rouge, nor of the Viet Cong, nor of anybody else."

A few kilometers before the intersection with the American Highway leading from Kompong Som to Phnom Penh, the countryside changed, becoming flatter now that they had gone around Elephant Mountain to the west. The jeep stopped and the truck followed suit. Suon Phan saw the paratroopers leap out and deploy without a single order having been given, as though they were on a maneuver they'd practiced over and over again.

"Out," Kao said to the colonel.

The colonel hesitated. Kao grabbed him by the shoulder, pulled him out of his seat, threw him out of the jeep. He blinked the headlights.

"Get going," he said to the colonel.

And as the colonel, frozen with terror, still made not the slightest move, Kao slowly shifted into gear and drove the jeep forward till the bumper was touching the officer's legs. A shiver ran up and down Suon Phan's spine.

"Get going. Straight ahead. Run. Very fast. Maybe you'll get away."

Kao turned to Suon Phan, who was still sitting in the back seat. "Come up here and sit alongside me."

As Suon obeyed, Kao shouted, "Run, Colonel, *Run!*"

The officer leapt forward, as though he'd been given an electric shock. He was still young, barely forty, and did his best to get away. The night was bright, but in any case the headlights of the jeep and the truck together formed a long rectangle of light, along the sides of which the paratroopers had taken up positions, squatting in a double row, with the colonel running down the lighted space between.

"*Run!*" Kao shouted once more.

And he put his foot to the floor.

The man being tracked down was already thirty or forty yards away. Kao came up on him as fast as the jeep would go, and for an instant Suon Phan thought he was going to knock his prey down, but at the very last second, with a slight twist of the steering wheel, Kao dodged the human obstacle, went around it, and drove on some ten yards farther. Then, turning the wheels of the jeep as abruptly as possible and braking as hard as he could, he put the jeep into a fantastic full-lock skid. *We're going to be killed,* Phan had just time enough to think in terror. But the dried crust of the rice paddy gave way and mud appeared beneath the cracked earth. The jeep turned two full circles. Kao roared with laughter. He revved the engine and took off again, heading straight for the colonel.

"Run, Colonel, run!"

The officer tried to dodge to one side, but immediately the impassive paratroopers, squatting down with their rifle butts buried in the dirt, stood up and pointed their guns at him. The jeep was already upon him. It missed him by a few inches, rushed on for a few seconds, and then went into another full-lock skid quite as insane as the first one.

The game went on, in the glaring yellow beam of the two sets of headlights that sliced through the pale moonlight of the forest clearing. Five times, ten times, Kao swept down upon his victim like a whirlwind, coming a little bit closer each time but never quite touching him, going by much too fast for him to get a handhold on the jeep being driven at full throttle. Each pass ended with two or three waltz turns, which made Suon Phan cling to his seat in desperate terror but wildly excited Kao.

The colonel fell two or three times, and the third time he refused at first to get up again, clearly prepared to die. Kao used his machine gun then, the large-caliber bullets raking the ground a handbreadth away from the colonel's sprawling body. He got up and started running once more, looking like a disjointed puppet, his knees almost doubled up, his head thrown back, and his wide-open mouth gasping for air. He took off again, but it was the last escape effort he had the heart to make. He slowed down, as though hesitating, then stumbled to a halt, remaining on his feet in one last surge of pride.

The roar of the jeep engine abruptly died, and in the suddenly returning silence the only sound was the soft throb of the vehicle as it moved forward at a deadly slow speed, heading straight toward the motionless silhouette.

"Well, that's that," Kao said. His wild excitement had vanished and there was a strange look of sadness on his face.

Little by little the hood of the jeep moved closer. The colonel's legs gradually gave way and he collapsed to his knees. The hood came closer still, till it was brushing his belly.

"Do you want to kill him?" Kao asked Suon Phan. "I'll let you finish him off if you like."

The colonel's mud-spattered face looked like a fright mask with two huge red-rimmed eyeholes. The jeep had stopped. Kao switched off the ignition. The barrel of the machine gun began to rise inch by inch, at once obscene and terrifying, until it was pointing directly at that inhuman face.

"Well?" Kao said to Phan. "Have you made up your mind?"

Suon Phan swallowed hard and finally answered in a hoarse voice, "No, sir. I can't do it."

Kao burst out laughing, a kindly, understanding laugh. He glanced around at the paratroopers, now all on their feet and moving indifferently out of the line of fire. His eyes came back to the colonel.

"Let's go," he said. "We're not going to spend all night here."

He squeezed the trigger, and the colonel's head literally exploded.

The FARK paymaster, officially in charge of disbursing the pay of soldiers in the province of Kampot, was a fat, short little captain who had brought his two wives and eight children to the camp with him.

"As you no doubt already know," Kao said to him, "our late-lamented colonel met a valiant death on the battlefield last night, the victim of traitorous-Khmer Rouge-lackeys-of-totalitarian-Communist-atheist-Vietnamese imperialism, and so on and so forth. In short, I'm taking command here until further notice. I've talked with men all over the camp and have learned that their pay is somewhat in arrears."

"Er, ah, yes, it's perhaps a month late, yes," the paymaster stammered.

"Four months," Kao corrected him. "Have you enough cash on hand to pay them what's owed them?"

"I don't have a cent," the captain said. "The colonel always took care of everything having to do with the men's pay."

Sitting at the wheel of his jeep, Kao was amusing himself by toying with the machine gun, pivoting it slowly back and forth with his index finger. He smiled. "You wouldn't lie to me, would you?"

"Oh, no, sir!" the captain replied in utter terror.

Kao nodded. "Give him the sack, Phan."

Phan handed the captain the canvas sack containing the money, which no one had touched.

"I want a precise accounting of what's in this sack," Kao said to the captain. "An exact one. Down to the very last riel. And then you are to proceed to disburse the men's pay that is in arrears, beginning with the privates. You are personally to render me an account of every riel paid out. If the contents of this sack are not enough, you are also to tell me. And I want the second lieutenant and the ten paratroopers who are with me to receive double pay. An execution."

The jeep took off again, followed by the truck. Kao was humming, casting an amused glance at Suon Phan from time to time. "You thought I was going to keep that money for myself, didn't you?"

"No sir," Phan said.

But that in fact was exactly what he had thought.

Kao shook his head. "In the old days, I would have. But not anymore. I don't give a damn about money now. I'm making war. And I like it a lot."

During the morning following his arrival at Kampot, on April 4, 1970, Kao called all the officers together. He told them what he expected of them: on the one hand, to fight the Viet Cong and pursue them to the border, aided by the South Vietnamese Rangers and in collaboration with them; and on the other hand, to track down, without pity or respite, the band or bands of Khmer Rouge hiding out in the forest, on the slopes of Elephant Mountain, and even in the Kirirom Range on the other side of the American Highway. Among his listeners there was not one who had the smallest doubt as to the real circumstances of the colonel's death. Not a single one of them dared to bring up the subject, however, and not one made the slightest comment about this sudden change in the way they were to occupy their time, which up to then had involved remarkably few duties. If Kao's frightening reputation alone had not sufficed to effect this change, there was also the certainty that he enjoyed the protection of the most influential figures in Phnom Penh.

"I know," Kao said to Phan as they left the meeting with the officers, "apart from two or three who are ready, willing, and able to fight, the rest are simply more afraid of me than of the Khmer Rouge. But do you want the truth, Phan? The truth of the matter is that I don't give a damn. This army is rotten to the core. It's not even an army. It's nothing: pure shit. The French have always said that we Cambodians can be made into first-rate soldiers; a Khmer in uniform is worth five Vietnamese. But only if he wants to fight, only if he knows what he's fighting for. I know why *I'm* fighting: to kill, for the pleasure I get out of making war. Do you understand that, Phan?"

"Yes, sir."

"No, you don't understand. But that doesn't matter. For pleasure, Phan. And those men up there—they, too, know why they're fighting. Maybe I've chosen the wrong side."

He was pointing to Elephant Mountain, where the Khmer Rouge were probably hiding. "Are you an anti-Communist, Phan?"

Phan hesitated, then cursed himself for doing so, glimpsing for a brief moment the possible consequences.

"I'm not one," Kao said. "I couldn't care less. Earlier on, yes, maybe. But not anymore. The only thing I care about now is this."

... The machine gun swaying up and down like a stiff penis ...

"I don't even care about women, Phan. But then I've never been very interested in women." He laughed. "Nor in boys either. You needn't worry on that score."

They had turned into the road to Kep.

"You did tell me, didn't you, that you'd never seen the sea? Well then, have a look at it. Do you know how to swim? We'll have time for that. Luckily, this war is going to be a long one. Lon Nol has agreed: I'm not going to remain here in command of clods from Kampot. Lon Nol has given me what I asked for: the chance to have my own unit, not depending on anybody else, with men that I'll be able to pick myself. And I'll go fight wherever I damn well please. The ten men behind us are the first ones, but there'll be others. Not all that many of them though. A commando unit of a hundred men, no more. You'll come with me; you'll be right at my side wherever I go. Don't argue—that's an order. Why do you think I took you with me last night to kill the colonel? But even so you'd rather leave me? I like you, Phan. I'm going to look after you. A hundred men and no more: We have to be able to move quickly from place to place without attracting attention to ourselves. We're going out to hunt down Khmer Rouge."

When they arrived at the beach at Kep, Kao, just for the fun of it, bashed in with the bumpers of his jeep the wooden shack that the pedal-boat owner had once operated from, and then drove the vehicle all the way down to the water's edge so that the waves lapped over the wheels. The great stretch of white beach dotted with coconut palms was completely deserted, and from a distance even the hotel-bungalow looked abandoned. Fascinated by the sea, Phan took his clothes off, as did the paratroopers, and warily tested the water with one toe. He was excited, almost hypnotized, not only by the vastness of the sea but by its fabulous transparency. The only place he'd ever gone for a dip was in the Mekong, on the outskirts of his native village in the province of Kompong Cham; he had never seen anything but muddy water in which you could no longer see your feet as soon as you had waded to ankle depth. He finally stretched out full length at the water's edge, excited by the slow shifting of the sand beneath his naked belly as the little warm waves washed in and out.

Kao laughed. "The fierce Khmer warrior needs a woman!"

In the days that followed, Kao began to recruit men for his commando unit, carefully selecting them one by one from among the candidates who presented themselves. A week later, having formed a group numbering forty-five men, he launched his first operation. It involved an exhausting four-day march through the forest, a steep and difficult climb that was real torture for Suon Phan, who was completely out of the habit of physical exercise and managed to hold up only because he was young. The operation ended with a brief skirmish, in the course of which nine Khmer Rouge—real ones, because they were all armed—were killed, while Kao lost only two of his men, and with the sacking and burning of reserves of rice and fish in the huts that had served as hideouts for the band of Khmer Rouge.

From that time on, Suon began to get a better idea of what sort of man Kao really was: There was no doubt he was a bloodthirsty madman, capable of the most insane cruelties and the worst butchery, but at the same time he unquestionably had extraordinary physical courage, and when it came to commanding his unit in battle, a remarkable sense of tactics along with a perfect knowledge of the forest. Kao was an instinctive hunter; the barrel of his weapon, whether a machine gun or an assault rifle, was simply an extension of his intelligence and, in fact, of everything experience had taught him in life. He was a born killer and the war had liberated him, refined his skills, so to speak.

Kao and his commando unit operated in the Kampot region during all of April, May, and June of 1970. At the beginning of July, with an enemy body count of three hundred to his credit—unlike the FARK troops, Kao's count included only real Khmer Rouge—Kao decided to shift his area of operations.

He spread the map out in front of Phan.

"Kampot's here. Just to the north of it, Elephant Mountain, which you no doubt are beginning to be acquainted with. Going still farther north: Between the Elephant and the Kirirom Range, where the Cardamomes begin, there's this sort of valley through which the American Highway passes. To the left, the bay of Kompong Som. To the right, some sixty kilometers and more away, the town of Kompong Speu. Kompong Speu's the territory of Prince Chancarangtsaï. Do you know who he is?"

"I know the name."

"He's a prince of the Norodom family, like Sihanouk, whose uncle he is; so his full name is Norodom Chancarangtsaï, and he's a real prince of royal blood. But he and his nephew Sihanouk don't get along and never have, even though Chanca is a friend of the Queen Mother's. Do you know why, Phan? Because in 1941, Prince Norodom Chancarangtsaï would have really liked to become the King of Cambodia, and had as solid a claim to the throne as Sihanouk. But the French preferred young Sihanouk, precisely because he was young and, for that reason they thought, could be more easily manipulated. Chancarangtsaï never forgave his nephew, and since 1949 he's always lived more or less apart from the regime and kept more or less to the forest. During the sort of war against the French, he joined the Issarak resistance, though at the same time remaining his own man. In reality, he's a pirate, the biggest pirate in Cambodia. During these last few years, he's been the one who's protected the gambling parlors and the opium dens in Phnom Penh. Do you know what "protection" means, Phan? The Americans call it racketeering. That's how he's made a tremendous fortune: gambling and opium.

"But make no mistake about it: He's a gangster but he's also, first and foremost, a war leader, a real Warlord, perhaps the last of them all. With his money he's gotten up a personal army that the general staff of FARK call the Thirteenth Brigade, so as to lead people to believe that it takes orders from Phnom Penh and the headquarters of FARK, and so as to persuade themselves that it does. But Chancarangtsaï doesn't take orders from anybody. He's the one who's recruited his men. There are seven or eight thousand of them, very loyal, very devoted, very well trained. He pays his men out of his own pocket and also with the money he managed to squeeze out of the generals of Phnom Penh, and he pays them well. Just as he pays his officers well. They're very good officers, moreover, and some of them have been in the forest for twenty years.

"The Thirteenth Brigade doesn't have any artillery, any air support, and it has practically no trucks, no heavy matériel. Its soldiers are often dressed in black, and they move from place to place very quickly, the way the Khmer Rouge they're fighting do, the way we ourselves are beginning to do and will continue to do. The soldiers of the Thirteenth Brigade are so much like the Khmer Rouge that they fool even the Khmer Rouge—who sometimes approach a detachment of the Thirteenth Brigade in all confidence, thinking they're other Khmer Rouge, and by the time they realize their mistake it's too late and they get their throats cut or get themselves shot and Chanca's detachment eats their livers.

"That's why nobody, neither the Khmer Rouge nor the Viet Cong nor the Rangers nor even the FARK troops, goes to Kompong Speu. Not even me, Phan. The people of Kompong Speu are the happiest people in Cambodia at the moment. They live in complete peace, and Chancarangtsaï, again with his own money or with the subsidies that the ministers in Phnom Penh give him more or less under duress, has wells dug, new irrigation ditches laid down, schools and public clinics built. The Kompong Speu area isn't Sihanouk's country or Lon Nol's; it's the exclusive territory of Chancarangtsaï and his Thirteenth Brigade and almost an independent country."

Kao tapped the map with his fingertips, a dreamy look in his eye. "I can't be another Chancarangtsaï, Phan. I'm not a prince and I'll never have eight thousand men under my command. And what's more, even if I could, maybe I wouldn't want to. For years and years, Phan, I dreamed of being a colonel. And now I don't give a damn about that either. . . ."

He had spread the map out on the hood of the jeep. All around them the commandos had set up a furtive, temporary camp, in the heart of the forest. Most of them were not even wearing uniforms; on the other hand, their arms and matériel were remarkable. Their numbers had steadily increased as the weeks and months passed, and the commando group was now much larger than a regular army unit, a savage horde of thin guerrillas resembling nothing so much as wolves on the prowl. There were now almost a hundred of them.

"We won't even set foot in Prince Norodom Chancarangtsaï's territory, Phan. But we're going to make use of him nonetheless, simply because he exists and because he's located precisely where he is. He's going to protect us on our right and prevent the Viet Cong from getting at us from that direction. To our left we'll still have the sea, which will protect us in the same way. Behind us, to the south, the garrisons of Kampot and of Takeo will more or less guard our rear. So that from now on we're going to be able to hunt in peace on what's going to be our territory and ours alone, where nobody can come check up on us and keep us from hunting.

"Look, Phan, do you see this area that includes the Cheko Peninsula and the offshore islands? That's it. That's our territory. It's an area where there are few villages, and the few there are, are almost all inhabited by Malay fishermen, just enough of them to keep us in food. And in front of us, up here, are the Cardamomes, the biggest Khmer forest of all. That's going to be our hunting preserve."

Kao was beside himself with excitement. "A hundred square kilometers and all mine! Just imagine, Phan!"

The last three months had toughened Suon Phan, both physically and psychologically. He nonetheless felt a shiver of anxiety, strangely mingled with wild enthusiasm, at the spectacle of this exultant savage beast now definitely on the loose, freed of all restraints, killing for the pleasure of killing, dreaming of nothing else, and having finally acquired the means to do so.

11

AFTER LEAVING PHNOM PENH, THOMAS AQUINAS O'MALLEY HAD headed for Manila, where he had a medical checkup that showed him to be in fine shape. He hadn't stayed in the Philippines long, contrary to his usual habits and preferences which ordinarily inclined him to linger for a while in any country he passed through, in order to get to know it better. He could easily have taken the time; they were not exactly waiting eagerly in Washington to heap glory upon him. His request for a transfer had come at precisely the moment when the U.S. Embassy in Cambodia was about to expand fantastically, both in size and in the scope of its activities. The clandestine maneuvers of a Price or others of his ilk in helping to plan and lead the Lon Nol/Sirik Matak coup d'état had already brought an extraordinary increase in staff among the many American missions operating in the country. But very soon, from the first days of April and to a greater degree in the weeks that followed, when the American State Department had been obliged to recognize that the Lon Nol regime would never be able to hold up by itself, when the principle of a more forcible and direct intervention had first been studied, then actually put into practice, the pressing need for a much more massive American presence had become evident.

At that point hordes of military advisers and technicians of every sort and description had been sent to Phnom Penh—not only Americans but also Formosans, Indonesians, Filipinos, and others. In the midst of all this, a cultural attaché, especially one who merely went on performing his usual functions, had rather the air of a ballerina on the roster of a football team. But that didn't matter. What counted was the principle of the thing, and nothing less than a general mobilization was called for.

In Washington they had made it abundantly clear to O'Malley that his asking for another assignment at such a time came close to desertion. And they had been in no hurry to give him another post. As a consequence, he was still in Washington on April 30 when Richard Nixon announced the U.S. military intervention in Cambodia. Enormous special funds had been granted by vote of Congress to cover the expense of the operation, which, according to Nixon, was to be a short-term one.

From his office overlooking the Potomac, the Kennedy Center under construction, and the Watergate complex, O'Malley had witnessed what his superiors called the reinforcement of the embassy in Phnom Penh. Like its counterpart in Saigon, it was necessary to turn it into something quite different from an embassy. The total ineffectiveness of Lon Nol, Sirik Matak, Cheng Heng and company, their incompetence, their inability to create a national consensus which might have rallied the country to resist the Viet Cong and the Khmer Rouge more vigorously, if not actually to expel them from Cambodia or annihilate them, made it necessary for the Americans to take over the army, communications, transport, logistics, aviation, ground operations, and all administrative functions. Not only would the Americans provide funds to shore up a Cambodian budget that was rapidly falling apart, they would even oversee the distribution of the tremendous sums invested by the United States, so as to try to limit the effects of an incredible amount of graft and collusion.

In other words, it was necessary for the U.S. Embassy in Cambodia to take over almost all the functions of the Cambodian government, and to do so as discreetly as possible. All of this in a country that had probably not been heard of by one American in a hundred thousand a short time before, a country whose language no one, or almost no one, was able to speak—there were not all that many Americans available who even knew French—and whose customs were familiar to a tiny handful at most.

In the light of what had been happening for years in Saigon, where America had gone about things in precisely the same fashion, this Cambodian operation already bordered on madness. It became sheer insanity when it was officially announced—and hence a fact impossible to ignore—that the American Senate had appropriated the requisite funds on the express condition that a time limit be placed on the operation, and therefore that it would end when this limit had expired, no matter what happened.

Having entered Cambodia at the end of April, the units that were 100 percent American were to be completely withdrawn from the country by the end of June. In principle, the South Vietnamese troops were to pull out on the same date. On May 21, however, thanks to the support of the CIA, which still had high hopes for the success of the operation, the Vice President of South Vietnam, Nguyen Kao Ky, announced that Saigon Marines and Rangers would continue to fight in Khmer territory as long as necessary. On May 26, the American Senate passed a resolution providing for the cessation of all military intervention on the part of the United States in Cambodia after June 30. On that same day, Nixon obtained for Lon Nol a new official grant of $7.5 million for military aid, a paltry sum in view of the huge funds that had already been granted and would continue to be granted for five more years.

American troops did in fact pull out on June 30. But only the ground troops were withdrawn, and even their departure was compensated for by the spraying of gases throughout the border zones of Southeast Cambodia that would make them uninhabitable for six months. For further security, heavy artillery was installed on the other side of the border, in South Vietnamese territory, with the same stubbornly pursued objective of cordoning off South Vietnam and ensuring it against infiltration from Giap's troops. And in addition, although the U.S. ground forces had in fact been withdrawn, air forces still remained in the country, Phantom jets and their napalm bombs in particular, capable of wiping out a column on the march in a matter of seconds.

All of these measures, along with the continued presence of troops from Saigon, would enable the war to go on.

O'Malley had no idea how long it would go on. That was the only thing he had no knowledge of: exactly when it would end. But he thought he knew, and with the naïveté of those who have always considered politics beneath their notice until the moment it explodes in their faces, he was driven wild to discover that he was apparently the only person around to foresee what was bound to happen sooner or later: A day would come when the tremendous war effort of his country would be brought to a halt, both in Vietnam and in Cambodia. He was certain of this, to the point of desperation. This crushing defeat of the United States, the first in its history, which he foresaw with utter certainty, filled him before the fact with shame, revulsion, and rage.

Even though he could not claim to know Vietnam, he did know Cambodia. Because he had lived in that country in peacetime and had loved it, and also because Lisa was still in Cambodia.

* * *

Just before he went off for vacation leave in Ireland, O'Malley had been told what his new assignment was. As he had expected, given the fact that he was not at all popular with his superiors, it was hardly a choice post. The list of countries to which the U.S. government deemed it necessary to send a new cultural attaché forthwith did not include France, although Belgium, Greece, and Tunisia were mentioned. O'Malley put them down in that order on the list of preferences he was invited to submit. He was then informed, with just a touch of sarcasm, that the post assigned him was Burundi. He was unaware that such a country even existed. By consulting an atlas, he learned that it was a country in central Africa inhabited by Hutus, Tutsis, and Twas, names that didn't mean a thing to him, that about half the population was Catholic, and that in addition to Kirundi and Swahili, French was spoken there. He was to report to his office in Bujumbura—apparently the capital of the country—by September 15 at the latest.

His two weeks in Ireland had cut him off from the world. He hadn't once read a newspaper. A few days before his departure for Africa, he left New York, where he had been visiting his family, and went to Washington for a day, where he dropped in on one of his friends in the State Department.

"What's going on in Cambodia?" O'Malley asked.

"What was the last chapter of the serial you read?" said his friend Slattery.

"As I remember, it was just about when the American cavalry was retreating north of the Rio Grande, leaving the good Indians of Saigon and Phnom Penh and the bad Apaches of Hanoi to fight it out."

Slattery was also of Irish origin. He was fond of Thomas Aquinas, whom he had known since childhood, and he had long hoped that his sister, who was mad about O'Malley's green eyes, would one day succeed in leading Thomas Aquinas to the altar and thus make him his brother-in-law.

"This business in Cambodia upsets you, doesn't it?"

"Yes," O'Malley replied.

"All right. Resumé of the preceding chapters: We've officially withdrawn from Cambodia as of June thirtieth. Nothing much has happened since then. The troops from Saigon and Lon Nol's army, supported by our air power and our artillery, are more or less holding their own. As for the story in detail, it goes more or less like this: Our Secretary of State, Bill Rogers, doesn't see eye to eye with our beloved President. Old Bill thinks that we would have been better off not to stick our noses in what was strictly Cambodia's business. He's not the only one to think so; the Senate does too. Not to mention what goes by the name of public opinion. Public opinion is beginning to be completely fed up. General Lon Nol asked Thailand for military aid and was sent packing; Sihanouk has been condemned to death in absentia by a military tribunal in Phnom Penh; his wife, Princess

Monique—she has Italian blood in her veins; did you know that?—was sentenced to hard labor for life, also in absentia since she's in Peking with her
man. Spiro Agnew, that impossible man who, I was informed by someone in
all seriousness, is our Vice President, has come out in favor of a defense of
the Lon Nol regime to the death of our very last man in Cambodia.

"And now for a few brief news flashes: Nearly thirty foreign journalists
have been killed in the line of duty in Cambodia; Georges Pompidou, the
President of France, who's almost as much of a pain in the ass as De Gaulle
was, is advising us to clear out of Indochina immediately; Melvin Laird, our
Secretary of Defense, has confidentially informed a hundred and fifty
American women, swearing them to secrecy, that the number of sorties by
the American air forces in Cambodia has doubled since August first; our
bombers are having great fun spraying napalm and are flying in formation
with Lon Nol's Cambodian MIGs."

"And on the ground?"

"A military secret."

"Damn," said O'Malley.

"Is there any place in particular that interests you?"

"Phnom Penh itself and the part of Cambodian territory that extends
from Phnom Penh to the Gulf of Siam, along what's known there as the
American Highway."

"I've got good news for you," Slattery answered. "Along with the road
to Saigon and the provinces in the Southeast, plus a few towns here and
there and a small area in the province of Battambang along the Thai border,
that's the only part of Cambodia still in Lon Nol's hands. According to a
declaration by Sihanouk dated August twenty-fifth, all the rest of the country is under the control of the provisional government that he's president of.
The thing that's most annoying is that that's very nearly true."

Slattery looked at Thomas Aquinas gravely. "Is it Cambodia itself that
interests you, or is there someone in particular?"

Thomas Aquinas hesitated before answering. "Both."

"Cambodians?"

"No. That is to say . . ."

"A man or a woman? I remind you that you're supposed to marry my
sister. She's been waiting for you at the door of Saint Patrick's Cathedral
clutching her little wedding bouquet in her hand for three years now."

Again Thomas Aquinas hesitated. Lisa. And Lara. And Roger Bouès
smiling at him over the bowl of Chinese soup at the Old Market. And the
frail and fragile silhouettes of Charles and Madeleine Korver, walking hand
in hand in the sunlight beneath the coral trees lining the Boulevard Norodom. All of a sudden he felt a lump in his throat.

"Men and women," he answered.

"If they live in Phnom Penh, there's nothing to worry about. Even though in certain places the Viet Cong and their little pals the Khmer Rouge have advanced to within ten or twenty kilometers of the city, I've heard. And if your friends want to go take a dip in the Gulf of Siam, they can doubtless still do so. Put yourself in Lon Nol's shoes. He has to deal with the problem of a city that had a population of six or seven hundred thousand a few months ago, but these days countless refugees keep pouring in. The nearby rural areas, most of which have been laid waste or have definitely fallen into Communist hands, can no longer provide adequate food supplies for the capital. Lon Nol, and consequently we ourselves, thus have no choice: Phnom Penh's two umbilical cords, the roads leading to Saigon and to the port of Kompong Som, must be kept functioning at all costs. What you call the American Highway has been cut off, not once but twice, for several days at the end of August, but traffic is now flowing again, as the cops say. According to the latest reports, things are more or less all right for the moment."

"Thanks," Thomas Aquinas said. He got to his feet.

"Shall we have lunch together?" Slattery asked.

"I'm on my way back to New York and still have to pack my bags. Give Bea a big hug for me, and tell her not to wait for me at the church door. Besides, I'm a Buddhist now."

"It would appear that you've been posted to Burundi."

"Um-hm."

Without further comment, Slattery offered O'Malley a cigarette, which he refused. Slattery got to his feet too.

"Come on, Tom. Don't let it worry you too much. If things were really going badly in Phnom Penh, we could always evacuate the Westerners. That sort of operation is beginning to be routine. It's all we've been doing lately."

He took a bottle of whiskey out of a desk drawer and the two of them, standing up and exchanging curiously embarrassed glances, had the traditional farewell drink together, in the no less traditional paper cups. And merely because they felt ill at ease, they thought they were obliged to spend a few moments talking of their childhood, of friends they'd lost track of, of women long forgotten, of Ireland, and of the streets of Brooklyn. And Slattery could see that Thomas Aquinas' eyes kept coming back to the map of Cambodia on the wall, to the point that Slattery too, by contagion, felt himself falling into a melancholy mood.

"Well, that's life," he said, accompanying Thomas Aquinas to the elevator.

"I doubt it," O'Malley replied.

12

THEY HAD SETTLED IN ON THE ISLAND ON MAY 17, EXACTLY TWO months to the day after Mathias' birth, as it happened. The fact that the baby was still so little had worried Lisa at first, and Lara himself had hesitated. Finally, on the day before they left Phnom Penh, they went to see one of the two French doctors who had looked after Lisa all during her pregnancy. The doctor laughed scornfully.

"You're American, aren't you?" he said to Lisa.

"I'm not quite sure anymore."

"Oh, she's American all right!" Lara commented, with just a touch of sarcasm in his voice. "She's hung the star-spangled banner over the head of our bed."

"What state in America are you from?"

"Colorado."

"That's in the West, isn't it? Indians, hardy pioneer stock, and all the rest. What did your grandmothers and great-grandmothers do when they were going to have a baby? Did they go back to Scotland every time? That creature you've brought into the world is doing marvelously well. He's a strapping young lad. At worst, he might get diarrhea or some other trifling thing of that sort. I'll give you the medicine you'd need in such a case. Moreover, you've got a Chinese amah. She probably knows more than I do about bringing up a child in countries such as this one. Besides, where is it you're going exactly?"

"We have a house at the seashore, near Kompong Som," Lara answered, deliberately vague.

"There's a public clinic in Kompong Som with a Cambodian colleague of mine, a midwife, and two male or female nurses—I don't remember exactly which. What more do you need? A complete hospital with Dr. Christiaan Barnard ready to operate before all the television cameras in the world? Clear out of here, you two, and take your kid with you. You're wasting my time."

They left the following morning, after a dinner at the Korvers'. Roger Bouès was also present at the dinner, in a gay, scintillating mood, just back from a trip to Hong Kong, a city he'd never been to before for lack of money. He was almost too gay and scintillating, and not quite able to conceal a nervousness bordering on feverishness, a mood none of them had previously seen him in.

The Laras took Seng, the kitchen boy, and the Chinese amah with them. Kutchaï was waiting for them aboard the sampan anchored to the little cove on the Cheko Peninsula, but despite Lara's insistence, he smilingly refused to come along with them. As arranged previously, he was to take the 504 back to Kompong Som, where he would turn it over to the guards in the harbormaster's office at the port, which was just a little over an hour away from Sré by boat.

"But I'll come to see you," Kutchaï said to Lisa. "That's a promise. I'll swim over if I have to."

It was Lisa who had wanted them to address each other in the familiar *tu* form when they spoke French together—as they usually did, since Kutchaï's English was rather rudimentary.

"Watch out for sharks if you do," Lisa said.

"It's sharks that are afraid of Kutchaï, not the other way around," Lara said. "Have you had a good look at the teeth on him? Every time Kutchaï goes swimming, the Shark Union lodges an official complaint."

It had been many months since Lisa had been to Sré. She had naturally taken part in the discussions concerning the improvements to be made on the island, but she hadn't seen the results of the decisions they had arrived at together. When, after a crossing that had taken forty minutes or so, the sampan-junk slipped gently into calm waters and Sré filled the entire horizon, she thought at first glance that nothing had been changed. The house was invisible, and no one would even have suspected there was one on the island. More than ever before, Sré appeared uninhabited, as wild as on the first day of Creation. It seemed to her that the vegetation had grown taller and denser.

"Are you certain we're not heading for the wrong island?"

Lara merely laughed in reply.

She had stretched out on the deck at her husband's feet as he sat at the tiller, the back of his neck resting on the gunwale of dark wood that smelled of spice and salt. All she had on since coming aboard was a thin sarong, underneath which she was naked. Lara placed his bare foot on her knee and slid it underneath the fabric; it mounted slowly along her thigh as though it were a hand.

"You're shameless!" Lisa said.

The foot crept farther up, inch by inch.

"There's Seng and the amah," she said. "And Mathias. And the sharks."

But an overwhelming flood of happiness came over her, setting her to trembling. She took Lara's ankle and guided it till the warm sole of his foot was resting square on top of the slit just below her belly.

"Let's not drop anchor right away. Nothing's hurrying us—we don't have any reason to hurry from now on."

"Aye aye, sir," Lara answered in English.

From time to time large, gleaming white birds with black webbed feet and wing tips that seemed to be tinged with gold flew by in the ultramarine sky. Lisa took them to be seagulls.

"No," Lara said, "they're *fous de Bassan*, or a closely related species. It seems to me they're called booby gannets in English."

Fous de Bassan . . . booby gannets . . . the name delighted Lisa. The big birds flew past in flocks numbering dozens, hundreds even, and at times several of these bands gathered in an immense, squawking airborne army. But most often, as they were doing now above the junk slowly making its way around the island, they soared in absolute silence, their wings spread wide some hundred feet above the water, and then suddenly swooped down in wild, dizzying dives. They disappeared below the surface of the water then, and leaning over the top rail, Lisa spied several of them plunge down a good two fathoms or more, straight to the fabulous coral bottom, scattering a multicolored school of fish before them and returning to the surface with dolphinlike undulations, their bloody prey clutched in their beaks.

"They come from Europe," Lara said, "and the world belongs to them."

Lisa assumed her original position. She closed her eyes. Silence.

"Do you know what I'd like to do? Really like to do?" she whispered.

"I haven't the faintest idea," Lara answered mockingly.

"You louse."

The narrow inlet that Kutchaï had made into a little anchorage was on the far shore of the island, the one opposite Thailand and Malaysia. The sampan-junk slid into it, fitting exactly, like a sword in a scabbard.

"How long will we be staying here?"

"As long as we want to. A hundred years."

"A hundred and fifty. We'll watch the booby gannets. I could watch them for centuries. Do they really come from Europe?"

"Yes, really."

Seng came out of the cabin, yawning, and prepared to lower the sail, furl it, and lay the mast along the deck.

"Let's leave everything," Lisa said. "All the rest. Absolutely everything."

Lara took her hand and kissed the palm of it. He also kissed the tip of her shoulder blade and gently stroked her cheek, then went to help Seng.

What was surprising, and to Lisa admirable, about all the things that had been done on the island was that nothing showed. Kutchaï had instructed the workmen to dig a food storage cellar and line its walls with cement, and then to put the earth they had removed back on top of the stone slab covering it, so that the hibiscus and wild orchids and bougainvillea had grown over it, covering everything except a nearly invisible wooden trapdoor. The Jaraï had likewise placed the generator underground, a hundred yards away, cleverly using a heap of rocks the same color as the stones of Angkor to conceal it from sight, and had buried the electric lines belowground.

"And what about the television station?" Lisa asked. "I haven't spied it yet. Where have you hidden it?"

"It's in the planning stage. Have you seen what's inside the cellar?"

"Enough to feed twenty babies and their family. Kutchaï's the man I should have married."

During the next five weeks they did not leave the island, not even for a boat ride. The presence of Seng and the amah did not disturb them, since the two Asians never went more than a few steps away from the house and, without having had to be asked, carefully avoided that part of Sré that Lara and Lisa had made their private preserve. And so the two of them lived from day to day exactly as they had dreamed of doing, alone and naked, spending hour after hour alone with each other or with Mathias, whose amah reported that he already knew Chinese.

Early in June, around the eighth or ninth, Kutchaï kept his promise and came to see them. Curiously enough, he chose to cross over to the island from the continent after night had fallen. They didn't hear a sound as the Malays' pirogue approached, and it was only when the Jaraï gave a shout from the beach that they discovered he had arrived.

Lisa greeted him with a hug and a kiss, something she'd never done before. "We missed you."

"Me pool wletched Khmel velly glad to see you. How's the Ninth Generation?"

"He's learning Chinese. With a billion possible people to talk to, he ought to have some very interesting conversations later on."

Charles and Madeleine were getting along nicely, Kutchaï reported. "They send you their love, and everything that goes with it. The *ti-nam* and her husband have left them and gone off to Saigon, but I've found Charles and Madeleine somebody to help out and they're very happy with him. They've decided to learn Cambodian and are spending four hours a day at it. Every time I drop in on them they drive me crazy with their questions about all the different possible pronunciations of the same word. I'd never realized that Cambodian was that difficult. I wonder how I ever managed to learn it."

"*Kniom sraleïn neak,*"* Lisa said.

Kutchaï raised his eyebrows in mock surprise. "It would appear to be some sort of contagious disease."

"She wants to marry you," Lara said.

"It must be because I look so Scandinavian. No woman can resist me."

"I've told her you already have twelve or fifteen wives and that you beat all of them, but it didn't discourage her in the least."

* Literally, "me love you."

"After you, any man would seem divine to this little lady."

"I suppose the two of you know what the little lady has to say to that?"

The three of them looked at each other without a word, smiling, pleased and happy to be together again.

"I trust you're not thinking of going back tonight?" Lara said at last.

Kutchaï began to laugh, as he always did when embarrassment or an even more overpowering emotion, such as anger, kept him from answering.

"It's completely out of the question," Lisa said forcefully. "And I'm not joking."

Kutchaï was still laughing, baring his impressive jawful of carnivore's teeth. He finally threw up his hands. "All right then, I'll stay."

Lara went off to tell the Malay fishermen.

"Thank you," Lisa said to Kutchaï. "Thank you for everything."

"Are you pleased with what's been done here?"

"More than that. A thousand times more."

She smiled at him with that mingled feeling of almost fraternal friendship and slightly intimidated shyness that he had always inspired in her, and then she asked abruptly, "Are bad things happening?"

He looked her straight in the eye. "Nothing's happening. The American troops will be leaving at the end of this month but that shouldn't change the situation much."

"Lots of dead?"

Kutchaï shrugged. Lisa glanced in the direction of the beach, where Lara had gone. "There's something I'd like to know, and I'd like a frank answer," she said. "He doesn't want to leave this country and I'll fight against asking him to with all the strength I have. But . . ." She paused, searching for words. "But what are his chances? What are our chances?"

She felt him hesitate and was suddenly overcome with emotion, as though her entire life depended on Kutchaï's answer.

"A Cambodia without Lara would no longer be my Cambodia," he finally said. "I just can't imagine such a thing. Not Lara. Anybody else, but not him. All the others, except him. If there had to be one last White in this country, it should be him. And his family."

13

KUTCHAÏ SPENT A WEEK WITH THEM, AND WITHOUT THE LEAST difficulty they shared once again that atmosphere of camaraderie, even of complicity, that they had already shared during evenings together in the villa on the Rue Phsar Dek in Phnom Penh, when they were all planning together the craziest, most far-fetched projects for improving the accommodations on the island. Those had been joyous, carefree days. To her vast surprise, Lisa discovered the Kutchaï had never really learned to swim, and at best could only paddle around in the water, that he was terrified of the sea and was even more afraid of sharks than she was. And when he mistook a drifting tree branch for a shark, and clung pitiably to a rock sticking out of the water, Lisa had never seen Lara laugh so heartily and unrestrainedly as he did at the expression on Kutchaï's face. The great tall Jaraï, perched on a rock the size of a kilometer-marker, looked like nothing so much as an old lady who'd climbed up onto a kitchen stool to escape a mouse. He would no doubt have remained cool and collected in the face of a dozen tigers or an equal number of cobras, but the mere sight of a moonfish scared him to death. And the extraordinary clearness of the water, which revealed to him whole schools of wriggling sea-creatures, didn't help matters in the least. Nor did Lara's peals of uncontrollable laughter, to which Lisa couldn't keep herself from adding her own.

"I'm a man of the forest," Kutchaï said gloomily. "I can't help it."

He stubbornly, almost violently, refused even to eat slices of grilled tuna, tuna that the Malays brought them regularly along with other fish they had caught. Kutchaï said it had an unpleasant taste and insisted that he preferred the mud-flavored fish of the Tonle Sap.

As for what was happening on the mainland, the war that was going on so near and yet so far away, Kutchaï spoke very little about it, but when he did he expressed himself frankly, and in French only, so that Lisa could follow his explanations. She had already noted that the two men no longer exchanged one word in Khmer when she was with them. This had been true since the day Lara had come back from the plantation after setting the house on fire. It was plain to see that since then, Lara had decided to lay his cards on the table; and though he never mentioned, any more than he had earlier on, what he had done in the past (for example, buying and delivering arms to Ieng Samboth), at least he no longer hid from her what he was doing at present. He had given up that irritating attitude that in the beginning had made him regard Lisa as a total stranger to the country, to its secrets and its labyrinthine intrigues, while treating her like an objet d'art so fragile that it was necessary to shelter her from the least little breeze.

She did not understand all Kutchaï's explanations. He mentioned the names of tiny villages that had become combat theaters, and men she knew nothing about, including which camp they belonged to. She gathered that the situation was extremely confused, in no way like a conventional war with a front, advance positions, an area behind the lines, a no-man's-land. At one moment Kutchaï described a hamlet in ruins, battered by shells and bombs, taken and retaken, but then the next minute he spoke of whole vast areas where calm reigned, where the peasants were working as always in their rice paddies or on the kapok or sugar-palm plantations.

"You must have seen planes," Kutchaï said. "American ones, naturally. They're the only ones in the sky."

Lara and Lisa had seen some, but only twice, and flying at such a high altitude that it had been impossible for them to make out their fuselage markings. More often, they had caught sight of freighters entering the Kompong Som harbor channel or leaving it. But they had not noticed any particular increase in maritime traffic since they had been on the island. Furthermore, the ships passed by far out to sea, usually at a distance of at least ten kilometers, and when they might have become identifiable as they came into Kompong Som, they disappeared behind Rong Island at the entrance to the bay.

"In any event, as far as the movement of supplies between Kompong Som and Phnom Penh is concerned, as usual it's the Chinese who are handling it. They furnish arms and rice and medical supplies to both camps; they have pull with bigwigs on both sides, confederates everywhere. If you want to go to Phnom Penh, Liu can be of far more help in getting you there than Sihanouk, Lon Nol, and Nixon put together. By the way, I have a message for you from your uncle, Lara: Liu has a confidential agent in Kompong Son, a certain Weï Ching Hi. If there's anything at all you need, go see Weï. The harbormaster will tell you where to find him."

Kutchaï left them around June 15, promising to come back the following month. Or before, depending on his movements. He did not say what these movements were—not in front of Lisa at least—nor what the purpose of them was. She didn't question him but she could not help wondering, and discovered in the process that she didn't even know where the sympathies of the giant Jaraï really lay in this conflict that had set Khmer against Khmer.

Finding themselves alone again—the amah and Seng were simply silent presences hovering in the background—made Lisa suddenly aware of a slight sense of loneliness and frustration, a feeling she had not had before and which lasted for several days. For the first time she realized fully what an extraordinary situation they were in, staying on an island just a few kilometers from a country at war. Lara must have sensed what sort of mood she was in, and suggested they go over to Kompong Som.

"In the sampan? By sea?"

"Unless you'd rather water-ski over there."

"And what about Mathias?"

"We could leave at dawn and come back the same night. It'd be best to leave him here."

She finally let Lara talk her into leaving her son in the amah's hands. The rainy season was just beginning, and it had already rained twice, although in theory at least the torrential downpours would not begin until later, in September and especially in October. The year before, when she'd

been in Phnom Penh with a great bulging shape that hadn't lent itself to
gallivanting about, she had not really been able to discover the marvels of a
tropical rain falling at last after months and months of drought. Except in a
few rare instances, she had never considered rain as anything but an annoying meterological phenomenon, forcing one to carry a ridiculous umbrella
or to wear a raincoat, and at best something of benefit to farmers. This year,
on Sré, she enjoyed it to the utmost, stretching out naked in pelting showers,
ecstatically opening every pore of her skin.

Rain at sea was another discovery. They left on one of the first days in
July, before first light, preferring like Kutchaï to stay out of sight of boats
passing by Sré in broad daylight and thus avoid the risk of betraying their
presence on the island. But just as dawn broke, the rain came in great silvery squalls blowing in off the sea. Beneath the storm clouds the sea became
dark violet, and less clear than usual. Despite its having only one sail, the
junk raced along in a furrow of white foam, pitching and rolling until the
moment it slipped beneath the shelter of Kas Rong.

Lara dropped anchor. "There's no use hurrying. It's too early still."

Lisa's wristwatch hadn't worked since the day she'd forgotten to remove it before taking her first swim, and Lara had left his waterproof chronometer behind on Sré. But they decided between the two of them that it
must be around six A.M.

The rain died down and then stopped altogether, and a timid sun finally pierced the clouds.

"Whose side is Kutchaï on?" Lisa asked out of the blue. "Politically, I
mean."

Lara's pale gray-blue eyes stared at her in surprise. "I'd say he's biding
his time."

"That doesn't keep him from traveling from one end of Cambodia to
the other while a war is going on, if I understand things rightly."

Lara gestured vaguely. He had stretched out on the deck and was licking the last drops of rain off his forearms.

Lisa pressed the point: "Let's suppose that there had never been a Lara
in Cambodia, or that Kutchaï had never met you. Would he be a Khmer
Rouge in that case?"

Lara yawned. "I know somebody who's going to be swimming home.
Somebody who has violet eyes, very beautiful breasts and round hips, and
speaks French with a funny accent."

She refused to be put off by his bantering. "I'm asking you an important question."

"In that case, it's one you'll have to ask Kutchaï."

A freighter appeared, coming from the port and flying the Japanese
flag; it passed within a few hundred yards of the junk. Up to that point,
Lisa had been lying on her back on the fragrant wood of the deck. She

now raised up on one elbow and then squatted on her heels, naked and deeply tan.

"Are you angry?" she asked.

"No."

"Yes, you are," she contradicted him curtly, almost aggressively.

He smiled, a far-off look in his pale eyes, his reserve of earlier days returning all of a sudden, withdrawing into himself and presenting to the outside world that courteous, mild-mannered façade that could be so exasperating.

"You should get dressed," he said calmly. "You're going to cause riots in Kompong Som. Those Japanese sailors with their binoculars got a real eyeful just now."

She was wearing only a necklace of fine-woven gold strands that came down between her breasts. Her pregnancy had left no trace on her body except for two or three almost invisible white stretch marks in the even, golden tan of her skin. In this blue and deep-purple light of dawn, still shimmering from the rain, her eyes seemed even more violet than usual, and she was breathtakingly beautiful.

"What did she look like? Your first wife, I mean."

"I really don't think there's any point to this sort of conversation."

"Why not? I can tell you about Bob, if you like."

"I'd rather you didn't."

He got to his feet and began to get dressed. Lisa didn't move. Still sitting on her heels, she stroked her naked body with the palms of her hands, brushing off the last drops of rain.

"Let's not talk about it," she said. "Let's not talk about anything. Let's never talk about anything. Let's pretend to know nothing of what's happened, what's happening, what's going to happen. Let's be blind. Is that what you want?"

Suddenly she saw herself from outside, naked on this junk, within sight of a tiny country in Asia where men were slitting each other's throats. A wildling. She felt almost cold, an odd sensation after a year.

"And I have a husband who has a Chinese uncle," she said.

She shook her head, and all at once, for no reason that she could explain, she burst into tears.

Weï was short and plump, so short that he was obliged to tip his head way back to see Lara's face and Lisa's as they stood before him. He had received the couple with all the marks of the profoundest respect.

"Monsieur Liu told me that you might honor me by paying me a visit."

"We merely want to find out whether it's possible to get through to Phnom Penh by road."

"In the near future?"

"In general."

"The road isn't very safe. At times it's very dangerous and even"—he searched for the right word—"unusable. At other times one can get through all right. The orders that Monsieur Liu has given me are very definite: If you wish to go to Phnom Penh, I am to do everything I can to help you. And I will help you. And you'll get through. At any time and in complete safety."

The battery of the Peugeot 504 was plugged into a recharger, but otherwise the car was in running order. Once the battery had been put back, the car started with no difficulty. Lara got behind the wheel and headed for Réam, fifteen kilometers or so away. The little restaurant run by a Corsican was still in business. They ate the inevitable roe deer, preceded by crab flamed in cognac, and drank a bottle of the Bordeaux that the Corsican bought directly from the freighters calling at Kompong Som. Lisa didn't say a word during the entire meal. Though she was trying her best, she still hadn't gotten over the fit of depression that had come over her on the junk.

"Do you want us to go back to Phnom Penh?"

She hesitated a moment, then shook her head. "That wouldn't change anything. No, I'd rather stay on at Sré."

She was sincere. At the time, because of what she had gathered from Kutchaï's explanation, she envisioned Phnom Penh as a city under siege. And later on, remembering this lunch at Réam, she was to discover that her idea of what things were like in the Khmer capital had not been all that mistaken, and indeed, in the course of the next five years, it was gradually to become even closer to fact.

"Tell me a little about Monsieur Liu. He strikes me as being a very important man."

"He is." Lara explained why. The Chinese in Cambodia, at least those who were at the very top of the social hierarchy, in fact held three quarters of the capital in Cambodia.

"You heard what Kutchaï said, just as I did. Two months ago, Lon Nol and Sirik Matak decided to attack the Chinese community, for the same reasons that had impelled them to attack the Vietnamese. But Peking immediately stepped in and threatened to withdraw all Chinese capital from Cambodia—that is to say, to wreck the entire economy of the country in forty-eight hours. And while Liu may not be the richest Chinese in Cambodia—though that remains a debatable statement—he's beyond all question one of the most influential."

"I don't understand. From Mao's point of view, Liu is a capitalist."

Lara burst out laughing. "But Mao, like Liu, is Chinese. Why do you think Hong Kong continues to be a British colony? Hong Kong is a *comptoir*, a trading post that enables China to buy and sell; whether this *comptoir* is predominantly yellow or white matters little, since in point of fact it belongs to men such as Liu. And that's not just a figure of speech: Two of Liu's brothers are in Hong Kong, and own, among other things, a fair number of the freighters you've seen going past Sré. Another thing: Liu has another brother in Manila, plus an uncle in Taipeh, and cousins, nephews, other uncles in Djakarta, Rangoon, Bangkok, and Singapore. In San Francisco, I met one of his sons, who's an American citizen thanks to his marriage to a Chinese-American girl from California. I've been to New Caledonia, the New Hebrides, and Tahiti, where I met family connections of Liu's. And likewise in South Korea, Japan, Hawaii. Liu even has a Nobel laureate in his family: the Nobel prize in physics in 1957. No, I'm not joking. But I've gotten a smile out of you nonetheless. Lisa, I love you and there are six hundred thousand Chinese in Cambodia."

"And you're a member of the clan."

"Not at all. But Liu and I have always gotten along very well together."

"Because you were once married to his niece. And then after that you married *me*. But I don't have nearly as much to offer you. Nothing but a brother who's a deserter and an elderly grandfather who grows flowers in his greenhouses in the wilds of Colorado."

"I find you physically far more attractive than Monsieur Liu," Lara answered.

He smiled, trying to make peace with her. She felt weary, sad, lost; she felt like a complete outsider, knowing nothing of this war, of this country, of Monsieur Liu, and even almost nothing of this man who was her husband. She looked at Lara and felt like bursting into tears once again.

"I'd like another cognac. A big glass of it this time."

She downed it in one swallow. The cognac was warm and burned her throat.

"I was forgetting something," she said. "I too have an uncle and an aunt by marriage. They live in Texas. But as far as I know, they don't own a single freighter. They didn't own one the last time I saw them, though it's quite possible they've bought one since. But that would surprise me. The last time I saw them, they were saving up for a trip to Italy. I've searched my mind, but those are the only people I come up with. Except for a girl friend from college days who's married to a not very important industrialist and is now living in North Dakota, or else in Montana. I can check which, if it interests you. And I don't think she can be of the slightest help in getting us from Kompong Som to Phnom Penh or vice versa. I'm afraid she doesn't even know where Kompong Som is. On the other hand, she has three children who can go outside on the streets, play in the garden with their friends, and eat ice-cream cones like everybody else."

"Calm down," Lara said.

"I don't feel like it."

"All right then, don't calm down."

"You're calm enough for both of us. There's no doubt of that!"

She reached over and grabbed her husband's full glass, which he hadn't yet touched, and downed her third cognac in one swallow. She rose to her feet. "Let's get out of here."

He paid the check and found her sitting in the car outside. She was gazing at the open forest to the right of the road and, a little farther off, the dark-green fleece of the Elephant Range.

"Look," she said to him. "It's swarming with Khmer Rouge. I can see their big eyes gleaming as they watch us. But naturally they won't do anything to us, right? They've surely recognized you. They're shaking their heads and saying to each other, 'But that's good old Lara and his nice little wife. Obviously we can't shoot down good old Lara and his nice little wife. In the first place, Lara is immortal—everybody in Cambodia knows that. And Lara's our friend. Lara is everybody's friend.' "

He slowed down and stopped the car.

"Lisa . . ."

She opened the door of the car, got out, and walked off a few yards.

"Lisa."

Apart from the car door slamming, not a sound had reached her ears, but Lara was now directly behind her.

"Don't touch me."

One or two minutes went by, amid an overwhelming silence. The morning light was slowly fading in the sky and great swollen gray and dark-purple clouds were drifting slowly down, hovering above the Elephant Range and enveloping the distant peaks of the Cardamomes, some four to five thousand feet high, gradually hiding them from sight. A strong odor of rain-soaked earth mounted in successive waves, spreading out in an almost palpable sheet. Lisa finally turned around, and after a few seconds pulled her eyes away from Lara's, refusing to see in them the great, touching tenderness he felt for her.

"Let's go back," she said. "I want to see my son."

After that, they spent another month on Sré in a strange atmosphere. Lara tried several times to talk things over with Lisa, but each time she refused, out of a stubbornness she herself thought stupid, or in any case pointless, though she nonetheless continued to give not an inch. She had no illusions as to the depth of the abyss that separated them. She had always known Lara would refuse to leave Cambodia, that he was unable even to conceive of such a thing. When she had married him, she had solemnly promised herself never to ask him to do so. She was still determined to keep this promise he had never sought from her. She had said as much to Kutchaï, and in so saying, she had been absolutely sincere.

She even reached the point of questioning her unconditional love for Lara, which she continued to feel with an intensity that frightened her at times. It was unquestionably a sexual love, so much so that she felt almost ashamed of it. In Lara's thin, nervous body, in his grave, slow voice, his often thoughtful gaze, the very smell of his skin, in his extraordinary way of moving about without appearing to budge an inch, in his way of making his presence felt without a word, there was something that touched her and melted her heart. On their return from Kompong Som and Réam, she had tried for ten days to refuse to make love to him, even though she knew what a feeble weapon this was, avoiding the smallest physical contact, knowing she would not have been able to resist him. He had not said or done a thing, remaining his usual charmingly polite and gentle self, waiting for her to get over the mood she was in. In the end she had given in, too honest with herself to believe her surrender was due to any sort of pity for him, or to her desire not to hurt him anymore. She gave in to him as one gives into hunger or thirst.

But the love she felt for him was not merely physical: Tenderness, affection, friendship played an equal role in it. It was quite likely that she loved Lara's weak points even more than his strong ones.

Kutchaï came back twice more, on July 10 first and then two weeks later, arriving and leaving at night each time. His comments on the war situation indicated, surprisingly, that it had changed very little. Phnom Penh and the Korvers apparently continued to live almost normally, though the capital was completely encircled and all communications cut off except those with Saigon, by road and by river, and, periodically, with Kompong Som. But as for the remainder of the country, though a city such as Kratie had long since fallen and even taken on the status of Khmer Rouge capital, Siem Reap, Kompong Thom, and in particular Battambang, not far from the Thai frontier, were still holding out, definitely secured by Lon Nol's forces, thanks to massive support from the U.S. Air Force, whose B-52 bombers and Phantom jets filled the sky.

Just three days after Kutchaï's last departure, at the very end of July, another visitor arrived as dawn was breaking.

Dominique Christiani had made the crossing on a very large cabin cruiser crewed by a half-dozen impassive Malays. As usual, the Corsican was in high spirits and full of energy. He seemed to regard the war in Cambodia and Vietnam as merely a slightly unpleasant turn of events. He was wildly enthusiastic about the conversions and improvements they had made on the island.

"It's paradise on earth!" he exclaimed.

He spent the entire day on Sré, anchoring his cruiser all the way inside one of the largest coves to the west of the island, completely out of sight of prying eyes on the mainland. His men unloaded a large crate which proved to be full of toys for Mathias. There was even an electric train, and Lisa couldn't help laughing.

"But he's only a four-and-a-half-month-old baby!"

"Don't worry, my dear little lady, he'll get over it. Everyone always gets over that sort of thing."

He explained that the boat had to get under way again that very night, but that he'd be back in two days. He had errands to do, he said. He was about to add something, but a look from Lara stopped him.

Lara then turned to Lisa and said, "I didn't say anything to you about it earlier because I didn't know when Kutchaï would be able to get together with Dominique. How do you think our friend here found us? And besides"—he smiled—"I didn't know if you'd like the idea or not. But I thought we might take advantage of Dominique's stopping by with his cruiser to go back with him and spend a little time in Bangkok. I'm very nearly out of razor blades. We'd take Mathias and the amah with us, of course. As for Seng, he'd rather stay here. In any event, if he wants to go over to the mainland while we're gone, he can always call on his Malay friends."

Lisa stared at her husband in open-mouthed amazement. Lara burst out laughing. He spread his hands, palms up. "I have to check things out to make sure this Corsican isn't cheating me. We're fifty-fifty partners, after all."

Christiani laughed.

14

IT WAS CHRISTIANI WHO FOUND THEM A VILLA IN BANGKOK, ON the west side of the Bang Rak district, on the edge of a large park with a little river running through it that recalled the Serpentine in Hyde Park in London, and not far from the University of Chulalongkorn and the Olympic stadium. Built just two years before, the villa had two floors and three superbly equipped bathrooms. It was doubtless these latter that most impressed Lisa on her arrival in the Thai capital.

But her biggest surprise came when she looked at herself in the enormous mirror in their bedroom. On Sré, one of the rare things that both Kutchaï and Lara, being men, had forgotten to bring to the island was a full-length mirror. She had been using a little pocket one and the last good look she had had at herself had been several months back, in Phnom Penh. She had not been particularly overjoyed then at the sight of a rather plump young woman with a prominent belly, the bosom of a wet nurse, and a complexion the color of a very ripe peach. She now found herself looking at a Lisa she had never seen before: so slender she was almost thin, though not quite, for her nicely rounded curves were still there, and her body in general firmly muscled and, above all, deeply tanned to a tawny bronze color that delighted her, a perfectly even tan from head to foot. Thanks to an ingenious, even acrobatic, juggling of mirrors, she managed to examine herself from the back as well. It was even worse, or rather, even better: not the slightest lighter patch left by a swimsuit, and for good reason.

"Tarzan love Jane?" she asked in a deep booming voice.

"Hubba hubba," Lara replied.

Lying on the bed, his hands crossed behind the nape of his neck, he was plainly enjoying the spectacle. "No doubt about it," he said. "It's really you. You're Lisa."

"And you love me when I look like this?"

"I guess so," he said with mock indifference. "Habit. On a desert island, you have to make do with what's at hand."

She leapt on top of him.

Most of the couple's personal belongings had been left behind in Phnom Penh, and her maternity dresses obviously wouldn't do now. Lisa made the rounds of every single shop in Bangkok, indulging in a buying orgy with a pleasure she had never known before, even in New York, even in Paris a few years earlier. Lara nonchalantly tagged along after her, with laughter in his eyes, and paid. Eventually a shadow of a doubt crossed her mind.

"Am I spending too much money?"

"We've saved lots of money recently."

She suddenly realized she'd never wondered how much money they had. "Are you . . . are we rich?"

He burst out laughing. "Neither rich nor poor. If you don't buy this many dresses every month, we'll very likely continue to have enough to eat."

From the moment Christiani's boat had begun cruising up the Chao Phraya to Bangkok, Lara had changed completely. It seemed to Lisa that he was again exactly as he had been in the months before Mathias was born: calm, certainly, but at the same time playful and full of life. He was not a man given to sudden outbursts, be they fits of anger or flights of fancy, and he kept his violent emotions entirely to himself—she simply could not imagine him singing his head off in the shower or cavorting madly about or screaming with rage—but at the same time he could be merry and gay and very funny, and he was now.

As for Lisa, she was happy as a lark. She adored the villa they had rented; she adored the incredibly tiny Thai servants with their gracious dancers' gestures who gave the amah a helping hand; she adored Bangkok. After all, it was the first country in Asia she had seen that was not at war or faced with the threat of war. She wanted to visit everything, from the inevitable Floating Market to the Temple of Dawn and even the Snake Farm, plunging into the crowds of Asians with a sort of sensuous pleasure, surprised that in days gone by she had found that experience overwhelming.

The minute they had moved into the villa, she had telephoned to Colorado. She was able to speak to Matthew Kinkaird and was touched by how deeply her grandfather was moved, having learned from him, not without remorse, that he had had no news of them for more than three months. Matthew had never received the letter Lisa wrote to tell him that they were about to leave for Sré, which she described in glowing terms, stressing that they would be completely safe there—a letter mailed two days before their departure from Phnom Penh, on May 15.

Matthew told her he had gone to Stockholm and had seen Jon there, so that she also had news of her brother and, at last, an address for him. She wrote him immediately to confirm the news that he now had a nephew. Three weeks later she had an answer from Jon, now apparently quite at home in Sweden. He mentioned the possibility of a trip outside the country as soon as his job permitted (he had been hired by a machine-tool company as a marketing executive), of a trip in fact to Thailand, once he got his Swedish passport. There was something else in Jon's letter that touched Lisa: the way he spoke of Lara, who had unquestionably impressed him and whose role in rescuing him he referred to with an emotion deeper than mere gratitude: "He's the older brother I've always dreamed of having."

Among the people Lara knew in Bangkok was an English couple who had lived there for years, Peter and Jodie Hayward. Peter was a photographer and worked for British and Australian publishers, and Jodie was a sculptress with a lack of talent which could only be described as miraculous, though that fact apparently troubled her not at all. The Haywards had often visited Cambodia, which they really liked better than Thailand, and Peter had built up an impressive collection of photographs of Khmer monuments, in his view the most beautiful in the world.

Thanks to the Haywards, the Laras met a number of people from the colony of Westerners who lived in Bangkok, English or American nationals for the most part, and through one of the U.S. embassy attachés Lisa learned that Thomas Aquinas O'Malley was about to leave America in September for his new post in a small African country called Burundi.

"Are you sure a country such as that exists?" she asked the attaché.

"All I know is that we have an embassy there."

She hesitated a long time, but in the end did not write to O'Malley, though later she felt a bit annoyed at herself for not having done so.

They stayed in Bangkok through the end of August, and then all of September, October, and November. Lara never spoke of Cambodia, and when the conversation at a cocktail party or a dinner turned to the war on the other side of the border, his face went blank and he took no part in it, or else, when he could, he left the group.

In September, Christiani brought them news of Charles and Madeleine Korver, as well as of Roger Bouès. All three of them were fine. Relieved and reassured at the time, on second thought Lisa wondered how Christiani, who lived in Bangkok and never went to Cambodia, could have spoken to Kutchaï, who had apparently not left his country, though he seemed to move about from one end of it to the other with the greatest of ease. After a few days, she came straight out and asked Lara.

"Christiani's trafficking in contraband goods," he answered.

She was dumbfounded by this piece of news and even more by Lara's frank reply. "But he's your partner!"

"As far as our absolutely straight and aboveboard import-export company is concerned, yes. But what Dominique does outside of his work with me is none of my business, at least in the present circumstances."

She stared at him intently, convinced he was hiding something from her. She told him as much.

He gave a slight shrug, with his usual imperturbable calm. "No. Not anymore."

They were in their bedroom on the upstairs floor of the villa, getting dressed to go to a dinner.

"What circumstances are you referring to? And what sort of contraband?"

"Cambodia is a country at war that lacks absolutely everything. There's always money to be made in such cases. And I wouldn't stop Dominique from making himself some, even if I wanted to."

"And you don't want to? How come? What's he selling?"

The light suddenly dawned on her. "Arms," she said. "Kutchaï said that the Khmer Rouge lacked arms, and that Hanoi wasn't eager to supply them, except in driblets."

"And medicine."

"And you've been involved in that trafficking, haven't you?"

He fastened the bow tie of his dinner jacket. "In the beginning, yes. But certainly not to make money. And I didn't make any."

In his grave, quiet voice, very calmly, as though it were the most natural thing in the world, he told her of his meeting with Ieng on the high plateaus and how, with $60,000 out of his own pocket, he had financed a part of the first shipment of arms to Ieng Samboth which Christiani had arranged.

"But they gave me back the money later on."

"Who do you mean by 'they'?"

"The Chinese."

"You mean to tell me that the Peking government, Mao Tse-tung and company, gave you back sixty thousand dollars?" Lisa was thunderstruck.

"That's precisely what happened."

"And why did they pay you back?"

"I suppose I owe the fact that they did to Ieng's stepping in on my behalf. He didn't want me to be out of pocket, knowing that that money represented a fair share of my financial resources."

She had just put on the dress she was going to wear that evening. She sat down on the bed, feeling shaky in the legs, with the zipper down the back of her dress gaping open.

"You bought arms and delivered them to the Khmer Rouge?"

"Not to the Khmer Rouge. To Ieng Samboth and to him alone."

"What's the difference?"

"There's a tremendous difference. The Cambodia of tomorrow is not going to be the Cambodia of Lon Nol. That's already a foregone conclusion. But I don't want it to be the Cambodia of a Saloth Sar or a Rath either."

"I don't know who those men are."

"They exist nonetheless," he said with his exasperating calm.

He turned around and saw that she was completely distraught. He walked over to her and sat down beside her. "Lisa, I've told you the truth. I'm not hiding anything from you." He zipped up her dress.

"Tell me, does it change anything at all now that you know?" he said. "What difference is there between right now and the minute before? Cambodia's my country, Lisa. I can't even imagine any other, and I've the right to try to help shape its destiny."

We always keep coming back to the same point, Lisa thought. Lara hadn't changed, and in her heart of hearts she had always known this, even if the departure for Bangkok, their long stay in Thailand, had allowed her to believe the contrary for a time. Lara hadn't changed and was as stubbornly and madly attached as ever to this country which already had begun to reject him and, when all was said and done, had never really accepted him. Lisa was convinced of that and a searing anger swept over her. Why did he refuse to face facts? How could he fail to realize that that money he had invested was a price he had been willing to pay? He had simply paid or tried to pay for his right to live in Cambodia, no matter what regime took over. And the fact that Ieng Samboth had done everything possible to see he was reimbursed could have only one meaning: Ieng himself, his friend since childhood, had given him back the forfeit he had been willing to pay. And refused to guarantee his right to stay.

That evening, for a few seconds, she very nearly exploded. But her rage did not last long. She controlled herself, in the name of the love she felt for Lara, and by virtue of a simple process of reasoning as well: After all, they were in Bangkok now and at no time since the moment they arrived had Lara spoken of a possible return to Phnom Penh. The truth was that time was on her side; this war was bound to be over sooner or later. She recovered her usual self-control and her good sense. She turned around and looked her husband square in the eye.

"And you have nothing to do with these arms deliveries anymore?"

"Absolutely nothing. And I won't get involved in them again."

She looked at him in silence, certain he was telling her the truth. She finally lowered her eyes to her new dress, distraught and very nearly overcome with a pity for him that made her sick at heart. She said in a dull voice, "You forgot to hook the clasp, just above the zipper."

The fact that Christiani or others could easily pass contraband supplies from Thailand to the Khmer resistance fighting Lon Nol, and operate almost openly, had surprised Lisa at first. But she was not surprised for long. All she had to do was walk through the streets of Bangkok a few times to realize that the Thai capital looked very much like the South Vietnamese capital in many ways. There were countless new nightclubs, bars, restaurants, not to mention massage parlors, a traditional local specialty, catering to a clientele that was practically the same as that in Saigon: her compatriots in uniform for the most part, small fry let loose for piranhas to devour, sent there for R and R, Rest and Recreation, between one battle and another in Vietnam, in Laos, in Cambodia before the American retreat on June 30, or else officially stationed in Thailand, since this was the end of 1970 and the beginning of 1971, when there were more than fifty thousand Americans, pilots, ground crews, and military advisers working at supposedly secret American bases. So secret that Peter Hayward was able to point their locations out to her on a map.

"But why has Thailand agreed to allow these bases on its soil?" Lisa asked the Englishman.

"First off, because when you add everything together, it brings them in a billion dollars a year, counting all the various sorts of aid that your country furnishes. Secondly, and perhaps even more importantly, because the Thais aren't crazy: Like the Khmers, they're convinced that when Hanoi has devoured Cochin China, as is bound to happen one day or another, the Tonkinese will swallow up Laos and Cambodia, an operation that's already well under way, and that after that it'll be their turn. It isn't easy to be an Asian in our day and age, Lisa. If you were one, you'd have only three solutions to choose among: accepting American dollars and aid from the West without having the least assurance that they'll be forthcoming forever, and that's not really freedom exactly; or else accepting Chinese domination, the religion of Peking, and its future but nonetheless predictable expansionism—don't forget that, while in Cambodia one inhabitant out of ten is Chinese, the proportion here in this country is one out of seven; there are five million Chinese in the country of the King of Siam, and a good half of the capital is in their hands. Or else, the last of the three solutions, submit to the stranglehold of North Vietnam, with the Russians behind the scene, or at any rate behind the scene for the moment—you need only ask the Kazaks and other Uzbeks, the Turkomans, and the Kirgiz what their thoughts on the subject are.

"Only three solutions, Lisa. Any other choice is a farce, and one that's not even funny. The Thais are the only people in Asia not to have officially undergone colonial tutelage, even though we English have exercised what I would modestly call a certain influence here. They've always been officially independent. I might add in passing that they don't seem to have gotten very much further ahead than the others because of that fact. . . . And they are determined to remain independent. For them, the immediate danger is Hanoi and its gluttony; the thrashing that the Vietnamese are giving the United States, after having thoroughly beaten the French, hasn't satisfied that ravenous appetite. Quite the contrary—it seems instead to have stimulated it, and if need be the Popoffs would help to stimulate it, just to give the Chinese trouble.

"Lisa, dear, beautiful, big, tall Lisa, there was a time when the whole world was White. Being White was the thing to be, and White civilization was the model. That was the situation for around four hundred years. Have you read the late lamented Jules Verne's *Around the World in Eighty Days*? In it there were two Englishmen, plus one Frenchman, who travel around the globe as though it belonged to them. And it really did belong to them. They could go anywhere and find at each crossroad, in front of each straw hut or each igloo, a bobby from Pontypool or Kilmarnock, or a gendarme born in Tarascon-sur-Ariège. That's all over and done with now, my dear lady. Today there are no more Welsh miners in the Army of the Indies; they're all out on strike, and the Scots are thinking of asking for their independence. Let's console ourselves as best we can: We British have invented the miniskirt and the Beatles, and your American Blacks carry off all the Olympic medals."

Just a few days before the end of November, Lisa discovered she was pregnant again. She welcomed the discovery with heartfelt joy, first of all because Lara and she had long since decided to have at least three children, secondly because Lara was so obviously delighted when she announed the news, and finally for a third reason, one far less clear in her mind: It immediately struck her that a second pregnancy was the surest possible way of avoiding a return to Cambodia in the near future. Moreover, she was determined to use it as an excuse for refusing to return to Phnom Penh. But as it turned out, it was not necessary for her to do so.

Lara needed to make contacts outside of Bangkok, after three months of hard work every day at the import-export company in which he and Christiani had been partners for many years, and which the Corsican had managed by himself up until then. In fact, Lara should long since have gone to Tokyo in particular, via Hong Kong. He suggested to Lisa that she come with him while she could still travel without too much discomfort, and little by little, as they talked about it and made their plans for it, what had begun as a simple business trip turned into a grand tour, whose principal aim was sightseeing rather than drumming up new trade for the company.

They left on December 2, 1970, heading first for Burma, where they spent four days visiting Rangoon and above all Mandalay, which was more typically Burmese and which Lisa liked far more. From there they took off for India, stopping as fancy struck them, at Calcutta, Benares, Delhi, and Agra, and even going as far as Srinagar in Kashmir. There were certain names the very sound of which had always set Lisa to dreaming. Kashmir was one of them, like Samarkand (but Samarkand was in the USSR and by mutual agreement they crossed it off their itinerary), like Bombay and Hyderabad, like Ceylon, all of which they visited.

They came back to Bangkok to spend Christmas and New Year's with the Haywards and found numerous letters from Matthew and Jon Kinkaird waiting for them there—Jon had just been granted Swedish citizenship and was talking of coming to Thailand, perhaps the following summer—and also from the Korvers and from Roger, who announced that he was counting on paying them a visit in Bangkok some time in February, perhaps the last two weeks of that month.

They left again on January 3, this time for Singapore and its venerable Raffles Hotel that was an all-time favorite of Lara's. They found there the traces of a past long dead and gone, peopled by the heroes of Joseph Conrad and Somerset Maugham and calling to mind *Lives of a Bengal Lancer* or *The Four Feathers*. Four days later, on the seventh, they landed in Hong Kong, where a veritable delegation of members of the Liu family was waiting for them, forewarning them, the moment they set foot in the crown colony, that the cousins (or the nephews, or the uncle, or the brother-in-law, or perhaps the son-in-law—Lisa always got lost amid the many ramifications of the family tree) had spread the word that they were on their way, that the Singapore network had confirmed the news, and that the entire Liu family would be forever dishonored, and even doomed to commit collective suicide, if Lara and his wife had any occasion to spend one single Hong Kong dollar during their entire stay, which was to last two weeks.

Once she recovered from her initial surprise, Lisa was delighted. These Chinese seemed to her absolutely charming. They owned banks and real estate, airline companies or shipping lines; they raced horses under their colors; they played cricket and rugby; they produced very amusing films in which heroes brandishing yataghans disemboweled seventy assailants with one backhand blow, moaning the while as though suffering from severe constipation and leaping into the air to altitudes mindful of stratospheric balloons taking off. They had marvelous villas, luxurious swimming pools, sublime yachts, and private marinas and beaches. They would probably not have hired Roger Boués as their interior decorator, or would have done so only because it amused them, and chose to hang Utrillos and Matisses on the walls of their living rooms, alongside Klees and Picassos, and not only knew who these painters were but also why they liked them. And yet they were Chinese, no doubt about it, faithfully worshiping their ancestors and respectful of the age-old social hierarchies. They were Chinese and proud of it, maintaining the closest ties with their mother country and priding themselves on being its representatives, even though they happened at the same time to be billionaires and knights of the British Empire, a dignity conferred upon them by the Queen herself.

The impression Lisa had formed on first meeting a member of the Liu family in Phnom Penh was confirmed: She was in the presence of an Asia whose culture, personality, intelligence, and fortunes were in every respect the equal of those of the Western world. They were far from the world of *beps* and *ti-bas,* of pedicab boys and latex collectors; they were far from Cambodia. Or so she thought. In any event, the two weeks in Hong Kong were like paradise, even after a long trip on which she had ecstatically contemplated Singhalese landscapes, the Himalayas, the gleaming whiteness of the Taj Mahal.

At the beginning of the last week in January, they took off again, for Tokyo this time. She was less entranced by Japan, but doubtless that was because, like Lara, she was beginning to feel pangs of regret at being separated from her son for so long. They decided to cut their trip short, and on their way back to Bangkok spent only two days in Manila, the time necessary for the business discussions Lara had planned on.

Peter and Jodie Hayward had been kind enough to bring Mathias and the amah to the airport with them. The Chinese nursemaid was thus the first person Lisa saw, and then, lowering her eyes, she spied her son, Mathias, on his feet and walking, held up by the amah and Jodie. He broke away from them and toddled toward her. Moved and amazed, Lisa nearly burst into tears. She hurried to him. Mathias had his mother's eyes, that was plain to see, but apart from that, he looked more like Lara: the same build, and certainly the same mouth and eyebrows and forehead.

They had landed in Bangkok around three in the afternoon. They left for the villa in Chulalongkorn two hours later, having finally managed to reclaim their luggage. Christiani was waiting for them at the villa. Lisa, who had felt ill at ease with the Corsican ever since she had learned of his trafficking in contraband goods, paid very little attention to him. She had eyes only for her son, calling him to come to her and holding out her hands, while the amah, as entranced as she was to see him walking, laughed in delight. After a few moments, however, Lisa looked around for Lara. He was an extremely affectionate father and she was surprised to see that he had disappeared.

"I'll be back," she said to the amah.

She called to Lara but there was no answer. She went upstairs. She found him in the bathroom next to their bedroom. He was leaning over the washbasin, his hands resting on the edge of it, deathly pale. She thought he had been taken ill.

"What's the matter?"

He had not heard her coming. He straightened up and shook his head, his mouth wide open as though gasping for air.

"It's Roger," he said. "They've killed him."

15

IN THE PLAIN, AFTER THREE MORE OR LESS HUMID MONTHS, THE rainy season was over by the end of October. On the peaks of the Cardamomes it was not yet ended, and would not be for several weeks more. That was what particularly surprised Ieng Samboth, a man from the plain and the Mekong—that and the silence, and even more than the silence, the loneliness. He had discovered another Cambodia here, deserted, wild, almost unexplored, still completely intact. The villages were few and far between, and consisted only of a few huts hidden in the bottom of a valley almost four thousand feet above sea level, just barely visible in their fields on burned-off land, where they grew a mountain rice with a particular, slightly bitter taste that seemed to preserve the smell of smoke.

The inhabitants were Khmer Loeu—literally Khmers from Up Above: a tribe called the Pears, of exactly the same racial stock as those who centuries earlier had settled around Kompong Thom on the other side of the Tonle Sap, yet different from them in that they had kept almost all their age-old customs, along with a fierce desire to live by themselves in their mountain fastnesses.

Ieng was beginning to know them, and to be known by them. He had earned their trust and even gained their friendship. It had taken him ten or twelve weeks to reach that point, and it had been an exhausting undertaking, in every sense of the word—because of the terrain, first of all, which everywhere was rough and steep, spongy, rugged, with vegetation so dense in places that it was stifling, and dangerous because of the countless snakes, and perhaps tigers and panthers as well (though in fact he was not nearly as afraid of them); and secondly, because of the reaction of the Pears, who vanished under cover like shadows the moment anyone came in sight. In this regard, Ouk had been of inestimable help. There was something about the giant Jaraï with the look and the strength of a great wild buffalo that won the mountain people's confidence immediately. Perhaps they recognized themselves in him. *Whereas I will always be an outsider to them,* Ieng thought to himself.

Looking back on this month of January 1971, when all was said and done Ieng was satisfied. He had attained all the goals he had set himself. The arms first of all. The initial delivery from Christiani had gone smoothly and the arms had been transported with an almost disconcerting lack of problems; this had been true of subsequent shipments as well, with one exception, when they had happened upon a unit of Thai soldiers who, after a few moments' hesitation, pretended they'd seen nothing, and after that had run into a FARK patrol with which they had exchanged a few desultory rounds of fire. In fact, the transporting of the arms had been almost a game, except when it came time to haul the cases up to the depot—the term did not designate any sort of building but simply a series of caves in the middle of the forest, at an altitude of almost 4,000 feet, in a spot that Ieng himself chose. To his knowledge, he was the only one who knew exactly where, within a radius of twenty kilometers from the headwaters of the Pursat River, they were located. The result of these multiple expeditions, eleven in all: enough individual arms and ammunition to supply three or four thousand men.

As for his men, there, too, everything had gone marvelously well. The intuition he had had on March 18 had not been mistaken: The principal effect of the coup d'état had been a spectacular increase in the number of Khmer Rouge recruits, to the point that it was hard to know what to do with this sudden influx. Ieng was unable to consider the possibility of keeping them all in the Cardamome Mountains, since provisioning them alone would have presented insurmountable problems. He had sent hundreds of them back to their native villages, with orders to hold themselves in readiness, and had kept with him only some thirty guerrillas, who he thought could be trained as cadres for the future army.

In June he had been visited by Hu Nim and several other representatives of the government of national union created by Sihanouk. His organization, almost too careful, had amazed them. He had shown them a few— just a few—of the caches where the arms and ammunition received from Christiani were stored, not really knowing why he was being so wary with them. He had also shown them the stocks of provisions.

"There's enough here for us to hold out for years, against the entire American Army if need be, and certainly against the troops from Saigon," they had said.

"We've no assurance that we won't be forced to go on fighting for years," Ieng had shot back.

They reconfirmed his standing orders: for the time being, no real military engagements. "The North Vietnamese are doing our fighting for us. So much the better. We've no objection to their getting themselves killed in our stead. In the meantime, let's get ourselves organized." Moreover, the latest news was rather encouraging, despite the fact that Lon Nol's partisans were putting up much stronger resistance than had been expected.

Certain units of the Phnom Penh army were even fighting with unquestionable valor, often under difficult conditions.

Hu Nim told Ieng how, during the battle of Srang (between Phnom Penh and Kompong Speu), on the American Highway near Kompong Som two battalions made up of high-school students from the capital had literally been hacked to pieces by their far more seasoned Viet Cong adversaries. "They sent those kids into battle with one rifle for every two of them, and very few automatic weapons. And the trucks that were to transport them had meanwhile been sold by their colonel to Chinese traders. The survivors were taken out in buses, buses that headquarters had to rent for the purpose, at an exorbitant price, from a company whose owner was none other than the colonel's brother. It's high time we got rid of such swine."

Ieng then brought up the problem of Rath with Hu Nim, who held the portfolio of Information and Propaganda in the provisional government. He did so cautiously, not knowing exactly what he might be getting into. Isolated as he'd been in his mountain refuge, he had not been able to follow in detail all the ins and outs of the relationship between the two major factions of the Khmer Rouge—the one led and personified by Saloth Sar, known now as Pol Pot, and backed by men such as Rath, and the other more "Sihanoukist." He had been so eager for the Sihanouk faction to win out that he was now beginning to wonder if he hadn't simply dreamed it.

"The moment hasn't yet come to discuss what the Cambodia of the future will be like," said Hu Nim. "We should have only one goal: victory, through the elimination of the traitor Lon Nol and his clique on the one hand, and through the retreat of all foreign troops, including those of Hanoi, from Khmer territory on the other."

It was the answer Ieng had expected. Once again he reproached himself for his naïveté. What other answer could he expect? Could he believe that before all else they were going to get rid of a madman like Sar, a crazy man like Rath, simply because he, Ieng Samboth, and they did not have the same concept of the future of the country? And besides, in what way were these concepts so different? The means, yes, most assuredly. Ieng did not believe that one could judge the value of a revolution simply by the quantity of blood shed. From all appearances, Saloth Sar and Rath, and probably Khieu Samphan too, believed this was a valid criterion. Yet all of them, including Ieng, agreed on the end to be achieved.

"Who's the Frenchman supplying you with arms?"

"A Corsican from Bangkok named Christiani."

"We know him. He was a friend of that other Corsican who was a tax collector at Kompong Cham around the end of the fifties."

There had indeed been a Corsican tax collector for the province of Kompong Cham for several years after independence. The whole thing had turned out badly. The man had died mysteriously in a car accident and when his state coffers were opened and his accounts gone over, a vast sum of money was missing. But certain ministers of that era had made huge fortunes at the same time, by sheerest coincidence supposedly.

"Christiani's not on the take. Furthermore, it's Lara who's behind the entire operation. So even if that was his intention, Christiani wouldn't manage to pull any funny stuff with Lara."

The visitors obviously knew Lara. They also knew that he and Ieng were close friends. They didn't press the point. They had gone off, repeating the same orders yet again: Wait, simply wait, taking cover behind the fifty thousand men Giap had moved onto Khmer soil to fight the Cambodian right backed by Saigon and Washington.

This visit left Ieng with mixed feelings. Something had made him hold back, had kept him from revealing to those who in principle were his superiors the extent of the stockpiles he had built up. The payments to Christiani were at present being made directly to the Corsican by representatives of Peking on the basis of information supplied by Ieng, so that he was probably the only man in all of Cambodia at the moment—and was long to remain so—who knew exactly where all the arms and provisions were located, and exactly how large these stores were. It was an ace he was unwilling to discard, even though he had no idea how he was going to use it.

Around the end of July, a man had succeeded in stealthily approaching him, in making his way to within a few yards of him without having once been spied either by the sentinels he himself had posted all around him, or even by the Pears: an extraordinary performance.

But Ieng had always known that Kutchaï was capable of all sorts of seemingly impossible feats.

"I came to make sure everything was going all right."

"Everything's fine."

"And to tell you that another shipment will be arriving soon."

They spread out the map drawn up ten years earlier by an engineer of the French National Geographical Institute who was also French despite his name, Kyryll Thikomiroff, and whom both Ieng and Kutchaï had often run across.

"Here," Kutchaï said. "Sixty kilos north of Sre Umbell." When speaking Cambodian, Kutchaï used the word *kilo* for *kilometer*. He pointed to the precise spot on the map. "At just about three kilos farther north than for the second delivery in June. Do you remember that outcropping of rocks?"

"Yes. But you didn't need to come all the way up here. We agreed we'd get in touch with each other through the intermediary of that man in Pursat."

"He's dead," Kutchaï said in an indifferent tone of voice. "They shot him last week. And besides, I felt like breathing some mountain air."

He looked around him. "I often used to come hunting·round about here in the old days. You've picked a good place. Even six armored divisions couldn't take you by surprise."

"You managed to."

"I'm not an armored division," Kutchaï said. "I'm Kutchaï the Jaraï."

"Were you with Lara?"

"When? Just now?"

"When you used to go hunting."

"In either case, the answer is yes," Kutchaï replied, his mind seemingly elsewhere.

Ieng looked at him again, with the same curiosity as ever. Whereas he trusted the Jaraï's younger brother Ouk absolutely, Kutchaï, to an equal degree, thoroughly disconcerted him. There was something maddeningly elusive about him. *He's more intelligent than his brother, with a personality ten times more complicated. Because of Lara?* Ieng wondered. As always, Lara's name came to his mind, almost obsessively. As it had a short time before, during Hu Nim's visit . . .

"Where is Lara exactly?" Ieng asked.

"Somewhere or other in Cambodia, as always."

"Is he all right?"

"He's fine. And Lisa and Mathias are fine too."

A silence. Some of Ieng's men happened by and stared at the Jaraï in surprise, as though he'd suddenly sprung up out of the ground.

"And what about my brother?" Kutchaï asked.

"He's down along the Tonle Sap. He should be back here tomorrow."

"I'll be gone by then," Kutchaï said.

"Is there anything you'd like me to tell him for you?"

Kutchaï didn't answer. He appeared to be lost in thought. His bloodshot eyes, with their strange animallike intensity, swept the heavily wooded slopes of the Cardamomes.

"I presume you hid the arms in the series of caves to the south of here—is that right? You couldn't have chosen a better place."

The expression on Ieng's face must have spoken volumes, for Kutchaï burst out laughing.

"Don't let it bother you. I told you I knew this region very well."

That silent laugh of his! Ieng thought, and remarked in a bitter tone of voice: "One of these days you're going to end up getting yourself killed, wandering about all over the place the way you do."

"Kutchaï pool wletched immoltal Khmel," he answered in his mock-Pidgin French.

A silence fell. The two men were in a sort of hut with a thatched roof of fan-palm, wedged between two outcroppings of rock on the mountainside. Before them lay a panorama of intersecting slopes, with deep gorges and valleys plunged in shadow, and mountain crests hidden in clouds tinged with violet. After having let up for a time, the rain had begun to fall again in a gentle, peaceful patter.

"Do you know where Rath is?"

"Somewhere around Kompong Thom," Ieng replied.

Kutchaï nodded, then said with the same absent-minded look in his eye, "Lon Nol's troops are in control of the city, but Rath has it very nearly encircled. He has at least four thousand men with him. And he's extended the territory he controls all the way to the north shore of the Tonle Sap, and perhaps even as far as Siem Reap. With the exception of the highway, where armored convoys still get through, he holds all of it. You're not very far from each other. He may already be in Angkor."

"Have you met up with him?"

Kutchaï stared intently at him with his eerie gaze, and Ieng felt a shiver run down his spine.

"No," Kutchaï answered with his great, silent, disconcerting laugh. "No, I haven't met up with him. Not yet."

He was squatting comfortably on his heels, his forearms resting on his knees, his strangler's hands with their spatulate fingers dangling down, a position suggestive of a monster in repose. All of a sudden, in one continuous movement that appeared to have neither a beginning nor an end, he rose to his feet, and Ieng was struck by the explosive force animating the huge bony body that seemed to be strung together with steel cables.

"I'm off," Kutchaï said. "I just dropped around to have a look at how things were going. Is your mother still in Phnom Penh?"

"I have no idea."

Ieng hadn't seen his mother for three years. And he'd never seen his father.

"If I can, I'll pay her a visit and tell her you're all right."

Ieng nodded. "Thanks."

His eyes followed Kutchaï for a long time as he walked off with his enormous, long, backwoodsman's strides, "as silently as a leaf falling." Where was he heading? An inexplicable certainty stole over Ieng: Nothing, ever, could kill Kutchaï. Kutchaï *was* most likely immortal, as he himself so often said.

His tall, powerful silhouette disappeared all of a sudden, as if by magic, swallowed up by the glistening rain-drenched foliage of the teak trees a hundred yards farther down the slope. And it was only then, as he happened to lower his eyes, that Ieng Samboth discovered the two cartons of Philip Morrises, his favorite brand of cigarettes, which the Jaraï had left at his feet.

16

"THAT," ROGER BOUÈS SAID, "IS ANGKOR WAT. OR RATHER, THAT was Angkor Wat. We've just gone past it, my good man. At the speed you're driving, we should be in Shanghai by nightfall. Wouldn't you care to slow down just a little?"

"Stones," Donaldson replied. "Nothing but a pile of stones."

Donaldson was wearing very dark sunglasses and a long-billed cap in the orange and white colors of the Broncos, the Denver football team. It seemed to Roger that the Englishman looked fatter than ever.

It was January 23, 1971, around three o'clock in the afternoon.

"Off there in the distance is Angkor Thom," Roger went on. "Angkor Thom is very beautiful. We should stop and see it. You should try to hoist your imperial buttocks out of the driver's seat of this powerful limousine and admire it religiously. If you like, I'll even take a color shot of you in Angkor Thom, standing right in front of Bayon. You could send it to your poor old mother in her tumbledown castle in Sussex. That would spoil her appetite and make her muffins stick in her throat."

Beneath the trees of the forest that the jeep was passing through, on both sides of the road that ran straight as a die from Angkor Wat to Angkor Thom, touches of color in the greenery attracted Roger's eye: three or four bonzes in saffron robes, squatting on their heels for an enigmatic conference—unless they were merely dropping figurative trousers, which they weren't wearing, to relieve themselves collectively, not even looking around as this lone car on the road passed by them.

"I am a renowned international journalist who enjoys the secret but effective protection of Her Gracious Majesty the Queen, hieratically seated in the shitter of Buckingham Palace, with her matutinal crown resting majestically on her august head," Donaldson said in his slightly affected Oxford accent. "If you take a close look behind you, you can make out the ghosts of gunboats that have followed me for centuries or catch a glimpse of the white leather fittings of grenadiers under the command of Kitchener or Wolseley or Roberts marching to the shrill sound of skirling bagpipes to chastise the Mad Mahdi in Khartoum or the Sepoys of Meerut. As a renowned international journalist, I have benevolently focused my attention on Koreans who were kicking off, on minor Malaysian maquisards madly murdering, on Mau Maus in Jomu slitting the throats of blond lady schoolteachers, on Balubas bolting down Belgians, on virulent Viet Minh and then on vicious Viet Cong, the latter in my eyes indistinguishable from the former. I am doubtless forgetting certain others, and I have cited those that I have without regard for chronological order or hierarchical precedence. I haven't in fact mentioned Cypriots, Palestinians, Jews, Congolese, Bolivians, Algerians, and dozens of others. So this is what you call Bayon?"

"This is what I call Bayon. And if the wheels of this car continue on a quarter of a turn farther, a revolutionary bullet is going to lodge itself in your imperial bum. I'm getting more and more nervous by the second. What do you say to clearing out of here with the speed of a falling meteor?"

"My dear Roger, I've been in this business for some thirty-four years, nineteen days, and fifty-six minutes. Each and every day of my life that hasn't been marked by a spurt of red Occidental blood is to be commemorated by a white stone. For approximately thirty-four years, nineteen days, and fifty-six minutes I've been keeping careful tabs on the kicks in the ass aimed indirectly at me by various parties and those aimed directly at my imperial bum by the revolution in its triumphant march. For more or less the same length of time I have been contemplating, with British unflappability, the heirs of Kitchener and Lyautey in the act of lowering their flags if not their trousers. To me, a day without bloodshed by my countrymen is like a pear without cheese. I am eager to write my piece on Khmer Rouge ambling about with ancient temples in the background. If you're feeling a charge of adrenaline that is too much for you—in other words, if you're experiencing a certain anxiety—in short, if you're scared stiff, you can always climb out of this limousine and make your way back to town on foot, running with a buoyant step."

He stopped the ancient Peugeot 403 convertible he had rented in Siem Reap and looked about him. "I don't see a single Khmer Rouge on the horizon."

"I don't either," Roger replied, still overcome by a vague feeling of anxiety.

Ten minutes earlier, as they were leaving Siem Reap, where they'd arrived in one of the armored cars of a convoy coming from Phnom Penh, they had called on the archaeologists of the Temple Preservation Commission and had found them going about their normal tasks, as though this war in progress had nothing to do with the century in which they were living. Their serenity had reassured Roger somewhat, for the moment at least, so that he had finally given in to the insistent Englishman who was eager to go on. But now their reassuring effect was wearing off—indeed, had disappeared completely—and his fear had come to the surface again.

"What's the most typical spot amid these ruins?"

"The Ta Prohm," Roger answered without even taking the time to ponder the question. "Or the Balustrade of Demons. Or the Prah Khan, or perhaps the Elephant Terrace or the Tower of the Rope Dancers. Not to mention others that are better still."

"Have you invented those ridiculous names on the spot or do they really exist?"

"To hell with you," Roger answered wearily.

Donaldson stood up on the seat of the Peugeot, his belly hanging out over his belt and his cigarette jutting out horizontally from his lips.

"Hey there, Khmer Rouge, where are you?" he yelled in French. "I'm Donaldson, the renowned international journalist whom Her Gracious Majesty has sent here for the express purpose of listening to your nonsense!"

The echo of his voice resounded in a tomblike silence; resounded, then died away.

"Oh, shit!" Roger said. "Shit shit shit shit!"

The car started off again, its horn blaring. It made one complete circle of the great monument, the sixty-four giant, impassive faces with closed eyes and stone smiles.

"Where are the bloody natives? What name did you say? The first one?"

"The Ta Prohm."

"And how do you get there?"

"Straight ahead and then to your right. Then right again, left, and right again. For the love of heaven, let's get the hell out of here!"

They left the Elephant Terrace and the five temples in Prah Pithu behind them on their left. But the faces of Bayon lingered on in Roger's inner eye.

"I know why they're smiling," he said all of a sudden, as though he'd just discovered something.

Donaldson wasn't listening, keeping his eyes peeled for human silhouettes. He was humming, nothing really musical, reciting, rather, the famous verses of Kipling's "Recessional"* on an improvised melody: "God of our fathers, known of old,/Lord of our far-flung battle-line,/Beneath whose awful Hand we hold/Dominion over palm and pine . . ."

"I know why," Roger said again. "They aren't smiling out of compassion and serenity. That's twaddle. One isn't compassionate and serene at the same time—that explanation won't hold water. They *know,* that's all. They're detached. They've stopped suffering the pain of living. They refuse to have anything to do with it. And they're smiling. To be compassionate is to care about others, to share their suffering. They couldn't care less. I'd even say that they're gloating. And their eyes are closed because there's nothing to see, period. You know, Donaldson, my asshole buddy, that in France, at Rheims, we've something of the same sort? An angel that's smiling. But not the same smile. Oh, no, the angel's happy, eternal bliss, the paradise of believers and of Santa Claus and of Allah all rolled into one, the reward at the end of the road, the lollipop after you've cleaned up your plate nicely. Here there's no lollipop, no harp combo with Lionel Hampton on vibes and Satchmo on trumpet. Nothing. Not a damned thing."

* Written in 1897 in celebration of the sixtieth anniversary of Queen Victoria's reign

"You're getting on my nerves, my good fellow," Donaldson said. "You promised me some Khmer Rouge."

"Nothing at all," Roger said. "Zero. That's why they're splitting their sides laughing. With good reason."

"Left or right?"

They were approaching the eastern *baraï*.

"Right," Roger said. "And then left. Angels don't have any peckers. That in itself should have made me smell a rat. Here, my good man, angels have cocks, tremendous ones. As big as interplanetary rockets and all of them likewise aimed at the sky. What a way of giving fate the finger, old buddy."

With a sudden feeling of warm friendship, of fraternity almost, he contemplated Donaldson's thick lower lip and flabby pink flesh. And then he looked straight ahead of him and his heart gave a leap.

"Stop. We're here, my dear Donaldson. Here we are. The end of the road. All set to give fate the finger."

He got out almost the minute the car stopped. For the last five hundred yards or so, the Peugeot had been driving slowly along a narrow, heavily shaded trail with traces here and there of what had once been a paved road.

"Note the splendid balustrade," Roger said. "Behind it you can see the second enclosure and the great reception hall with three intersecting naves. Follow the guide."

He was walking along without paying any attention to Donaldson and speaking in a loud voice. "You can see from here the one hundred eight monks' cells, each one with its laterite portico. And farther on, the marvelous courtyard in the shape of a cross decorated on the outside with admirable false portals . . ."

He went back out into the open air, or what passed for such. Everything was bathed in a murky sea-green light because of the millions of dust particles suspended motionless in the air. The giant tentacles of the kapok trees ran along the ground like creeping white monsters. He sat down on a stone that had toppled over and stroked the warm, smooth trunk of the tree. He watched Donaldson walk toward him, his cigarette stuck in his mouth like a spur.

"We won't have to go any farther. We've arrived, my brother."

"I saw them," Donaldson whispered, his pale-blue eyes bulging.

Roger smiled. "You can shout at the top of your lungs. It won't change much of anything."

He grabbed his Rollei, adjusted the settings, and began taking photos showing the minuscule doors, the rubble, the massive walls that had tumbled down, the jungle. And at one moment three motionless figures who had not been there a second before appeared in his lens, Kalashnikovs resting on their bellies. Roger took the photo, then raised his head. There weren't just three of them now, but twenty-five or thirty.

"Do any of you speak French?" Donaldson asked.

Thirty impassive faces, empty eyes. They were thin and dressed all in black, the only spot of color the red and white checkered scarves knotted around their necks.

"*Parlez français?*" Donaldson asked again. "Do you speak English? *¿Hablan español? Sprechen Sie Deutsch?*"

Roger almost burst out laughing.

"Journalists. Press," the Englishman said. He waved a tricolor card encased in plastic bearing the word PRESS in large red letters, an official permit allowing him to park his personal car in a special lot at the London airport.

Silence. He might as well have been addressing the trunk of a kapok tree.

"They're downright unfriendly," Donaldson said to Roger.

The green underwater light made his eyes seem an even paler blue.

"Lodge a complaint," Roger said. He rose to his feet and stepped back a few paces so as to have both Donaldson and the guerrillas in his field of focus. As he was about to snap the photo, he had the feeling there was someone behind him. He turned around. There were more of them, come out of nowhere as silently as the first ones.

"I'm an English, British journalist," Donaldson went on. "And this person with me, though French, is a photographer gentleman."

Others kept arriving and the dark tide of men dressed all in black slowly invaded the ruined buildings of the Ta Prohm. Roger turned all the way around and faced these new arrivals. He took a whole series of photos in rapid succession. Donaldson's voice purred at his back, with its irritating English accent and his no less irritating manner of speaking French as though he found it extremely distasteful to express himself in that language.

"English journalist. Me friend of you. Me speak in big newspaper. Khmer Rouge be known in whole universe. Very well known. Publicity, great glory. Tell why you fight."

If only that fucking Anglo-Saxon would shut his big mouth, Roger thought. Facing him now, a bare two yards away, was a veritable wall of men in black. He took one last photo, then tried to reload the Rollei. No one made the slightest move, everything was absolutely still, and even Donaldson had finally shut up. The familiar odor of rot came back again, at the same time as the memory of his first visit to this place which, like all the other temples, he had explored by following the Henri Parmentier guide that the Saigonese publisher Albert Portail had just brought out back in those days. He had read and reread it so often that he could cite the first lines of it from memory: "The Cambodians call themselves 'Khmers';

foreigners call them Kambujas, the sons of Kambu, from the name of a legendary ancestor. . . ."

"Hello there, sons of Kambu," Roger said. He finished reloading his camera and shut the case again.

"Roger, do something," Donaldson said behind him.

"You wanted some Khmer Rouge."

The wall facing Roger finally quivered almost imperceptibly; then a break appeared in it and it parted. A short, stocky man with closely cropped hair stepped into view.

"My name is Roger Bouès," Roger said. "I've lived in Cambodia for almost twenty-five years. Ieng Samboth and Lara are friends of mine."

"I don't speak a word of French," the newcomer said in French. He held out his hand. "Your camera."

Roger removed the Rollei from around his neck and gave it to him.

"The other one too."

The Canon changed hands.

"The rolls of film. All of them."

The thickset man placed the two cameras and the unwound rolls of film on a stone block and gave an order. The wooden butts of the Kalashnikovs manufactured in China, recognizable by their sights, came crashing down, smashing the two cameras and pounding the film to pieces.

"That's not nice," Roger said.

His eyes met those of the thickset man. He suddenly realized, with absolute certainty, what was going to happen. He wasn't even afraid. On the contrary, he felt extraordinarily, almost miraculously calm. His gaze traveled over their heads, through the jungle vegetation and the trees whose tops looked white in the sunlight, and lit upon a stone face, at the summit of a towering temple gateway eaten away by green mold. He remembered a trip to Benares that he had taken with Lara in the fifties, the people dying in the streets, of starvation or something else, whom one simply stepped over when there was no way of going around them, victims of their bad karma whom no one among the living was really obliged to help unless he desired to acquire merit for a next life in another form. But in Asia one could keep an account of these merits—one had the right and practically the duty to do so—and as soon as a person calculated that he had accumulated enough of them to assure himself a good personal reincarnation, what use was it to show any more pity for others? No, that enigmatic smile could not be a smile of compassion. Compassion, charity, were words devoid of all meaning here, since one could weigh them and keep an account of them. Hence that fantastic indifference to the death of others . . .

"Roger, I have a most disagreeable feeling," Donaldson said in English. "For the first time in my ostentatious life as a great international foreign correspondent, it seems to me that I've gone just a bit too far."

The kick in the ass that's the last straw, Roger thought. He was still contemplating the stone face far overhead in the yellow-green sea of foliage, and almost unconsciously trying to form his lips, beneath his Gascon musketeer mustache, into an identical smile.

"My fault, Roger. Sorry." The Englishman's voice was calm.

Roger lowered his gaze, which came to rest once again on the thickset man. "He's short, broad-shouldered, with a bull neck and a nose so flat it looks almost broken, and he has a scar on his right cheek, at the corner of his jaw. . . ." The exact words that Oreste had used. "Roger, his name is Rath. He's a madman. If Ieng hadn't been right there on the spot, he'd have finished me off. Roger, if you ever meet up with him, stay out of his way, clear out, fast. That guy is death on the march. . . ."

Roger smiled. "Did you hear what my English friend just said? He thinks you're planning to kill us."

The heavyset man stared at him.

"I believe you're Rath. I've heard of you."

In the silence that ensued, there was an enormous, terrifying, muffled blow, immediately followed by a choked gasp; there was a sort of rustling noise and then a body fell to the ground.

"Nobody spoke well of you," Roger went on. "They all told me you were completely, totally, incurably nuts."

Other muffled blows, falling in a slow, fatal rhythm. *I won't turn around. Absolutely not. Not under any circumstances. I won't turn around.* And he stared straight back into Rath's dull eyes as though everything depended on it.

"In short, a hopeless case," Roger said.

Behind him, a death rattle. And more blows. Roger turned around.

"Oh, God!" the Englishman said, struggling to get the words out clearly. "God, no bagpipes . . ."

There were four of them who went for him, raising stones and then letting them fall, stones that must have weighed seventy or eighty pounds apiece, lifting them to shoulder height, then suddenly letting go of them. And as they fell the stones crushed Donaldson's feet and legs. The rest of his body seemed to be intact. He was lying on his side. With the barrels of their rifles they rolled him over onto his back, spreadeagled him, and shattered his arms and hands. He tried to spit in their faces and managed to smile at them. Then they put his head in a transparent plastic sack which they fastened around his neck with a tight cord. He tried to turn over but they held him pinned to the ground for a few moments, his arms and legs crushed and bloody. At one moment, he managed to free one of his hands and the horrible pulp of flesh and bones tried to tear the plastic. Without managing to do so. The stump slid down over his chest, lay there motionless for a brief moment, then slid down to the ground. Then the whole body ceased to move.

Roger closed his eyes and opened them again. He slowly pivoted round, hearing the men approaching him. He stared Rath square in the eye. He smiled, his teeth so tightly clenched they were about to shatter.

"Colonized," he said.

Part Five

THE CHEKO PENINSULA

1 AT SIEM REAP, KUTCHAÏ RAN INTO ONE OF HIS FRIENDS, A CAMBODIAN teacher of about his own age whom he had sometimes taken hunting with him. The teacher told him he'd seen Roger Bouès with his Englishman.

"But I'm worried," the man said. "They left yesterday morning to visit Bernard Groslier at the Preservation Commission and nobody's seen them since."

For a brief moment, Kutchaï's enormous hand holding his glass of cognac-and-soda halted midway to his mouth.

"Not since yesterday morning?"

That made more than thirty hours.

"That's right. Not since yesterday around eleven-thirty or twelve."

"And you're certain they haven't come back?"

Kutchaï impassively finished his cognac, thanked his friend, promised to come back to have dinner with him some day soon, and got behind the wheel of the plantation Land-Rover. The Temple Preservation Commission of the École Française d'Extrême-Orient had its headquarters four kilometers from Siem Reap and two kilometers from Angkor Wat. Kutchaï stopped there for only a few minutes, just long enough to verify that the teacher's information had been correct.

Just as he was leaving, someone remarked, "It could be that they headed directly southeast to rejoin the road to Phnom Penh."

"Of course," Kutchaï said. "They might have gone back that way."

He drove to the Auberge des Temples and left his car there. He set out on foot, avoiding the paved road that led directly to Angkor Thom, seeking instead the cover and the shade of the trees. He made rapid headway, without running and without the slightest sound, all his senses on the alert, sniffing the stifling hot air, the pupils of his huge black eyes wide open.

There was not a soul in sight on the great esplanade of Bayon. He made his way along the edge of it without stepping out onto it, carefully avoiding venturing into terrain where there was no cover. A little farther on he reached the forest clearing opposite the Elephant Terrace that constitutes the great open square of Angkor Thom; Phimeanakas and Baphuon to the left, Prah Pithu on the far side, the two Kléangs to the right. Here, too, there was not a soul in sight. A city forever dead, for centuries now, completely silent in the filtered sunlight. The temples left Kutchaï indifferent and had never interested him; it rather surprised him that anyone could attach any great importance to them, and he found it even more surprising that anyone could find them beautiful. All he could see in them were stones set one atop the other for no good reason, by distant ancestors he wasn't even sure were his.

He hesitated. Should he continue straight on, passing in front of the Leper King, in the direction of the Great Circuit? Or should he veer off to his right, in the direction of the Gate of the Dead?

He chose the second solution, since that route would afford him better cover.

Some twelve hundred yards farther on, he discovered the first tire tracks. According to the teacher in Siem Reap, Roger and the Englishman had been in an old Peugeot 403 that one of the French teachers at the local high school had sold just before he returned to France. Kutchaï remembered having seen the vehicle. And these tire tracks he had spotted might well have been the Peugeot's. He followed them, more and more alert now.

He crossed the river leading to Siem Reap about one kilometer south of the Chausaÿ bridge, so that he was now on the other side of the road, directly opposite the entrance to the Ta Prohm. Again, almost invisible on the hard dry ground, the same tire traces as before. Extremely reluctant to venture out into the bright sunlight beating down on the paved road of the Lesser Circuit, he waited almost forty minutes in the frightful heat, hidden in a roadside ditch, not moving a muscle and on the alert for the slightest telltale sound, breath, odor.

He finally screwed up his courage, crossed the road in a few swift strides, scaled like a shadow the outermost wall surrounding the temple complex, glided into the unbelievable jumble of kapok-tree roots, toppled stones, and partially ruined galleries, a number of which had been blocked off by the archaeologists and posted with threatening signs warning people to keep out.

He spied the car.

Once again he took his time, with unfailing animal patience. At length he drew closer, stirring not a single leaf as he passed. But the car was empty, as was all the area around it, although its four tires had been punctured.

He slipped into the temple itself then, allowing the wide-open pupils of his eyes to adjust to the almost total darkness inside. He stole from gallery to gallery, from cell to cell, obliged at times to step across what appeared to be bottomless black holes, with something writhing and slithering in their depths, making his way along nearly doubled over so as to get through doorways scarcely four feet high, his shoulders and head brushing against living ceilings formed by thousands of sleeping bats hanging suspended, awaiting the night and quivering in the half-light like rustling silk. The powerful, almost intoxicating odor of rot and stones decaying in the damp air enveloped him like a sort of fog.

He came upon the Englishman first—or what remained of him. The mouth of his fat, chubby-cheeked face was gaping open, his eyes bulged out of their sockets, and a monstrous column of insects was already at work on the arms and legs smashed to a bloody pulp.

Roger lay ten yards farther on.

At first Kutchaï was unable to see his face. The plastic sack covering it had been left in place, no doubt because they had decided it couldn't be used again. The plastic was smeared with a stomach-turning pus, and Kutchaï thought he could imagine what had happened when Roger's crushed hands had ridiculously attempted to tear it away.

Kutchaï loosened the thin cords looped around Roger's neck, not tightly enough to strangle him, their sole purpose being to prevent air from getting into the sack. He uncovered the face. For a long moment he remained squatting on his heels contemplating it, unable to tear his eyes away from the familiar features, on which there was not the slightest expression of horror, anger, or even fear. Lying there dead, almost smiling, Roger Bouès seemed merely to be sleeping. Except that his eyes were wide open, still eerily filled with life, and hard as he tried, Kutchaï could not manage to close his eyelids.

Kutchaï thought of Lara. And his big spatulate fingers trembled.

He finally took Roger's body in his arms, insensible to the horrible sight of flesh reduced to a pulp with splinters of bone sticking out and the unbearable stench of rotting meat. Rescuing him from the army of ants, he picked him up and carried him for five or six hundred yards to the river, plunging into it, completely immersing the corpse and washing himself clean.

He took off his shirt and tore it into strips with which he tied the body to a fallen tree trunk, and taking advantage of the thin stream of water flowing past—it was because the Stung Siem Reap never ran completely dry that centuries earlier the ancient Khmers had built their first capital here—he set his improvised raft afloat as best he could. It took him four hours to traverse the six kilometers that separated him from Siem Reap, where he handed Roger's body over to a French priest who had lived there all his life.

He then sought out again his friend the teacher, who was terrified by the look on his face, and with almost no word of explanation Kutchaï downed one glass of cognac after another, finishing two bottles. Even so he did not mange to pass out.

He kept thinking of Lara. Lara alone.

✿   ✿   ✿

On February 2, 1971, Kutchaï returned to Phnom Penh.

He noted the first signs of what was eventually to become a veritable migration toward the capital. In the first months of the war the movement had been exactly the opposite: People had fled Phnom Penh to escape conscription, or out of fear of the Khmer Krom units that had been responsible for the massacre just outside the city the year before, on March 29, or else simply in obedience to that atavistic reflex that causes a Khmer in difficulty, for whatever reason, to head immediately for the forest.

But in Phnom Penh the exodus had soon slackened and little by little people had returned en masse to the city, or were at least beginning to do so. The inconveniences of the general mobilization were admittedly constant and real (over the months Lon Nol's army had increased in size from 30,000 to 140,000 men), but after all, being in uniform did not necessarily mean being obliged to fight to one's last drop of blood—or even to the first, for that matter. There was always the possibility of deserting and of quietly stealing back home after selling one's rifle. The going price being paid for an M-14 was now 2,000 riels, and an M-16 would bring heaven only knew how much—but unfortunately not everyone was issued one.

These inconveniences were luckily very largely compensated for by multiple advantages: Phnom Penh was beginning to become almost as amusing a city as Saigon. The American Army had of course been officially withdrawn—after being a "presence" in the country for only two months—to the great disappointment, indeed the despair, of hordes of pimps and madams who had been beside themselves with joy on seeing them arrive. But the military advisers of all the countries belonging to SEATO (the Southeast Asia Treaty Organization) were still around, and that made a goodly number of customers, Buddha be praised. And there were journalists still around as well, all of them convinced they were doing *the* job of reporting of the century, or at the very least of their careers: "I am writing at this moment in the heart of a city under siege. . . ." The thrill of a lifetime. And pawing the Chinese whore with a touch of Khmer blood, just enough to give her skin a dark velvet sheen and endow the celestial breed with the ample breasts it did not always have if not mixed with other strains. "I am writing at this moment in the heart of a city under siege. . . ." There were approximately a hundred and fifty of them who seized upon this lead sentence with voluptuous delight.

The mass exodus had also become a mass return because the situation was growing more and more risky outside the cities. You risked getting killed, for one thing, if you happened to find yourself in the midst of a battle between Giap's men on the one hand and those of Khieu and Lon Nol on the other. Or underneath American planes launching bombs and napalm. But that wasn't all: People were gradually discovering that a strictly Khmer resistance movement, aimed at overthrowing Lon Nol and based in the forest, was bending all its efforts to establish an implacable organization that made one's blood run cold. Though it was not yet common knowledge that it was called the Angkar Loeu, the Organization from Up Above, the effects of its inexorable progress were already beginning to be felt....

Kutchaï brought the Korvers the news of Roger Bouès' death. He was well aware of the long-standing, almost paternal friendship that Charles and Madeleine had had with Roger, and had expected them to be grief-stricken. But the Korvers greeted the news almost with indifference.

"Who killed him? Government troops, the Viet Cong, or the Khmer Rouge?" Charles asked.

"The Khmer Rouge. But what difference does that make?"

Charles nodded in agreement. "You're absolutely right. It really makes no difference whatsoever. Do you know if he died a painful death?"

"Yes," Kutchaï answered simply.

"Have you had dinner?" Madeleine asked in her piping little-girl voice.

Kutchaï replied that he had, thank you. His gaze traveled from one to the other of these two elderly people. It seemed to him that they had in fact aged very little since he had last seen them, and yet they struck him as having changed radically; they had always been tiny, frail creatures, but now they were diaphanous, their complexions lighter and lighter, the skin of their faces and hands as pale as translucent wax. On arriving at their villa, Kutchaï had found them playing gin rummy, sitting opposite each other in their far too large living room, where a film of dust, for the first time in nearly forty years, slightly dimmed the luster of the statuettes and of the hundreds of objets d'art that covered every inch of the occasional pieces and the shelves against the walls.

"You don't have any servants left?"

"We have Yuan, that cook you found for us. He's very nice and very neat, and his wife is too. But the poor things don't have very deft hands, and after they inadvertently broke two or three little things, we thought it best not to ask them to dust anymore. Oh, please don't scold him, whatever you do! The two of them do the very best they can, you know."

"I'm going to try to find you somebody else."

"There's no use going to the trouble," Charles said. "Really not."

"We're certain you've a thousand things more important to do," Madeleine said, tilting her head with its blue locks.

"Do you have any news of Lara and Lisa? And of the baby? What's his name again? Oh yes, Mathias! How's Mathias?" they asked him, almost in chorus.

Kutchaï answered that they were all fine and the Korvers nodded, pleased to hear it.

"They're still in Bangkok," Kutchaï added, "and I'm fairly certain that Lisa's expecting another baby."

"Really? Do you know when she's expecting it?"

"In June or July, I think."

Sitting there in that living-room museum where time stood still, he looked immense and terribly alive, from another time, another world than Charles and Madeleine.

"Why don't you go to Bangkok?" he asked them.

They stared at him as though he had suggested they go to the moon.

"And leave our house? No, thank you very much," Madeleine replied.

"We won't leave here ever again," Charles said firmly. "When did you last see Lara and Lisa?"

"Last July."

"And . . . they haven't been back since?"

Kutchaï shook his head. A thoughtful look came into Charles' eye.

"I didn't think Lara would ever leave here."

"He hasn't left," Kutchaï answered.

A silence. Kutchaï started for the door.

"For my part I think they'd be better off staying in Bangkok," Madeleine said. "Far better off. You ought to tell them so."

Kutchaï didn't bat an eye. When he had entered the room, the Korvers had politely laid their gin-rummy hands face down on the bridge table's green baize cover. He surmised that the moment he'd left they'd go on playing. *And they'll keep on playing to the end of time,* Kutchaï thought to himself. He realized at that moment how self-absorbed and withdrawn Charles and Madeleine had become. If he had announced to them that Lara and Lisa were dead, they would doubtless have wept, but wept fewer tears than they would have six months before. *They've reached the point where they're hardly even here,* he thought.

"I'll come back and see you. The next time I'm in Phnom Penh."

They nodded in unison, each with the same polite bob of the head and the same absent expression; it was almost as though they couldn't wait for him to leave.

"Give Lisa and Mathias a big hug for us when you see them. And Lara too, of course."

He nodded and left. Nearly all the neighboring villas were deserted, abandoned by their occupants, who had fled Cambodia. Some of them had obviously been looted; doors stood wide open, untended gardens were being overrun with weeds, and the echo of his footsteps resounded in an eerie silence. *The end of a world,* Kutchaï thought with complete indifference. Just as he was about to get back into the Land-Rover, he spied Yuan, the Korvers' Cambodian cook, at the end of the street. Kutchaï looked like a giant standing in the middle of the street waiting for him.

"Listen to me," he said to Yuan. "Listen to me carefully. I want you to look after them. If something happens to them, if you leave them in the lurch, you'll have me to deal with. I'll find you, wherever you are, and I'll cut off your head. Do you understand, Yuan?"

"Yes, I understand," he answered. He would no doubt have been less afraid of a cobra sitting on his chest.

Kutchaï was almost a foot taller than he was. His huge hand reached out and patted Yuan on the head.

"That's good," Kutchaï said.

Kutchaï had various ways of getting messages to and from Christiani. The surest way was obviously via the embassy of the People's Republic of China, and he had already used that route several times; another was to take advantage of the mysterious, long-established communications network set up by Chinese traders and traffickers and maintained despite the vicissitudes of war; a third was to use his own network, an even more discreet one, which had taken him more than two years of patient work to organize; and finally, there was Boudin's plane.

As a result, the message sent by the Corsican reached him via three different routes. It came more or less in answer to the news concerning Roger Bouès' death, and read: "Robinson 3." "Robinson" was their code name for Sré, and "3" meant February 3. The fact that the message was not signed "Christiani" indicated that it was Lara himself who had arranged for them to rendezvous there.

That didn't give Kutchaï much time. He made some rapid calculations. Going directly to Kompong Som via the American Highway was more than risky, and at that particular juncture it would be sheer madness to try to get through. He could surely get to the Gulf of Siam by slipping through the combat zone disguised as a peasant; it was a feat he'd managed many times in the course of the preceding months, but there wasn't time enough for that now. That left Boudin's plane. He set out to look for him.

The Strasbourg Sausage was making a fortune these days and flying a brand-new Cessna 180 of his very own, plus being part owner, along with Chinese and Corsicans, of two others.

"Clear out of here!" Boudin yelled. "Flying you anywhere is out of the question. I've just gotten back. I'll shoot you down like a dog if you don't get the hell out of here!"

One of Kutchaï's hands reached out, gripped the irascible pilot's wrist, and took the Colt away from him. His other hand followed, grabbed Boudin by his shirt collar, lifted him up, and held him against the wall with his feet flailing the air a good eighteen inches off the ground.

"Sometimes you annoy me," Kutchaï said with his terrifying wolf's smile.

"I'll kill you," Boudin growled.

Kutchaï's enormous spatulate fingers tightened their grip around his throat just slightly.

"Kutchaï! Kutchaï!"

The fingers loosened their hold.

"We'll be leaving tomorrow morning at four A.M."

Boudin's tongue was sticking out between his teeth. He slid slowly down the wall and his feet touched the ground again.

"Good God, whatever got into you? You very nearly killed me!"

"Not really," Kutchaï said with his silent laugh. "You're imagining things."

"At four A.M., you say? And where is it we're going?"

"Kompong Som."

"I don't even know where the damned landing field is there."

"You'll set down on the roof of a hut. You could land on top of a coconut palm if necessary. And we both know it. Four A.M."

Boudin rubbed his throat. "Can't you take a joke?" he said. "Is it something to do with Lara? Why didn't you tell me so straight off? You need only have said it was for him. I'd have understood."

Kutchaï put his forefinger on the Alsatian's chest and gave him a poke. "See you tomorrow morning."

He then went to see Ieng Samboth's mother, who lived in a little wooden house just beyond the Silver Pagoda. He spoke to her for several minutes, with his head bowed respectfully and his palms joined at the level of his lips, and when he left he slipped five thousand riels into her hand. He then went back into the center of town and stopped in briefly at the Zigzag. Albert Vandekherkove recognized him the moment he came in and insisted on standing him to his first cognac-and-soda.

"Nobody's seen Lara around for some time," Albert remarked.

"Oh, is that so?" Kutchaï replied noncommittally.

He had two cognac-and-sodas and left again, paying no attention to the three or four Filipino sailors who were anxious to pick a fight with him for some reason only they knew. He then went to the hut near the stadium where he slept when he was in Phnom Penh and where he had a wife and three or four children. He left some money there too. He went to bed, dropping off to sleep immediately even though it was still daylight outside, and despite the din all around him—women chattering, children squealing.

Without need of an alarm clock, he opened his eyes again at two-thirty A.M. He climbed into the Land-Rover and headed for Pochentong Airport, eating, as he drove along, big hunks of his favorite delicacy, *an sam chruk*, a fat roll of sticky rice filled with soybean cake and little bits of pork; it was the specialty of his wife in Phnom Penh and she always added little bits of pineapple and even banana to it. To tell the truth, a person needed a stomach like an ostrich's to digest more than a small helping of it. According to legend, *an sam chruk* had been invented by Buddha himself: Noting that the first woman and the first man on what at the time was virgin earth hadn't even thought of getting together and had no idea how to go about cozying up to each other, Buddha had gotten out his recipe book, made a roll of *an sam chruk,* and suggested to the couple that they eat it, each beginning at one end. Mr. First Man and Ms. First Woman had met in the middle, and whammo! humanity was born.

Boudin was there waiting at Pochentong, muttering something unintelligible but most likely disagreeable. The Cessna took off at four A.M., greeted a few moments later by salvos from Viet Cong in the front lines who were being just a touch overoptimistic as to the range of their weapons.

At Kompong Som, on the other hand, just as dawn was beginning to break, everything was calm.

"And what do I do now?" Boudin asked, in a voice filled with hatred, the moment he'd switched off the ignition.

"You shut your trap and wait. We'll meet again at the state inn."

"I had work to do today in Phnom Penh."

"You have work to do in Kompong Som."

Kutchaï was obliged to awaken Weï from a sound sleep. But the Chinese understood the situation instantly.

"I have two boats, a big one and a small one."

"Which is faster?"

"The smaller one. It really flies over the water."

Kutchaï nodded. "That one."

Weï seemed relieved. "You can handle it all by yourself. I would have had to find you a crew for the other one."

The one-man craft in question was a sleek motorboat with two 100-horsepower engines. It had been imported into Cambodia for use on the Tonle Sap and the Mekong to tow water-skiers, but the war had broken out and it had remained on the dock where it had been unloaded; Liu had bought it very cheaply. Weï filled the tank all the way to the top and put several spare cans of fuel aboard as well. He explained how the controls worked. At approximately 4:40 A.M., Kutchaï set a course for Kas Rong and, once beyond it, for Sré, keeping well clear of the Cheko Peninsula. The sea was calm and beautiful, with patches of light fog here and there, and it was barely daylight.

There was no one on Sré and no sign that anyone had been there recently. Kutchaï made the rounds of the entire island, closely inspecting everything and making certain everything was all right. The sampan-junk was snugly anchored in its sort of rocky sheath, carefully covered with its camouflage net, so that it was impossible to spot unless it was right under one's nose. Kutchaï continued his inspection: The house was clean and in perfect order; Seng had obviously come there regularly, and doubtless the cook had gone off for a while to the mainland, thanks to the Malay fishermen, rather than staying all alone on the island.

As this thought crossed his mind, Kutchaï glanced over at the mainland through the curtain of trees. The Cheko Peninsula was directly opposite him. He noticed a column of smoke, much too thick and high to be coming from a mere campfire. He hadn't seen it as he was crossing over to the island in the motorboat, but he remembered that at the time fog had hidden most of the coast from sight. He decided that American planes must have dropped napalm at one point or another before he arrived on the scene and set fire to a few acres of forest. It worried Kutchaï for a brief moment, but the next minute, as he looked once again at the peninsula on the horizon, he noted that the smoke was gradually dissipating and finally it disappeared altogether.

He went down into the cellar and methodically checked the provisions stored there. Although some of them had been affected by the dampness, in general the food reserves were in good condition, enough to enable those on the island to hold out for several months.

He refilled the fuel tank of the generator with kerosene and started it up again. Thus there was cooled beer on hand when, an hour later, one of Christiani's cruisers appeared on the horizon, approaching from the northwest.

Lara was aboard. And Lisa was with him, her face completely expressionless, obviously fighting hard to control an icy anger.

2

THE CHEKO PENINSULA IS QUITE ISOLATED FROM THE REST OF CAMBO-dia, being hemmed in on one side by the Gulf of Siam and on the other by the great mountainous barrier formed by the Elephant, Kirirom, and Cardamome ranges, which cut it off from any major means of communication with the east except for the American Highway threading through the narrow gap of Phnom Pich Pass. It encircles the northern end of the bay of Kompong Som, and rises to form two slight peaks, one broader than the other, each of them only a few hundred meters above sea level. The Khmer Rouge base was located on the slopes of the peak farther west.

At first glance, Kao didn't see a thing.

"Lower down," the scout said. "A little to the left and below that cluster of rocks that looks like a herd of wild cattle."

From a distance of twelve hundred yards or so, Kao's powerful field glasses finally revealed a slight movement, and the usual excitement of the hunt flooded through him, causing him almost to tremble.

"They've dug in," the scout said. "We can move still closer to them if you like. We've been able to creep up so close to them that we could hear them talking together."

"There's no point in that," Kao replied. And he thought to himself, *It's not going to be all that difficult.* He almost regretted that fact. He didn't like it when his prey enabled him to take it too easily. What proof was that of a hunter's skill?

After a moment, Kao raised his field glasses and swept the horizon in a vast arc of more than 180 degrees, starting from the port of Kompong Som within his direct line of sight to the left, then examining one by one each island, some of them just tiny dots strung out like beads of a rosary a few kilometers off the coast, and ending his inspection off to his right, in the direction of Koh Por Krom. Most of these islands were said to be uninhabited. For the first time since he had learned of their existence, he began to wonder if this were true. Through an association of ideas, it occurred to him that for months now he had not seen the Malay fishermen who had lived along the coast since time immemorial.

He would perhaps have followed the vague intuition taking shape in his mind to its logical conclusion, except that the scout who was with him asked a question that brought him back to the immediate reality before him: the engagement of the enemy that he was about to embark upon and the splendid butchery he hoped would result from it.

"What time is the attack scheduled to begin?" the scout asked.

"At twenty hundred hours tonight."

That is to say, the night of February 2, 1971.

Kao had said, "You'll see the massacre from up here, Phan, my boy. Feast your eyes."

Phan saw. In the gathering darkness, the fearful yellow-orange flames of the napalm leapt into the sky and a sound something like hissing moans came to him above the regular chatter of submachine guns and all the other automatic weapons spitting fire at the same time. The burning vegetation lit up ignoble crawling things, the bodies of men writhing and rolling on the ground, caught by the tongues of flaming napalm and trying desperately to put out the fire searing their sticky oil-covered flesh.

This lasted for several minutes, after which the line of troops laying down an impenetrable barrage of machine-gun fire or napalm began to move forward. Little by little the distance separating this line of fire from the crest where Phan stood diminished until it was barely two hundred yards away. A few minutes more went by and then the firing ceased.

"Phan!"

Kao's voice.

"Yes, sir."

"Did that please you, Phan? Did you like that? Go down there with your men now. Spread out and search each nook and cranny in the rocks. Don't let a single soul escape. Do you understand, Phan? Not a single soul!"

Thanks to the trees set on fire by the napalm, it was still nearly as bright as day even though night had fallen.

They found a whole series of hideouts, linked together by hand-dug tunnels just large enough to permit one body to wriggle through. A few grenades and more dazzlingly bright napalm torches forced out the last occupants: ten women and two children, whom they herded together with the twenty-some Khmer Rouge who had surrendered, almost all of them because they had been wounded.

"Make a count, Phan. The dead and the living."

They continued to search the terrain. They found a miscellaneous collection of arms, the majority of them Kalashnikovs of Chinese manufacture. A little farther on, they came across a hundred or so cans of gasoline, probably stolen from somewhere around the port.

It took Suon Phan only a few seconds to realize what Kao was going to do with this gasoline. He tried to intervene. "I beg you . . ."

"No survivors," Kao said. "Get the hell out of here."

Phan went off, climbed back to the top of the crest, crossed it, and sat down facing the sea. He sat there contemplating its dim, milky phosphorescence, unable to stifle the deep sobs that were making his chest heave, without knowing exactly what it was he was weeping for: for himself, who just that day had turned twenty; for a Cambodia that was dying; or simply for the great barbecue fire he was expecting to see flame up at any second, able already to smell the hideous odor from it and hear the screams that were going to fill the air. And in fact it flamed up a few moments later, even more atrocious than he had imagined, giving off an indescribable stench.

The barbecue fire of which nothing was left in the morning except a towering column of smoke, the very one that Kutchaï, inspecting Sré, spied on the following day.

"Phan!"

Someone was shaking him by the shoulder. He opened his eyes and recognized Chau, one of the Khmer Krom officers second in command after Kao.

"Yes."

"Kao wondered what had happened to you."

Phan stood up, His cheek and his entire right side were numb. He had fallen asleep on his rifle and ached all over.

"Kao wants us to finish searching the hill. He thinks there may be other caches," Chau said.

Phan nodded, still too sleepy even to think of arguing. He discovered that it was barely light; in fact dawn had just broken on this morning of February 3, 1971. It was around five-thirty. He took a look out over the sea. From where he was, at about a thousand feet above sea level, he saw a great stretch of water as smooth as a mirror, with delicate wisps of fog hovering just above the surface, leaving gaps here and there as clouds do. To his left was Kas Rong and opposite him, at a distance of approximately four kilometers, dimly silhouetted in the faint light of this dawn, other smaller islands.

"You coming or not?"

He was about to turn around when something caught his eye: a sort of large triangle, with perfectly regular sides, standing out clearly above the surface of the sea in one of the spots where the water was visible amid the wisps of fog, and growing bigger by the minute as it came toward him.

"What's that?" he asked in a dull voice.

Chau had field glasses hanging around his neck. He raised them to his eyes and gave a yelp of surprise.

"Go get Kao! Quick! He wanted us to report any boat movements. And that's a boat!"

Several minutes went by before Kao located in the double circle of the field glasses the outline of the sleek motorboat cleaving the water, because three quarters of the time the fog hid it from sight. But from the moment he finally spotted it, he never once let it out of his sight.

"One of those motorboats like the ones they used to have at the Club Nautique. The Barangs used them to go water-skiing. Have you ever gone water-skiing, Phan?"

"No, sir."

Kao laughed, but his eyes were ice-cold. His face was drawn with fatigue after a sleepless night, a sleepless night spent avidly watching gasoline-drenched men, women, and children burning to death.

A few moments earlier, they'd brought Phan some rice seasoned with *prahoc* and rolled in a banana leaf; but at the very first mouthful the young man nearly vomited, already sick to his stomach from the hideous smell that still floated in the air and seemed to have impregnated him.

Kao's eyes were still following the motorboat. "It's really flying along. I wonder where it's going. There's only one man in it."

After three or four minutes he rose to his feet, disappointed. The boat had definitely disappeared, swallowed up by the fog; at one moment it had seemed to be heading toward a small island, and no doubt was passing behind it on the seaward side. Kao waited patiently for it to reappear. Nothing. Finally he gave an order. Among the men in the commando unit, Chau looked for and found someone who knew that section of the coast. He brought him to Kao, who asked him the name of that island in particular.

"Sré," the man said. "It's deserted. The only people who ever go there are Malays fishing for shark. But they don't stay there."

"We'll wait," Kao said.

And that was how they happened to see the cabin cruiser arrive, approaching from the north. It proceeded around to the far side of the island, remained invisible for some twenty minutes, then reappeared and headed out to sea on a course straight west.

"Do you see what's going on?" Kao asked Phan.

Kao's eyes were gleaming despite his fatigue and he was wildly excited. He was certain that the rendezvous he had just been witness to bore some relationship to the presence of the Khmer Rouge camp he had just destroyed on this hill on the Cheko Peninsula.

"Chau, you stay here. If the motorboat leaves, if other boats approach, note it down. Note everything down."

Kao left, almost at a run. His jeep was parked four kilometers away, as close to the spot where the engagement with the Khmer Rouge would be taking place as he could get it the evening before. He could alert Kompong Som on the jeep radio, and they would send someone out to the island to search it. That was one possibility. But there was another. He remembered the Malay fishermen. Their pirogues could take him out to the island, him and a few of his men.

He ran on, almost in sight of his jeep now. He hadn't yet made up his mind which of the two solutions he would choose.

3 "TELL ME ABOUT IT," LARA SAID.

From the moment their eyes had met, Kutchaï had known something was wrong, something not altogether due to Roger's death and perhaps having nothing at all to do with it. Christiani and his Malayan crew hadn't even set foot on land; their cruiser had spent twenty minutes at most anchored just off the island and then immediately set out to sea again. Kutchaï knew where it was going: On the following night, February 3–4, 1971, the Corsican, at the head of a veritable flotilla of similar cabin cruisers, was to meet a Japanese freighter whose hold was full of weapons, and the day after that these arms would be handed over to Ieng Samboth's men. Once Christiani had delivered the arms to them, he was to return to Sré, at dawn on the sixth. Then he would take Lara and Lisa back with him on the cruiser to Bangkok.

"There's not much to tell," Kutchaï said. "That Englishman he'd teamed up with always took incredible risks. They had to be out of their minds to go wandering around the temples like that. Everybody had warned them, the guys from France-Presse and from UPI, the photographer from Gamma, the people at the Preservation Commission. But there was no way to talk them out of going."

"What was the Englishman's name again?"

"Donaldson."

Lara nodded, his pale eyes staring off into space.

He's barely listening to what I'm saying, Kutchaï thought. "They ran into a band of guerrillas led by Rath."

This time Lara's eyes showed signs of life. He stiffened. "How do you know that?"

"Who's Rath?" Lisa asked.

"That it was Rath? I made inquiries," Kutchaï said in answer to Lara's question. "Some bonzes saw Roger and the Englishman go by. And two hours before that, they'd seen Rath. And they saw him again afterward. There's no question."

"Who's Rath?" Lisa asked again, a note of irritation in her voice.

Kutchaï turned his eyes toward her, hesitating to answer, preferring to leave that up to Lara. But Lara didn't say a word, absorbed once again in his own thoughts. *The two of them have had a fight,* Kutchaï said to himself. *A serious one.*

"Somebody we know," Kutchaï finally answered. "He never was one of our friends, and he's even less of one now."

"Where did it happen?" The question came this time from Lara.

"The whatdoyoucallit overrun by kapok roots, near the eastern *baraï.*" This was not a linguistic affectation on Kutchaï's part. He really did not know the names of most of the temples at Angkor.

"The Ta Prohm?"

Kutchaï nodded.

"Where are the bodies?"

"I took Roger back to Father Aguirre's in Siem Reap. As for the Englishman, it was the army that came to pick up his body."

Why did the two of them come back? Kutchaï was thinking. *Why didn't they stay in Bangkok?* Then he corrected himself: *No, the real question is, why did Lara come back?* That surely must have been what the fight was about: on the one hand Lara's stubborn determination to come back, if not to the mainland of Cambodia, at least to the island, and on the other hand Lisa's determination, equally if not more stubborn, not to return. Kutchaï looked closely at the young woman. There were now obvious signs that she was pregnant, and it was plain to see she was nervous, tired, furious. It was surely not Lara who had asked her to leave Bangkok; hence it was Lisa herself who had decided to accompany her husband, probably in order to force him by her mere presence, in the state she was in, to make his trip a short one and not linger along the way.

Kutchaï smiled at Lisa. "How's the future mother doing?"

"She's in great shape," Lisa answered, in a vaguely sarcastic tone.

"A boy or a girl this time?"

She shrugged. She was wearing a loose-fitting silk dress, the predominant color of which matched the violet of her eyes; she was literally breathtakingly beautiful. After a moment she rather reluctantly returned his smile.

"I'm happy to see you again," she said to him. "But were you really so busy you couldn't have come to visit us in Bangkok?"

"Kutchaï pool wletched Khmel wolk velly velly hard."

"You could have come all the same."

"You're right. I'm ashamed of myself."

"The Korvers?"

"I saw them just yesterday. They're still playing cards. They send you a big hug."

Up to that point, they hadn't gone any farther than the sand of the cove, facing the sea and not the mainland, where Christiani's cabin cruiser had dropped them off. But suddenly Lara strode off toward the house. After a few steps, however, he turned around, intending to help his wife along the steep narrow path that wound its way amid the rocks and the brush up to the palm grove in the center of the island. Lisa followed him, seeming not to see the hand he held out to her. Finally all three of them reached the veranda. Lisa sat down on a rattan bench and the two men remained standing, facing her.

"I started the generator up again," Kutchaï said. "Are you thirsty by any chance?"

No reply. Lara's face was set in an impassive, completely inscrutable expression that Kutchaï had seldom seen, but the Jaraï knew what it meant: a stubbornness, a force of will that no one could divert. *No one except this woman, who has tried and is still trying, and who is not someone who gives in easily either,* he thought.

"I'm going for a swim," Lara suddenly announced.

He didn't wait for a reply from his wife or from Kutchaï but strode off, removing his shirt as he went and heading for the southern tip of the island, their usual swimming spot. They caught a glimpse of the old scar on his bare shoulder. Kutchaï sat down on the veranda steps.

"Well, I imagine you've realized what's going on. Haven't you?"

Kutchaï ran his huge hand through his mop of black hair. "I don't know what's going on at all, Lisa."

He glanced in her direction, but there was a faraway look in her violet eyes.

"It's been going on for months," Lisa said. "Since the beginning, rather. There hasn't been one single day, one single minute without this problem between us, even though we pretended to shut our eyes to it. I've tried to understand—I've really tried. It's quite natural that he should be attached to this country; he was born here, and so was his father and all those generations before him. That's something not at all hard to understand, especially for an American like me whose forebears arrived in America long after the first Lara landed here. But the situation has changed now. The country is at war. We may be killed at any moment. And it's at war because . . ."

She paused for a second. "I'm American. Do you resent me because I'm American, Kutchaï?"

"You're talking nonsense now," Kutchaï said in a low voice, not realizing that he had gone back to addressing her in the formal *vous*.

A silence.

"This war may last for years and years," Lisa went on in a distant voice. "And I for my part want to live in a country at peace, where my children can grow up normally, go to school normally, cross a street normally. We've traveled a great deal during these last months. We've been in all sorts of marvelous places, but we've never set foot out of Asia. We've never talked of Cambodia during all that time, but I knew, of course, that he never stopped thinking of it. I knew that one day or another he'd bring up the subject of coming back here. I was expecting it and I shouldn't have been so taken by surprise. Day before yesterday, on receiving the news about Roger Boues' death, he told me that he was leaving with Christiani. What good was that going to do? Roger was dead. He answered that if he, Lara, had been in Cambodia, which he never should have left, Roger would no doubt still be alive. That's totally, monstrously absurd. I warned him; I swore to him that if he came back to Cambodia I would too, and that if he refused to take me there with him, as soon as he'd left I'd take a plane for Phnom Penh. If we're going to be absurd, let's be altogether absurd. But I didn't have any choice: It was either that or going home to the U.S., taking my son with me. I was ready to do that and I still am. This situation simply can't go on."

She fell silent for a few moments, and Kutchaï very nearly got up to go join Lara. But then she went on.

"I said horrible things to him that I'll regret for a long time, but they were true things, things I secretly think. I told him that the Cambodia he'd once known doesn't exist anymore, and that it never will again. I told him that there's no place for him here anymore. And he must choose now, right away: Cambodia or me. It's as simple, as stupid, as insane as that. But I won't give in. I can't give in, not anymore."

Kutchaï rose to his feet and stood there at the bottom of the four steps of black wood leading up to the veranda. Immediately alongside him, the hibiscus he himself had planted a year and a half earlier had grown amazingly, its branches intermingling with the bougainvillea spilling over the veranda railing, hiding it almost completely. A little lower down were cannas, and the frangipani that Lisa had wanted above all else, along with

jasmine, the same sort of jasmine whose flowers were fashioned into necklaces and bracelets sold by children, for a smile almost, in the markets of
Phnom Penh or on the terraces of the cafés.

"Oh, dear God!" Lisa said. "How can he not understand?"

Kutchaï stood there, not knowing exactly what to do. A minute earlier,
he would no doubt have joined Lara without the slightest hesitation. But
now he wasn't really certain what he ought to do, or even what he felt like
doing.

"Go on, go join him," Lisa said in a harsh voice. "What are you waiting
for?"

4 SUON PHAN MADE THE CROSSING IN THE SECOND PIROGUE ALONG
with three other men in the commando unit. He didn't feel particularly at
home on the water, his only previous experience aboard a boat having been
limited to two trips to Kratie on the big steamer plying the Mekong.
But once the first anxious moments were over, he had begun to enjoy the
crossing.

The Malays had proved strangely reluctant when Kao had demanded
they put themselves and their pirogues at his disposal. At first even the barrels of the M-16 rifles pointed at them had not been sufficient to persuade
them. It had been necessary to work them over, and thoroughly.

Trembling like a hunting dog scenting deer, Kao had left first, with
three of his men, his thin face tense. "I'm certain there's something or someone hidden on that island. I'm going to head right and go around to the
other side of it from the north. And you, Phan, are to head straight for it and
land on this side of it, facing the mainland. If you see a boat trying to make a
getaway, shoot first and ask questions afterward. If possible, take those trying to escape alive. If you can't, too bad for them."

The island was there ahead, two yards away. Phan leapt out onto the
shore. The pirogue carrying Kao had disappeared from sight behind the
northern tip of the island some minutes before.

Phan sank deep into the burning sand, which struck him as being even
finer than that at Kep, but of the same bright gold color and mingled with
the same tiny, sparkling particles of mica. Everything was completely silent, and though he listened attentively, he could hear no sound from Kao's
side of the island. The three men with Phan deployed in extended order.
Only the two Malays remained motionless, their faces impassive beneath
their black turbans, but when his eyes met theirs, Phan realized beyond
any doubt that indeed there was something hidden on the island, and they
knew it.

We're going to be spotted, he thought, nearly allowing himself to be carried away, like Kao, by the excitement of the chase.

After several yards of gently sloping beach the terrain rose abruptly, forming a veritable wall of dense vegetation, through which they found it rough going in the beginning. Phan was the first to get his rifle caught in it, and he almost fell. He had just recovered his balance when the characteristic reports of an M-16 rang out.

"Quick!"

He urged his men on and reached the top of the steep slope in one bound. A path appeared on his right. He took it on the run and came out in the middle of a palm grove where someone had hung marvelous embroidered hammocks with scalloped edgings and set up an immense rattan boat with a high pointed prow. He finally spied two of the men who had set out with Kao standing twenty yards away. Just to see them calmly standing there reassured him. *And there were only three shots,* he thought. He slowed down almost to a walk as he approached them.

"Who was it you were shooting at?"

Without a word they pointed to a great mass of hibiscus, bougainvillea, and jasmine, with the branches of a young frangipani making a still thicker screen of vegetation. It was then, and only then, that Phan spied the house, completely invisible until one came within a few yards of it.

"Where's Kao?"

He climbed up four steps, found himself on a veránda, and then saw, inside a huge room, Kao standing with the barrel of his M-16 pointing downward, Kao with the blood-spattered body of a young woman, quite plainly a white woman, lying at his feet, Kao who said: "Okay, I made a mistake. So what?"

The moment he heard the first of the three shots, Kutchaï leapt into action. Not the slightest doubt ever crossed his mind. It could only be Lisa they were shooting at. Or, worse still, Lara.

To reach the beach he'd been heading toward the second before, he would have to scale the tall rocks covering the last few yards, or else wade out into the water and go around them. And then he heard Lara's footsteps on his left, breaking into a run on the path leading up from the southern tip of the island to the house. A second of instinctive relief: *It wasn't Lara they'd been shooting at!* And the very next second: *But he's going to get himself killed!* He plunged like a madman through the vegetation cutting him off from the path, and lost time disentangling himself from the brush. When he came out onto the path, Lara was already a long way ahead of him. He rushed after him.

He heard Lara call out to his wife. Then, he, too, bolted into the palm grove. He saw Lara there, and Lon Nol's soldiers leaping on him, hitting him, knocking him to the ground, overpowering him. Shouting in murder-

ous fury, Kutchaï almost literally flew over the last few yards. He flung his
vast bulk upon the six men, hit to kill, crush, grind to bits. The first bullet hit
him in the thigh, sending him crashing to the ground. He got up again, returned to the attack, smashed a throat with a backhand blow, was hit in the
upper back by a second bullet, and a third somewhere around his hip. He
fell again and managed once more to get to his feet despite a blow from a
rifle butt that grazed his skull. He hit out, received another blow, and then
someone thrust a rifle barrel into his mouth and down his throat.

"One more move and you're dead."

He froze, his eyes blazing with rage, his huge hands clawing the
ground, his jaws yawning open as though to bite; terrifying.

A sudden calm.

A young officer with a boyish face came running out of the house toward them. "Who else is on this island?"

Despite the two M-16 rifle barrels thrust into his chest pinning him to
the ground, Lara moved.

"What have you done to my wife?"

"Who else?"

"I'll kill you," Lara said. "Where is she?"

"Answer my question first."

"There are only three of us here."

The officer hesitated, his adolescent face tense. "You can get up, providing you calm down. Okay? Your wife is in the house."

The moment he was free, Lara bolted off. The officer turned to Kutchaï, plainly impressed by this huge body contorted with rage and hatred.

"Don't try anything," he said. "I don't want to kill you. I really don't.
Cool it. Let him go," he ordered the men.

They let go of Kutchaï very warily, keeping their rifles trained on him
every second. Two of the soldiers were lying on the ground with broken
necks.

"Keep calm," the officer said.

"*Kutchaï!*" Lara's voice, calling from the house.

"Okay," the officer said. "But keep it nice and slow and easy. Or we'll
kill all of you."

Three of the soldiers followed Kutchaï as he entered the house and saw
Lisa lying on the floor. Lara's face was chalk-white, but so abnormally calm
that it was frightening.

"She's alive. She's got a bullet in her belly," Lara said. "We'll have to
take her to Kompong Som. Help me carry her."

"It was a mistake."

Kutchaï recognized the voice even before he recognized the face.

Kao was standing at the far end of the room, lurking in the dark with his back to the wall; the only things visible were the characteristic flat planes of his cheekbones and his gleaming eyes. But his assault rifle was aimed at them, his finger on the trigger.

"A simple error. I made a mistake, that's all."

"For God's sake, let's be quick about it!" Lara said.

They used one of the double doors as a stretcher. Outside, Kutchaï stumbled, his thigh and his chest streaming with blood. Thus far none of the soldiers had made the slightest move to help them carry Lisa. It was the young officer who made up his mind to give them a hand. He stepped forward, slinging his rifle over his shoulder.

"I'm going to help you."

"Get the hell out of here," Kutchaï said in a fierce animal snarl.

He managed to get to the motorboat, he too losing blood. He started the engine. It was only after they had put out to sea and were speeding madly away from the island that he took off his shirt and bound it around the worst of his wounds, the one in his upper back; the bullet must have perforated his lung. A pinkish froth was beginning to show at the corners of his mouth as he shouted to Lara, "Boudin at Kompong Som with his plane."

Lara turned his head in Kutchaï's direction for a brief moment. He was sitting with his face pressed to Lisa's, weeping.

The Cambodian doctor in Kompong Som, a young man of about thirty, shook his head. "Two bullets. But the wound in her abdomen is the only one that's serious, especially in view of her condition. I could operate on her but I'd prefer not to perform the operation myself. You have time to take her to Kompong Thom, but it appears that they're firing on the airport."

"And what about Bangkok?" Lara asked impassively.

The doctor shook his head again. "That means a flight of at least thirty to forty minutes more. But if she remains under perfusion . . ."

"Yes or no?" Lara was glacially calm.

"She'll make it."

Outside, plump little Weï was waiting, having even managed to find an ambulance. "I'll look after Kutchaï. And Boudin's ready to take off."

They flew out less than three minutes later.

Alerted by radio, an American Army helicopter was waiting in Bangkok to take them the rest of the way.

Lara telephoned the Haywards from the hospital to tell them the news.

5

PETER HAYWARD HAD BEEN BORN IN INDIA, IN LAHORE, AND IT WAS HIS considered opinion that in order to be at all interesting, every man ought to have had at least one Great Adventure in his past. What he meant by Great Adventure wasn't very clear. According to him, it might be a question of setting up a factory to turn out trouser buttons and making a success of it; or a grand passion, preferably with a tragic ending; or a glorious war, providing that one came out of it alive; or being Rembrandt, for example (he conceded that this was not within the range of every man's possibilities), and applying the last brushstroke to "The Night Watch."

As far as he himself was concerned, he maintained that he had had two Great Adventures in his life: his participation in the Burma campaign under the command of the celebrated General Wingate, firstly, and secondly the fact that he had been personally present in India and in Pakistan at each and every crucial moment of their struggle for independence. He had even photographed Mahatma Gandhi five seconds before he was assassinated (though unfortunately somebody had stepped on a corn on one of his toes at the very second Gandhi was murdered, so that as a result he hadn't seen a thing). Before that and after that, according to him, nothing worthy of note had ever happened to him, save for having had mumps at the age of seven and having received a ticket for being parked illegally the one time in his life he had visited London. But he willingly admitted that the two latter events were perhaps a trifle less spectacular than the other two.

As for Lara, Peter did not share his wife's opinion of him. Jodie Hayward found Lara madly attractive: secretive, mysterious, handsome, romantic, but as cold as an Eskimo who'd forgotten to put on his long johns before going outside for a bit of air. "Lara's polite and considerate, amazingly cultivated for a rubber planter, with a good sense of humor. His eyes are as fascinating as he himself is, and in a word, if I were just a bit younger, let's say six months younger"—Jodie was fifty-two at the time—"it would take a crane and a battalion of paratroopers to get me out of his bed. But marry him! Good gracious! Lisa must have been out of her mind!"

About Lara's irresistible romantic charms, Peter Hayward did not venture an opinion. But beneath Lara's unfailing reserve, that reserve that might well appear to be indifference, Peter had discerned, almost at first glance, a violent, desperate, total passion, a passion that Peter could understand. He himself had suffered the tortures of the damned the day that the India of Kipling, of his youth, had ceased to exist, though at the same time he had recognized the fact that this turn of events was at once logical and inevitable. He had indeed felt such pain that he had finally left India, though nothing had really forced him to do so. He had settled first in Ceylon, and soon afterward in Thailand, as a bitter last resort to which he would never wholly reconcile himself. Twenty-one years had gone by since without his ever once setting foot on Indian soil again, despite the fact that it was only a short distance away. How could he have failed to understand Lara, and what Jodie called "his madly stubborn determination to stay on there amid those savage Khmers, no matter what"?

Peter respected Lara, admired him, and beyond question looked on him as a close friend. Though Peter was a good twenty years older, he thought of Lara as an alter ego, with a strength, a singlemindedness, a tenacity that to his regret he himself had never had. "Whereas I left what I considered my country, overcome with self-pity, he wants to stay on in his country. And God knows that things in Cambodia are far different from what they were in India when I left."

As for Lisa, there too he and his wife had very different opinions. For his part he did not see her as a victim. When she had married Lara, she had no doubt known exactly what she was up against, and he regarded her as being quite capable, if need be, of standing her ground just as obstinately as Lara.

But all that was before the dramatic events that had taken place on the island of Sré. That drama, and above all its consequences, had reinforced his convictions. He had sized up the situation correctly, but felt no gloating self-satisfaction at having done so. In all truth, it pained him to have seen things so clearly.

One of the two bullets that had hit Lisa had killed the child she had been carrying for over four months. This was the first question she asked as she came out of the anaesthesia after the operation, even before she thought to ask where she was. It was plainly impossible to hide the truth from her. Lara himself answered her question. She closed her eyes again and did not say a word for a few moments.

"And what about you?"

"I wasn't hurt at all."

"Kutchaï?"

"Who's ever going to be able to kill Kutchaï?"

She lowered her eyelids again, and then, with her eyes closed, asked in the same even tone of voice, "Who were those men?"

"Officially, regular army troops. They shot you by mistake."

He explained to her what had happened.

"So then I'm in Bangkok now," she said.

Until that moment, Lisa had not noticed that Jodie Hayward was also there in her hospital room, and that was what struck Jodie most of all: her almost total lack of reaction.

"And what about Mathias?"

"There's no reason for you to worry about him at all," Lara answered slowly. His tone of voice was dull, fainter than usual, but the expression on his face was perfectly calm.

"Hi there, Lisa," Jodie said.

Lisa turned her head and gave her a wan smile. "It's so nice of you to have come."

"Mathias wasn't on the island, remember," Lara added.

Later, recounting the scene at the hospital, Jodie Hàyward emphasized the importance, as she saw it, of these last words of Lara's. "They're a proof at least of how responsible he feels for everything that happened," she explained to Peter. "He feels guilty. That's something anyway, but it's not enough. Did you know it's not at all certain that Lisa can ever have another child? That's awful, just awful. If I were in Lisa's place . . ."

"But you're not in Lisa's place."

She shrugged, annoyed at such a feeble argument.

On leaving the hospital, Lisa went directly to the villa in Chulakong-korn. Peter Hayward had the impression that she had put off as long as possible the moment when she would find herself all alone with her husband. In any event, however, she recovered quickly from her wounds. She went out for the first time at the end of March, he remembered later, to attend a cocktail party given by the representatives of UNESCO in Thailand, and spent the evening, constantly aided, supported, and protected by Jodie, who acted as a minesweeper clearing the way for an aircraft carrier. (The two women had very different builds: Jodie was as short and plump as Lisa was tall and slender.) After the cocktail party, the Laras, the Haywards, and an American couple, the Greens, went to have dinner together at the Normandie, the terrace-restaurant of the Hotel Oriental, from which one had a splendid view of the sampans on the *menam* and the Temple of the Dawn.

The first time Peter and Jodie had met Lisa, she had just come from that two to three months' stay on the paradisiacal island in the Gulf of Siam; she had gotten herself a beautiful tan, which made her extraordinary violet eyes seem even more striking. Her stay in Bangkok and then in the hospital had made her lose the tan, but in Peter Hayward's view that was no great loss. In fact, he found her more beautiful than ever, and what was more, he was not the only one.

To Freddy Green, Lisa Lara was the prettiest young woman in all of Southeast Asia, or even in California and the entire Far East, and no doubt east of the Rockies as well. Freddy Green, a producer who was in Bangkok supervising the making of a film—a spy story with a superhero based on a script that Peter couldn't make head or tail of—said to Peter in a tone of voice that brooked no argument: "She's Lauren Bacall twenty years ago.

And perhaps something else besides. Do you remember that scene in *To Have and Have Not* with Bogey? God, she'd be fantastic in it!"

"Offer her a role," Peter suggested, with a slight sarcastic edge in his voice. "With her husband in the Bogart role. According to Jodie, Lara isn't bad-looking either."

Green was the sort who went wildly overboard with enthusiasm and all through the dinner out on the terrace above the river-lights gleaming in the dark, Hayward witnessed, not without a certain sardonic pleasure, the idea irresistibly taking hold in the producer's mind.

Green launched his attack as they were having after-dinner whiskeys or cognac-and-soda in the Bamboo Bar on the downstairs patio of the Oriental. He first approached Lara, who answered with a "Thanks very much, but I don't believe I'd be interested," in a quiet, polite tone that was nonetheless unmistakably firm. As for Lisa, she simply burst out laughing, though it was laughter that sounded to Hayward just a bit nervous and made him feel vaguely ill at ease.

He noticed that Lara and Lisa never spoke to each other directly and did not even look at each other these days, living parallel lives, so to speak. He was familiar with symptoms of this sort, having shown them once or twice himself after the bitter conjugal fights he and Jodie sometimes had. The differences between Lisa and her husband were, naturally, a more serious matter, but in their case, too, he did not believe they were irreparable.

Around this same time, something happened that more or less diverted his attention from the Laras' marital difficulties. He learned of the discovery, on the Philippine island of Mindanao, of a tribe that up until that moment no one had known anything about, the Tasaday, who were still living in the Stone Age, in the true meaning of that term. In April of '71 he made his first journey to the remote corner of Mindanao where they lived, and brought back photographs of cave dwellers lighting a fire—they did at least have knowledge of fire—by rubbing two sticks of wood together, never using salt in their food and enjoying excellent health, although the tallest member of the tribe was barely five feet tall and afflicted with a gigantic goiter. He was able to sell his photos immediately and received assignments for a more complete report on these cave dwellers from magazines such as *National Geographic* and from anthropology departments of various universities. He spent the month of May getting ready for his expedition, and on June 10 left on a trip that was to take him away for a little over two months. In addition to his films and photos of the Tasaday, he also sold in advance several pieces on the peoples of the Celebes Sea, the Torajas of Sulawesi in particular.

On June 9, the evening before his departure, he and Jodie had dinner at the Laras'. (Jodie was staying behind in Bangkok; anthropology left her absolutely cold.) Peter Hayward saw no particular signs that the relations between his host and hostess had improved, but neither did he see any notable signs that they had worsened. If anyone had asked him, however, he would have been willing to bet they would eventually have a definite reconciliation, perhaps because that was what he was hoping for, in the name of the sincere friendship he felt for them.

But he would have lost his bet.

Peter Hayward returned to Bangkok on August 12, 1971, and through an inexplicable error in transmission in the cable he had sent from Manila announcing his arrival, there was no one at the airport to meet him when he got off the Air India plane. This did nothing to put him in a better mood. During the last few days fate had consistently been against him, in the most idiotically perverse way: His stay in the year-round humidity of the Celebes had caused him to have an attack of the recurrent malaria he had contracted long ago in his colonial days; part of his baggage had unfortunately been sent on to Istanbul or some equally preposterous destination; the seat next to him on the plane had been amply occupied by a nymphomaniac from New Zealand who had maintained that he reminded her of David Niven and had done her best to put her hand down his trousers; and last but not least, it was raining when he arrived in Bangkok. Though he was English, he detested rain. Alerted by telephone—he likewise detested taxis and airport buses—Jodie had finally come to pick him up. They bickered a little, out of habit, and made up as usual.

Jodie then announced that Lisa had left for the United States and taken Mathias with her. "And Lara naturally refused to go with her. I think that this time it's all over between them."

Well, that's the straw that broke the camel's back, Peter thought. He looked at his wife. If Jodie had shown the slightest sign of gloating at that point, he would have been strongly tempted to hit her. But Jodie had traces of tears in her eyes.

The Bangkok rain beat hard against the windshield, in such torrents that every so often it momentarily stopped the windshield wipers.

"I find that very sad," Jodie finally said and began to cry.

"Yes," Peter said. "I do too."

6

IT WAS MORE THAN A MONTH AND A HALF LATER THAT PETER Hayward saw Lara again. Peter had done everything possible to get in touch with him before that and had telephoned the offices of the import-export company on New Road several times. But each time he managed to reach only Dominique Christiani, Lara's partner, or the other Corsican,

Christiani's nephew or cousin. Napoleon's two compatriots had assured him that Lara was not even in Bangkok, and they didn't know when he'd be back.

"Maybe he's gone off to the United States," Jodie suggested hopefully.

Peter didn't believe so. He thought it more likely that Lara was in Cambodia. He went to the Bang Rak villa in the Chulalongkorn district and discovered not only that it was deserted but that there was a For Rent sign on it. He finally managed to get together with Christiani and learned from him that Lara had dismissed the Thai servants and that the amak who had come with them from Cambodia, on being offered the choice of going back to Phnom Penh if the now-uncertain airline connections permitted or of staying on to live in the Chinese colony of Bangkok, had opted for the latter solution.

"What did I tell you?" Jodie said. "Lisa's in the United States and Lara's gone back to Cambodia, his lousy fucked-up Cambodia. It's all over between the two of them."

"You don't absolutely have to use such vulgar language."

"If that madman went back there, he may be dead by this time."

Peter shook his head. "Lara's not an easy man to kill."

And Lara came back to Bangkok, on September 29. He turned up unexpectedly that evening, in the Peugeot 504 he'd bought when he first arrived there a year earlier. He looked much thinner and terribly tired to Peter and Jodie. He gradually broke into the characteristic slow, almost timid smile that was one of his charms.

"I thought maybe you might invite me to dinner."

"Well, how do you like that?" Jodie said. "Where do you think you are, anyway? In a hotel?"

Whereupon she threw herself into his arms and burst into tears.

"Don't pay any attention to her," Peter said. "She's had complexes ever since I explained to her that in the social hierarchy of a certain tribe in Borneo, a woman's place is immediately below a pig's and just slightly above a dog's. A cognac-and-soda as usual?"

Lara nodded. In the brightly lighted living room, he looked not merely very tired but absolutely exhausted. He appeared to be unable to focus his pale gray-blue eyes on anything in particular, and his habitual tic of massaging his shoulder and neck with his long thin fingers was more pronounced than ever.

"Come and sit down," Peter said. "I needn't remind you that our house is your house."

He didn't dare ask Lara any questions, and to fill the gap in the conversation he began to talk of the Celebes and the trip he'd taken there. With a tact so exceptional that it left Peter nonplussed, Jodie rose to the occasion and joined in with a will. She discussed anthropology as though the subject had fascinated her since earliest childhood. Skipping gaily from one

thing to another, she babbled on endlessly about a book she'd just read by
the American writer L. Sprague De Camp, a work that bore more or less
the same relation to serious archaeology as a recipe for buttered noodles
bears to haute cuisine.

"Are you acquainted with a Turkish admiral by the name of Piri Reis?"
she asked Lara.

"By sight, perhaps," Lara answered with a smile. "No, I don't believe
I've ever been formally introduced to him."

"I'd be surprised if you had," Jodie crowed. "He was hanged in the
year 1515. And do you know why? Because he made maps showing
America, at a time when it hadn't yet been discovered by Columbus, and
not only America but also the Antarctic—or maybe the Arctic, I don't remember exactly which—and in precise detail, moreover, as we're only now
beginning to learn from aerial surveys. What do you think of that?"

"Extraordinary," Lara said. He had not touched his cognac-and-soda.

The conversation at dinner was in the same vein, and as soon as they
left the table Jodie excused herself on the pretext that she had phone calls to
make, so as to leave the two men alone together. *My wife's sudden tact is
not simply surprising; it's downright amazing,* Peter Hayward thought to
himself.

"I've been in Cambodia," Lara said to Peter.

"I suspected as much."

"I crossed the border last night."

"Was it easy?"

"No."

"But that doesn't mean you've left Cambodia for good, does it?"
Hayward was certain what Lara's reply to that would be.

"Absolutely not," Lara answered. "I wouldn't ever think of such a
thing."

His clear gray-blue eyes looked straight into Hayward's as though de-
fying him to argue the point. *He's not only physically exhausted; his nerves
are all on edge,* Hayward thought.

"What were things like over there?"

"Terrible."

Peter Hayward would have followed events in Cambodia in any case,
since Cambodia was less than two hours away by car, he knew the country
well because he'd been there a hundred times, and he liked it so much that
at one point he had even considered going there to live, and only his command of French, so shaky that it would have made a Swiss German die of
laughter, had kept him from doing so. Since he had met Lara, he had yet
another reason to be deeply interested in what was happening there. The
ousting of Sihanouk from power had struck him as a catastrophic turn of
events which would bring war to a country that until then had been miraculously spared. He had not doubted for a moment that Lon Nol would inevi-

tably be defeated, any more than he doubted that Thieu, in Saigon, was doomed to defeat in the near future. He was not particularly eager to see them overthrown; he merely intuited that such an outcome was inevitable. It was not necessary to be an editorial writer for *The New York Times, Le Monde,* or *The Washington Post* to foresee this and imagine what would happen afterward: The Americans would try to save face (Mission Impossible) and then would sneak off exactly as the French had done—with their tails between their legs. And immediately after that, the entire country would fall apart.

"And do you still think it won't be the Viet Cong who will parade down the streets on V-Day?" Peter asked.

"I'm more certain than ever. Eighteen months ago, there were four thousand Khmer Rouge. Today there are more than twenty-five thousand of them. And their numbers and their strength are growing day by day."

Lara had entered Cambodia via the coast of the Gulf of Siam and then crossed the Cardamomes from the south; as Hayward unfolded a map and spread it out before them, Lara traced on it the route he had followed.

"It reminds me of my rambles with General Wingate."

"I'm not a soldier," Lara had replied in a rather curt voice. A remark immediately followed by a smile. "Begging your pardon."

Several days later, in the company of a Khmer named Kutchaï, whose name he had mentioned before to the Haywards, Lara had reached the rail line linking Phnom Penh to Thailand. Heavy fighting was going on there, they discovered, and they had been obliged to swing south, where they had entered a more or less quiet zone held by the Thirteenth Brigade under the command of the prince-colonel, Norodom Chancarangtsaï.

"I've already told you about him."

"I remember."

From Kompong Speu, Lara had finally slipped into Phnom Penh, where he had remained for ten days.

"Has the city changed very much?"

"People have begun pouring into it and it's being attacked by North Vietnamese artillery barrages. Lon Nol has turned his villa into a veritable bunker."

"Like Hitler in Berlin."

"If you like," Lara answered with a shrug.

Hayward gave him a searching look, as always thunderstruck by the tremendous, monolithic indifference that Lara had always shown with regard to the Second World War in Europe. For Lara, the main enemy in 1945 had been the Japanese, the major war that in the Pacific. He knew, or gave the appearance of knowing, as little about Hitler as a Frenchman from Savoy or a Belgian from Liège knew about Tojo. Hayward remembered Lara's total lack of reaction in the face of the events of May '68 in France: an eruption on Mars.

From Phnom Penh, Lara and his friend Kutchaï had made their way to the north of Cambodia.

"We climbed the eastern slope of the Cardamomes, via Pursat."

"You went to your old plantation?" *I shouldn't have asked him that,* Peter Hayward thought.

"No," Lara answered.

A silence. Lara puffed on his cigarette, his eyes staring into space.

He had crossed the Khmer-Thai border south of the Cambodian town of Pailin. He recounted how he had witnessed an engagement, almost a pitched battle, between Khmer Rouge and Viet Cong troops.

"Do you mean to tell me they're fighting each other?"

"That's precisely what I mean. And I think it's only a beginning."

Hayward drank a sip of his cognac. Despite his deep feelings of friendship for Lara, he wondered what part wishful thinking had played in what he had recounted. "And that's exactly what you wanted to see happen, right?"

"That's what I saw," Lara shot back coldly.

Hayward felt uncomfortable. He got up to get a cigar and held out the box to Lara, who refused one with a shake of his head.

"Very well," he said. "I'm only an idiot of an Englishman born in Lahore. Simply an idiot of an Englishman who hasn't been back to Punjab or to India for almost twenty-five years."

He was familiar with Lara's theory, on which Lara was stubbornly, desperately basing his future: the collapse of the Lon Nol regime once it no longer enjoyed the support of America and South Vietnam, and the coming to power, in a new Cambodia, of the men now organizing in the Khmer forest. Not of all these men, but of the more moderate among them.

"A revolution is something dreamed of by idealists and carried out by fanatical madmen who sooner or later disappear and are replaced by moderates. I'm counting on that 'sooner or later' not being too long a time. I'm acting on the principle—trying to act on the principle—that it will be short," Lara was saying.

Lara had not said much about these moderates in whom he was placing all his hopes. *Doubtless he knows them personally, and he may even have helped them. And in return, he's expecting them to allow him a place in this new Cambodia. Hence the absolute necessity for him never to go very far away from Cambodia, where matters are bound to come to a head at any moment, where he must go, no matter what the dangers are, to prove to himself that he's right and keep up the contacts he's made. It's the most insane endeavor imaginable. I might perhaps have dreamed of doing such a thing, but as for actually going through with it . . . !* Peter Hayward felt a shiver run down his spine.

There was Lisa, first of all.

Since her departure, the Haywards had received two letters from her;

she had written that she was in Colorado for the moment but intended to go to New York in order to find work and perhaps go back to her old job in the ad agency if they were willing to take her on again. There was not one word about her husband in either of the two letters.

Lara, sitting opposite Peter, had buried himself deeper and deeper in one of the leather armchairs which had cost a small fortune to import from England and were Jodie's pride and joy. He had closed his eyes.

"You'll stay the night here of course, and as many nights as you like," Peter said.

At first Lara did not appear to have heard him. Then he raised his eyelids. "I won't be staying," he said. "Just tonight, if I may—I haven't slept for three days. And I have to catch a plane tomorrow."

He gave a sad little smile. "Yes, a plane to the United States."

He left on September 30 and came back five days later. Alone. It was only by sheerest chance that Peter Hayward learned he had come back; it happened that the star of the film Freddy Green was producing had flown in on the same plane from San Francisco as Lara. Green had gone to meet her at the airport, seen Lara, and said hello to him. Lara gave the impression that he was both deaf and blind to everything going on about him.

Both Jodie and Peter immediately understood what Lara's return meant. Lisa had said no.

"What did I tell you!" Jodie exclaimed with breathtaking inconsistency. "That idiot of a Lisa is never going to give in!"

Two weeks went by before Peter Hayward was able to locate Lara. But despite the fact that Bangkok had a population of two million, it was not a city in which a White could pass unnoticed for very long. Hayward finally learned that Lara had taken a room at the Hotel Erawan. He resisted Jodie's insistent chiding for two days and then gave in. To his surprise, Lara immediately accepted an invitation to dinner on the evening of October 22.

Peter was extremely eager to avoid a confrontation and above all to keep Jodie from putting her foot in her mouth, since she was consumed with curiosity about what had happened in the course of the couple's last meeting in the United States and would probably not have hesitated to put the question directly to Lara. So he invited the Greens to the dinner as well, and three members of the cast of Freddy's film, two beautiful young women and the male lead, a tall, handsome Anglo-Irish devil who soaked up Scotch like a sponge.

The dinner turned out to be a lively, gay affair, and Lara, surprising as always, gave every appearance of being completely at his ease, with his diabolical courteous reserve that could hide most anything, including whatever tortures of the damned he might well be suffering. The two actresses' reaction to him was unmistakable: Like Jodie, they found him fascinating. But despite their insistence, he declined their invitation to have a last drink with them at their hotel, accompanying his refusal with his usual slow smile. He was the first to leave, shortly after midnight, and Peter, for some reason he couldn't explain, went on to drink more than he should have, something he hadn't done for more than twenty years.

Over two months went by before the Haywards saw him again. They never knew whether or not he went to Cambodia, or even to the U.S., during this time. Peter did learn, once again from Christiani, that Lara had left Thailand several times. But as usual the Corsican was the soul of discretion and said not one word regarding any of the details.

In fact, it was Lara himself who finally got in touch with Peter. He telephoned on New Year's Day to wish him and Jodie good luck in the coming year and invited the two of them to lunch, an invitation they naturally accepted. But to Jodie's vast disappointment, Lara was not alone. A Chinese from Hong Kong and another who lived in Bangkok were also present at this lunch. The two Chinese were both named Liu, and Lara introduced them as old friends of his, with whom he would be working more often than he had in the past.

"I intend to open offices in Hong Kong. So I won't be in Bangkok as often."

It was apparently a way of saying good-bye. At least that was how Peter Hayward interpreted it.

In those days Jodie Hayward's mornings were spent running a little school of painting and sculpture sponsored by UNESCO. Peter took advantage of his wife's absence to phone Lara on the day after the lunch.

"I was afraid you'd already have left."

"I won't be leaving till tomorrow."

Where is it you're going? Peter was dying to ask him. But all he said was, "May I see you?"

A moment's hesitation. Then Lara's voice: "All right. Come on over."

They met in the bar of the Erawan.

"Are you really going to settle in Hong Kong?"

"Yes and no."

"Half in Hong Kong, half in Cambodia. When are you leaving for Cambodia?"

A thoughtful look in the pale gray-blue eyes, and the slow smile. "Why? Do you want to come with me?"

The idea suddenly appealed to Hayward. "If Christiani is taking you there, I'd like to go with you. I won't get off the boat, naturally."

Lara shrugged.

They put out to sea the following evening and it was already quite late by the time they came in sight of the Khmer coast, between the mainland and the island of Kong ten kilometers or so to the north of the village of Koh Por Krom, where Krom colonists had been settled.

The boat stopped dead in the water and for a long time there was no other sound than the slapping of the light swell of the Gulf of Siam against the hull. Then someone on shore gave a series of brief signals. The cabin cruiser slowly started up again and soon Peter Hayward caught sight of the very tall silhouette of a Khmer dressed entirely in black standing on some flat rocks.

The boat came closer inshore.

The man was still taller and more solidly built when seen close up than he had looked from afar: a giant. He was carrying two assault rifles and a sack full of ammunition; he was bony and had an extremely impressive face, with very prominent cheekbones, the dark, dilated eyes of an animal, and a mute smile that had something terrifying about it.

"Kutchaï," Lara said in his grave, melodious voice. "Ah, it's true, you've never met him."

The cabin cruiser, slowly losing way, came alongside the rocks.

"Here we are," Lara said. "Hug Jodie for me."

He shook Peter's hand and leapt ashore. Kutchaï handed him one of the rifles. There were movements on the rocks higher up and Hayward noticed men whose presence he had not even suspected until that very moment, all of them dressed in black and armed, standing guard. Lara was about to leave.

"Lara!" Hayward pointed to his camera. "May I?"

Peter Hayward took some photos without a flashbulb and then, changing cameras, took others with one, as the cruiser backed water.

On his return to Bangkok, when he developed the photos in his darkroom, he noted that the first series of photos was the best. The contrast between Lara's thin, handsome face and his pale eyes was striking. As were Kutchaï's carnivorous smile and the barely visible silhouettes of the guerrillas in the background. *A ghostly vision.* As always, Peter Hayward noted the date and the hour on the back of the prints: January 5, 1972, 2 A.M.

Part Six

THE MANGO RAIN

1 "YOU'RE LYING," THE BLOND WOMAN SAID WITH A REPROVING LOOK. "Burundi doesn't exist. People would have heard of it if it did."

"Curses! I've been unmasked!" O'Malley said. "It's true: Burundi doesn't exist. You have incredible breasts. How do you manage to sleep on your belly? Do you rock back and forth?"

To his great disappointment, the blond woman didn't even cry rape. On the contrary, she gave him a come-hither look that scared him half to death. He turned tail and lost himself in the crowd. Twenty yards and nine ambassadors farther on, he came upon Slattery, his friend from the State Department. Slattery took him by the arm and led him behind a thicket of diplomats.

"I have to talk to you."

"Not me," said O'Malley. "I'm drunk as a skunk. I feel like pissing on the left leg of the Secretary of State."

"That can wait. I want to talk to you about your appointment tomorrow."

"Tomorrow doesn't exist."

But Slattery dragged him outside, onto Virginia Avenue. They were in Washington, on a day early in April 1973. They climbed into Slattery's car.

"Where are we heading?"

"We're going to a bar on L Street where we have a date with two really stacked Washington chicks, one of whom is already dreaming about your green eyes. Then to a French restaurant on Wisconsin Avenue, and after that to the Tidal Basin where we're going to contemplate the six hundred fifty Japanese cherry trees that have just bloomed, while we try to make out with the really stacked Washington chicks. But let's talk first. I know what they're going to offer you tomorrow."

"As my next post?"

"Yawohl."

A pause.

"Saigon."

A silence. With incredible, fantastic vividness, Thomas Aquinas suddenly discovered on his tongue the exact taste of the soup, the many bowls of soup he'd eaten in the Old Market of Phnom Penh with a Frenchman named Roger Bouès. *What's become of Roger, I wonder?* he thought to himself.

"You're going to laugh," he said to Slattery at length. "I could have sworn you said Saigon."

"You're not all that drunk after all. Tom?"

"Yes."

"You spoke to me one day of somebody there. Not in Vietnam, in Cambodia. Right?"

"Right."

"Any news on that score?"

"Nothing. Not one thing. Zero. Nothing."

As far as he knew, Lisa was still in Phnom Penh. The remembered pain came back, and an old French verse he'd learned by heart when he was young and foolish: *"un amour éternel en un instant conçu"*—an eternal love born in the space of an instant. . . . *O'Malley, you wretched fool, you should have hanged yourself.*

"Might that be a prime reason, for you, for going back to Indochina?"

Thomas Aquinas closed his eyes. "Would there be other reasons for me to accept?"

"Your career. People in the Foreign Service aren't exactly pushing and shoving to get themselves assigned to Saigon at this stage in the game. To be frank with you, I'm having a devil of a time finding volunteers. And you've yet to be forgiven for your impulsive request to be transferred out of Cambodia. Are you still dreaming of that post in Paris? Well then, it's tit for tat."

"You bastard," O'Malley said softly.

Slattery nodded.

"And it'll be Paris after that?"

"It's a promise, I swear, cross my heart and hope to die. Two years, Tom. To the day—not one hour more. You'll leave on the thirtieth. And you'll be back here on April 30, 1975. Two weeks later, and even sooner if you like, you'll be on the Champs-Élysées. Paris in the spring is mighty pretty."

"Dirty bastard," O'Malley said. "Miserable, dirty bastard."

Who do I mean by that: Slattery or me? he asked himself.

Slattery started the engine. "Okay then. Shall we go try to make out with those Washington chicks?"

On his return to Washington from a vacation leave in the Bahamas, O'Malley went through the usual week's briefing period, in the course of which they explained to him exactly where on the globe Vietnam was located, what the capital of the country was, the diseases venereal and otherwise that one risked catching there, and the situation with regard to the war in progress. He was informed that the "Vietnamization" so close to the heart of Richard Nixon was in full swing and taking place exactly according to plan. This last statement worried him more than all the rest of the briefing put together. He was told about the Kissinger–Le Duc Tho agreements of October 1972, and the Paris Accords of January 27, 1973. In brief, peace was in sight.

"And what about Cambodia?" he asked.

"The same goes for Cambodia," he was informed. There too, as seen from on the spot, the stabilization of the situation was obvious. Nothing was happening, and next to nothing had changed for almost three years, since the triumphant (the adjective was obviously Nixon's) American intervention in the spring of 1970. Phnom Penh was still holding out and Lon Nol as well, although the real reins of power were now in the hands of Sirik Matak, since Lon Nol was ill and being cheered on, principally by his astrologers (as the Dallas Cowboys are cheered on by their Cowgirls), as he propelled himself back and forth across a few yards of concrete in a wheelchair.

O'Malley's briefing ended on April 19. On the twentieth, after methodically laying in a fresh supply of cotton undershorts (the manual of the perfect tropical diplomat officially advised against wearing nylon), he left for New York, having in front of him ten days or thereabouts before boarding the plane which would take him, via San Francisco, to the Tan Son Hut-Saigon airport.

He visited Brooklyn and in waves of melancholic nostalgia rediscovered his childhood, along with his retired uncles, the potatoes and the pudding of his aunt on his father's side, and the joyous wheezing accordion of the elderly shopkeeper in Flatbush. There was a Matisse show at the Museum of Modern Art and he decided to visit it, but before going in, he took advantage of the warm spring air and went for a stroll along Third Avenue. As he was walking along, his eye was caught by a plaque bearing the name of a certain ad agency. On an irresistible impulse, he went up to the second-floor office.

"Lisa Kinkaird? Yes, of course we remember her. But she isn't here any more."

"I know. She's in Cambodia."

A surprised look from the receptionist. "She did go there for a while."

He was advised to have a word with a man named Kerner, who wasn't doing anything at the moment and was somewhere around, or else he was out having coffee at Joe's or Mario's or Beppe's on the corner of Sixty-seventh Street. He went back downstairs, with his heart in his mouth. He learned from Kerner that Lisa had been back in the United States for around eighteen months, that she'd worked at her old job for a time at the agency in New York, but that she'd left Manhattan the summer before and gone back to Colorado, where she had relatives.

"She left on account of her son. It's hard to work in this godforsaken town if you've got a kid on your hands. The boy must be three years old by now. A beautiful boy—as beautiful as six angels put together. I don't know who his father was; she's never said a word about him, but the guy's out of his mind to have left her by herself. Unless he's dead."

The receptionist found him the number of a Kinkaird in Colorado Springs, but nobody answered there. And that same day, O'Malley took a plane to Denver.

Above them, on their left, the towering green and brick-red bulk of Pikes Peak, dotted with patches of cloud, and the territory of the Gold Rush prospectors of old. Much closer, just below them, the red clay cathedrals of the Garden of the Gods.

"Have you ever been to Colorado before?"

"This is my first visit. I should have come sooner, rather than just following the crowd and wandering off to Greece or the Loire Valley."

She burst out laughing. "You haven't changed."

"I certainly hope not. I feel young and full of vim, vigor, and vitality and all the rest."

"Younger than ever."

"I'm the youngest Irishman ever to have blessed New York by choosing to be born there. Can't we sit down somewhere?"

They were on a little wooded lookout point with a view of the entire Garden of the Gods below them. It was not O'Malley who had chosen this spot, whose existence he had known nothing of a quarter of an hour before; he had simply allowed the young woman to take her car out of the underground parking lot of the Civic Center of Colorado Springs and drive him there.

"Or else we could go somewhere to have lunch."

"All right," Lisa said. They got back into the car. "Tell me everything," Lisa said.

"I spent two whole years in darkest Africa, and then I came back. As simple as that."

"An exciting story, the way you tell it."

"A born raconteur, that's me!" O'Malley said. "But let's talk about you instead."

"I had a job for a while in New York in an ad agency, and the only work I could find here was in the municipal administration, and that was only thanks to my grandfather. Did you know I have a son?"

"Yes."

"He's three years old."

"I know."

She was driving along very slowly. Thomas Aquinas cleared his throat. "Are you divorced?"

"No," Lisa answered. "And I'm not a widow either."

"I shouldn't have asked you that."

"Oh, why not?" she said softly.

"All right, then. Do I have the right to ask you another question?"

"Twenty of them if you like."

"Are you thinking of getting a divorce some day?"

"I really don't know."

"But you've thought about it."

"Yes."

They were driving back toward Colorado Springs, looking for a place to lunch, along a narrow winding road that threaded its way among pines and wooden houses, some of them simple cabins and others luxurious dwellings, and one motel after the other.

"Where is he?"

"My son?"

"No, not him."

"I'd rather not talk about it," Lisa said in an even voice.

"O'Malley's handiwork," Thomas Aquinas said. "Bulldozer O'Malley: wherever he passes, nothing ever grows again."

"I'm fond of him," Lisa answered.

"He can go to the devil," Thomas Aquinas said.

As it turned out, they were unable to find a single restaurant that was open—the skiing season was about over and the summer tourists yet to come—except for hamburger joints which O'Malley refused to set foot in. They ended up back in Colorado Springs and went to a restaurant on El Paso Boulevard where they lunched on an almost-rare steak and a specialty of the restaurant, its Famous French Mint Pie.

"I've never heard of a French mint pie," O'Malley remarked. "And I presume the French haven't either."

He looked at Lisa and for a few seconds was literally paralyzed by the emotion that overcame him.

"Oh, Lord, I haven't stopped thinking of you for one second during all this time! That's idiotic, isn't it?"

She lowered her head for an instant, then raised it again and gave him a kind, slightly sad smile. "What can I say?"

"Don't say anything. If you go on to say that you're fond of me, that you love me like a brother, I'll swallow this fork crossways and maybe this sugar dispenser with the pouring spout as well. No, don't say a word. Or rather, do say something. I remember you told me about your grandfather who raises flowers in his greenhouses. How is he?"

"He's just fine. He'd be delighted to meet you. What's more, you saw that he immediately recognized your name over the phone. I've often talked to him about you."

"Really?" For a second he felt ridiculously happy.

"Why not come to dinner? No, wait a second, not tonight—that was dumb of me. We're going out to dinner at some friends'. How about tomorrow night?"

"I have to leave before that," Thomas Aquinas said, inventing an excuse on the spur of the moment. "I have to be back in New York right away—or rather, in Washington."

"Do you know what your next assignment is?"

He hesitated a bare hundredth of a second. "Not yet."

The Famous French Mint Pies were brought them. They did indeed have a faint taste of mint, and were loaded with sugar. They had drunk a bottle of California Burgundy and were now drinking coffee in red earthenware mugs decorated with a picture of the funicular railway leading to the top of Pikes Peak. Lisa opened her handbag and took out a package of cigarettes. O'Malley, who didn't smoke, happened to catch sight of some photographs of a little boy in the half-open handbag.

"Your son?"

"Yes, that's Mathias."

"May I see them?"

She handed him the photographs. The little boy was indeed an extraordinarily handsome child, but one thing in particular struck Thomas Aquinas: Though his eyes were the same deep violet color as Lisa's, their calm, thoughtful, attentive, grave expression was Lara's. As was the strange stillness of the body, the characteristic tilt of the head. He almost expected to see the little boy's hand move up to the back of his neck to massage it. The resemblance was so striking it was eerie. He handed the snapshots back to Lisa without a word and slid his hands underneath the table so she wouldn't see how badly they were trembling.

"Must you really leave?"

"What would Kissinger do without me?"

"What would the United States of America do without you?"

He paid the check and they left the restaurant together.

"Where's your car? I'm quite sure you didn't walk here from Denver."

He halted in his tracks on the sidewalk, staring down intently at it. "Lisa, I'll wait as long as necessary. Ten years, if I have to."

He straightened up and looked her square in the eye. "Lisa, Lisa!"

She looked at him with her huge violet eyes, and the beauty, the sweetness of her face made him tremble. She shook her head. "Don't wait," she said. "There wouldn't be any point in it. Oh, Tom, I'm so sorry!"

She walked to his car with him and then went on her way.

On the flight back east he thought up twenty or thirty strategies, excuses, or schemes whereby he would announce to Slattery that he was refusing the appointment to Vietnam. The most spectacular, but also the simplest of them, consisted of handing in his resignation from the Foreign Service.

He went directly to Washington, where no matter what happened, he still had packing to do. On the second evening, after swearing to himself that he wouldn't drink anymore, he called Shelley, the Washington chick, and by some miracle or other found she was free. He rented a small trailer and went off with her to Shenandoah National Park, so as to spend his last hours on American soil contemplating lynxes, bears, and birds amid the thick fog of the Blue Ridge Mountains. In the language of the Indians of the region, Shenandoah meant Daughter of the Stars. Thomas Aquinas O'Malley dreamed of America—not the one he knew, the one he lived in, but the one where 360 years earlier, white men had first ventured, discovering a virgin land and thus enjoying the right to dream of re-creating there a world that had none of the imperfections of the old world, for it was a time when illusion was still possible.

He came to realize that he felt a definite affection, if nothing else, for sweet, gentle Shelley, though the young woman confessed that her feelings for him went further than that.

Hence it turned out that there was someone to weep tears for him after all when he left for Saigon on the date agreed upon.

2

IN APRIL 1973, FOR THE FIRST TIME IN THREE YEARS AND THREE months spent mostly in Peking, Norodom Sihanouk came to Cambodia.

Sihanouk's very existence, his many long years as Chief of State, his extraordinary popularity in the countryside and among those who went by the name of "the little people," the very fact that he had been ousted from power (and by the likes of Lon Nol and Sirik Matak!), his appeal to his people that had reached the ears of almost everyone in the country, were all factors the Khmer Rouge leaders skillfully exploited. And while there had been other factors as well, such as the glaringly obvious incompetence, the lies, and even the stupidity of the Lon Nol/Sirik Matak regime, Sihanouk's prestige had served as an essential element contributing to the success of the Khmer resistance movement.

For almost three years, from the end of March 1970 to January 1973, the Khmer Rouge combatants had been displaying Sihanouk's pictures on their "uniform" of black trousers and tops and scarves with little red and white squares. This had been the sign of their rallying around Sihanouk and had played a role that was far from negligible in swelling the ranks of the resistance fighters. Furthermore, they did not officially speak of themselves as the Khmer Rouge; that was a nickname meant for journalists. They called themselves the Popular Armed Liberation Forces of Kampuchea, or the FAPLK, with that passion for initialese of countries that are discovering or rediscovering their identity.

For a long time the FAPLK troops had engaged in almost no armed combat. They had recruited men first, and then organized. They had left most of the fighting up to Giap and his divisions, though the war effort had involved very little violent combat, since both in Phnom Penh and in Saigon no one seemed particularly eager to go track down Viet Cong or Khmer Rouge units in rough terrain, or anywhere else for that matter. Both sides had been content for the most part merely to occupy cities.

But from January 1973 on, everything changed.

The FAPLK now considered itself ready for combat, and insisted on carrying on the fight alone. The Paris Accords acted as one of the detonators; they made it fairly evident that Washington and Hanoi would soon settle their differences. The Khmer Rouge and the pro-Chinese faction pretended to believe that these accords constituted a betrayal of the revolutionary cause, and to the degree that they presaged a stopping of the American bombing of Cambodia (although in fact it did not stop until August 1973), they removed all justification for the deployment on Cambodian soil of Giap's North Vietnamese divisions, a deployment that thus far had served as the pretext for the American bombing raids. In reality, for Khieu Samphan and Saloth Sar, the moment had come to take command. Up until then, over two thousand Tonkinese advisers had served as cadres for the Khmer Rouge. Khieu and Saloth demanded that they be withdrawn. They also demanded that the forty thousand North Vietnamese troops withdraw beyond the borders of Cambodia, toward Annam and Laos. And when this withdrawal did not take place rapidly enough, they did not hesitate to give their own troops orders to attack their official allies, who were scarcely eager to depart from the scene inasmuch as they were trying to establish a Vietnamese—that is to say a pro-Russian—brand of Communism in Cambodia, whereas the Khmer Rouge leaders had, temporarily at least, declared their loyalty to Peking. The skirmish that Lara had witnessed in September 1971 near Siem Reap, between North Vietnamese and a detachment commanded by Rath, later took on the proportions of a major battle in this same region of Siem Reap, ending with more than 350 dead and at least 1,000 wounded.

For it was not only a question of taking over responsibility for the conduct of the war and demanding the expulsion from the country of Giap's forty thousand men, who, though they were Communist co-religionists, were nonetheless also Vietnamese and thus hereditary enemies. The Khmer Rouge leaders also wanted to embark upon large-scale maneuvers whose aim was the political, administrative, and social reorganization of the entire country. Khieu Samphan, Saloth Sar, Hu Nim and others of their persuasion, considered that the hour had come to apply to the letter the theories elaborated in Paris many years earlier, in the white-hot fury of youth. The hour had come for Angkar Loeu, the Supreme Organizaton.

In Peking, although still officially invested with revolutionary power, Sihanouk had seen a formidable adversary spring into being before his eyes and gradually grow in stature and strength; a certain Ieng Samboth, the representative of the most hard-line faction of the FAPLK, the representative in fact of Saloth Sar, alias Pol Pot. In April 1973, Ieng had just laid his cards on the table: He declared that henceforth he was to be the only, the supreme commander of the revolution taking place in the forest.

Without Chou En-lai's support, Sihanouk would perhaps have resigned himself to handing over his power, to withdrawing from the scene—although on the other hand. . . . On certain days, he was almost persuaded that this was the course he ought to take. But having recovered his fighting spirit thanks to continual Franco-Chinese encouragement, he resolved to gamblé everything on one throw of the dice: going back to Cambodia and appearing in person before the "little people" before they were definitely regimented by the Angkar. Confident of his power, of his charisma, he believed sincerely in the possibility of his unleashing a formidable wave of popular support for himself that would change everything. He saw himself overwhelmed once more by the applause of huge crowds, making his way through a sea of palms joined at the level of the forehead in respectful greeting, the very trees of the Khmer forest seeming to bow as their king passed by.

He left Peking, taking with him his wife and his movie-making equipment. He was Charles de Gaulle reentering Paris in August of '45. But a Charles de Gaulle disguised as John Ford or Alfred Hitchcock.

3

IN THAT SAME MONTH OF APRIL 1973, AROUND THE TWENTIETH, LARA was also in Phnom Penh, having just arrived from Hong Kong in immediate response to a call for help from his old friend Liu. The Chinese had had a severe heart attack, and curiously enough, instead of one of his four sons (two of whom were in the United States, another in Japan, and the youngest taking a training course in Germany), he had asked for Lara the moment he had recovered his powers of speech. As it happened, he recuperated so quickly he begged Lara to forgive him for having troubled him.

"To tell you the truth," Lara told him, "I was very eager to get back to Phnom Penh in any case."

Liu lived in an enormous, luxurious villa between the Boulevard Norodom and the Rue Pasteur, in a residential district that was more or less the counterpart of the French quarter on the other side of the city. There were countless rooms and they had been magnificent; they seemed almost empty now, for most of the furniture and the objets d'art had long since been shipped off to Hong Kong.

"By requesting your presence in such a grossly selfish fashion—and my only excuse was that I was not entirely myself at the time—I now discover that I merely expressed clearly what I had been confusedly aware of all along," Liu said. "My brothers have spoken to me of you. There is no one they esteem and love more. I know that your business dealings with them in Hong Kong are going along perfectly. I also know that you haven't settled in Hong Kong, that you were in Bangkok before that, but you didn't stay there for good any more than you did in Manila or Singapore. And where will you go next? Why not simply come back here? We could work together. And you would live here with me. You know very well that we Chinese have a foot in both camps. My brothers and my cousins help Sihanouk and his revolutionary friends, and I'm a friend of Khieu Samphan's. And though Lon Nol may have contemplated using us the way he used the Vietnamese, that is to say as scapegoats, even he now knows that we can't be touched. Come and work with me. I'm not talking about dealing in contraband, but about a straightforward business proposition: Let's help these people, regardless of which side they're on. Cambodia's going to change masters sooner or later, Lara. You know it and I know it. One might as well make ready for the change, and you won't find any better way than this. And you'll be right here on the spot."

The day after his return, on dropping in at the Zigzag, Lara ran into Kutchaï, who had suddenly reappeared like a ghost. The two men hadn't seen each other for at least two months. They sat down to have a drink together as though they'd last seen each other only the evening before. Lara told Kutchaï about the offer Liu had just made him.

"You're going to accept." The words were not put as a question.

"Before I do, I want to see Ieng," Lara said. "Where is he?"

"Still in the Cardamomes, keeping an eye on his supplies. Or at least he was still there three weeks ago. The Strasbourg Sausage can take you as far as Battambang, and from there that Corsican who traffics in opium in that neck of the woods could easily get you through to Ieng. Tomorrow morning?"

Lara nodded, and looked intently at Kutchaï. "Is everything all right with you?"

Kutchaï laughed. "The same as ever. Ambling around here and there."

Albert Vandekherkove brought them their cognac-and-sodas himself.

"Want to come with me?" Lara asked the Jaraï.

"Why not?" Kutchaï answered.

As they left the Zigzag, Lara wanted to pay a call on the Korvers, but it was already late at night and there were no lights on in their villa. He went back to see them the next morning, just two hours before Boudin's Cessna was due to take off.

"When will you be back?" Charles Korver asked.

Lara smiled at him. "Very soon. That's a promise."

"It's one you'd better keep," Madeleine said.

She walked all the way around him, looking him up and down as she always had. "You've gotten even thinner, haven't you?"

"No, I haven't. I'm in great shape."

"You really look it, I must say." She sniffed sarcastically. She had not once mentioned Lisa's name, or Mathias' either, and consequently the tension between her and Lara was almost palpable.

"I'll see you to your car," Charles said.

They walked down the drive to the end of the garden and out onto the street. The Korvers' villa was the only one in the district still being lived in; the others had been abandoned and were standing empty, their gardens deserted. The contrast between this emptiness, this abandonment, and the men, the women, the children squatting on the sidewalks amid abnormal silence was spectacular, even heartrending. These people were refugees fleeing the fighting, the government troops, the Viet Cong, the Rangers from Saigon, the Khmer Rouge, the American planes, fleeing everything, having left everything they possessed behind them and contenting themselves for the moment with a tiny stretch of sidewalk staked out for themselves alongside marvelous, patiently laid-out gardens, bordering mansions they didn't dare enter, in a quarter of Barangs and *louk thom*, important men, mansions which for an entire century people of their sort had never been inside, except perhaps as servants. From time to time soldiers came to chase them out, and the little street lined with frangipanis and scarlet coral trees was once again silent and deserted. But that state of affairs did not last long. One night a new family would arrive, settling down fearfully, as mute as the one that had been there before it, with the animal stubbornness of rats taking refuge on the topside of a sinking ship. And soon there were others. . . .

"We try to help them," Charles said. "We give them all our rice, but even rice isn't that easy to find anymore."

"I know," Lara said.

"But we really have nothing to complain about. That Monsieur Liu whom I went to see had enough rice and fish delivered to us to feed quite a few people. And besides that, those Cambodians that Kutchaï found for us to replace poor Monsieur Bê are very devoted."

"If they weren't, Kutchaï would chop their heads off."

American planes flew over regularly; every so often they heard a rocket exploding in the distance and the rumble of North Vietnamese 105's firing from the other side of the Chrui Chang War Peninsula, beyond the Mekong. But since the beginning of the year the bombing raids were becoming less frequent with each passing day, as the North Vietnamese artillery began to withdraw under pressure from the Khmer Rouge, who were now undertaking their own siege of the city. Thus Phnom Penh seemed calmer than it had for a long time.

"There's something I wanted to talk to you about," Charles said. "Madeleine and I have made our will. . . ."

He raised one hand to stop Lara from interrupting him. "Shhh, let me finish. We're not going to live forever and we've never had children. Our money is mostly in Hong Kong and in Switzerland. And there must be about five million French francs, what they call new francs, in France. I don't know exactly how much that amounts to. In fact, I don't have the least idea. . . ."

"Too much, in any case."

"Our will is all in order. There's a certified copy of it at the Chartered in Hong Kong and another one at the Crédit Suisse. The original is filed with a notary in Bordeaux. Everything's in order. Our sole heir is Mathias, your son. I know you; *you* would have refused."

"There's no doubt whatsoever of that."

"Mathias will receive the interest on the principal until he's twenty-one and then after that he can dispose of the entire estate as he sees fit. I hope he'll spend it lavishly and a bit foolishly. That money isn't worth a whole lot."

He bent over, slowly and with difficulty, to clear weeds away from around a canna.

"How long will it be before Phnom Penh falls?"

Lara didn't answer.

"Ask a foolish question and . . ." Charles said. "Be off with you, my boy, and please don't get yourself killed. . . ."

Boudin was still flying, flying in fact more than ever. He transported whatever anyone asked him to or, as he put it, "preferably anything and everything." The week before, he had flown a group of nuns from Phnom Penh to Bangkok . . . and two hours later brought them back to Phnom Penh, the sisters having in the end refused to abandon their flock.

"I couldn't care less who or what I fly where. I'm just feathering my nest. And where is it we're going?"

"Battambang," Lara answered.

Boudin looked at him intently, then leaned his head even farther back to stare up at Kutchaï's face. "You guys really like to travel, don't you?"

"Doesn't he get on your nerves?" Kutchaï said to Lara. "He certainly gets on mine. What say we sell him to the Khmer Rouge?"

The little Alsatian leapt at him, boiling with rage, his hand already on the butt of his pistol. Lara's hand grabbed his wrist.

"Let's get going, Lindbergh."

After a moment, Boudin walked off toward his plane, growling angrily to himself.

"Can you imagine? That little monster would have shot me!" Kutchaï laughed.

"Stop needling him, okay?" Lara said.

There had been a time when Pochentong was one of the quietest airports in the world. Practically the only plane that had landed there was the weekly Air France flight, and people had turned out to stand in the shade of a customs buildings that looked like a fisherman's shack and watch the plane fly in on Sundays, as though its arrival were some sort of special event. But now the airport was another world entirely. The French Boeing still set down each Sunday, but it was no longer queen of the runway and did its best to touch down discreetly, timidly, amid gigantic squadrons of C-130's, cargo planes of all sorts, screaming fighter-bombers, swarms of helicopters flying under the name of Air America, a substitute for the U.S. Air Force, bringing in wounded troops, some of them in enormous nets suspended from the helicopters' sides, sometimes with bloody arms and legs hanging out.

"We're off!" Boudin yelled so as to drown out the high-pitched whine of the rotor of a Sikorsky S-58 settling down its human cargo with the delicate touch of a goldsmith. Zigzagging down the runway pitted with great holes from rockets and shells, Boudin lifted the plane off as soon as he could in a breathtaking chandelle, thus avoiding being hit by small-arms fire. Once they were airborne, the usual miraculous peace and quiet of the sky overhead enveloped them.

At the last minute, with Lara's permission, the Strasbourg Sausage had taken aboard a journalist disguised as a paratrooper who had outfitted himself on Fifth Avenue. His name was Halley and he explained that the war was of no interest to him except, as he put it, as an epiphenomenon.

"I'm doing research on the opium trade. Did you know that despite the war the traffic in opium is still going on? Even the Khmer Rouge aren't doing anything to stop the deliveries coming in from Laos."

He explained that he was going to Battambang because informers had sworn to him that the governor was one of the kingpins of the traffic in opium. "What's your opinion on the subject?"

"I couldn't care less," Lara answered.

"This is the first time I've been in Cambodia," Halley said. "For that matter, it's the first time I've been in the Far East."

"You've come at the right moment," Kutchaï said. "You'd be hard put to find a better time."

Lara looked out at the Cardamomes on his left, remembering a time four years before when he had been heading for Saigon to search for a youngster named Jon who was hiding out there. The sky above the mountain peaks was leaden, with a greenish tinge at times and a violet one at others; the cloud bank seemed this time to be determined to drift down the western side of the central Cambodian basin that lay between the Cardamomes and the Moï highlands far to the east. It had not rained in central Cambodia for nearly six months.

"It looks as though this time we're going to get some rain," Lara said to Kutchaï. The Jaraï leaned over to have a look and nodded.

"The Mango Rain. It's very late this year."

"What's the Mango Rain?" Halley asked.

Lara yawned. "The first rain of the year. Before it comes, it's the dry season, and after it too. It falls before the heavy monsoon rains from June to October."

"Like a warning sign," Halley said, delighted by his own phrase.

"Right," Lara answered. "A shot across the bow."

The lead-colored storm front stretched out for hundreds of kilometers. The Cessna skirted it, as though it were an unknown coast. The clouds advanced, slowly, inexorably.

The Corsican in Battambang cast curious glances at Lara and Kutchaï in the rearview mirror.

"Dominique Christiani's told me about you. About both of you."

"Where in Corsica are you from?" Lara asked him.

"From Bastia. Well, not really. I'm from Brando, on the Cape."

"Do you know a place called Piedicorte di Gaggio?"

"Sure. It's in the mountains. Why do you ask?"

"No particular reason," Lara said, thinking of Oreste, whom he hadn't heard a word from. "Somebody mentioned it to me once."

They entered Battambang. The Cambodian city with the second largest population after Phnom Penh, it was also important because it was a center for the rice trade, which was controlled by Chinese; because of its factories processing the fish from the Tonle Sap, factories set up and directed by Chinese; because of other factories, established by the French and taken over by Chinese through Cambodian front men, which processed rubber, gold, sulphur, and precious stones extracted from the nearby region of Païlin. It was also important in a somewhat less aboveboard way, as the center through which the opium of the high plateaus passed, the purchase, transport, and resale of which was in the hands of Corsicans . . . and Chinese.

"There are two possibilities," the Corsican said. "The hotel, where I've reserved a room for you, or else at my house."

"Where do you live?"

"On the road to Païlin. It's a nice quiet place."

Lara turned halfway round. Kutchaï nodded his head, and Lara said, "At your place, if you don't mind."

"*Indeh,*" the Corsican replied in his native dialect. "On the contrary."

It was a small concrete-block villa, three-quarters hidden by greenery, past which the Stung Battambang flowed, two hundred yards away. They entered a dining room that might well have been situated in an apartment on the Rue César-Campinchi in Bastia. Not a single detail was missing: the waxed oak table and sideboard with six matching chairs; on the walls, in addition to a map of Corsica, watercolors representing, according to the titles handwritten in purple ink, the valley of the Bebbiu, the seafront of Pietracorbara and that of Porticciolu; on the sideboard, photos of a boy and girl, both around twenty.

"My son and my daughter. My boy's going to be a doctor; he's almost through medical school."

He offered them some Casanis with religious gestures. After that they waited for nightfall over a dinner of bamboo-hen accompanied by rice and a rosé from Provence. They left the villa at ten-thirty and drove some twenty kilometers in the direction of Païlin, in a car with all the lights out. Then the Corsican stopped the car.

"Here we are. Do you see that embankment to your left? Follow it and you'll end up in a grove of sugar palms. Walk straight through it and wait. Don't talk and don't smoke; there'll be soldiers a hundred yards from you. Good luck."

Lara shook hands with him.

"Watch the doors when you get out. Don't slam them, please."

The grove was a kilometer from the road. For almost an hour, Lara and Kutchaï heard the voices of soldiers passing back and forth in front of the flames of their campfire. Then there was an almost imperceptible sound of footsteps and two men appeared. Not a single word was exchanged. All four of them left together, amid the same silence; they walked for about an hour, and then crossed the Stung Battambang. A truck was waiting on the far bank of the river, and started off the moment they climbed aboard.

The road soon began to climb steeply, as the night grew darker. The sky became more and more overcast and the forest on both sides of the road hemmed the truck in.

"Is Ieng Samboth up there?" Kutchaï asked one of the two guides.

"*Até.* No."

"Where is he?"

The man stared at Kutchaï. "You haven't heard?"

"Haven't heard what?"

The man's eyes gleamed brightly. "Samdech Sihanouk," he said. "Samdech Sihanouk is back."

There was a sort of movement forward. The clan of Khmer Rouge leaders had started marching, and the groundswell thus unleashed gradually began to spread in a long, slow surge among the hundreds of men around them. On either side of Ieng and Ouk, the human tide parted and began to flow in the direction of a great open space, surrounded by trees, in direct view of the five towers of Angkor Wat. It was eleven o'clock in the morning, and the sky was becoming more overcast by the minute, rapidly darkening as deep purple and black clouds kept rolling in, thicker and thicker.

"The Mango Rain," Ouk said.

Around Ieng Samboth and Ouk, the tide of black-clad men continued to surge forward with irresistible power, new waves continually emerging from the forest. Ieng resisted this advancing sea for some time, then gave in and let himself be carried along by it, in a sort of daze that was almost a stupor. He moved forward two or three hundred yards to the edge of the trees, where he found his way blocked by the continuous line of Kamaphibals who formed an impassible barrier, prohibiting him from taking a step farther.

"This way." Ouk led him toward a burial mount on which a number of people were already standing. The two men hoisted themselves up onto it, too, and from this vantage point a few feet higher, they found an unobstructed view of the entire scene. The middle of the vast clearing directly in front of them was completely empty. On its longest side, however, approximately twelve hundred men and women, all of them dressed in black and wearing around their necks the red and white checkered scarves that served as their emblem, were lining up with no other sound than a muffled stamping of feet, without a single order being given, obviously executing a maneuver long since planned.

Along a second line, a circular one this time, thousands more men and women were assembled, defining the arena, lugubrious black spectators with impassive faces, like birds of prey awaiting permission to begin the slaughter.

A minute went by and then total silence fell. Even the sound of stamping feet stopped and there was no sound exept a gigantic, collective mute breathing, tense and anxious. In this oppressive silence, the rumble of a truck gradually became audible, an almost ridiculous sound by comparison. The truck came into sight, approaching from the east along a trail through the forest. It came slowly closer and stopped in front of the group formed by Khieu Samphan and Saloth Sar and their comrades, standing slightly apart from all the others. Norodom Sihanouk stood up and leapt out of the truck. He too was dressed in black and wearing a checkered scarf. He was trying his best to smile. But his eyelids were blinking, his face was pale, and his hands were trembling.

The mere sight of this plump little figure—so very familiar, calling up so many memories, almost mythical—left Ieng breathless for the space of a few seconds. But he mastered his feelings enough to look around him, and saw that all the men and women were gripped by the same irrepressible emotion. It was true that almost every one of these thousands of combatants gathered together here had not yet been born when Norodom Sihanouk ascended the throne of Cambodia. He himself, Ieng Samboth, could not remember a time when Samdech Sihanouk's face had not invariably been displayed on the walls of buildings, in the pages of the newspapers, on the woven-straw-matting walls of the most isolated huts. Twenty-nine years . . . for twenty-nine years this little man had not only governed but been the very incarnation of Cambodia.

Hou Yuon's words, speaking to him ten minutes earlier: "Ieng, in two weeks Sihanouk has been taken from one end of the country to the other, at any rate to all the places he's been permitted to go. And the only people he's seen are Saloth Sar's men and Khieu Samphan's, nobody but them, not a single peasant capable of being deeply moved by the sight of his Samdech, nobody but indoctrinated soldiers and Kamaphibals. Even I haven't really been able to speak to him. He's finished, even though he still refuses to believe it. You know him: He always thinks he's going to be able to get out of trouble. But this time he's wrong. He asked—almost begged—that ordinary people, thousands of them, be called together for him. He wants to talk to them one last time and thinks that he's going to touch their hearts. He believes that the mere sound of his voice will make them burst into tears. He believes he's still their god-king. He doesn't know what's in store for him. . . ."

Norodom Sihanouk walked toward the group of Khmer Rouge leaders in his familiar way in such situations, a fixed smile on his lips, moving forward with tiny little steps, slightly bent over, with one shoulder thrust forward, his head leaning on that shoulder, his two cupped hands held out before him. The men opposite smiled back at him and vaguely went through the motions of offering him the greeting of respect, the *laï*, their palms joined at the level of their foreheads. But despite the fact that he was a fair distance away, Ieng could see that their faces remained cold, even icy.

After speaking with them for a few moments, Sihanouk was led to a little wooden platform with a single microphone at the front of it. As was his habit, he made one or two joking remarks; they fell flat, amid a dead silence. Finally he began speaking, in a voice hoarse with emotion at first, his tone almost grave, and then as he became more sure of himself, it became shriller, with those brusque, strident rises in pitch that sounded almost like yelps which he had never been able to avoid, even when he was speaking in French.

What he had to say was in no way surprising. He praised the courage and stubbornness of the Khmer forest people, their unfailing valor; he berated the men in Phnom Penh and their allies in Washington and Saigon; he rendered homage to the wisdom, the intelligence, the faith of the leaders of the revolution, whom he mentioned by name, following each name with a laudatory remark but not failing to remind his listeners that several of them, such as Khieu Samphan and Hou Yuon, had been his ministers and that he had already granted them his trust in the past. It was a way of stressing the allegiance they owed him, yet he did it skillfully and with that sly, calculating humility whose uses he knew so well. He stated his desire to be nothing but an ordinary man from now on, resigned to living in the shadow in silence, having no other ambition and no other hope save to see his country no longer in need of him, although he would continue to hold himself in readiness to answer any appeal that might be made him. It was perfectly obvious that this peroration was a hint that such an appeal *should* be made him, in the form of a tremendous ovation, the very next second, as his last word died away, now.

He fell silent, and not one voice was raised.

It was pathetic and poignant, so much so that tears came to Ieng Samboth's eyes. Directly opposite Sihanouk, who stood on his platform silent and desperately watching for the least sign, the thousands of men and women dressed in black were moving not a muscle, continuing to stare at their former prince with empty eyes, in an icy indifference that was a thousand times worse than jeers.

What happened next was really the coup de grâce. Saloth Sar stepped out of the group of leaders and walked slowly to the platform. He did not mount it, as though he wished to further emphasize Sihanouk's isolation. For a long moment he contemplated his troops, for once allowing his mask of simple, slightly effeminate goodheartedness to fall. He smiled slowly, his eyes half closed, then raised his right arm, fist clenched. Scrupulously obeying this signal, the thousands burst into cheers. The cheers poured out for some ten seconds. Until the instant Saloth Sar lowered his arm. Then they broke off with the same incredible simultaneity, as though a radio had been abruptly turned off.

And total silence again fell.

Badly shaken, Ieng Samboth finally succeeded in tearing his eyes away from Sihanouk's pale face and trembling lips as he struggled, with a courage that was enough to break one's heart, to go on smiling. Ieng's eyes traveled over the thousands of frozen, completely impassive faces that by contrast with the tortured features of this little, lonely man standing all by himself, made his blood run cold. He couldn't bear it a moment longer and slid to the ground, followed by Ouk. They made their way through the motionless groups together and left.

Less than twenty minutes later, the Mango Rain began to fall.

4

ON MAY 2, 1973, THE SAME RAIN WELCOMED THOMAS AQUINAS O'MALley on his arrival in Saigon.

"I don't think you'll have much to do here as cultural attaché," Ambassador Martin said to him. "In the short run, at any rate. This country is at war, as you know. But the long run is another matter. Hence it is going to be vital to implant American culture and our ideals of freedom even more firmly. That will be your role. The long run, O'Malley: That's your problem."

Slattery was right: He's nuts, Thomas Aquinas thought to himself.

"Yes, sir," he said aloud. "The long run. I understand exactly what you mean."

"And I've another reason besides for asking for you to be sent here: In the present circumstances, and despite—and I would even go so far as to say, above all, because of—the Geneva Accords, we must make it clear that we are determined to maintain our position here, in every realm, including the cultural."

"Yes, sir."

And another minute's time out for observation: Martin's eyes scrutinized him closely.

"Do you like trees, greenery, O'Malley—Tom?"

Here we go.

"Come over here," the ambassador said, leading him to a window. "Do you see that tree? Do you see it, O'Malley?"

"Very distinctly," O'Malley replied. One of its branches was right under his nose.

"They tried to cut it down, maintaining that it was in the way of helicopters. I formally objected. I did even better that that: I've posted sentries to keep watch on it night and day, ever since they tried to cut it down in the middle of the night. A commando unit with saws, O'Malley, can you imagine? Luckily I was on my guard, and their attempt failed. Do you realize what that tree means for America and for Vietnam, O'Malley? Do you realize what great symbolic value it has?"

Good Lord Almighty! O'Malley thought. *Can things have possibly gotten to this point?*

After June 1973, Thomas Aquinas O'Malley was to spend his time working on the ambassador's "plan for the long run," as he called it, an elaborate, murky program for "a firmer implantation of American culture in the Mekong Delta." Thomas Aquinas was tempted more than once to hand in his resignation. But in the end he did not do so. He had discovered that, for some inexplicable reason, he did not enjoy the detachment, the somnambulistic obliviousness to everything going on around them with which almost all of his compatriots living the same life that he was in Saigon seemed so richly blessed. He came close to reproaching himself for a flagrant lack of patriotism, and his pessimism made him feel ashamed of himself. The military officers he happened to meet at parties told him with a straight face that the war might very well go on for two hundred years more but that it was already won.

Several times he found out everything he could about the situation in Cambodia and particularly in Phnom Penh, and was even tempted to go there. After all, it was only two hundred miles away. He could doubtless have easily made arrangements to get there if he'd taken the trouble; there was now a veritable airlift with daily military flights linking the two capitals. He never made up his mind to take the necessary steps, however, and simply arranged to have a letter delivered to the Korvers announcing that he was in Vietnam, and asking for news of Roger Bouès.

In fact, outside of a brief trip to the Philippines in August of '74 to recover from an amoebic infection, Thomas Aquinas O'Malley was to remain in Saigon to the end.

5

IN RECENT MONTHS, CHARLES AND MADELEINE KORVER HAD RE-sumed an old habit of theirs: walking each morning to the Taï-San's outdoor terrace bordered with dwarf palms, on the corner of Yukanthor and Ouk Loun. They had their personal table there that the Chinese waiters religiously reserved for them, and spent two and three hours there on many a morning sipping iced coffee or iced tea with lime to recover from the walk of almost two kilometers that took them up the Avenue des Français first, then across the esplanade of the Phnom, and finally halfway up the Boulevard Norodom. Just after the death of Bê and the other Vietnamese servants they had given up this rite, which admittedly tired them but which forced them out of their shell. For a time they had fallen into a self-imposed isolation. But one morning, almost without discussing the matter with each other, they had decided to put an end to their cloistered life.

They had gone out expecting to find a Phnom Penh reduced to rubble by bombs, shattered by plastic explosives, torn apart by rocket bursts—at any event, at war. They had kept up sufficient contact with the outside world to be aware that the city had been under siege for very nearly three years and that the siege was growing heavier by the day.

They were amazed to discover that things were not like that at all: Unbelievably, Phnom Penh looked more or less as it had in peacetime, despite the rumble of artillery fire, to which they were so accustomed by now that they didn't even notice it, despite the countless soldiers and the hordes of refugees, and despite, admittedly, a few traces here and there of plastic bomb explosions and shellfire.

Reaching the terrace of the Taï-San, they sat down at their table, the second one from the entrance on the Rue Yukanthor (the first one being reserved, as always, for the magistrate with the pocket handkerchief scented with human excrement). The chief magistrate greeted the Korvers graciously; the drunker he was the more gracious he was, and that day he was extremely so.

"I have a message for you," he mumbled. "Monsieur Lara passed by here an hour ago and will be back. He would like you to wait for him."

"Thank you ever so much," the Korvers answered in chorus, pleased to learn that Lara had returned to Phnom Penh.

When he joined them shortly afterward, Lara told them the story Ieng had recounted to him: the scene at Angkor Wat.

"Poor Sihanouk," Madeleine said. "He didn't deserve that."

Charles looked intently at Lara. "And what does Ieng Samboth think?"

Lara's long thin fingers delicately removed a minuscule thigh from a glazed roast squab and dipped it in the lime juice seasoned with *nuoc-mam* and green peppercorns from Kampot.

"He thinks we're all going to be driven out of the country."

"Ieng has always been extremely excitable," Madeleine said, in the tone of a schoolmarm speaking of one of her pupils.

"But you don't think so," Charles said, looking deep into Lara's pale gray-blue eyes.

Lara licked his fingers and then reached for the hot perfumed towel the waiter was holding out to him. "Only up to a certain point. But I think you and Madeleine should leave."

There was a sudden silence.

"Anything else?" Madeleine asked indignantly.

"All of us will let ourselves be driven out, but not you—that's what you mean, isn't it?" Charles remarked bitterly.

Lara smiled, a faraway look in his eyes. "That's right," he answered.

He told them of the offer Liu had made him, and informed them he'd decided to accept. He seemed to think that Liu's proposal settled everything. *He really seems to think that,* Charles thought, his mind in a daze. He felt very old and very tired; it was all too much for him.

He had heard of the atrocities, real or imagined—how was one to know?—committed by the Khmer Rouge. Was there anyone in Phnom Penh who didn't talk of them? People seemed to enjoy scaring themselves. The war correspondents and innumerable refugees were full of frightful stories. To hear them tell it, half of Cambodia was busy slitting the throats of the other half.

But they had said very nearly the same thing about Mao's Communists in the months and weeks that had preceded Chiang Kai-shek's flight to Formosa. And how many Europeans had stayed in Hanoi after Ho Chi Minh's troops had entered the city? They hadn't been slaughtered, however. At worst, they'd been expelled from the country. How many abandonments, retreats, and withdrawals in the world's history had been caused by panic, a panic that in most cases was unjustified? From a distance of thousands of kilometers away, Charles had followed the grotesque mass exodus of the French during the summer of 1940. People always abandon ship too soon. Lara was right. Immutable; Phnom Penh and Cambodia were immutable. Saigon, too, which had seen many an invader come and go.

The association of ideas between the fate of Saigon and that of Phnom Penh was inevitable, and it was not the first time it had occurred to Charles Korver to make the comparison. There was no doubt in his mind that both would fall some day. For him, the one question was which of them would fall first. For a long time, he would have bet it would be Saigon, but now . . . *Or else the two of them will fall together, on the same day, at the same hour. And why not?* he thought to himself. *History is illogical and mad, equally capable of celebrating its great events with a savage, superb clash of cymbals, or by a low mass whose meaning does not become clear until long afterward. . . .*

Charles Korver was gradually pulling himself together. He had always struggled with his last ounce of strength against this sort of depressed feeling, this dull despair that sometimes came over him. Once again, he was getting the best of it. He smiled at Lara. "If I understand you correctly, since you'll now be staying on in Phnom Penh, we'll be seeing each other more often?"

"You poor things," Lara said, smiling back at him. "You'll be seeing me constantly."

And so, now that Lara had returned to Phnom Penh and was determined to stay there, and now that O'Malley had arrived in Saigon, everything was in place for the last act. At the time, naturally, things were not all that evident, but a race to catastrophe had in fact begun. Charles Korver had been right: The only real question was which of the two would fall first, Phnom Penh or Saigon.

As things turned out, it was Phnom Penh just fourteen days before Saigon.

Part Seven

THE LAST WHITE MAN

1 IN SEPTEMBER OF 1974, WITH PETE'S HELP, MATTHEW KINKAIRD FINALLY finished enlarging still further the first of his three greenhouses, the one immediately adjoining the house. He took advantage of the work going on to add two small bedrooms, one for Lisa and one for Mathias, onto the house. The enlarged conservatory was the one kept at the highest temperature, the one with the aviary; Matthew had added fifteen feet onto it, bringing its total length up to ninety feet, with an overall width of twenty-seven feet, as before.

Singlemindedly pursuing his passion, to which he was devoting every last cent of his retirement pension, Matthew was sinking into the blissful self-centeredness of old age. He had ceased to have any real relation with his son, Jon and Lisa's father, except for a card with the usual season's greetings and best wishes that he received from him at the end of each year and which he didn't even take the trouble to answer. On the other hand, he had news of Jon fairly often; the young man regularly wrote to him every two months or so. In the most recent letter, written three weeks before, he announced his coming marriage to a tall blonde studying sociology in Stockholm and urged his grandfather to come to the wedding, which was to take place in that city on April 30. Matthew hadn't answered the letter yet, but he'd already made up his mind. He would not go to Sweden, being too advanced in years now to undertake such a long journey. That at least was the excuse he was about to resort to, though the real truth lay elsewhere, as he himself vaguely realized. Sweden really seemed to be a long way off, and he'd always been a homebody, but what was essentially weighing more heavily in the balance was the fact that this grandson he had loved so dearly had become, curiously enough, almost a stranger to him now that he was no longer an American citizen and had found a safe niche in life.

In all truth, the only real problem still confronting Matthew, doubtless because their living together in Colorado made him aware of it almost every day, was the one posed for him by Lisa. Not that his granddaughter complained in any way. On the contrary, she never spoke of her troubles. On one and only one occasion had she ventured to offer an explanation for what Matthew still hesitated, despite everything, to call the breakup of her marriage to Lara: Lara's insane determination to remain in a country where there was no longer any place for him. She had explained herself once and for all and after that he had refused to discuss the matter again.

He suspected she was having financial difficulties. Her job at City Hall probably brought her some $15,000 a year, and the money she paid out to the Hunter sisters for taking care of Mathias and providing his meals doubtless amounted to a third of that, so that once her income tax was deducted from her salary, she most likely had just enough left to live on; even though she had no rent to pay, the old Powder Cache house required more and more frequent repairs. On one of the rare occasions when Matthew had dared mention the subject to Lisa, he had learned that even though Lara persisted in sending money to his wife and son, Lisa stubbornly continued to refuse to draw one cent of the sums transferred from Hong Kong or Bangkok, so that they simply accumulated in a bank account, untouched. "I don't need that money. And I don't want any of it. I'm perfectly capable of supporting and raising my son all by myself."

For a long time Matthew had thought that Lisa's adamant refusal was probably another means she was resorting to in order to bring pressure to bear on her husband to give in, a stratagem complementing her original one of leaving Asia and taking Mathias with her. But as the months and years went by, the old man no longer understood what was going on between them. (When Lara had come to see his wife, Matthew had not met him, and as a matter of fact knew nothing of his attempts to patch things up with Lisa until months later.)

As for Mathias, his great-grandson who was almost his namesake, Matthew at times felt a wonderstruck love for him. The little boy was so beautiful he took your breath away; he was extraordinarily intelligent; he could be very affectionate and was usually sweet and gentle, though he tended to have sudden flareups of boisterous exuberance, not to mention fits of temper which were early evidence of an extremely willful character. But he was Lara all over, to an unbelievable degree, and in the youngster's least little gesture, in every one of his attitudes, in everything about his behavior, Matthew was forcibly reminded of this man he had once known, whose gift of a black wooden statuette still stood in Matthew's own bedroom.

During the morning of this Friday, September 20, Matthew received a phone call. He immediately recognized the voice of Jubal Wynn, the San Francisco attorney. Since his visit in the spring of 1969, more than five years earlier, Wynn had never altogether lost contact with Matthew. He had bought a chalet near Aspen, a few hours away by car, and often went there in winter to ski.

"May I drop by to say hello?" he asked Matthew.

"You know you're always welcome."

"Around six this evening?"

"Don't even consider having dinner anywhere but here with me."

It was only after he hung up that Matthew remembered it was Friday, and that therefore Lisa and Mathias would be coming for dinner and to spend Saturday and Sunday with him. And only then did he also remember that Lisa and Wynn had never met.

One word above all others would have best described Wynn: elegance. His elegance had to do not only with his physique, his dress, or his way of life; the moment one set eyes on him, one instinctively knew he was rich, accustomed to being rich, and regarded it as only natural to be rich. That evening, Friday, September 20, 1974, Pete and Ruth Martinez left just after dinner was over; past eight o'clock, especially after a chicken in *mole* sauce, Pete was ready for bed. Wynn stayed much later, until almost one in the morning in fact, in front of a fire he had insisted on lighting himself, giving proof of undeniable charm and even succeeding in making Lisa burst into wholehearted laughter.

Two weeks later, he turned up in that part of the country again, this time telephoning Lisa directly at her office in City Hall, asking her to have dinner with him in Colorado Springs, and inviting her and Mathias to go with him for an airplane ride the following day. Of course he had his own private plane. Lisa accepted the dinner invitation but declined the offer of a plane ride. This did not discourage Wynn in the least: He came back to Colorado again at the end of October, and then again in November, and this time he came straight out and told her of his intentions, which as always he acknowledged frankly and forthrightly.

"I haven't the least desire to meddle in your private life, I beg you to believe me. I merely know what sort of work you did in New York, what important responsibilities you had in that advertising agency. And I also know what sort of job you have here. Among my good clients and friends in California are several directors of one of the national television networks. What they call your professional profile fits their needs exactly, and they are certain of your capabilities. And because I'm eager to lay all my cards on the table so that there will be no misunderstanding between us, allow me to add also, it's true that there are very few things in this world that I would like more than to see you come to live and work in San Francisco, which is where I live. But if you accept this proposal I'm making you, you won't owe me anything. You won't be obliged to see me again, or to accept the invitations I'm planning on extending you, to share for instance a sunny afternoon with me on my black-hulled ketch, the most beautiful one ever to have sailed the Pacific. . . ."

The apartment Lisa rented in San Francisco occupied the entire upper floor of an old two-story house; there was even a garden with magnolia trees, on a quiet, steep street on Nob Hill, where the only sound was the charming clatter and clang of the ancient cable car swaying up and down California Street. Lisa and Mathias moved into the apartment on January 14, 1975, along with a young Chinese girl born in Taipeh. And Lisa did accept the first of the invitations to dinner extended her by Jubal Wynn.

2

LIU RETURNED TO PHNOM PENH ON MARCH 29, 1975. THE AIR FRANCE Boeing that brought him back managed to land on the runway at Pochentong Airport without being hit by a single rocket, a feat that seemed like a genuine miracle, or would have seemed one to anyone ignorant of the fact that the Khmer Rouge artillerymen had actually done everything possible to avoid hitting the aircraft. But an accident, naturally, is always within the realm of possibility.

"One always has an anxious moment or two," Liu said to Lara. "Seen from the window next to my seat, Pochentong appears to be completely surrounded by Khmer Rouge trenches. I caught glimpses of men standing looking up at my plane, which they could very easily have riddled with projectiles. A very unpleasant sensation. What exactly is the situation here at present?"

Three months earlier, Lara's Peugeot 504, along with other vehicles, had been destroyed by a rocket while it was parked in the Rue Pasteur. The two men therefore climbed into a big Mercedes belonging to Liu, no doubt one of the few civilian vehicles in Phnom Penh that still had gas available, thanks to the 1,800-liter capacity storage tank that in September of 1973 Liu and Lara had had installed in the garden of the house on the Rue Phanouvong.

Lara got behind the wheel. Since his heart attack Liu had refused to drive a car. In this month of March 1975, the Chinese was looking forward to celebrating his sixtieth birthday, on April 17.

"The Khmer Rouge are about to take Neak Luong," Lara said in answer to Liu's question. "It's only a matter of days now, or maybe even of hours. As soon as Neak Luong has fallen, they'll be in control of both shores of the Mekong between Saigon and us and will keep any boat bringing in supplies from South Vietnam from getting through. Boats that are still trying to go up the Mekong are already being machine-gunned at point-blank range, and it's suicide. They obviously won't be trying to get through much longer. Sooner or later, one of them will sink athwart the channel and block it. And that'll be the end of that."

"There's naturally no traffic getting through by road anymore?"

"Naturally."

Silhouettes of tanks were framed in the windshield of the Mercedes, their gun turrets aimed toward Pochentong, the direction from which the enemy might appear, but the tanks themselves aimed in the direction of Phnom Penh, so as to be able to take off more quickly when the time came.

"And how about traffic to and from Kompong Som?"

"Nothing's getting through now," Lara said. "Phnom Penh is completely cut off by road. There's no possible way to get in or out of the city overland. As far as the rest of the country is concerned, to my knowledge and at this moment, Kompong Cham and Kompong Thom are still holding out, but doubtless not for long. They're isolated islands, completely surrounded. And the same goes for Kampot and Kompong Speu. The only actual territory still officially held by Lon Nol is the city of Battambang, along with about half the province. Boudin flew there just yesterday."

"And in Phnom Penh itself? Don't forget that I've been gone for two months."

"You shouldn't have come back."

Liu smiled. He was a rather tall, slender man with silver temples, who for some time now had been thought by many people to bear a marked resemblance to Chou En-lai, and indeed he did have the same intelligent and penetrating gaze and the rather aristocratic manner.

"Don't forget that I was born in this country, just as you were," Liu said.

They were now entering Phnom Penh, and Lara turned into the Rue Pasteur, leaving behind on his right the Boulevard Norodom, recently renamed the Boulevard du 18 Mars, in commemoration of the 1970 coup d'état. Lara drove along without a word, impassive and calm.

Liu started to laugh. "There are times when I wonder if you aren't even more Chinese than I am. All this is so like you: You come out to the airport to get me, at the risk of being blown sky-high by a rocket. You know very well that I'm bringing back important news, and you don't say a word, you don't make a single remark, you don't ask me the least question."

Lara nodded, and said with a smile, "All right, then, I'll ask you a question: Was the weather nice in Peking?"

Liu had been one of the very first residents of Phnom Penh not only to consider the ousting of Sihanouk a monstrous, stupid mistake but to do everything he could to see that this error was rectified just as soon as possible. From the very first minute of life of the new regime, he had decided that Lon Nol's chances of survival in power were nil. He had taken his first trip to Peking during the summer of 1970, met Samdech there, and had a long talk with him. He had not gone to China in his own interests alone; he had gone there also in the name of the Chinese community of Phnom Penh and of all Cambodia.

And the plan, which was not solely of his devising, had slowly taken shape over the years. It was based on the assumption that the elimination of Lon Nol and the return of Sihanouk to a position of power were the two fundamental goals to be achieved. The Watergate affair and Nixon's disappearance from the American political scene in 1974 had allowed the plan's proponents to foresee for a short time the possibility of removing the essential stumbling-block: Washington's stubborn, almost fanatic refusal to see Sihanouk resume his prerogatives and his responsibilities. But this hope did not last long. The CIA had devoted more than fifteen years to the task of driving Norodom Sihanouk, its personal enemy, from power; and they had not done so merely to open the door amiably for him again and facilitate his triumphant return. In the final analysis, it was a question of pride.

So that even though time was pressing, since the military situation was becoming more and more critical, they had wasted months that soon became years trying to remove this stumbling-block. Recently, however, Kissinger's trips to Peking, where he had been privately upbraided by Chou En-lai, the multiple representations made to Gerald Ford, who really had no firm policy, by the French, by the British, by Bouteflika the Algerian after being urged on by Boumedienne, by Tito, and by just about everyone, including even Mokhtar Ould Daddah of Mauretania, had at last very nearly convinced Washington.

"They're going to give in," Liu said to Lara. "In principle, the United States is going to announce tomorrow, very officially, that it will no longer support Lon Nol."

The Mercedes slowed down, threading its way between two wrecks of burned cars. Liu eyed Lara intently. "It's a pleasure to see you looking so enthused," he said.

"Sorry," Lara answered.

"You think it's too late—is that it?"

"I don't know."

The entry to the garden of Liu's villa was closed off by a wooden gate. When the car drove up, a Cambodian servant who must have been watching for it hurried to open the gate, forcing the refugees camping on the earthen sidewalk to clear out of the way by yelling at the top of his lungs and kicking them. Lara drove the Mercedes through the gate and up to the entrance to the garage, which contained three other cars, two more Mercedeses and a jeep. He switched off the ignition before driving the car inside, and sat lost in thought.

"And what about Ieng Sary?" he asked.

"He's still in Peking," Liu replied. "I saw him last Tuesday but we talked together for only a very short time. He's more virulent than ever."

"Does he know what's brewing? Sihanouk's return here and all?"

The two men's eyes met.

"It would be hard for him not to know," Liu answered.

More than ever the adversary of Sihanouk, of the monarchy, of the old regime that Sihanouk represented, in his personal fight against Samdech, Ieng Sary had managed to obtain the support of some of the most influential leaders in Peking, all of them adversaries of Chou En-lai's, and foremost among them Mao's own wife.

Liu finally made a move to get out of the car. He was obligated to lean far over to speak to Lara, who had remained at the wheel. "Will you have dinner with me?" he asked.

Lara shook his head. "The Korvers are waiting for me. If I could use this car . . ."

"Everything I have is yours," Liu said. "You know that."

It was not just a polite formula. For almost twenty years, Liu had felt genuine friendship and affection for Lara.

That evening at the Korvers', there was another guest at dinner besides Lara: an Australian journalist named Walter Brackett. Brackett was a veteran of the wars in Indochina; he prided himself on his friendship with Sihanouk and Souphanouvong, the Laotian Communist prince, and with Ho Chi Minh as well when he was still alive. It was a mania with him to explain everything, even the flooding of the Mekong Delta and plagues of locusts, as the fault of what he called American imperialism. A nice chap nonetheless, despite his obsession; each time he visited Phnom Penh, he made it a point to bring with him, all the way from Melbourne, an enormous box of a special kind of liqueur-filled chocolates that Madeleine adored.

It was an almost normal dinner, and would have been completely so had it not been for the incessant heavy artillery fire and the sort of powerful, omnipresent, persistent, dim roar that reached their ears from all over the city. Phnom Penh, which might have had 600,000 inhabitants before the coup d'état, now had a population of 3 million, and perhaps even more. In fact, half the population of Cambodia had now taken refuge in the city. It was as though one Frenchman or Britisher out of two had swarmed into Paris or London, which would thus have sheltered 26 million or 30 million men, women, and children.

"Heaven only knows how happy I was to learn that you were here in Phnom Penh and how happy I am to see you again," Brackett said to the Korvers. "But why in the devil have you stayed on? There can't be more than a few hundred Westerners at most left in the entire city. . . ."

"The people from the embassy came to see us twice," Madeleine said in her tiny voice. "They would have liked to see us fly out on one of those planes, or if worse came to worst to plan to come stay at the embassy. What a ridiculous idea!"

Delicately stroking the blue lock on her milky-white forehead, she turned to her husband for confirmation. Charles nodded his head approvingly. He was nonetheless thinking over the development that Lara had informed him of a few moments earlier: the change in attitude on the part of the Americans, who were finally about to stop supporting Lon Nol and were perhaps preparing to go along with the return of Sihanouk.

"And you think it's probably too late?" he asked Lara.

"Yes," Lara replied. "But one can always believe in miracles."

"I find you very pessimistic. You aren't taking sufficiently into account the enormous, the fantastic popularity of Norodom Sihanouk. I'd wager you can't even imagine what his return to Phnom Penh would mean. There are three million Cambodians in this city; there isn't a single one of them who doesn't dream of peace, and it's Samdech Sihanouk who represents peace, since the war didn't begin till after he'd been removed from power. If the imperialists in Washington really do finally abandon Lon Nol, and if Sihanouk really does return, Cambodia is saved."

"The one thing you're forgetting is the Khmer Rouge," Lara said with a calm bordering on seeming indifference.

"They've officially recognized Samdech Sihanouk as their Chief of State," said Brackett. "They've accepted him as President of a government of which they are the ministers. Why, and above all how, would they be opposed to him? And besides, three million Cambodians will be on the scene to acclaim and defend their prince."

Barely listening to what the Australian was saying, Charles Korver searched Lara's face intently. "But China supports Sihanouk, isn't that true?" he asked him.

"Chou En-lai, yes. But there's another faction in Peking that supports Ieng Sary and Pol Pot."

"You're a victim of Western propaganda," Brackett said. "China acts and thinks as one man, following Mao's lead. The supposed tensions between Peking and Moscow are nothing but a fiction invented by American journalists. On the plane coming here, I almost had a fight with a man who swore to me that Hanoi is dreaming of conquering all of Indochina. I knew Ho Chi Minh very well and I assure you that's completely untrue. If the two Vietnams one day become one again, it will be as a result of a perfectly democratic vote."

Lara turned his pale eyes Brackett's way, gave him a lingering look, then turned away.

"Good heavens, all that is certainly complicated!" Madeleine said. "I don't have any coffee left, but would anyone like some tea?"

"No, thanks," Brackett answered.

"I'd prefer a bit of cognac if you have any left," Lara said with a smile.

"A marvelous idea," the Australian said with a conspiratorial wink.

"You drink too much," Madeleine said to Lara.

He smiled again. "I know. And I smoke too much too." He lit a Bastos.

"I follow you," Charles said. "In effect, it's a race between Sihanouk and the Khmer Rouge to see who'll take over the city: Sihanouk by his mere presence, or the others by force of arms." He was silent for a moment, listening to the heavy artillery fire.

"That's why those gentlemen seem to be in such a rush to get inside the city all of a sudden, whereas during the last three years they've taken all the time in the world."

Unable to remain seated in his chair any longer, Charles rose to his feet. In just a few steps, he was outside in the garden, where many of the flower plantings were dying for lack of sufficient care. Standing there in the garden, he listened to the shelling, which was loud enough to drown out the sound of Brackett's voice as he went on with the conversation inside, and, even louder than the shelling, the immense, monstrous roar of the teeming city. It seemed to him to be a single, giant sound of breathing, like the syncopated panting of millions of people waiting in terror for the blows to descend. To his great surprise he found himself breathing in exactly the same rhythm.

He came back into the vast living room. The Australian and Lara had their backs turned to him, and his eyes met Madeleine's as she looked his way with tender affection. The love he felt for his wife, stronger than ever, gripped his heart.

"You don't know Sihanouk the way I know him," Brackett was saying. "He's the man of destiny, of last-second one-hundred-and-eighty-degree turns, of moments of genius and carefully staged sensational surprises. Even if—as you fear, and I must add that I don't share your fears—even if Saloth Sar and Khieu Samphan want to steal his victory from him by taking Phnom Penh before he returns, they won't be able to. Our friend Charles here spoke of a race against the clock. Samdech Sihanouk will win it."

Sihanouk lost it.

On April 1, the huge base at Neak Luong, the last remaining link between Saigon and Phnom Penh, fell. Worse still, a violent push by literally fanaticized Khmer Rouge allowed them to take over Pochentong Airport.

This was to doom Phnom Penh itself to fall, and within a very short time; it would no longer be possible to provision the city except by dropping supplies by parachute, and the only way in or out would be by helicopter. But this was not really the most important objective of the push: Controlling Pochentong meant that a plane flying Sihanouk into the country from Peking would not be able to land.

In the race against the clock that was a favorite metaphor of Brackett's, the Khmer Rouge scored a decisive point that day.

On March 30, finally, the United States had announced that it would no longer support Lon Nol. The United States did not agree, however, to lend its endorsement to Sihanouk's return. A representative at the American Embassy whom Brackett interviewed stated that anything, including a crushing defeat, was better than the victory of a man who, according to the official in question, was entirely responsible for the whole frightful mess, not only in Cambodia but in all of Southeast Asia.

"Without him, without Snookie, we would long since have settled things in Vietnam. Let him come back now? We'd die first! It's a point of honor."

The official was tall and blond, with a receding hairline and thick sideburns; he had the build of a truck driver, and the sleeves of his shirt rolled up past his bulging biceps. His name was Price. Lara had clued Brackett in about him: "He's the man who came here specifically to lay the groundwork for the coup d'état of March 18, 1970."

On April 1, Lon Nol left Phnom Penh for Indonesia, whose experts had lent him such precious help five years earlier. He was succeeded by a certian General Saukham Khoy, a figurehead who announced when Brackett went to see him: "If it were the will of the people, nothing could prevent a conditional surrender." That was tantamount to giving Sihanouk official permission to come back to Cambodia; all that would be needed would be a street demonstration demanding his return—a demonstration that for once would not have to be planned carefully so that it would be "spontaneous." But since Washington still had at its beck and call tough Khmer Krom and Khmer Sereï units quite capable of shooting Sihanouk on sight, it continued to beat about the bush, and the CIA fought a last-ditch battle, in the teeth of everything and everyone and in defiance of all reason, to prevent the situation from being saved by its personal enemy, "Snookie."

On April 11, Gerald Ford nonetheless managed to assert his authority. He sent Sihanouk a cable informing him of the "conviction of the American people" that Norodom Sihanouk represented the "unanimous choice of the Cambodian people," notifying him that he was taking every possible step to transfer to Sihanouk himself the "leadership of Phnom Penh," and advising him that nothing now stood in the way of his return to Phnom Penh, "with the aid of the Chinese government"—that is to say, providing Peking was willing to back Samdech and repatriate him.

Eighteen hours later, on April 12, Mao Tse-tung, finding himself obliged to arbitrate between Chou En-lai, who supported Sihanouk, on the one hand, and on the other the clique, headed by Mao's own wife, who supported Ieng Sary, Saloth Sar (also known as Pol Pot), and Khieu Samphan, chose, in view of his precise knowledge of the situation in Cambodia, to back the Khmer Rouge.

Sihanouk had lost out and knew that he had. He therefore answered Ford that he was no longer in a position to accept the responsibilities he was being asked to assume. He could not have failed to know that Saloth,

Khieu, and Ieng Sary were, or would one day be, the all-powerful masters of his country. He nonetheless considered that his rightful place, and his chances of one day influencing the course of events, lay in Cambodia itself, at the side of the Khmer Rouge, at whatever cost. And he added this sentence to his letter to Ford in reply: "I shall never betray the ties forged with the revolutionaries."

3

ON APRIL 17, 1975, SHORTLY BEFORE FIVE A.M., KUTCHAÏ ARRIVED AT A spot just outside the Central Market, the corner of the Rue Samdech Souk and the Boulevard Monivong, within a few steps of the entrance to the small hotel called the Kirirom. He stood there without moving for several minutes, impressed despite himself by the extraordinary calm, the heavy silence that had suddenly descended on the city at the second the war had ended.

There wasn't the slightest sign of life. He left again, passing in front of the gaudy façade of a movie theater; a little farther on, he turned into the Rue Pasteur, where he found himself obliged to step into the street to keep from awakening the hordes of refugees sleeping on the sidewalk.

He did not open the wooden gate barring the entrance to Liu's villa, but merely stepped over it. All the lights in the house were out, and in the early morning darkness it seemed to be completely deserted. He walked through the garden, more or less feeling his way along, and finally came upon the steps leading up to the stone veranda.

He went up onto the veranda and was about to knock at the door.

"I'm over here," Lara said, cupping his lighted cigarette in the palm of his hand.

Kutchaï wheeled halfway around. Lara was sitting, almost invisible, in one corner of the terrace.

"I was detained," Kutchaï said.

"A beer?"

Kutchaï nodded. He walked over to Lara, who handed him a bottle he fished out of the portable ice container at his feet. Kutchaï leaned his back against the wall, removed the cap of the bottle of Tsing Tao beer with his teeth, and began downing it.

"Are they very far away?" Lara asked.

"They could well arrive here within the hour. But they're taking their time. They've got everything all planned."

He drained the rest of the bottle. "Is there any more?"

Lara fished out another bottle.

"They're going to clear out the entire city," Kutchaï said. "Empty it completely."

For a second, Lara froze, just as he was handing the bottle to Kutchaï. A silence fell.

"There are three million people in Phnom Penh," Lara finally said.

Kutchaï lowered his chin to his chest and burped. "They don't give a damn. They're terrified at the thought that Sihanouk might land in the midst of all these millions. The best parry is to empty the whole city. If there's nobody left in it, there can't be any demonstration. Simple logic."

He took the bottle of Tsing Tao that Lara was still holding out to him and sat down alongside his friend on the little wooden bench, stretching out his arms and legs.

"And what about foreigners?" Lara asked.

Kutchaï knew that when Lara said "foreigners," he was in no way referring to himself but rather to people such as the Korvers.

"It's all been carefully planned," Kutchaï answered. "All the houses are going to be searched, all the buildings, public or private. A fine-tooth comb. No traffic, nothing."

Once again he performed the amazing feat of removing the bottle cap with his teeth. "I was dying of thirst. In principle, the plan is that everybody—the foreigners, I mean—will be rounded up and shut inside the French Embassy. Everybody, even the journalists."

He emptied two thirds of the bottle in a single swallow.

"Even the Swiss and the Russians." He began to laugh, his white teeth gleaming, relishing the thought that the Soviets were about to undergo the same fate as the French, the British, the Americans, the Germans, and even the Swiss.

"But not the Chinese," Lara said.

"No. Not the Chinese."

By sheer coincidence, at that same moment there was the sound of footsteps and a door slamming inside the villa, and Liu appeared on the veranda. "I heard you two talking down here. I was quite sure it was you," he said to Kutchaï.

The Chinese had chosen not to dress himself in his usual business suit tailor-made for him in Rome or Paris and was wearing only a shirt and a pair of khaki pants. In his hand was an equally modest khaki bag containing a few basic necessities; he was prepared to head for the embassy of the Popular Republic of China as planned. He glanced at the two men with a thoughtful look in his eye and finally asked, "When will they be here?"

"On the twenty-third, according to the battle plan."

"Why the delay? Today is the seventeenth, so that leaves six days. What are they waiting for?"

"They need time to round up all the political commissars they'll be needing. And they're going to be needing quite a few of them."

Kutchaï quickly explained what was going to happen: the total evacuation of Phnom Penh, down to the very last one of its three million inhabitants.

"Incredible!" Liu exclaimed, dumbfounded.

From the terrace of the villa they could see, very distinctly, the huge shantytown to the west of Phnom Penh burning to the ground. And dawn was just breaking in the east, beyond the Tonle Sap and the Mekong, illuminating in its ever-brighter crimson light the rest of the city still plunged in darkness.

"By the way, happy birthday," Lara said to Liu.

The first men dressed in black appeared at the very end of the Boulevard Norodom around seven A.M. The broad avenue laid out in earlier days by the French was totally deserted at this moment; the entire city seemed to be dead.

They numbered a few hundred at most, and after firing a dozen shots in the air, they began to advance slowly up the middle of the boulevard, the barrels of their rifles aimed at the silent façades of the buildings, dotted here and there with white flags. Lara and Kutchaï spied them just as they themselves were about to turn into the boulevard, across from the Hotel Raja. For a second Kutchaï halted dead in his tracks in surprise. Then he said, "Look at their arms."

The assault rifles brandished by the little band were American M-16's, with the characteristic tote grip mounted on top of the breech. The detachment passed by, their faces a bit tense but not really threatening otherwise. These faces were all very young; one could see in them the excitement of great events, but anxiety as well. They went by and continued up the boulevard, headed in the direction of the center of Phnom Penh; a little farther on, at the intersection of the Rue Dekcho Damdin, another group joined the first, this one arriving from the east of the city, from the Quai Sisowath beyond the Royal Palace.

"Let's go," Lara said.

He crossed the boulevard with Kutchaï at his side, and took the Rue Makhavan, which runs past the former Musée Albert Sarraut. The little square, where once upon a time the Venerables and members of the royal family were cremated, was deserted, but just as the two men started across it the towering figure of Mueller, the Swiss liquor salesman who lived just a few steps away, loomed into view. Mueller was relieved to see them.

"You couldn't have come along at a better time!" he exclaimed. "So the war is over, is it?"

"Something like that," Lara said, gently massaging the nape of his neck. Mueller must have dressed a little too hastily. His shirt was buttoned wrong.

"I saw the first Khmer Rouge go by," he said excitedly. "They don't look all that terrifying."

"They aren't Khmer Rouge," Lara said in his slow drawl. "They're students playing at revolution. They won't be playing long."

"Are you sure? Are you certain of that, you two?"

Kutchaï poked him in the chest with his enormous broad forefinger. "Certain," he replied.

Lara had already walked off, and Kutchaï followed him. After standing stock-still for a moment in the middle of the little square, Mueller ran after them.

"Where are you going?"

"To the Korvers'."

Mueller grabbed Lara's arm, forcing him to stop. "Listen, I really don't have any idea what to do. . . ."

He did look completely bewildered. Lara nodded distractedly. "Okay, then. In theory the Khmer Rouge were to wait a few days before entering the city, but it's probable that those idiot students will precipitate matters and bring them here sooner. In other words, they may arrive today; in fact, they're quite likely to do so. Pack a suitcase, a small one, and get yourself over to the French Embassy as fast as you can."

"But I'm Swiss!"

Kutchaï was the only man in all of Cambodia to deal with this particular Helvetian as an equal from the point of view of sheer physical height. He tapped him on the cheek and smiled. "Do what Lara says," he told him. "The French Embassy. And get your Swiss ass in gear."

It began less than a hundred yards farther on, in the Rue Yukanthor, after they'd left behind the Swiss, with his tall thin frame and his air of utter confusion. At the windows of the crowded apartment buildings, at each door, on the metal grilles of the Chinese shops, a sea of white flags had gradually appeared. The population of Phnom Penh, at first timid and anxious, then little by little reassured, had begun to pour out into the streets, surrounding these black-clad youngsters who didn't look at all like the monsters they'd been described as—who, on the contrary, were smilingly explaining that they weren't really bloodthirsty revolutionaries but, rather, fervent supporters of Samdech Sihanouk, Sihanouk who was about to return, who was nearly there, who would fix everything and restore peace forevermore. Sihanouk. The name rang out all along the streets and soon was being chanted in unison, as the population came out of hiding, poured out of their dwellings, and gathered on the streets and sidewalks.

On the Rue Khemarak Phomin, Lara and Kutchaï almost had to fight their way through a joyous crowd already starting to celebrate the end of the fighting, the arrival of these good-natured conquerors, the return of peace and of Samdech. They struggled through the mob and finally came out in front of the Eden movie theater.

"You were right," Kutchaï said. "They're going to be forced to intervene. So much the worse for their battle plan. They can't allow the city to get carried away with excitement. Just look at those stupid idiots!"

A group of boys and girls ran by, holding aloft an enormous portrait of Norodom Sihanouk like the ones that, six years earlier, the Khmer Royal Socialist Youth had carried in their parades.

It was nearly eight-thirty by the time they arrived at the Korvers', but they found the house empty. Yuan, the Cambodian servant, informed them that the couple had left some twenty minutes before.

"I trust they weren't crazy enough to go out and mingle with that crowd, were they? Might they have gone to the French Embassy?"

Yuan had no idea. Lara slowly walked through all the vast rooms on the ground floor, contemplating the countless statues and objets d'art that Charles and Madeleine had collected in their sixty years of patient and costly research. Each one of these pieces, selected from among tens of thousands of others, was fabulously beautiful and undoubtedly priceless. Lara fingered a little T'ang statuette, which must have dated from the seventh or eighth century: It represented a marvelous young woman of the Imperial Court, in a dress with a long train, wide flowing sleeves, and high pointed shoulders. Alongside it, and dating from the same period, a falconer on horseback; farther on, a group of girl musicians in yellowed ivory, breathtakingly graceful, next to a sumptuous collection of ivory and jade pieces chiseled by the hand of a sculptor born four centuries before the building of Angkor and its temples.

"And what are you doing, may I ask? We don't have all that much time." There was a note of irritation in Kutchaï's deep booming voice.

"The Taverne," Lara said. "They sometimes go there to have breakfast."

They left again, this time at a run.

Empty a quarter of an hour earlier, the Avenue des Français was now teeming with a crowd apparently identical to the one that had filled the streets of the center of town to overflowing, but this crowd, less urban, made up for the most part of refugees and more uncertain of its own feelings, was also more anxious. It moved aside with dull resignation to let the two men through, impressed by the size of the enormous Jaraï and the look of violent exasperation on his face, and also by the fact that Lara was a *Barang*, a *Barang* who was running.

In front of the Palace of Government a number of soldiers had been positioned behind sandbags, but there was no commanding officer in sight and they were content merely to remain at their posts, with stupid looks on their faces, listlessly pointing the barrels of their submachine guns more or less in the direction of five or six pedicab boys, who were standing there perfectly calm and relaxed with their funny little conical straw hats perched on their heads and barelegged. They had plainly decided that all this commotion in no way concerned them, since they had nothing to lose and probably nothing to gain no matter what change might be in the offing.

The Taverne was closed, but the Korvers were sitting at one of its outdoor tables, all by themselves, calmly holding hands. The Main Post Office was closed, as were the French pharmacy, the Banque d'Indochine, and even the commissariat of police; but here the Korvers were, on this deserted square that had been so full of life once upon a time, the two of them looking as tiny and as cheerful as ever, a frail old couple whose combined ages added up to something close to 160 years.

"Were you looking for us?"

"That's right," Lara said, his long thin hands thrust into the pockets of his canvas bush jacket.

He walked over, took Madeleine by the hand, and gently but firmly pulled her to her feet.

"But we haven't had our breakfast yet!" she protested indignantly.

"I think there are certain things that are more pressing," Lara answered softly. "And anyway, the Taverne's closed."

They went back to the villa. By then it was approximately ten A.M.

"It seems to me that you haven't quite realized what it is that Madeleine and I really want to do. The two of us have had a long talk about it together," Charles said.

"Exactly. We've talked it all over together," Madeleine put in.

"And we both agree perfectly as to what we want to do. We're certainly not going to go to the French Embassy."

"Oh, no!" Madeleine said. "In fact, we're not going to go anywhere. We're going to stay here."

And as proof of her determination, she sat down at her usual place at the big table, facing the tall filing cabinet where she kept her index cards.

Lara exchanged glances with Kutchaï and then, pulling out a chair, sat down astride it. "You know, don't you, that Kutchaï and I could take you away from here simply by tucking you under our arms?"

Madeleine gave him a sly condescending smile. "You most certainly wouldn't do a thing like that," she said. "We've known you ever since you were born. Both of you. You were really awful, both of you, in those days, and not very big at all."

Charles sat down, too, opposite his wife, and began thumbing through index cards. "We're not going to leave this house," he said. "Absolutely not. We were driven out of Shanghai. We were driven out of Hanoi. This time is once too many. We're not going to leave all these things that are our whole life."

"I beg you, I implore you," Lara said in a gentle, sad voice. "I swear to you that there's no hope left. None."

He raised his eyes, meeting Kutchaï's. Kutchaï's face was deliberately blank, completely impassive.

"These men who are going to come aren't just ordinary revolutionaries," Lara went on. His eyes never left Kutchaï's as he spoke. "They're going to make a charnel house of this country. You can't even imagine what they're getting ready to do. They're going to do something that's never been done before in all of history."

Charles Korver nodded amiably and began to consult a large register bound in white leather in which he had noted the principal characteristics of each of the pieces in their collection.

"And what about you?" he asked as he turned the pages. "Will you go to the embassy?"

"No," Lara answered. "As soon as you're safe and sound, I'm going to take off to the Cardamomes."

Madeleine had started to write, in her fine English hand with its exquisitely formed thick-and-thin characters. She gently shook her head and said in her tiny schoolmarm's voice, "You can see very well that all that isn't reasonable. This time you won't have that amusing little Boudin to take you off in his plane, and if the situation is as dreadful as you say, how are you going to get through the lines of the hundred thousand Khmer Rouge who have us surrounded?"

"Because Kutchaï is a leader of the Khmer Rouge," Lara said in a weary voice, still gazing intently at the Jaraï. "And because we're leaving together."

There was a silence. After having sat there for a second with their pens suspended in the air, Charles and Madeleine began writing again.

"I see," Charles said. "But that doesn't change anything as far as we're concerned."

"Go along with you," Madeleine said, as she would have said "And now go off and play" to children. "It's so very nice of you to have come."

For the first time since they had come back into the vast living room following their return from the Taverne, Kutchaï moved. In just two strides he reached one of the glass cases on the wall opposite them. As Lara had done an hour or so before, he opened it and picked up the T'ang statuette, more than twelve centuries old, in his enormous fingers. He turned around, facing the Korvers, and at the very second that Charles cried out, he smashed it to bits with one sharp blow on the edge of the cabinet shelf. He let the pieces fall to the floor and crushed them beneath his heel.

"No! No!" Charles screamed, rushing over to him.

Without being brutal but with irresistible strength, Kutchaï lifted Charles up off the floor and set him down again out of his way. He took a long Samurai saber down from the wall and began to lash out with it at random, pulverizing the priceless porcelains and terra cottas, wielding it with a sort of suppressed, cold, absolutely implacable violence, as though it were not only a question of shattering something but of killing it as well. Madeleine began to scream too.

"Lara, stop him!" she shouted.

For a few interminable seconds Lara remained rooted to the spot, motionless, his pale eyes almost completely shut, and then he moved toward Kutchaï. But instead of trying to overpower the towering Jaraï, he, too, grabbed a saber and began lashing out with it, his face livid and contracted in a horrible grimace, smashing everything in a ruthless frenzy, and crushing the debris underfoot in hopeless rage.

4

KOMPONG SOM HAD FALLEN.

The great bay was empty and the port deserted. Through his field glasses, for the third time, Suon Phan had just witnessed a mass execution. This time, after some hundred officers of the former garrison had been mowed down with machine guns, after their wives and children had been slaughtered in the same way, it had come the turn of several hundred civilians, apparently technicians and workers from the refinery and the port. Led by their Kamaphibals, the Khmer Rouge had forced them to tie each other up so as to form a compact group, a hideous tangle of trunks, limbs, and heads, and then, with great bursts of machine-gun fire aimed only inches from this human swarm, they had very slowly driven it toward the sea, compelling it to advance along the northern jetty and then finally forcing it over the edge into deep water and firing on everything that came back to the surface.

Suon Phan knew he should have long since abandoned the lookout post where he had hidden, on one of the points of the Cheko Peninsula. Terrified that the enemy might discover them, the four men Suon Phan had with him kept urging him to do so. But, no longer fascinated but literally overwhelmed, stupefied by the excess of the massacre he was watching, he could not bring himself to leave. Ever since he had joined Kao, the former student from Phnom Penh had admittedly witnessed the basest sort of mass murders often enough—he remembered the way in which Kao had wiped out the Khmer Rouge camp, only a little distance from the spot where he was at this moment—but it seemed to him that an even greater degree, an inconceivable degree, of horror and madness had been reached now. The last batch of prisoners they had captured had willingly, almost complacently, explained in detail what the Angkar Loeu not only planned to do but had actually begun doing: systematically killing off monks, small tradesmen, civil servants, students, teachers, intellectuals—anyone who knew how to read and write was regarded as an "intellectual"—officers, noncommissioned officers, even buck privates guilty of zealously carrying out the orders of the supercorrupt supertraitor Lon Nol, doctors, nurses, engineers, architects; all those who, in any way, shape, or form had exercised the least responsibility under the old order. It was necessary to raze, or at the very least to empty of any sort of human presence, the largest cities and eliminate all those who had lived there, because they were people who had denied their origins: the land and the forest, which alone allowed the Khmer people to remain pure. It was necessary to eliminate all those who, because they were old, because they were more than thirty, because they had known the rottenness of the old order, could not really accept the new Kampuchea. It was necessary to eliminate the sick and the infirm, and the half-breeds who had contaminated the age-old Khmer race, especially if they had in their veins the blood of the hereditary enemies of Kampuchea, the Vietnamese and the Thais. It was necessary to return to the pastoral purity of the Khmers of old, to seal the country off and live in proud and terrible isolation for as long a time as it would take to do so to achieve that purity, refusing even to acknowledge the existence of the outside world and rejecting, without pity or regret, everything it had created.

Suon Phan was lying on his belly. Someone brushed against his leg. He turned around and at that precise moment heard the sound of an engine which, the very next second, in the space of a single pounding heartbeat, he recognized. At last, he stopped watching. Taking care not to stand silhouetted above the crest of the hill that until then had hidden him from sight, he cautiously crawled backward and soon was able to stand up again. He ran down the slope. As he was skirting a dense patch of forest, he caught sight of Kao's jeep, with his machine gun still mounted on the hood, and Kao himself, who grumbled, "What in hell were you doing? We've been spotted. A column is headed straight this way."

Besides the jeep, they had two trucks left, but after about twenty kilometers on what was not even a trail, one of the trucks stopped for good, having run out of gas. The sixty-odd men still alive out of the hundred who had made up the original commando unit clambered up onto the two vehicles still able to proceed and hung on as best they could. They drove on for another hour over terrain that was still not very heavily wooded but increasingly rugged, climbing higher and higher as they made their way deeper into the foothills of the Cardamomes. Turning around at regular intervals, Kao and

his men could now see their pursuers, as tenacious and fully as well trained
as they themselves were at this deadly game. At the wheel of his jeep, Kao
was humming an old Sinatra song, or at least Suon Phan thought he recognized the melody.

"And where is it we're going—if we managed to get away from them?"

Phan kept turning around more and more often, and each time he discovered that the three or four hundred Khmer Rouge pursuing them, with
an even larger detachment following behind, were regularly gaining
ground. *It's this truck and this jeep that are holding us up. We'd make better
time on foot.* But he didn't dare to imagine what Kao's reaction would be if
he suggested to him that he abandon his beloved jeep.

"We'll get away from them," Kao said with a laugh. "What are you
worried about?" He began humming again.

"And where will we go then? To Thailand?"

Phan couldn't believe the things that were happening. He had no idea
what fate had befallen Phnom Penh, the other cities, the enclave of Battambang. The last prisoner they had tortured till he talked before executing
him like the others seemed convinced that the end of the capital was near.
According to him, it was only a question of days, if not of hours. So Phnom
Penh had already fallen by now, a dead, destroyed city. Phan was suddenly
overcome by a painful nostalgia at the memory of the little tables of the Old
Market in the balmy, fragrant darkness of a Phnom Penh evening, the
young girls with splendid bodies in their clinging silk *sampots*, their hips
swaying, their breasts moving freely underneath their close-fitting bodices.
That was one of the things he had learned from the foreign films of the
West: the beauty of girls' breasts and how pleasing it was to stroke them
with the palm of your hand or simply to look at them, whereas in the countryside so many women went about with bare breasts that nobody ever
dreamed of paying any attention to them.

"What would you want to go to Thailand for?" Kao said, bursting into
laughter. "Are you tired of the war already? No, Phan, we're going to go on
fighting the way we always have. I thought about it last night, and I've even
found a name for us: the Black Cobras. You've seen cobras, haven't you?
Sure you have. We even killed one a couple of months ago. Phan, where
we're going, there are cobras all over the place. It's a forest such as you've
never seen in your life. The Kirirom and the Elephant forests are just little
woods by comparison. It's another world, Phan, dense, dark, unknown.
We're going to seek refuge there, and we'll come out every so often to strike
like cobras: just once, quick but deadly."

Ten minutes later, the second truck stopped dead, too, its gas tank
empty. It was time: The Khmer Rouge were a bare eighteen hundred yards
away now, and less than five hundred feet below. The truck was set on fire
like the first one, with an incendiary grenade, and destroyed. They started

off again and the grade became steeper still, so steep that sometimes the jeep balked like a horse refusing a jump. More and more often, a dozen men had to get out and push to get it past a rocky stretch. Phan, who was sitting alongside Kao, wanted to get out and walk but Kao wouldn't let him.

"Stay where you are. This'll get us through. It's never failed me yet." And he stroked the barrel of the machine gun that was like a sort of prick.

As they climbed, the panorama became more and more vast and grandiose. It was an unusually clear day and a light, almost cool, breeze blowing off the sea made for an astonishing range of visibility, so that Suon Phan saw Elephant Peak slowly rising on his left, the Thai coast on his right, and when he turned around to look down the slope they had just climbed, the chains of large and small islands, like rosaries, in the violet waters of the Gulf of Siam. For a second, the memory of that very beautiful white woman, wounded by mistake on one of those little islands, flashed through his mind. He wondered if she had died. For a brief instant, the memory of the faces of the two men also came back to him: the White with his pale eyes and that enormously tall Cambodian with the wild, terrifying grin.

And then these memories vanished from his mind; the Khmer Rouge were now a mere twelve hundred yards away.

"They're catching up with us."

"Damn!" Kao said, his teeth clenched and his forehead dripping with sweat.

He clutched the wheel of his fetishistic jeep, forcing it to the limit, no longer able to keep it headed straight up the steep slope, zigzagging back and forth and gaining almost no ground.

"Push!" Kao screamed.

The jeep had gotten stuck on a rock again. The men got behind it, their faces drawn with exhaustion, their eyes wary. This insanity was beginning to worry them, though after five years they had had every occasion to realize what a madman their leader was.

"Push!"

They pushed, and the jeep took off again with a screech of ripped metal. At the same instant, someone gave a sharp cry. Phan turned around once more and saw that one of the commandos had been hit in the thigh by a bullet.

"PUSH!" Kao screamed.

The nose of the jeep was tilted at such an angle that Phan had to grip the windshield frame so as not to tumble backward.

"PUSH, YOU GODDAMNED BUNCH OF BASTARDS!"

Phan scrutinized the terrain in front of him and saw a sort of ascending slope vaguely crisscrossed with little gullies made by the rain, with sharp tops of buried rocks sticking out here and there. The forest was only 150 yards away now. *And then what? Even if we manage to push this fucking jeep up there?* The forest seemed literally impenetrable: a barrier as hermetic, as formidable as a solid wall.

"PUSH OR I'LL SHOOT EVERY LAST ONE OF YOU DOWN!"

Once more the men bent their backs and pushed, amid a strong odor of oil dripping out of the cracked crankcase. They gained ten, then twenty yards. The bullets were now falling all around them in a terrifyingly steady hail, burying themselves in the clay soil or shattering the tops of the rocks. Other wounded men collapsed on the ground.

"PUSH!"

Suon Phan leapt out of the jeep in one bound. He pointed his M-16 straight at Kao.

"Come on, get out!"

For a second that lasted an enternity Phan really thought he was going to have to pull the trigger. And then the murderous gleam in Kao's eyes went dead, he lowered his gaze, and nodded his head.

"Okay, kid, okay."

He set the hand brake and climbed out. The jeep slid three feet or so downhill and then collided with a boulder that kept it from sliding farther.

"Okay," Kao said again. "Clear the hell out of here, all of you."

"Into the forest!" Phan shouted.

He broke into a run, as others fell all around him. Very soon, much sooner than he expected, they reached the solid green wall towering before them. Someone hacked out an opening in it with a machete and he disappeared through it.

"This way!"

The men filed past him, as though passing through a doorway, a number of them covered with blood, limping, or dragging a more seriously wounded comrade after them. In rapid succession, two bullets hit the trunk of the teak tree behind which he had taken cover. The flow of men past him slowed to a trickle, then stopped altogether. Phan stuck his head out and saw that the slope was deserted, with the exception of five or six men lying on the ground motionless, none of them giving the slightest sign of life.

And with the exception of Kao.

Kao was leaning over the hood of the jeep, and with an extraordinary, inhuman calm, despite the bullets riddling the ground and pinging on the sheet metal all around him, was patiently unbolting his machine gun.

"KAO! QUICK! OVER HERE!"

Why am I shouting? The guy's completely mad! Phan thought. But a wild, inexplicable pride came over Suon Phan on seeing the courage of this man at whose side he had fought for so long. He had always believed, he had always been convinced, that he hated Kao, that he had stayed with him for the sole reason that Kao terrified him. But at this moment he found himself praying with desperate fervor that Kao would reach him still alive. Kao removed the last bolt, flung the cartridge belt over his shoulder, lifted the machine gun up, and cradled the barrel of it in the crook of his left arm. He began to yell and at the same time to shoot at the dozens of Khmer Rouge storming up the slope, no more than three or four hundred yards away from him now. Kao began to climb up the slope toward the forest then, walking backward, shouting defiantly and still shooting.

Still walking backward, he covered step by step the seventy or eighty yards separating him from Suon Phan without being hit, without the slightest scratch, still bellowing defiantly and firing his last bullets when the forest closed around him and swallowed him up.

5

AT ALMOST EXACTLY THE SAME HOUR—ON APRIL 17 AT TWO O'CLOCK in the afternoon—Walter Brackett came out of the Hotel Royal where he had managed to have lunch served him and resolutely stepped into the burning-hot sunlight to cross the broad esplanade of the Avenue Daun Penh, with the Catholic cathedral on his right, the Lycée Descartes opposite him, the Phnom on his left. He was aware of the fact that for several hours people had mistaken for Khmer Rouge mere students playing at reenacting May '68. From this turn of events, which he flattered himself corroborated his judgment as to the fabulous popularity of Sihanouk, he nonetheless drew the same conclusion as Lara: He expected to see the Khmer Rouge arrive at any moment. The real ones.

And he had to admit he was scared.

At the Rue Ang Non, he recognized a French photographer he knew from the Sygma agency. He raised his hand to wave at him and yelled "Serge!" but the Frenchman didn't turn his head, and something about his very attitude alerted Brackett. He looked in the same direction, toward the south, and saw too.

They were there.

Walter Brackett had been born in Adelaide and was now sixty-two years old. He had been a witness, on the battleship *Missouri*, of the formal surrender of the Japanese; he had covered the war in Korea and been wounded twice, first as he followed the retreat of the First Marine Division at Chosin Reservoir, and then again several months later at the time of the battle of the Iron Triangle; he was present at Dien Bien Phu on May 7, 1954, a few hours after the end of the fighting and the capitulation of the last French defenders, and then on July 9 of that same year, he had been on the scene as French civilians left Hanoi.

Walter Brackett had never really been a card-carrying Communist, but he had always considered himself a Communist sympathizer. He thought he had seen everything that a war or a revolution could bring in the way of courage, baseness, monstrosities, horrors. The next few hours brought him incontrovertible proof that he still had everything to discover.

Close to three million inhabitants of Phnom Penh were driven out in four days. Four days during which—counting the men, women, and children murdered outright, those who were strangled to death, those who died of thirst, those who perished as the result of wounds received in preceding battles, those who committed suicide or succumbed to various epidemics during what was the largest exodus in the history of the world in such a short period of time—there were probably between 100,000 and 200,000 dead. Not counting the hundreds of thousands, perhaps even a million or more, victims whose corpses piled up in the days that immediately followed.

The nearly three million inhabitants of Phnom Penh were driven out onto the highways and the roads, fleeing in any and every direction, so long as it was somewhere else. There was no possibility whatever of escaping the campaign to clear out the entire city. Every house was searched, every administrative, commercial, or community building, and those who had hoped to be able to hide out in them were murdered on the spot without a chance to offer one word of explanation in their own defense. Frenzied hordes of Khmer Rouge, very young usually, many of them as young as twelve or thirteen but all armed with Kalashnikovs, M-16's, Colts, submachine guns, or machetes, burst into all the public hospitals and private clinics, even into the operating rooms where surgeons were at work. They smashed everything to bits, from the scialytic lamps to the cabinets full of medicines that soon were to be so cruelly missed, from the most costly medical apparatus to the beds on which amputees, dying patients, or women in labor were lying. Often they shot off their firearms at random, ordering everyone out and pushing those patients who were hesitant, mad, or helpless out the windows when the order was not obeyed promptly enough to suit them.

In conformity with the tradition marking total defeats, the officials of the large banks, the National Bank, the Khmer Commercial Bank, Inadana Jati, held themselves in readiness from one P.M. on that same day, April 17, to hand over to the conquerors the keys to their vaults. They were almost all slaughtered on the spot and the bloody survivors watched as hundreds of millions of riels, dollars, francs, pounds sterling, roubles, all the money still on hand in Phnom Penh, was stuffed into sacks which were then drenched with gasoline and burned.

Obviously obeying a precise order, the invaders also set fire to every book, pamphlet, newspaper, manuscript, and in general any bit of paper of any sort with writing or printing on it to be found in the entire city. In certain places, these autos-da-fé set whole buildings on fire, with no one bothering to put them out.

The incredible frenzy of destruction did not end there. Everything the dwellings, the warehouses, and the stores of the city contained in the way of furniture, household equipment of any sort, clothing, lamps, knickknacks, radio sets, record players, mechanical devices of all kinds, was methodically tossed out onto the streets in the course of the next few days and likewise consigned to the flames, sprayed with napalm, blown up.

In the first twelve hours following the fall of Phnom Penh, no more than ten thousand Khmer Rouge entered the city. This was already a large number, inasmuch as each one of these ten thousand men and women was ready to murder, and set about doing so with a will. It was not, however, a large enough number to empty the city completely and channel the gigantic human torrent that had to be forced out immediately. During the night of the seventeenth and the early morning hours of the eighteenth, reinforcements arrived, approximately 25,000 new killers, no less bloodthirsty than the first wave but, on the contrary, sent into a frenzy of excitement at the sight of the carnage their predecessors had already wreaked. They used rockets and bazookas, flamethrowers captured from Lon Nol's troops, and to speed the exodus up, they used them at point-blank range.

It was right in the middle of the dry season, there was not the slightest drop of water in the rice paddies, and during the afternoon of the seventeenth, either because of an accidental rupture of a main conduit or because it was deliberately cut off, the Phnom Penh municipal water system ceased to function. As a result, with the thermometer at over 100 degrees Fahrenheit, the three million inhabitants of the capital were forced to abandon their dwellings and set out without water or any other provisions, in a fantastic crowd so dense that it took some people, so jampacked together they nearly smothered to death—as thousands of others in fact did—four days to cover two kilometers.

On April 23, the day officially set by Saloth Sar (who had meanwhile become Pol Pot) and Khieu Samphan, in their battle plan, for the taking of Phnom Penh, an American reconnaissance plane—a Phantom!—flew over the city and spied absolutely no sign of life except for dogs devouring corpses in the streets.

There was one place in the city, however, where there were people still alive: the French Embassy, at the very end of the Boulevard Monivong. All the foreigners left in Phnom Penh in its last hours had assembled there, making of it a strange caravanserai. Besides French citizens, inside its walls were English, Germans, Italians, Belgians, the handful of Americans who had not been evacuated at the last minute by the Air America helicopters, Koreans, Pakistanis, Indians. Even the Soviet chargé d'affaires and his aides,

after the door of their legation had been blown off by a bazooka, had been
gagged and then shoved to this island surrounded by a desert.

Walter Brackett regained consciousness and for a few seconds had no idea
where he was or how he had gotten there. Then there flashed into his mind
the memory of the young Khmer Rouge advancing toward him and lashing
out at him with the butt of his Kalashnikov, just as he, Brackett, was trying
to explain that he was a leftist journalist, a personal friend of Ho Chi Minh.
Someone told him how he and the photographer from Sygma had been literally delivered, like parcels, at the French Embassy.

Brackett explored his forehead gingerly with his fingertips and could
find only a big lump and a slight wound. They even did him the honor of
bandaging his head. Soon he could walk normally again and he began to
search for the Korvers.

He met up with schoolteachers, professors, French *co-opérants* who, in
the name of the sacred alliance of revolutionaries of all countries, had been
all set to welcome the Khmer Rouge in proper fashion, donning revolutionary garb in the form of a red scarf from the Belle Jardinière in Paris, or
even Cardin. They had been literally booted in the ass straight into their
embassy, like so many plain ordinary colonialists. Their indignation at not
having been understood knew no bounds. Their Khmer Rouge "comrades"
had not even deigned to join in the chorus of the "Internationale" that six of
them had sung in front of the Bank of Indochina.

Brackett spotted Mueller, the Swiss, sitting on a suitcase.

"I don't know what I'm doing here," Mueller said. "I'm Swiss."

Farther on, he came across Albert Vandekherkove and his trombone.

And still farther on, he came across the Korvers. Or rather, Madeleine
Korver. The little old lady was sitting on one of the front steps of the embassy, her delicate, diaphanous hands resting on her knees, hands one would
almost have expected to see encased in embroidered mitts. She was frail and
tiny, meticulously dressed as usual, more reminiscent than ever of those
pastel pink and blue eighteenth-century porcelains.

"Thank heaven," Brackett said, his voice full of emotion. "Thank
heaven you're here."

He sat down beside her, as always dumbfounded at how extraordinarily
slender and graceful she was. Madeleine raised her forget-me-not-blue eyes
and looked up at him.

"Charles is here too," she said in her little voice. "But he's dead. He
had a heart attack an hour ago."

She was gazing straight ahead of her now. With a great lump in his
throat, Brackett tried to take her hand in his, but she gently pulled it away.

"Thanks, Walter, but he was very old, you know. And he was a very
sentimental man."

Brackett's eyes misted over. Finally he said, "Is there anything I can do?"

"I don't believe so," Madeleine replied. "Thank you very much."

She opened her eyes wide, as though she were having difficulty seeing. Then she added, in a perfectly calm, even voice, "I'd really like to die, too, now. I hope it won't be too long before I do."

Someone from the embassy came to get her and, holding her gently beneath the arm, helped her to her feet and then led her inside.

After a moment Brackett rose to his feet too. Through the dazed crowd he walked in a stupor strangely mingled with feelings of shame and sadness such as he had never felt before. He caught sight of several of his fellow journalists who, from just inside the wall surrounding the embassy and marking its extraterritorial limits, were contemplating with a shiver of horror the monstrous human torrent beginning to flow past. He walked over to exchange impressions with them. He learned from them that all the Whites in Phnom Penh, and not only all the Whites but all non-Khmers except for the Chinese, were grouped, gathered together, cooped up around him in this embassy.

All but one.

6

OUTSIDE THE MAIN GATE OF THE AMERICAN EMBASSY IN SAIGON, AN almost battle was going on. Those who managed to get inside, after having their papers carefully inspected by the Marine guards on duty, had left their Cadillacs and their Mercedeses parked in the street, and hordes of looters, some of the most rapacious of whom were policemen, had immediately set to work ripping them apart, removing the tires, the radios with built-in cassette players, the seats, the brake linings, all the engine and body parts, screaming and cursing and kicking each other as they quarreled over the spoils.

O'Malley left the Vietnamese girl in front of the entrance to a store, a hundred yards from the scene of the big fight, smiled at her, went inside the embassy and straight up to the office of Ambassador Graham Martin. The ambassador grabbed him by the arm.

"O'Malley, my dear Tom, I'm counting on you. You alone can understand, you alone have realized what this tree means to me, to the America that we love, to the Free World. Tom, I implore you and order you to take care of it. I know I can count on you, can't I?"

The ambassador was downing one cup of coffee after another, with trembling hands and dark circles under his red eyes, and swallowing heaven only knew what sort of pills. O'Malley finally left and wandered about from one office to another, finding them all empty. Eventually he came across someone, a great hulking bald fellow with the chest of a bull who, O'Malley seemed to remember vaguely, was from Security, from the CIA, or one of that breed at any rate, the sort your nose told you instantly was either a military officer or a duly appointed undercover agent. O'Malley explained his problem. The great hulking brute turned out to be a colonel. And just the person he needed to see.

"And you never drew up a list?* Never?"

"Never," said O'Malley

The colonel was utterly imperturbable, with the cold, unyieldingly skeptical stare of the veteran police officer. "All the names you give will be carefully checked out, you may rest assured of that."

"I have complete confidence in the authorities," O'Malley replied, trying his best to be sardonic.

The colonel reached into a drawer and took out a series of papers which he promptly stamped, apparently at random.

"Sign here. And write down the names in this column, with the numbers of their identification cards or their passports. With no mistakes, please. You don't have all of them? All right, you can add them later. Provided there are not more than eight names in all, not a single one more. Are they friends of yours? Your little sister, maybe?"

O'Malley looked him straight in the eye. "A mistress of mine, as everybody knows."

He had the satisfaction of seeing the colonel's cold, hard eyes cloud over for a brief moment. He recopied onto the printed form the girl's whole name, just as she had given it to him some ten minutes earlier. He left the other seven lines blank. At the last second, he underlined the only name he'd written down.

"It's no use underlining it. That won't change a thing," the colonel remarked.

"You can go to hell," O'Malley said blandly. "You can go fuck yourself, at the bottom of hell for all eternity."

The colonel burst out laughing. He put the paper O'Malley had signed, a sort of receipt for the safe-conduct pass for the girl, in a briefcase.

"You got here just in time. I was about to leave myself. In an hour, I'll be aboard one of the aircraft carriers lying offshore. The people on your list have a choice: a seat on the plane taking off from Tan Son Hut, or one on a helicopter flying out from here in the city. Is she pretty?"

"The helicopter. Very pretty."

---

* The list that employees of the State Department and military personnel had the privilege of drawing up, indicating the names of Vietnamese nationals whom they wished to see safely evacuated from the country.

"And is she a hot number in bed? In general they're cold fish, worse than my wife, and that's saying quite a lot. I like you, O'Malley. If they erect a statue one of these days to the Unknown Civilian, I'll have to remember you. You're one of the most civil civilians I've ever had the distinct lack of pleasure of meeting. And now you can get the fuck out of here. You don't realize how lucky you were to find me still in my office. You take it entirely for granted! And what do you have to say to the obliging gentleman?"

"To hell with you, doubled in spades," O'Malley answered.

He put the papers in the right inside pocket of his suit coat and even went so far as to button it. He felt a sort of joy, a glow of pleasure and tenderness. He would at least have been useful for something. He walked down the ice-cold air-conditioned corridor lined with wide-open doors, breathing in the dusty smell of papers in the process of being shredded by special machines to be used in case of evacuations, retreats, irremediable defeats. He came upon groups of CIA agents searching each office, one after the other, calmly and methodically, in order to make sure nothing had been left behind that might incriminate the United States of America. They were even searching the lavatories and inspecting the toilet paper.

O'Malley walked off, with the strong feeling that he was leaving the combat theater for good. He didn't intend to be caught there ever again, no matter what. He thought of Paris, of this or that chair or this or that narrow outdoor terrace on the Rue des Saints-Pères, that he loved almost as much as he loved the Brooklyn Bridge—Paris, where Slattery had promised-sworn-crossed-his-heart that he would be given a post, where he would perhaps end up eventually, if he didn't resign first.

He went outside, passing from the cool sixty-eight-degree temperature inside the embassy to the hundred degrees and more outside. The sky was full of rolling dark purple clouds.

"Where are you going?" Kearns, the commanding officer of the Marine guards attached to the embassy, called after him. "This is no time to leave here. Can't you see we're about to clear the hell out of here? It's not a question of hours now, but of minutes."

Without turning around, O'Malley waved a hand to indicate that he'd heard. He walked through the embassy grounds, had the guards open the main gate, on the other side of which the same mob was still fighting tooth and nail, went out onto the street, threading his way like a sleepwalker between the cars that the looters were gutting. He did not see the girl at first; she was no longer where he had left her. Without knowing what he really wanted, he walked on for ten yards or so, amid a group of South Vietnamese soldiers who had just climbed out of trucks and were beginning, right there in the middle of the street, to shed their uniforms and get rid of their equipment, turning again into civilians then and there. Above the din, he heard someone calling his name. He caught sight of her motioning to him. He crossed the street, amid jeeps and trucks racing along at full throttle, sidestepped a torrent of Honda motorcycles, and joined her in the doorway of the store where she was standing.

"I was so afraid you wouldn't come back. I was so afraid, I prayed all the time you were gone. Have you got the papers?" She leaned over and kissed O'Malley's hand with her cool, fresh lips.

"Listen," he said.

All of a sudden he wanted her badly.

"My name is O'Malley," he said. "I'd like . . ."

"Have you got the papers?"

Helicopters flew past in an unending stream overhead. He drew her inside the store and stood there, not letting go of her arm.

"Have you got the papers?"

His left hand was gripping her arm, and he reached his right hand out, not knowing exactly what he intended to do, perhaps merely to stroke her cheek. She stepped back two paces. Still gripping her arm, he also took two paces, so that he, too, was now well inside the store. And it was then that he caught that glance over his shoulder, meant for someone behind him, that slight conspiratorial raising of her eyebrows. He tried to turn around but didn't have time to. The first knife-thrust slashed the nape of his neck and his face. He collapsed, not yet unconscious.

The girl said in a perfectly calm voice, "He's got the papers in his pocket. Kill him."

The second blow pierced his back, and others followed. This time he completely lost consciousness, but it was still light outside when he opened his eyes again. The first face he spied was Kearns'.

"How lucky you were, you bastard!" the Marine commandant said in his effeminate voice. "How lucky you were!"

"It didn't take you long to come get me," O'Malley managed to say.

They must have given him an injection of morphine or some such drug. He felt no pain, only a slight twinge on one side of his face, and he even had the feeling he was floating on air.

"Didn't take long!" Kearns exclaimed. "Six of my men looked for you all night long, even though heaven only knows they had other things to do. If it hadn't occurred to one of them to search through the sacks in that store, you'd still be there and you'd have kicked off by now. Didn't take long! That's really a laugh! You poor miserable Irish nut. It's Wednesday, April 30, 1975, and it's eight-forty A.M. You're in the last Chinook helicopter to leave that fucking city, along with the very last Americans. Me and my guys were the ones who locked the door and left the key under the mat, so to speak. You've got a few fingers and an eye missing, and a rather good-sized hole in your lower back, and just below you is the nice overcrowded deck of the *Blue Ridge,* an aircraft carrier merrily sailing over the China Sea. And when I say merrily ... Smile, pal. We've lost. And you're not going to die."

7

IT HAD BEEN RAINING WITHOUT LETUP FOR TEN DAYS IN THE CARDA-mome Range, at least on the slope that faced the Gulf of Siam and descended abruptly to it. A warm wind blowing in from the southwest constantly stirred and roiled the newly formed clouds of the monsoon, driving them before it into the mountain peaks, though they crossed them only rarely. It was a tropical rain, most often gentle and silent, with occasional sudden angry squalls that lashed the trees and bent their tops.

"You're the last White," Ieng Samboth said, shaking with fever. He stared into Lara's pale eyes. "The last one. It's been more than a month since they evacuated all those people from the French Embassy. They piled them into trucks and drove them off to the Thai border. I don't know if the Korvers were among them."

"They most likely were," Lara said.

Ieng nodded. "No doubt. There's no White left in Cambodia except you. Not one, not anywhere. Phnom Penh is empty, totally deserted, a dead city. So are Kompong Cham, Kompong Thom, Kampot, Battambang."

He fell silent and for a very long moment the only sound was the endless, peaceful, soft patter of the rain, which after a while they were not even aware of anymore; every so often irregular splashing noises rose above it, from rivulets of water running down the fan-palm roof or clefts in the rocks, or rain falling on leaves stirring in the wind, with musical changes of pitch varying from a deep bass to a thin treble.

They sat in a simple shelter in a hollow recess in the rock a few yards below the summit, at an altitude of about 4,000 feet. In front of it was a short, slightly sloping promontory, with more rocks at the far end of it. Immediately below the rocks there was nothing but empty space, a precipice plunging straight down for more than six hundred feet, opening out onto a panorama of long valleys stretching down like scars to the sea. The curtain of rain was so thick at the moment that the sea was invisible.

Lara was sitting underneath the overhanging fan-palm roof smoking, his legs stretched out, his hand holding the cigarette resting on his knee. He, Kutchaï, and the five Jaraïs with them had been at this hideaway for almost four weeks now, ever since their long, stealthy escape on the run from Phnom Penh to this spot in the Cardamomes. How Lara had managed to leave the encircled capital less than an hour before the Khmer Rouge entered it, Ieng Samboth knew next to nothing of. Neither Lara or Kutchaï was by nature inclined to confide in others. Ieng presumed that Kutchaï had played an essential role in this escape, no doubt taking advantage of the rank to which he had risen in the resistance, a rank he had now given up. *Doubtless for the same reasons I gave up mine,* Ieng thought to himself.

He turned his head to look around for the Jaraï. He was sitting at the very edge of the precipice, naked except for a sarong, allowing the rain to pour down on him with the stoic indifference of an animal. The other Jaraïs were inside the shelter, and most of them were asleep, or seemed to be. Ieng, too, closed his eyes, all of a sudden feeling the effect of the rapid climb he had just made, the endless hours of walking and running in recent days. His muscles ached, and he still seemed to be in the grip of a sort of spasmodic nervous tension that made him eager to talk, as did the fever that was spiking more and more frequently now.

"I've counted," he said. "Between the moment when Phnom Penh fell and the one when Saigon was taken over by the North Vietnamese, precisely twelve days and twenty-two hours elapsed. Twelve days and twenty-two hours! After thirty years of uninterrupted fighting. It's almost unbelievable."

His eyes and Lara's met, and he went on: "I've been struck by another thing: The Indochina war began at a time when all of Asia, all the Orient, all of Africa, and even Latin America were part of the White world. And during the time that the war went on, the White world has collapsed—a certain White world, which no doubt began with Christopher Columbus or even before, with the Portuguese, I don't remember exactly. The war in Indochina was the first of the great wars of colonial liberation to begin and the last to end."

"There'll be other wars in Indochina," Lara said coolly.

Ieng shook his head. "Between Cambodians and Vietnamese, between Vietnamese and Chinese. Or with the Thais. But among ourselves. Even the Russians won't dare to risk getting mixed up in another war here. Things will never be the same again."

He had sat down very close to Lara, so as to shelter himself as much as possible under the overhanging thatch of palm fronds. He reached out his hand and took a cigarette from the package sticking out of Lara's breast pocket, then borrowed Lara's cigarette to light his own. Suddenly there was an almost imperceptible movement some sixty yards away, at the edge of the forest; a Jaraï appeared, making his way toward them at the slow trot of the long-distance runner. Kutchaï stood up and walked slowly toward the newcomer along the edge of the precipice, oblivious to the dizzying void just below, his great, heavily muscled body glistening with rain.

"The English in India and everywhere else, the Dutch in Indonesia, the Belgians in the Congo, the French in Africa and here, even the Portuguese in Angola and Mozambique have all left," Ieng said. "Four hundred years of

history have just ended, Lara. It was only in Indochina that the White
world refused to let go for some reason or other. It was beaten a first time at
Dien Bien Phu. It still wouldn't give up. Whereupon its great champion, its
superpowerful champion, the greatest power on the face of the earth, never
once beaten in two hundred years, came to the rescue. The Great White
Knight. In the West, white is synonymous with purity; here in the Orient,
it's the color of mourning. The great White champion was beaten. Not only
beaten, humiliated. Humiliated."

He handed Lara back his cigarette. "Do you really want to go back
down, you and Kutchaï?"

Lara nodded.

"Where will you go?"

"We can't spend our whole life in these mountains," Lara said in his
slow drawl.

"On Mount Tippadeï, they shot to death more than three hundred officers brought there from Battambang. And two hundred more at O Taki.
And hundreds more at Mongkol Boreï, at Veal Trear, at O Koki, plus thousands of men, women, and children who had been deported from Battambang, near the Japanese Center for Agricultural Research at Mey Chbar.
Because they're not content to kill Lon Nol's commissioned and noncommissioned officers only; they also kill their families. Near the temple of
Chamcar Khnor, just outside of Sisophon, they clubbed only the women to
death, accusing them of having been prostitutes. They set up a concentration camp at the monastery of Wat Ek, and another at Kpor; they herded
more than three thousand schoolteachers in all, men and women, into the
two camps, and when they'd had enough of hacking at them with axes, they
then did their best to literally work them to death without giving them any
food—and most of them *did* die. I have dozens, hundreds of other examples
I could cite. I can give you an account of tens of thousands of dead. And I'm
speaking only of what I myself have seen, with my own eyes, in just a small
part of my country. I don't know what's happening in the rest of Cambodia—I'm afraid to find out. I'm afraid and I'm ashamed, and full of endless
despair. And that's where you're thinking of going?"

Kutchaï had gone to meet the Jaraï who had emerged from the forest a
few moments earlier. He had spoken to him, listened to him, then gone over
to one of the lookouts posted at the northern tip of the promontory and
given him an order. He was now walking slowly back toward the shelter,
with great lithe strides, his bare feet firmly gripping the clay soil. And the
black sarong he wore was like a sort of second skin, emphasizing the explosive, feline power of his huge body.

Ieng's eyes followed Kutchaï.

"Lara, a long time ago, last year or even longer ago, you and Kutchaï
and I made a deal with each other: If things turned out really badly, if Sa-

loth Sar took power, we were all to meet here, on this promontory where we are right now. We thought we'd foreseen the very worst of cases. The worst! I was to turn up at our rendezvous with all the men I could muster and Kutchaï was to do the same. I came, Lara, but I'm all alone. There's nobody behind me. Nothing but shadows."

"You have arms. You still have arms," Lara said, his pale eyes painfully, intently searching Ieng's face.

"Yes, I have arms. The ones you procured for me. I still have them."

Lowering his head, Ieng contemplated the glowing tip of his cigarette and then slowly stubbed it out in the mud.

"I have enough arms to equip two battalions. All I have to do is find the two battalions."

"You should be able to do that. There are men who will try to escape these massacres. They'll come to the forest. Pick the best of them, form combat units, train them, equip them—you could certainly do that."

"Yes, I should be able to," Ieng said. He stubbornly continued to bury the cigarette butt deeper in the mud with the tip of his index finger, even though the butt had long since disappeared from sight.

"Ieng Samboth, the new Warlord. Do you remember Kamsa? He too was a Warlord, or thought he was one. And then came the Corsican with the blue eyes who hanged him. I know—Kamsa was nothing but a stupid killer, nothing but a stupid petty killer. . . ."

"So I'm to pay for him too," Lara said in a quiet, even voice.

Kutchaï was only a few yards from them now, walking very slowly, like a film in slow motion.

"You wanted to tell me something else," Lara said. "Tell me."

"Rath. There's still that old account to settle with Rath. Lara, there are four men that Rath dreams night and day of finding: me, Kutchaï, a certain Kao, and you. He knows that all four of us are still in Cambodia. He knows that you're still here."

"Kao?"

"Kao, the former army captain, the one who was in charge at Pochentong Airport. In the last few years he led a commando unit hunting down Khmer Rouge in the region of Kompong Som and Kampot."

"I remember," Lara said.

Kutchaï had joined them. He stood there in front of them, enormously tall, just beyond the protection offered by the overhanging roof.

"Rath will allow himself no rest till he's found us," Ieng said. "He'll spend years tracking us down if necessary."

He hesitated, his head still lowered, staring at the spot where he'd buried the cigarette. Up until that moment Lara's eyes had never left him; now he turned away and gazed intently at the curtain of rain hiding the sea from view.

"You above all, Lara," Ieng went on. "Because of what you represent."

"What Ieng Samboth means," Kutchaï said, laughing his strange laugh, "is that your presence in Cambodia is dangerous. For you, naturally. But for him, Ieng Samboth, too—for Ieng Samboth and his future army. Ieng Samboth thinks that if you were no longer here, if you were in Europe or in America, Rath might possibly weary of the hunt or pursue it less stubbornly and viciously. Ieng Samboth thinks that you should clear out, leave Cambodia. He thinks your place is no longer here in this country."

"I had already realized all that," Lara said in his slow, seemingly drowsy voice. He turned his head and stared intently at Kutchaï. "And what about you?"

The silence that followed seemed endless to Ieng. Kutchaï squatted down on his heels, his face impassive. He reached out and picked up one of the M-16 assault rifles next to Lara. It was equipped with a forty-millimeter grenade launcher, with its own sight and firing mechanism. Kutchaï examined it in silence, put it down again, and picked up a Winchester 70 carbine with a special barrel and a large Unerti sighting telescope of the sort used by elite sharpshooters. He stroked the stock, meticulously wiping off the tiny drops of water on it, and then asked Ieng, "Where is Rath? Did he come into the forest behind you?"

"Yes."

"He's on your trail?"

"Yes."

Kutchaï nodded. "How far ahead of him were you?"

"Six, maybe eight hours."

A silence.

"He can't have many men with him," Kutchaï said, as though he were thinking aloud. "There's no point in that in the forest. And besides, they have other things to do, murdering all those people. Rath's working on his own."

With amazing agility and skill, he shouldered the Winchester and held Ieng's face directly in his line of sight for a second. Then he lowered the carbine and his silent laugh bared all his teeth. He turned his head finally and looked at Lara "You want us to go meet him, is that it?"

"I don't know."

"Yes, you do," Kutchaï said. "Of course you do. You know very well."

"You didn't answer me," Lara said to him.

Kutchaï laid the Winchester down and when he shook his head his long black hair sent little drops of water flying. He began to laugh again—the laugh that served to hide his feelings of friendship, his rages, his most violent emotions.

"I don't know where Rath is," he said. "Maybe he's already spotted us. Maybe he's on the crest, somewhere up above there, patiently waiting to kill us."

"You haven't answered me."

"He may very well be up there on the crest," Kutchaï went on. "And in an hour, or tomorrow, we may all be dead, with our heads in a plastic sack. I don't know where Rath is, but on the other hand I do know where Kao is. That fire we saw five nights ago was Kao. He's been advancing since then. He's not very far from us right now. He's got fifty men with him, he's following the crest line, and he's heading straight for us."

The next morning at dawn, another of the Jaraï scouts spied Rath's column without being spotted himself. Rath had two groups of sixty men each with him, advancing in a pincer movement; he was proceeding west-southwest, heading up the Pursat toward its headwaters and therefore keeping to the bottom of the valley, though it kept climbing at an ever-steeper angle. Meanwhile the riverbed grew narrower and narrower, until finally there was only a thin trickle of water at the bottom.

Driven out of their hideout by Kao's approach, Lara, Kutchaï and Ieng, and the handful of men with them had moved northwest, so that on the third day, having made camp with their backs to the Gulf of Siam and the Thai border, they had Rath on their left and Kao on their right, around twenty-five kilometers separating the detachments of the two men—who were enemies of each other as well.

The idea of pitting Kao and Rath against each other took hold in their minds. It was perfectly logical, and moreover, the prospect fascinated them.

The afternoon was drawing to a close. Three of the scouts returned, and all confirmed what up until then had been mere conjecture: The two columns, Kao's and Rath's, were going to pass within five or six kilometers of each other, at different altitudes, probably without catching sight of each other.

Kutchaï left at nightfall, taking with him an M-16, the Winchester 70, a machete, and spare ammunition in a haversack slung over his shoulder. He whispered a few words in Jaraï to his men, nodded in Ieng's direction, and just barely touched Lara's fingertips with his own as their eyes met. Ten seconds later he had disappeared, swallowed up at once by the forest and the darkness.

8

FOR THREE DAYS KAO HAD GIVEN HIS MEN STRICT ORDERS TO MAKE not so much as a small campfire. He couldn't have explained why; his instinct alone had put him on his guard, for none of his six scouts had spotted anyone but them in this vegetable world, which the continual downpour had transformed into a cloaca crawling with millions of creatures. But some intuition kept him on the alert; he sniffed the saturated air and thought he detected faint smells that were not normal. Several times he felt as though eyes were watching him, and some of his men—among them young Suon Phan, who had by now become a much more seasoned guerrilla fighter—had had the same sensation. Some sixth sense told them so. They had all had too much experience of pursuing and being pursued to be mistaken.

As he almost always had done since they came up into the Cardamomes, Kao had ordered a halt about an hour before sundown—if one could still speak of sun, if the sun still in fact existed beyond the endless damned rain. It was now pitch dark, and Kao, huddled in the lee of a boulder and wrapped in his plastic poncho, was trying to sleep. The men of his detachment were huddled about him, not even trying to fight the rain anymore, but dejectedly resigning themselves to it. Kao looked around once more to make sure the sentinels were at their posts. There were more of them than usual, spaced at regular intervals, and each was in his proper place. He closed his eyes again. Images out of the past filed by in his mind: those women and children burned alive on the Cheko Peninsula. The war. *I'm a man made for war.* He saw nothing, heard nothing.

Just a giant hand over his mouth, an ice-cold blade against his throat. A voice in his ear: "You're dead, Kao. Don't move."

The steel nicked the flesh of his throat at the level of his Adam's apple, but sank in no farther.

"I'd like to kill you, Kao. I'd really like to. But I'm not going to. I need you."

The giant palm was removed from his mouth.

"Can I move?" Kao asked in a low voice.

The blade moved away from his throat. Kao turned around and saw, as he had guessed, that it was Kutchaï.

"What is it you want me to do?"

"What you know how to do best," Kutchaï said. "Kill."

Ieng's voice, weary and feeble, quavering from the fever that had raged for three days now: "We're not going to get out of here alive. It's all over. It was bound to end some day. I'm happy that it's happening with you here, Lara. The only reason I came to this rendezvous was to see you again, to say good-bye to you. You should leave Cambodia and you know it."

"Shut up," Lara said softly.

His eye caught that of the Jaraï lookout. The highlander nodded his head almost imperceptibly. It was now more than twelve hours since Kutchaï had left with the intention of putting Kao on Rath's tail, and dawn had just broken.

"Years. It's gone on for years," Ieng was saying. "Years."

Lara put his long thin hand on Ieng's shoulder and gave it a slight, friendly squeeze to calm him. He said in a low voice, "Sam, please shut up. Somebody's coming."

The same fever that had been making Ieng Samboth shiver for several days had now overtaken Lara, too, and his whole body was shaking in long tremors. Every so often his vision blurred and he would then fight fiercely against his own body. Nonetheless he slipped out of the shelter in the cleft of the rock, and the chill rain on the back of his neck and his face made him a bit more clearheaded. He joined the lookout. His lips formed the name without really uttering it aloud: "Kutchaï?"

A shake of the head, a light in the dark pupils of the highlander's animal eyes. "No. Enemy." This accompanied by a silent waggling of the fingers of one hand, while the other held an M-16 with the charger in place.

Twenty or thirty men approaching, climbing up the north slope of the butte, and already less than two hundred yards away. It became evident that, contrary to their expectations, a small group of men had separated from the rest of Rath's detachment on the valley floor and, either by sheer chance or thanks to information brought back by its own scouts, was headed straight for this mountaintop where Lara and Ieng had taken refuge.

A second Jaraï joined Lara, then two more; there was only one of them missing now. He was doubtless posted somewhere in this extraordinarily dense vegetation, which only a snake—or a Jaraï—could have slipped through without causing a single leaf to stir. Perhaps he was perched in a tree—they often did that—in which case this unexpected approach of the enemy had probably taken him by surprise and cut him off from any possible avenue of retreat.

Stretched out flat on top of a boulder, Lara hesitated only a few seconds. To his right was the fault scarp, a towering, nearly vertical cliff overlooking the fog-blanketed ravine from which, at any moment, the shots from the detachment lying in ambush might ring out—provided that Kutchaï had managed to reach Kao and persuade him to go for Rath. To his left and thus to the north was a steep, bare slope that would be very difficult to climb and provided no cover whatever. The enemy—for who else could be coming except Rath's men?—was approaching from the north. Only one possible solution remained then. He signaled to the Jaraïs, his index finger circling, then pointing south.

"We're pulling out."

He crawled back toward the rock shelter from which he had just emerged. Ieng was lying curled in a ball, trembling from head to foot, his eyes closed, his face deathly pale.

"Come on, on your feet, let's go."

"I can't."

"Come on."

"Leave me here."

Lara slung his AR-18 carbine over his shoulder, grabbed Ieng by the shoulders, and dragged him outside. At the same instant, a thousand yards below in the ravine, the first bursts of machine-gun fire rang out and then all hell broke loose.

"Try to walk."

"I can't."

Ieng was burning with fever, despite the cold and the rain pouring down, heavier than ever. He did not even have strength left to hold his head up, and it lolled to one side, resting on his shoulder. Lara managed to get him on his feet, but he immediately collapsed. Crawling on their hands and knees for a time and then rising to their feet and running, the four Jaraïs reached the two men.

"Khmer Rouge coming. Twenty men."

Above the din of machine-gun and rifle fire mounting from the ravine in a steady roar, they heard the much closer bark of an M-16—that of the Jaraï who was missing—several bursts before the sound of his assault rifle was drowned out by the heavy answering fire from many Kalashnikovs. In one swift motion Lara hoisted Ieng onto his back and began to run straight up the slope to the south. One of the Jaraïs tried to give him a hand.

"No!"

He ran fifty or sixty yards up the slope. A hail of bullets spattered around him, almost between his legs. Someone at his side stopped to return the fire, and then suddenly cried out. Though tottering on his feet, Lara did not slow down, staring intently with blazing eyes at the green wall that seemed to take such a long time to reach, but which finally opened up before him. He plunged into it, staggering amid the low-hanging branches and nearly falling but catching himself just in time, the barrel of his Armalite hitting him in the face. He began to run again, zigzagging between the trees and thickets, bursting through immense spider webs, aware that another of his Jaraï comrades was staying behind him and beginning to fire, not in wild, panicked bursts, but calmly and deliberately, an experienced hunter who counts his bullets carefully and shoots only to kill.

A hundred yards of jungle, a hundred and fifty. Lara felt as though he were smothering to death in this suffocating closeness made more stifling still by the pouring rain. The terrain stopped its abrupt downward slope; it formed gentle hollows now and, after a few dense patches of forest where it was almost flat, began to climb upward again. It was a gentle incline, and ordinarily Lara would have found it barely perceptible. But to his strained legs it seemed steep. He fell, or rather collapsed, panting for breath.

Thirty, forty seconds.

Ieng's eyes opened. "I'm done for," he said. "Leave me here."

On his knees, his mouth wide open gasping for air, Lara had already unslung his rifle. He nearly forgot to release the safety catch. At the same time he looked behind him, his eyes rapidly retracing the passage up the slope that he himself had just opened. He saw two figures following from below, dressed in black, their checkered scarves fluttering in the wind. For the first time in fifteen years, for the first time since he had last gone hunting, he raised his rifle to his shoulder, aimed, fired off one lightning-quick burst. One of the men fell to the ground with a bullet through his throat; the other one dived for cover, though he, too, had obviously been hit.

"Done for," Ieng repeated in a surprisingly clear voice, though it was plain to see he was nearly unconscious.

He had not stirred from the spot and the position in which Lara had left him when he himself had fallen. He was lying on his side, one arm underneath him, his cheek resting on the sticky mud, the rain making his long black hair glisten. Though he was past thirty-five, he looked twenty years old at most, and heartbreakingly frail. Lara looked about: There were only two Jaraïs with him now.

In a whisper: "The others?"

"Two dead. One wounded, stayed behind." Gesture of a throat being slit. "He same thing dead."

Like Lara, the two highlanders were crouching with one knee resting on the ground, leaning slightly forward, their index fingers on the triggers of their rifles. They opened their red-rimmed eyes wide in the pouring rain, like drowned men, their gaze constantly searching the sea-green world in front of them. The echo of the battle in progress in the ravine, between Kao and the Khmer Rouge column, was farther away now, almost unreal, though there was still a constant roar of gunfire. Outside of that and the patter of rain, the forest was silent. Too silent. Then strange rustling sounds reached their ears.

Lara went back to where Ieng was lying. "We're pulling out again."

"Clear out without me. If you're by yourselves, you have a chance. Without me, Lara."

Lara smiled. "Yes, right."

Someone tapped him lightly on the shoulder as he was leaning down to hoist Ieng to his shoulders again. One of the Jaraïs acted out in sign language: "You and my comrade leave first with Ieng Samboth. I'll stay behind to delay our pursuers."

Lara shook his head vehemently.

But he finally gave in. What other solution was there? He gave one charger of his remaining three to the highlander who was staying behind and then took off, with the other Jaraï helping him carry Ieng. Repeatedly Ieng would regain consciousness just long enough to struggle and try to force them to leave him behind.

They slipped and crawled through dense forest growth dripping with water, splashed about in a low-lying flooded area on the edges of which

Lara mechanically noted the tracks of several panthers and a tiger. A snake slithered into sight a few yards distant but glided away. Two minutes later, they heard the first sharp report of the M-16: The Jaraï behind them had begun shooting. From that moment on, the firing never stopped, separate shots when it was the American rifle, and furious bursts when it was the Kalashnikovs returning fire. The gun battle lasted some twenty minutes; then, with a last hail of Russian bullets, an eloquent silence fell.

They quickened their pace even more, moving ahead as fast as they were able, and finally emerged into a sort of glade, planted with teaks whose trunks looked black and shiny in the rain, with fairly well cleared spaces between the trees in spots and extending for several hundred yards up the gentle slope of another mountainside. They climbed to the top. When they arrived at the crest, they were about three kilometers from the ravine where the ambush had taken place, to the southwest of it. They could no longer hear the sound of gunfire from the ravine, but the forest, which swallowed up everything, could also have muffled the sounds of a battle which might still be going on.

Ieng Samboth was delirious now, mixing French and Khmer as he spoke of a hotel on the Rue de l'Estrapade, of a girl named Françoise, of Lara.

"Ieng? Can you hear me?"

No intelligible answer. Lara turned to the Jaraï. "You stay here. You take care of him, you protect him, you look after him."

With these words, he took off, back down the slope they had come up, but just to the left of the clearly visible trail he and the Jaraï, carrying Ieng, had left in the drenched earth, where the rain formed miniature watercourses. He moved very fast, often running, and reached the edge of the forest clearing where it gave way to denser cover, six hundred yards lower down. He made his way into the thick brush and installed himself behind the shelter of a stump, leaning the barrel of his rifle on it. Chilled to the bone, struggling to keep himself from shivering uncontrollably with fever, and trying to fight off the torpor slowly stealing over him, he stretched out on his belly. He was about 350 yards from the place where he and the Jaraï had come out into the clearing a little earlier. From his lookout post, he could see perfectly the slight track he had made with his heel in the soft ground. Deliberately.

He waited.

After making certain that Kao and his men would really join battle with Rath's party, Kutchaï had set out before first light to meet Lara and Ieng again. Because of the steep incline of the ravine, and in order not to find himself caught in the crossfire of the two columns when they engaged each other, he chose to skirt the ravine by heading around to the north of it. He thus passed close to the rear guard of Rath's detachment, and soon came across the traces of some twenty men who had evidently opted to follow along the crest line, leaving most of the men in the Khmer Rouge column to move forward along the bottom of the ravine—straight into the ambush that Kao had set up for them.

Kutchaï instantly realized what a grave danger these twenty-odd men represented. He rushed after them, almost at their heels (just as Kao, down below, was opening fire, just at the second when Lara, with Ieng on his back, was beginning to withdraw). He reached the edge of the escarpment by climbing the same north slope as Rath's men. Kutchaï picked up their trail again and also came upon the first corpses, even before he reached the little rock shelters at the summit: two Khmer Rouge and one of his Jaraï friends, the latter so ripped to pieces by the bullets that he was nothing but a hunk of bloody meat hanging grotesquely from the branches of the tree in which he'd been perched.

Farther on, past the empty rock shelters, a second Jaraï, and lying in front of him the three men he had killed before being killed himself. Still farther on, a third highlander, this one with a bullet in his back and half decapitated by the machete blow that had finished him off.

And then, right in the middle of the trail hacked out of the vegetation, a sixth Khmer Rouge with a bullet clean through his throat.

A hundred fifty yards more and four other bodies scattered over thirty square yards, one of them a fourth Jaraï who had clearly taken a heavy toll of the enemy before being killed. *He sacrificed himself for the others,* Kutchaï thought to himself. Nine Khmer Rouge and four Jaraïs: a real bloodbath. *But Lara, Ieng, and Rath are still alive.* Kutchaï hesitated; there were so many footprints on the ground before him now that they were hard to read, and the flooded area he came upon a little later further complicated his task, since even though the water was not very deep it hid the tracks from sight.

His face completely impassive, all his animal instincts on the alert, listening, scrutinizing, sniffing the jungle, he finally found a bootprint of Lara's. He was about to hurry on when his ear caught the distinct sound of a rifle being cocked. He sank to his knees, squeezed off a shot. When silence had fallen once again, he advanced with his rifle at his side, and discovered a tenth Khmer Rouge, less than fifteen yards distant, who must have been wounded and left behind; in any case, Kutchaï's shot had finished him off.

He had just started off again when he heard to his right, at a distance of about fifteen hundred yards, the unmistakable chatter of Lara's Armalite.

There were eleven of them, and he gave them time to step out into the open space amid the trunks of the teak trees. Rath was among them, the third in the line, short, stocky, with close-cropped hair. Lara had never seen him—Kutchaï had merely described Rath to him—but the moment he laid eyes on him, he was certain this was the man who had tried to kill Oreste and who had killed Roger.

Lara had unfolded the stock of his Armalite 18, a light machine gun, superior even to the M-16, which could fire 750 rounds a minute. He had loaded it with a full charger containing twenty cartridges and had another one ready.

The eleven men advanced, spreading out, though not too far apart. Their eyes were fixed on the crest six hundred yards higher up, where the trail of footprints led, and they were using the trees as cover against gunfire coming from that direction. They were already eighty yards away from the heavy cover they had come out of when Lara opened fire.

His first bullet was for Rath, and though he realized immediately that he had not hit his target squarely, he did not have the time, or did not take the time, to aim a second bullet at him. The most important thing was to kill the maximum number of men, and he did so. Shifting the barrel of the gun a few fractions of an inch each time, he aimed successively at each of the men in the group. He mowed down six of them, firing eight bullets in less than ten seconds.

The answering fire came with terrifying suddenness, in the form of a hail of bullets that ripped the leaves and branches around him to pieces, riddled the tree stump and the trunk of the tree at whose foot he was lying. A first grenade exploded without hitting him. He answered with a burst of fire that sprayed the terrain, then bounded to his feet and slipped into an immense patch of dense forest where coiled serpents were lurking. He crawled rapidly for a distance of seven or eight yards, found the embankment he had spotted, and threw himself over it.

It was only about four feet to the bottom of the embankment, but it saved him from the second and third grenades which burst at that moment, and also allowed him to run to one side for a distance of about a hundred yards. He ran crouched over, shaking with fever, all his strength exhausted, remaining on his feet only by a prodigious effort of will.

He came back to the trail he and the Jaraï, carrying Ieng Samboth, had made twenty-five minutes earlier. The rain-soaked earth now bore the traces of Rath and his men as well. With the slow caution of a reptile, he crawled to the edge of the forest clearing. The green light took on a yellower tinge and the curtain of rain parted.

He counted the bodies strewn on the ground; there were five of them. *Plus two others that I only wounded, one of them Rath himself,* he thought. He tried to make out some sign of life at the top of the slope, where he had left Ieng and the Jaraï, but saw nothing.

Where are Rath and his men? He would have expected six of them to be still on his trail. But there was no visible sign of their presence or any movement on their part. Yet they were there somewhere, as cunning as he himself was at moving about in this hell; he could feel their silent presence. He glanced one last time in the direction of the crest, overcome for a brief instant by the mad desire to stand up and run to the one Jaraï still alive, who might have been able to help him. But finally he turned around and plunged into the jungle again.

There was a burst of automatic rifle fire and two of the bullets buried themselves in his left side, almost pinning him to the ground. He spied the man standing thirty yards away, already convinced he had won. Lara shot and distinctly saw his bullet hit his adversary in the face.

Another burst of fire, this one from his right. *They're surrounding me.* The fever kept making him shiver and shake. He fired back blindly, tried to stand up and run. But a paralyzing pain gripped him. He stumbled and after a few yards fell to the ground, curled up in a ball like a stunned rabbit. Perhaps his fall saved him, or delayed the end; they were firing at him from two directions, and the bullets laid down a pattern of rifle fire above him.

Lara lifted himself out of the mud, his mind even cloudier now and reacting only out of instinct. Dragging himself along on his knees, he passed beneath a succession of rotting stumps dotted with marvelous orchids which the fat raindrops set to trembling. He crouched there, savagely biting his own arm in the hope that the intentional pain would enable him to control himself. His entire body was one great wound now, and dozens of leeches were avidly clinging to it. He noted that he had been hit in the leg, twice, and also in the back, very close to the twenty-year-old scar.

Minutes went by in total silence. But he knew there were eyes watching him. At length, he chose to move again. He dragged himself along on his side, pulling his numbed leg after him, nearly losing consciousness every so often but continuing his attempt to escape with the insane stubbornness of an animal refusing to let itself be cornered by the pack closing in for the kill.

The sound of a waterfall came to his ears. He realized he had reached a riverbed, perhaps the very river that flowed through the ravine in which Kao was fighting.

He took a drink, and then three-quarters submerged himself in the river, leaving above the surface only his head and his right arm holding the rifle. He was unable to go any farther and he knew it. Little by little a deathly cold stole over him, oddly associated with the burning sensation from the fever and from his wounds, and with the incessant pounding of his temples. His eyelids drooped shut more and more often, and several times he plunged his face in the water to clear his head for a few seconds.

He was aware of a body gliding into the water very close to him. A voice said in Khmer, "He's here."

The torso of a man appeared in his field of vision, black with the little red and white squares of the scarf. Using his rifle as though it were a pistol,

Lara squeezed the trigger. Two bullets went off, the last two in the charger. The man fell as though struck by lightning.

Reload, I must reload. The entire left side of his body was paralyzed now, but he was still holding the Armalite up out of the water. He was falling into a stupor. His left hand slowly mounted along his leg in the direction of the charger still attached to his belt, but this slight movement was enough to put an end to the resistance his body had until then been offering the flow of the stream. He began to glide slowly with the current, his face turned toward the sky from which the rain still poured down.

A few yards downstream, he set the nape of his neck against a stone to keep from drifting farther, and so was able to see Rath coming toward him, striding unhurriedly through the rust-colored running water, his little hard eyes staring at him without blinking. Rath covered the last few yards separating them. He stopped, leaned down, grabbed Lara's American rifle out of his hand and flung it onto the bank of the stream. He was not smiling, and his face was not at all that of the excited hunter who has at last managed to corner his prey. It was cold and impassive, almost indifferent, just as he was indifferent to the deep furrow Lara's bullet had opened down one side of his face, tearing his ear and doubtless shattering his jaw. He took a plastic sack out of his breast pocket.

"Lara. Lara, the last one."

He was having difficulty talking, seemingly spitting his words out rather than pronouncing them.

"It's been a long time," he added, in French.

He slung his rifle over his shoulder and breathed into the sack to separate the edges.

It was at that moment that Kutchaï chose to open fire.

Kutchaï did not shoot to kill. His first shot, from a distance of less than twenty yards, shattered the Kalashnikov and made Rath's body pivot around; his second bullet pierced Rath's hand. Then Kutchaï advanced almost nonchalantly, he, too, walking in the water, and with the same terrifying calm, the same contempt, he pushed Rath's left hand away as Rath tried to hit him with the blade of his machete. He seized Rath's wrist, pried loose one by one the fingers gripping the handle, grabbed Rath by the scruff of the neck, and flung him onto the bank. He tied him to a tree, arms circling the trunk. He came back to Lara then.

"You okay?"

"I'm still alive."

"That's pretty good going already."

Kutchaï leaned over, then straightened up with Lara in his arms, and carried him over to the bank.

"Ieng," Lara said. "Ieng and one of your Jaraïs, on the crest."

"I found them," Kutchaï said, in an oddly distant voice. "But Rath's men had found them before I did. They're both dead."

Lara closed his eyes but opened them again immediately to watch Kutchaï, who was searching in the water for the machete. His huge hand reappeared holding the knife. Kutchaï turned around slowly, looking at Rath.

"Don't do that," Lara said. "I beg you. I implore you." His voice was trembling, and not only from raging fever.

"*Khniom khmer,*" Kutchaï said in a deep-throated animal growl. "I'm a Khmer."

"Kutchaï, I beg you."

Kutchaï began to laugh silently, his bloodshot eyes gleaming with savage hatred.

"*Khniom khmer.*"

In two strides he reached Rath and effortlessly ripped off his clothes, baring his belly and chest. The blade sliced through Rath's skin and the muscles of his abdomen. The enormous fingers reached in, searching for something.

The liver. Which he removed.

And ate, the blood on his lips mingling with the rain.

And that was how the story ended.

On Tuesday night, March 17, and in the early hours of Wednesday, March 18, 1975, Dominique Christiani landed his last contraband shipment on the Khmer coast. The last because he was now afraid. During the preceding weeks, he had gone close inshore to the Cambodian coast, without landing, and picked up refugees who had escaped from the indescribable hell the former little kingdom had become. Their stories had terrified him, even though he was not a man who allowed himself to be easily frightened. But he had finally given in to his fear and had sworn that in no case, even if he were offered his own weight in gold, would he make another trip there.

But on the eleventh, a Chinese came to see him and uttered the only name that could possibly have changed his mind: Lara. And so he left once more, with his usual Malay crew aboard and also Kutchaï's brother Ouk, who a month earlier had managed to cross the Thai border but now wanted to rejoin his elder brother.

Things went very fast, for they knew that Khmer Rouge detachments constantly patrolled the beaches and rocky stretches along the coast in order to intercept people attempting to flee.

Christiani took on board a Lara who was so thin it frightened him, who was unquestionably wounded, and ill as well; but what impressed Christiani even more was his face, like the face of a living corpse. Lara was a mere shadow now, and had just enough strength to drag himself to a bunk in one of the cabins. He stretched out on it, his face to the wall, and never once stirred after that.

On top of the rocks along the shore, around Kutchaï, and Ouk now with him, were a dozen men, a number of them still wearing the uniform blouses of the Lon Nol army. They all looked extremely tough; they were fully armed, as cold and dangerous as cobras. Among them was a young man with an emaciated face who introduced himself as Lieutenant Suon Phan and who asked the Corsican to send on news of him to his family, especially to his uncle, whose name he wrote down; he hoped that all his family had been able to flee to Thailand. Christiani looked at the youngster intently.

"Weren't you with Kao?"

"Kao's dead. Kutchaï's our leader now. Other men will be coming to join us soon."

As he left, Christiani tried to shake Kutchaï's hand, but the giant didn't even seem to notice the hand held out to him. His eyes were fixed on the cabin into which Lara had just disappeared, and his dilated pupils had in them that wild, blind look that the stone demons of Angkor trained on visitors. Dominique Christiani had always realized that there was something savage about Kutchaï, a sort of primitive, age-old barbarism. That night, the last time he ever saw the Jaraï, it seemed to him that the wildness in Kutchaï's nature had taken him across some invisible new threshold, with no hope of his ever returning.

"We'll meet again one of these days," the Corsican said, just to fill the silence.

"*Até,*" Kutchaï answered. "No."

He was still staring intently at the cabin, and the last word he said was probably not addressed to Christiani and his crew alone.

"*Tao,*" he said. "Clear out."

9 MADELEINE KORVER TILTED HER HEAD SLIGHTLY AND PATTED THE lock of blue hair over her forehead. "I came here for the first time in July 1913," she said in her gentle little voice. "I was just thirteen years old. You no doubt remember . . ."

"I'm terribly sorry, but I don't," the hotel manager said, in a tone meant to suggest that this lapse of memory was driving him to the edge of an attack of nervous depression and perhaps even suicide.

"That was over sixty-two years ago, I admit. Perhaps you weren't here back then?"

"I don't believe so," the manager of the Hotel Peninsula said with impeccable courtesy.

"I remember that we'd just left Shanghai—or was it perhaps Peking?—because of that frightful General Yüan Shih-k'ai who was determined to remove that good Dr. Sun Yat-sen from power. Did you ever meet Dr. Sun Yat-sen personally? What a pity! You missed meeting a marvelous man if you didn't, an altogether admirable person, despite his theories. He often came to dinner at my parents'. All Chinese are extremely intelligent."

The Chinese manager of the Hotel Peninsula spread his hands apart and smiled, as though he could only respectfully bow to the evident truth of such a remark.

"We've always been very fond of your hotel," Madeleine said.

The Hotel Peninsula had long been the glory of Hong Kong in the old days, even though it was less so at present. The Korvers had put up there dozens of times, and had even stayed there for several months in a row in the happy days of the twenties, at the time when Pierre and Nancy Lara, who had just been married in this city where they had first met, were still living in the crown colony. The Korvers had always liked the indolent, quietly genteel, undoubtedly snobbish and unquestionably refined atmosphere of the Peninsula, where each day at five in the afternoon the froth of Hong Kong's White society, Englishmen in straw hats and immaculately turned-out colonials, had dropped in to take high tea beneath its flamboyant, brightly gilded nineteenth-century ceilings.

"When I say 'we,' I mean my husband and myself. But my husband is dead now, as you may know. He died in Phnom Penh, where his body was laid to rest. That was really best after all; it's my opinion that he wouldn't have liked to be buried anywhere else, since Phnom Penh was the city he loved best in all the world. Certainly not in France. We once tried, several years ago now, to reacclimate ourselves back there. You've never been to Bordeaux? Never mind. Furthermore, it wasn't particularly Bordeaux that we couldn't get used to. We really did try. Good heavens, it was frightful! All those people rushing all over the place like madmen, all those dark houses all shut up, those humid afternoons and those freezing evenings, those faces that never smiled. We very soon came back."

The Hotel Peninsula was located in Kowloon at the very tip of the Chinese mainland, just opposite Victoria on the island of Hong Kong. To the right of it were the ferries of the Star Line, whose docks continually swarmed with people meeting others as they arrived or departed. The hotel had no swimming pool and its plumbing sometimes tuned up and vibrated most irritatingly, but the Rolls-Royce from the hotel was always there when one got off a plane at Kai Tak, a P. and O. liner, or the MS *Paipoosek* bringing you from Singapore. And at the mere mention of the name Korver, they had immediately thrown out the vulgar businessman occupying the $1,000-a-day suite that Madeleine and her husband had always stayed in, with its ten windows overlooking Wanchai, Victoria Peak, and Happy Valley, and installed her in it.

"I'm seventy-five years old today," Madeleine Korver announced. "That is to say, it's my birthday and my wedding anniversary as well, and though I don't usually take tea, I will today. I'd like, if you please, that narcissus and chrysanthemum tea recommended by Luk Yué about two centuries ago. Charles, my husband, adored it. He used to drink quarts of it, and claimed it would make him live to be a hundred. There are certain days, you see, when it's hard for me to get used to the fact that he's passed on. Today especially, since it's my seventy-fifth birthday. Long ago, he had such a nice idea: I was eighteen years old the day we were married, and that day he gave me eighteen of the finest pearls that could be found in China at the time. Afterward, every July twenty-first, he gave me another pearl. He swore to me that I'd one day have a hundred of them and he'd be there to give me the last one. He was a man full of sentimental ideas like that. I don't hold it against him in the slightest for not having been able to keep his promise. Poor Charles, it isn't his fault. . . ."

She was served the tea with a ceremony they probably wouldn't have tendered the Queen herself, had she appeared on the scene from London. Madeleine Korver took a delicate, discerning sip of it and individually thanked each of the maîtres d'hôtel who had thronged about her, simply to keep her company and surround her with their beaming smiles. She drank it slowly, a tiny old lady dressed from head to foot in black lace, with a cameo on a ribbon encircling her neck, her pastel-blue porcelain eyes lost in a sea of memories. Beneath that resplendent high ceiling, she appeared to have been washed up on the shore by an immense tide that had long since ebbed. And when someone came and sat down beside her and the boys poured tea into the extra cup that had been laid out, she did not even turn her head but merely said, "Charles was absolutely right. This tea is really delicious."

"Happy birthday," Lisa said, with a lump in her throat and her eyes nearly brimming over with tears.

The big luxurious Mercedes with curtains at the windows stopped in front of the door for departing passengers at Hong Kong's Kai Tak Airport.

"You drive very well," Liu said. "Almost as well as my usual chauffeur. Or very nearly."

"You should have had him drive you. You're the one who insisted on my taking his place. But I presume you wanted to keep from paying him overtime."

"One doesn't economize when it comes to such small sums," Liu said, in a very serious tone of voice. "That's how a person realizes that he's fairly well off."

A silence. The two men exchanged a friendly glance.

"In any event," Liu went on, "I'll only be staying in Peking for four days, since I should be in Manila on Friday morning, the twenty-fifth. I'll telephone you from there as soon as I arrive."

"I still don't understand why you insisted on going to the Philippines yourself. I could have gone there, and should have. Or failing that, the two of us could have met there."

"I prefer having you right here. Just imagine what would happen if Chou En-lai asked me a question I couldn't answer: I'd have no other choice than to join my favorite associate in Hong Kong, since he knows everything."

"In a pig's eye," Lara answered.

Liu held out his hand. "I'll call you Friday morning."

He got out of the car and headed for his plane, escorted by the directors of the airline company, in which he happened to have a number of shares of stock. After a moment, Lara drove off again in the Mercedes. Near the main railroad station he entered the tunnel that had been finished the year before and drove over to Causeway Bay on the Hong Kong side. It was six P.M. by the time he arrived, and he decided there was no point in going to his office in the Hong Chong Building, on Queen's Road. He headed straight toward Repulse Bay, crossing the whole length of the island.

The house he had rented two years earlier from one of Liu's sons had neither the extravagant dimensions nor the ostentatious luxury of the other great mansions in that district; it was located, moreover, on the heights overlooking Stanley Bay, in a zone where the terrific real estate and tourist boom had not yet wreaked its ravages. The beach far below the garden was almost deserted. He changed into swimming trunks, and two minutes after his arrival was stroking lithely in the blue-green waters of the South China Sea. His scars were still visible, paler marks on skin that was otherwise superbly tanned.

He swam out for several yards, then turned over on his back, gently paddling his legs to keep from finding himself upright in the water. He had never managed to float, as Roger Boués, a poor swimmer, had never failed to point out to him in a triumphant tone, since that was the one and only aquatic skill Roger had ever acquired.

Roger. And Ieng. And those Jaraïs dying one after the other, and Oreste's crushed body, and the flames running the length of the marvelous black wood veranda.

And Lisa. And Cambodia murdered, Cambodia in the process of immolating itself, plunging into a mad delirium of self-destruction before, doubtless, conquerors came from Hanoi in pursuit of their logical, age-old ambition, to finish it off once and for all. Cambodia forever dead, with the one exception perhaps of Kutchaï the Jaraï, immense and black, gone back to his forest, to his primitive state of barbarism. Kutchaï could survive, should survive—he had to. At least Kutchaï, Kutchaï for himself, without Lara—even without Lara—forever. He had to. Or else no such thing as hope existed any longer.

He began to swim again, very slowly at first, then faster and faster, in a cold, desperate rage. He swam out toward the open sea. After a few hundred yards more, he was forced to stop, his muscles failing him. A piercing pain gripped his side where the two bullets had hit him. He regained partial control of himself.

His own house was directly in his line of sight, about a kilometer away. It was not very large, really, just three small bedrooms, five rooms in all. A few minutes before, during the few seconds it had taken him to walk through it and change out of his white linen suit into his swimming trunks, he hadn't seen or heard Cheng, his cook and only servant. The villa had seemed to him to be empty. Ordinarily, Lara dined early, and outside of the two or three times he had received Liu and one or another of the members of Liu's family, he dined by himself. He ate his meals on the little terrace overlooking the sloping garden and the sea below, with Cheng serving in silence as Lara read, paying no attention to what was on his plate. On two or three occasions, Liu had spoken out against such complete solitude, which he regarded as very nearly tragic.

"Come, come, you're exaggerating."

"Lara, I don't like it. I assure you it worries me."

"Mind your own business," Lara had finally said, softening the rudeness of his remark and even causing it to pass unnoticed by accompanying it with his slow, warm smile.

He stopped kicking his legs and they slowly descended to a vertical position in the dark water. All Lara would have had to do was raise his arms above his head for his entire body to disappear beneath the surface, sinking straight down six feet. He turned about so that he was facing out to sea. Straight in front of him, beyond the thousand kilometers of the South China Sea, was the immense Pacific, stretching out to infinity. One night not so long before, when he was swimming about as he now was, he had had to struggle against a fierce desire to strike out into this absolute emptiness till his strength gave out, leaving Asia behind him forever.

He plunged his face into the water, opening his eyes wide in a laughable attempt to see something at the bottom, almost three thousand feet below. Finally he began swimming slowly back toward the beach and the house.

"You can still get out of this car if you like" Madeleine said in the acid tone of a schoolmarm taking one of her pupils to task. "There's nothing keeping you from it. I'm not going to round you up with a lasso or anything as ridiculous as that. I need merely ask this chauffeur to stop and he'll do so, even though he's Chinese and therefore naturally inclined to be contrary."

A little farther on, as the Rolls-Royce from the Hotel Peninsula was driving through Happy Valley past the race course, Madeleine also said, "And dry your eyes, you big gangling girl. I didn't go all the way to San Francisco to get you, I didn't spend hours waiting outside that house on Nob Hill listening to that cable car swaying up and down while Madame lounged about on a sailboat, I didn't travel all those millions of miles at my age to bring back a pitiful sniveling girl. By the way, I want to see something. It's been preying on my mind for some time."

She leaned over and stuck her nose down the neckline of Lisa's dress, even opening it a little farther, exactly as she would have gone about searching for something in her sewing basket.

"Even your breasts are tanned. It's shameful. No, don't bother trying to blush: You're so tan it wouldn't show in any case. What was that man's name again?"

"Wynn."

"He was quite a handsome man, I'll admit. Why did I say 'was'? After all, he's not dead, as far as I know."

She looked at Lisa intently. "Did you . . . did you and he . . . er, well, did you . . ."

At that moment, most surprisingly, it was Madeleine Korver who turned bright red.

Lisa smiled. "No," she said. "No."

She laughed wholeheartedly, harder and harder, for the first time since they had left San Francisco together, at the expression on the old lady's face.

"Oh, that's naughty of you!" Madeleine said.

A silence fell again, and neither of them said a word till the Rolls-Royce stopped. The liveried chauffeur opened the door for Lisa and she got out.

"This house, Madame," he said.

He did not have time to say anything else, for Madeleine was already calling him back inside. He put his cap on his head, took his place behind the wheel once more, and started off again.

"To the hotel," Madeleine said. "And please step on it."

She didn't even turn around to take one last look at the silhouette of the tall young woman in a white dress, a forlorn look about her, whom she had just abandoned at the entrance to a villa on the heights overlooking Stanley Bay.

Once back at the Peninsula, she declined the invitation to dinner extended by some British friends who had always lived in Hong Kong and had just learned of her arrival there; she did not even bother to read the numerous messages waiting for her at the reception desk which had come from other old friends she and Charles had made over the years.

"I'll have dinner in my room. With my lover, Mathias Lara, as soon as he's finished his oatmeal porridge."

On the way upstairs in the elevator, she said in French to the elevator boy—who didn't understand one word: "What do you think of that? She said to me: 'No, I don't want our son to be there. Not before he and I have had a frank talk together.' A talk together! Now I ask you! That darling Monsieur Liu was right: The one of them is as stupid as the other."

In her room, she sat down in an armchair facing the panoramic view of the most beautiful bay in the world. She wept a few tears, very few, in the way she had been taught to weep seventy years before, merely dampening one corner of her lace handkerchief. She didn't spy immediately the little package lying on a low occasional table. She caught sight of it just as she was getting up to fetch young Mathias and his amah.

She opened it, found a jewelry box inside, and within the box, a single pearl of miraculous luster. Accompanied by these words: "With all my love and happy birthday. Lara."

When he came back into the house from the beach, contrary to his usual habit, he did not pass by the terrace and the living room that opened out onto it. Instead, he entered his bedroom by way of a French door at one side of the villa. He took a shower and changed into a white evening jacket. He lit a cigarette but stubbed it out in an ashtray after the first puff. The house was completely silent and night was falling. He hesitated a few seconds more, his pale gray-blue eyes staring into empty space. Then he went out onto the terrace. There were two places laid at the black teakwood table.

He raised his head and saw her violet eyes gazing at him.

"You knew I was in Hong Kong, didn't you?" she asked.

For a moment, he couldn't get a word out. Finally he said, "I knew that Madeleine was coming. Dominique Christiani told me so. That was all I knew, and I certainly had no idea that you and Mathias would be with her. Is Mathias here?"

"He's at the hotel, with Madeleine."

He slowly massaged his shoulder. "I only caught on a few minutes ago, while I was out swimming. Liu and Madeleine, plotting together."

He sat down on the table top, his long, tan fingers clutching the wood as though he were trying to crush it, so as to keep her from noticing they were trembling. But she was trembling at least as hard as he was.

"You've gotten thinner," she said.

"You're very beautiful."

She sat down in one of the chairs at the table.

"Everything will be fine from now on," Lisa said at last. "We'll live together. You and Mathias and I, together. And our other children, if you want us to have more. We'll live wherever you want to. Here in Hong Kong, if you like. Oh, my love, everything will be fine from now on."

"Yes," Lara said.

He gave a toss of his head. He rose to his feet, stepped toward her, took her in his arms, put his cheek against hers, and closed his eyes.